★"Duffy and Jennings have done justice to Butler's work, losing none of the story's richness and adding an exciting visual element that makes the reading experience even more visceral and engrossing."

> **—Forward Reviews**, starred review

"Jennings's work in the book is beyond stunning, with a woodcut quality that gives it an effective folkloric feel that is appropriate for the story of a religious movement during the end times. But this stylistic approach doesn't undercut the presentation of the characters as individual people with inner lives, and Jennings is able to extend the emotional quality of their experience through the world around them."

> **—The Beat**

"John Jennings's work succeeds as sequential storytelling and approaches the level of iconography regularly."

> **—The Believer**

"Jennings and Duffy are some of the most skilled and hardest working comics creators doing the work to radically transform and diversify the comics scene."

> **—Comicosity**

"Jennings has captured [Butler's] words with visual imagery in such an afrofuturistic, horror-esque way that the images jump off the page with every turn."

> **—Flickering Myth**

"There's a good reason to revisit Butler's Nebula Award-nominated classic: the new graphic novel adaptation of it by Damian Duffy and illustrator John Jennings—the same team who adapted *Kindred*, another of Butler's books. *The Parable of the Sower* graphic novel is as faithful an adaptation as you can get. Not only does it hit all the plot points, it perfectly portrays Butler's balancing act in regard to how far society has fallen apart. At the same time, it offers readers a bit more in fleshing out the horrors of a decaying society. The pictures, drawn with dark tones to match the serious mood of the story, often give subtext to the words. By the end, it's not hard to imagine the journey of Lauren and her growing congregation, because you've walked with them through the hardships and the pain."

> **—Kirkus**

"Duffy and Jennings—who also adapted Butler's book *Kindred* into graphic novel form—have done a masterful job at converting this story into a new medium."

> **—MuggleNet**

"Jennings's gift for channeling the color boldness of a Faith Ringgold or the energy of a Basquiat, while further expanding a distinctive Black comics visual aesthetic for which he has become a curator, propagator, promoter, and creator, get exhibited in *Parable*."

> **—Multiversity Comics**

"An inspired addition to Butler's story."

> **—The Portland Book Review**

"The graphic novel is faithful to Butler, yet still fresh in its world building."

> **—USA Today**

"This nimble graphic adaptation of Butler's 1993 novel of capitalism-ravaged California feels alarmingly prescient and relevant. Duffy and Jennings (*Kindred*) skillfully rework the tale told through the eyes of teenage empath Lauren Oya Olamina, who navigates a world transformed by drought, gun violence, and exploitation. . . . This accessible adaptation is poised to introduce Butler's dystopian tale to a new generation of readers."

> **—Publishers Weekly**

A Graphic Novel Adaptation by Damian Duffy and John Jennings

OCTAVIA E. BUTLER'S

PARABLE OF THE SOWER

Introduction by Nalo Hopkinson

ABRAMS COMICARTS · NEW YORK

ALSO AVAILABLE

Kindred: A Graphic Novel Adaptation

COMING SOON

Parable of the Talents: A Graphic Novel Adaptation

Editor: Charlotte Greenbaum
Designer: Pamela Notarantonio
Managing Editor: Amy Vreeland
Production Manager: Erin Vandeveer

Library of Congress Control Number 2020944173

ISBN 978-1-4197-5405-0

Printed and bound in China

10 9 8 7 6 5 4 3 2 1

ABRAMS The Art of Books
195 Broadway, New York, NY 10007
abramsbooks.com

CONTENTS

INTRODUCTION

Octavia Estelle Butler, the author of the original prose novel *Parable of the Sower* (1993), famously described herself as "a pessimist if I'm not careful, a feminist, a Black, a former Baptist, an oil-and-water combination of ambition, laziness, insecurity, certainty, and drive."[*]

Though we lived in different countries, Octavia and I were colleagues, fellow Black women science fiction authors with the same publisher. Older than I was, she started writing and publishing well before I did. She and Samuel R. Delany illuminated the path for we who would follow them. Her novel *Fledgling* was released in 2005, the same year the first edition of my novel *The New Moon's Arms* was published. Our publisher decided to send us on a U.S. tour together, and I was thrilled. Then came the news of Octavia's death as a result of a stroke. I'd known she wasn't well, but I hadn't anticipated this. At some level, we think our touchstones will always be there, perpetually living guiding lights.

Our editor at the publishing house, Jaime Levine, phoned from New York to speak with me in Toronto. She had first encountered Octavia's writing as a university student in feminist studies. She'd been deeply touched by it. It meant the world to her when she became Octavia's editor. Jaime and I wept and mourned on the phone for a solid three hours, trying to console each other.

A pessimist if I'm not careful. That phrase kept coming to mind as I read the inspired adaptation of Octavia's prose into a graphic novel at the hands of Damian Duffy and John Jennings. "If I'm not careful" implies repetition. Octavia didn't just reject pessimism once and become a sunny Pollyanna thereafter. It was an impulse she had to quell over and over. It was a dynamic and continuous act, a hard-nosed practice of staring down the worst of humanity's evils and refusing to live in denial, all the while choosing to remember that humanity is also capable of great good. It's part of what made her fiction so life-changing for her readers. And it is a quality evident in Lauren Oya Olamina, the young protagonist of *Parable of the Sower*.

---

[*] From *Conversations with Octavia Butler*, Consuela Francis (ed.). Jackson, MS: University Press of Mississippi, 2010.

One of the central frustrations of youth is being able to clearly see what the world is doing wrong while chafing at adults' apparent unwillingness to fix it. One of the capitulations of adulthood is the recognition that social change toward equitable communities is difficult and almost never seen in the course of one's lifetime. Lauren, a teenager on the verge of adulthood, stands on the cusp of both states. She's doing so while her world goes to hell around her: irresponsible big pharma testing drugs with harmful side effects on Black, brown, and poor bodies; exponentially extreme divisions between haves and have-nots; food and water scarcities as our depredation of the environment comes home to roost; communities tearing themselves apart from within; and corporations given legal carte blanche to reenact slavery under the guise of company towns. Octavia's vision of the nightmare of social ills that is Southern California in 2032 even presciently includes a U.S. presidential candidate who promises to "make America great again" by making the situation worse.

Lauren sees all this clearly. She thinks she knows what she must do to resist it. And it terrifies her.

I won't recapitulate Lauren's adventures after she escapes the walled and besieged community where she lives. The Duffy and Jennings version does so quite masterfully, through skillful use of captioning, strong dialogue selections, and excellent artwork, color, and panel/page design. This book *lives*. It breathes, moves, feels, clamors for your attention, insists on bearing witness, insists on being heard.

Nalo Hopkinson

February 2020

Nalo Hopkinson is Jamaican Canadian. Her 1998 novel, *Brown Girl in the Ring*, won the Warner Aspect First Novel contest. Her 2013 novel, *Sister Mine*, won the Andre Norton Award for Young Adult Science Fiction and Fantasy. She has also received the Campbell and Locus Awards, the World Fantasy Award, and the Sunburst Award for Excellence in Canadian Literature of the Fantastic. She is a professor of creative writing at the University of California–Riverside.

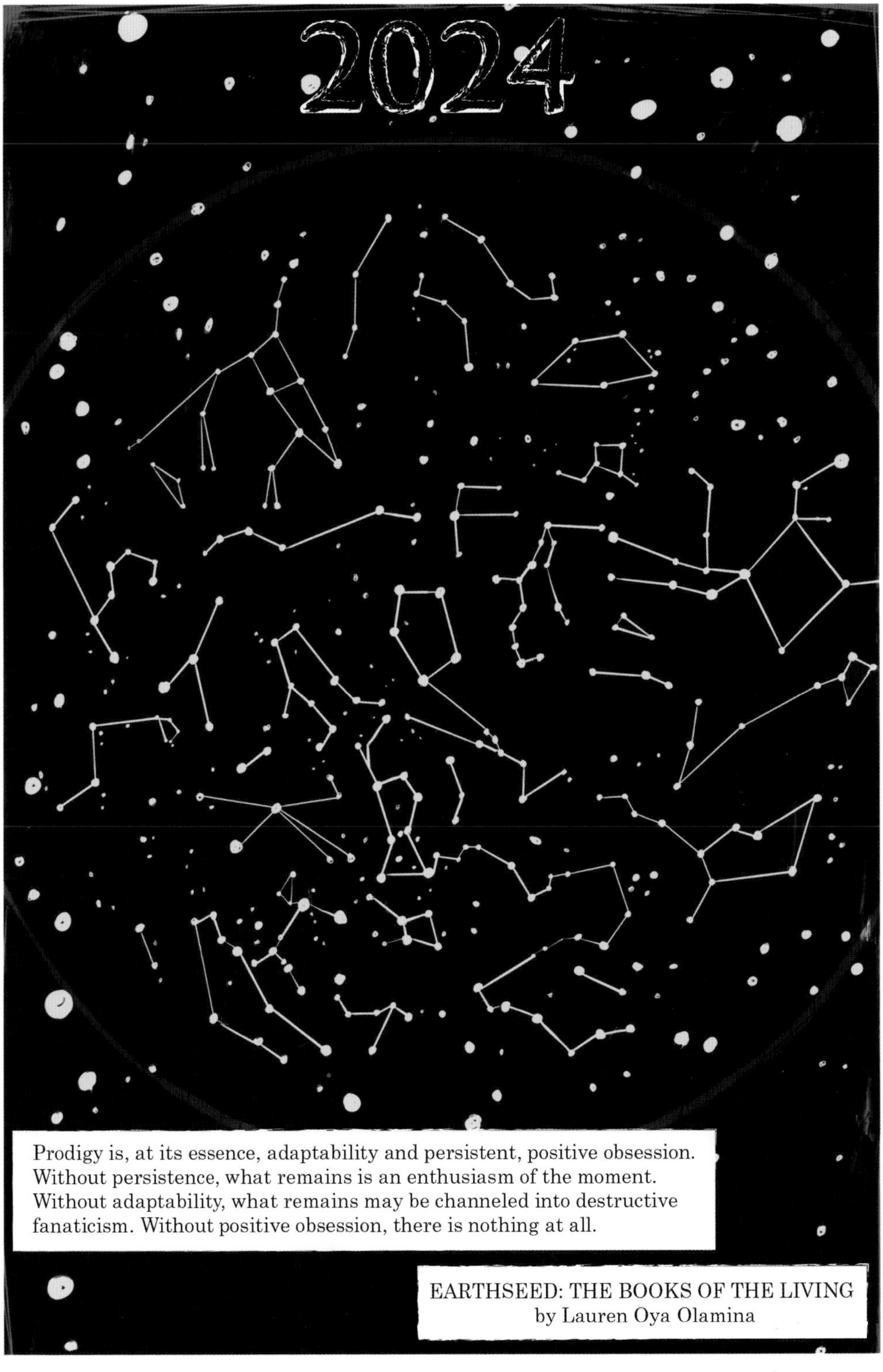
2024

Prodigy is, at its essence, adaptability and persistent, positive obsession. Without persistence, what remains is an enthusiasm of the moment. Without adaptability, what remains may be channeled into destructive fanaticism. Without positive obsession, there is nothing at all.

EARTHSEED: THE BOOKS OF THE LIVING
by Lauren Oya Olamina

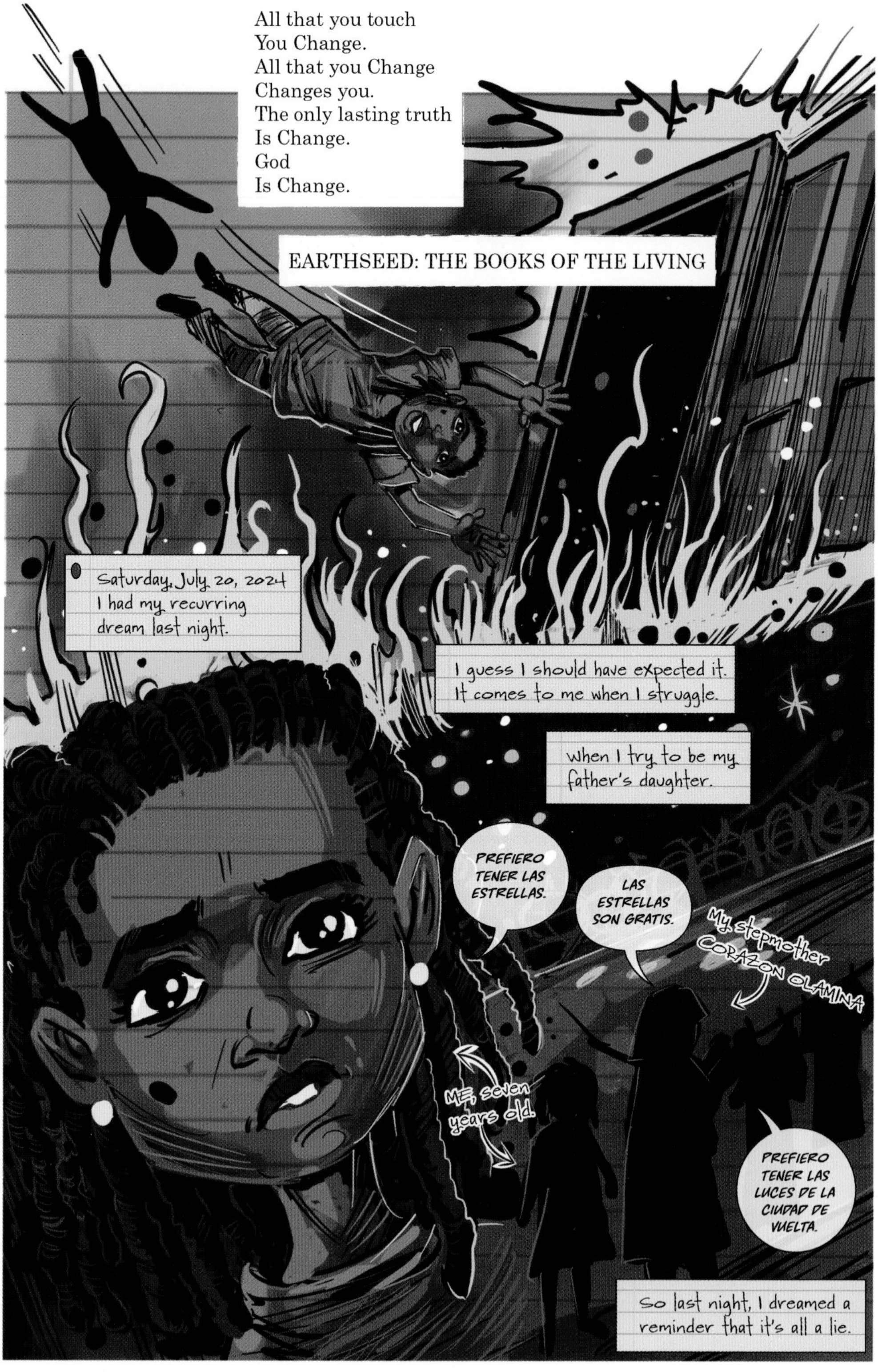
All that you touch
You Change.
All that you Change
Changes you.
The only lasting truth
Is Change.
God
Is Change.
EARTHSEED: THE BOOKS OF THE LIVING
Saturday, July 20, 2024
I had my recurring dream last night.
I guess I should have expected it. It comes to me when I struggle.
When I try to be my father's daughter.
PREFIERO TENER LAS ESTRELLAS.
LAS ESTRELLAS SON GRATIS.
My stepmother CORAZON OLAMINA
ME, seven years old.
PREFIERO TENER LAS LUCES DE LA CIUDAD DE VUELTA.
So last night, I dreamed a reminder that it's all a lie.

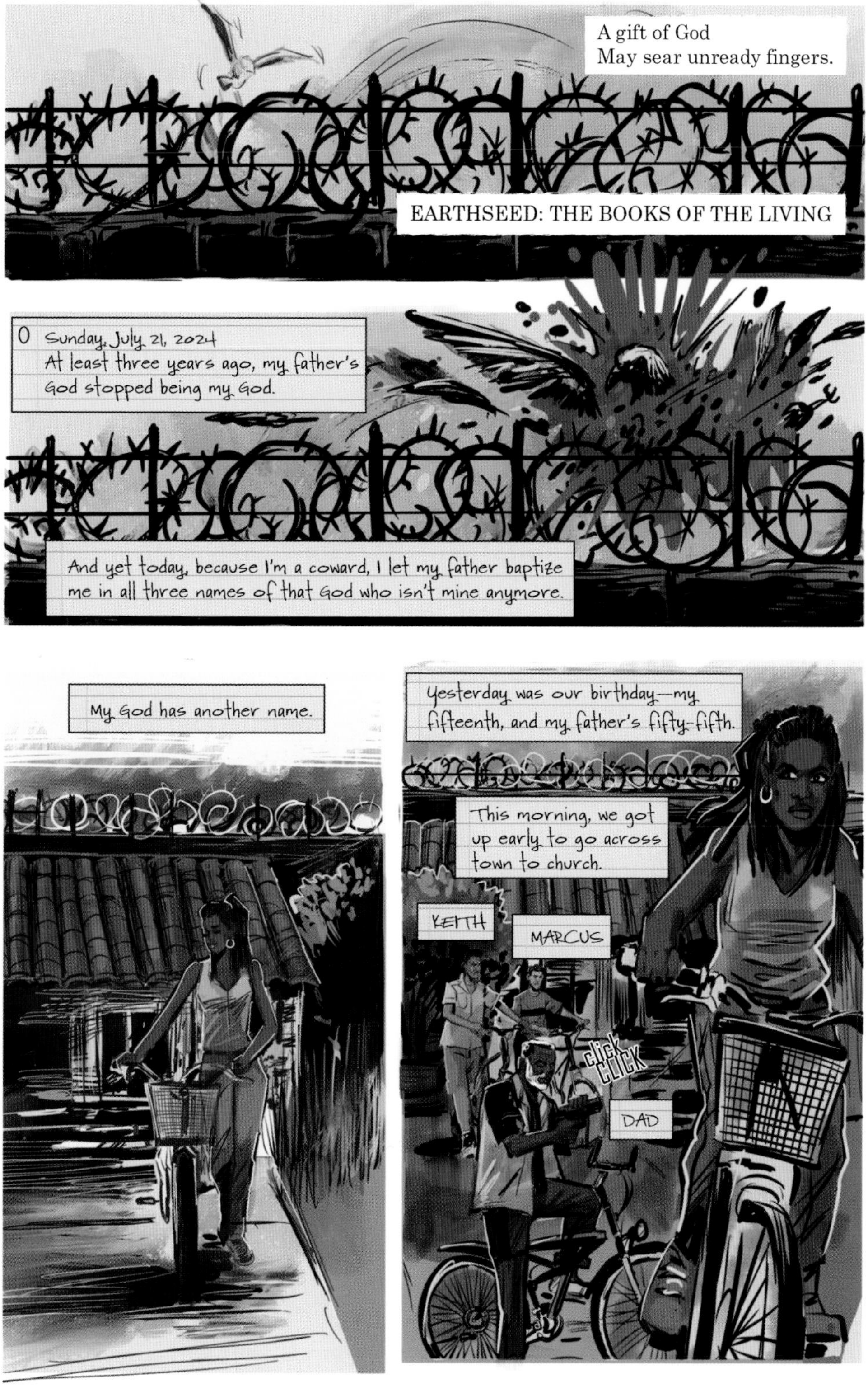
A gift of God
May sear unready fingers.
EARTHSEED: THE BOOKS OF THE LIVING
0 Sunday, July 21, 2024
At least three years ago, my father's God stopped being my God.
And yet today, because I'm a coward, I let my father baptize me in all three names of that God who isn't mine anymore.
My God has another name.
Yesterday was our birthday—my fifteenth, and my father's fifty-fifth.
This morning, we got up early to go across town to church.
KEITH
MARCUS
click CLICK
DAD

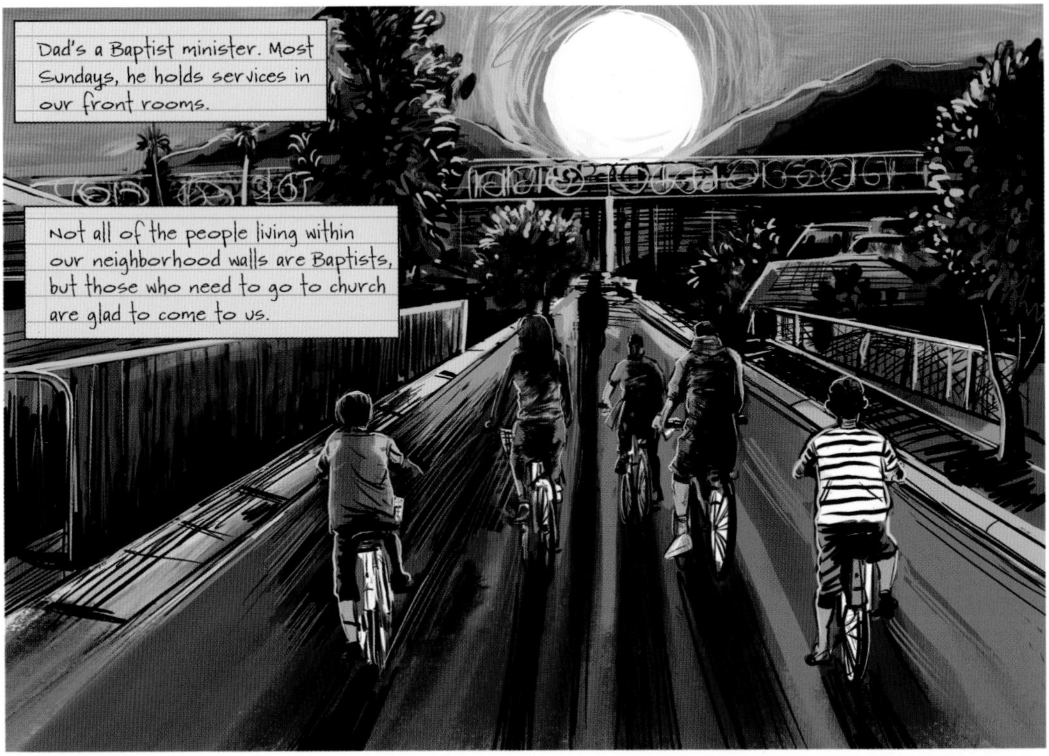
Dad's a Baptist minister. Most Sundays, he holds services in our front rooms.
Not all of the people living within our neighborhood walls are Baptists, but those who need to go to church are glad to come to us.

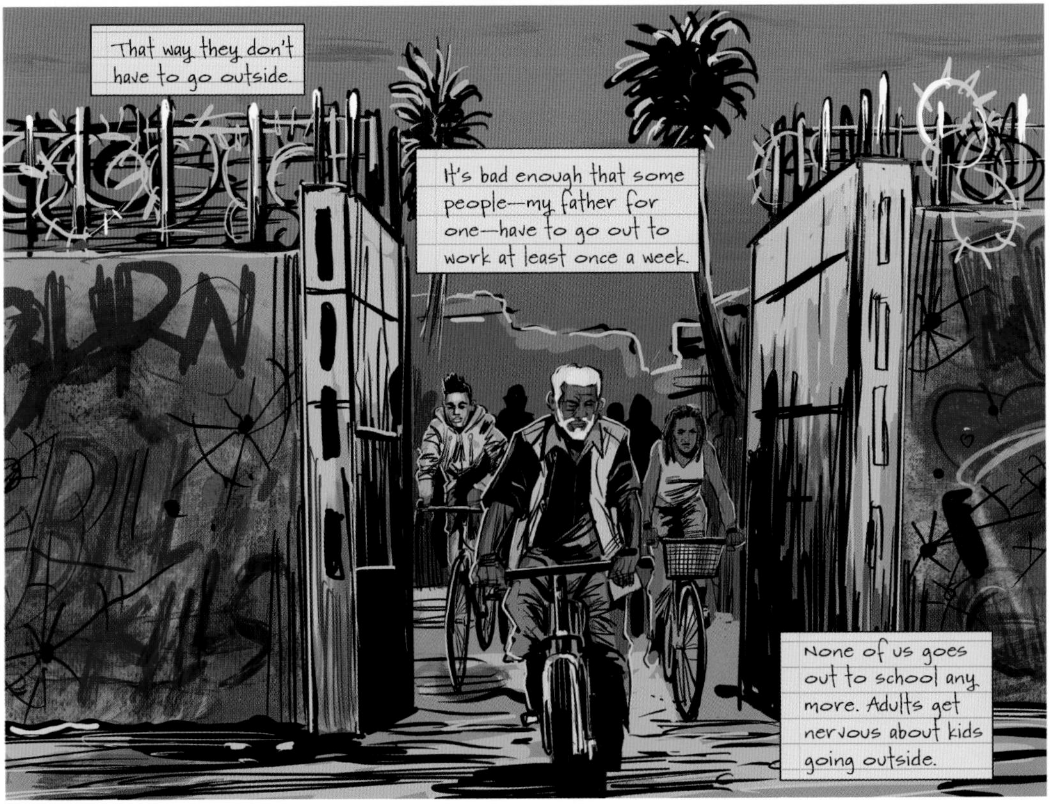
That way they don't have to go outside.
It's bad enough that some people—my father for one—have to go out to work at least once a week.
None of us goes out to school any more. Adults get nervous about kids going outside.

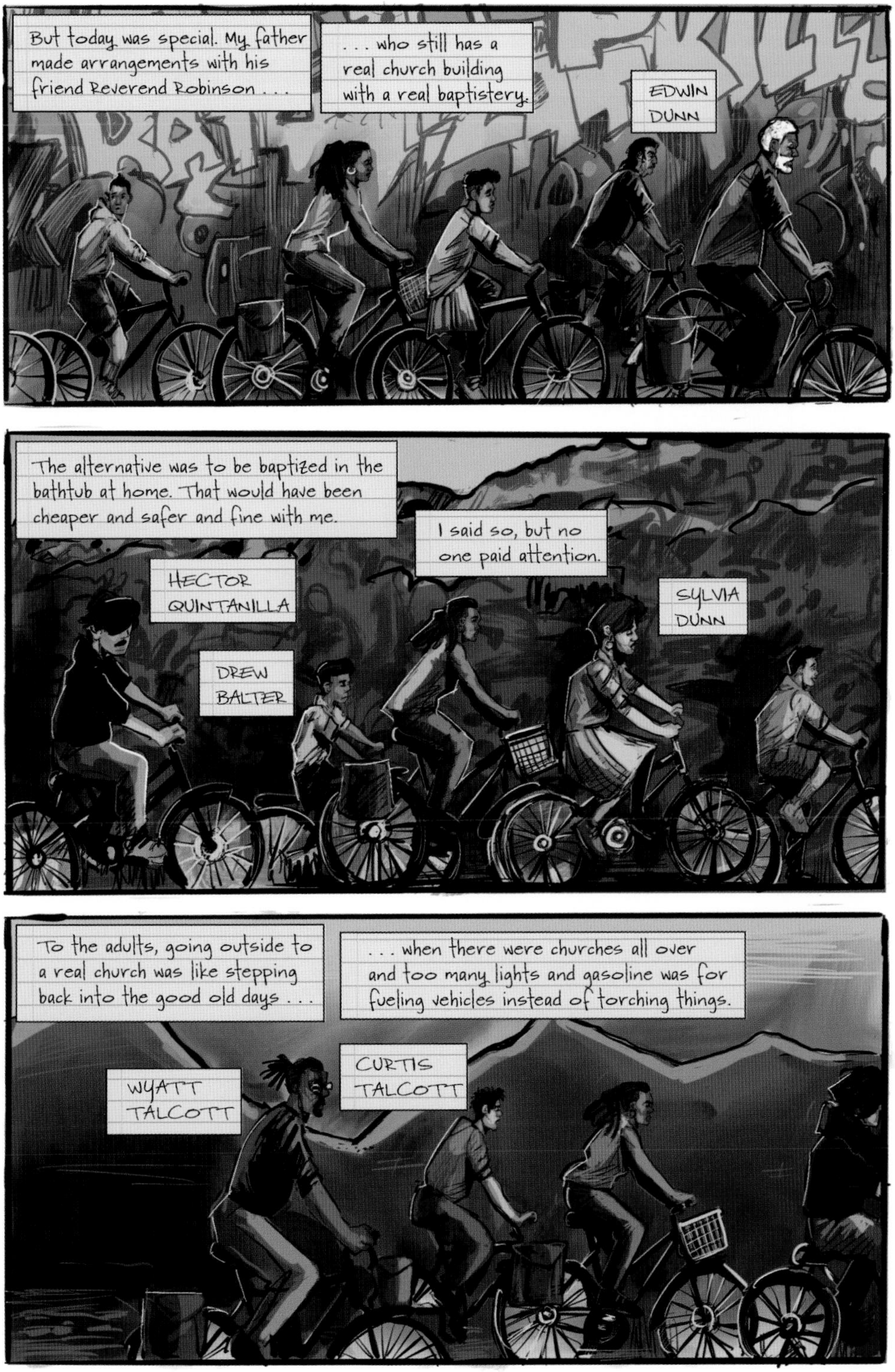

But today was special. My father made arrangements with his friend Reverend Robinson . . .
. . . who still has a real church building with a real baptistery.
EDWIN DUNN
The alternative was to be baptized in the bathtub at home. That would have been cheaper and safer and fine with me.
I said so, but no one paid attention.
HECTOR QUINTANILLA
DREW BALTER
SYLVIA DUNN
To the adults, going outside to a real church was like stepping back into the good old days . . .
. . . when there were churches all over and too many lights and gasoline was for fueling vehicles instead of torching things.
WYATT TALCOTT
CURTIS TALCOTT

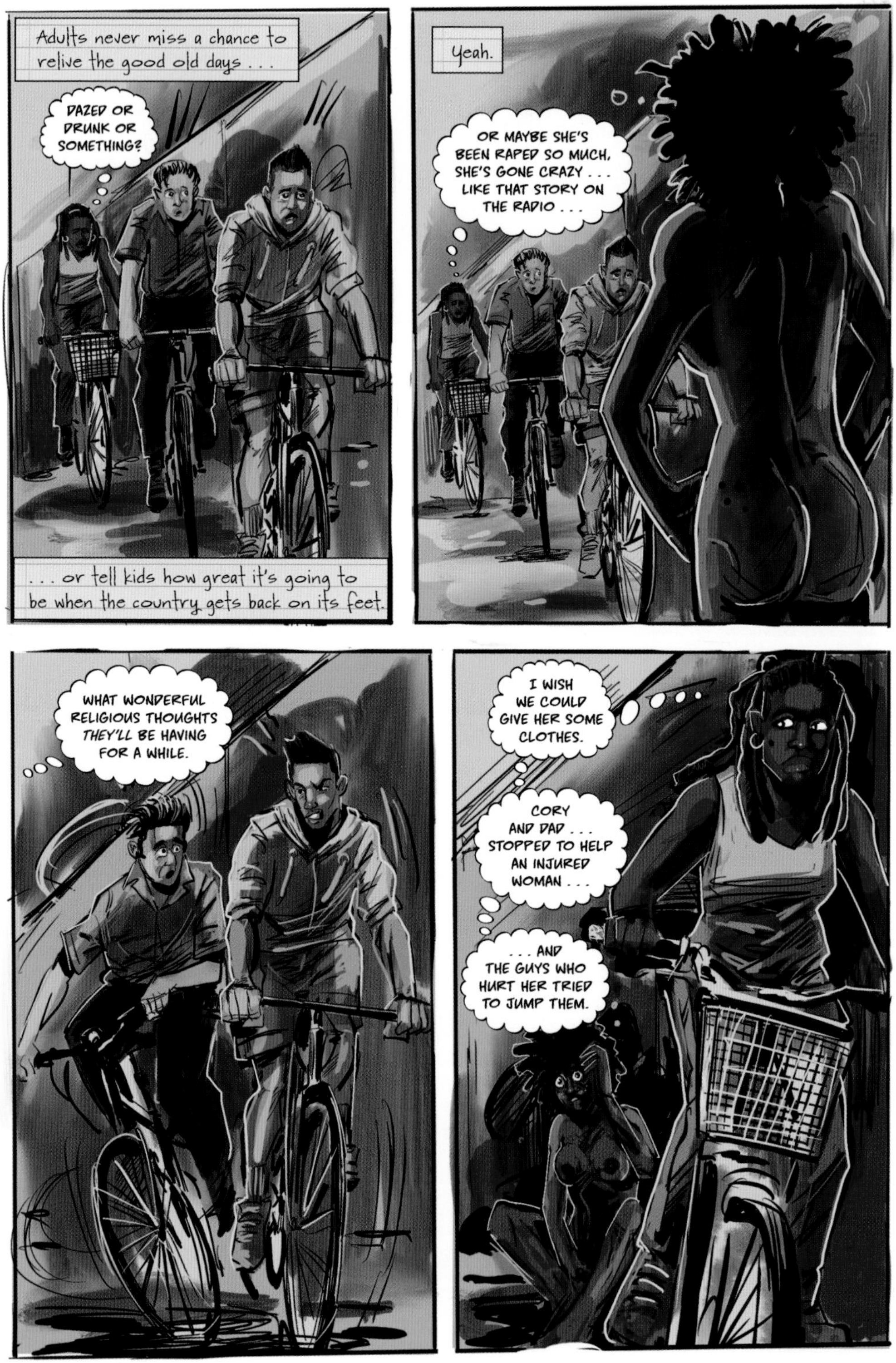
Adults never miss a chance to relive the good old days . . .
DAZED OR DRUNK OR SOMETHING?
. . . or tell kids how great it's going to be when the country gets back on its feet.
Yeah.
OR MAYBE SHE'S BEEN RAPED SO MUCH, SHE'S GONE CRAZY . . . LIKE THAT STORY ON THE RADIO . . .
WHAT WONDERFUL RELIGIOUS THOUGHTS THEY'LL BE HAVING FOR A WHILE.
I WISH WE COULD GIVE HER SOME CLOTHES.
CORY AND DAD . . . STOPPED TO HELP AN INJURED WOMAN . . .
. . . AND THE GUYS WHO HURT HER TRIED TO JUMP THEM.

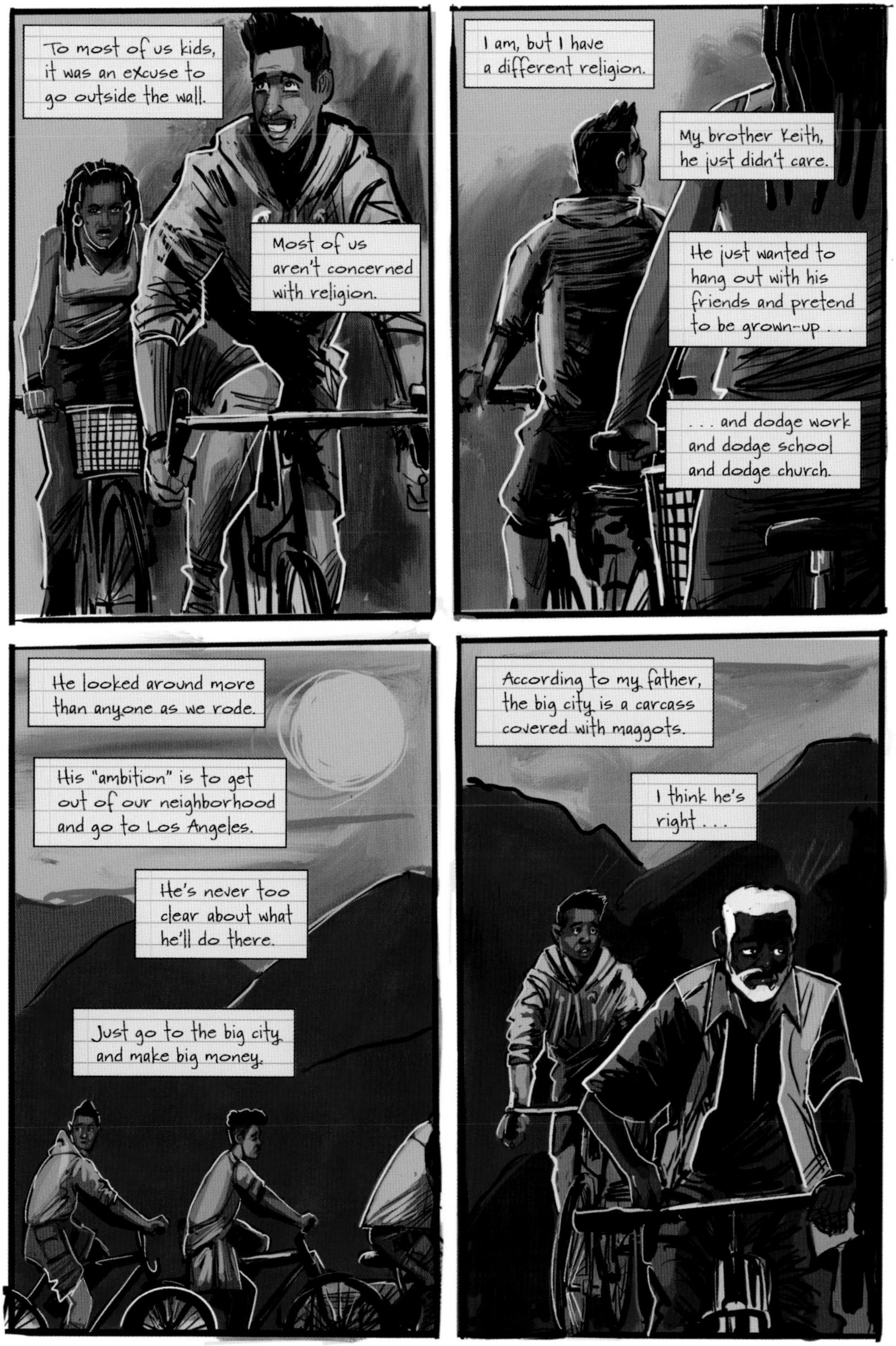
To most of us kids, it was an excuse to go outside the wall.
Most of us aren't concerned with religion.
I am, but I have a different religion.
My brother Keith, he just didn't care.
He just wanted to hang out with his friends and pretend to be grown-up . . .
. . . and dodge work and dodge school and dodge church.
He looked around more than anyone as we rode.
His "ambition" is to get out of our neighborhood and go to Los Angeles.
He's never too clear about what he'll do there.
Just go to the big city and make big money.
According to my father, the big city is a carcass covered with maggots.
I think he's right . . .

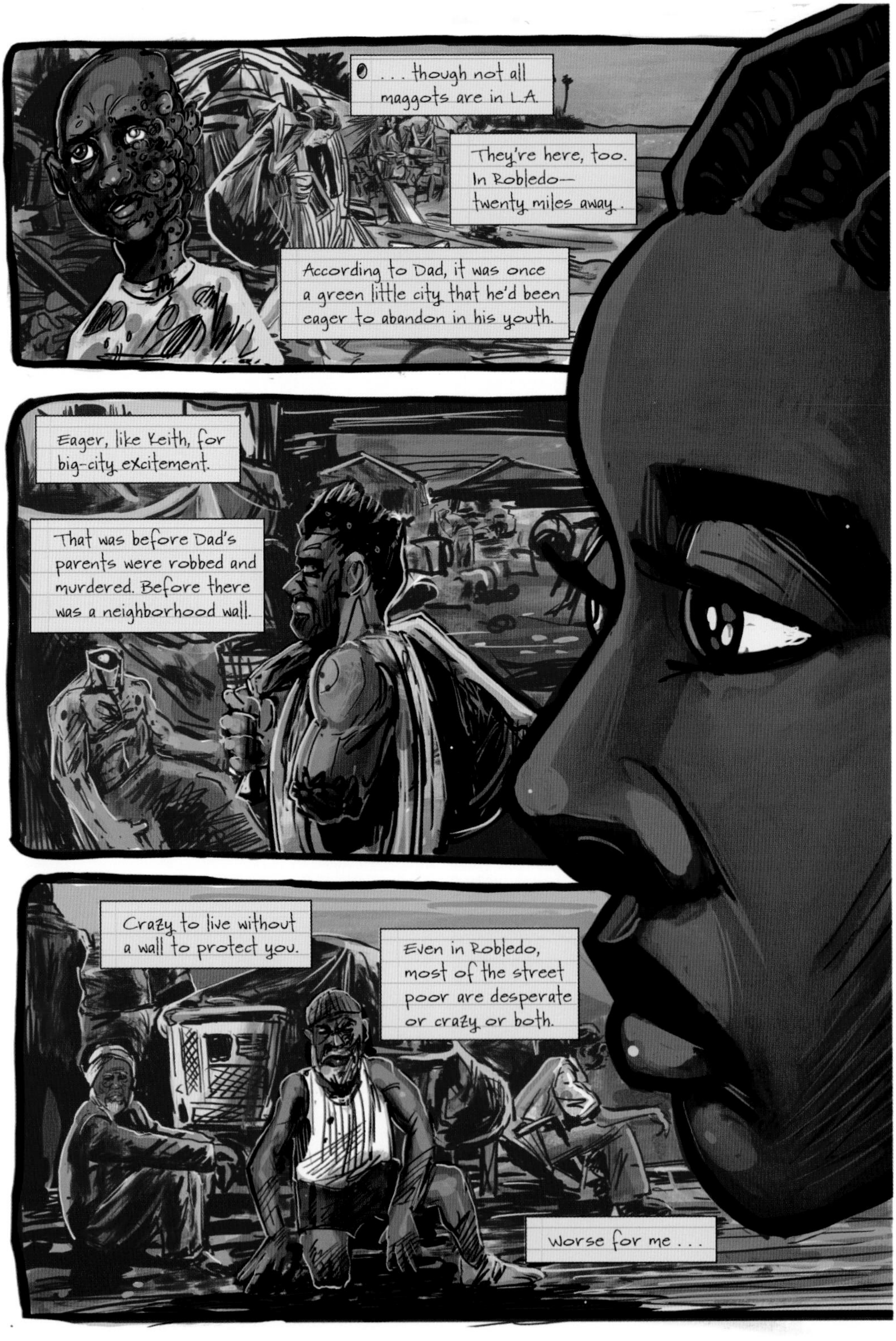
. . . though not all maggots are in L.A.
They're here, too. In Robledo— twenty miles away.
According to Dad, it was once a green little city that he'd been eager to abandon in his youth.
Eager, like Keith, for big-city excitement.
That was before Dad's parents were robbed and murdered. Before there was a neighborhood wall.
Crazy to live without a wall to protect you.
Even in Robledo, most of the street poor are desperate or crazy or both.
Worse for me . . .

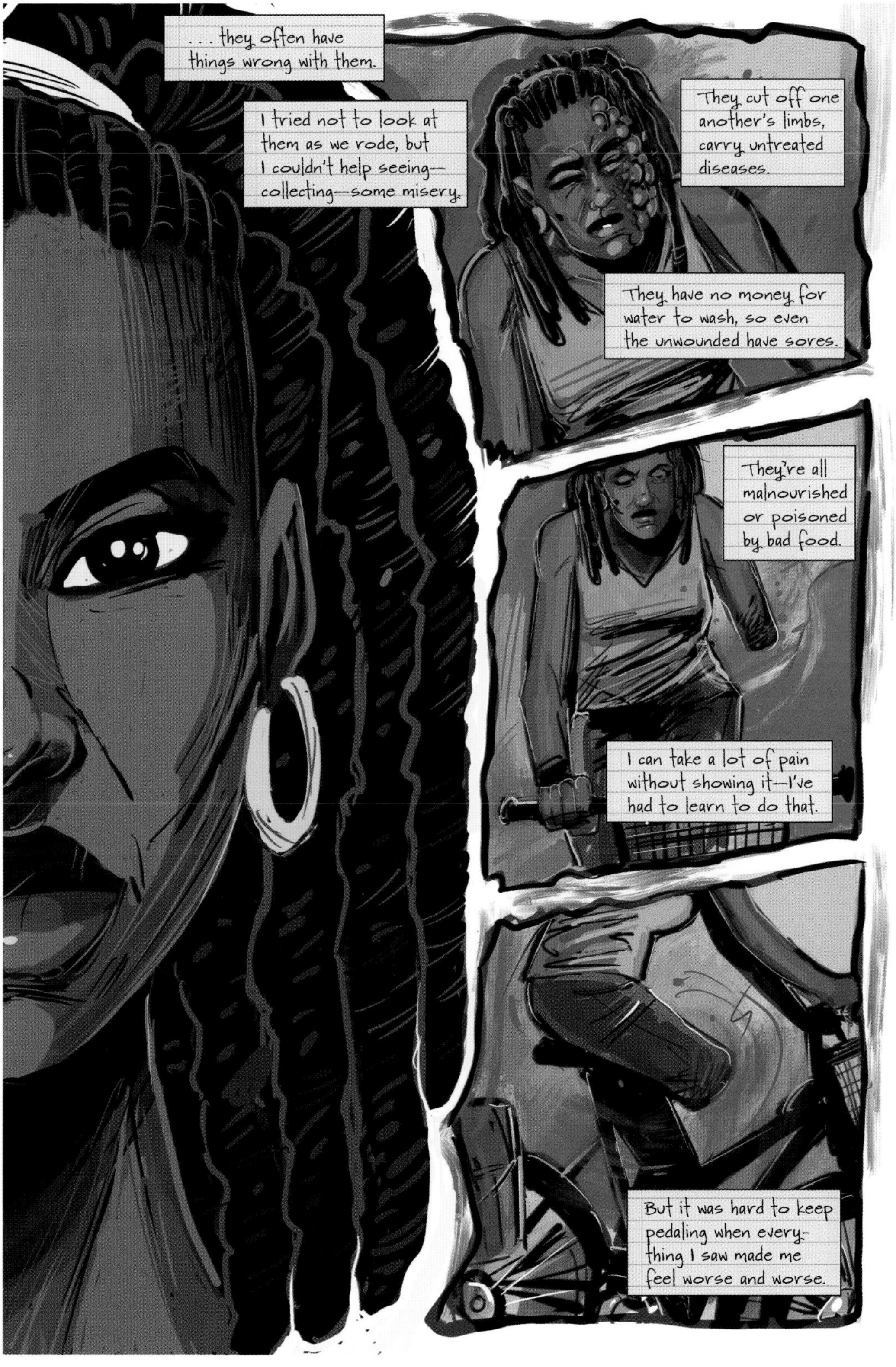
. . . they often have things wrong with them.
I tried not to look at them as we rode, but I couldn't help seeing—collecting—some misery.
They cut off one another's limbs, carry untreated diseases.
They have no money for water to wash, so even the unwounded have sores.
They're all malnourished or poisoned by bad food.
I can take a lot of pain without showing it—I've had to learn to do that.
But it was hard to keep pedaling when every-thing I saw made me feel worse and worse.

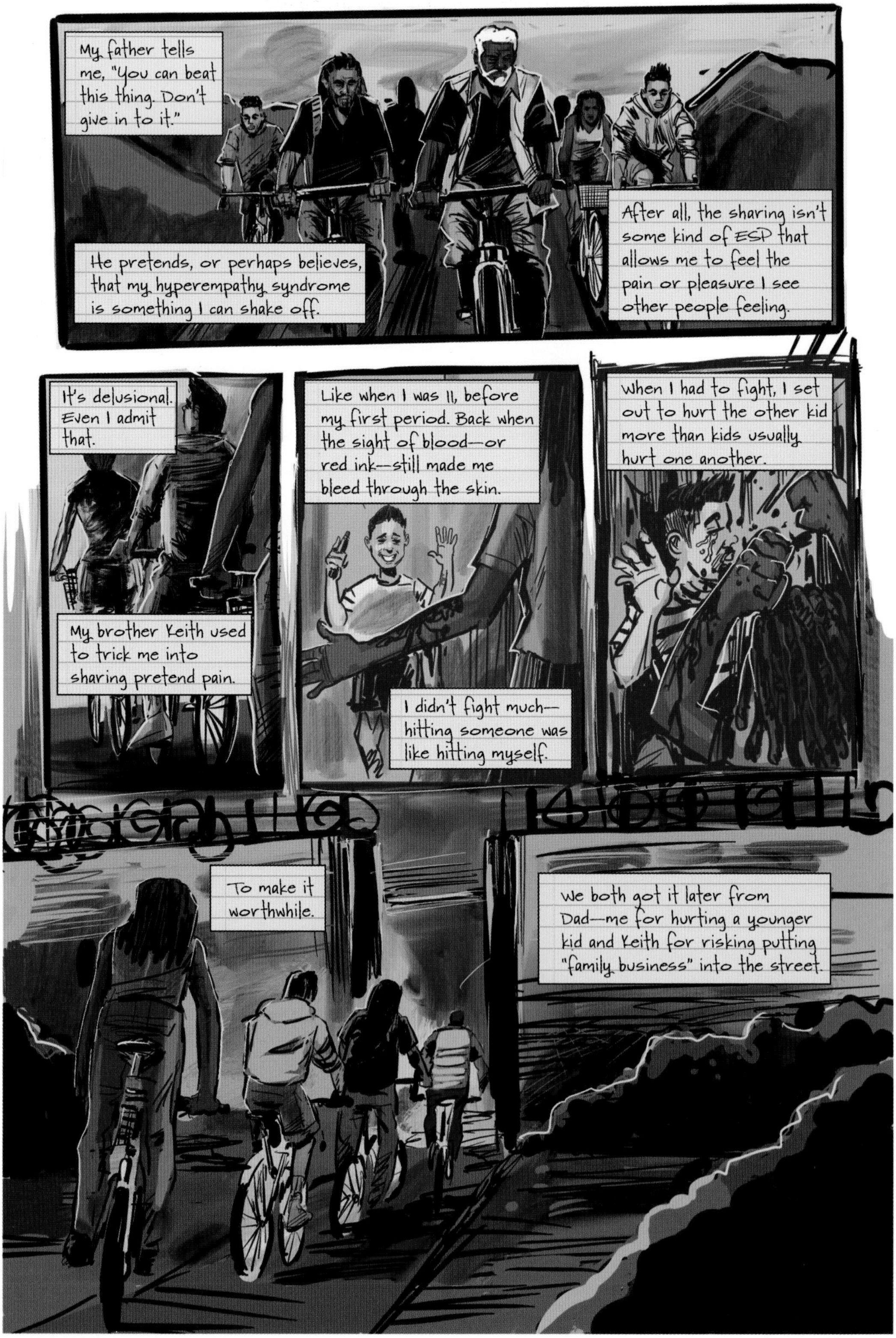
My father tells me, "You can beat this thing. Don't give in to it."
He pretends, or perhaps believes, that my hyperempathy syndrome is something I can shake off.
After all, the sharing isn't some kind of ESP that allows me to feel the pain or pleasure I see other people feeling.
It's delusional. Even I admit that.
My brother Keith used to trick me into sharing pretend pain.
Like when I was 11, before my first period. Back when the sight of blood—or red ink—still made me bleed through the skin.
I didn't fight much—hitting someone was like hitting myself.
When I had to fight, I set out to hurt the other kid more than kids usually hurt one another.
To make it worthwhile.
We both got it later from Dad—me for hurting a younger kid and Keith for risking putting "family business" into the street.

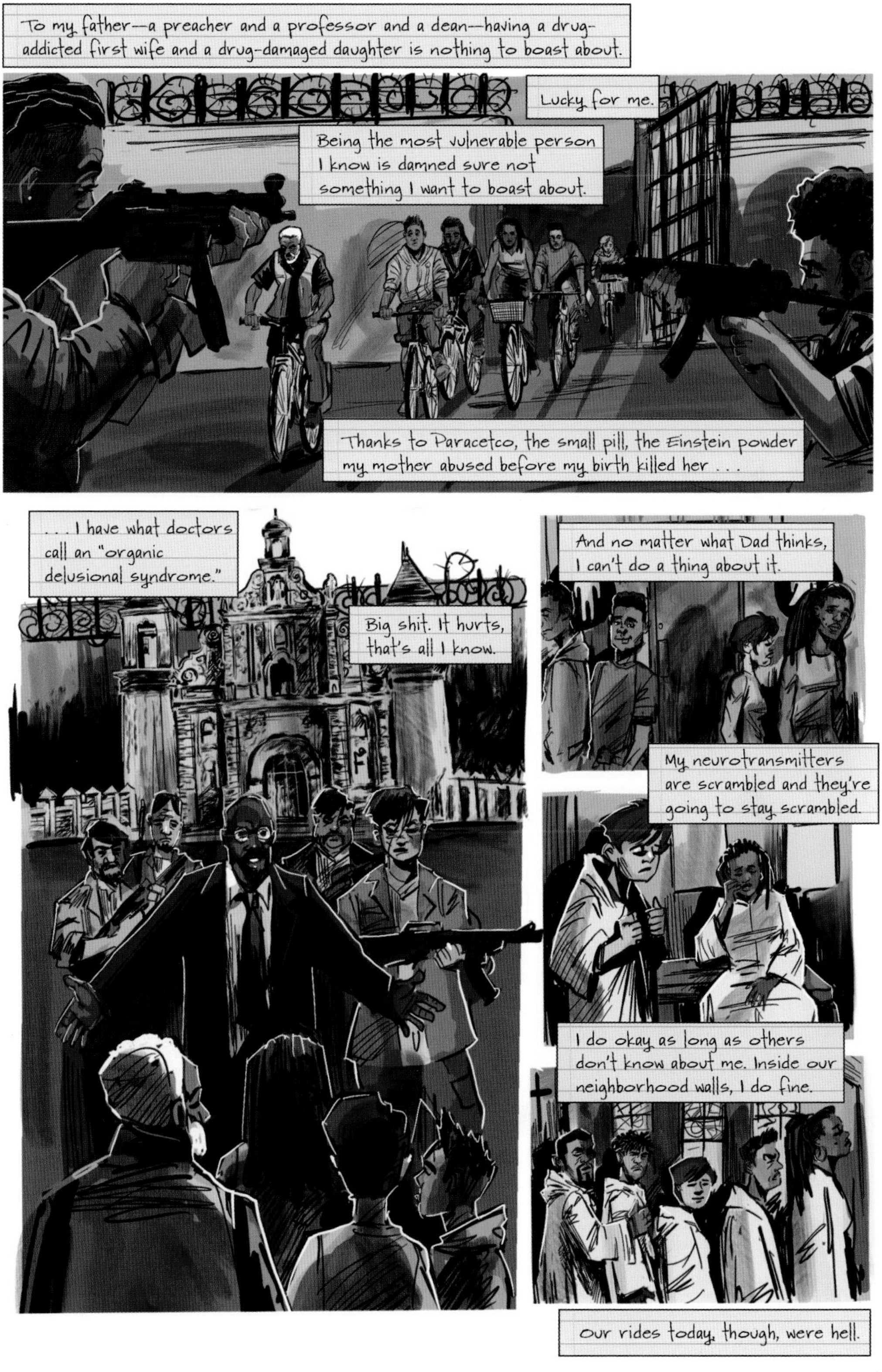
To my father—a preacher and a professor and a dean—having a drug-addicted first wife and a drug-damaged daughter is nothing to boast about.
Lucky for me.
Being the most vulnerable person I know is damned sure not something I want to boast about.
Thanks to Paracetco, the small pill, the Einstein powder my mother abused before my birth killed her . . .
. . . I have what doctors call an "organic delusional syndrome."
Big shit. It hurts, that's all I know.
And no matter what Dad thinks, I can't do a thing about it.
My neurotransmitters are scrambled and they're going to stay scrambled.
I do okay as long as others don't know about me. Inside our neighborhood walls, I do fine.
Our rides today, though, were hell.

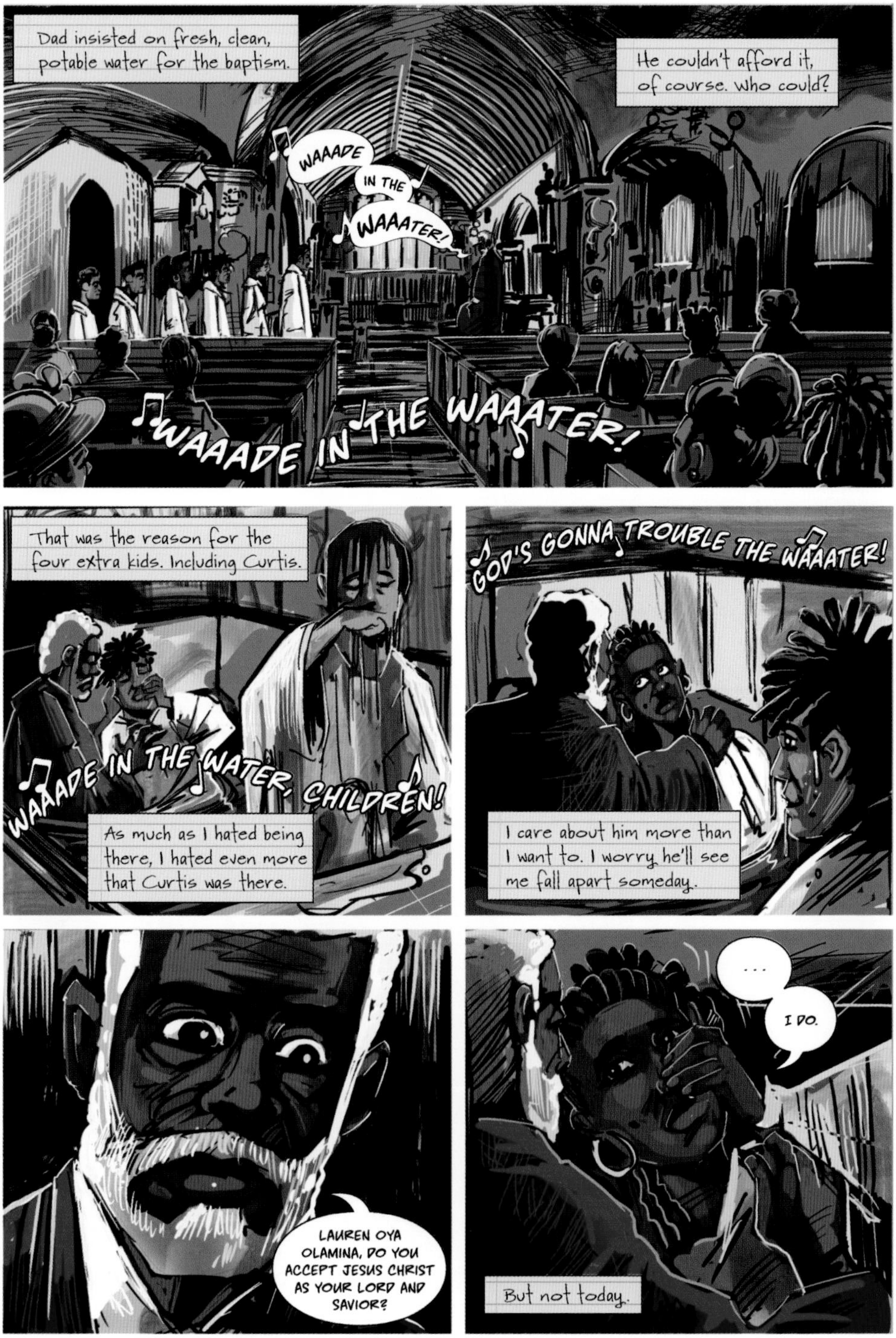
Dad insisted on fresh, clean, potable water for the baptism.
He couldn't afford it, of course. who could?
WAAADE IN THE WAAATER!
WAAADE IN THE WAAATER!
That was the reason for the four extra kids. Including Curtis.
WAAADE IN THE WATER, CHILDREN!
As much as I hated being there, I hated even more that Curtis was there.
GOD'S GONNA TROUBLE THE WAAATER!
I care about him more than I want to. I worry he'll see me fall apart someday.
LAUREN OYA OLAMINA, DO YOU ACCEPT JESUS CHRIST AS YOUR LORD AND SAVIOR?
. . .
I DO.
But not today.

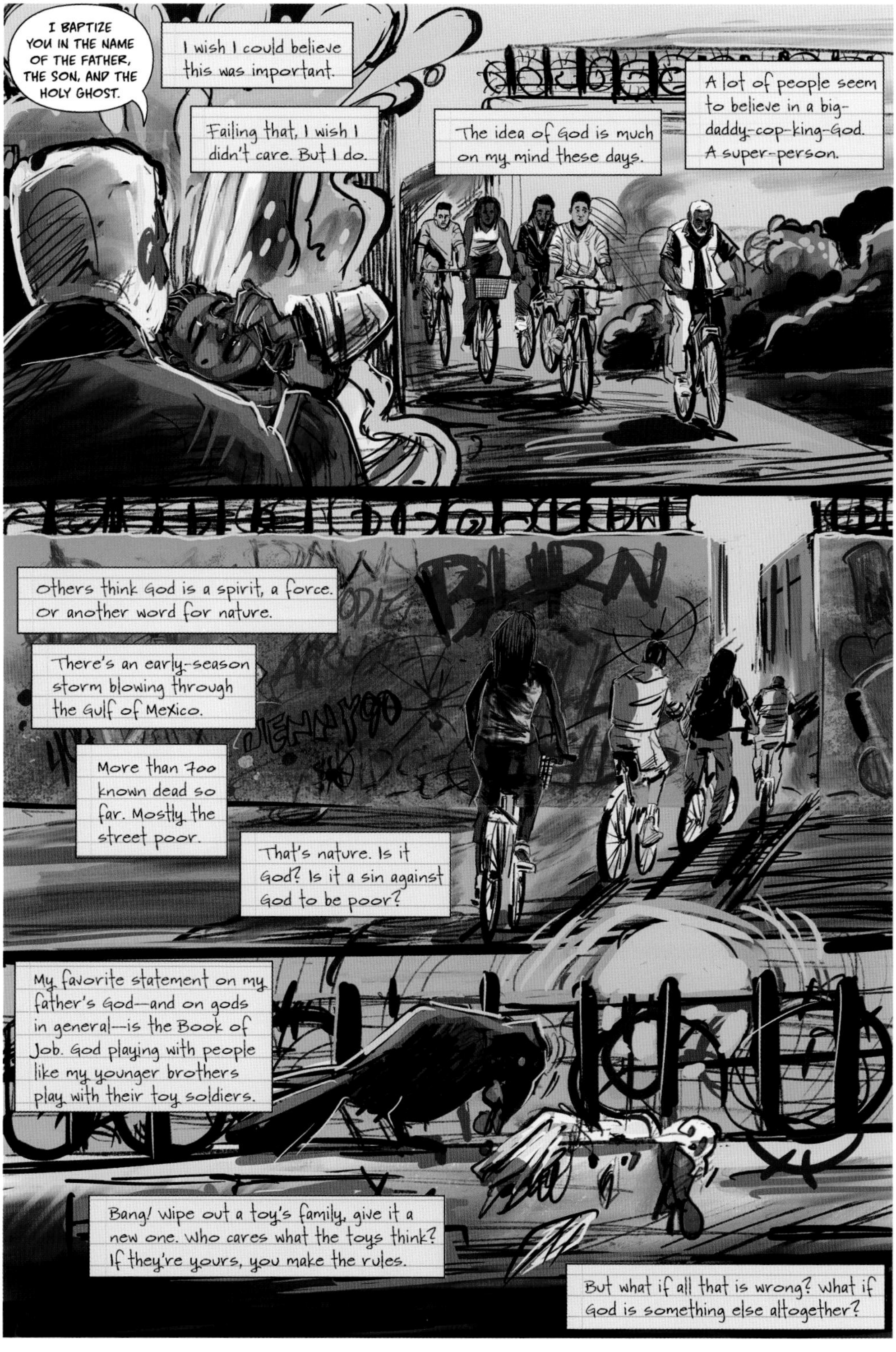
I BAPTIZE YOU IN THE NAME OF THE FATHER, THE SON, AND THE HOLY GHOST.
I wish I could believe this was important.
Failing that, I wish I didn't care. But I do.
The idea of God is much on my mind these days.
A lot of people seem to believe in a big-daddy-cop-king-God. A super-person.
BURN
Others think God is a spirit, a force. Or another word for nature.
There's an early-season storm blowing through the Gulf of Mexico.
More than 700 known dead so far. Mostly the street poor.
That's nature. Is it God? Is it a sin against God to be poor?
My favorite statement on my father's God—and on gods in general—is the Book of Job. God playing with people like my younger brothers play with their toy soldiers.
Bang! Wipe out a toy's family, give it a new one. Who cares what the toys think? If they're yours, you make the rules.
But what if all that is wrong? What if God is something else altogether?

We do not worship God.
We perceive and attend God.
We learn from God.
With forethought and work,
We shape God.
In the end, we yield to God.
We adapt and endure,
For we are Earthseed
And God is Change.

EARTHSEED: THE BOOKS OF THE LIVING

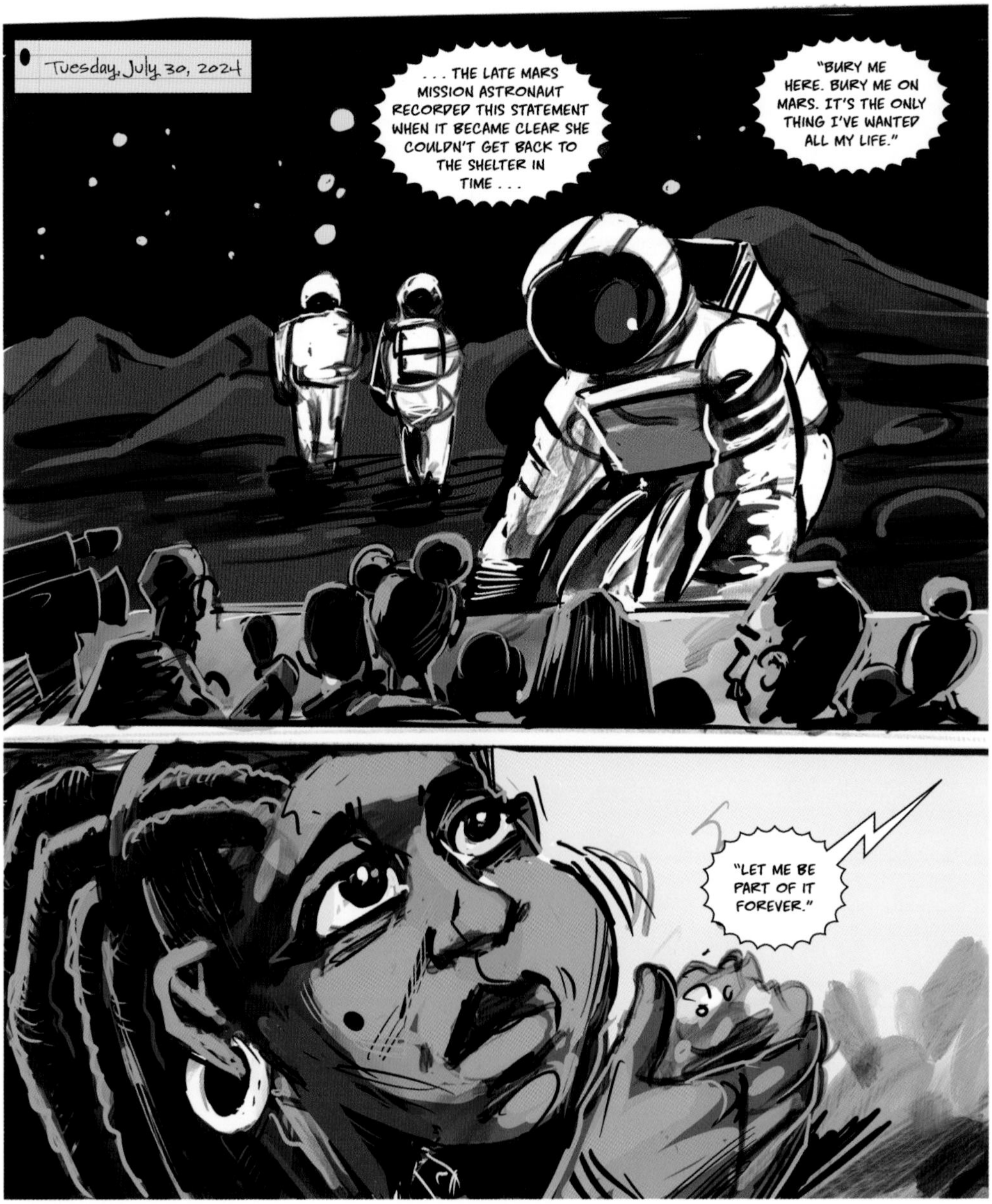
Tuesday, July 30, 2024
. . . THE LATE MARS MISSION ASTRONAUT RECORDED THIS STATEMENT WHEN IT BECAME CLEAR SHE COULDN'T GET BACK TO THE SHELTER IN TIME . . .
"BURY ME HERE. BURY ME ON MARS. IT'S THE ONLY THING I'VE WANTED ALL MY LIFE."
"LET ME BE PART OF IT FOREVER."

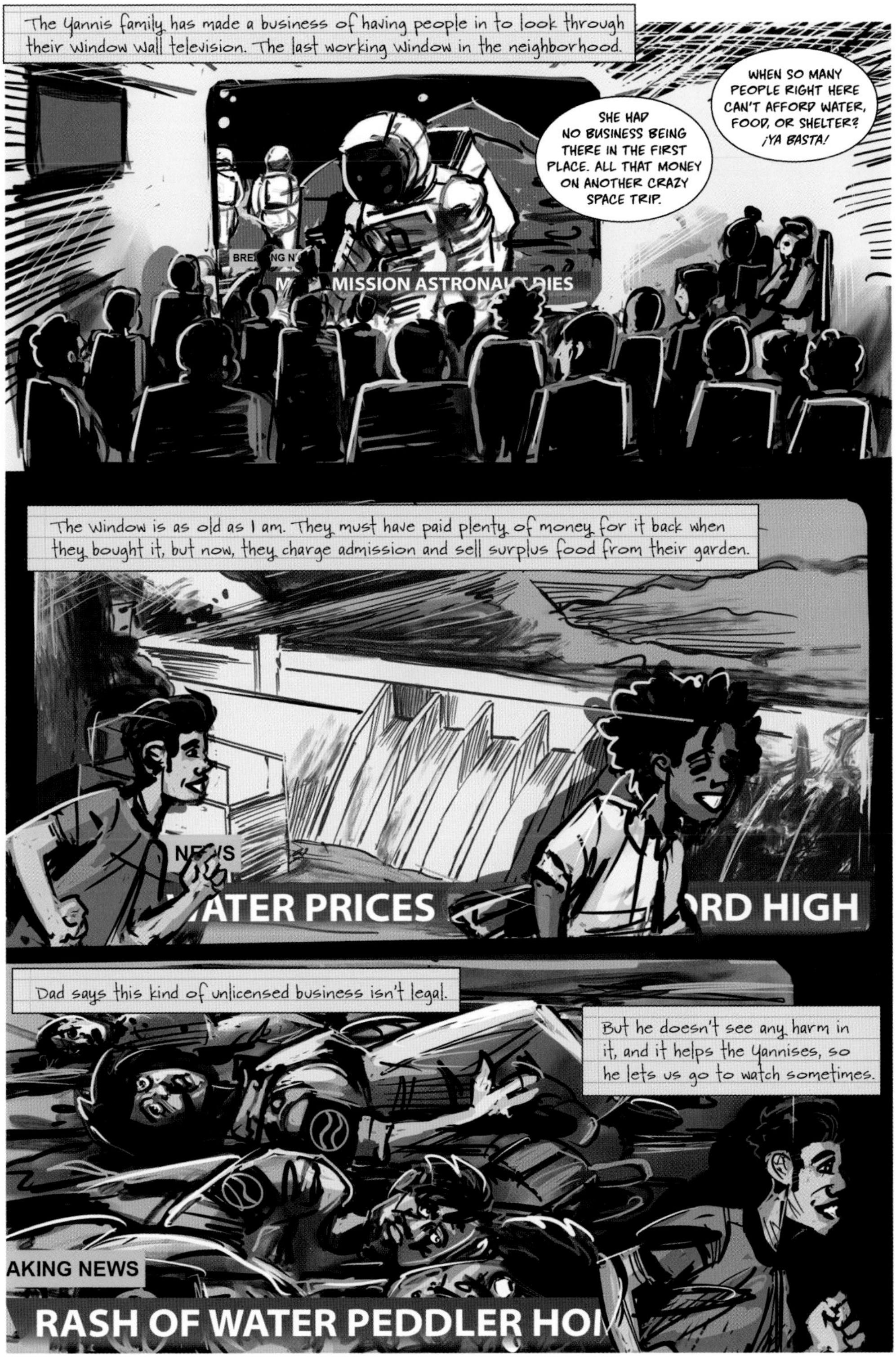
The Yannis family has made a business of having people in to look through their window wall television. The last working window in the neighborhood.
MISSION ASTRONA
DIES
SHE HAD NO BUSINESS BEING THERE IN THE FIRST PLACE. ALL THAT MONEY ON ANOTHER CRAZY SPACE TRIP.
WHEN SO MANY PEOPLE RIGHT HERE CAN'T AFFORD WATER, FOOD, OR SHELTER? ¡YA BASTA!
The window is as old as I am. They must have paid plenty of money for it back when they bought it, but now, they charge admission and sell surplus food from their garden.
NEWS
ATER PRICES
RD HIGH
Dad says this kind of unlicensed business isn't legal.
But he doesn't see any harm in it, and it helps the Yannises, so he lets us go to watch sometimes.
AKING NEWS
RASH OF WATER PEDDLER HO

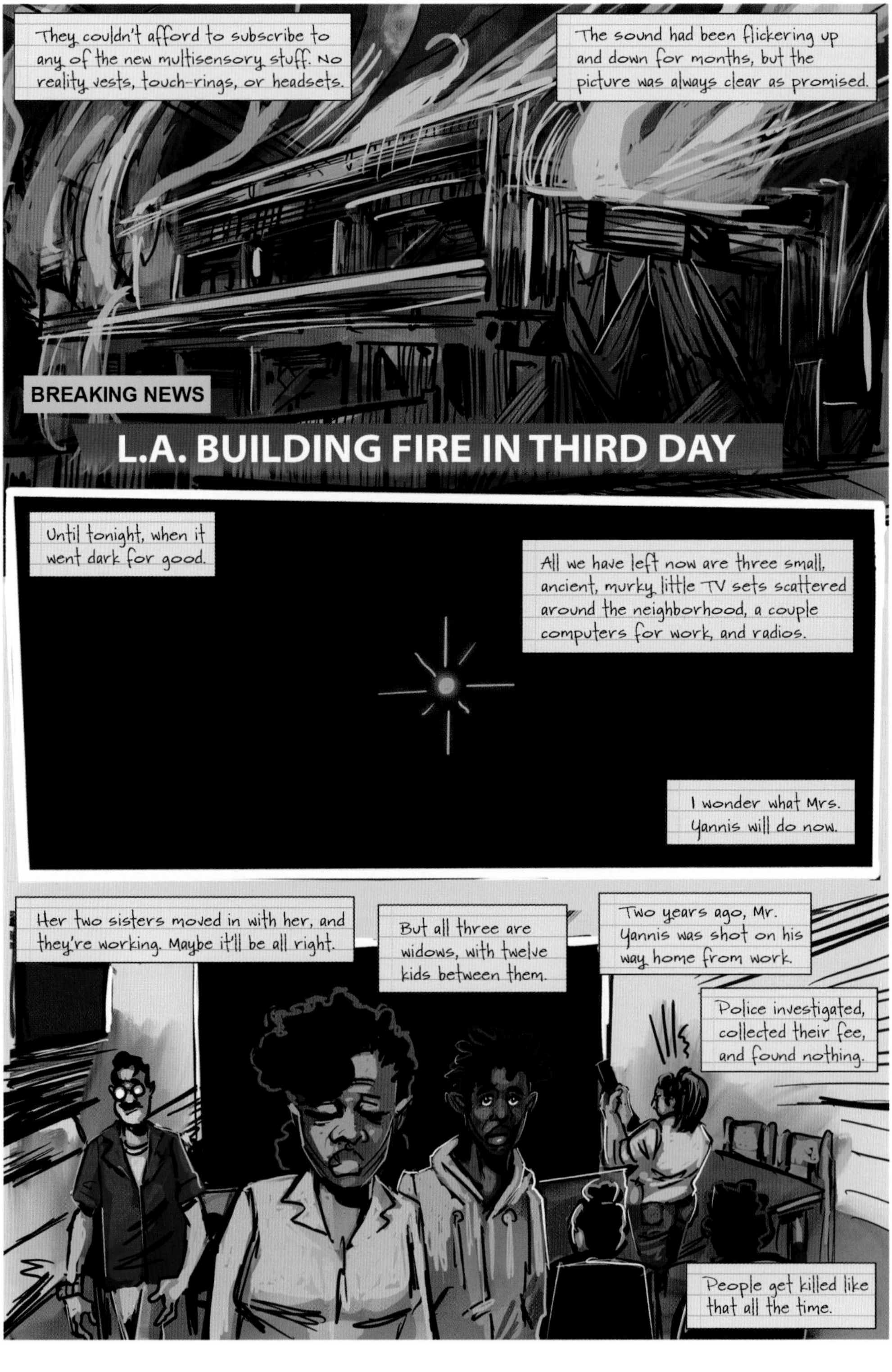
They couldn't afford to subscribe to any of the new multisensory stuff. No reality vests, touch-rings, or headsets.
The sound had been flickering up and down for months, but the picture was always clear as promised.
BREAKING NEWS
L.A. BUILDING FIRE IN THIRD DAY
Until tonight, when it went dark for good.
All we have left now are three small, ancient, murky little TV sets scattered around the neighborhood, a couple computers for work, and radios.
I wonder what Mrs. Yannis will do now.
Her two sisters moved in with her, and they're working. Maybe it'll be all right.
But all three are widows, with twelve kids between them.
Two years ago, Mr. Yannis was shot on his way home from work.
Police investigated, collected their fee, and found nothing.
People get killed like that all the time.

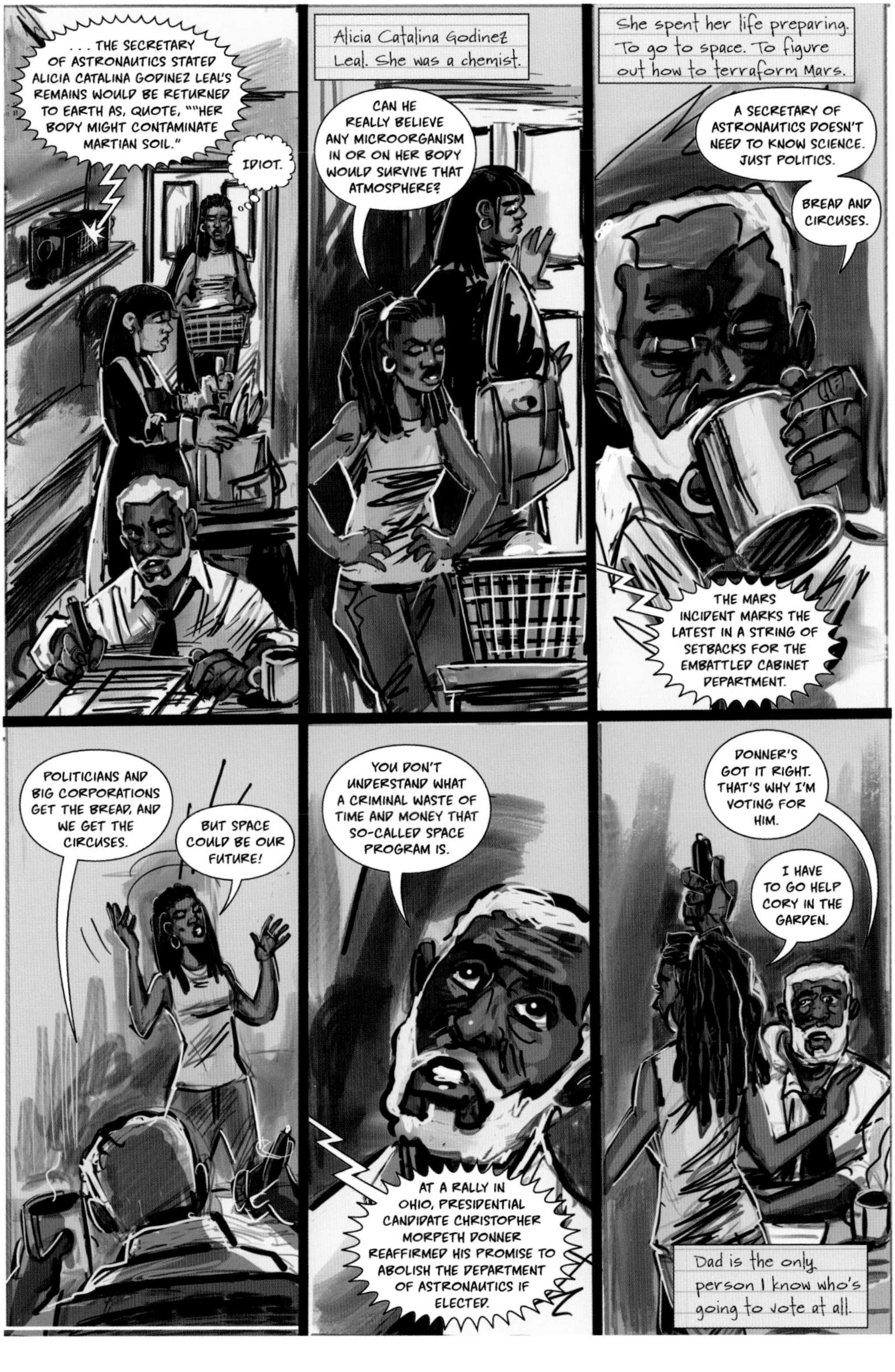
. . . THE SECRETARY OF ASTRONAUTICS STATED ALICIA CATALINA GODINEZ LEAL'S REMAINS WOULD BE RETURNED TO EARTH AS, QUOTE, ""HER BODY MIGHT CONTAMINATE MARTIAN SOIL."
IDIOT.
Alicia Catalina Godinez Leal. She was a chemist.
CAN HE REALLY BELIEVE ANY MICROORGANISM IN OR ON HER BODY WOULD SURVIVE THAT ATMOSPHERE?
She spent her life preparing. To go to space. To figure out how to terraform Mars.
A SECRETARY OF ASTRONAUTICS DOESN'T NEED TO KNOW SCIENCE. JUST POLITICS.
BREAD AND CIRCUSES.
THE MARS INCIDENT MARKS THE LATEST IN A STRING OF SETBACKS FOR THE EMBATTLED CABINET DEPARTMENT.
POLITICIANS AND BIG CORPORATIONS GET THE BREAD, AND WE GET THE CIRCUSES.
BUT SPACE COULD BE OUR FUTURE!
YOU DON'T UNDERSTAND WHAT A CRIMINAL WASTE OF TIME AND MONEY THAT SO-CALLED SPACE PROGRAM IS.
AT A RALLY IN OHIO, PRESIDENTIAL CANDIDATE CHRISTOPHER MORPETH DONNER REAFFIRMED HIS PROMISE TO ABOLISH THE DEPARTMENT OF ASTRONAUTICS IF ELECTED.
DONNER'S GOT IT RIGHT. THAT'S WHY I'M VOTING FOR HIM.
I HAVE TO GO HELP CORY IN THE GARDEN.
Dad is the only person I know who's going to vote at all.

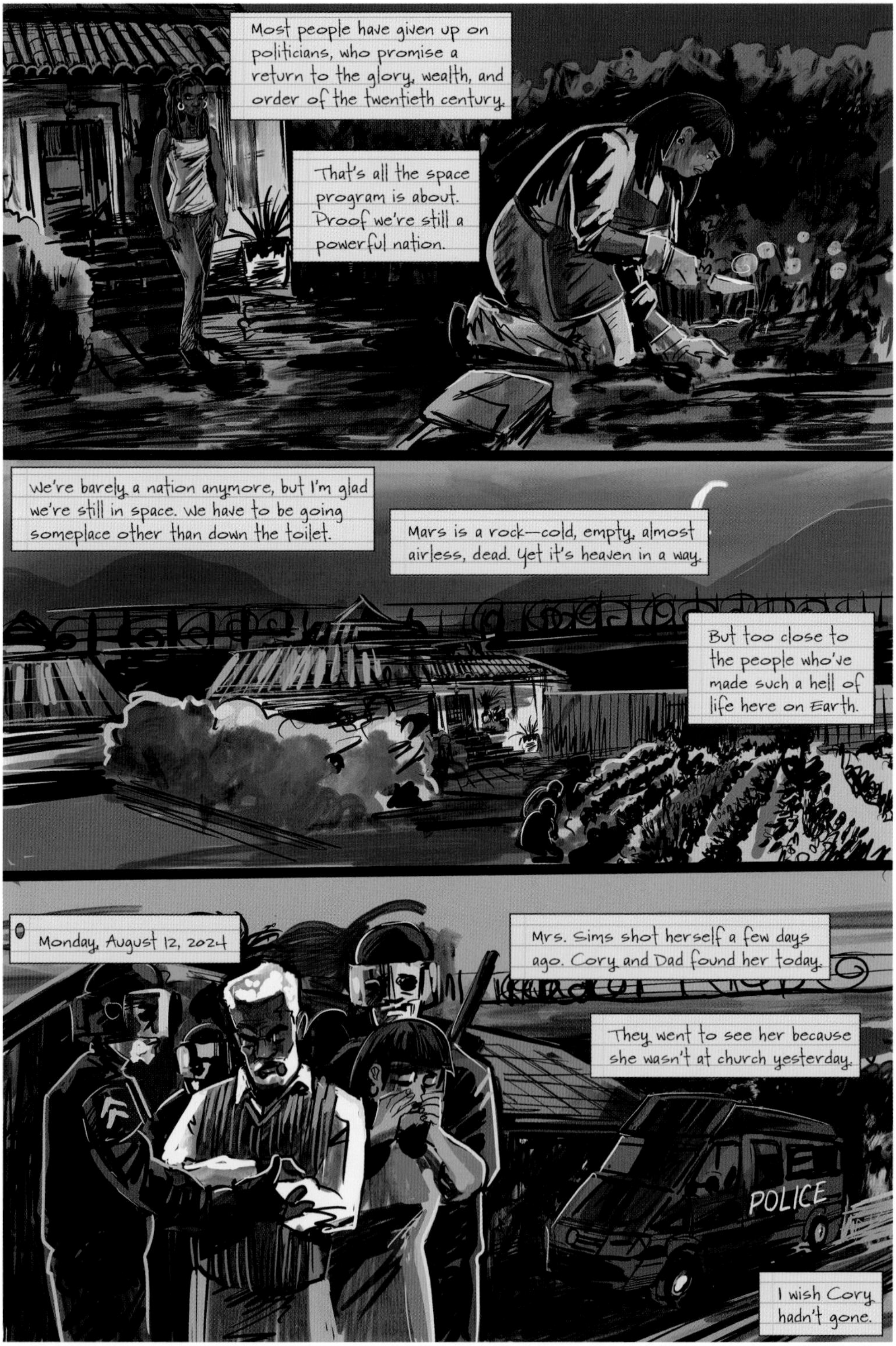
Most people have given up on politicians, who promise a return to the glory, wealth, and order of the twentieth century.
That's all the space program is about. Proof we're still a powerful nation.
We're barely a nation anymore, but I'm glad we're still in space. We have to be going someplace other than down the toilet.
Mars is a rock—cold, empty, almost airless, dead. Yet it's heaven in a way.
But too close to the people who've made such a hell of life here on Earth.
Monday, August 12, 2024
Mrs. Sims shot herself a few days ago. Cory and Dad found her today.
They went to see her because she wasn't at church yesterday.
POLICE
I wish Cory hadn't gone.

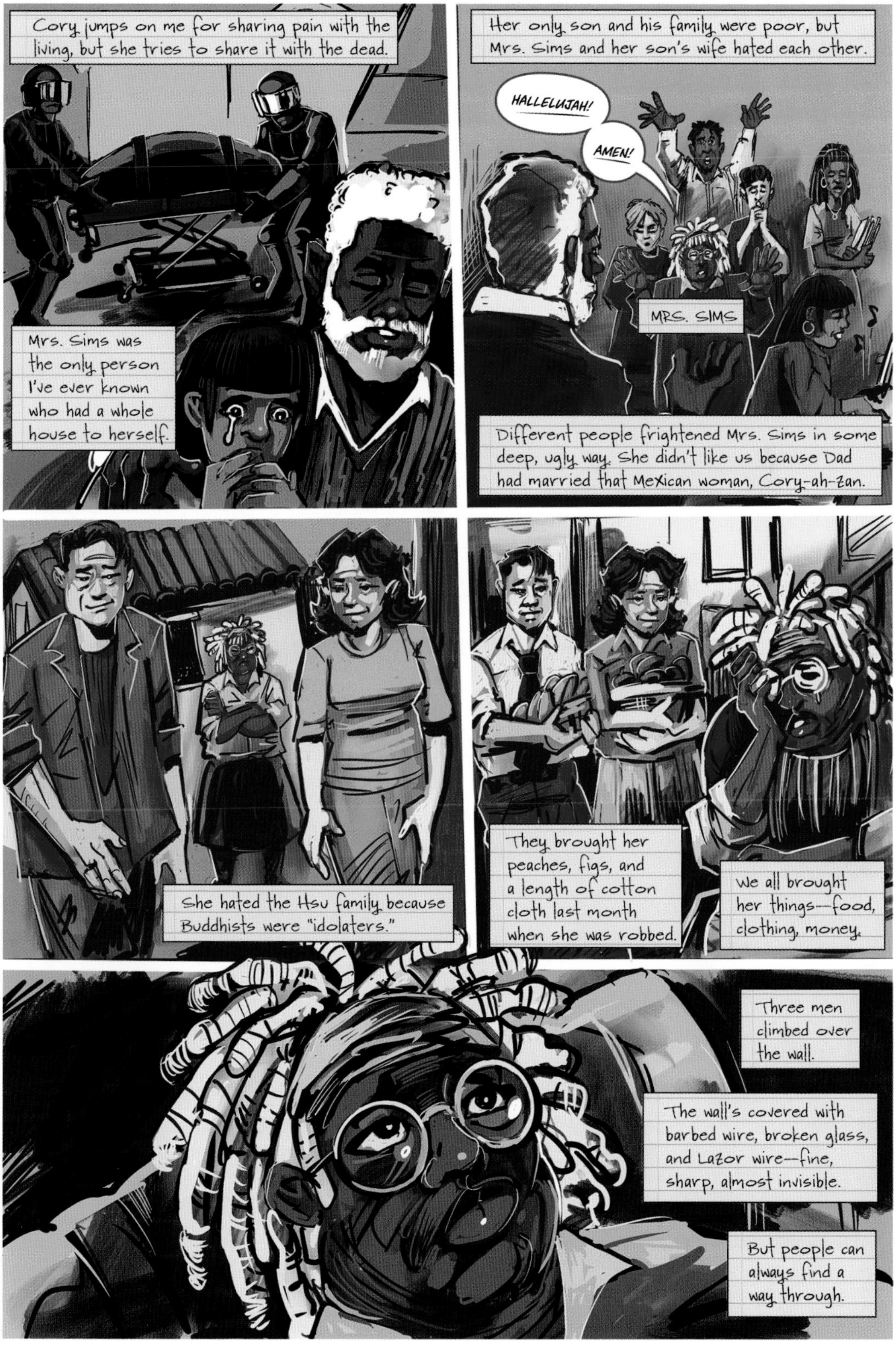
Cory jumps on me for sharing pain with the living, but she tries to share it with the dead.
Mrs. Sims was the only person I've ever known who had a whole house to herself.
Her only son and his family were poor, but Mrs. Sims and her son's wife hated each other.
HALLELUJAH!
AMEN!
MRS. SIMS
Different people frightened Mrs. Sims in some deep, ugly way. She didn't like us because Dad had married that Mexican woman, Cory-ah-zan.
She hated the Hsu family because Buddhists were "idolaters."
They brought her peaches, figs, and a length of cotton cloth last month when she was robbed.
We all brought her things—food, clothing, money.
Three men climbed over the wall.
The wall's covered with barbed wire, broken glass, and Lazor wire—fine, sharp, almost invisible.
But people can always find a way through.

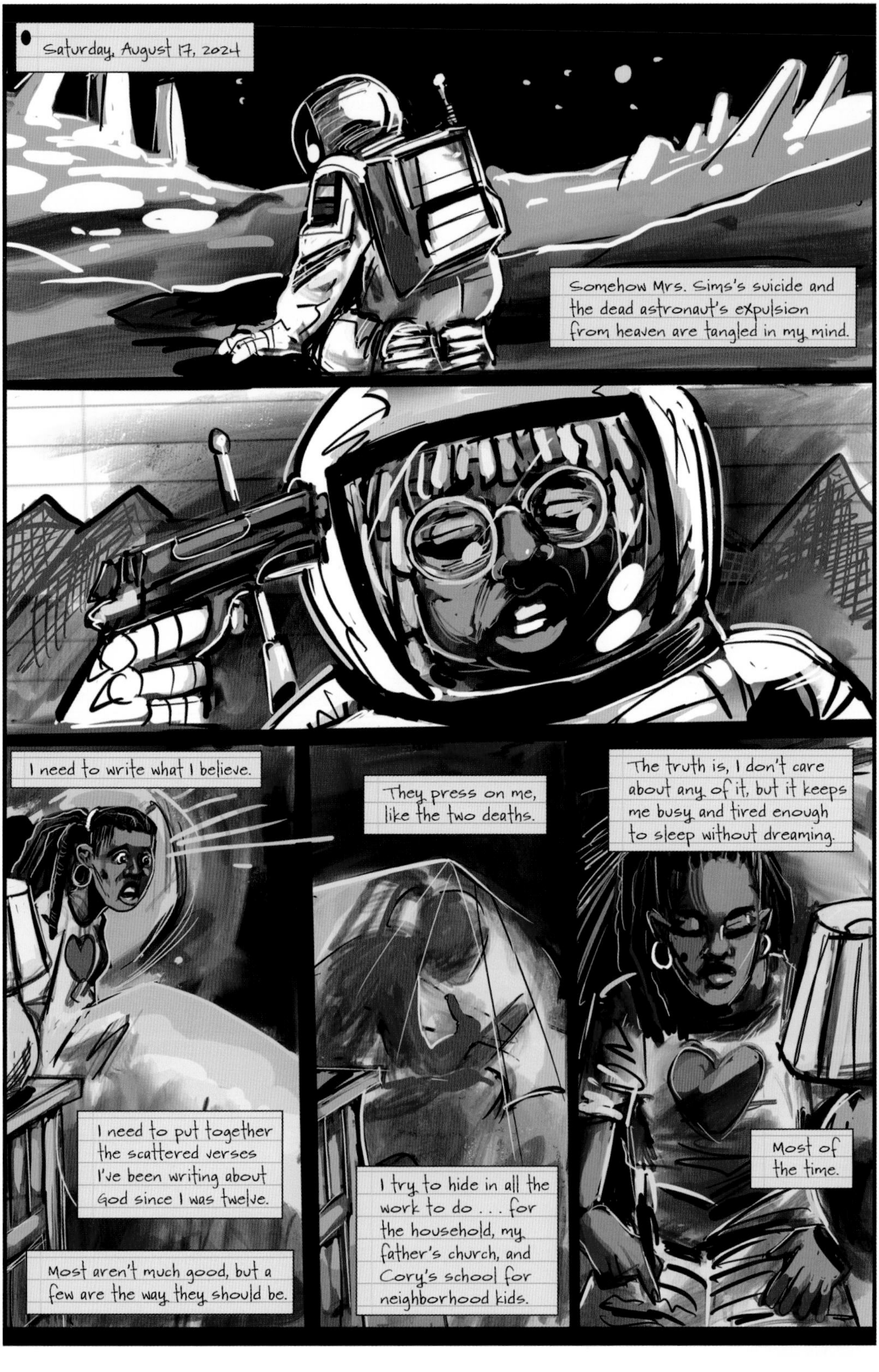
Saturday, August 17, 2024
Somehow Mrs. Sims's suicide and the dead astronaut's expulsion from heaven are tangled in my mind.
I need to write what I believe.
I need to put together the scattered verses I've been writing about God since I was twelve.
Most aren't much good, but a few are the way they should be.
They press on me, like the two deaths.
I try to hide in all the work to do . . . for the household, my father's church, and Cory's school for neighborhood kids.
The truth is, I don't care about any of it, but it keeps me busy and tired enough to sleep without dreaming.
Most of the time.

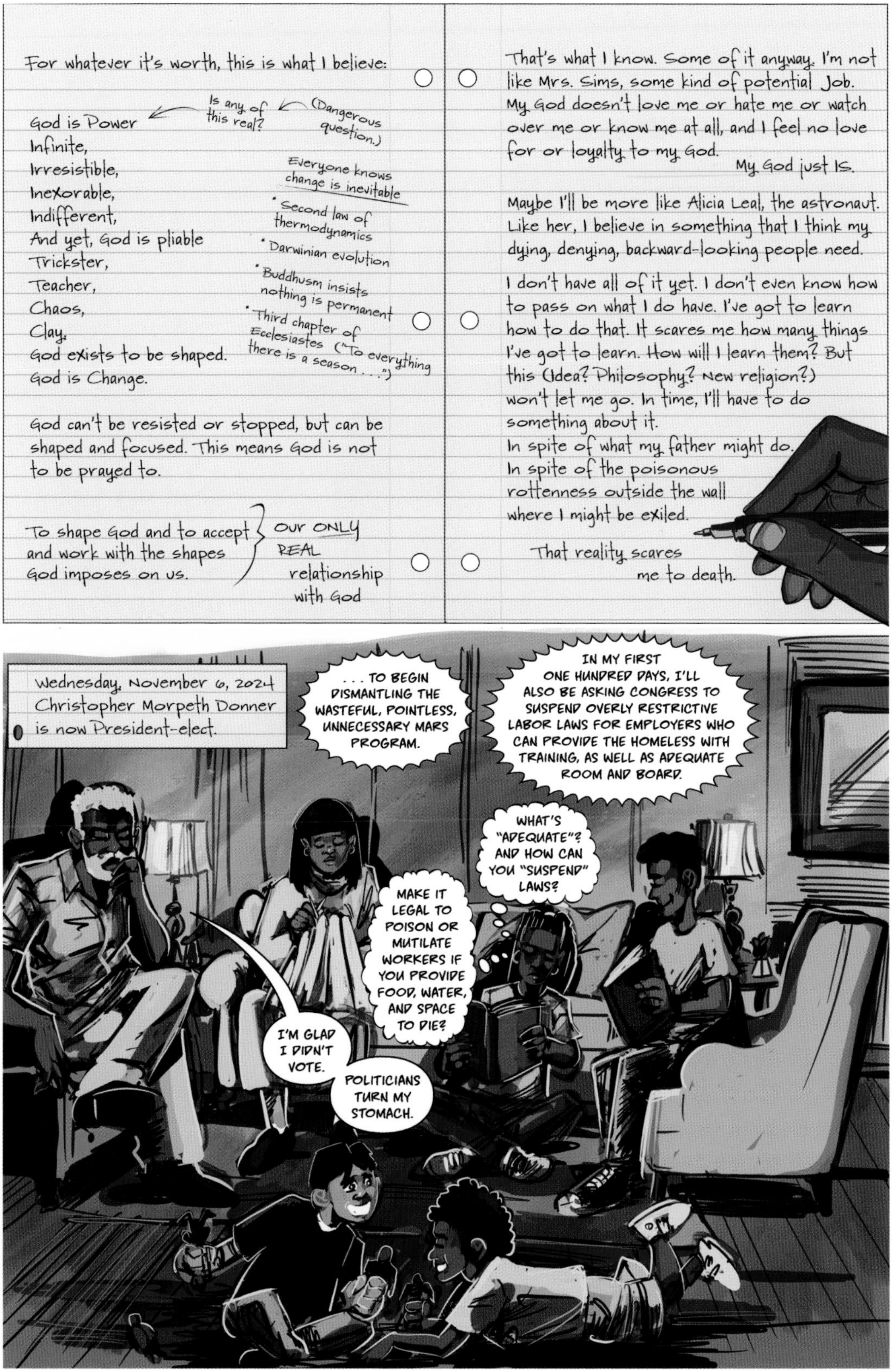
For whatever it's worth, this is what I believe:
God is Power
Infinite,
Irresistible,
Inexorable,
Indifferent,
And yet, God is pliable
Trickster,
Teacher,
Chaos,
Clay,
God exists to be shaped.
God is Change.
Is any of this real?
(Dangerous question.)
Everyone knows change is inevitable
• Second law of thermodynamics
• Darwinian evolution
• Buddhusm insists nothing is permanent
• Third chapter of Ecclesiastes ("To everything there is a season . . .")
God can't be resisted or stopped, but can be shaped and focused. This means God is not to be prayed to.
To shape God and to accept and work with the shapes God imposes on us.
Our ONLY REAL relationship with God
That's what I know. Some of it anyway. I'm not like Mrs. Sims, some kind of potential Job. My God doesn't love me or hate me or watch over me or know me at all, and I feel no love for or loyalty to my God.
My God just IS.
Maybe I'll be more like Alicia Leal, the astronaut. Like her, I believe in something that I think my dying, denying, backward-looking people need.
I don't have all of it yet. I don't even know how to pass on what I do have. I've got to learn how to do that. It scares me how many things I've got to learn. How will I learn them? But this (Idea? Philosophy? New religion?) won't let me go. In time, I'll have to do something about it.
In spite of what my father might do.
In spite of the poisonous rottenness outside the wall where I might be exiled.
That reality scares me to death.
Wednesday, November 6, 2024
Christopher Morpeth Donner is now President-elect.
. . . TO BEGIN DISMANTLING THE WASTEFUL, POINTLESS, UNNECESSARY MARS PROGRAM.
IN MY FIRST ONE HUNDRED DAYS, I'LL ALSO BE ASKING CONGRESS TO SUSPEND OVERLY RESTRICTIVE LABOR LAWS FOR EMPLOYERS WHO CAN PROVIDE THE HOMELESS WITH TRAINING, AS WELL AS ADEQUATE ROOM AND BOARD.
WHAT'S "ADEQUATE"? AND HOW CAN YOU "SUSPEND" LAWS?
MAKE IT LEGAL TO POISON OR MUTILATE WORKERS IF YOU PROVIDE FOOD, WATER, AND SPACE TO DIE?
I'M GLAD I DIDN'T VOTE.
POLITICIANS TURN MY STOMACH.

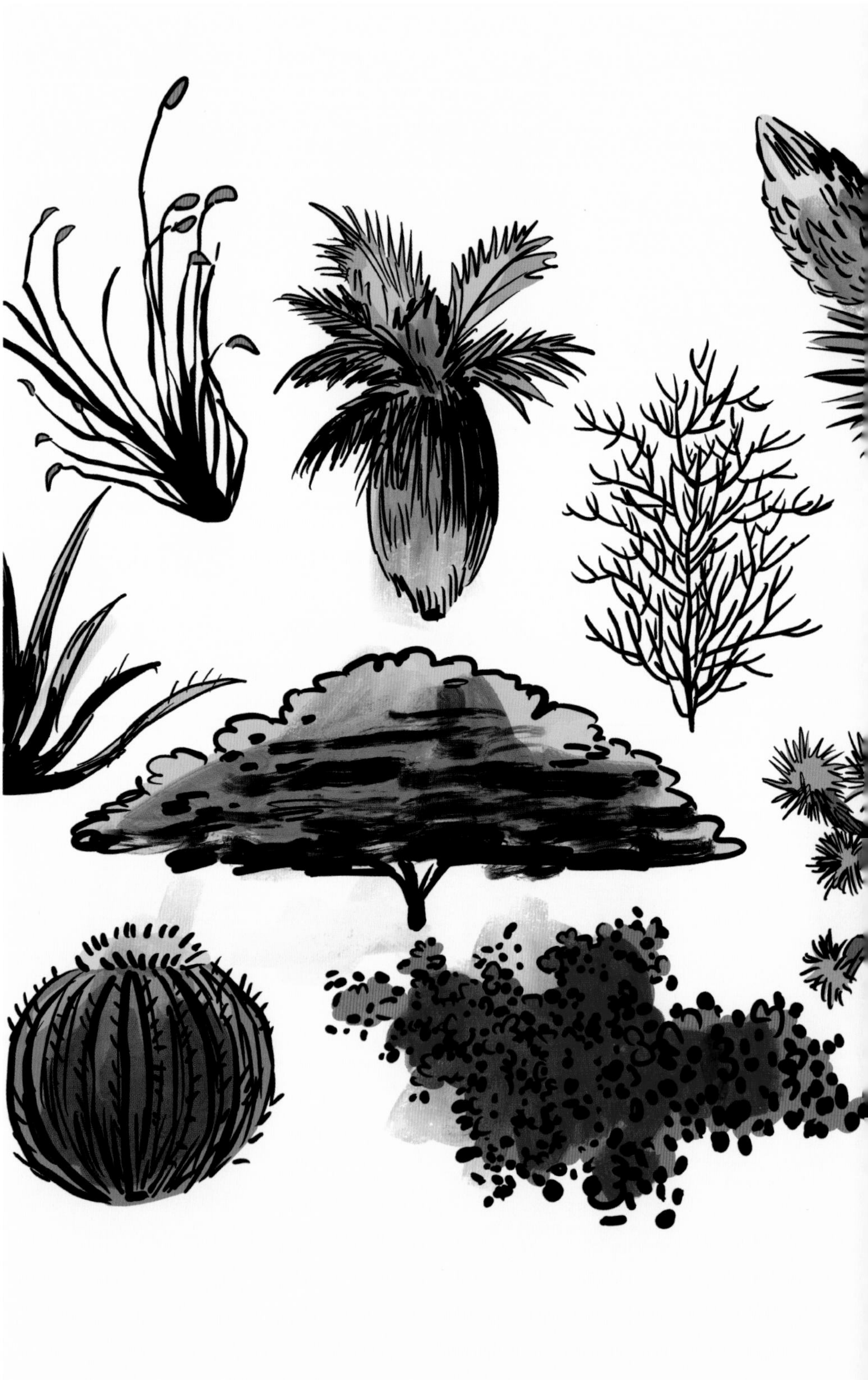

2025

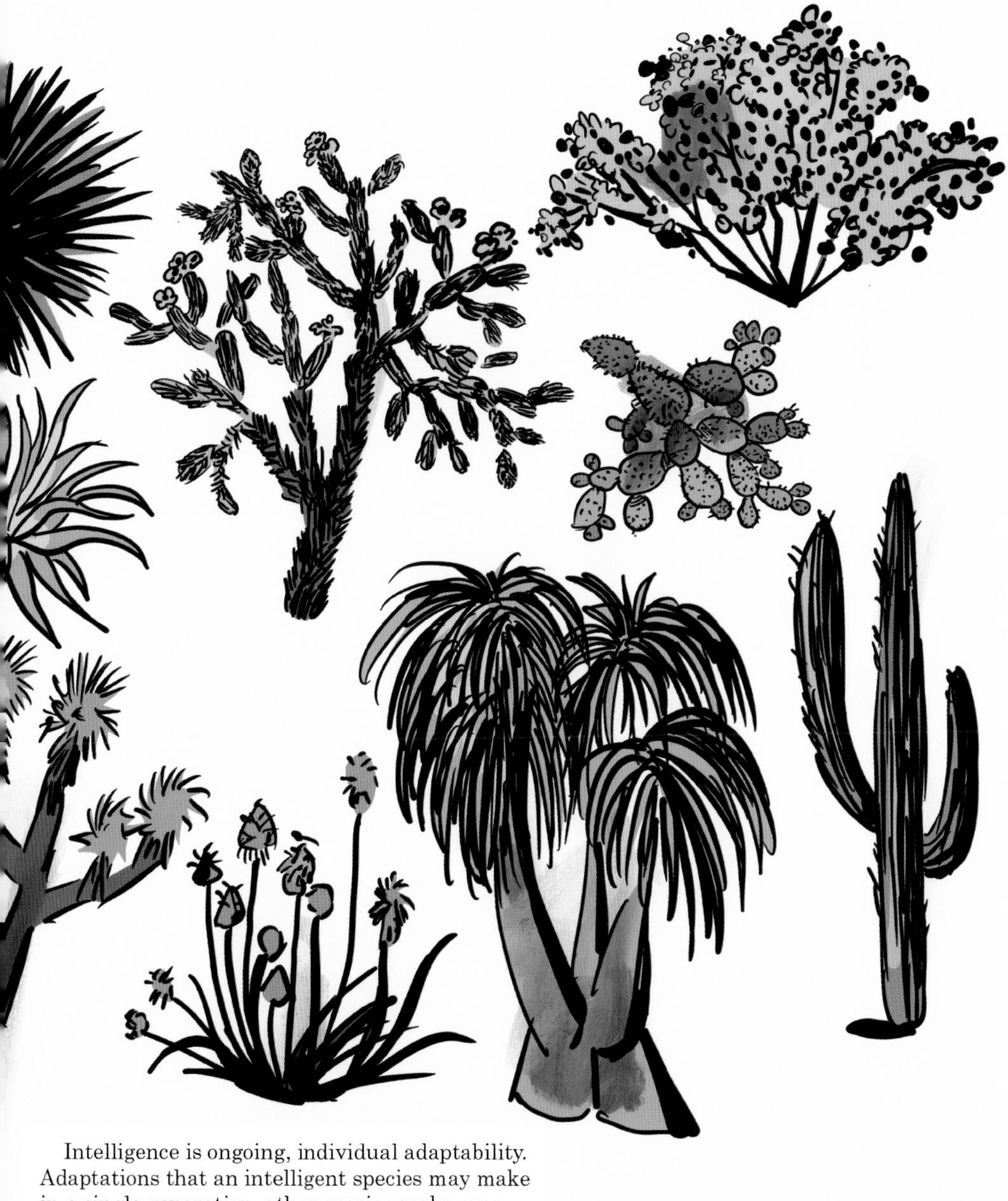

Intelligence is ongoing, individual adaptability. Adaptations that an intelligent species may make in a single generation, other species make over many generations of selective breeding and selective dying. Yet intelligence is demanding. If it is misdirected by accident or by intent, it can foster its own orgies of breeding and dying.

EARTHSEED: THE BOOKS OF THE LIVING

A victim of God may,
Through learning adaption,
Become a partner of God,
A victim of God may,
Through forethought and
planning,
Become a shaper of God.
Or a victim of God may,
Through shortsightedness and
fear,
Remain God's victim,
God's plaything,
God's prey.

EARTHSEED: THE BOOKS
OF THE LIVING

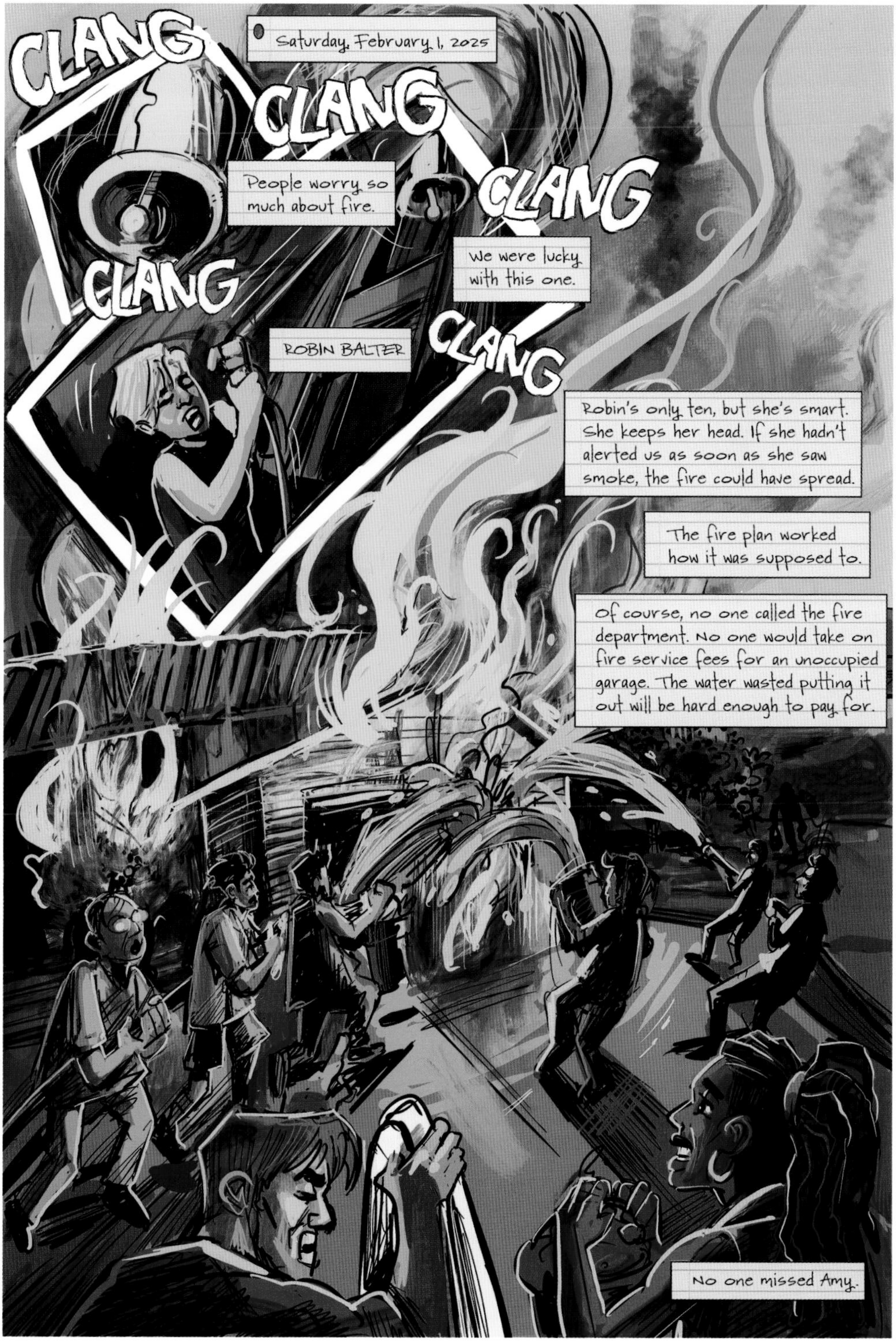
CLANG
Saturday, February 1, 2025
CLANG
People worry so much about fire.
CLANG
CLANG
We were lucky with this one.
ROBIN BALTER
CLANG
Robin's only ten, but she's smart. She keeps her head. If she hadn't alerted us as soon as she saw smoke, the fire could have spread.
The fire plan worked how it was supposed to.
Of course, no one called the fire department. No one would take on fire service fees for an unoccupied garage. The water wasted putting it out will be hard enough to pay for.
No one missed Amy.

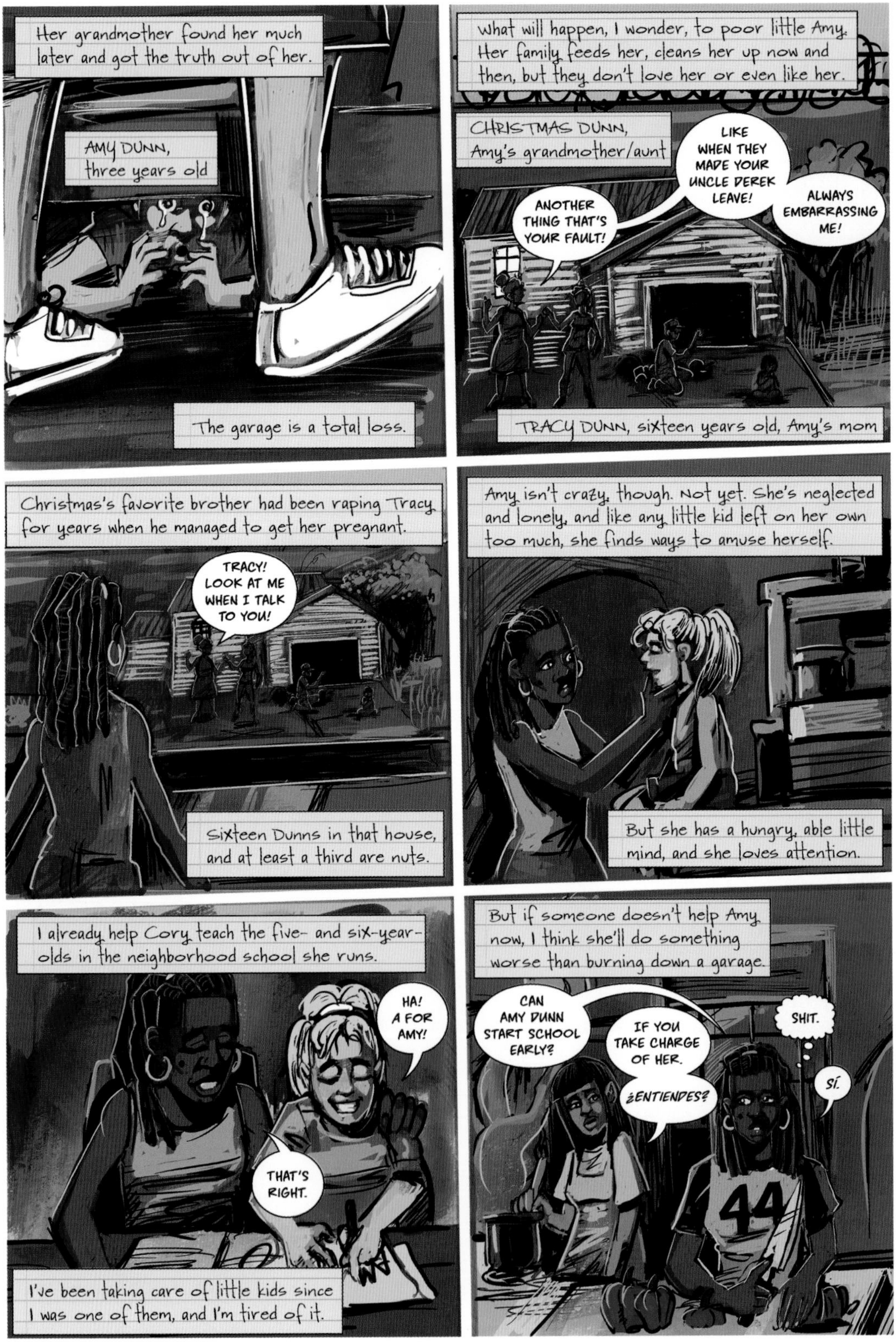
Her grandmother found her much later and got the truth out of her.
AMY DUNN, three years old
The garage is a total loss.
What will happen, I wonder, to poor little Amy. Her family feeds her, cleans her up now and then, but they don't love her or even like her.
CHRISTMAS DUNN, Amy's grandmother/aunt
ANOTHER THING THAT'S YOUR FAULT!
LIKE WHEN THEY MADE YOUR UNCLE DEREK LEAVE!
ALWAYS EMBARRASSING ME!
TRACY DUNN, sixteen years old, Amy's mom
Christmas's favorite brother had been raping Tracy for years when he managed to get her pregnant.
TRACY! LOOK AT ME WHEN I TALK TO YOU!
Sixteen Dunns in that house, and at least a third are nuts.
Amy isn't crazy, though. Not yet. She's neglected and lonely, and like any little kid left on her own too much, she finds ways to amuse herself.
But she has a hungry, able little mind, and she loves attention.
I already help Cory teach the five- and six-year-olds in the neighborhood school she runs.
HA! A FOR AMY!
THAT'S RIGHT.
I've been taking care of little kids since I was one of them, and I'm tired of it.
But if someone doesn't help Amy now, I think she'll do something worse than burning down a garage.
CAN AMY DUNN START SCHOOL EARLY?
IF YOU TAKE CHARGE OF HER.
¿ENTIENDES?
SHIT.
SÍ.

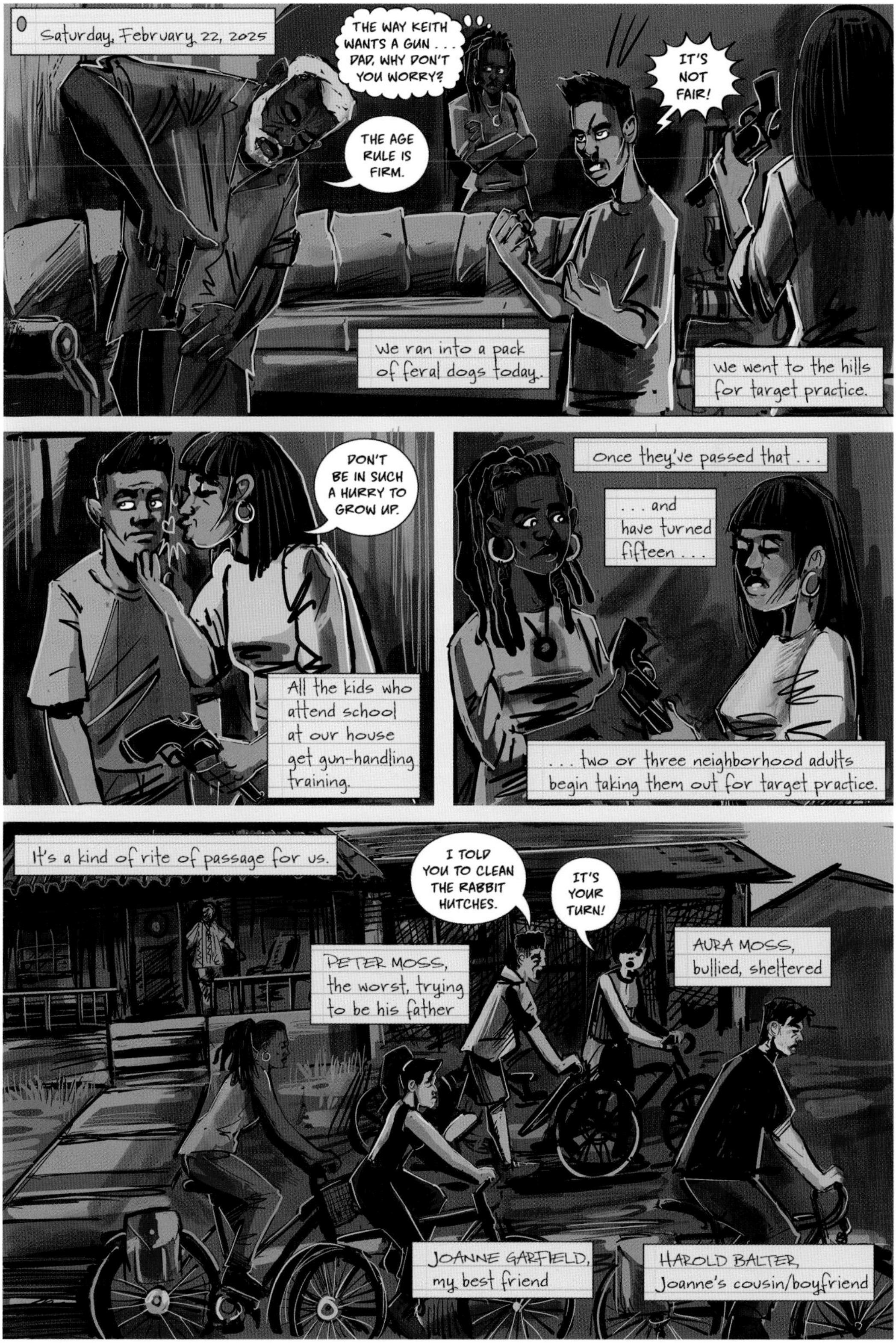
Saturday, February 22, 2025
THE WAY KEITH WANTS A GUN . . . DAD, WHY DON'T YOU WORRY?
THE AGE RULE IS FIRM.
IT'S NOT FAIR!
We ran into a pack of feral dogs today.
We went to the hills for target practice.
DON'T BE IN SUCH A HURRY TO GROW UP.
All the kids who attend school at our house get gun-handling training.
Once they've passed that . . .
. . . and have turned fifteen . . .
. . . two or three neighborhood adults begin taking them out for target practice.
It's a kind of rite of passage for us.
I TOLD YOU TO CLEAN THE RABBIT HUTCHES.
IT'S YOUR TURN!
PETER MOSS, the worst, trying to be his father
AURA MOSS, bullied, sheltered
JOANNE GARFIELD, my best friend
HAROLD BALTER, Joanne's cousin/boyfriend

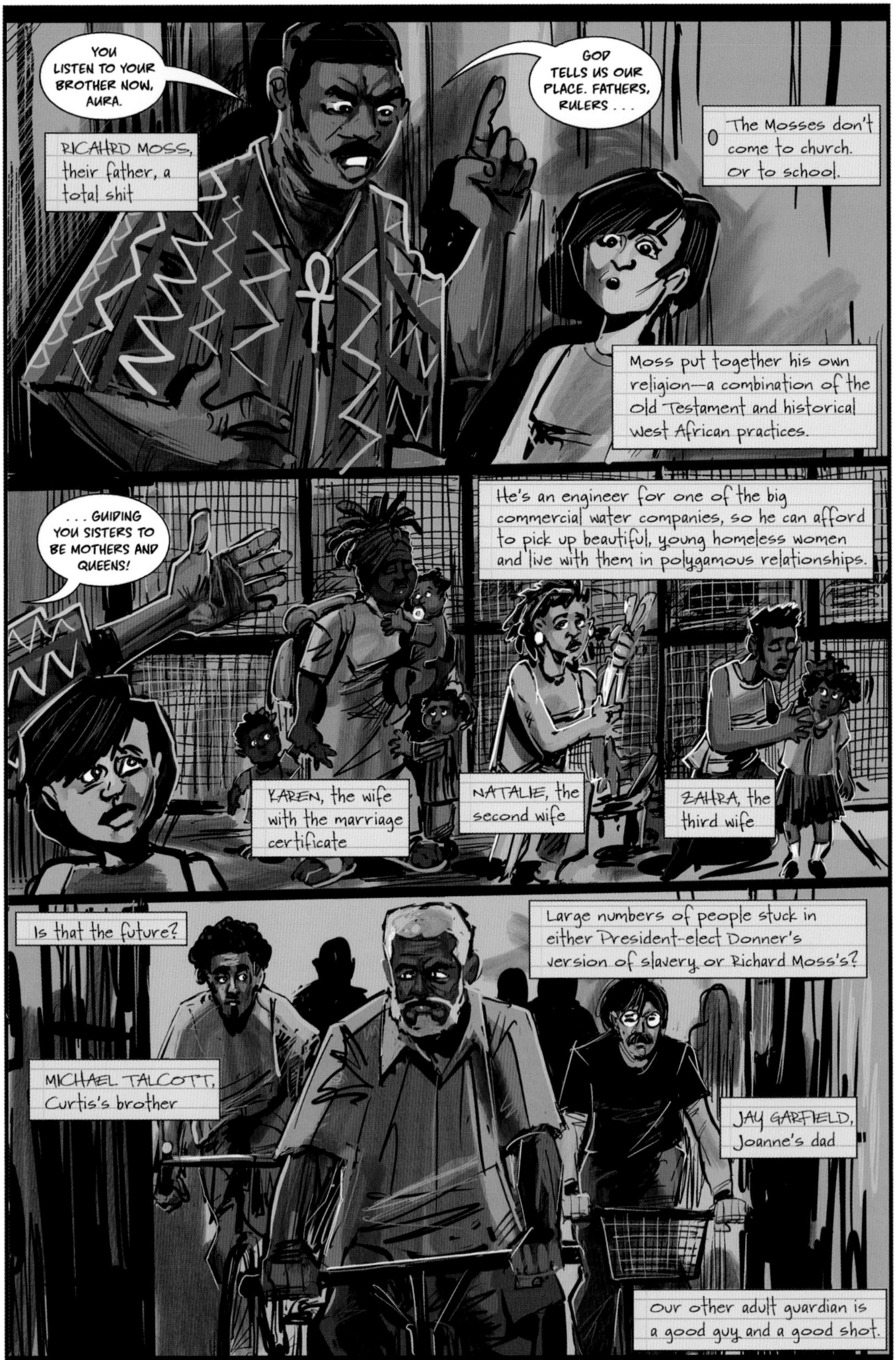
YOU LISTEN TO YOUR BROTHER NOW, AURA.
RICAHRD MOSS, their father, a total shit
GOD TELLS US OUR PLACE. FATHERS, RULERS . . .
The Mosses don't come to church. or to school.
Moss put together his own religion—a combination of the old Testament and historical west African practices.
. . . GUIDING YOU SISTERS TO BE MOTHERS AND QUEENS!
He's an engineer for one of the big commercial water companies, so he can afford to pick up beautiful, young homeless women and live with them in polygamous relationships.
KAREN, the wife with the marriage certificate
NATALIE, the second wife
ZAHRA, the third wife
Is that the future?
Large numbers of people stuck in either President-elect Donner's version of slavery or Richard Moss's?
MICHAEL TALCOTT, Curtis's brother
JAY GARFIELD, Joanne's dad
Our other adult guardian is a good guy and a good shot.

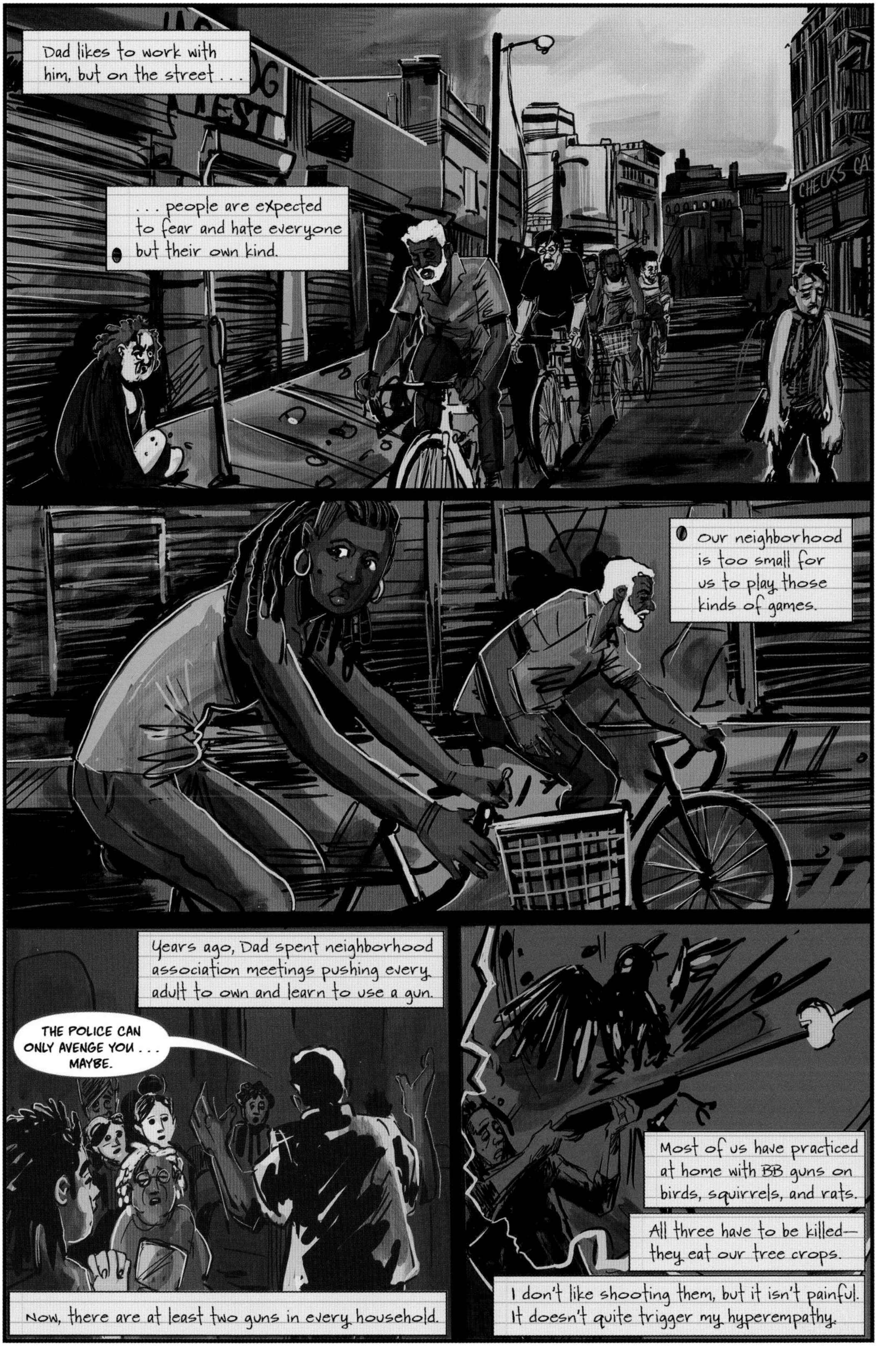

Dad likes to work with him, but on the street . . .
. . . people are expected to fear and hate everyone but their own kind.
Our neighborhood is too small for us to play those kinds of games.
Years ago, Dad spent neighborhood association meetings pushing every adult to own and learn to use a gun.
THE POLICE CAN ONLY AVENGE YOU . . . MAYBE.
Now, there are at least two guns in every household.
Most of us have practiced at home with BB guns on birds, squirrels, and rats.
All three have to be killed—they eat our tree crops.
I don't like shooting them, but it isn't painful. It doesn't quite trigger my hyperempathy.

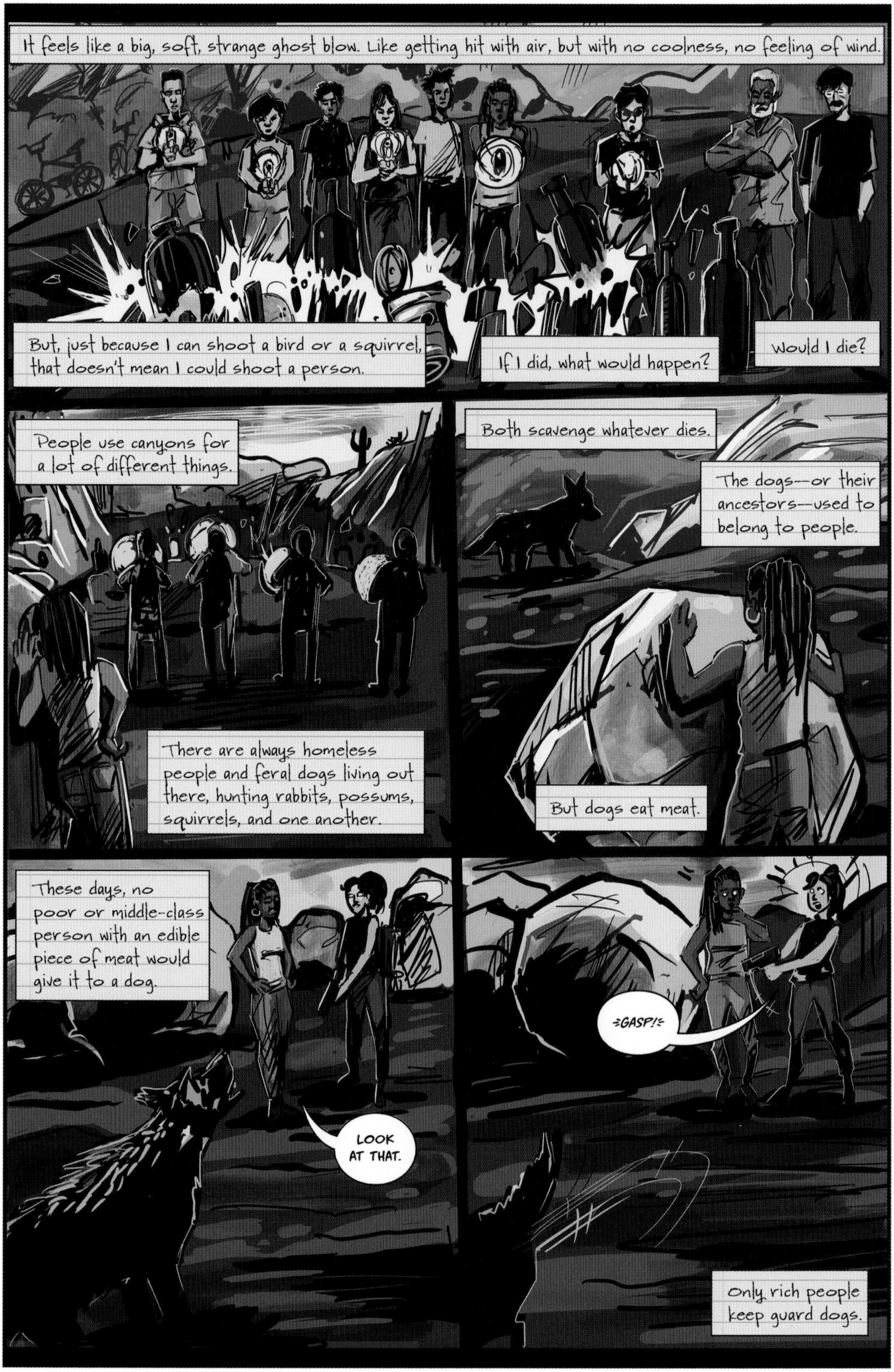

It feels like a big, soft, strange ghost blow. Like getting hit with air, but with no coolness, no feeling of wind.
But, just because I can shoot a bird or a squirrel, that doesn't mean I could shoot a person.
If I did, what would happen?
Would I die?
People use canyons for a lot of different things.
There are always homeless people and feral dogs living out there, hunting rabbits, possums, squirrels, and one another.
Both scavenge whatever dies.
The dogs—or their ancestors—used to belong to people.
But dogs eat meat.
These days, no poor or middle-class person with an edible piece of meat would give it to a dog.
LOOK AT THAT.
GASP!
Only rich people keep guard dogs.

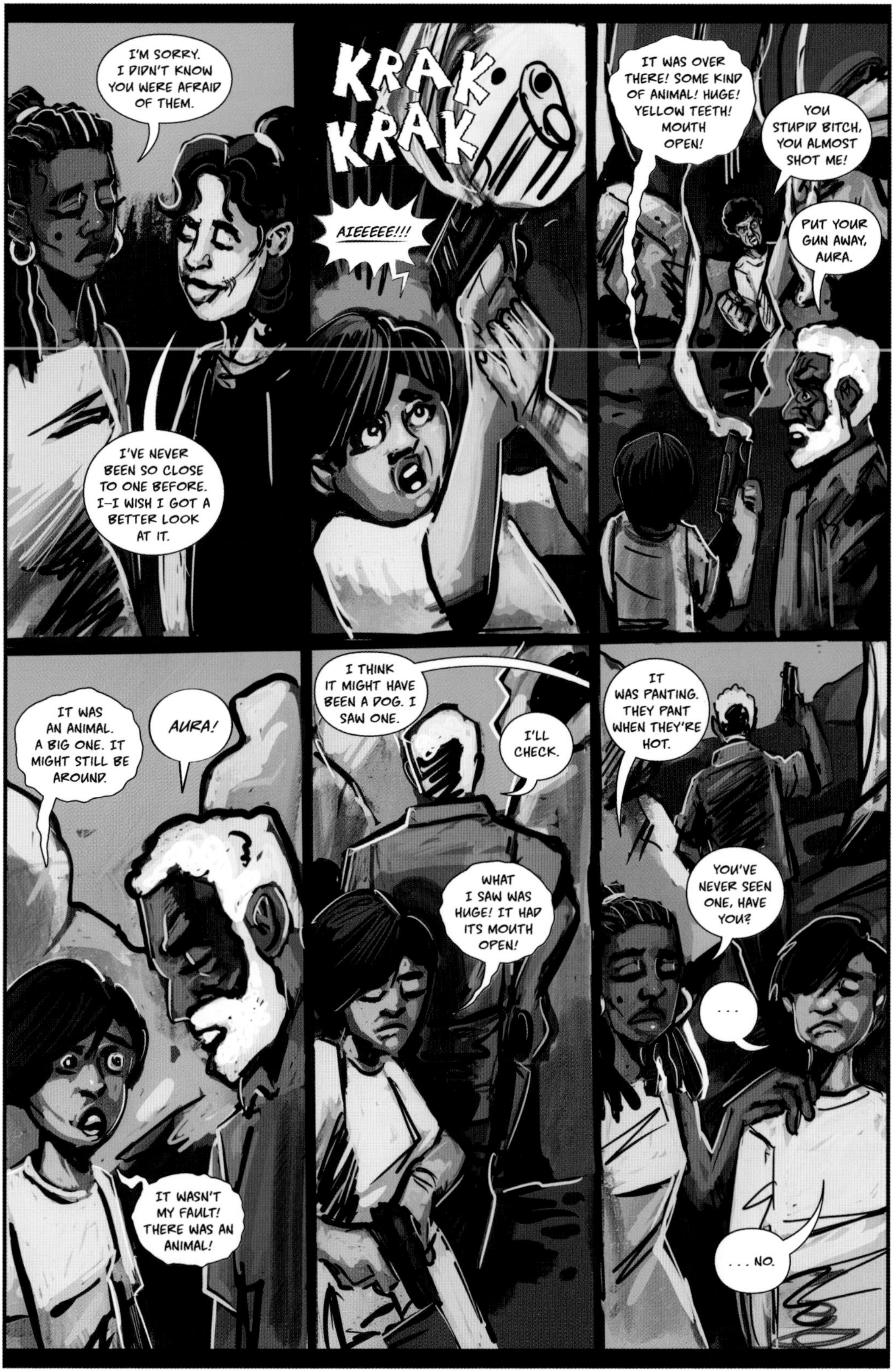
I'M SORRY. I DIDN'T KNOW YOU WERE AFRAID OF THEM.
I'VE NEVER BEEN SO CLOSE TO ONE BEFORE. I–I WISH I GOT A BETTER LOOK AT IT.
KRAK KRAK
AIEEEEE!!!
IT WAS OVER THERE! SOME KIND OF ANIMAL! HUGE! YELLOW TEETH! MOUTH OPEN!
YOU STUPID BITCH, YOU ALMOST SHOT ME!
PUT YOUR GUN AWAY, AURA.
IT WAS AN ANIMAL. A BIG ONE. IT MIGHT STILL BE AROUND.
AURA!
IT WASN'T MY FAULT! THERE WAS AN ANIMAL!
I THINK IT MIGHT HAVE BEEN A DOG. I SAW ONE.
I'LL CHECK.
WHAT I SAW WAS HUGE! IT HAD ITS MOUTH OPEN!
IT WAS PANTING. THEY PANT WHEN THEY'RE HOT.
YOU'VE NEVER SEEN ONE, HAVE YOU?
. . .
. . . NO.

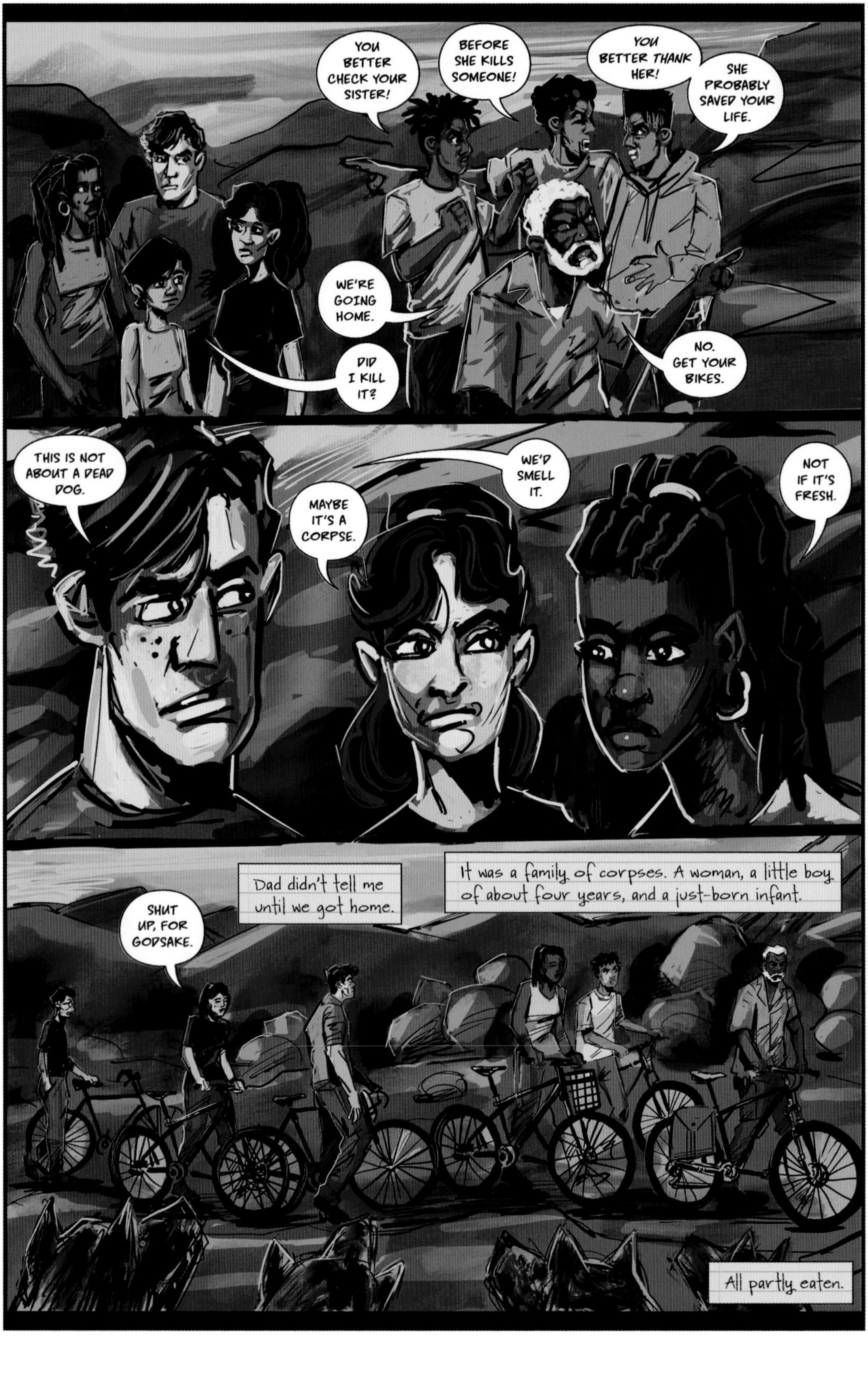
YOU BETTER CHECK YOUR SISTER!
BEFORE SHE KILLS SOMEONE!
YOU BETTER THANK HER!
SHE PROBABLY SAVED YOUR LIFE.
WE'RE GOING HOME.
DID I KILL IT?
NO. GET YOUR BIKES.
THIS IS NOT ABOUT A DEAD DOG.
MAYBE IT'S A CORPSE.
WE'D SMELL IT.
NOT IF IT'S FRESH.
Dad didn't tell me until we got home.
It was a family of corpses. A woman, a little boy of about four years, and a just-born infant.
SHUT UP, FOR GODSAKE.
All partly eaten.

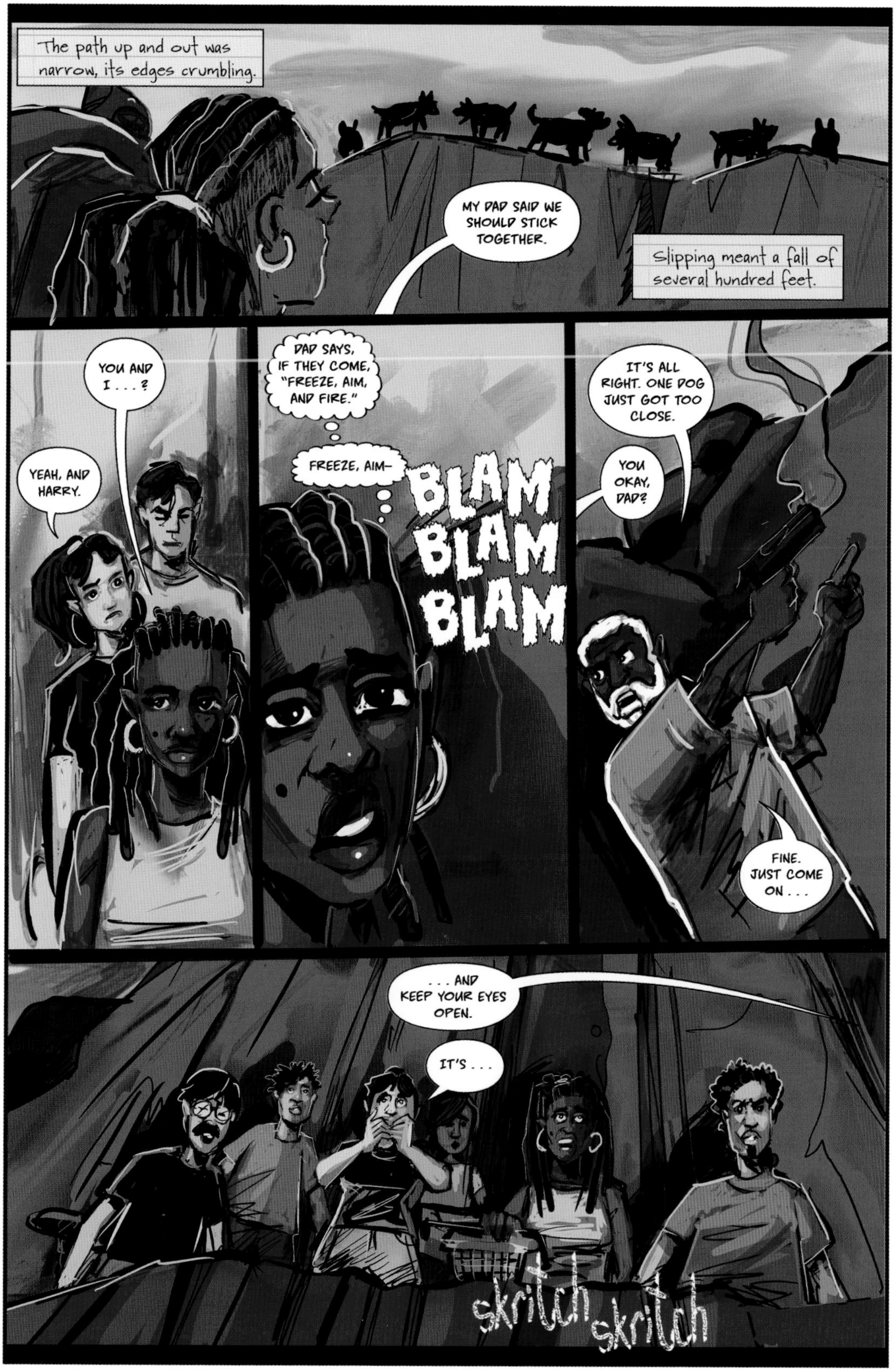
The path up and out was narrow, its edges crumbling.
MY DAD SAID WE SHOULD STICK TOGETHER.
Slipping meant a fall of several hundred feet.
YOU AND I . . . ?
YEAH, AND HARRY.
DAD SAYS, IF THEY COME, "FREEZE, AIM, AND FIRE."
FREEZE, AIM—
BLAM BLAM BLAM
IT'S ALL RIGHT. ONE DOG JUST GOT TOO CLOSE.
YOU OKAY, DAD?
FINE. JUST COME ON . . .
. . . AND KEEP YOUR EYES OPEN.
IT'S . . .
skritch skritch

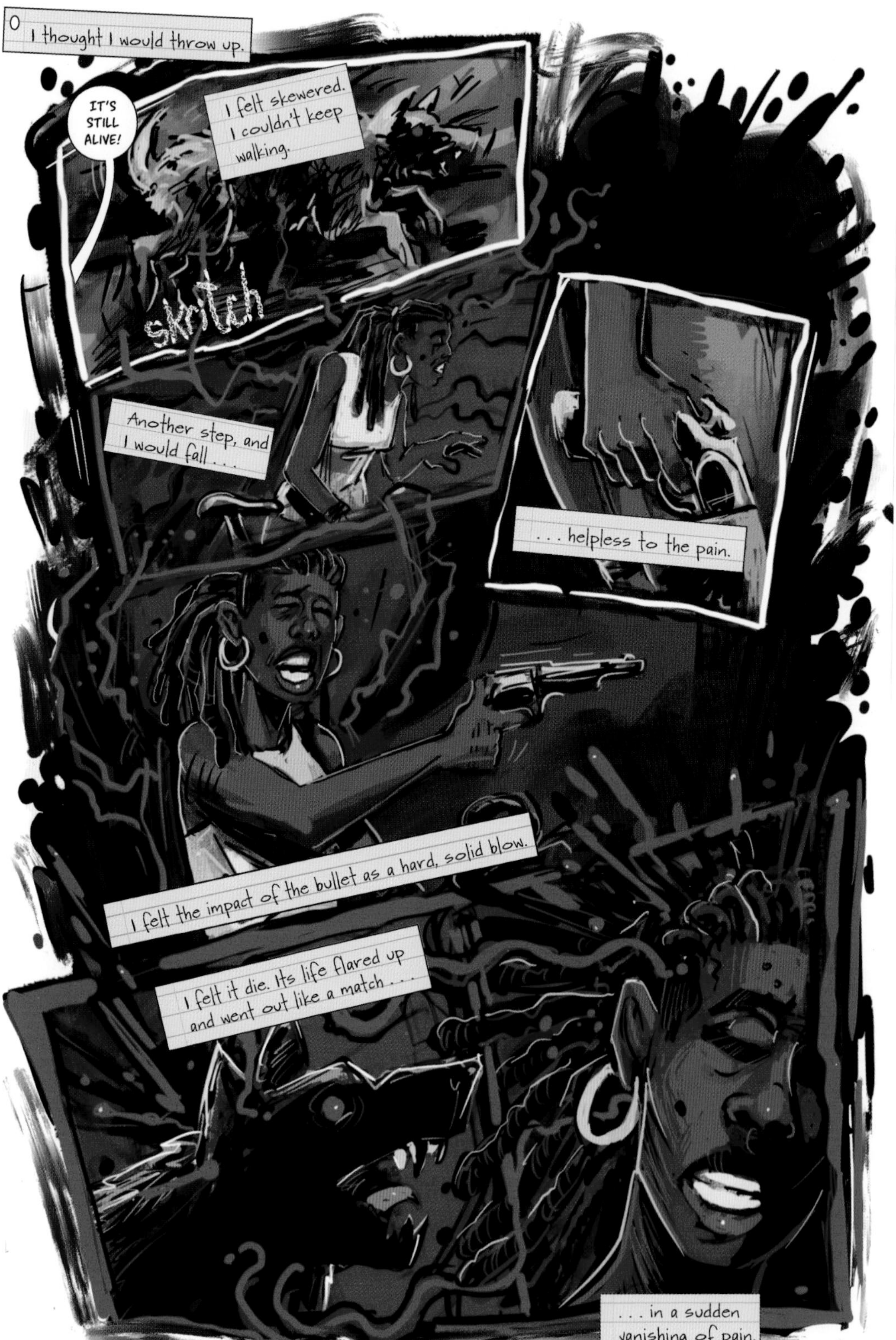
I thought I would throw up.
IT'S STILL ALIVE!
I felt skewered. I couldn't keep walking.
skritch
Another step, and I would fall . . .
. . . helpless to the pain.
I felt the impact of the bullet as a hard, solid blow.
I felt it die. Its life flared up and went out like a match . . .
. . . in a sudden vanishing of pain.

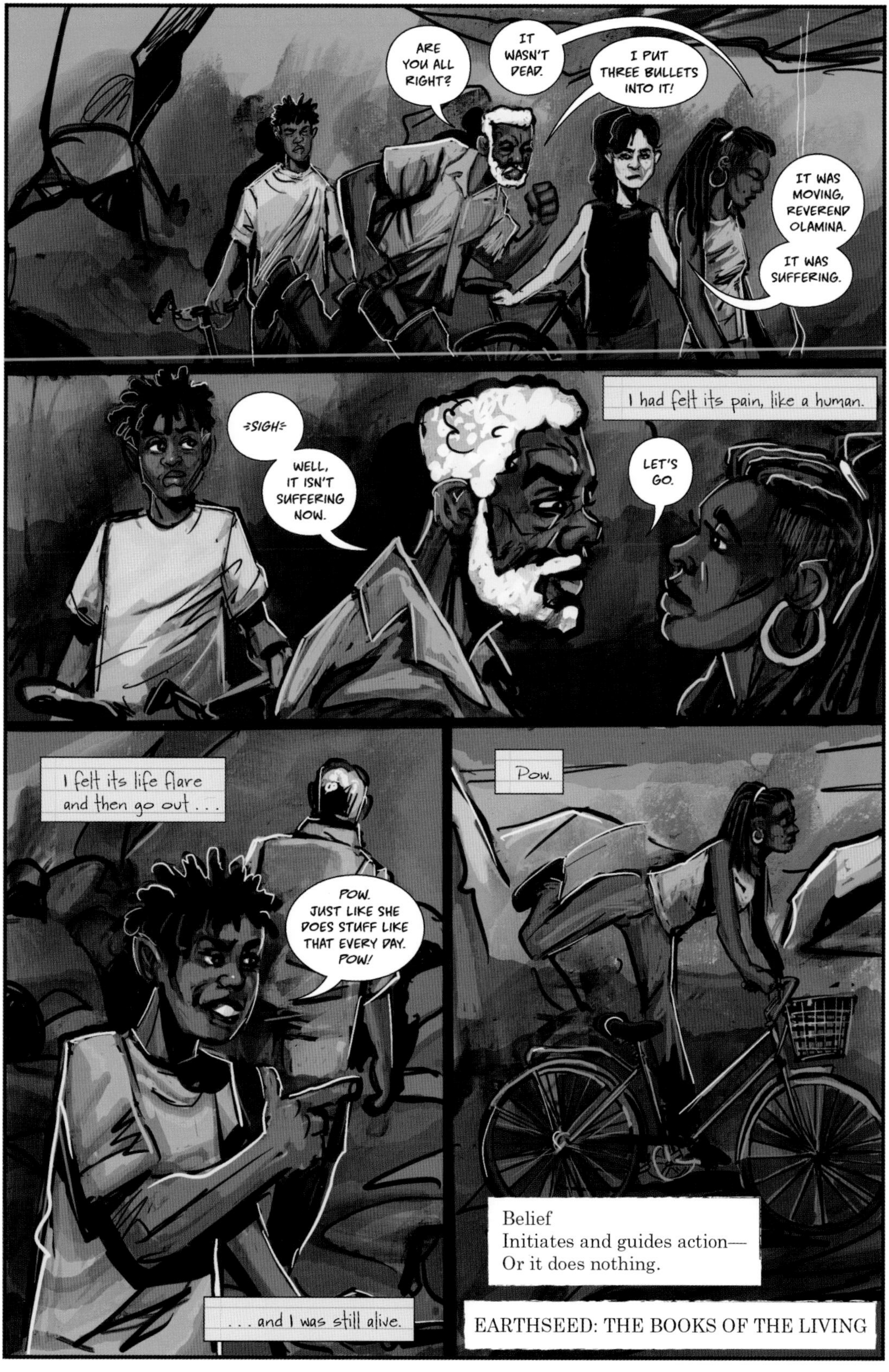
ARE YOU ALL RIGHT?
IT WASN'T DEAD.
I PUT THREE BULLETS INTO IT!
IT WAS MOVING, REVEREND OLAMINA.
IT WAS SUFFERING.
I had felt its pain, like a human.
SIGH
WELL, IT ISN'T SUFFERING NOW.
LET'S GO.
I felt its life flare and then go out . . .
POW. JUST LIKE SHE DOES STUFF LIKE THAT EVERY DAY. POW!
. . . and I was still alive.
Pow.
Belief
Initiates and guides action—
Or it does nothing.
EARTHSEED: THE BOOKS OF THE LIVING

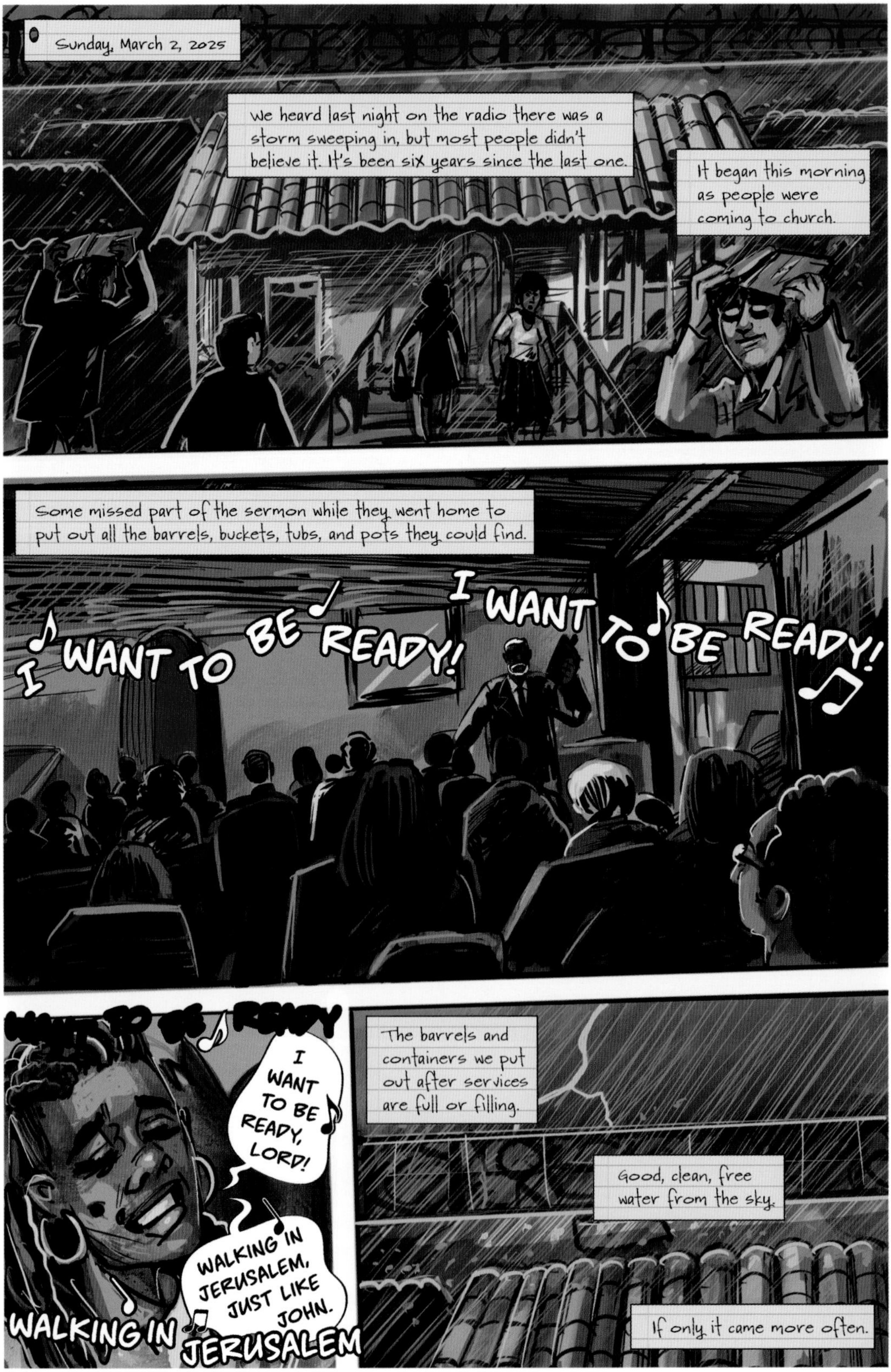
Sunday, March 2, 2025
We heard last night on the radio there was a storm sweeping in, but most people didn't believe it. It's been six years since the last one.
It began this morning as people were coming to church.
Some missed part of the sermon while they went home to put out all the barrels, buckets, tubs, and pots they could find.
I WANT TO BE READY!
I WANT TO BE READY!
I WANT TO BE READY, LORD!
WALKING IN JERUSALEM, JUST LIKE JOHN.
WALKING IN JERUSALEM
The barrels and containers we put out after services are full or filling.
Good, clean, free water from the sky.
If only it came more often.

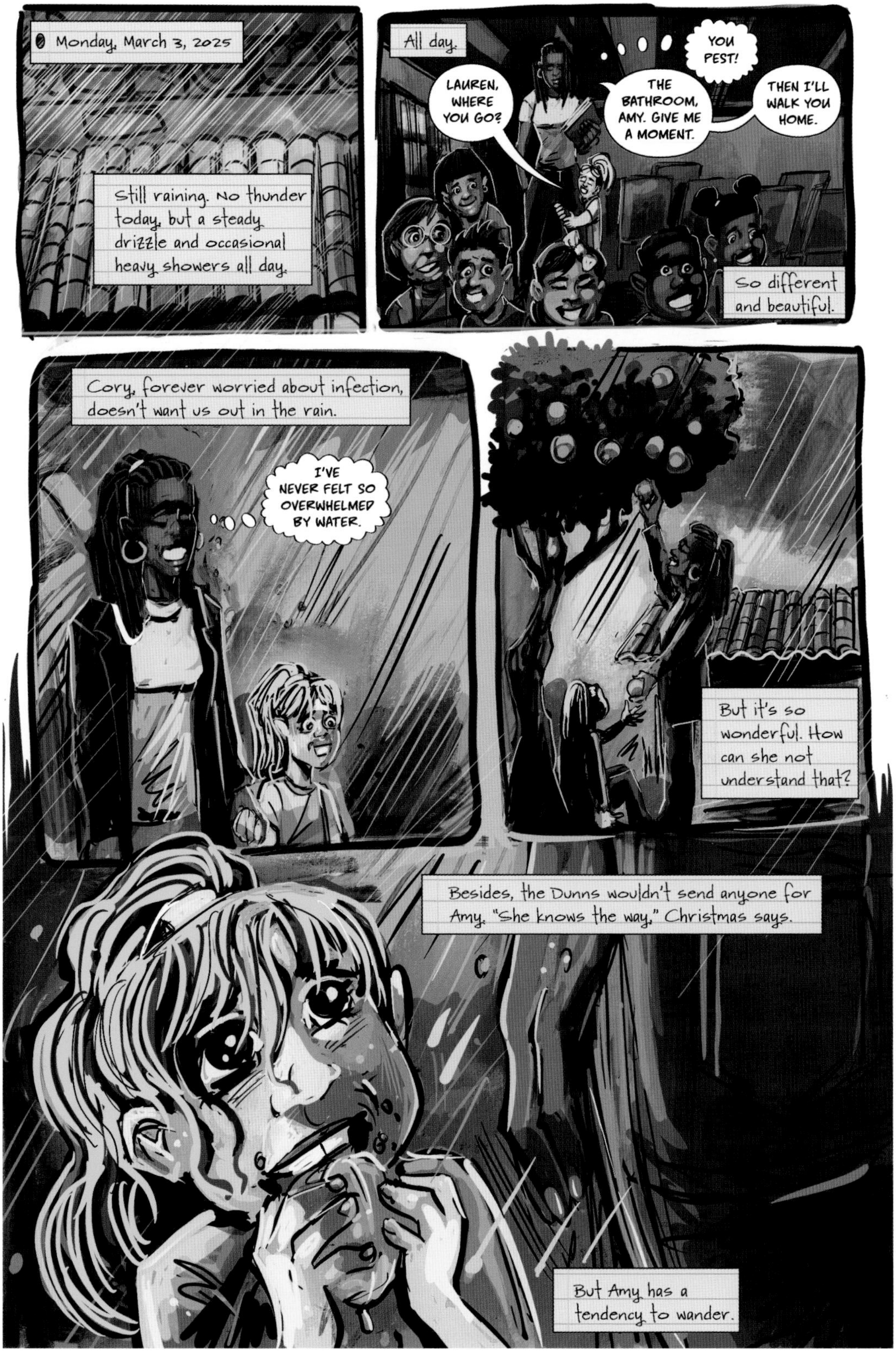
Monday, March 3, 2025
Still raining. No thunder today, but a steady drizzle and occasional heavy showers all day.
All day.
LAUREN, WHERE YOU GO?
THE BATHROOM, AMY. GIVE ME A MOMENT.
YOU PEST!
THEN I'LL WALK YOU HOME.
So different and beautiful.
Cory, forever worried about infection, doesn't want us out in the rain.
I'VE NEVER FELT SO OVERWHELMED BY WATER.
But it's so wonderful. How can she not understand that?
Besides, the Dunns wouldn't send anyone for Amy. "She knows the way," Christmas says.
But Amy has a tendency to wander.

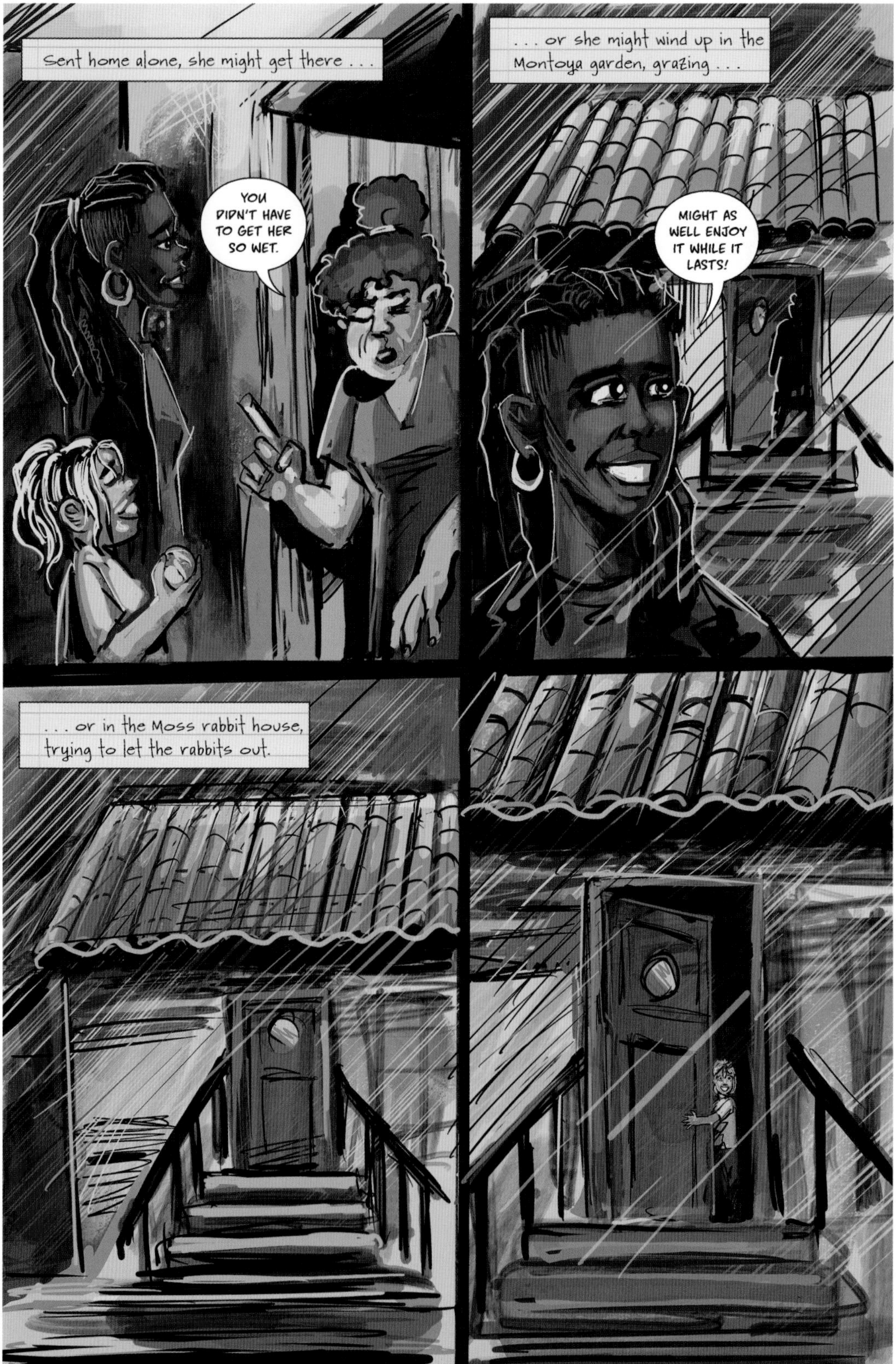
Sent home alone, she might get there . . .
YOU DIDN'T HAVE TO GET HER SO WET.
. . . or she might wind up in the Montoya garden, grazing . . .
MIGHT AS WELL ENJOY IT WHILE IT LASTS!
. . . or in the Moss rabbit house, trying to let the rabbits out.

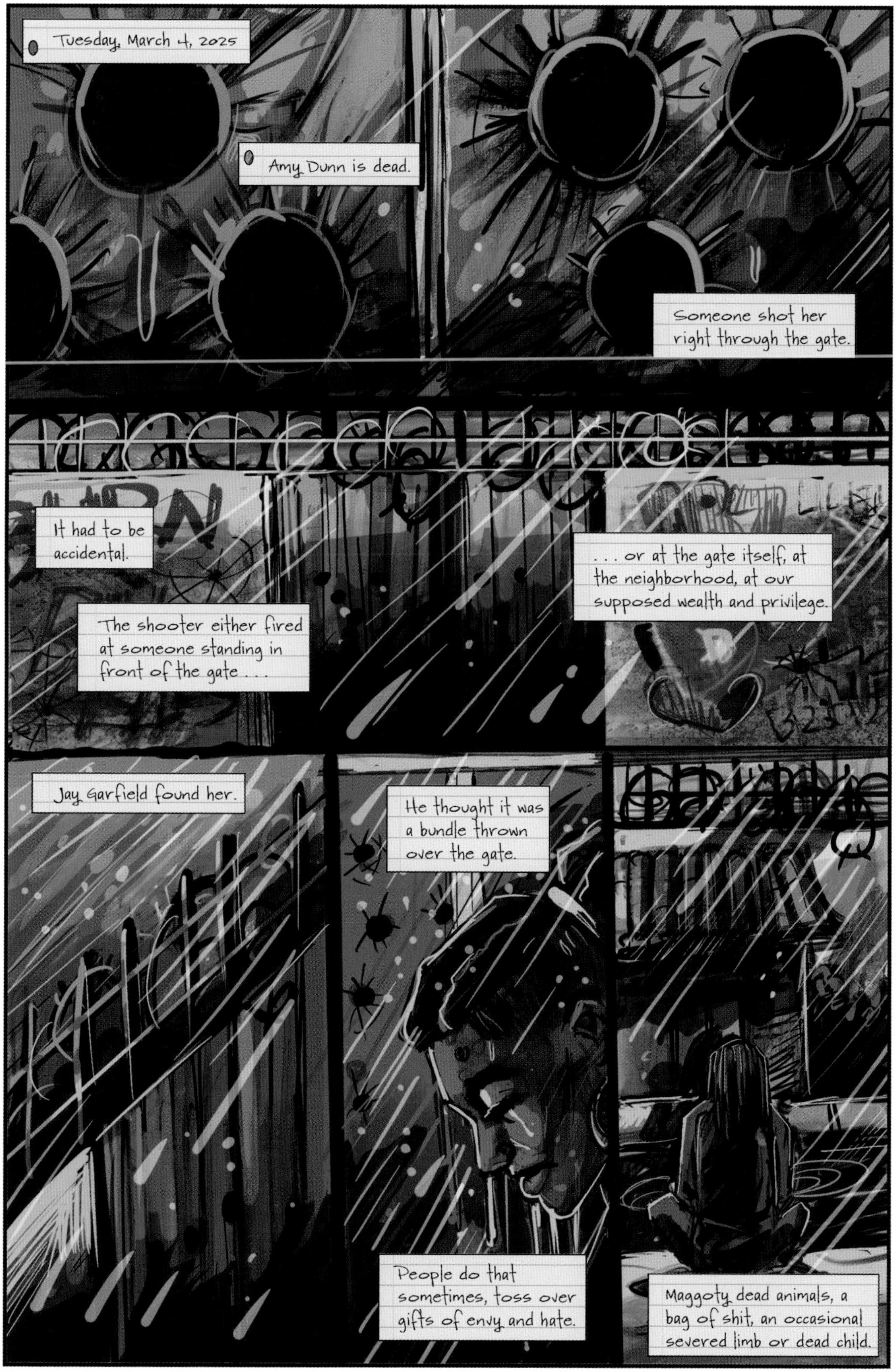
Tuesday, March 4, 2025
Amy Dunn is dead.
Someone shot her right through the gate.
It had to be accidental.
The shooter either fired at someone standing in front of the gate . . .
. . . or at the gate itself, at the neighborhood, at our supposed wealth and privilege.
Jay Garfield found her.
He thought it was a bundle thrown over the gate.
People do that sometimes, toss over gifts of envy and hate.
Maggoty dead animals, a bag of shit, an occasional severed limb or dead child.

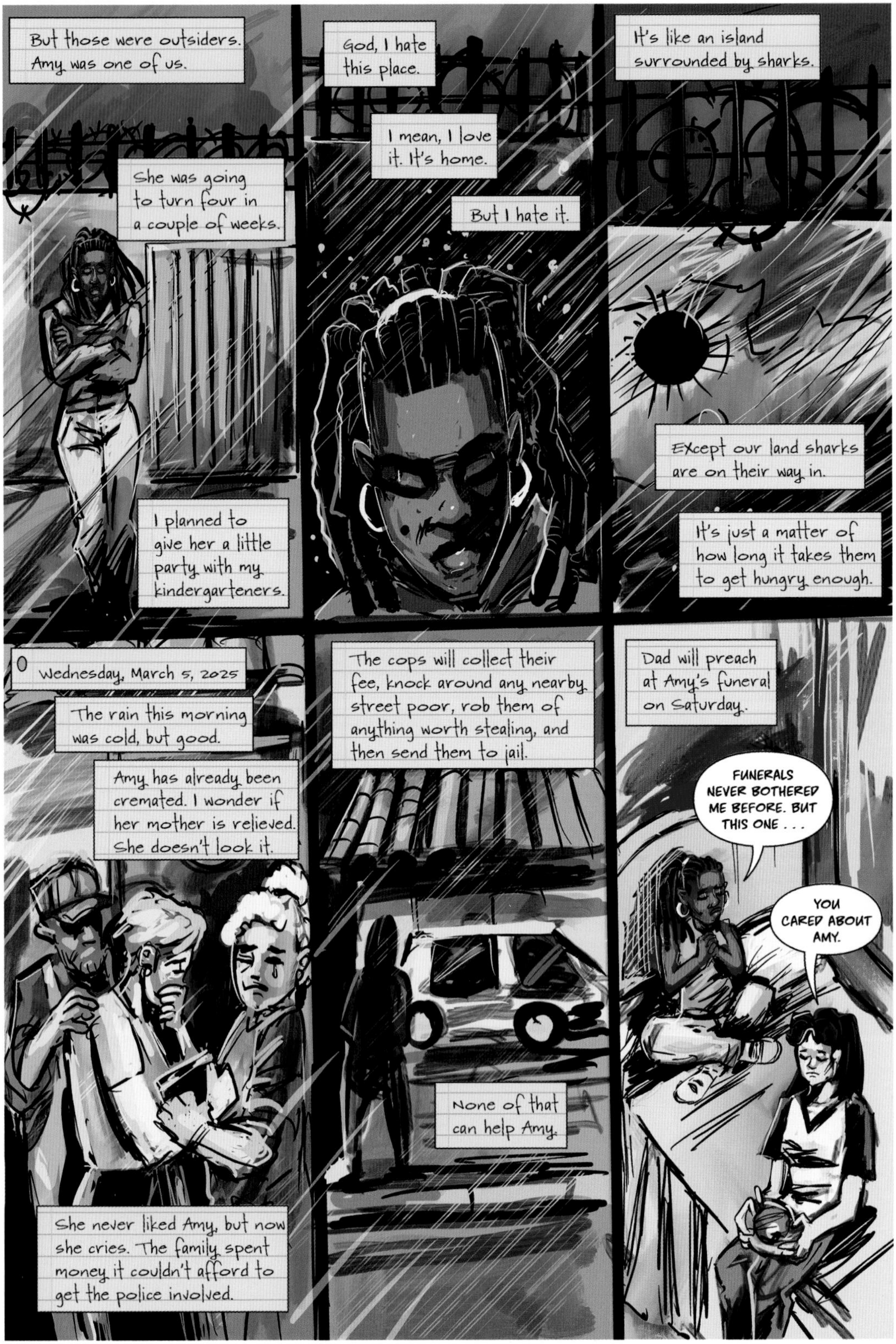
But those were outsiders. Amy was one of us.
She was going to turn four in a couple of weeks.
I planned to give her a little party with my kindergarteners.
God, I hate this place.
I mean, I love it. It's home.
But I hate it.
It's like an island surrounded by sharks.
Except our land sharks are on their way in.
It's just a matter of how long it takes them to get hungry enough.
Wednesday, March 5, 2025
The rain this morning was cold, but good.
Amy has already been cremated. I wonder if her mother is relieved. She doesn't look it.
She never liked Amy, but now she cries. The family spent money it couldn't afford to get the police involved.
The cops will collect their fee, knock around any nearby street poor, rob them of anything worth stealing, and then send them to jail.
None of that can help Amy.
Dad will preach at Amy's funeral on Saturday.
FUNERALS NEVER BOTHERED ME BEFORE. BUT THIS ONE . . .
YOU CARED ABOUT AMY.

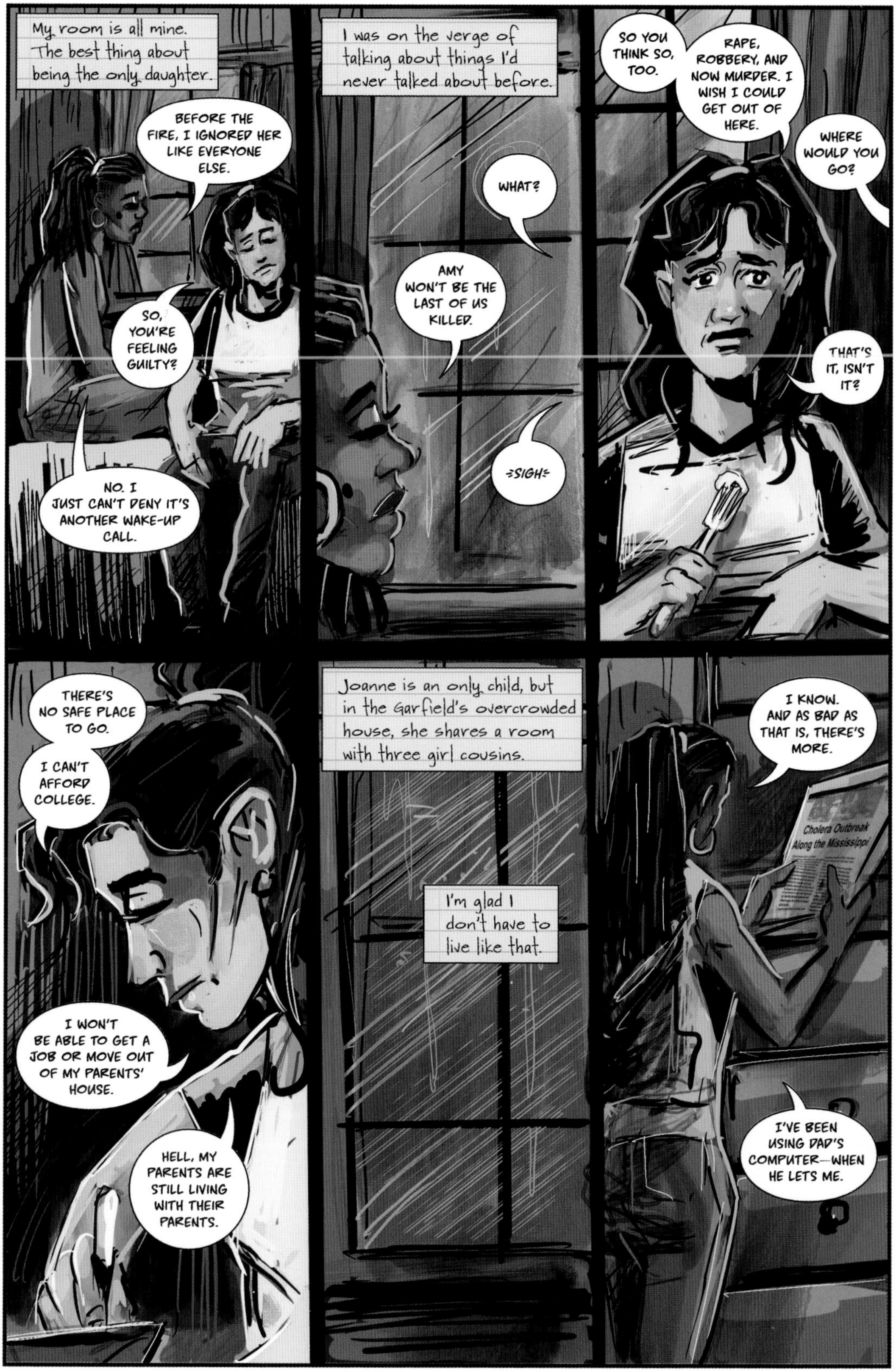
My room is all mine. The best thing about being the only daughter.
BEFORE THE FIRE, I IGNORED HER LIKE EVERYONE ELSE.
SO, YOU'RE FEELING GUILTY?
NO. I JUST CAN'T DENY IT'S ANOTHER WAKE-UP CALL.
I was on the verge of talking about things I'd never talked about before.
WHAT?
AMY WON'T BE THE LAST OF US KILLED.
SIGH
SO YOU THINK SO, TOO.
RAPE, ROBBERY, AND NOW MURDER. I WISH I COULD GET OUT OF HERE.
WHERE WOULD YOU GO?
THAT'S IT, ISN'T IT?
THERE'S NO SAFE PLACE TO GO.
I CAN'T AFFORD COLLEGE.
I WON'T BE ABLE TO GET A JOB OR MOVE OUT OF MY PARENTS' HOUSE.
HELL, MY PARENTS ARE STILL LIVING WITH THEIR PARENTS.
Joanne is an only child, but in the Garfield's overcrowded house, she shares a room with three girl cousins.
I'm glad I don't have to live like that.
I KNOW. AND AS BAD AS THAT IS, THERE'S MORE.
Cholera Outbreak Along the Mississippi
I'VE BEEN USING DAD'S COMPUTER—WHEN HE LETS ME.

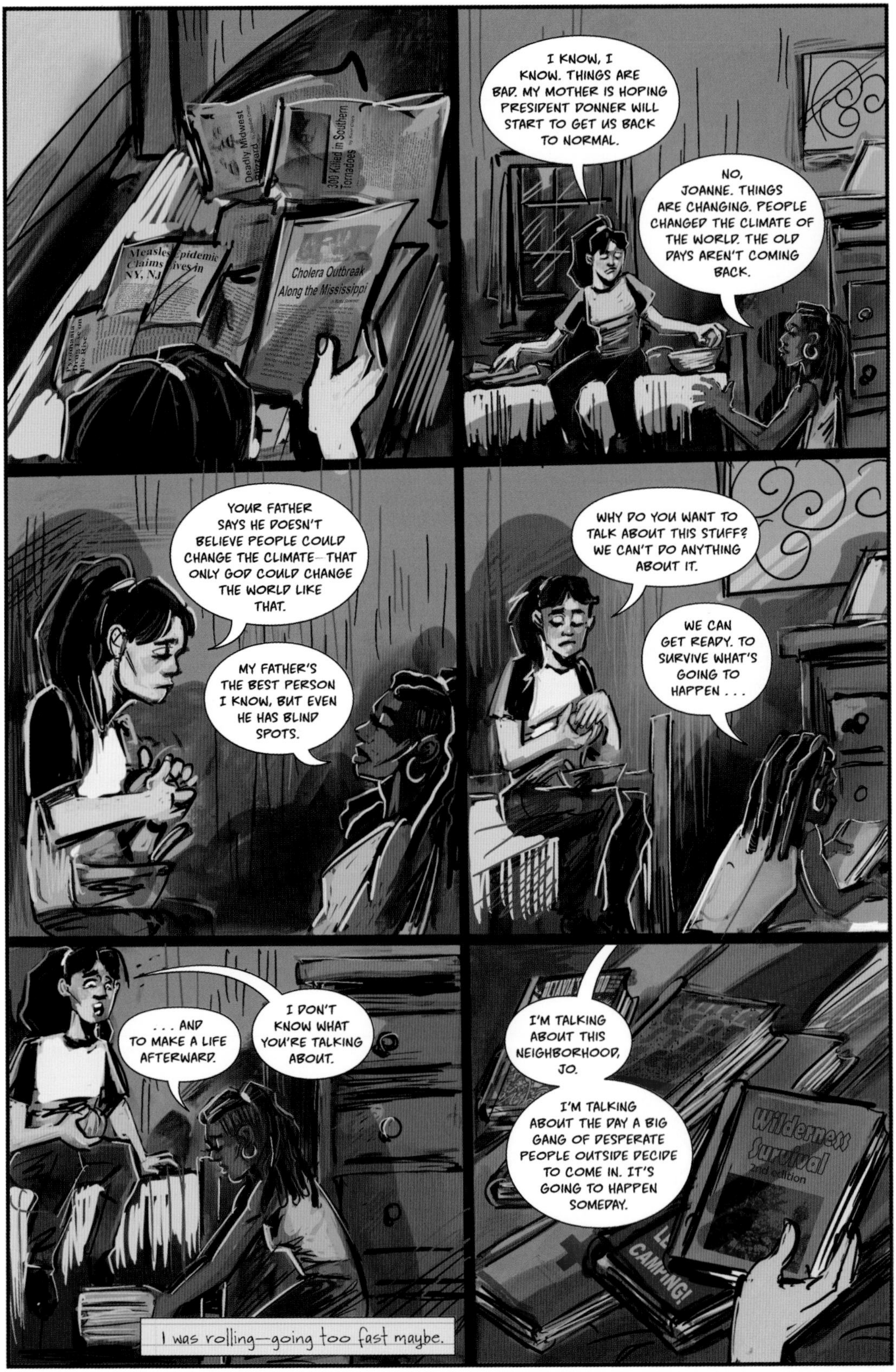

Deadly Midwest Blizzard
300 Killed in Southern Tornadoes
Measles Epidemic Claims Lives in NY, NJ
Cholera Outbreak Along the Mississippi
I KNOW, I KNOW. THINGS ARE BAD. MY MOTHER IS HOPING PRESIDENT DONNER WILL START TO GET US BACK TO NORMAL.
NO, JOANNE. THINGS ARE CHANGING. PEOPLE CHANGED THE CLIMATE OF THE WORLD. THE OLD DAYS AREN'T COMING BACK.
YOUR FATHER SAYS HE DOESN'T BELIEVE PEOPLE COULD CHANGE THE CLIMATE—THAT ONLY GOD COULD CHANGE THE WORLD LIKE THAT.
MY FATHER'S THE BEST PERSON I KNOW, BUT EVEN HE HAS BLIND SPOTS.
WHY DO YOU WANT TO TALK ABOUT THIS STUFF? WE CAN'T DO ANYTHING ABOUT IT.
WE CAN GET READY. TO SURVIVE WHAT'S GOING TO HAPPEN . . .
. . . AND TO MAKE A LIFE AFTERWARD.
I DON'T KNOW WHAT YOU'RE TALKING ABOUT.
I was rolling—going too fast maybe.
I'M TALKING ABOUT THIS NEIGHBORHOOD, JO.
I'M TALKING ABOUT THE DAY A BIG GANG OF DESPERATE PEOPLE OUTSIDE DECIDE TO COME IN. IT'S GOING TO HAPPEN SOMEDAY.
Wilderness Survival
2nd edition
CAMPING!

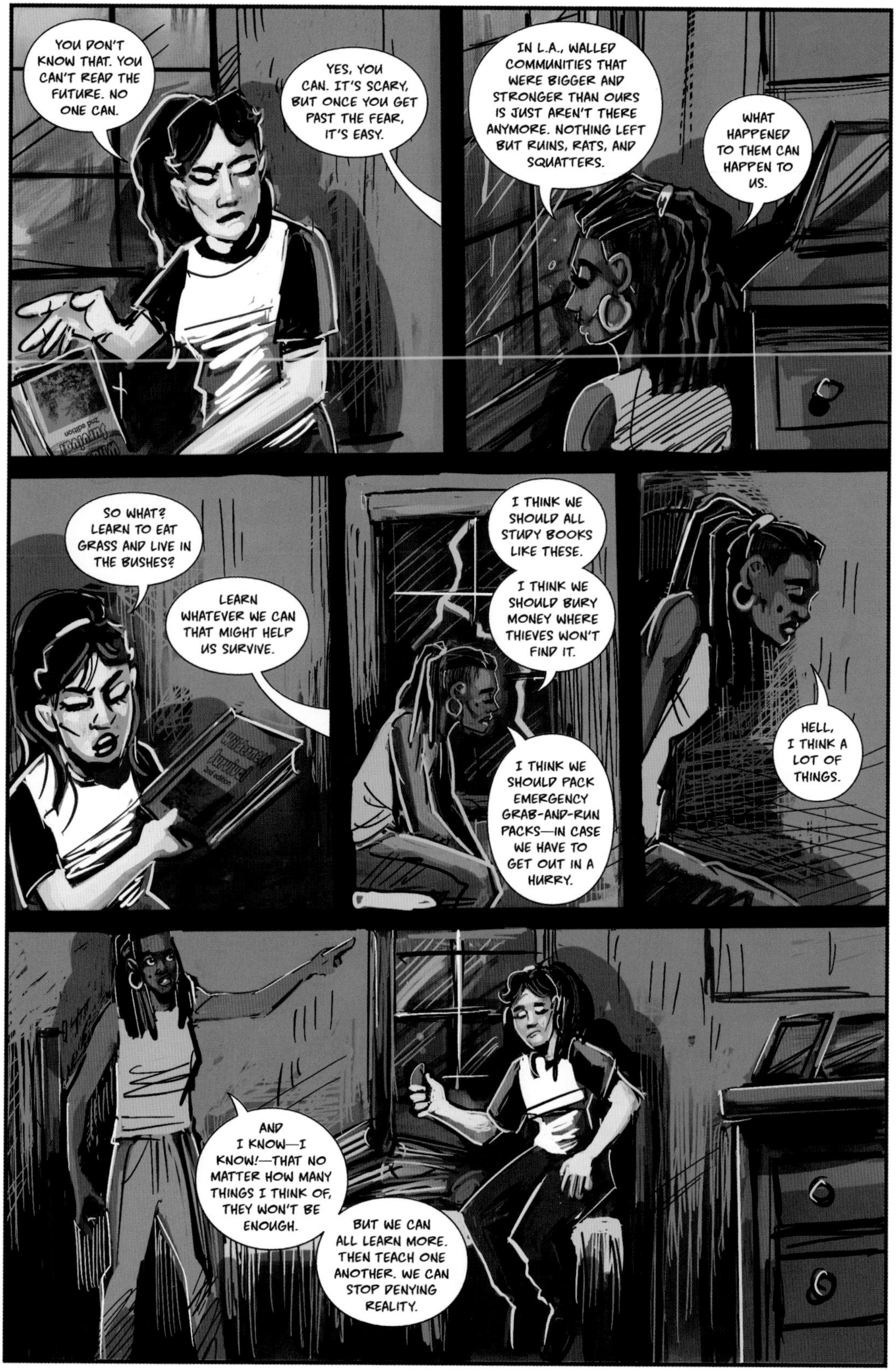
YOU DON'T KNOW THAT. YOU CAN'T READ THE FUTURE. NO ONE CAN.
YES, YOU CAN. IT'S SCARY, BUT ONCE YOU GET PAST THE FEAR, IT'S EASY.
IN L.A., WALLED COMMUNITIES THAT WERE BIGGER AND STRONGER THAN OURS IS JUST AREN'T THERE ANYMORE. NOTHING LEFT BUT RUINS, RATS, AND SQUATTERS.
WHAT HAPPENED TO THEM CAN HAPPEN TO US.
SO WHAT? LEARN TO EAT GRASS AND LIVE IN THE BUSHES?
LEARN WHATEVER WE CAN THAT MIGHT HELP US SURVIVE.
I THINK WE SHOULD ALL STUDY BOOKS LIKE THESE.
I THINK WE SHOULD BURY MONEY WHERE THIEVES WON'T FIND IT.
I THINK WE SHOULD PACK EMERGENCY GRAB-AND-RUN PACKS—IN CASE WE HAVE TO GET OUT IN A HURRY.
HELL, I THINK A LOT OF THINGS.
AND I KNOW—I KNOW!—THAT NO MATTER HOW MANY THINGS I THINK OF, THEY WON'T BE ENOUGH.
BUT WE CAN ALL LEARN MORE. THEN TEACH ONE ANOTHER. WE CAN STOP DENYING REALITY.

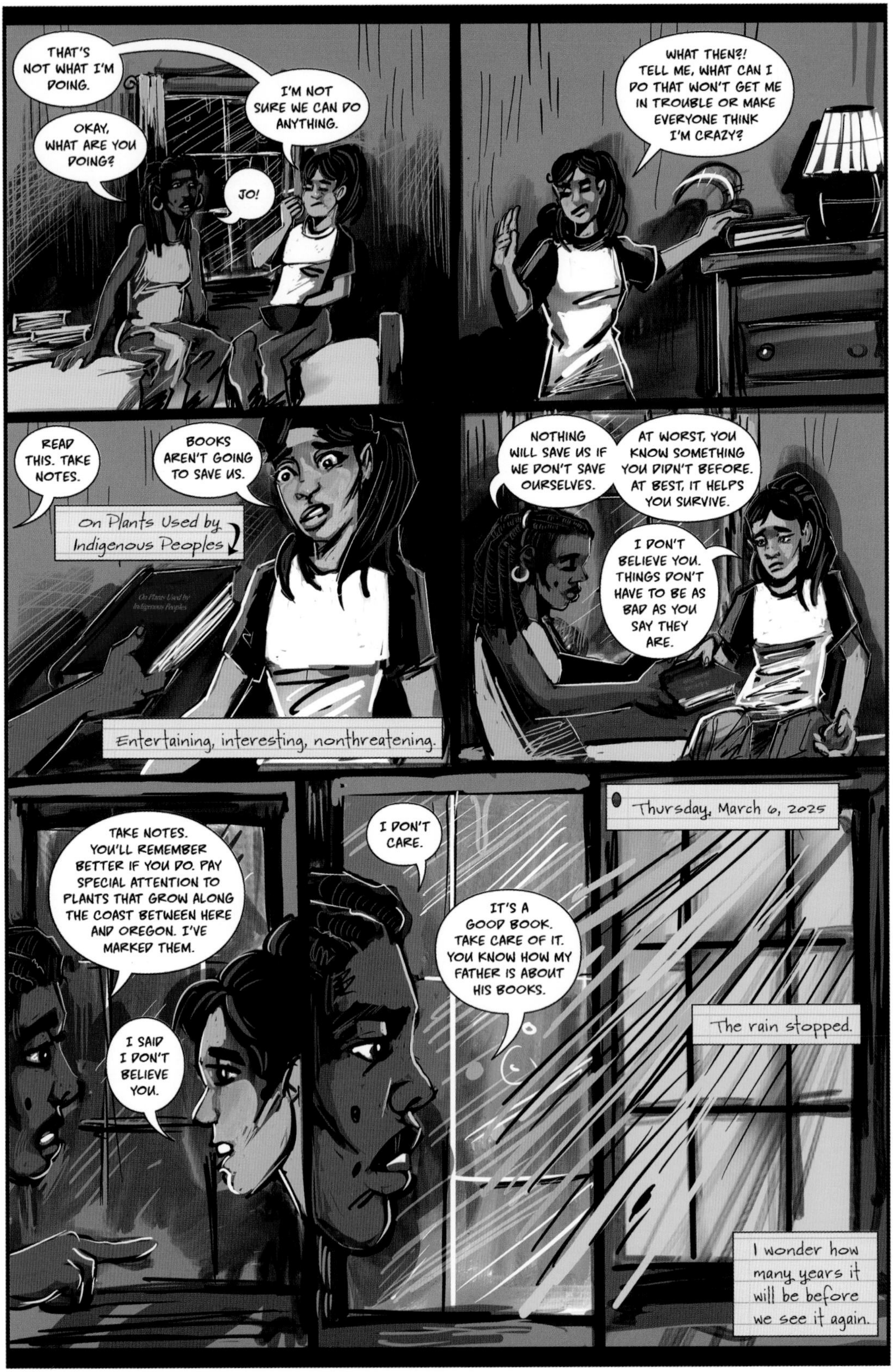
THAT'S NOT WHAT I'M DOING.
OKAY, WHAT ARE YOU DOING?
I'M NOT SURE WE CAN DO ANYTHING.
JO!
WHAT THEN?! TELL ME, WHAT CAN I DO THAT WON'T GET ME IN TROUBLE OR MAKE EVERYONE THINK I'M CRAZY?
READ THIS. TAKE NOTES.
BOOKS AREN'T GOING TO SAVE US.
On Plants Used by Indigenous Peoples
On Plants Used by Indigenous Peoples
Entertaining, interesting, nonthreatening.
NOTHING WILL SAVE US IF WE DON'T SAVE OURSELVES.
AT WORST, YOU KNOW SOMETHING YOU DIDN'T BEFORE. AT BEST, IT HELPS YOU SURVIVE.
I DON'T BELIEVE YOU. THINGS DON'T HAVE TO BE AS BAD AS YOU SAY THEY ARE.
TAKE NOTES. YOU'LL REMEMBER BETTER IF YOU DO. PAY SPECIAL ATTENTION TO PLANTS THAT GROW ALONG THE COAST BETWEEN HERE AND OREGON. I'VE MARKED THEM.
I SAID I DON'T BELIEVE YOU.
I DON'T CARE.
IT'S A GOOD BOOK. TAKE CARE OF IT. YOU KNOW HOW MY FATHER IS ABOUT HIS BOOKS.
Thursday, March 6, 2025
The rain stopped.
I wonder how many years it will be before we see it again.

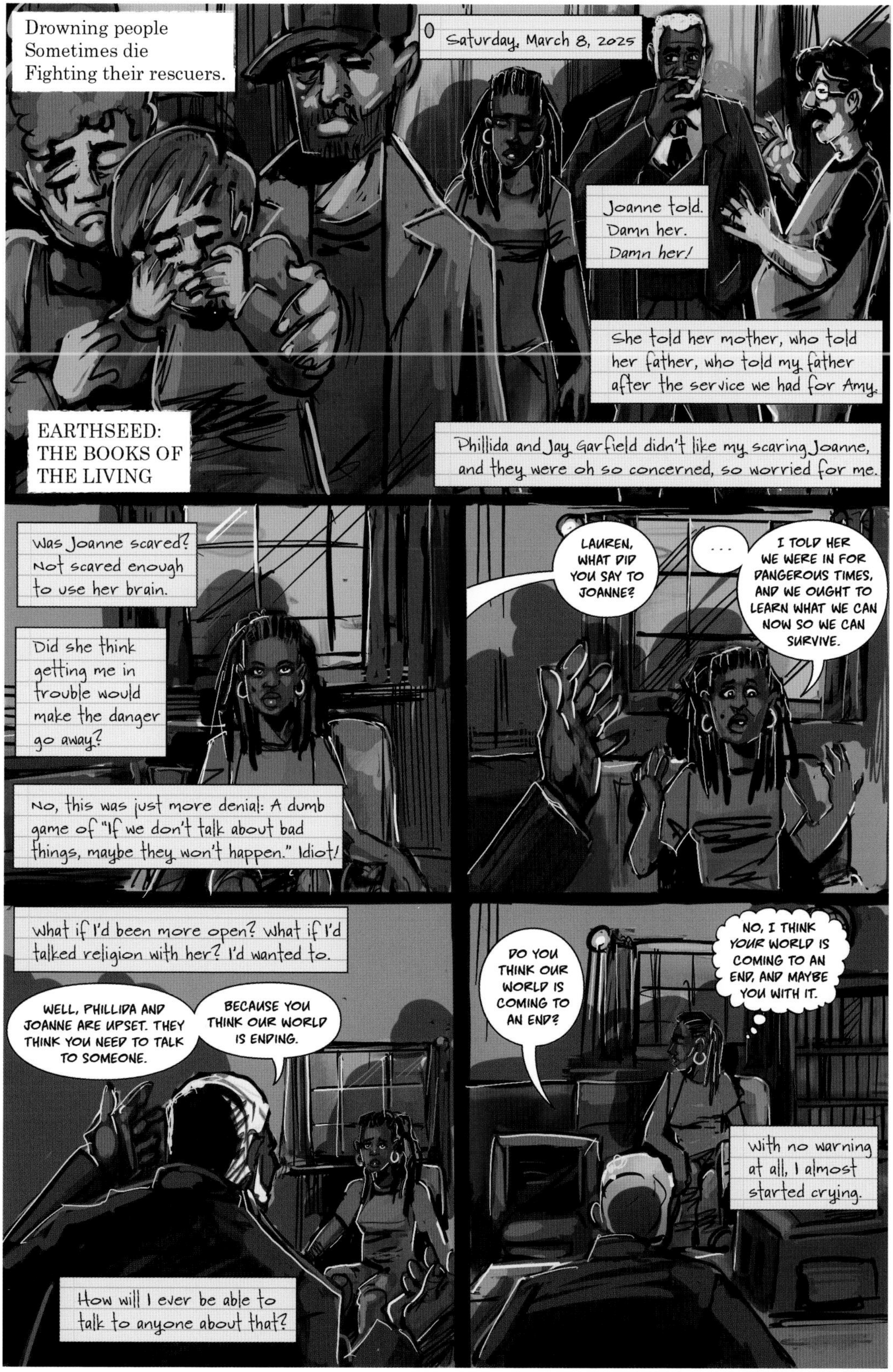

Drowning people
Sometimes die
Fighting their rescuers.
EARTHSEED: THE BOOKS OF THE LIVING
Saturday, March 8, 2025
Joanne told. Damn her. Damn her!
She told her mother, who told her father, who told my father after the service we had for Amy.
Phillida and Jay Garfield didn't like my scaring Joanne, and they were oh so concerned, so worried for me.
Was Joanne scared? Not scared enough to use her brain.
Did she think getting me in trouble would make the danger go away?
No, this was just more denial: A dumb game of "If we don't talk about bad things, maybe they won't happen." Idiot!
LAUREN, WHAT DID YOU SAY TO JOANNE?
. . .
I TOLD HER WE WERE IN FOR DANGEROUS TIMES, AND WE OUGHT TO LEARN WHAT WE CAN NOW SO WE CAN SURVIVE.
What if I'd been more open? What if I'd talked religion with her? I'd wanted to.
WELL, PHILLIDA AND JOANNE ARE UPSET. THEY THINK YOU NEED TO TALK TO SOMEONE.
BECAUSE YOU THINK OUR WORLD IS ENDING.
How will I ever be able to talk to anyone about that?
DO YOU THINK OUR WORLD IS COMING TO AN END?
NO, I THINK YOUR WORLD IS COMING TO AN END, AND MAYBE YOU WITH IT.
With no warning at all, I almost started crying.

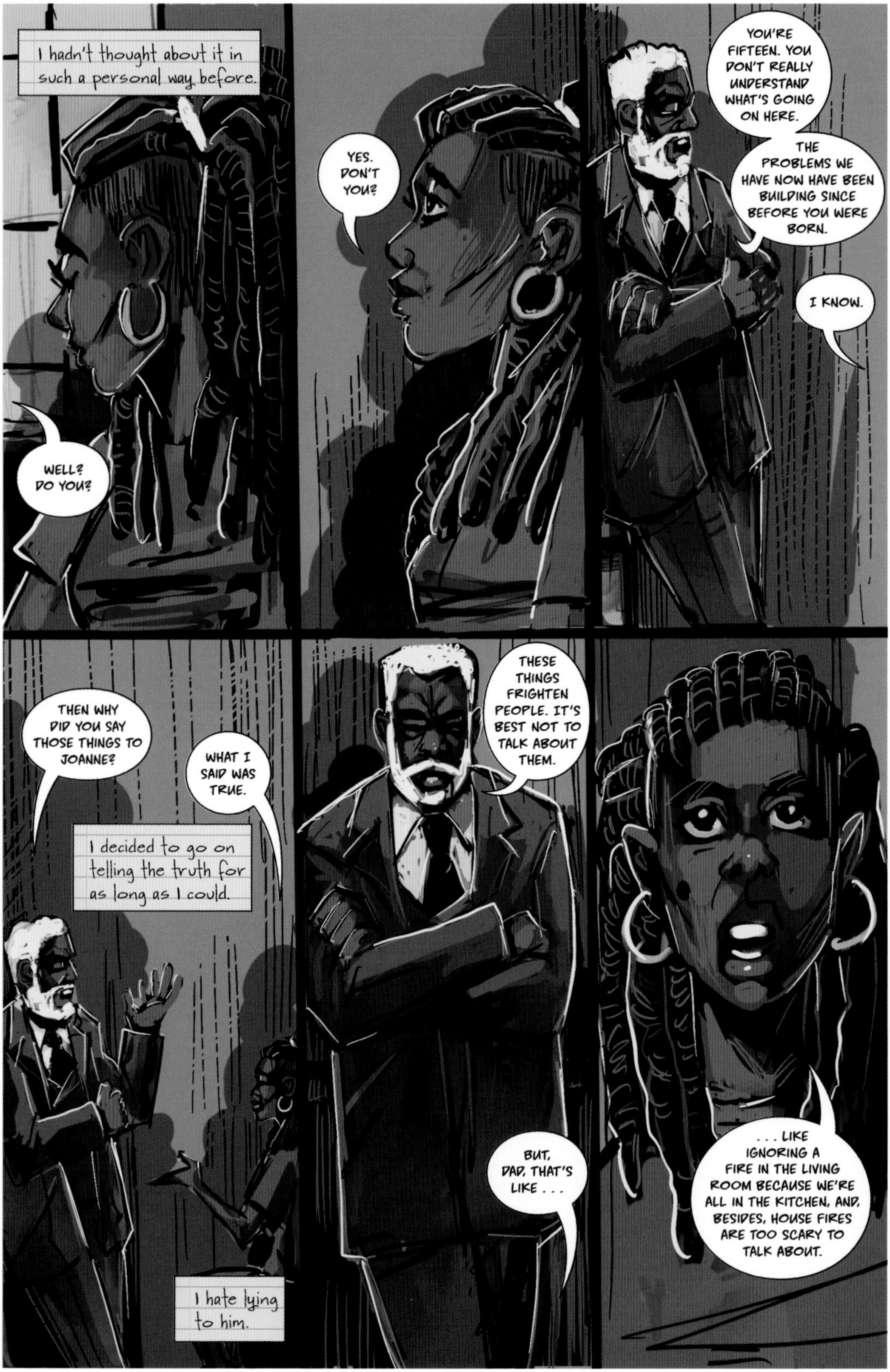
I hadn't thought about it in such a personal way before.
WELL? DO YOU?
YES. DON'T YOU?
YOU'RE FIFTEEN. YOU DON'T REALLY UNDERSTAND WHAT'S GOING ON HERE.
THE PROBLEMS WE HAVE NOW HAVE BEEN BUILDING SINCE BEFORE YOU WERE BORN.
I KNOW.
THEN WHY DID YOU SAY THOSE THINGS TO JOANNE?
WHAT I SAID WAS TRUE.
I decided to go on telling the truth for as long as I could.
I hate lying to him.
THESE THINGS FRIGHTEN PEOPLE. IT'S BEST NOT TO TALK ABOUT THEM.
BUT, DAD, THAT'S LIKE . . .
. . . LIKE IGNORING A FIRE IN THE LIVING ROOM BECAUSE WE'RE ALL IN THE KITCHEN, AND, BESIDES, HOUSE FIRES ARE TOO SCARY TO TALK ABOUT.

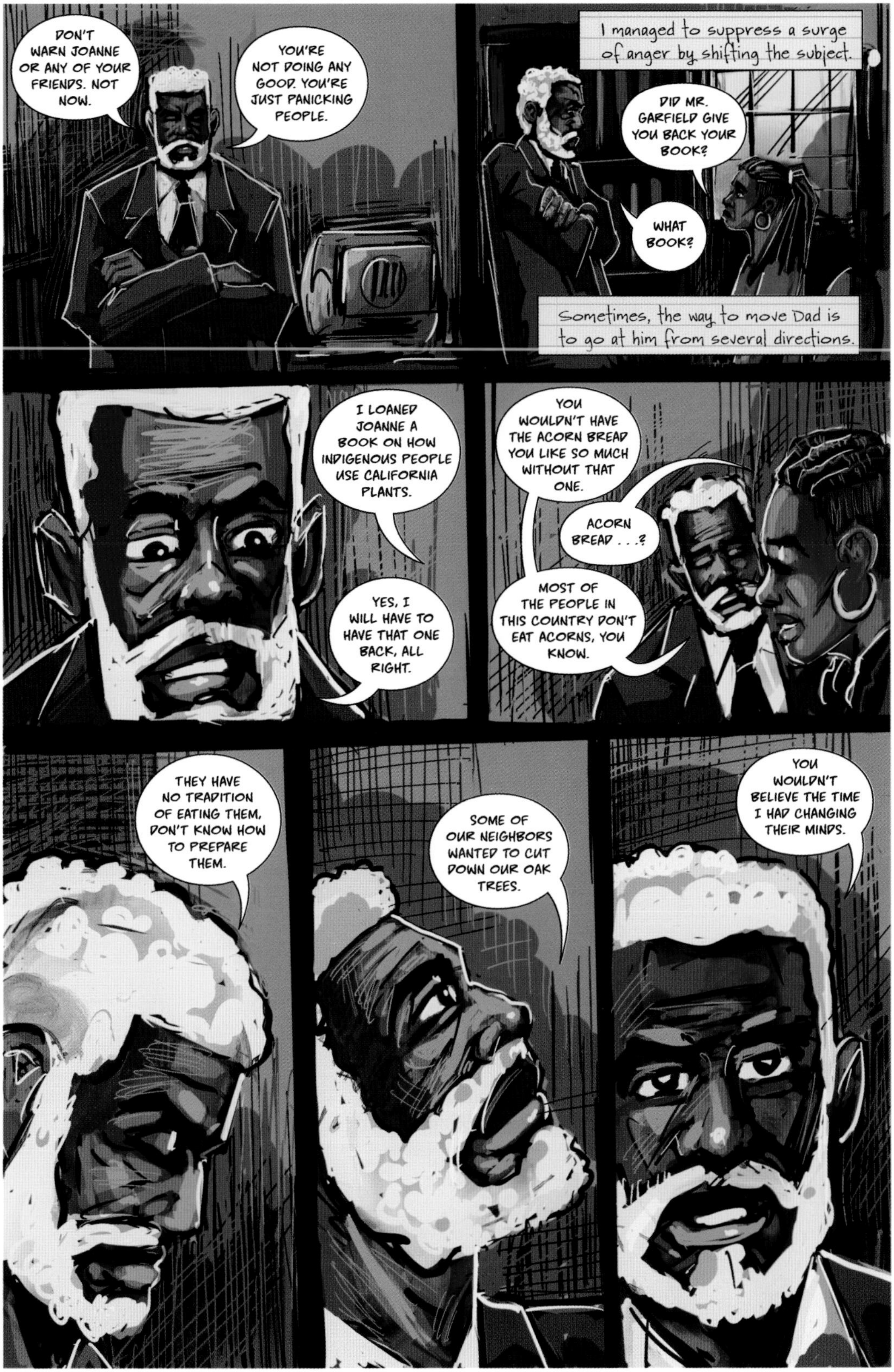
DON'T WARN JOANNE OR ANY OF YOUR FRIENDS. NOT NOW.
YOU'RE NOT DOING ANY GOOD. YOU'RE JUST PANICKING PEOPLE.
I managed to suppress a surge of anger by shifting the subject.
DID MR. GARFIELD GIVE YOU BACK YOUR BOOK?
WHAT BOOK?
Sometimes, the way to move Dad is to go at him from several directions.
I LOANED JOANNE A BOOK ON HOW INDIGENOUS PEOPLE USE CALIFORNIA PLANTS.
YES, I WILL HAVE TO HAVE THAT ONE BACK, ALL RIGHT.
YOU WOULDN'T HAVE THE ACORN BREAD YOU LIKE SO MUCH WITHOUT THAT ONE.
ACORN BREAD . . .?
MOST OF THE PEOPLE IN THIS COUNTRY DON'T EAT ACORNS, YOU KNOW.
THEY HAVE NO TRADITION OF EATING THEM, DON'T KNOW HOW TO PREPARE THEM.
SOME OF OUR NEIGHBORS WANTED TO CUT DOWN OUR OAK TREES.
YOU WOULDN'T BELIEVE THE TIME I HAD CHANGING THEIR MINDS.

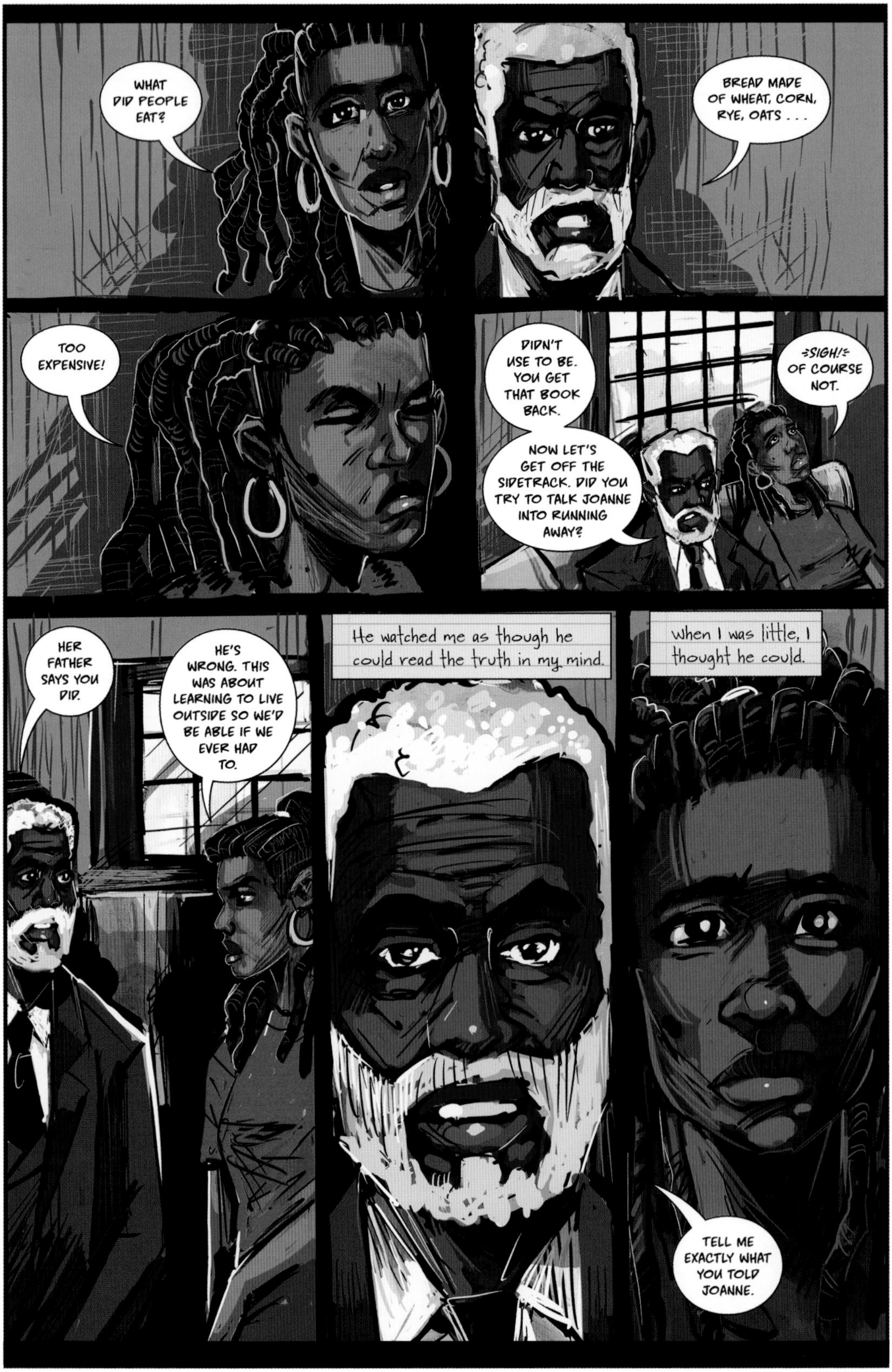
WHAT DID PEOPLE EAT?
BREAD MADE OF WHEAT, CORN, RYE, OATS . . .
TOO EXPENSIVE!
DIDN'T USE TO BE. YOU GET THAT BOOK BACK.
NOW LET'S GET OFF THE SIDETRACK. DID YOU TRY TO TALK JOANNE INTO RUNNING AWAY?
SIGH! OF COURSE NOT.
HER FATHER SAYS YOU DID.
HE'S WRONG. THIS WAS ABOUT LEARNING TO LIVE OUTSIDE SO WE'D BE ABLE IF WE EVER HAD TO.
He watched me as though he could read the truth in my mind.
When I was little, I thought he could.
TELL ME EXACTLY WHAT YOU TOLD JOANNE.

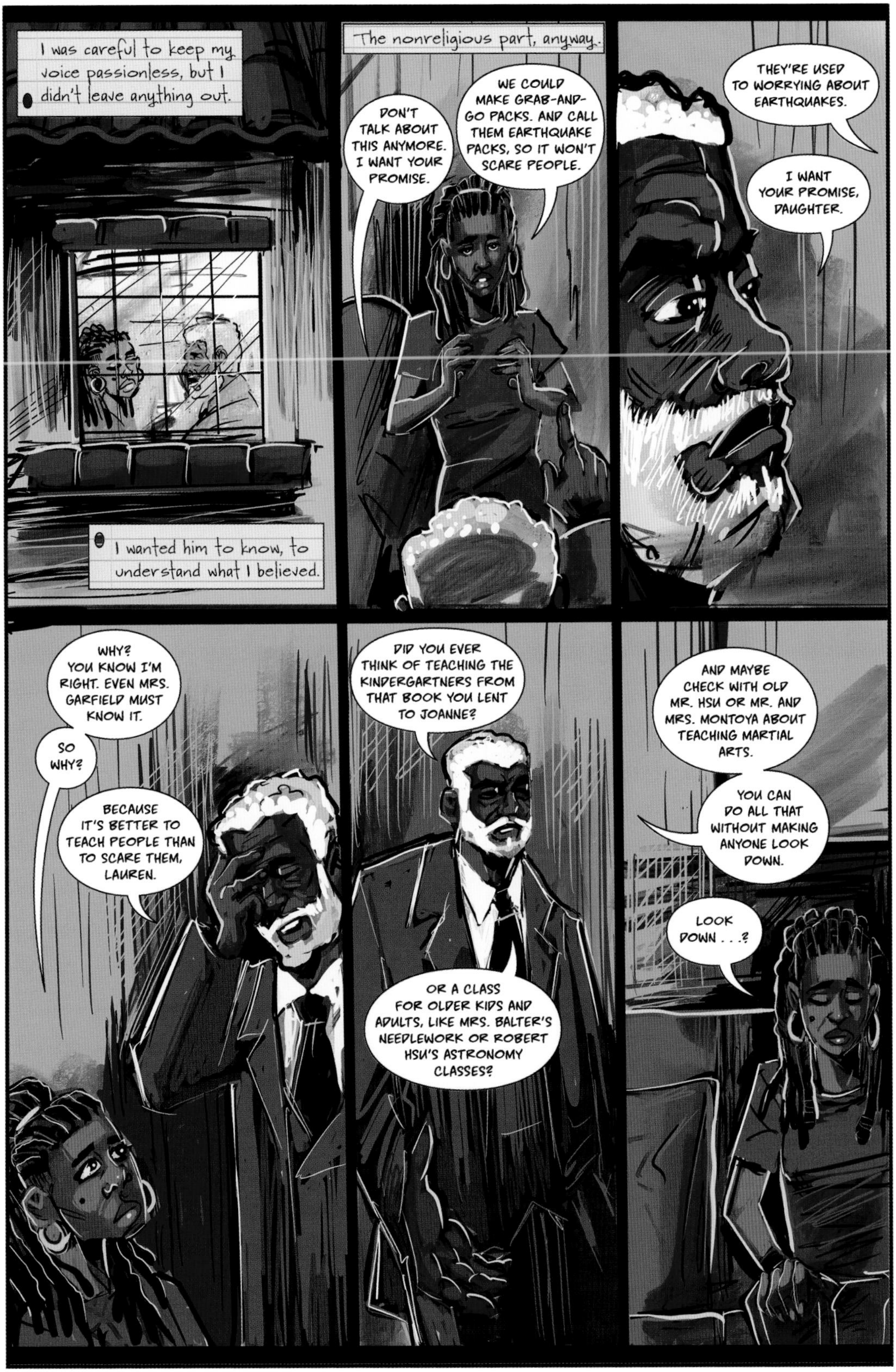
I was careful to keep my voice passionless, but I didn't leave anything out.
I wanted him to know, to understand what I believed.
The nonreligious part, anyway.
DON'T TALK ABOUT THIS ANYMORE. I WANT YOUR PROMISE.
WE COULD MAKE GRAB-AND-GO PACKS. AND CALL THEM EARTHQUAKE PACKS, SO IT WON'T SCARE PEOPLE.
THEY'RE USED TO WORRYING ABOUT EARTHQUAKES.
I WANT YOUR PROMISE, DAUGHTER.
WHY? YOU KNOW I'M RIGHT. EVEN MRS. GARFIELD MUST KNOW IT.
SO WHY?
BECAUSE IT'S BETTER TO TEACH PEOPLE THAN TO SCARE THEM, LAUREN.
DID YOU EVER THINK OF TEACHING THE KINDERGARTNERS FROM THAT BOOK YOU LENT TO JOANNE?
OR A CLASS FOR OLDER KIDS AND ADULTS, LIKE MRS. BALTER'S NEEDLEWORK OR ROBERT HSU'S ASTRONOMY CLASSES?
AND MAYBE CHECK WITH OLD MR. HSU OR MR. AND MRS. MONTOYA ABOUT TEACHING MARTIAL ARTS.
YOU CAN DO ALL THAT WITHOUT MAKING ANYONE LOOK DOWN.
LOOK DOWN . . .?

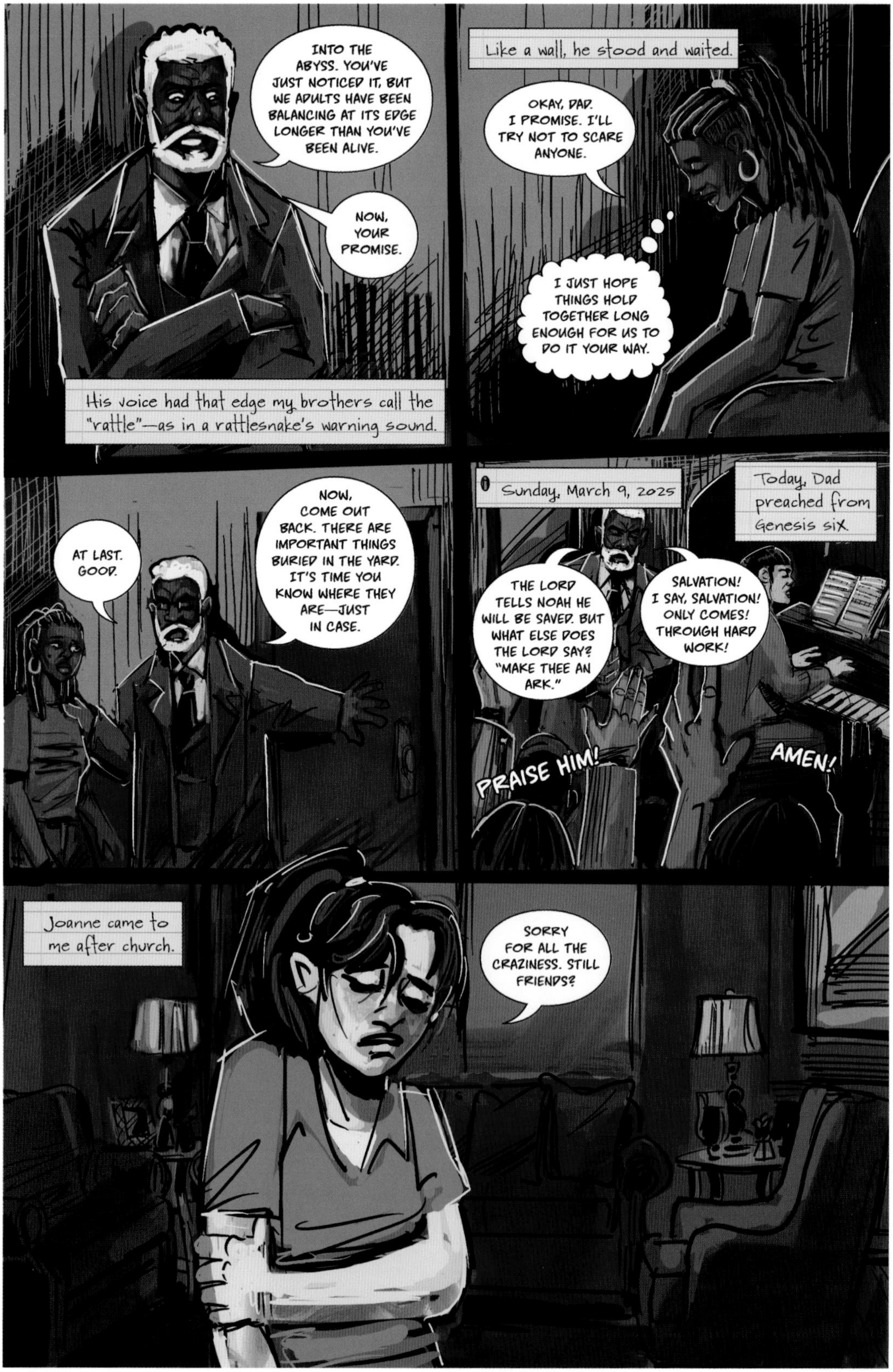
INTO THE ABYSS. YOU'VE JUST NOTICED IT, BUT WE ADULTS HAVE BEEN BALANCING AT ITS EDGE LONGER THAN YOU'VE BEEN ALIVE.
NOW, YOUR PROMISE.
His voice had that edge my brothers call the "rattle"—as in a rattlesnake's warning sound.
Like a wall, he stood and waited.
OKAY, DAD. I PROMISE. I'LL TRY NOT TO SCARE ANYONE.
I JUST HOPE THINGS HOLD TOGETHER LONG ENOUGH FOR US TO DO IT YOUR WAY.
AT LAST. GOOD.
NOW, COME OUT BACK. THERE ARE IMPORTANT THINGS BURIED IN THE YARD. IT'S TIME YOU KNOW WHERE THEY ARE—JUST IN CASE.
Sunday, March 9, 2025
Today, Dad preached from Genesis six.
THE LORD TELLS NOAH HE WILL BE SAVED. BUT WHAT ELSE DOES THE LORD SAY? "MAKE THEE AN ARK."
SALVATION! I SAY, SALVATION! ONLY COMES! THROUGH HARD WORK!
PRAISE HIM!
AMEN!
Joanne came to me after church.
SORRY FOR ALL THE CRAZINESS. STILL FRIENDS?

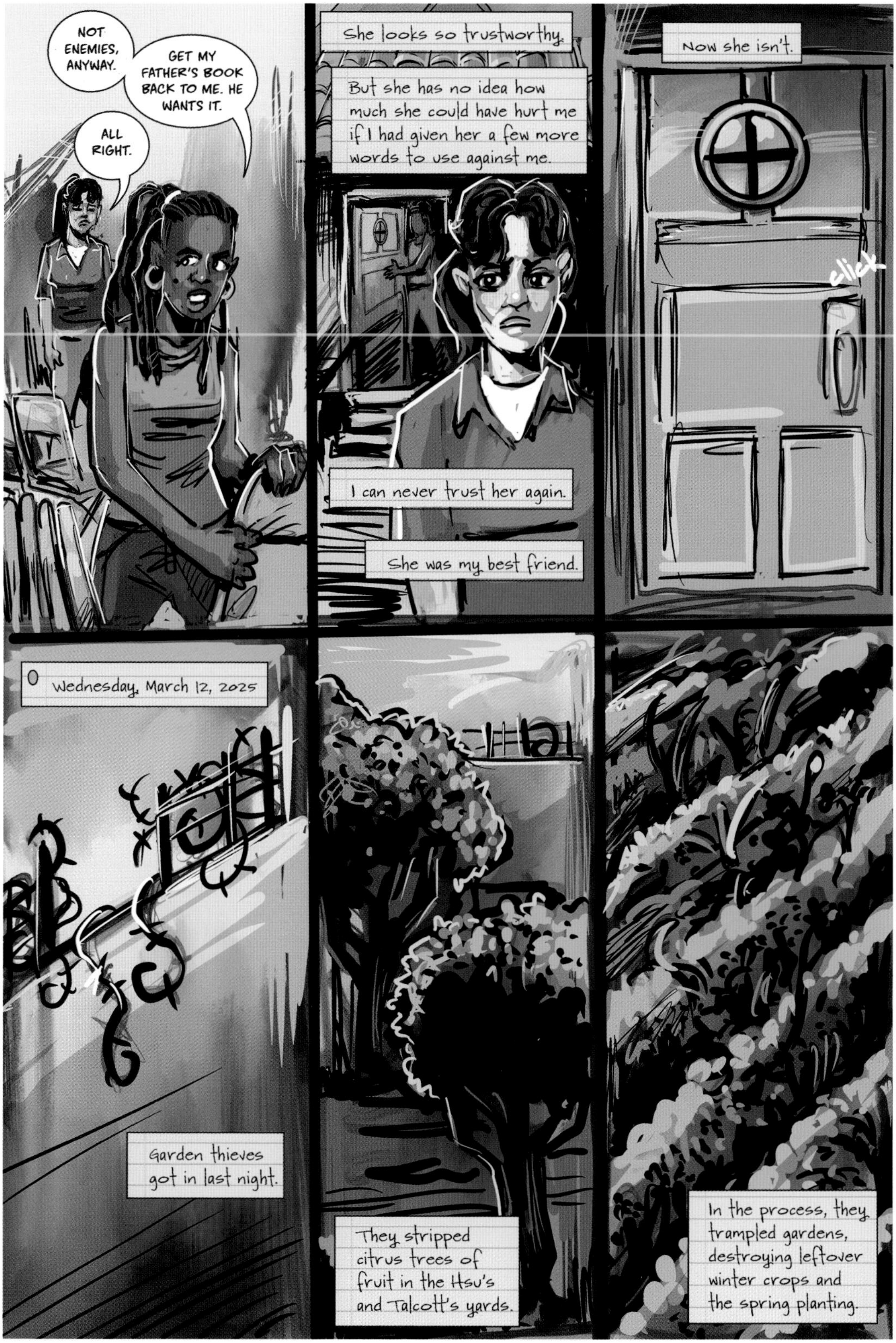
NOT ENEMIES, ANYWAY.
GET MY FATHER'S BOOK BACK TO ME. HE WANTS IT.
ALL RIGHT.
She looks so trustworthy.
But she has no idea how much she could have hurt me if I had given her a few more words to use against me.
I can never trust her again.
She was my best friend.
Now she isn't.
click
Wednesday, March 12, 2025
Garden thieves got in last night.
They stripped citrus trees of fruit in the Hsu's and Talcott's yards.
In the process, they trampled gardens, destroying leftover winter crops and the spring planting.

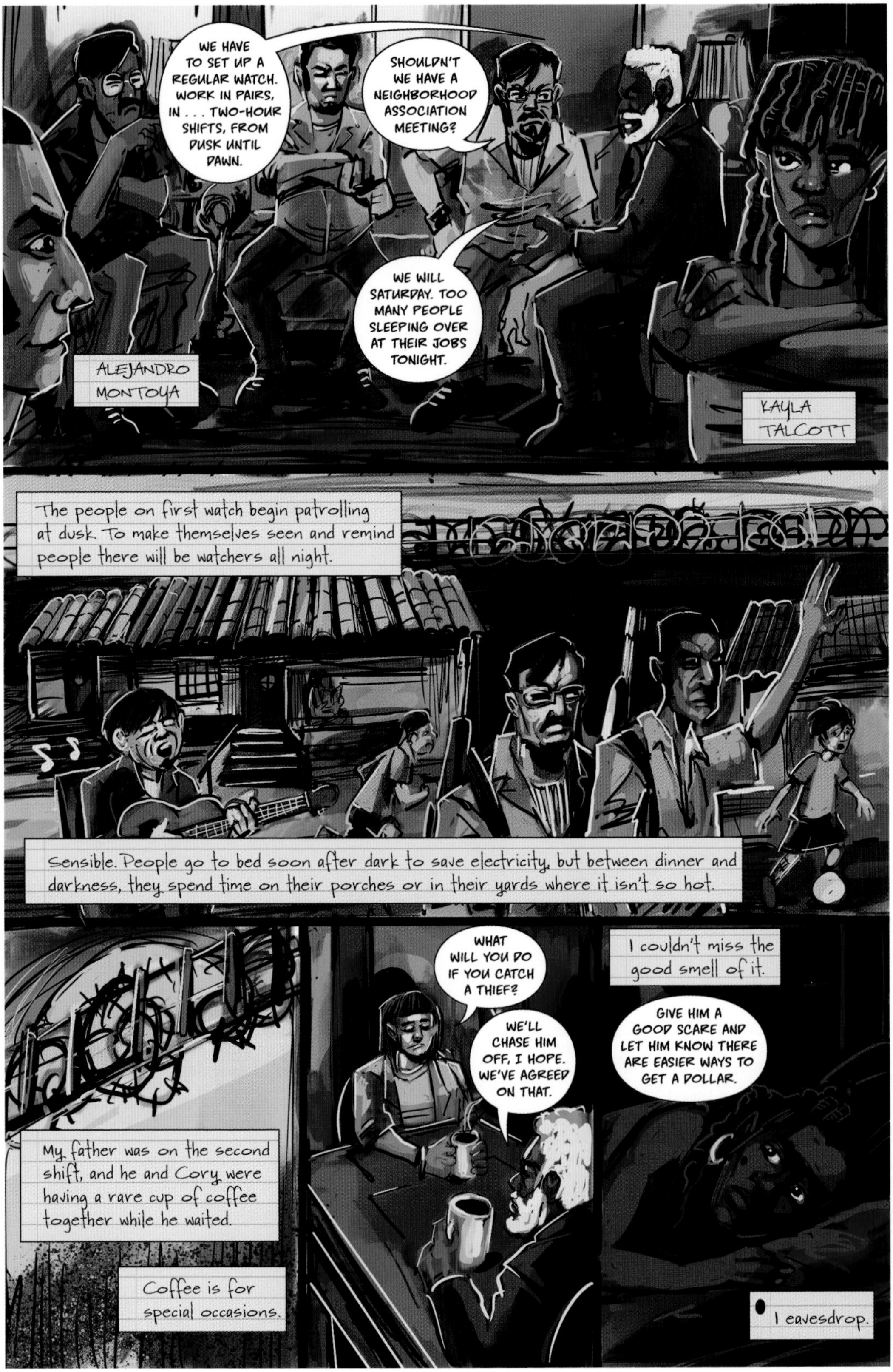
WE HAVE TO SET UP A REGULAR WATCH. WORK IN PAIRS, IN . . . TWO-HOUR SHIFTS, FROM DUSK UNTIL DAWN.
SHOULDN'T WE HAVE A NEIGHBORHOOD ASSOCIATION MEETING?
WE WILL SATURDAY. TOO MANY PEOPLE SLEEPING OVER AT THEIR JOBS TONIGHT.
ALEJANDRO MONTOYA
KAYLA TALCOTT
The people on first watch begin patrolling at dusk. To make themselves seen and remind people there will be watchers all night.
Sensible. People go to bed soon after dark to save electricity, but between dinner and darkness, they spend time on their porches or in their yards where it isn't so hot.
My father was on the second shift, and he and Cory were having a rare cup of coffee together while he waited.
Coffee is for special occasions.
WHAT WILL YOU DO IF YOU CATCH A THIEF?
WE'LL CHASE HIM OFF, I HOPE. WE'VE AGREED ON THAT.
I couldn't miss the good smell of it.
GIVE HIM A GOOD SCARE AND LET HIM KNOW THERE ARE EASIER WAYS TO GET A DOLLAR.
I eavesdrop.

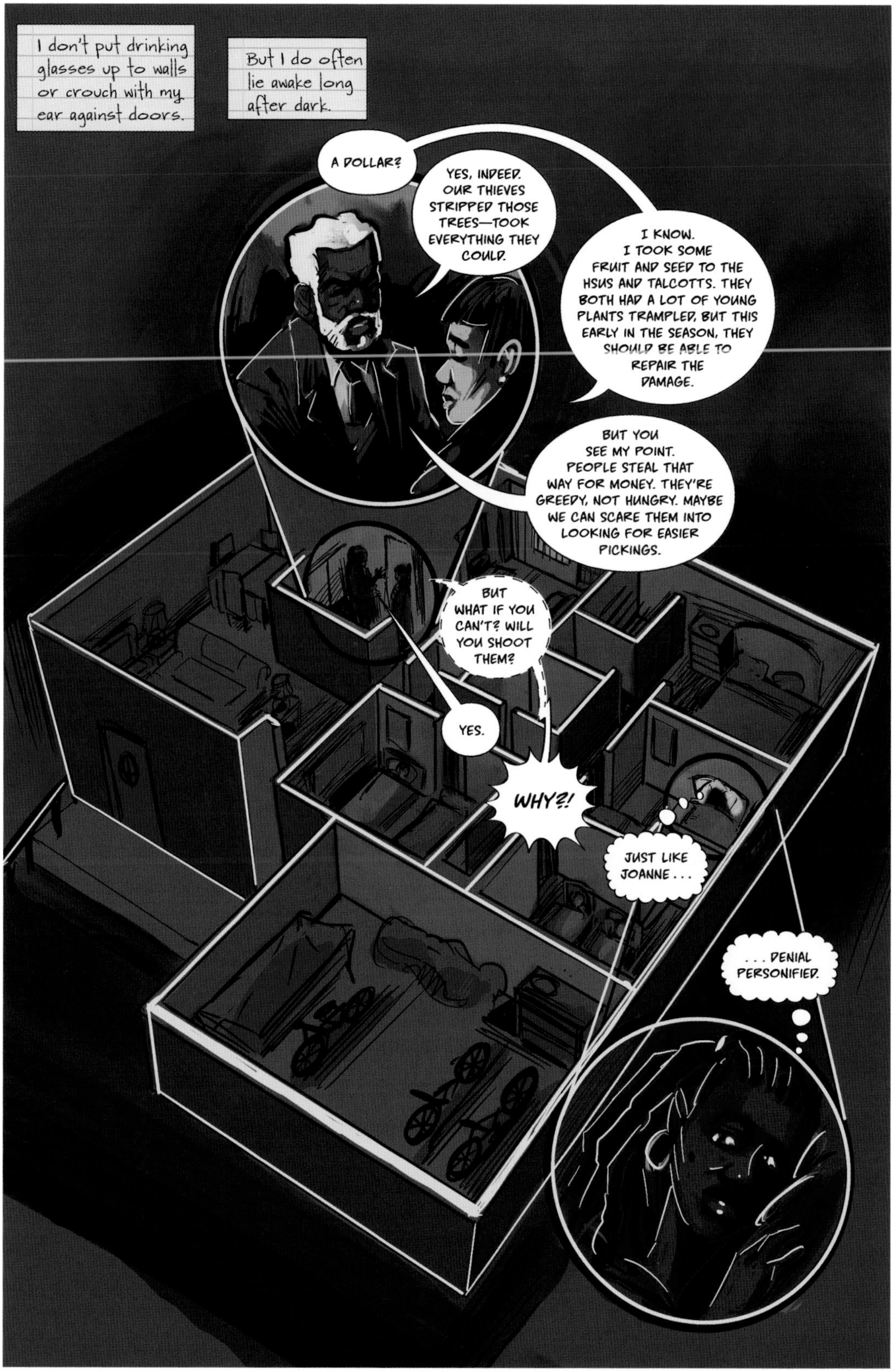

I don't put drinking glasses up to walls or crouch with my ear against doors.
But I do often lie awake long after dark.
A DOLLAR?
YES, INDEED. OUR THIEVES STRIPPED THOSE TREES—TOOK EVERYTHING THEY COULD.
I KNOW. I TOOK SOME FRUIT AND SEED TO THE HSUS AND TALCOTTS. THEY BOTH HAD A LOT OF YOUNG PLANTS TRAMPLED, BUT THIS EARLY IN THE SEASON, THEY SHOULD BE ABLE TO REPAIR THE DAMAGE.
BUT YOU SEE MY POINT. PEOPLE STEAL THAT WAY FOR MONEY. THEY'RE GREEDY, NOT HUNGRY. MAYBE WE CAN SCARE THEM INTO LOOKING FOR EASIER PICKINGS.
BUT WHAT IF YOU CAN'T? WILL YOU SHOOT THEM?
YES.
WHY?!
JUST LIKE JOANNE . . .
. . . DENIAL PERSONIFIED.

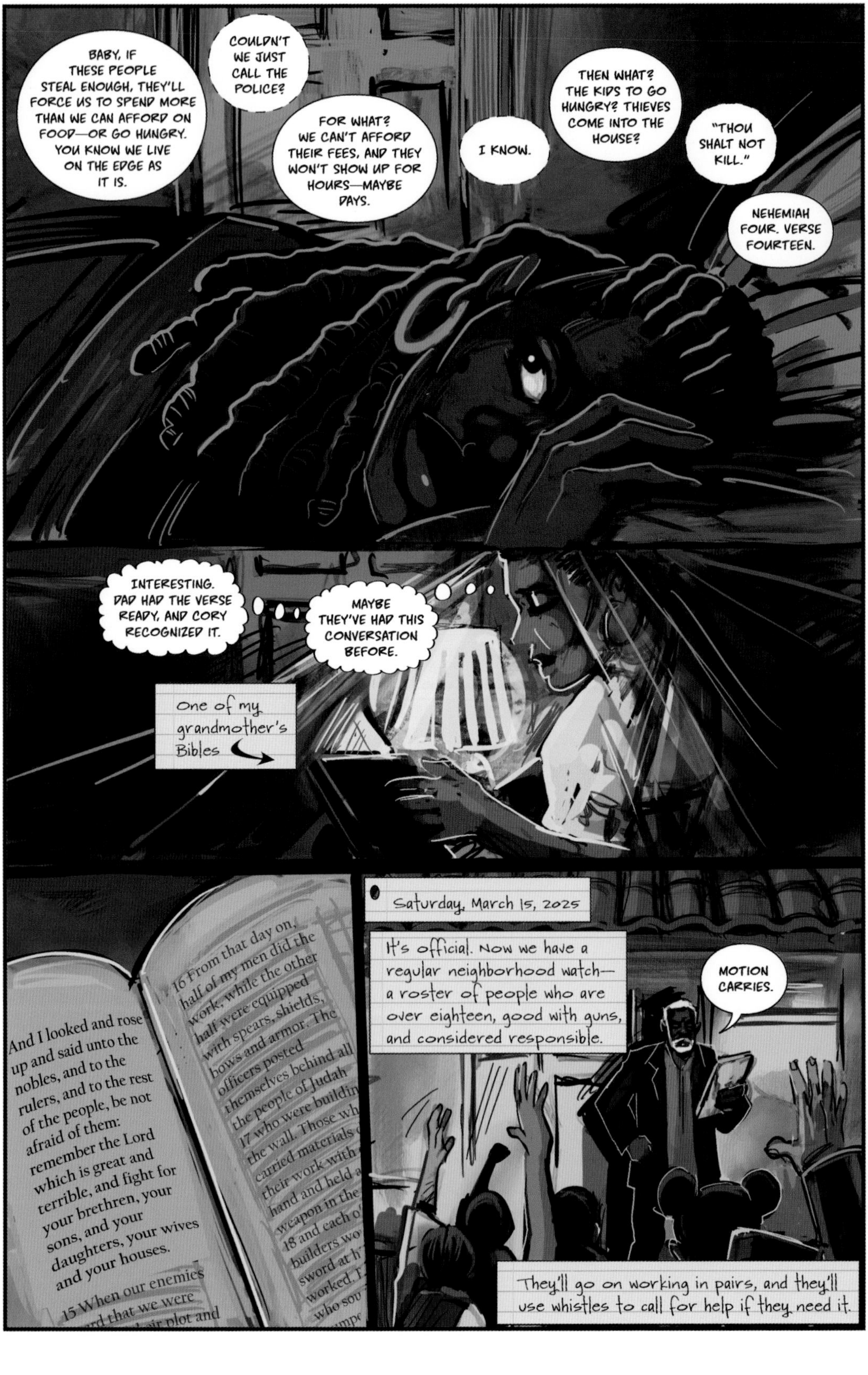
BABY, IF THESE PEOPLE STEAL ENOUGH, THEY'LL FORCE US TO SPEND MORE THAN WE CAN AFFORD ON FOOD—OR GO HUNGRY. YOU KNOW WE LIVE ON THE EDGE AS IT IS.
COULDN'T WE JUST CALL THE POLICE?
FOR WHAT? WE CAN'T AFFORD THEIR FEES, AND THEY WON'T SHOW UP FOR HOURS—MAYBE DAYS.
I KNOW.
THEN WHAT? THE KIDS TO GO HUNGRY? THIEVES COME INTO THE HOUSE?
"THOU SHALT NOT KILL."
NEHEMIAH FOUR. VERSE FOURTEEN.
INTERESTING. DAD HAD THE VERSE READY, AND CORY RECOGNIZED IT.
MAYBE THEY'VE HAD THIS CONVERSATION BEFORE.
One of my grandmother's Bibles
And I looked and rose up and said unto the nobles, and to the rulers, and to the rest of the people, be not afraid of them: remember the Lord which is great and terrible, and fight for your brethren, your sons, and your daughters, your wives and your houses.
15 When our enemies
16 From that day on, half of my men did the work, while the other half were equipped with spears, shields, bows and armor. The officers posted themselves behind all the people of Judah
Saturday, March 15, 2025
It's official. Now we have a regular neighborhood watch—a roster of people who are over eighteen, good with guns, and considered responsible.
MOTION CARRIES.
They'll go on working in pairs, and they'll use whistles to call for help if they need it.

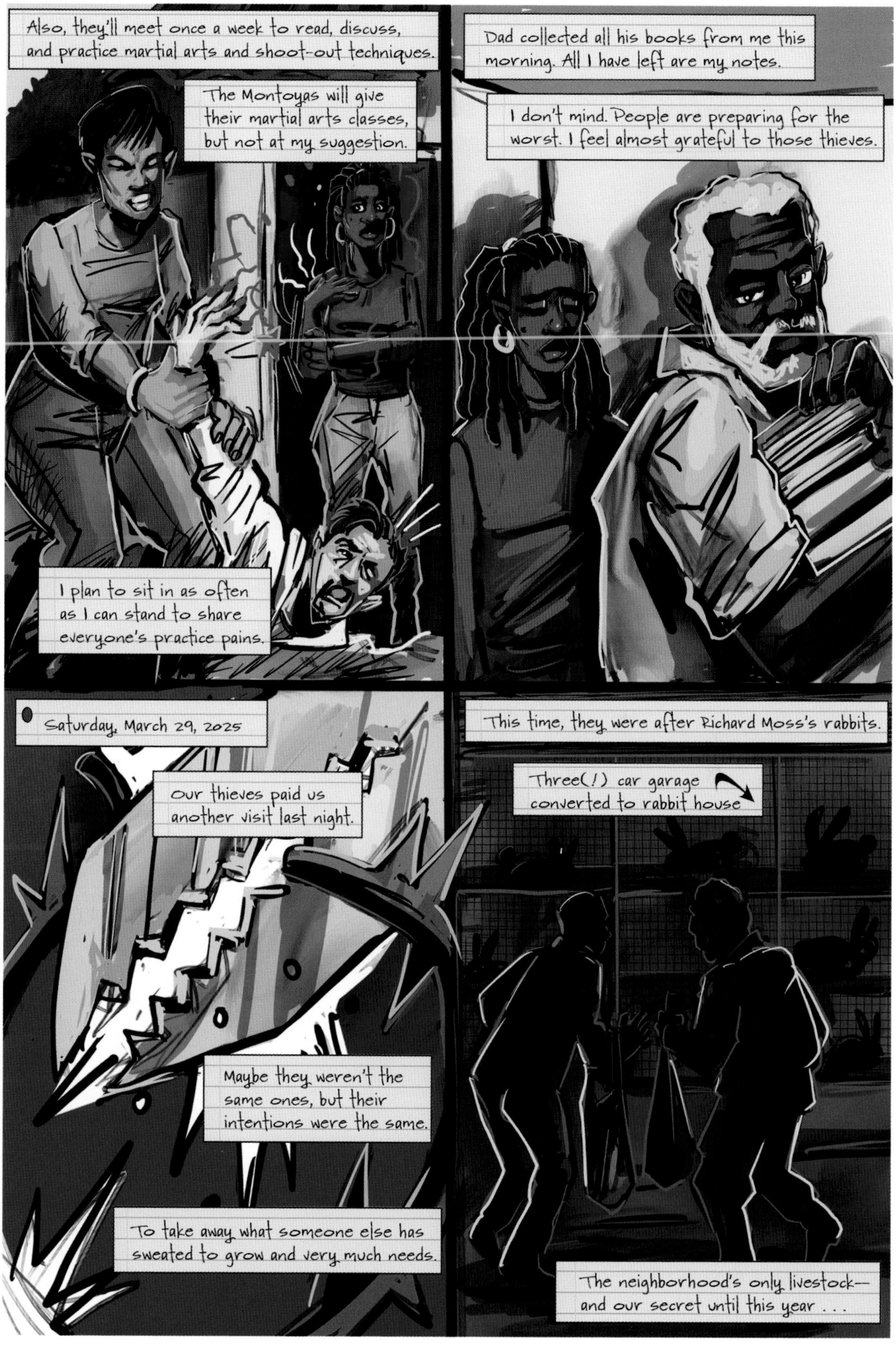
Also, they'll meet once a week to read, discuss, and practice martial arts and shoot-out techniques.
The Montoyas will give their martial arts classes, but not at my suggestion.
I plan to sit in as often as I can stand to share everyone's practice pains.
Dad collected all his books from me this morning. All I have left are my notes.
I don't mind. People are preparing for the worst. I feel almost grateful to those thieves.
Saturday, March 29, 2025
Our thieves paid us another visit last night.
Maybe they weren't the same ones, but their intentions were the same.
To take away what someone else has sweated to grow and very much needs.
This time, they were after Richard Moss's rabbits.
Three(!) car garage converted to rabbit house
The neighborhood's only livestock— and our secret until this year . . .

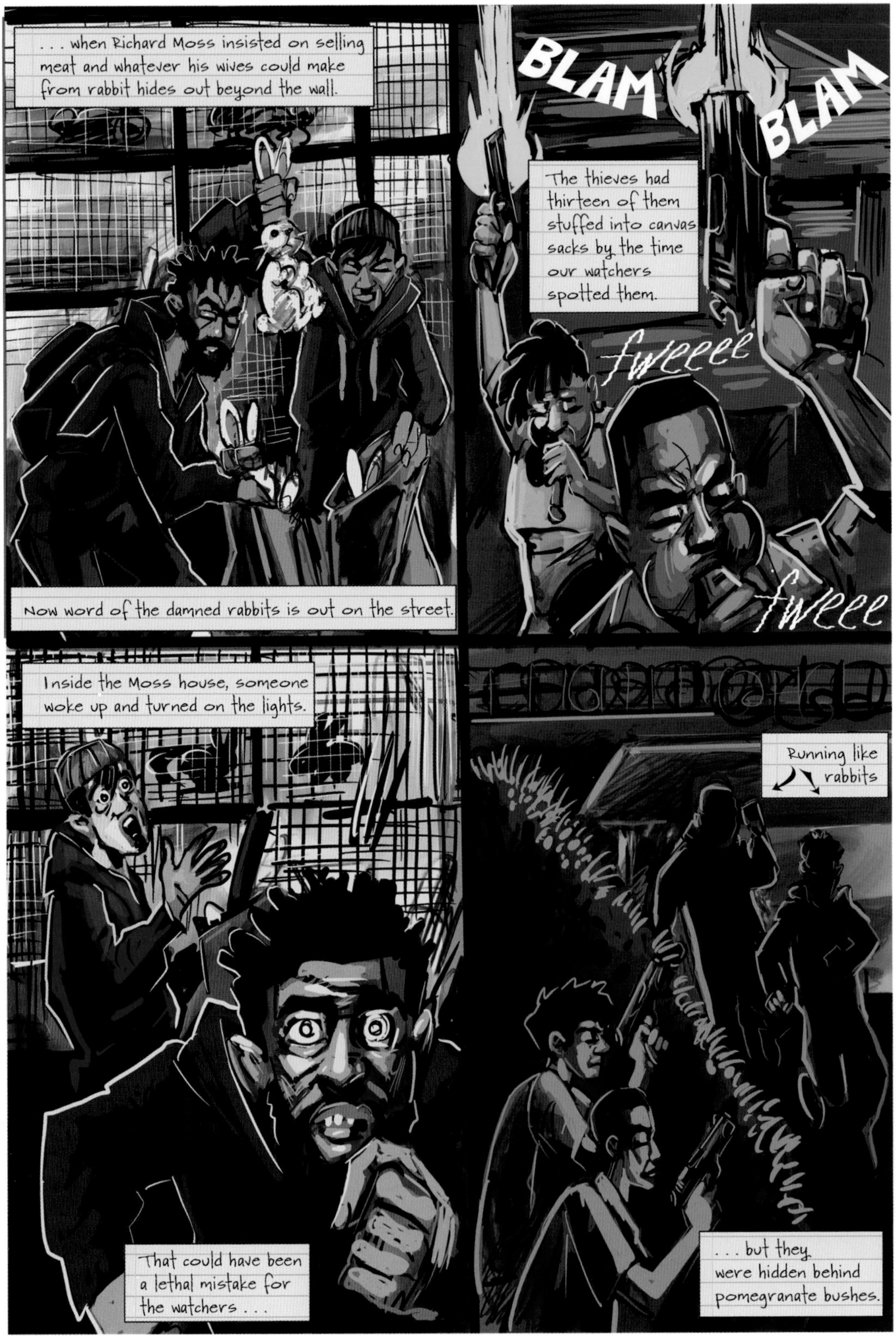
. . . when Richard Moss insisted on selling meat and whatever his wives could make from rabbit hides out beyond the wall.
Now word of the damned rabbits is out on the street.
BLAM
BLAM
The thieves had thirteen of them stuffed into canvas sacks by the time our watchers spotted them.
fweeee
fweee
Inside the Moss house, someone woke up and turned on the lights.
That could have been a lethal mistake for the watchers . . .
Running like rabbits
. . . but they were hidden behind pomegranate bushes.

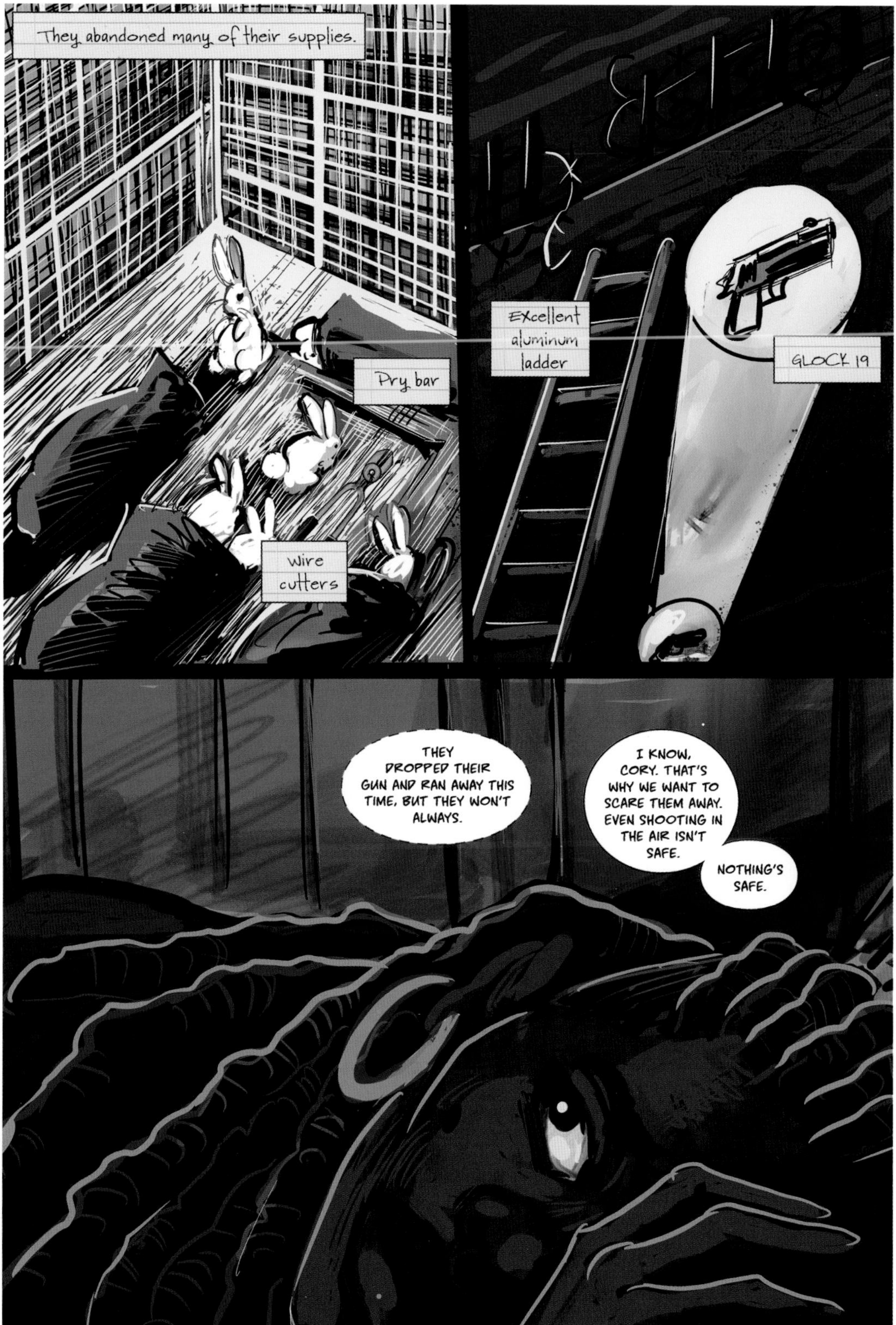
They abandoned many of their supplies.
Pry bar
wire cutters
Excellent aluminum ladder
GLOCK 19
THEY DROPPED THEIR GUN AND RAN AWAY THIS TIME, BUT THEY WON'T ALWAYS.
I KNOW, CORY. THAT'S WHY WE WANT TO SCARE THEM AWAY. EVEN SHOOTING IN THE AIR ISN'T SAFE.
NOTHING'S SAFE.

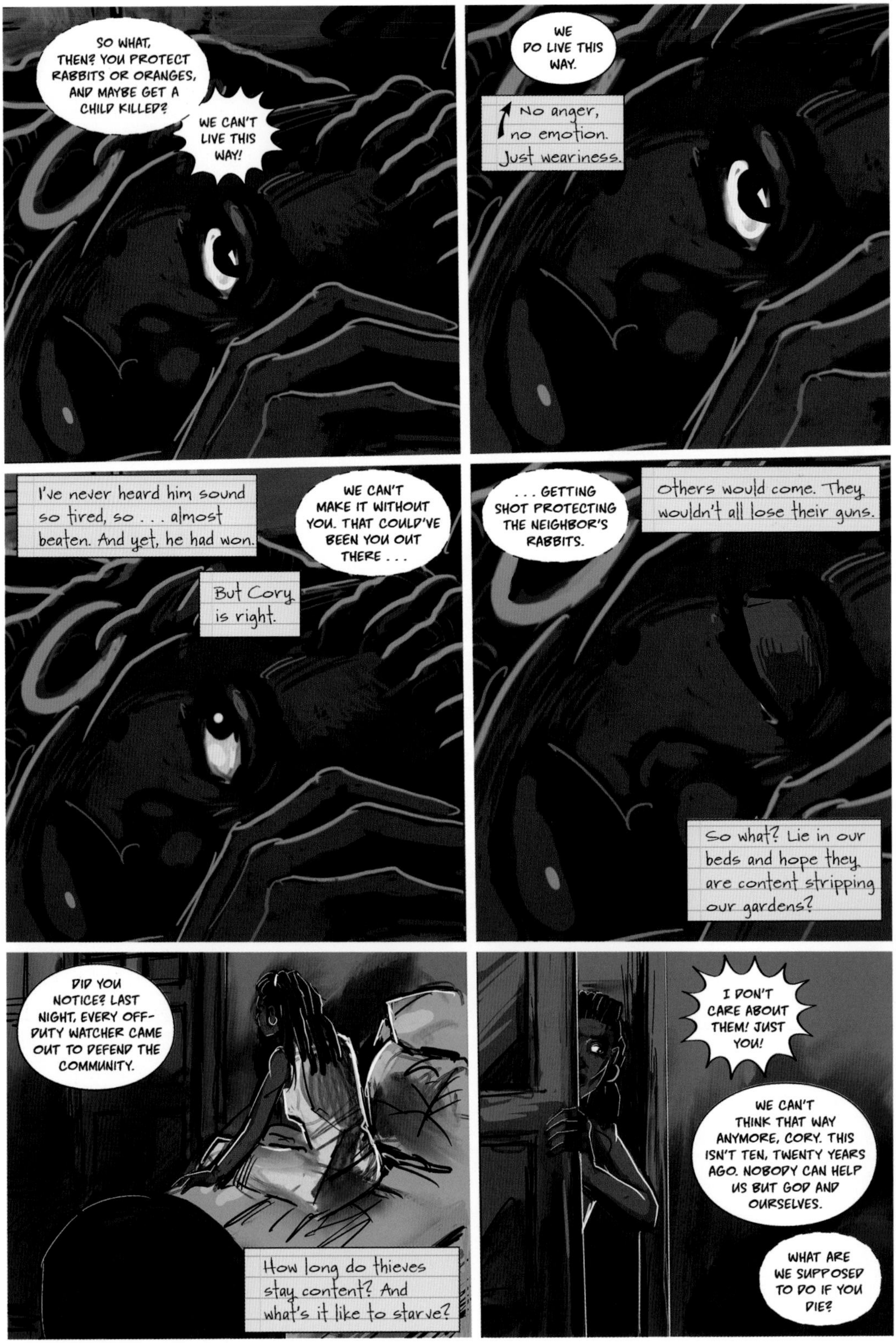
SO WHAT, THEN? YOU PROTECT RABBITS OR ORANGES, AND MAYBE GET A CHILD KILLED?
WE CAN'T LIVE THIS WAY!
WE DO LIVE THIS WAY.
No anger, no emotion. Just weariness.
I've never heard him sound so tired, so . . . almost beaten. And yet, he had won.
WE CAN'T MAKE IT WITHOUT YOU. THAT COULD'VE BEEN YOU OUT THERE . . .
But Cory is right.
. . . GETTING SHOT PROTECTING THE NEIGHBOR'S RABBITS.
Others would come. They wouldn't all lose their guns.
So what? Lie in our beds and hope they are content stripping our gardens?
DID YOU NOTICE? LAST NIGHT, EVERY OFF-DUTY WATCHER CAME OUT TO DEFEND THE COMMUNITY.
How long do thieves stay content? And what's it like to starve?
I DON'T CARE ABOUT THEM! JUST YOU!
WE CAN'T THINK THAT WAY ANYMORE, CORY. THIS ISN'T TEN, TWENTY YEARS AGO. NOBODY CAN HELP US BUT GOD AND OURSELVES.
WHAT ARE WE SUPPOSED TO DO IF YOU DIE?

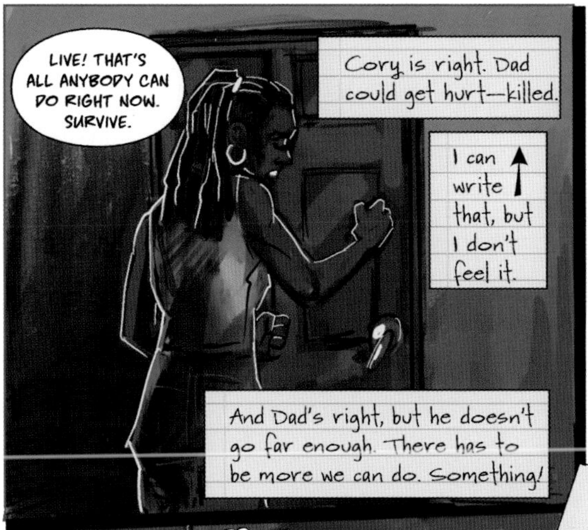

LIVE! THAT'S ALL ANYBODY CAN DO RIGHT NOW. SURVIVE.
Cory is right. Dad could get hurt—killed.
I can write that, but I don't feel it.
And Dad's right, but he doesn't go far enough. There has to be more we can do. Something!

We are all Godseed, but no more or less so than any other aspect of the universe. Godseed is all there is—all that Changes. Earthseed is all that spreads Earthlife to new earths. The universe is Godseed. Only we are Earthseed. And the Destiny of Earthseed is to take root among the stars.

EARTHSEED: THE BOOKS OF THE LIVING

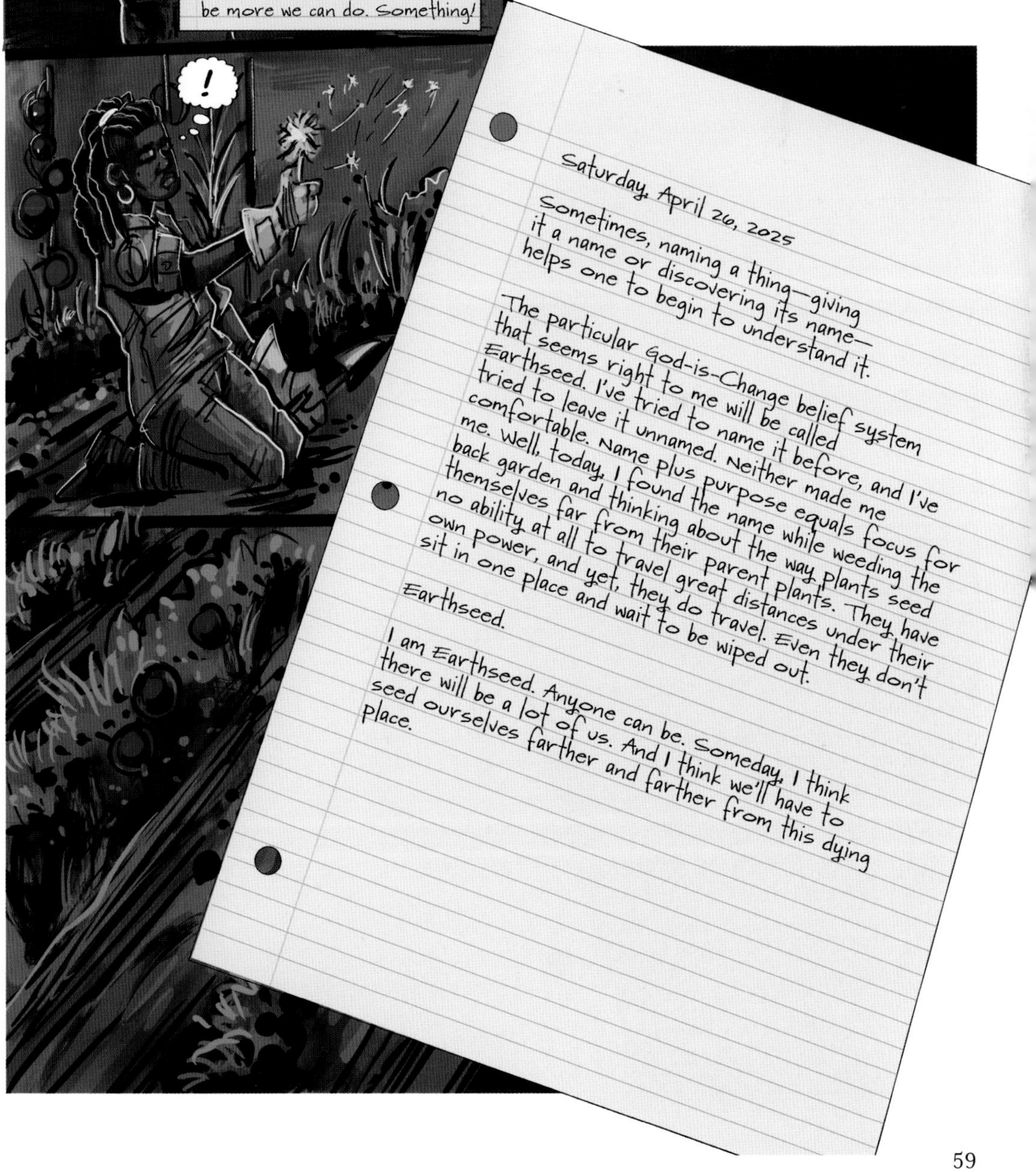

!

Saturday, April 26, 2025

Sometimes, naming a thing—giving it a name or discovering its name—helps one to begin to understand it.

The particular God-is-Change belief system that seems right to me will be called Earthseed. I've tried to name it before, and I've tried to leave it unnamed. Neither made me comfortable. Name plus purpose equals focus for me. Well, today, I found the name while weeding the back garden and thinking about the way plants seed themselves far from their parent plants. They have no ability at all to travel great distances under their own power, and yet, they do travel. Even they don't sit in one place and wait to be wiped out.

Earthseed.

I am Earthseed. Anyone can be. Someday, I think there will be a lot of us. And I think we'll have to seed ourselves farther and farther from this dying place.

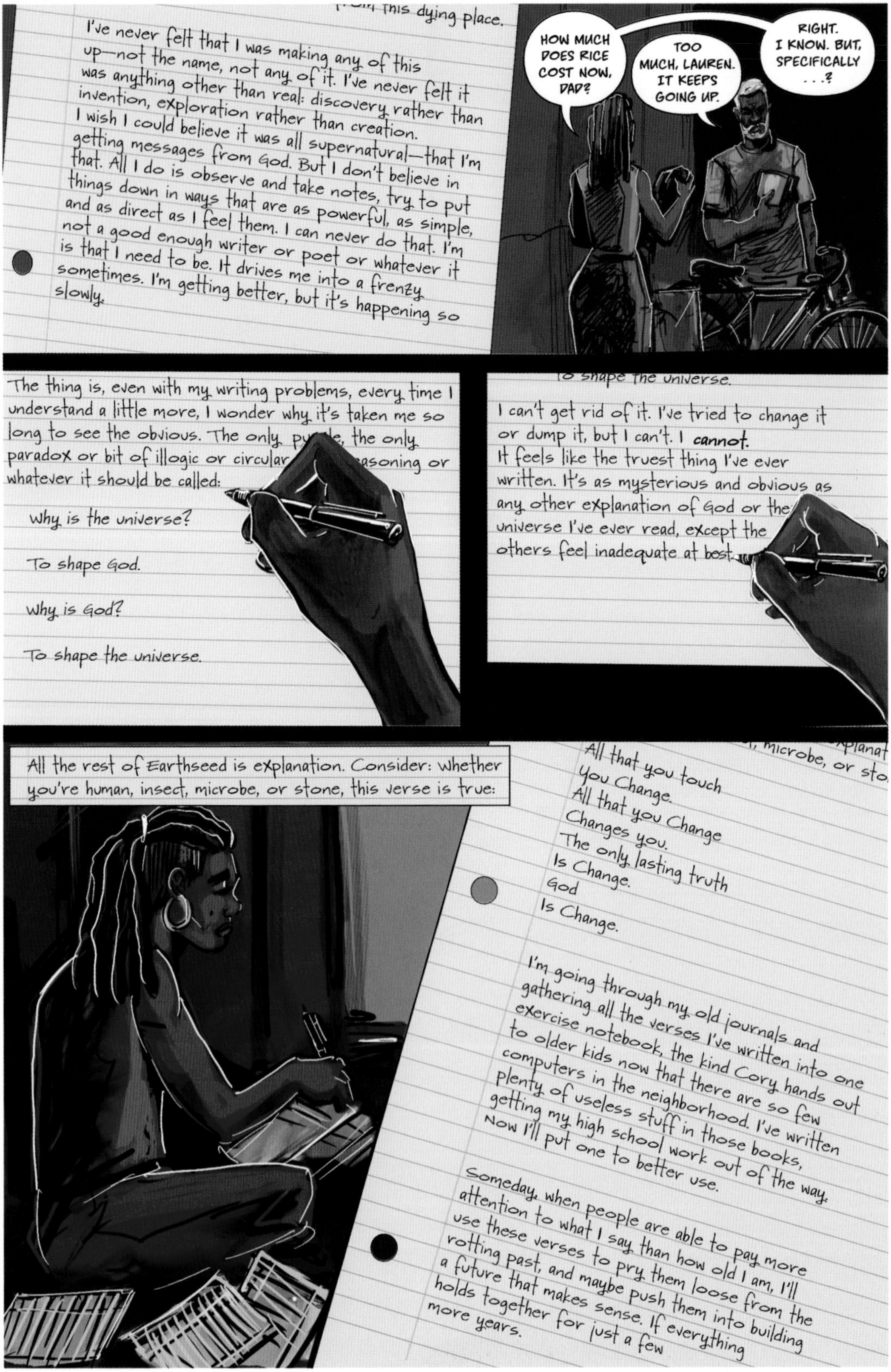
this dying place.
I've never felt that I was making any of this up—not the name, not any of it. I've never felt it was anything other than real: discovery rather than invention, exploration rather than creation.
I wish I could believe it was all supernatural—that I'm getting messages from God. But I don't believe in that. All I do is observe and take notes, try to put things down in ways that are as powerful, as simple, and as direct as I feel them. I can never do that. I'm not a good enough writer or poet or whatever it is that I need to be. It drives me into a frenzy sometimes. I'm getting better, but it's happening so slowly.
HOW MUCH DOES RICE COST NOW, DAD?
TOO MUCH, LAUREN. IT KEEPS GOING UP.
RIGHT. I KNOW. BUT, SPECIFICALLY . . .?
The thing is, even with my writing problems, every time I understand a little more, I wonder why it's taken me so long to see the obvious. The only pu le, the only paradox or bit of illogic or circular asoning or whatever it should be called:
Why is the universe?
To shape God.
Why is God?
To shape the universe.
shape the universe.
I can't get rid of it. I've tried to change it or dump it, but I can't. I **cannot**.
It feels like the truest thing I've ever written. It's as mysterious and obvious as any other explanation of God or the universe I've ever read, except the others feel inadequate at best.
All the rest of Earthseed is explanation. Consider: whether you're human, insect, microbe, or stone, this verse is true:
microbe, or sto
All that you touch
You Change.
All that you Change
Changes you.
The only lasting truth
Is Change.
God
Is Change.
I'm going through my old journals and gathering all the verses I've written into one exercise notebook, the kind Cory hands out to older kids now that there are so few computers in the neighborhood. I've written plenty of useless stuff in those books, getting my high school work out of the way. Now I'll put one to better use.
Someday, when people are able to pay more attention to what I say than how old I am, I'll use these verses to pry them loose from the rotting past, and maybe push them into building a future that makes sense. If everything holds together for just a few more years.

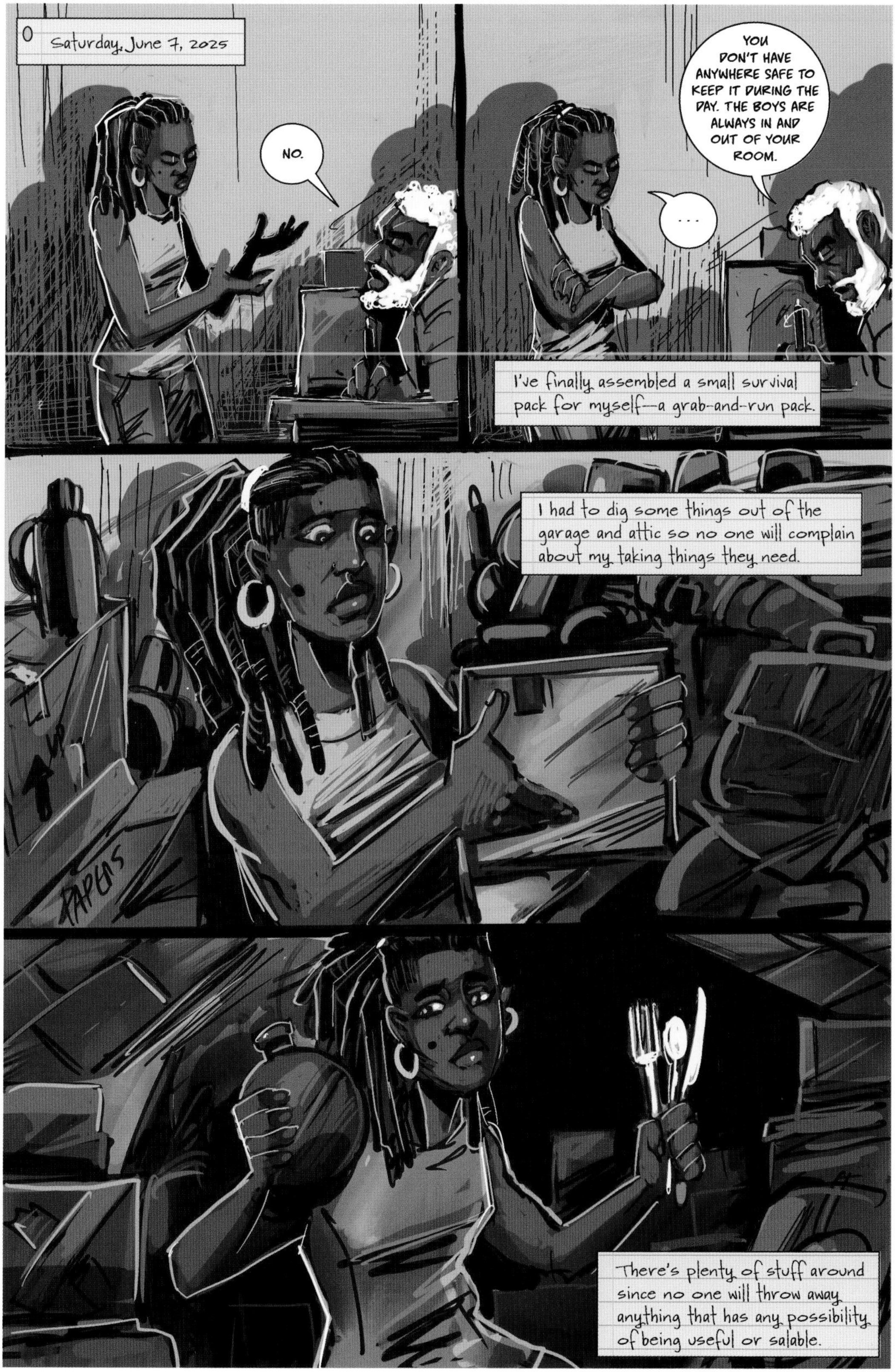
Saturday, June 7, 2025
NO.
YOU DON'T HAVE ANYWHERE SAFE TO KEEP IT DURING THE DAY. THE BOYS ARE ALWAYS IN AND OUT OF YOUR ROOM.
. . .
I've finally assembled a small survival pack for myself—a grab-and-run pack.
I had to dig some things out of the garage and attic so no one will complain about my taking things they need.
PAPERS
There's plenty of stuff around since no one will throw away anything that has any possibility of being useful or salable.

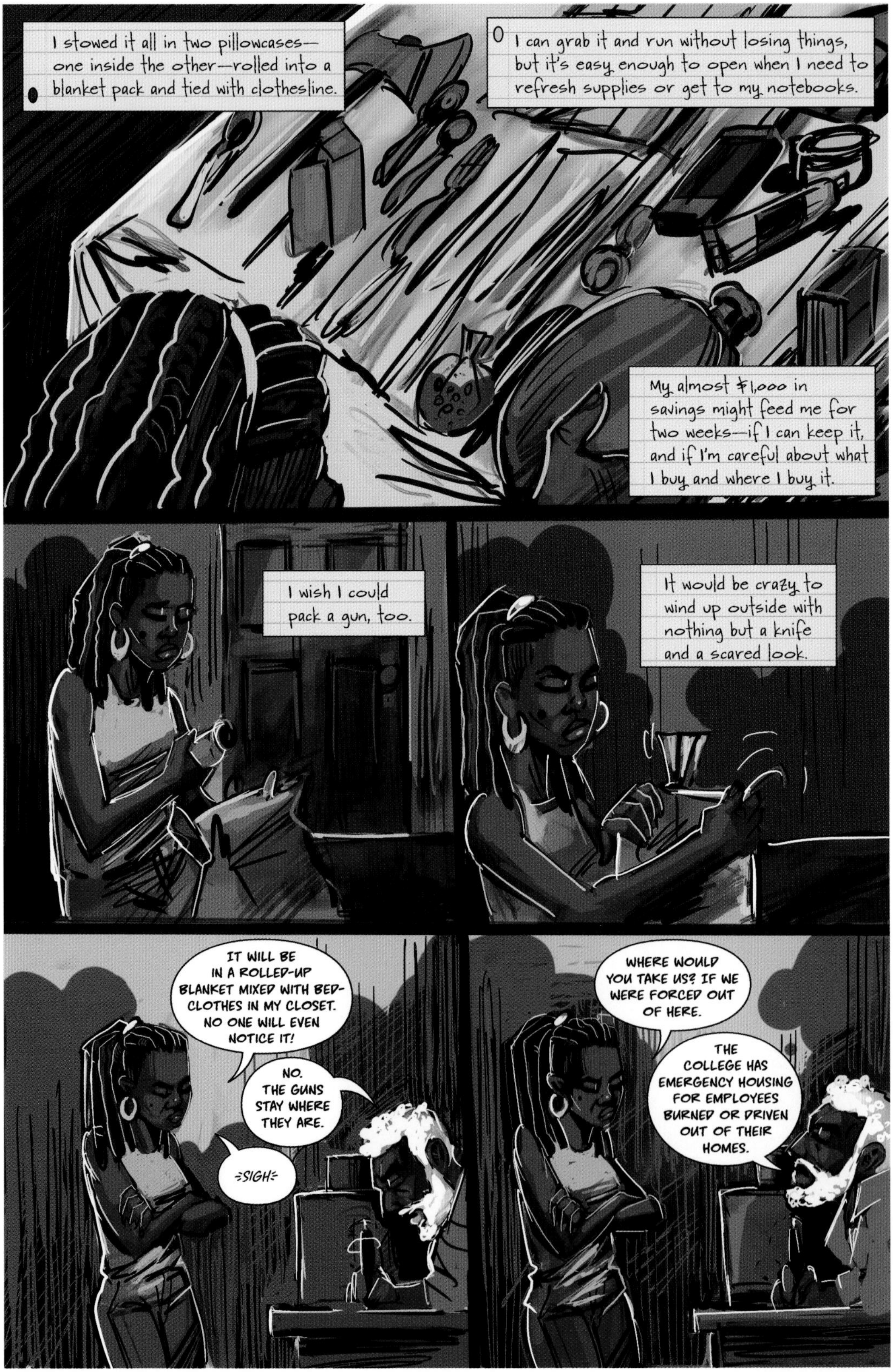
I stowed it all in two pillowcases—one inside the other—rolled into a blanket pack and tied with clothesline.
I can grab it and run without losing things, but it's easy enough to open when I need to refresh supplies or get to my notebooks.
My almost $1,000 in savings might feed me for two weeks—if I can keep it, and if I'm careful about what I buy and where I buy it.
I wish I could pack a gun, too.
It would be crazy to wind up outside with nothing but a knife and a scared look.
IT WILL BE IN A ROLLED-UP BLANKET MIXED WITH BED-CLOTHES IN MY CLOSET. NO ONE WILL EVEN NOTICE IT!
NO. THE GUNS STAY WHERE THEY ARE.
=SIGH=
WHERE WOULD YOU TAKE US? IF WE WERE FORCED OUT OF HERE.
THE COLLEGE HAS EMERGENCY HOUSING FOR EMPLOYEES BURNED OR DRIVEN OUT OF THEIR HOMES.

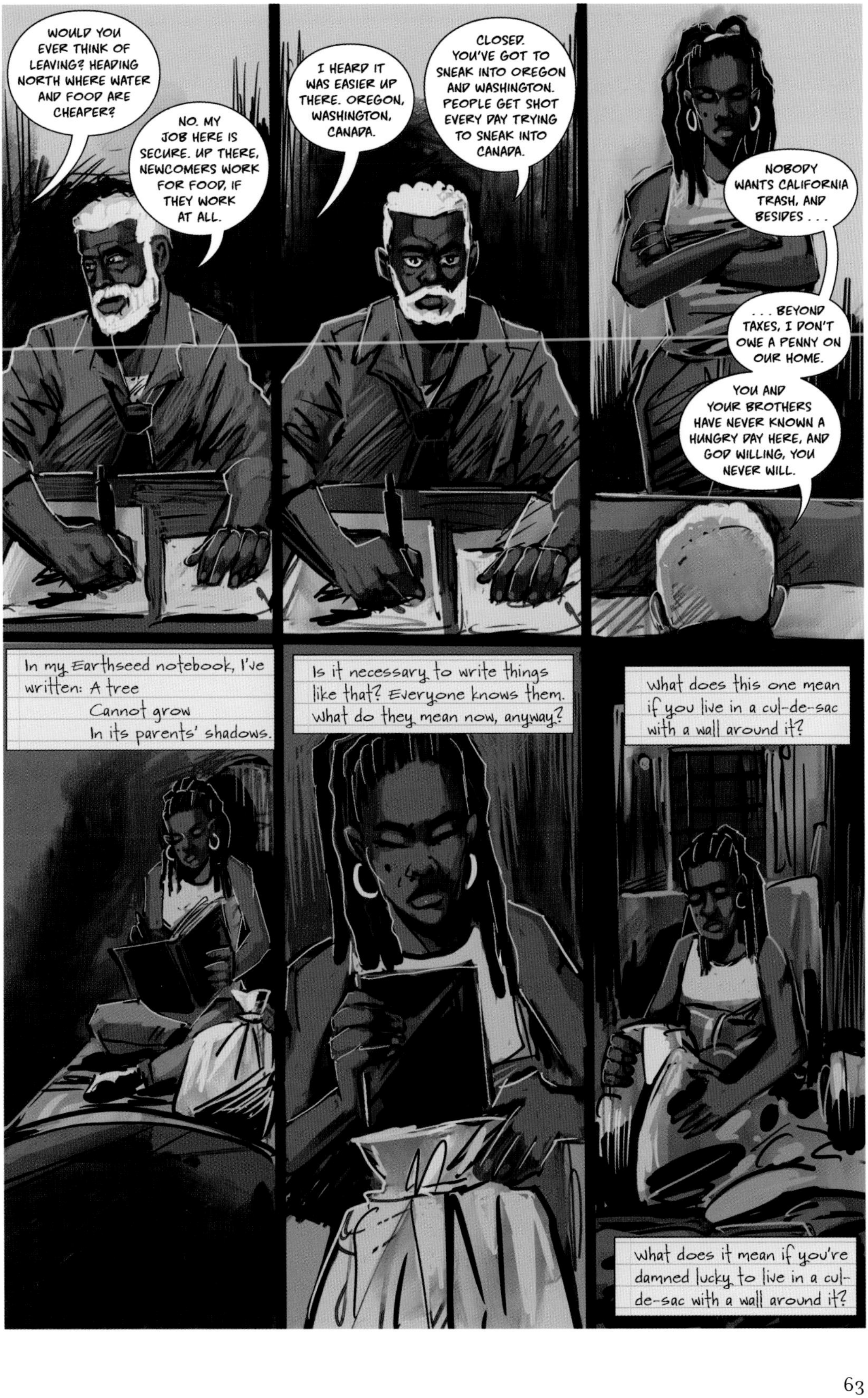
WOULD YOU EVER THINK OF LEAVING? HEADING NORTH WHERE WATER AND FOOD ARE CHEAPER?
NO. MY JOB HERE IS SECURE. UP THERE, NEWCOMERS WORK FOR FOOD, IF THEY WORK AT ALL.
I HEARD IT WAS EASIER UP THERE. OREGON, WASHINGTON, CANADA.
CLOSED. YOU'VE GOT TO SNEAK INTO OREGON AND WASHINGTON. PEOPLE GET SHOT EVERY DAY TRYING TO SNEAK INTO CANADA.
NOBODY WANTS CALIFORNIA TRASH, AND BESIDES . . .
. . . BEYOND TAXES, I DON'T OWE A PENNY ON OUR HOME.
YOU AND YOUR BROTHERS HAVE NEVER KNOWN A HUNGRY DAY HERE, AND GOD WILLING, YOU NEVER WILL.
In my Earthseed notebook, I've written: A tree
Cannot grow
In its parents' shadows.
Is it necessary to write things like that? Everyone knows them. What do they mean now, anyway?
What does this one mean if you live in a cul-de-sac with a wall around it?
What does it mean if you're damned lucky to live in a cul-de-sac with a wall around it?

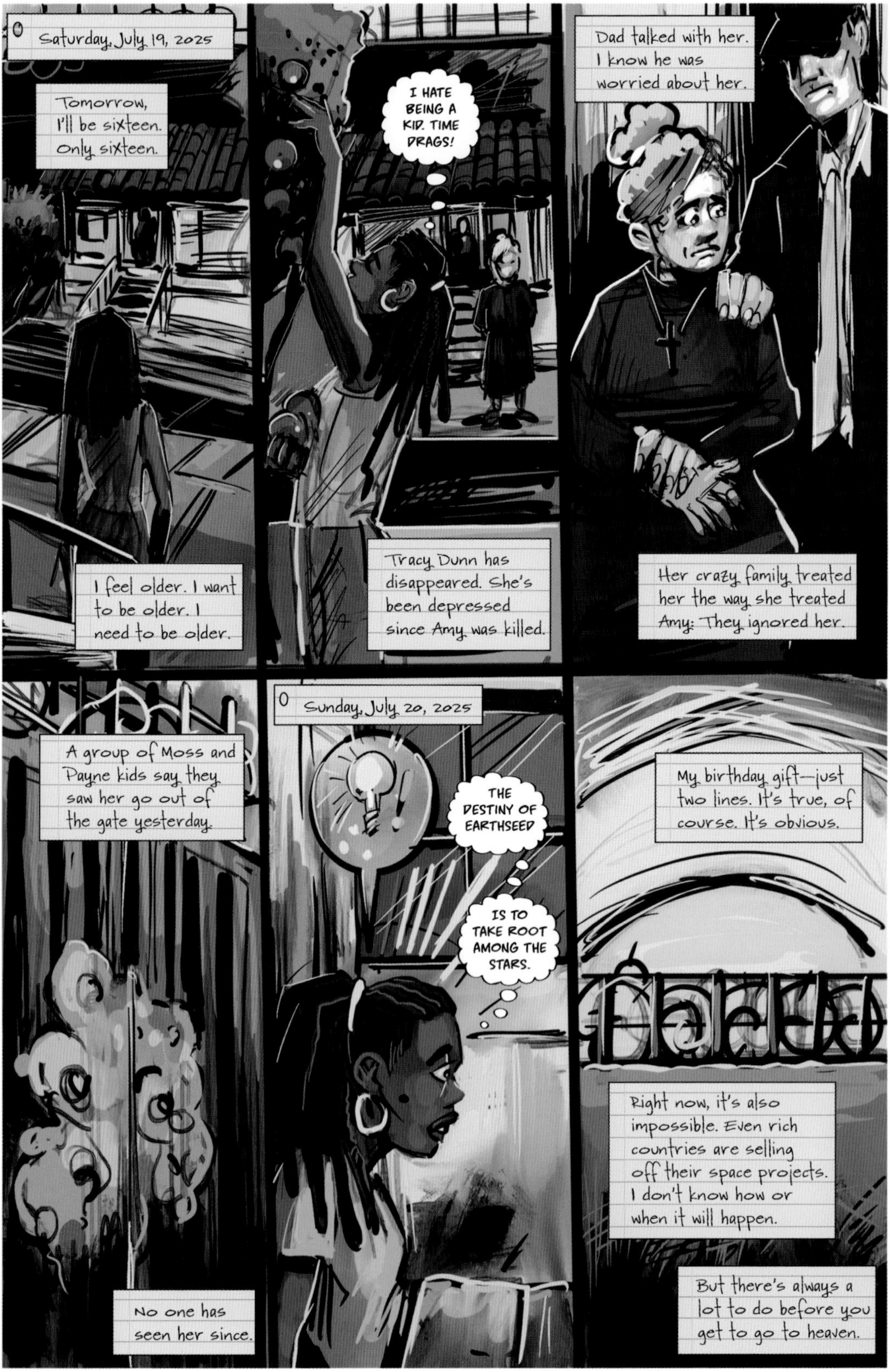
Saturday, July 19, 2025
Tomorrow, I'll be sixteen. Only sixteen.
I feel older. I want to be older. I need to be older.
I HATE BEING A KID. TIME DRAGS!
Tracy Dunn has disappeared. She's been depressed since Amy was killed.
Dad talked with her. I know he was worried about her.
Her crazy family treated her the way she treated Amy: They ignored her.
A group of Moss and Payne kids say they saw her go out of the gate yesterday.
No one has seen her since.
Sunday, July 20, 2025
THE DESTINY OF EARTHSEED
IS TO TAKE ROOT AMONG THE STARS.
My birthday gift—just two lines. It's true, of course. It's obvious.
Right now, it's also impossible. Even rich countries are selling off their space projects. I don't know how or when it will happen.
But there's always a lot to do before you get to go to heaven.

To get along with God,
Consider the consequences of your behavior.

EARTHSEED: THE BOOKS OF THE LIVING

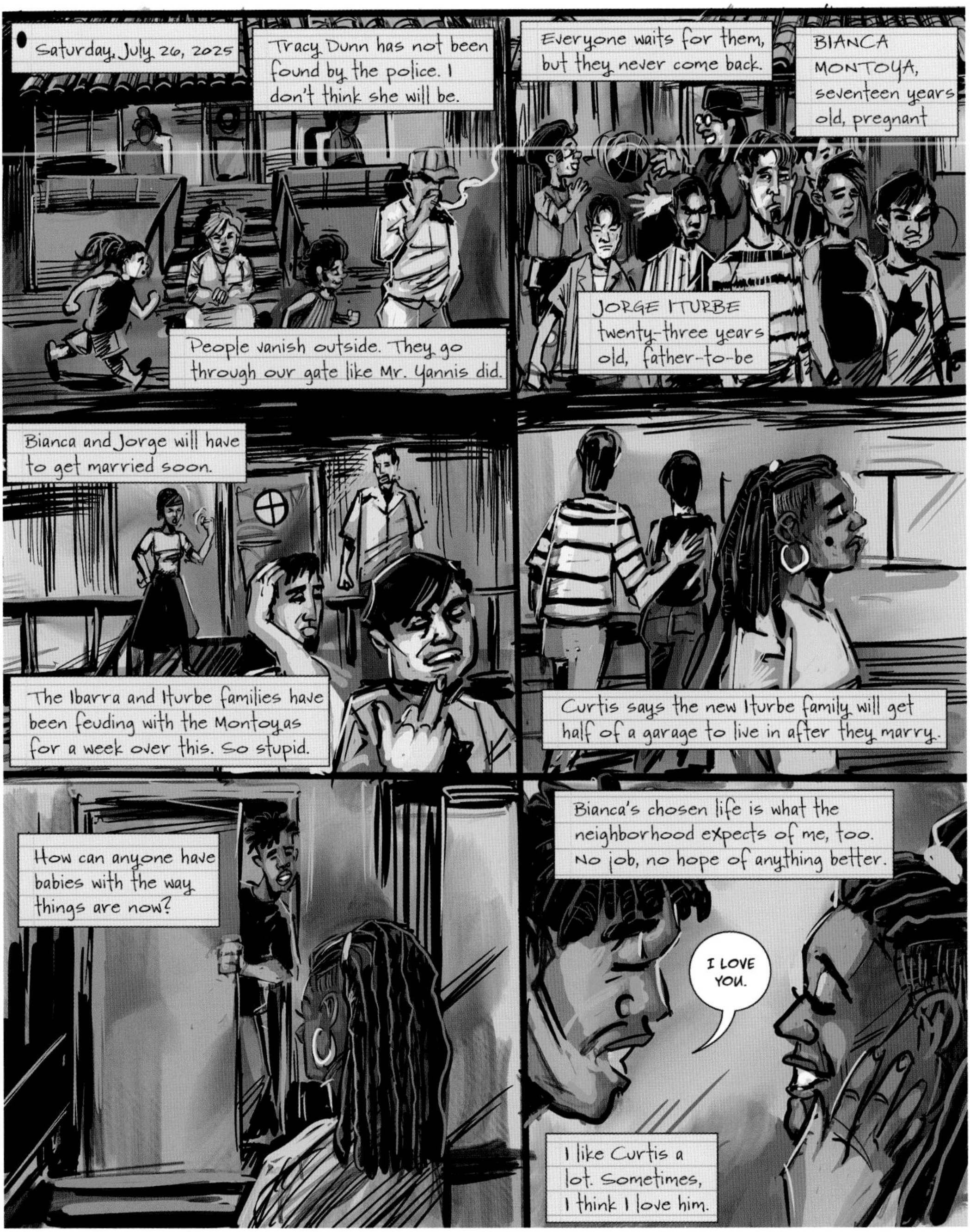

Saturday, July 26, 2025
Tracy Dunn has not been found by the police. I don't think she will be.
People vanish outside. They go through our gate like Mr. Yannis did.
Everyone waits for them, but they never come back.
BIANCA MONTOYA, seventeen years old, pregnant
JORGE ITURBE twenty-three years old, father-to-be
Bianca and Jorge will have to get married soon.
The Ibarra and Iturbe families have been feuding with the Montoyas for a week over this. So stupid.
Curtis says the new Iturbe family will get half of a garage to live in after they marry.
How can anyone have babies with the way things are now?
Bianca's chosen life is what the neighborhood expects of me, too. No job, no hope of anything better.
I LOVE YOU.
I like Curtis a lot. Sometimes, I think I love him.

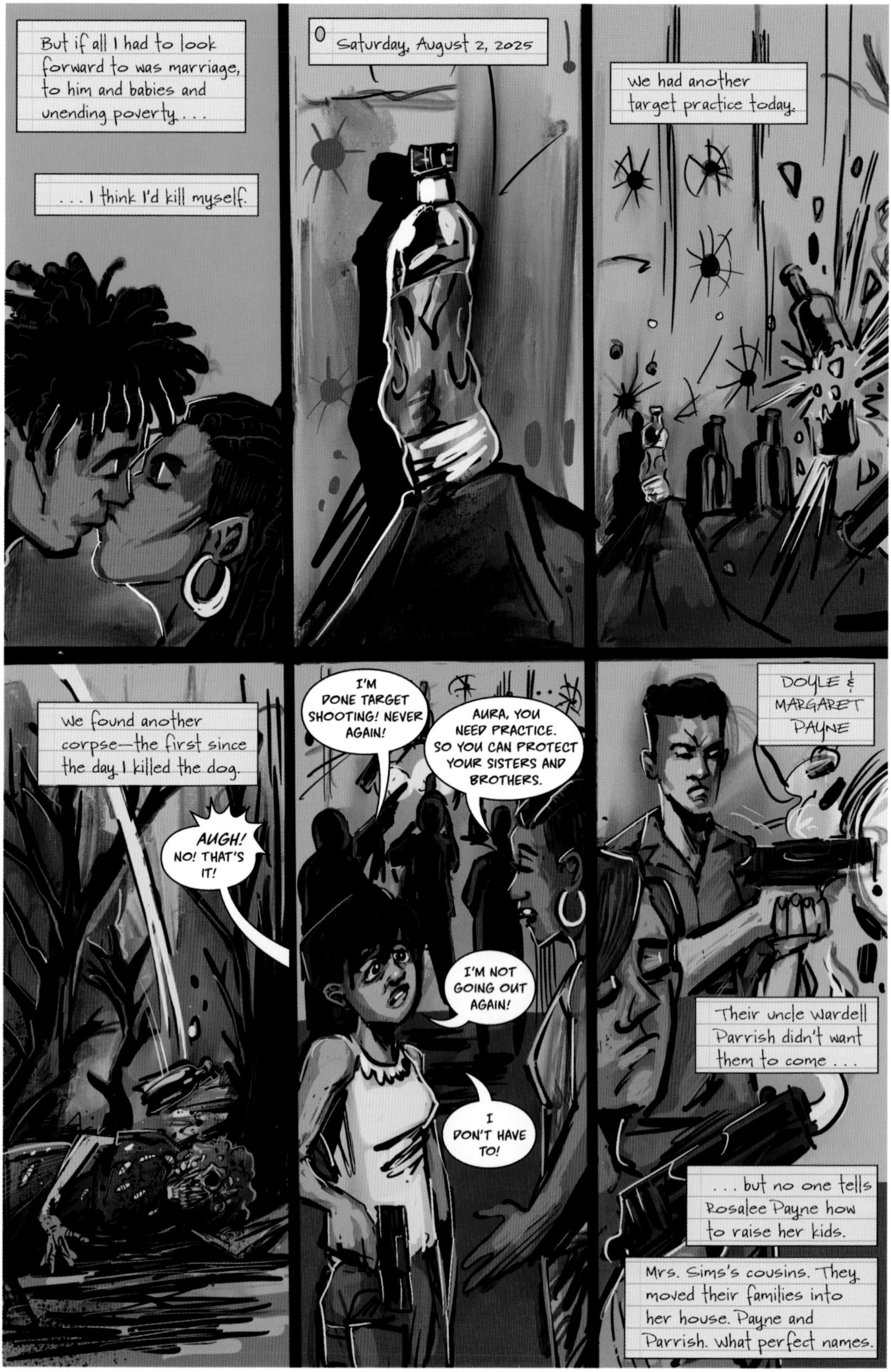

But if all I had to look forward to was marriage, to him and babies and unending poverty . . .
. . . I think I'd kill myself.
Saturday, August 2, 2025
We had another target practice today.
We found another corpse—the first since the day I killed the dog.
AUGH! NO! THAT'S IT!
I'M DONE TARGET SHOOTING! NEVER AGAIN!
AURA, YOU NEED PRACTICE. SO YOU CAN PROTECT YOUR SISTERS AND BROTHERS.
I'M NOT GOING OUT AGAIN!
I DON'T HAVE TO!
DOYLE & MARGARET PAYNE
Their uncle Wardell Parrish didn't want them to come . . .
. . . but no one tells Rosalee Payne how to raise her kids.
Mrs. Sims's cousins. They moved their families into her house. Payne and Parrish. What perfect names.

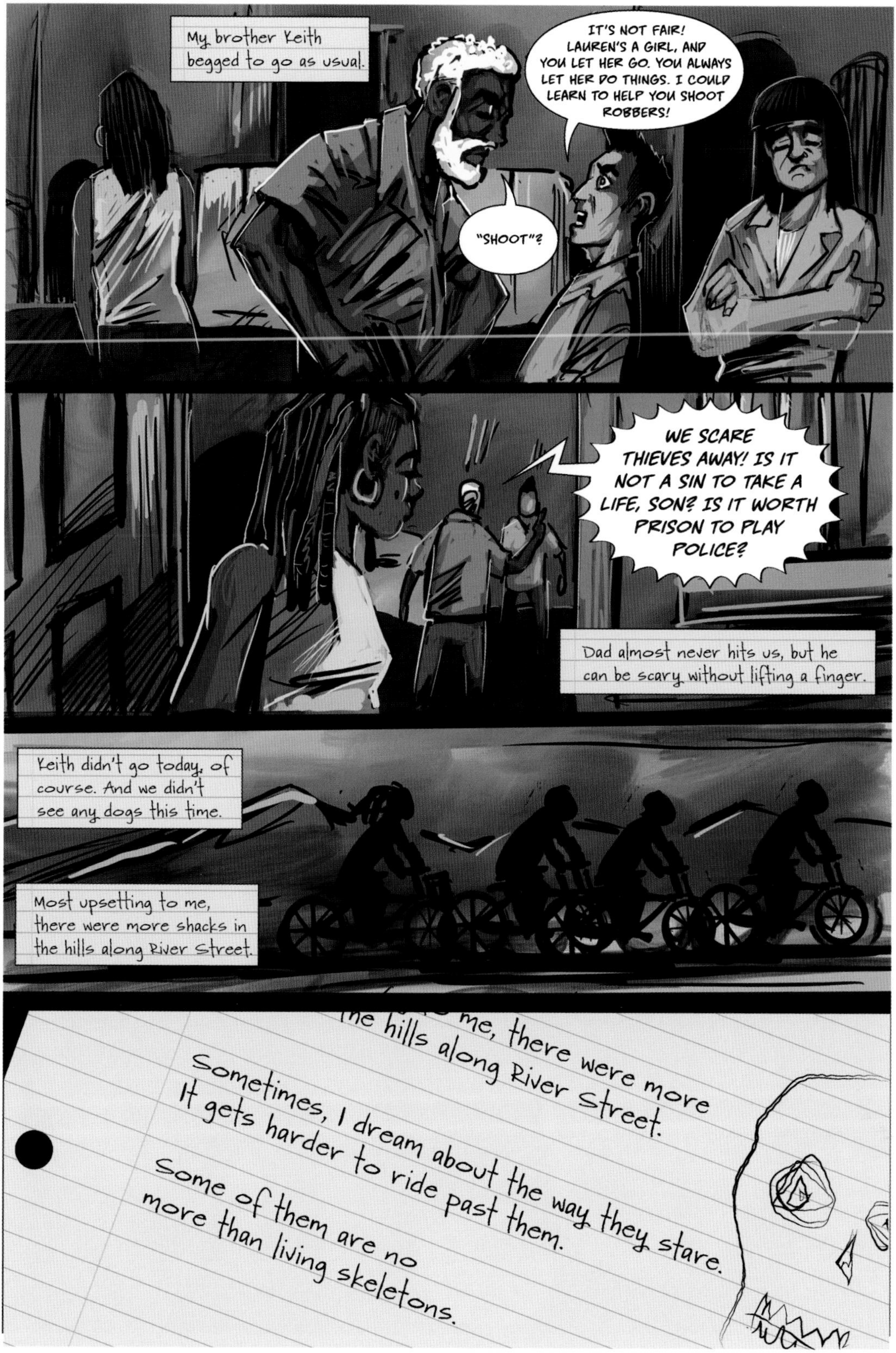
My brother Keith begged to go as usual.
IT'S NOT FAIR! LAUREN'S A GIRL, AND YOU LET HER GO. YOU ALWAYS LET HER DO THINGS. I COULD LEARN TO HELP YOU SHOOT ROBBERS!
"SHOOT"?
WE SCARE THIEVES AWAY! IS IT NOT A SIN TO TAKE A LIFE, SON? IS IT WORTH PRISON TO PLAY POLICE?
Dad almost never hits us, but he can be scary without lifting a finger.
Keith didn't go today, of course. And we didn't see any dogs this time.
Most upsetting to me, there were more shacks in the hills along River Street.
me, there were more
the hills along River Street.
Sometimes, I dream about the way they stare.
It gets harder to ride past them.
Some of them are no more than living skeletons.

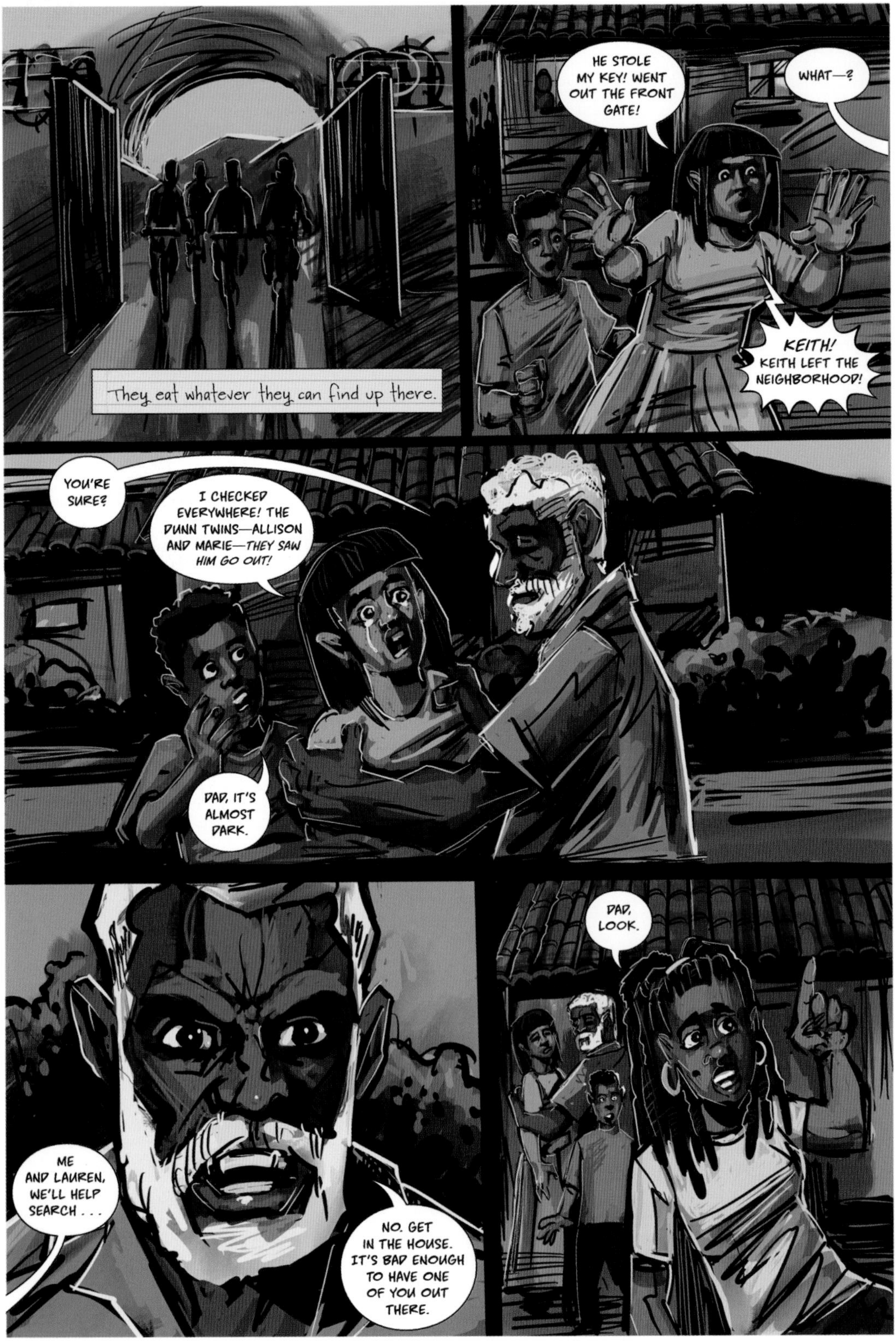
They eat whatever they can find up there.
HE STOLE MY KEY! WENT OUT THE FRONT GATE!
WHAT—?
KEITH! KEITH LEFT THE NEIGHBORHOOD!
YOU'RE SURE?
I CHECKED EVERYWHERE! THE DUNN TWINS—ALLISON AND MARIE—THEY SAW HIM GO OUT!
DAD, IT'S ALMOST DARK.
ME AND LAUREN, WE'LL HELP SEARCH . . .
NO. GET IN THE HOUSE. IT'S BAD ENOUGH TO HAVE ONE OF YOU OUT THERE.
DAD, LOOK.

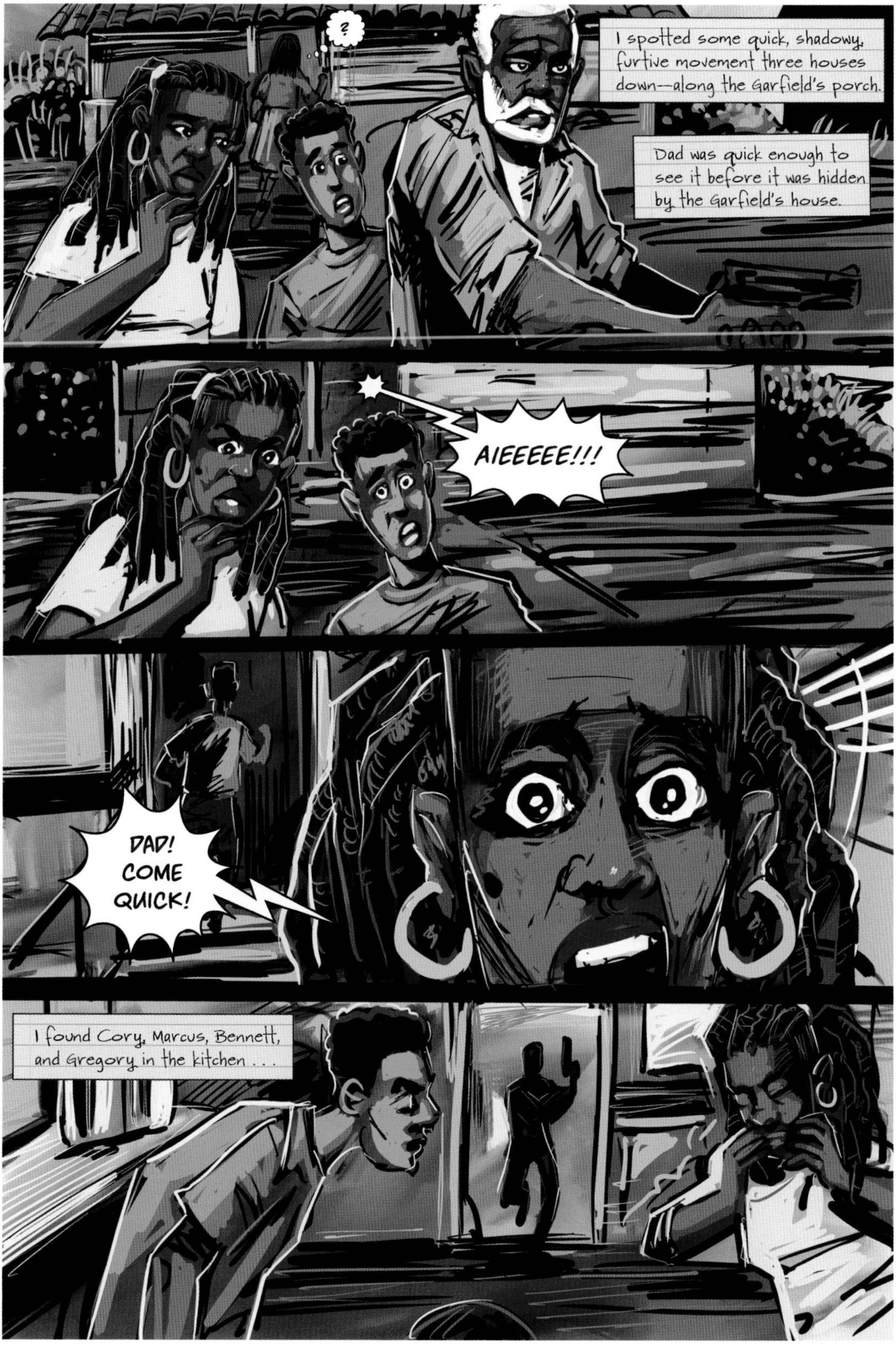
?
I spotted some quick, shadowy, furtive movement three houses down—along the Garfield's porch.
Dad was quick enough to see it before it was hidden by the Garfield's house.
AIEEEEE!!!
DAD! COME QUICK!
I found Cory, Marcus, Bennett, and Gregory in the kitchen . . .

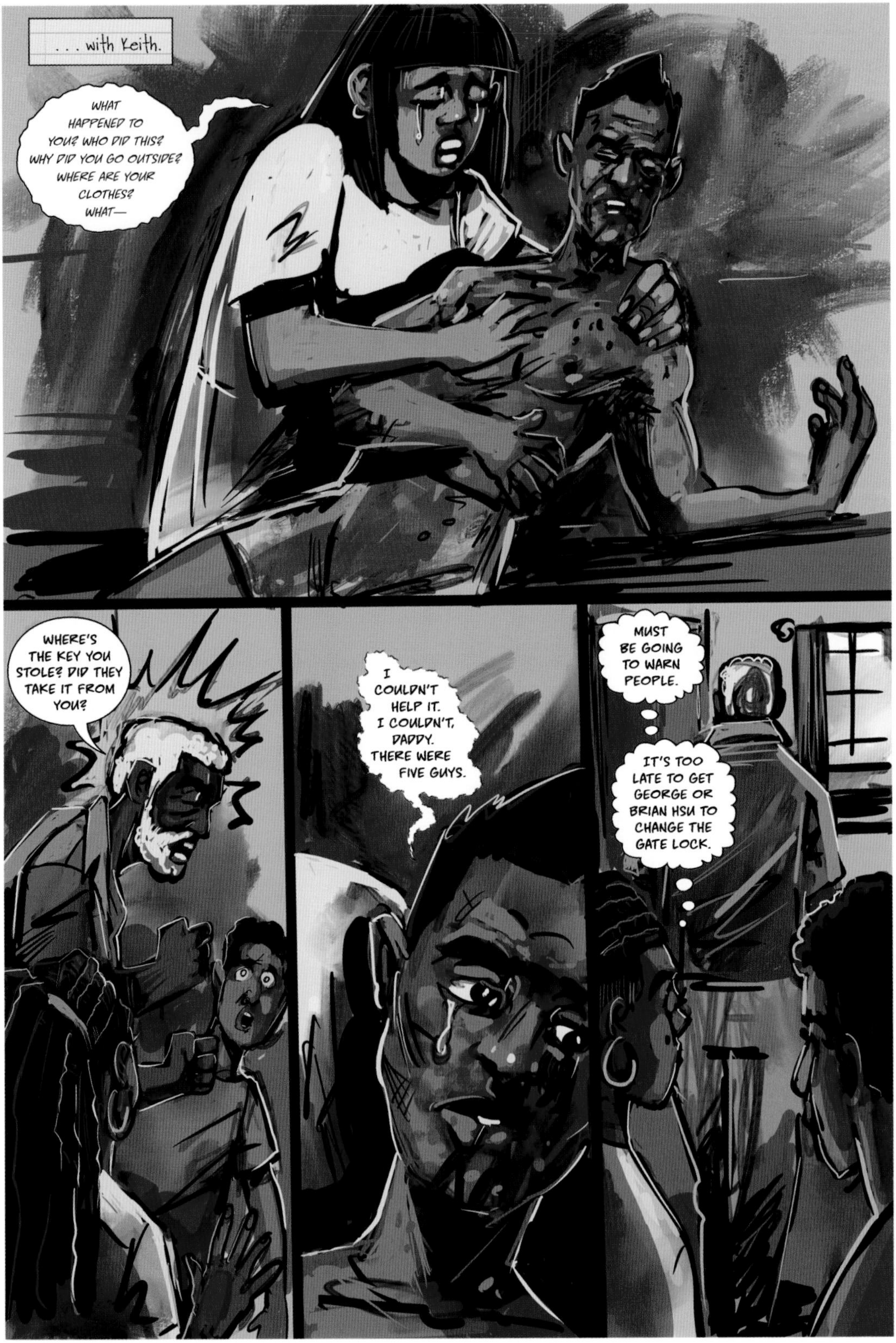
. . . with Keith.
WHAT HAPPENED TO YOU? WHO DID THIS? WHY DID YOU GO OUTSIDE? WHERE ARE YOUR CLOTHES? WHAT—
WHERE'S THE KEY YOU STOLE? DID THEY TAKE IT FROM YOU?
I COULDN'T HELP IT. I COULDN'T, DADDY. THERE WERE FIVE GUYS.
MUST BE GOING TO WARN PEOPLE.
IT'S TOO LATE TO GET GEORGE OR BRIAN HSU TO CHANGE THE GATE LOCK.

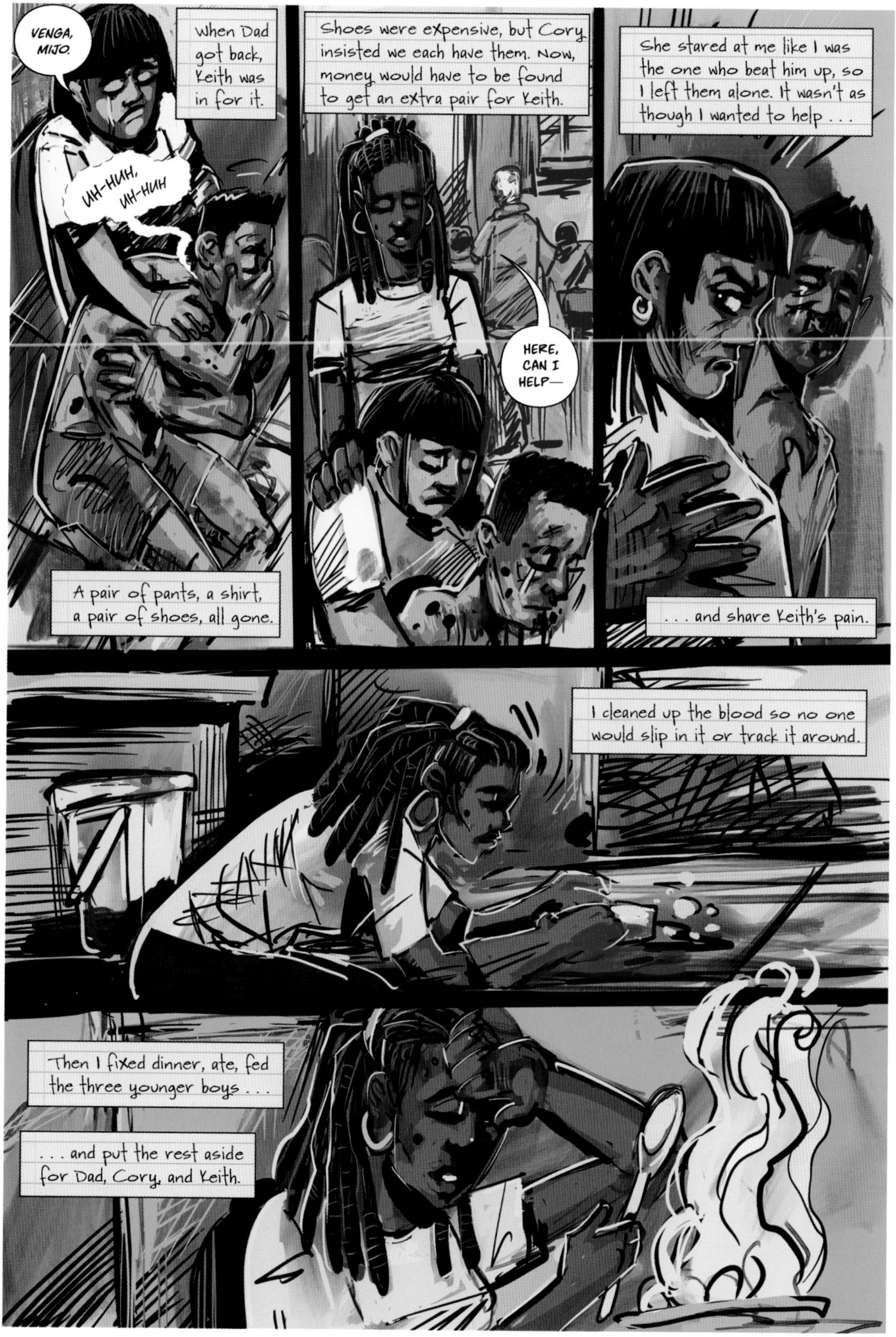
VENGA, MIJO.
When Dad got back, Keith was in for it.
UH-HUH, UH-HUH
A pair of pants, a shirt, a pair of shoes, all gone.
Shoes were expensive, but Cory insisted we each have them. Now, money would have to be found to get an extra pair for Keith.
HERE, CAN I HELP—
She stared at me like I was the one who beat him up, so I left them alone. It wasn't as though I wanted to help . . .
. . . and share Keith's pain.
I cleaned up the blood so no one would slip in it or track it around.
Then I fixed dinner, ate, fed the three younger boys . . .
. . . and put the rest aside for Dad, Cory, and Keith.

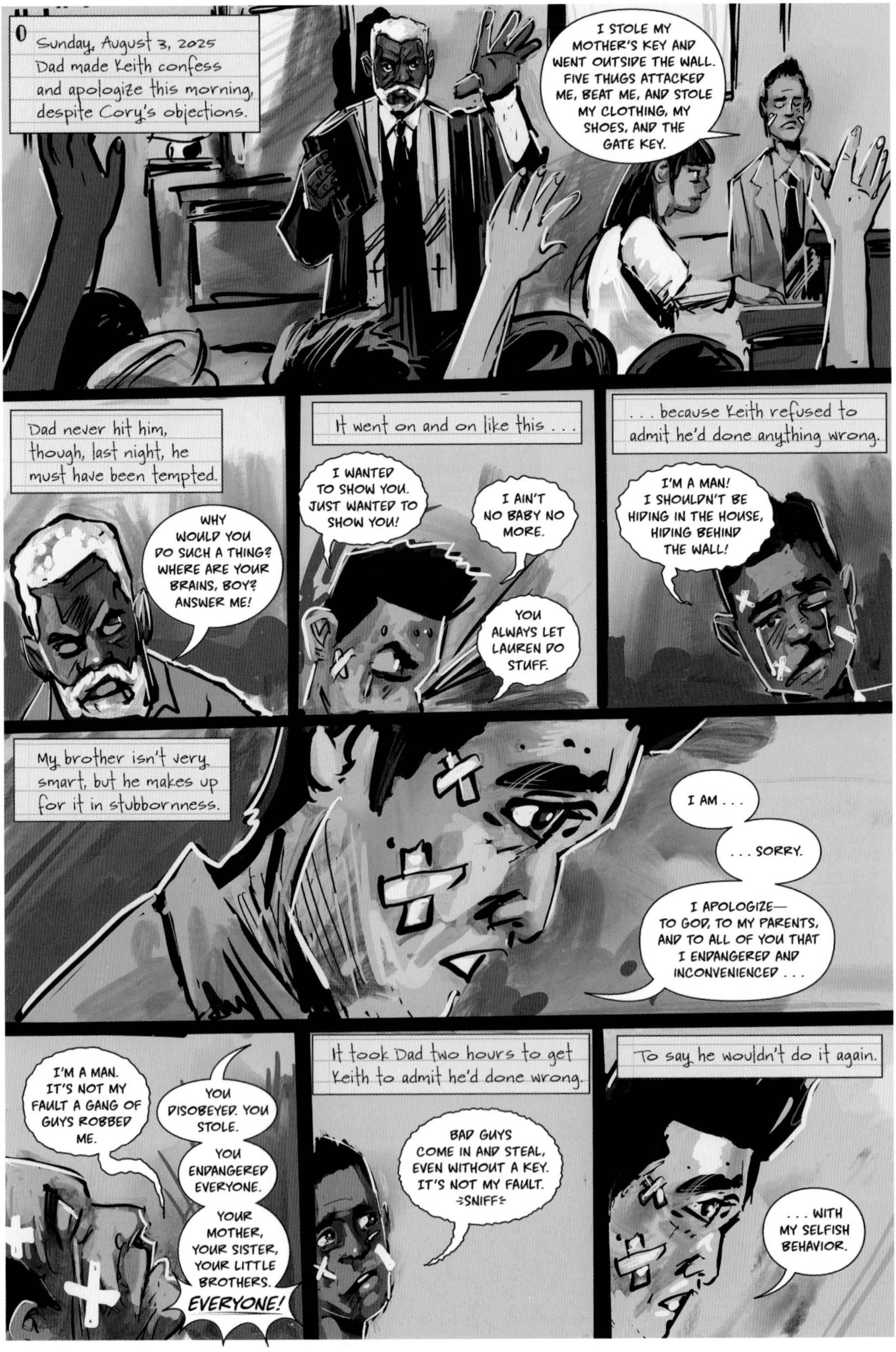

Sunday, August 3, 2025
Dad made Keith confess and apologize this morning, despite Cory's objections.
I STOLE MY MOTHER'S KEY AND WENT OUTSIDE THE WALL. FIVE THUGS ATTACKED ME, BEAT ME, AND STOLE MY CLOTHING, MY SHOES, AND THE GATE KEY.
Dad never hit him, though, last night, he must have been tempted.
WHY WOULD YOU DO SUCH A THING? WHERE ARE YOUR BRAINS, BOY? ANSWER ME!
It went on and on like this . . .
I WANTED TO SHOW YOU. JUST WANTED TO SHOW YOU!
I AIN'T NO BABY NO MORE.
YOU ALWAYS LET LAUREN DO STUFF.
. . . because Keith refused to admit he'd done anything wrong.
I'M A MAN! I SHOULDN'T BE HIDING IN THE HOUSE, HIDING BEHIND THE WALL!
My brother isn't very smart, but he makes up for it in stubbornness.
I AM . . .
. . . SORRY.
I APOLOGIZE— TO GOD, TO MY PARENTS, AND TO ALL OF YOU THAT I ENDANGERED AND INCONVENIENCED . . .
I'M A MAN. IT'S NOT MY FAULT A GANG OF GUYS ROBBED ME.
YOU DISOBEYED. YOU STOLE.
YOU ENDANGERED EVERYONE.
YOUR MOTHER, YOUR SISTER, YOUR LITTLE BROTHERS.
EVERYONE!
It took Dad two hours to get Keith to admit he'd done wrong.
BAD GUYS COME IN AND STEAL, EVEN WITHOUT A KEY. IT'S NOT MY FAULT. =SNIFF=
To say he wouldn't do it again.
. . . WITH MY SELFISH BEHAVIOR.

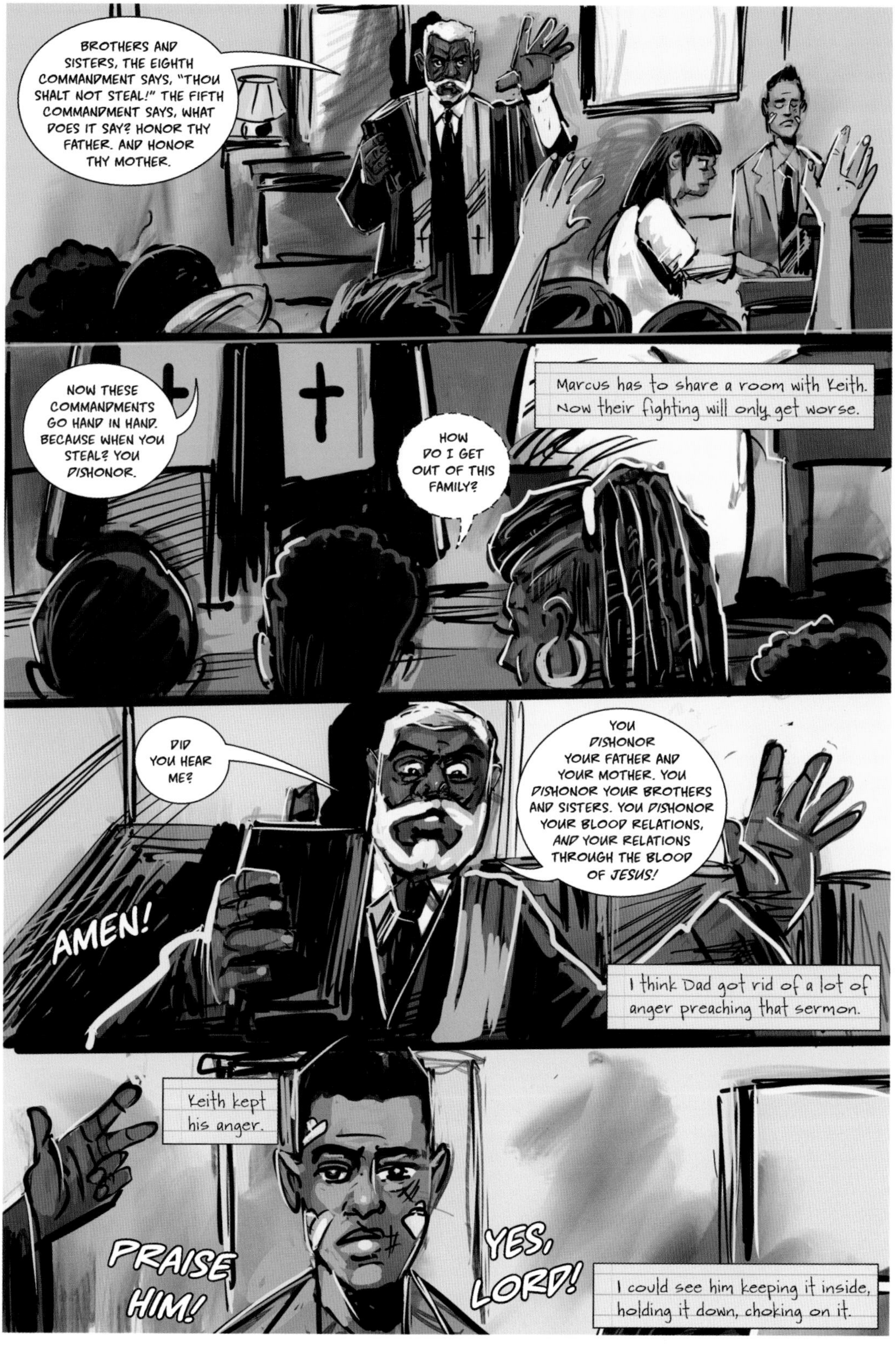
BROTHERS AND SISTERS, THE EIGHTH COMMANDMENT SAYS, "THOU SHALT NOT STEAL!" THE FIFTH COMMANDMENT SAYS, WHAT DOES IT SAY? HONOR THY FATHER. AND HONOR THY MOTHER.
NOW THESE COMMANDMENTS GO HAND IN HAND. BECAUSE WHEN YOU STEAL? YOU DISHONOR.
Marcus has to share a room with Keith. Now their fighting will only get worse.
HOW DO I GET OUT OF THIS FAMILY?
DID YOU HEAR ME?
YOU DISHONOR YOUR FATHER AND YOUR MOTHER. YOU DISHONOR YOUR BROTHERS AND SISTERS. YOU DISHONOR YOUR BLOOD RELATIONS, AND YOUR RELATIONS THROUGH THE BLOOD OF JESUS!
AMEN!
I think Dad got rid of a lot of anger preaching that sermon.
Keith kept his anger.
PRAISE HIM!
YES, LORD!
I could see him keeping it inside, holding it down, choking on it.

All struggles
Are essentially
power struggles.

Who will rule,
Who will lead,
Who will define,
refine,
confine,
design,
Who will dominate.

All struggles
Are essentially
power struggles,

And most
are no more intellectual
than two rams
knocking their heads together.

EARTHSEED: THE
BOOKS OF THE LIVING

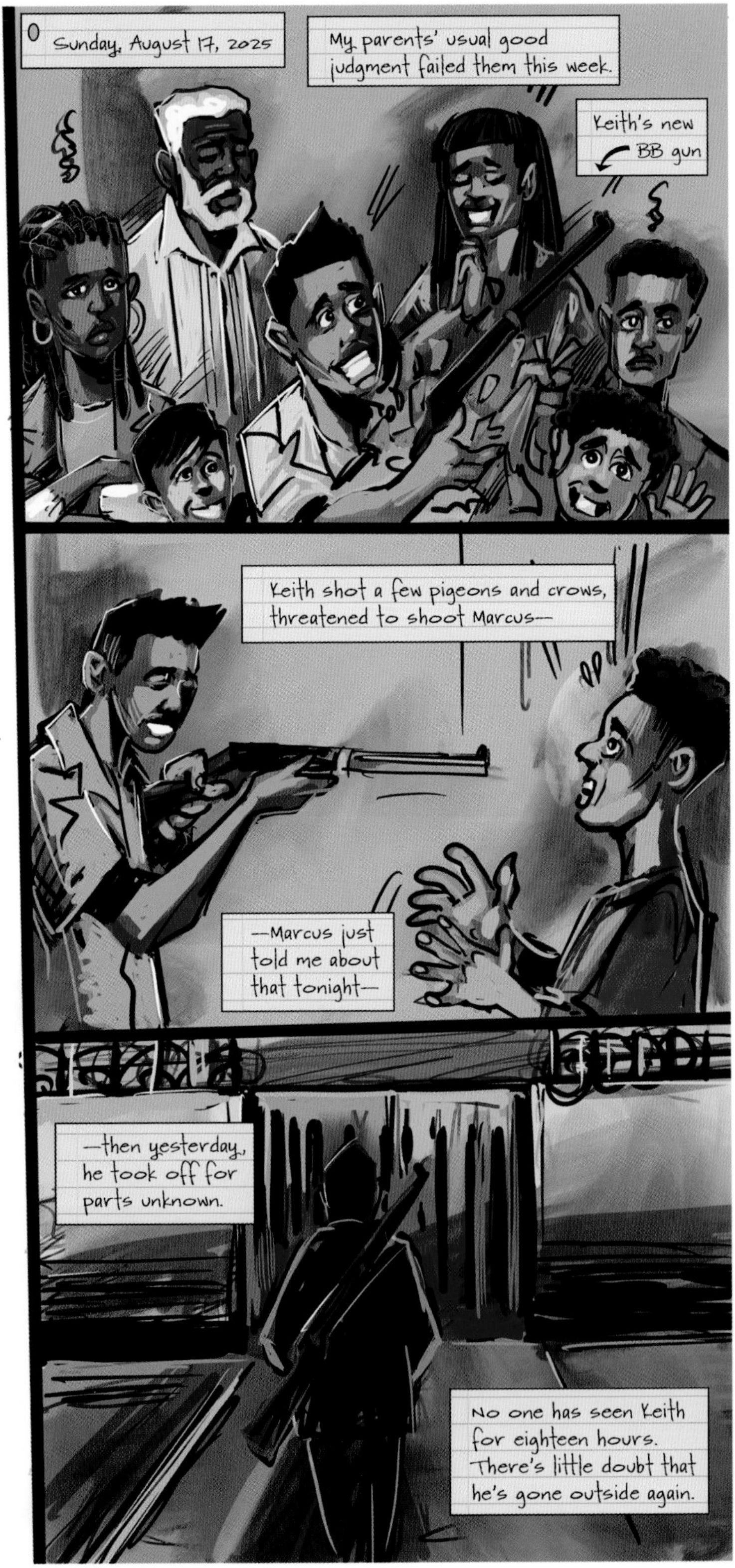
Sunday, August 17, 2025
My parents' usual good judgment failed them this week.
Keith's new BB gun
Keith shot a few pigeons and crows, threatened to shoot Marcus—
—Marcus just told me about that tonight—
—then yesterday, he took off for parts unknown.
No one has seen Keith for eighteen hours. There's little doubt that he's gone outside again.

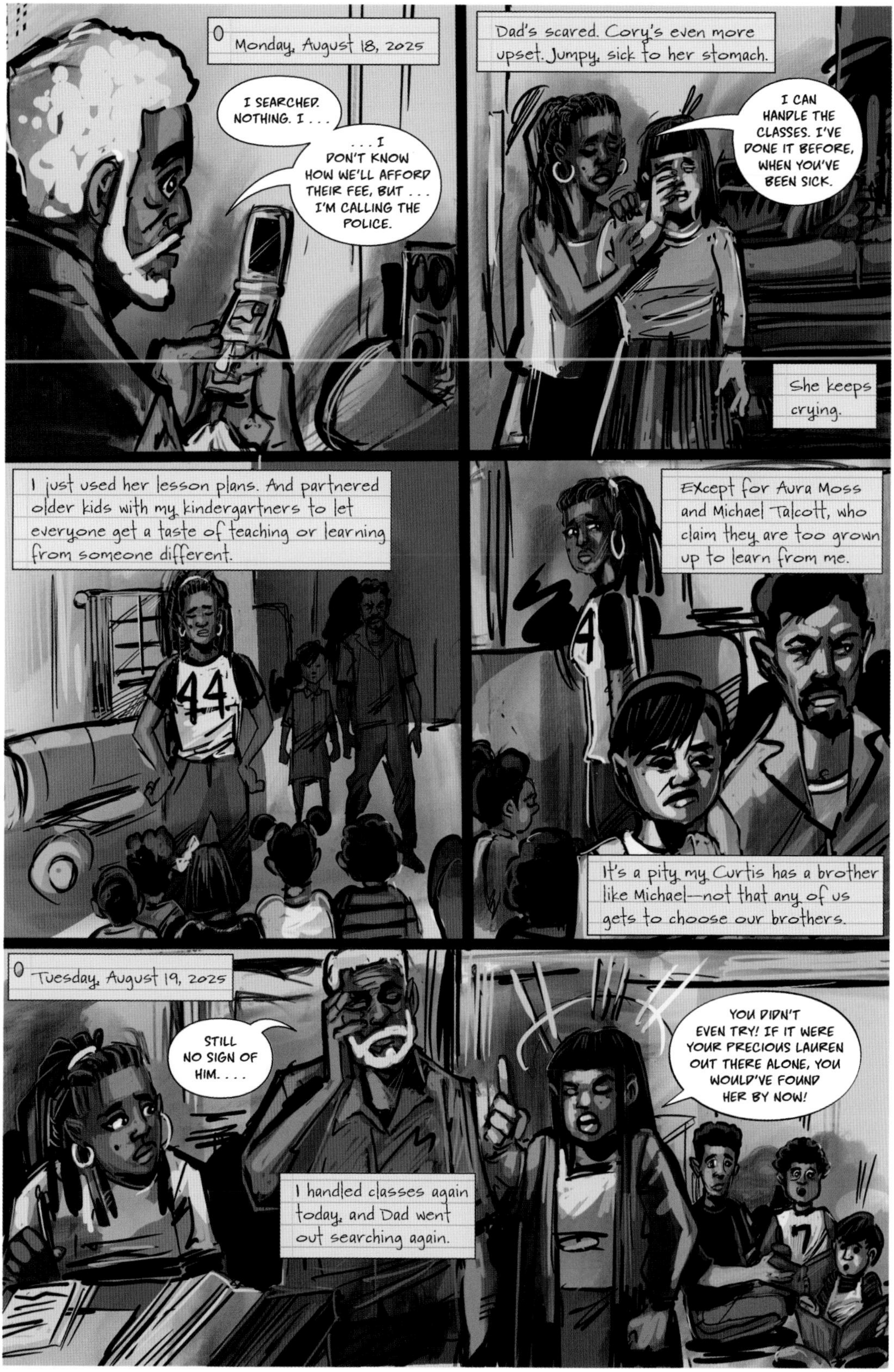
Monday, August 18, 2025
I SEARCHED. NOTHING. I . . .
. . . I DON'T KNOW HOW WE'LL AFFORD THEIR FEE, BUT . . . I'M CALLING THE POLICE.
Dad's scared. Cory's even more upset. Jumpy, sick to her stomach.
I CAN HANDLE THE CLASSES. I'VE DONE IT BEFORE, WHEN YOU'VE BEEN SICK.
She keeps crying.
I just used her lesson plans. And partnered older kids with my kindergartners to let everyone get a taste of teaching or learning from someone different.
44
Except for Aura Moss and Michael Talcott, who claim they are too grown up to learn from me.
It's a pity my Curtis has a brother like Michael—not that any of us gets to choose our brothers.
Tuesday, August 19, 2025
STILL NO SIGN OF HIM. . . .
I handled classes again today, and Dad went out searching again.
YOU DIDN'T EVEN TRY! IF IT WERE YOUR PRECIOUS LAUREN OUT THERE ALONE, YOU WOULD'VE FOUND HER BY NOW!

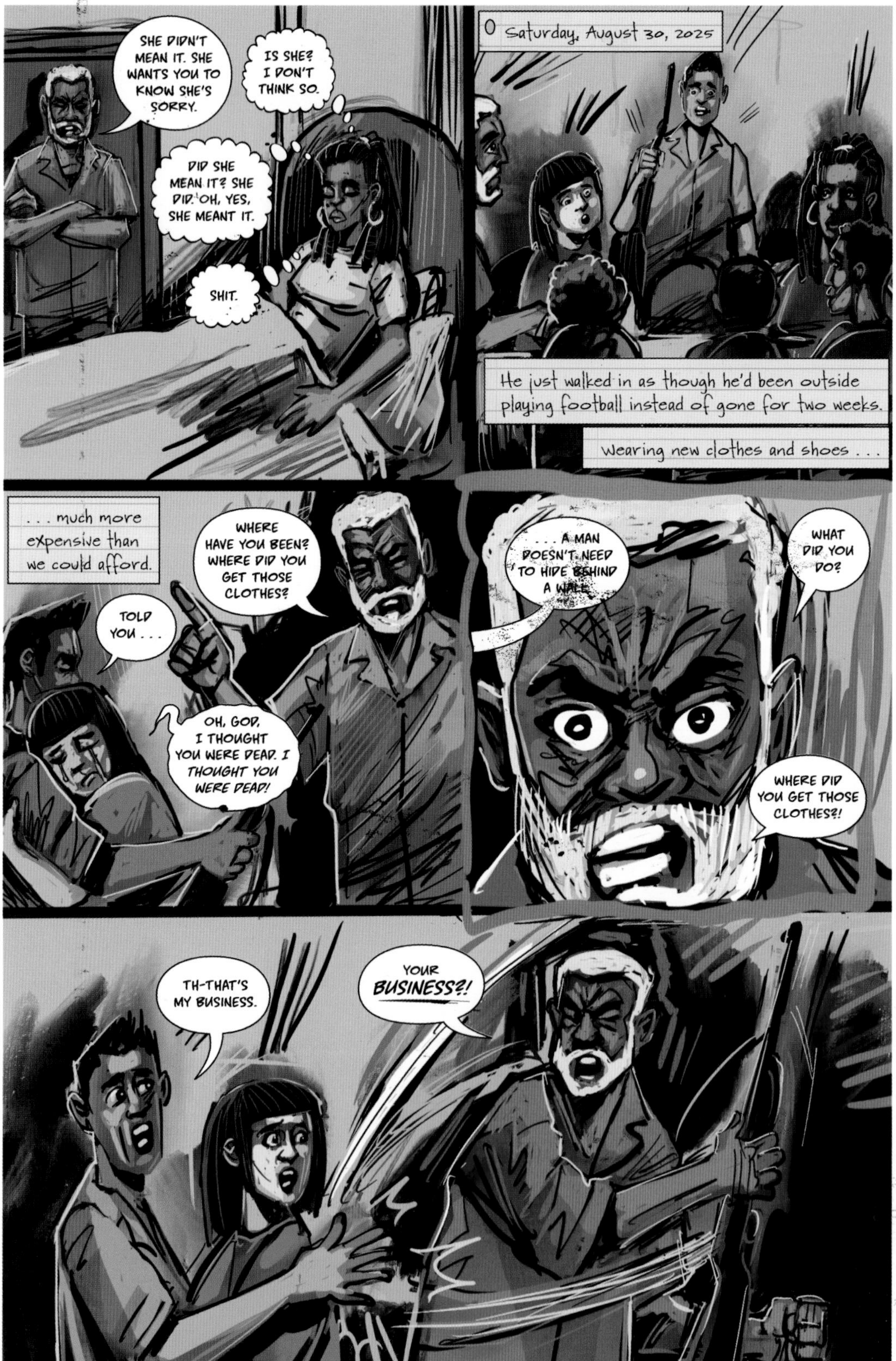
SHE DIDN'T MEAN IT. SHE WANTS YOU TO KNOW SHE'S SORRY.
IS SHE? I DON'T THINK SO.
DID SHE MEAN IT? SHE DID. OH, YES, SHE MEANT IT.
SHIT.
Saturday, August 30, 2025
He just walked in as though he'd been outside playing football instead of gone for two weeks.
Wearing new clothes and shoes . . .
. . . much more expensive than we could afford.
WHERE HAVE YOU BEEN? WHERE DID YOU GET THOSE CLOTHES?
TOLD YOU . . .
OH, GOD, I THOUGHT YOU WERE DEAD. I THOUGHT YOU WERE DEAD!
. . . A MAN DOESN'T NEED TO HIDE BEHIND A WALL.
WHAT DID YOU DO?
WHERE DID YOU GET THOSE CLOTHES?!
TH-THAT'S MY BUSINESS.
YOUR BUSINESS?!

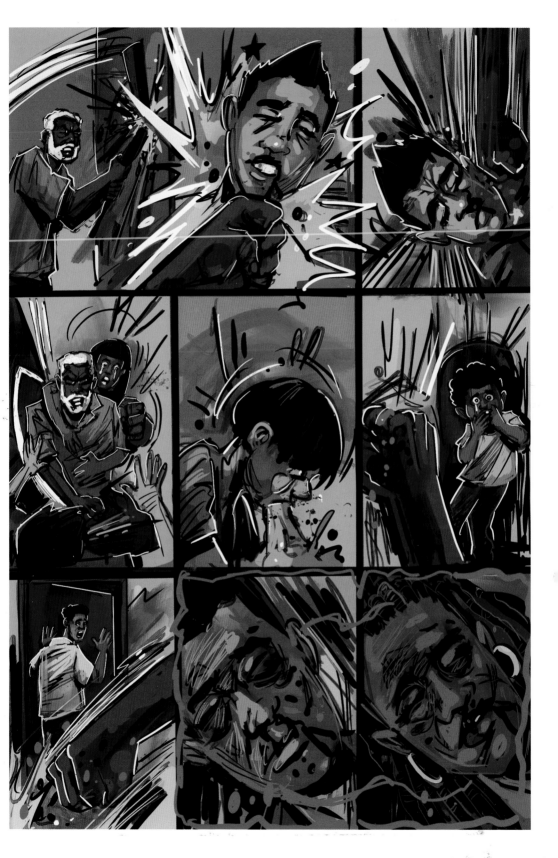

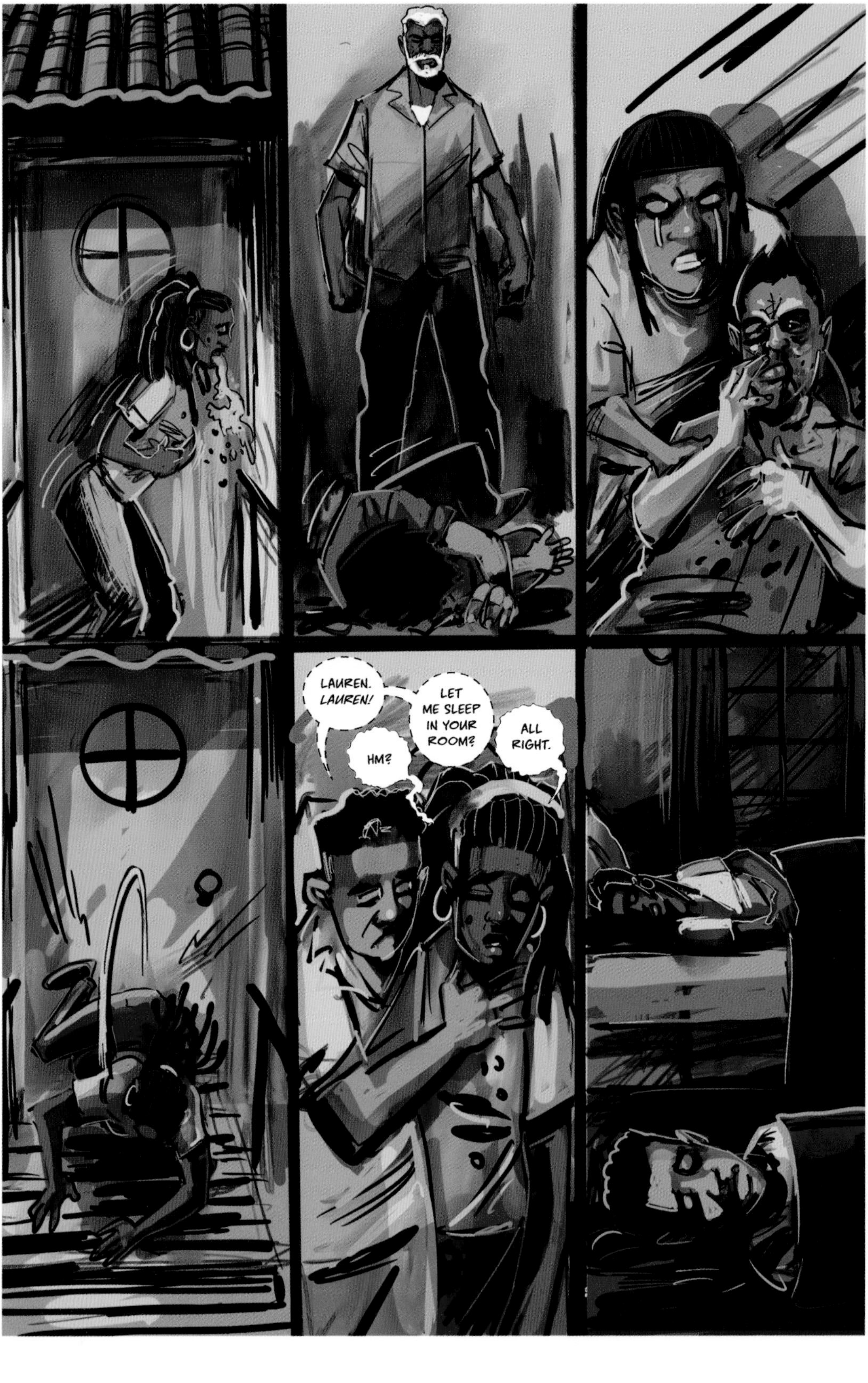
LAUREN. LAUREN!
HM?
LET ME SLEEP IN YOUR ROOM?
ALL RIGHT.

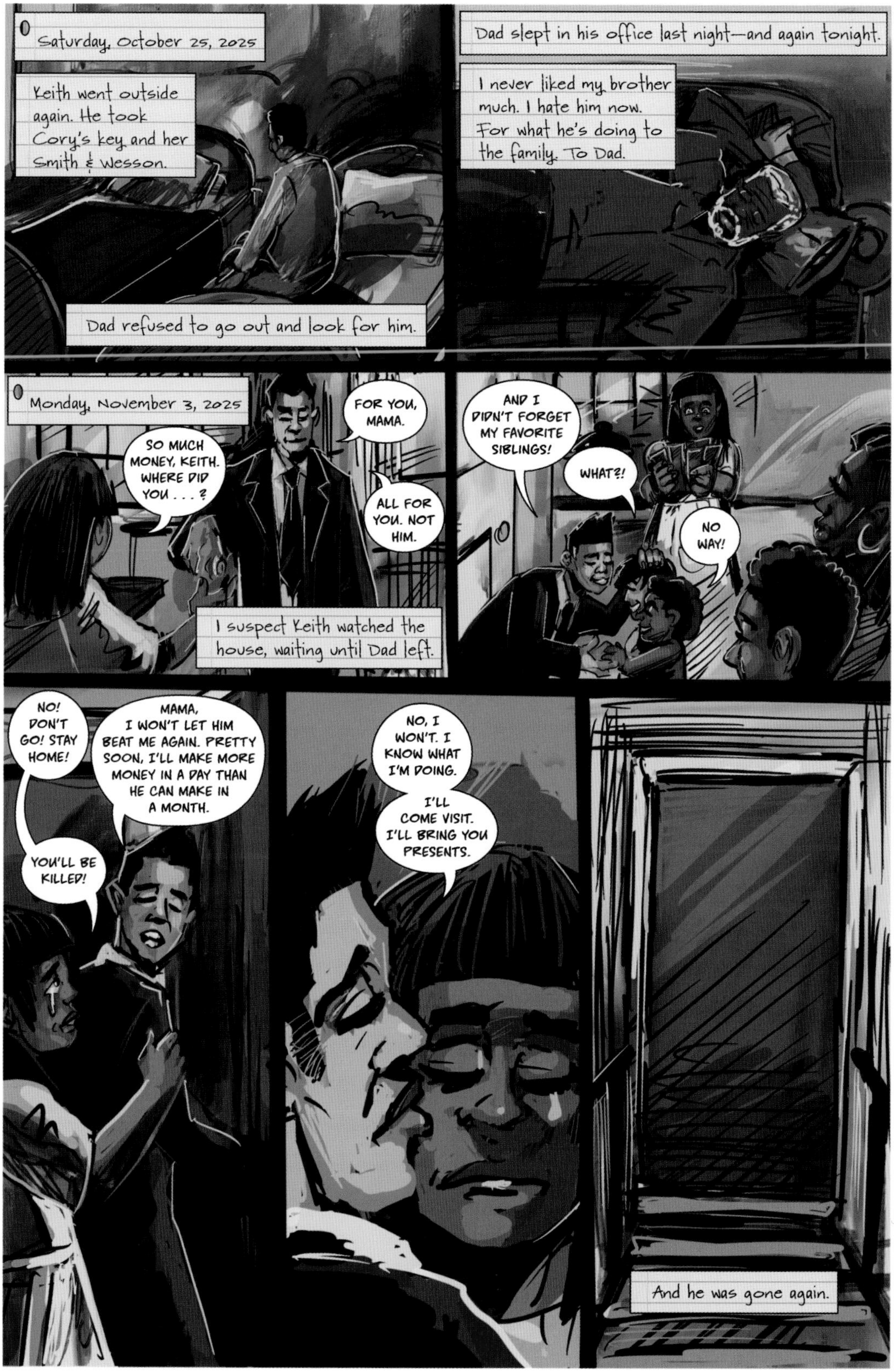
Saturday, October 25, 2025
Keith went outside again. He took Cory's key and her Smith & Wesson.
Dad refused to go out and look for him.
Dad slept in his office last night—and again tonight.
I never liked my brother much. I hate him now. For what he's doing to the family. To Dad.
Monday, November 3, 2025
SO MUCH MONEY, KEITH. WHERE DID YOU . . . ?
FOR YOU, MAMA.
ALL FOR YOU. NOT HIM.
I suspect Keith watched the house, waiting until Dad left.
AND I DIDN'T FORGET MY FAVORITE SIBLINGS!
WHAT?!
NO WAY!
NO! DON'T GO! STAY HOME!
MAMA, I WON'T LET HIM BEAT ME AGAIN. PRETTY SOON, I'LL MAKE MORE MONEY IN A DAY THAN HE CAN MAKE IN A MONTH.
YOU'LL BE KILLED!
NO, I WON'T. I KNOW WHAT I'M DOING.
I'LL COME VISIT. I'LL BRING YOU PRESENTS.
And he was gone again.

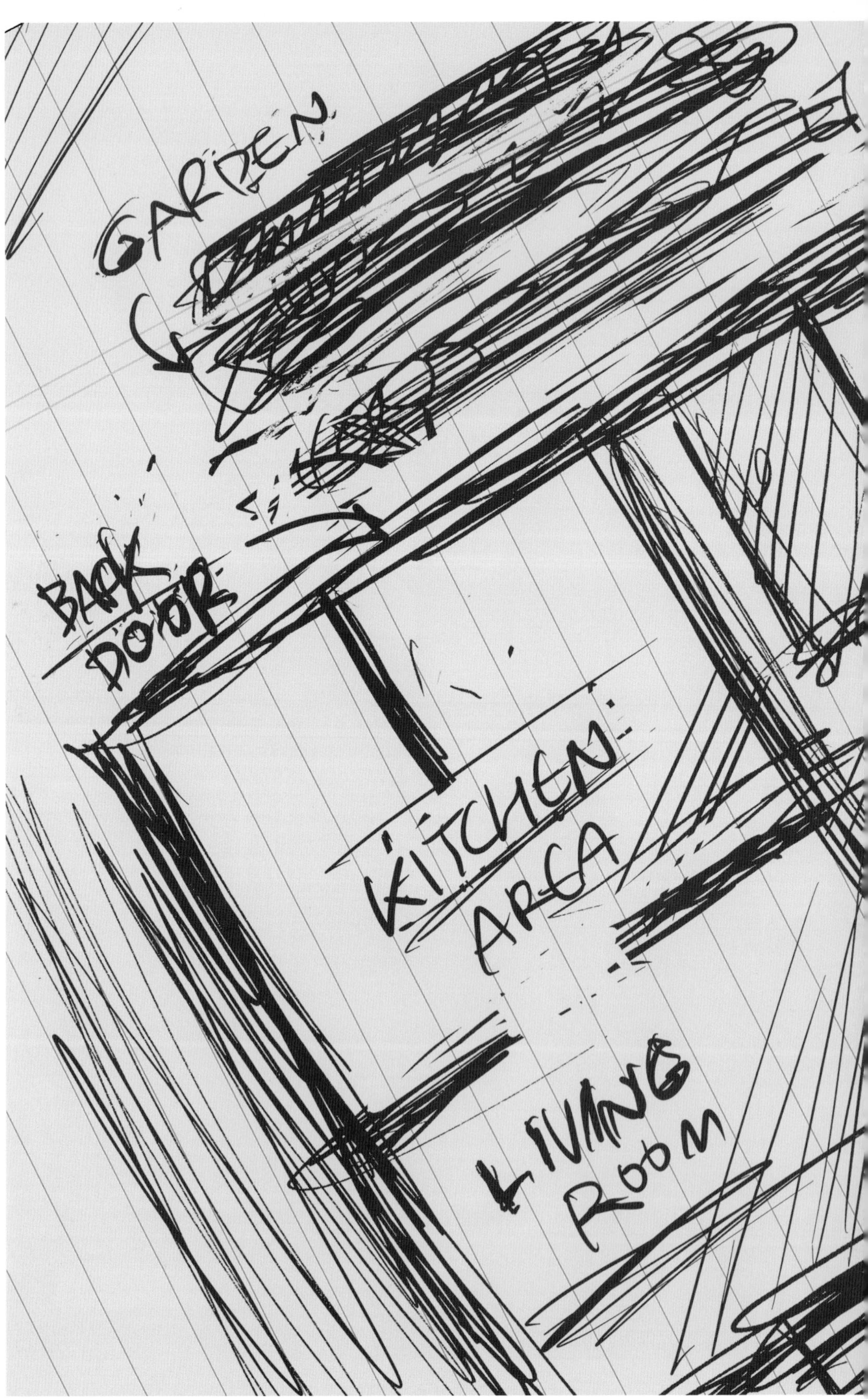
GARDEN
BACK DOOR
KITCHEN AREA
LIVING ROOM

2026

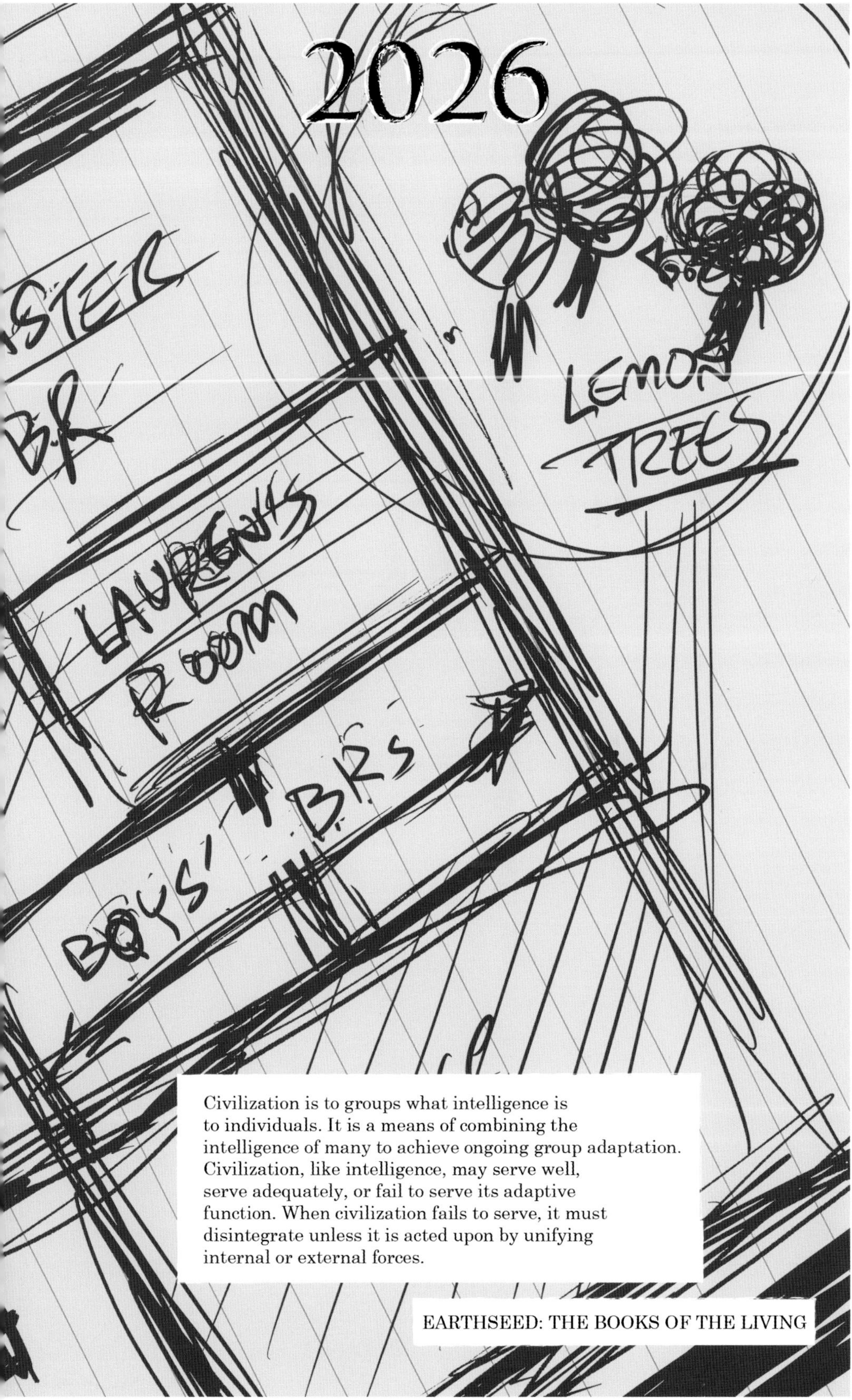
STER
BR
LAURENS ROOM
LEMON TREES
BOYS' BRS

Civilization is to groups what intelligence is to individuals. It is a means of combining the intelligence of many to achieve ongoing group adaptation. Civilization, like intelligence, may serve well, serve adequately, or fail to serve its adaptive function. When civilization fails to serve, it must disintegrate unless it is acted upon by unifying internal or external forces.

EARTHSEED: THE BOOKS OF THE LIVING

When apparent stability disintegrates,
As it must—
God is Change—
People tend to give in
To fear and depression,
To need and greed.
When no influence is strong enough
To unify people
They divide.
They struggle,
One against one,
Group against group,
For survival, position, power.
They remember old hates and generate
new ones,
They create chaos and nurture it.
They kill and kill and kill,
Until they are exhausted and destroyed,
Until they are conquered by outside
forces,
Or until one of them becomes
A leader
Most will follow,
Or a tyrant
Most fear.

EARTHSEED: THE
BOOKS OF THE LIVING

Thursday, June 25, 2026

Keith came home yesterday, bigger than ever. He's not quite fourteen, but he looks like the man he wants so much to be.

We're like that, we Olaminas—tall, sturdy, fast-growing.

I GOT A ROOM IN A BUILDING WITH SOME PEOPLE.

MEANING PROSTITUTES, THIEVES, OR "ASTRONAUTS" HIGH ON DRUGS?

DO YOUR FRIENDS KNOW HOW OLD YOU ARE?

Cory was with Dorotea Cruz, who just had another baby. The other boys were playing outside. Dad went to the college at dawn and would come home at dawn the next day. When it's safest.

Yet, Keith lives outside.

HELL, NO. WHY SHOULD I TELL THEM THAT?

IT DOES HELP TO LOOK OLDER SOMETIMES.

YOU WANT SOMETHING TO EAT?

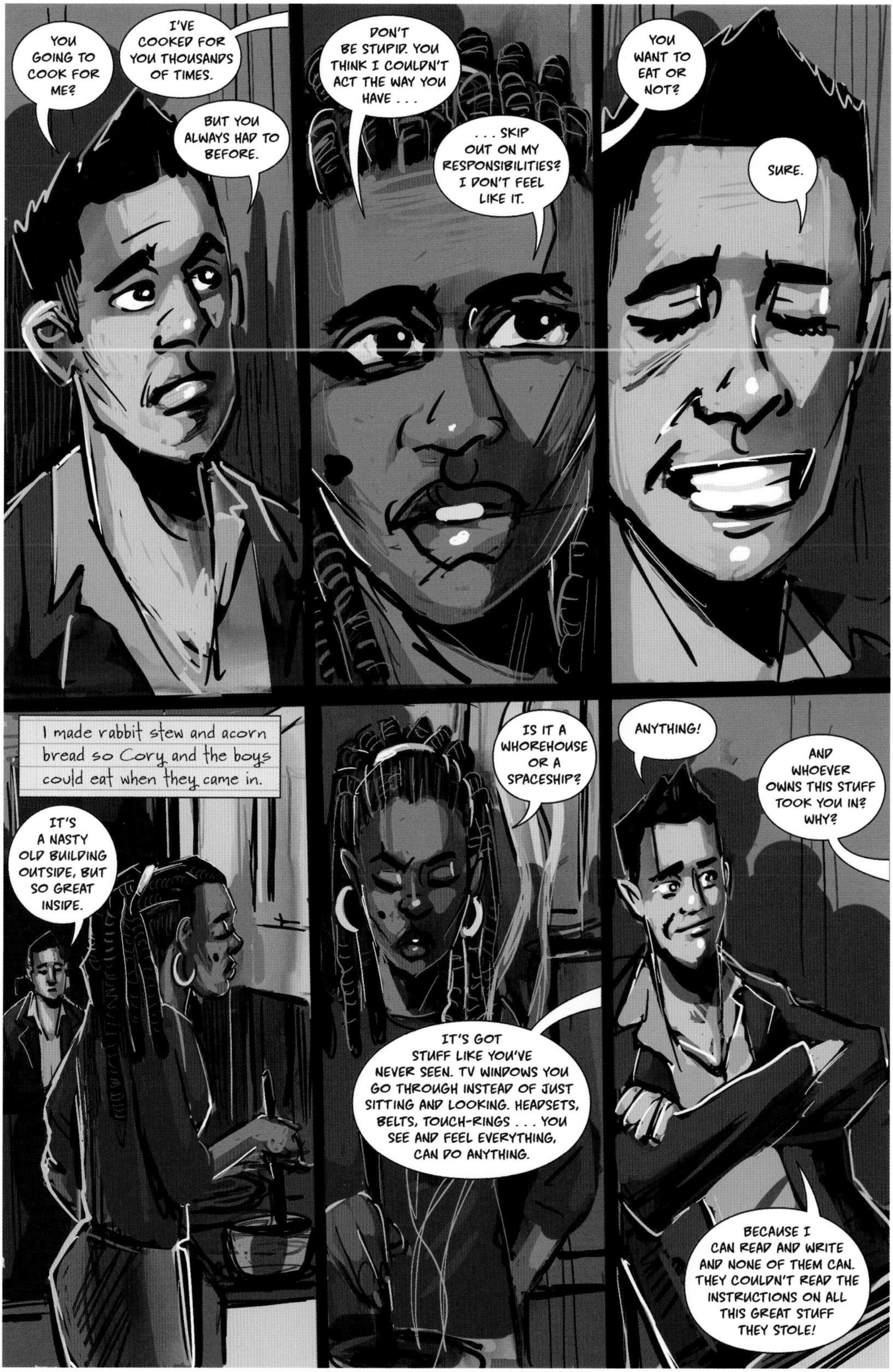
YOU GOING TO COOK FOR ME?
I'VE COOKED FOR YOU THOUSANDS OF TIMES.
BUT YOU ALWAYS HAD TO BEFORE.
DON'T BE STUPID. YOU THINK I COULDN'T ACT THE WAY YOU HAVE . . .
. . . SKIP OUT ON MY RESPONSIBILITIES? I DON'T FEEL LIKE IT.
YOU WANT TO EAT OR NOT?
SURE.
I made rabbit stew and acorn bread so Cory and the boys could eat when they came in.
IT'S A NASTY OLD BUILDING OUTSIDE, BUT SO GREAT INSIDE.
IS IT A WHOREHOUSE OR A SPACESHIP?
IT'S GOT STUFF LIKE YOU'VE NEVER SEEN. TV WINDOWS YOU GO THROUGH INSTEAD OF JUST SITTING AND LOOKING. HEADSETS, BELTS, TOUCH-RINGS . . . YOU SEE AND FEEL EVERYTHING, CAN DO ANYTHING.
ANYTHING!
AND WHOEVER OWNS THIS STUFF TOOK YOU IN? WHY?
BECAUSE I CAN READ AND WRITE AND NONE OF THEM CAN. THEY COULDN'T READ THE INSTRUCTIONS ON ALL THIS GREAT STUFF THEY STOLE!

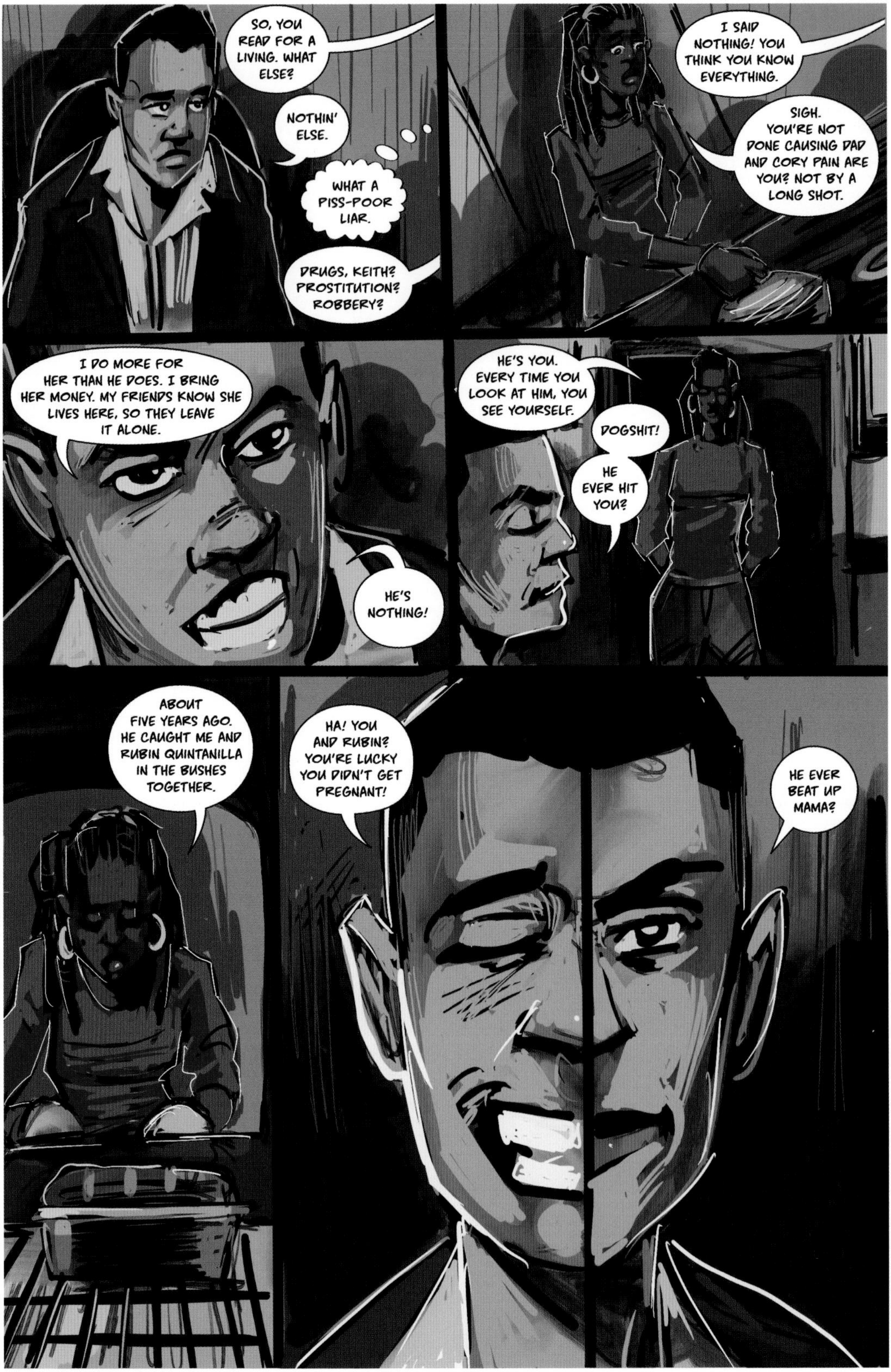
SO, YOU READ FOR A LIVING. WHAT ELSE?
NOTHIN' ELSE.
WHAT A PISS-POOR LIAR.
DRUGS, KEITH? PROSTITUTION? ROBBERY?
I SAID NOTHING! YOU THINK YOU KNOW EVERYTHING.
SIGH. YOU'RE NOT DONE CAUSING DAD AND CORY PAIN ARE YOU? NOT BY A LONG SHOT.
I DO MORE FOR HER THAN HE DOES. I BRING HER MONEY. MY FRIENDS KNOW SHE LIVES HERE, SO THEY LEAVE IT ALONE.
HE'S NOTHING!
HE'S YOU. EVERY TIME YOU LOOK AT HIM, YOU SEE YOURSELF.
DOGSHIT!
HE EVER HIT YOU?
ABOUT FIVE YEARS AGO. HE CAUGHT ME AND RUBIN QUINTANILLA IN THE BUSHES TOGETHER.
HA! YOU AND RUBIN? YOU'RE LUCKY YOU DIDN'T GET PREGNANT!
HE EVER BEAT UP MAMA?

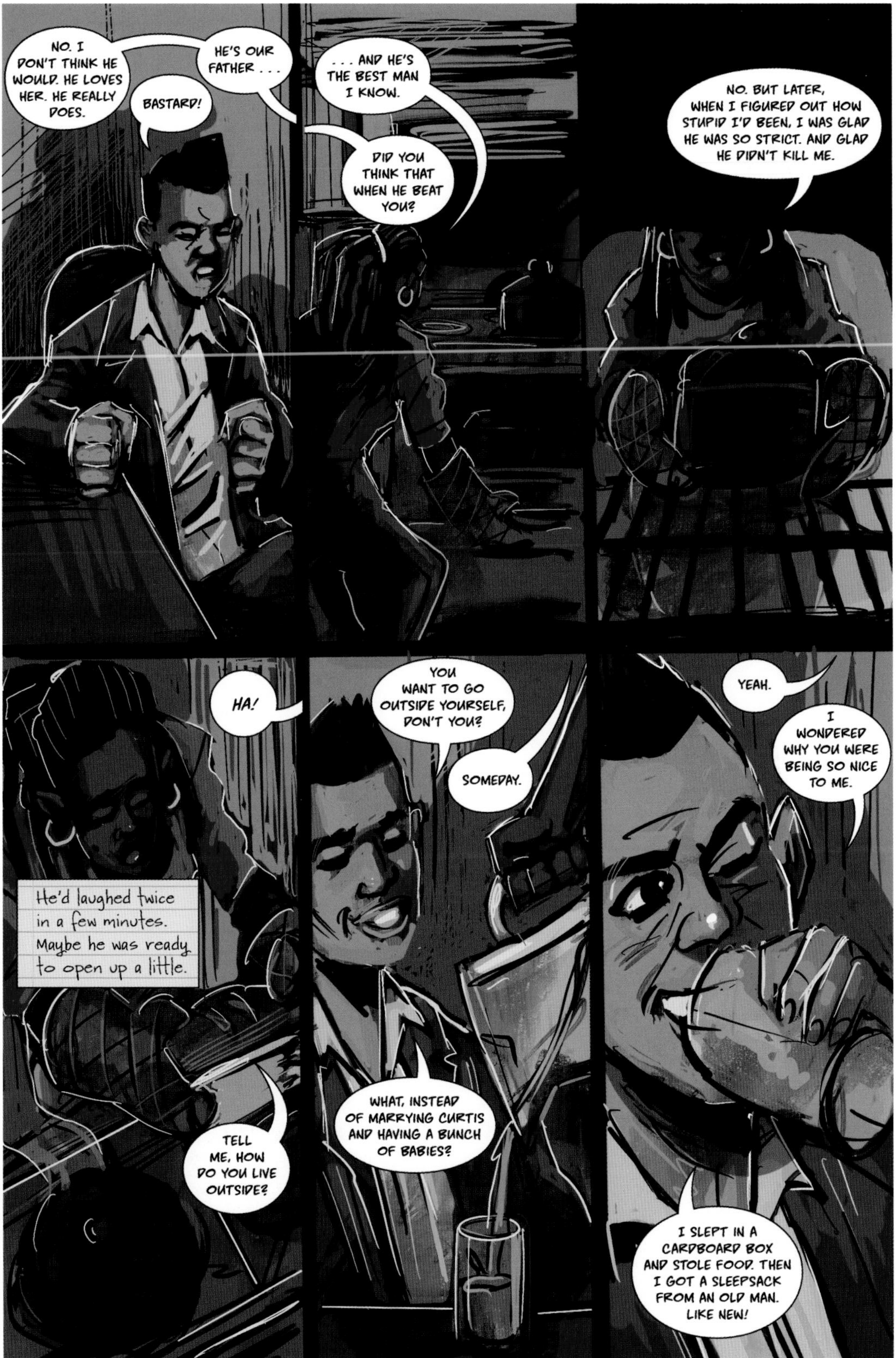
NO. I DON'T THINK HE WOULD. HE LOVES HER. HE REALLY DOES.
BASTARD!
HE'S OUR FATHER . . .
. . . AND HE'S THE BEST MAN I KNOW.
DID YOU THINK THAT WHEN HE BEAT YOU?
NO. BUT LATER, WHEN I FIGURED OUT HOW STUPID I'D BEEN, I WAS GLAD HE WAS SO STRICT. AND GLAD HE DIDN'T KILL ME.
HA!
He'd laughed twice in a few minutes. Maybe he was ready to open up a little.
TELL ME, HOW DO YOU LIVE OUTSIDE?
YOU WANT TO GO OUTSIDE YOURSELF, DON'T YOU?
SOMEDAY.
WHAT, INSTEAD OF MARRYING CURTIS AND HAVING A BUNCH OF BABIES?
YEAH.
I WONDERED WHY YOU WERE BEING SO NICE TO ME.
I SLEPT IN A CARDBOARD BOX AND STOLE FOOD. THEN I GOT A SLEEPSACK FROM AN OLD MAN. LIKE NEW!

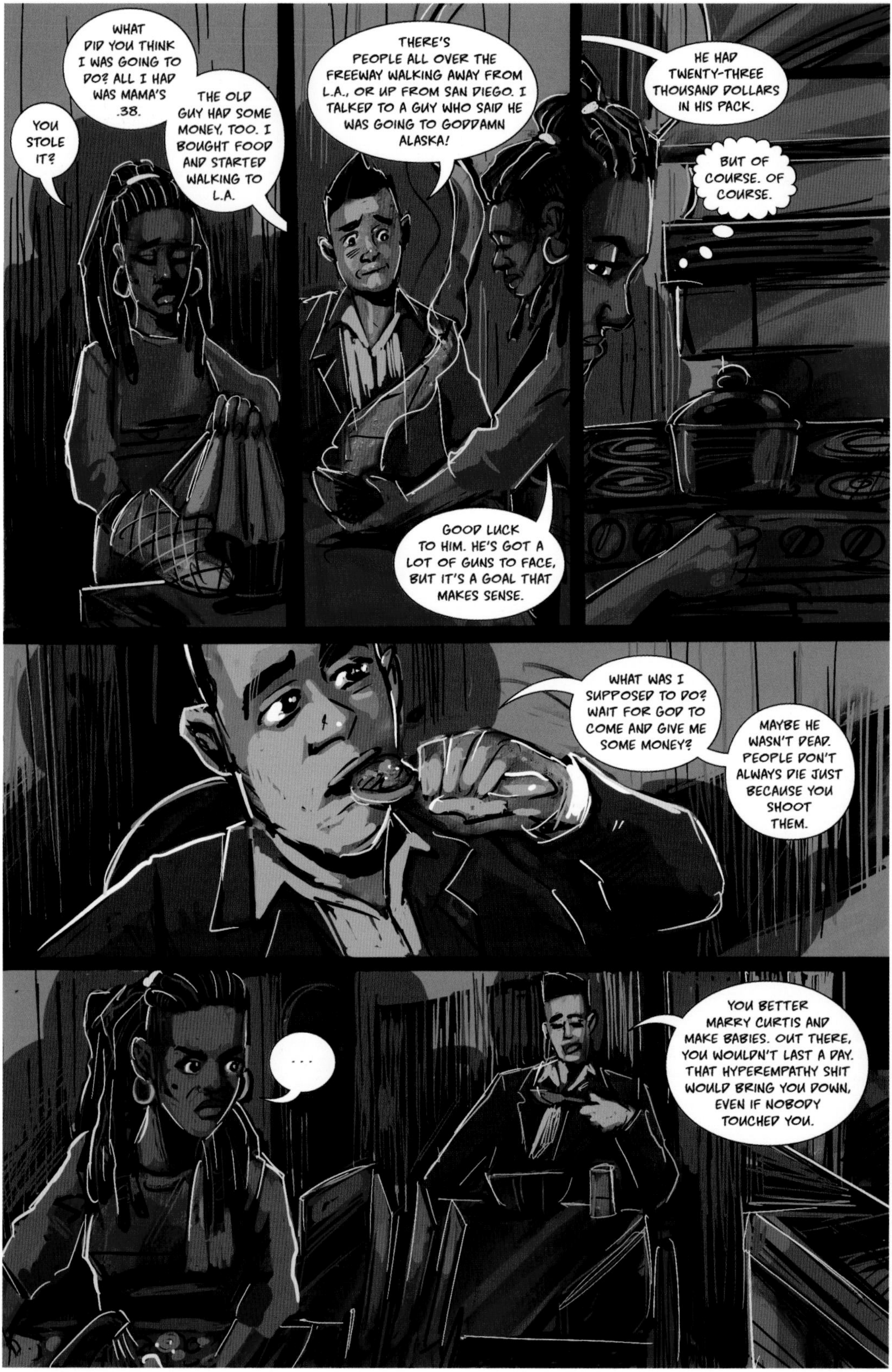
WHAT DID YOU THINK I WAS GOING TO DO? ALL I HAD WAS MAMA'S .38.
YOU STOLE IT?
THE OLD GUY HAD SOME MONEY, TOO. I BOUGHT FOOD AND STARTED WALKING TO L.A.
THERE'S PEOPLE ALL OVER THE FREEWAY WALKING AWAY FROM L.A., OR UP FROM SAN DIEGO. I TALKED TO A GUY WHO SAID HE WAS GOING TO GODDAMN ALASKA!
GOOD LUCK TO HIM. HE'S GOT A LOT OF GUNS TO FACE, BUT IT'S A GOAL THAT MAKES SENSE.
HE HAD TWENTY-THREE THOUSAND DOLLARS IN HIS PACK.
BUT OF COURSE. OF COURSE.
WHAT WAS I SUPPOSED TO DO? WAIT FOR GOD TO COME AND GIVE ME SOME MONEY?
MAYBE HE WASN'T DEAD. PEOPLE DON'T ALWAYS DIE JUST BECAUSE YOU SHOOT THEM.
...
YOU BETTER MARRY CURTIS AND MAKE BABIES. OUT THERE, YOU WOULDN'T LAST A DAY. THAT HYPEREMPATHY SHIT WOULD BRING YOU DOWN, EVEN IF NOBODY TOUCHED YOU.

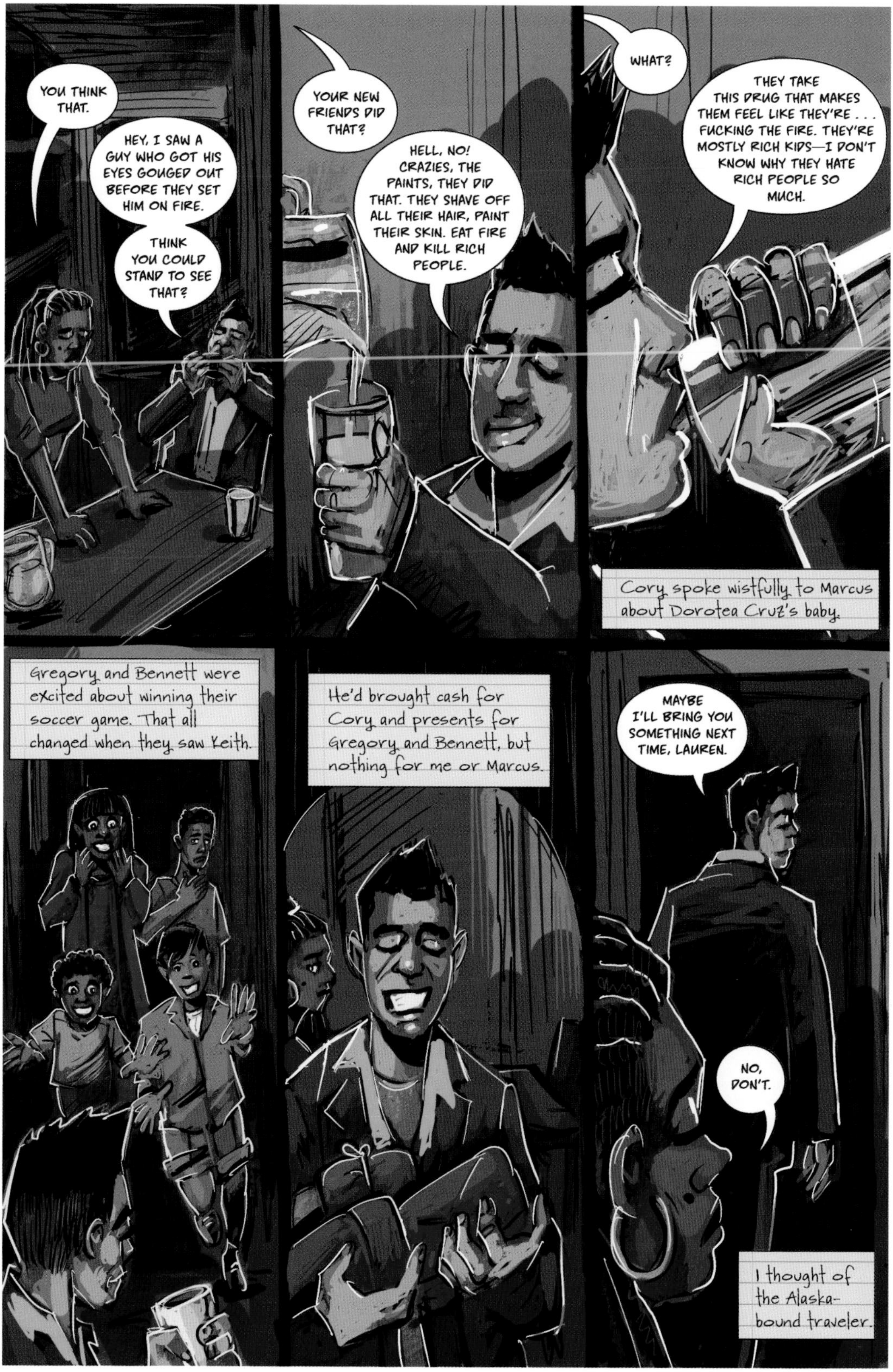
YOU THINK THAT.
HEY, I SAW A GUY WHO GOT HIS EYES GOUGED OUT BEFORE THEY SET HIM ON FIRE.
THINK YOU COULD STAND TO SEE THAT?
YOUR NEW FRIENDS DID THAT?
HELL, NO! CRAZIES, THE PAINTS, THEY DID THAT. THEY SHAVE OFF ALL THEIR HAIR, PAINT THEIR SKIN. EAT FIRE AND KILL RICH PEOPLE.
WHAT?
THEY TAKE THIS DRUG THAT MAKES THEM FEEL LIKE THEY'RE . . . FUCKING THE FIRE. THEY'RE MOSTLY RICH KIDS—I DON'T KNOW WHY THEY HATE RICH PEOPLE SO MUCH.
Cory spoke wistfully to Marcus about Dorotea Cruz's baby.
Gregory and Bennett were excited about winning their soccer game. That all changed when they saw Keith.
He'd brought cash for Cory and presents for Gregory and Bennett, but nothing for me or Marcus.
MAYBE I'LL BRING YOU SOMETHING NEXT TIME, LAUREN.
NO, DON'T.
I thought of the Alaska-bound traveler.

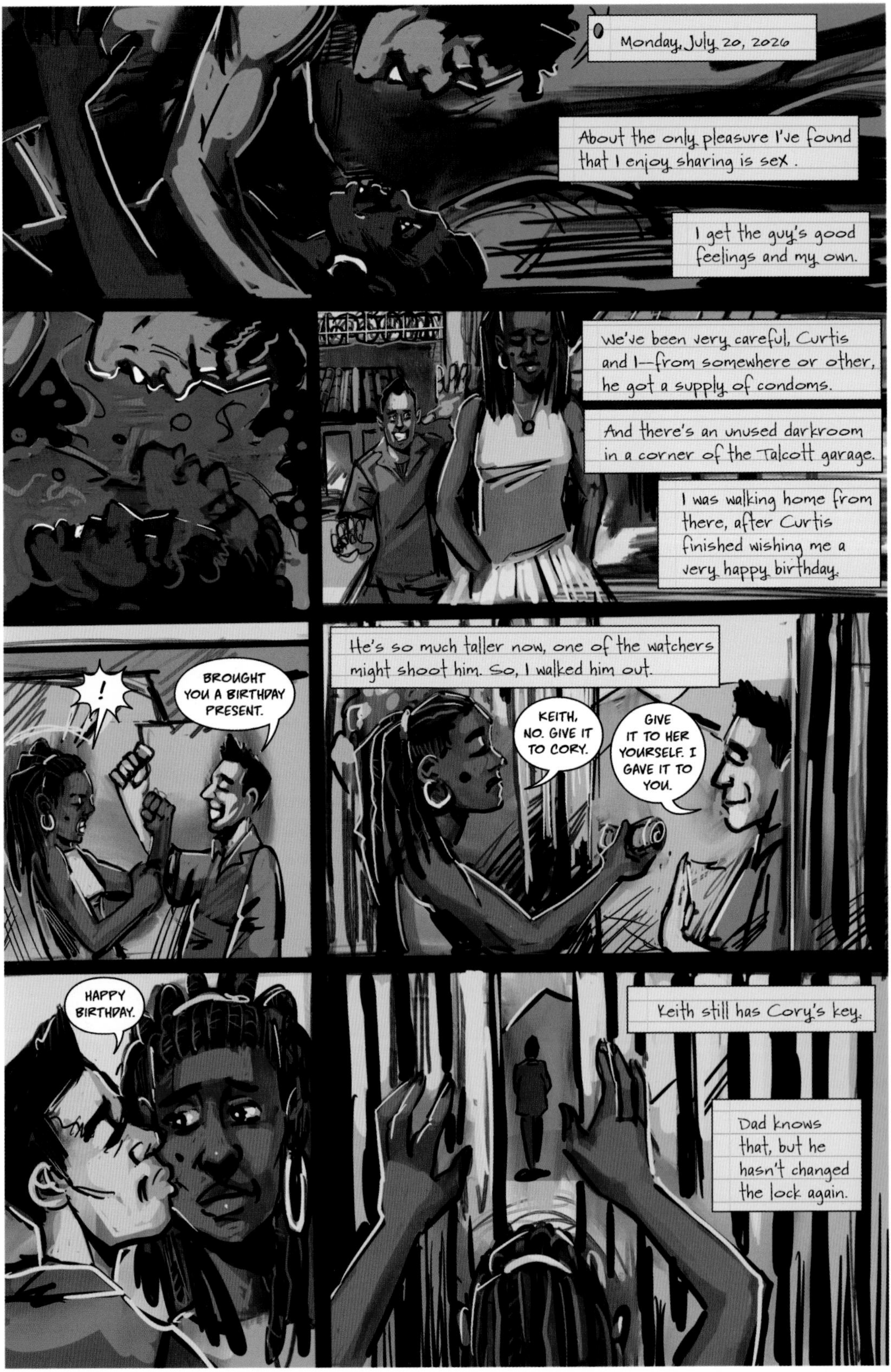
Monday, July 20, 2026
About the only pleasure I've found that I enjoy sharing is sex.
I get the guy's good feelings and my own.
We've been very careful, Curtis and I—from somewhere or other, he got a supply of condoms.
And there's an unused darkroom in a corner of the Talcott garage.
I was walking home from there, after Curtis finished wishing me a very happy birthday.
!
BROUGHT YOU A BIRTHDAY PRESENT.
He's so much taller now, one of the watchers might shoot him. So, I walked him out.
KEITH, NO. GIVE IT TO CORY.
GIVE IT TO HER YOURSELF. I GAVE IT TO YOU.
HAPPY BIRTHDAY.
Keith still has Cory's key.
Dad knows that, but he hasn't changed the lock again.

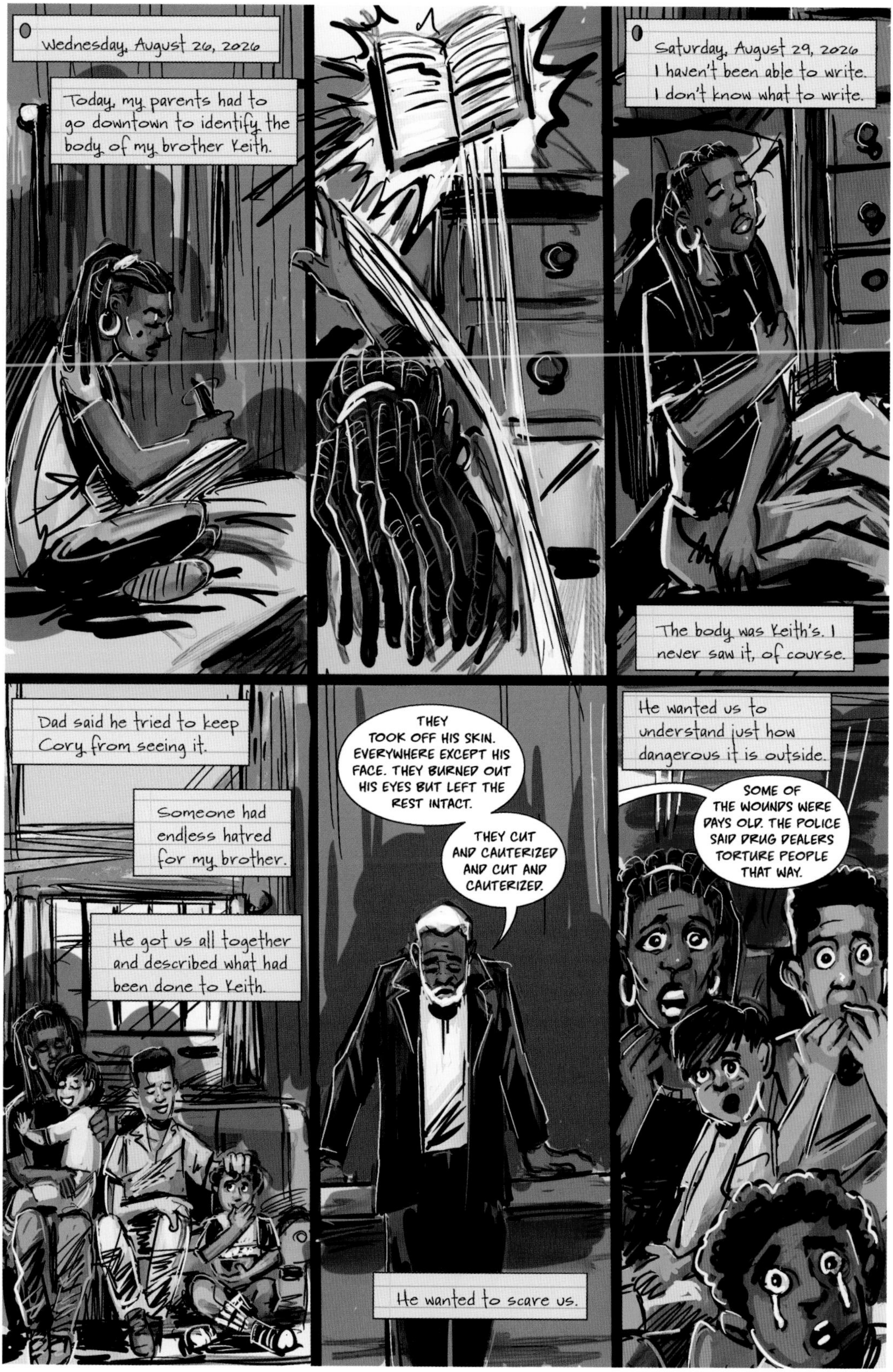
Wednesday, August 26, 2026
Today, my parents had to go downtown to identify the body of my brother Keith.
Saturday, August 29, 2026
I haven't been able to write.
I don't know what to write.
The body was Keith's. I never saw it, of course.
Dad said he tried to keep Cory from seeing it.
Someone had endless hatred for my brother.
He got us all together and described what had been done to Keith.
THEY TOOK OFF HIS SKIN. EVERYWHERE EXCEPT HIS FACE. THEY BURNED OUT HIS EYES BUT LEFT THE REST INTACT.
THEY CUT AND CAUTERIZED AND CUT AND CAUTERIZED.
He wanted to scare us.
He wanted us to understand just how dangerous it is outside.
SOME OF THE WOUNDS WERE DAYS OLD. THE POLICE SAID DRUG DEALERS TORTURE PEOPLE THAT WAY.

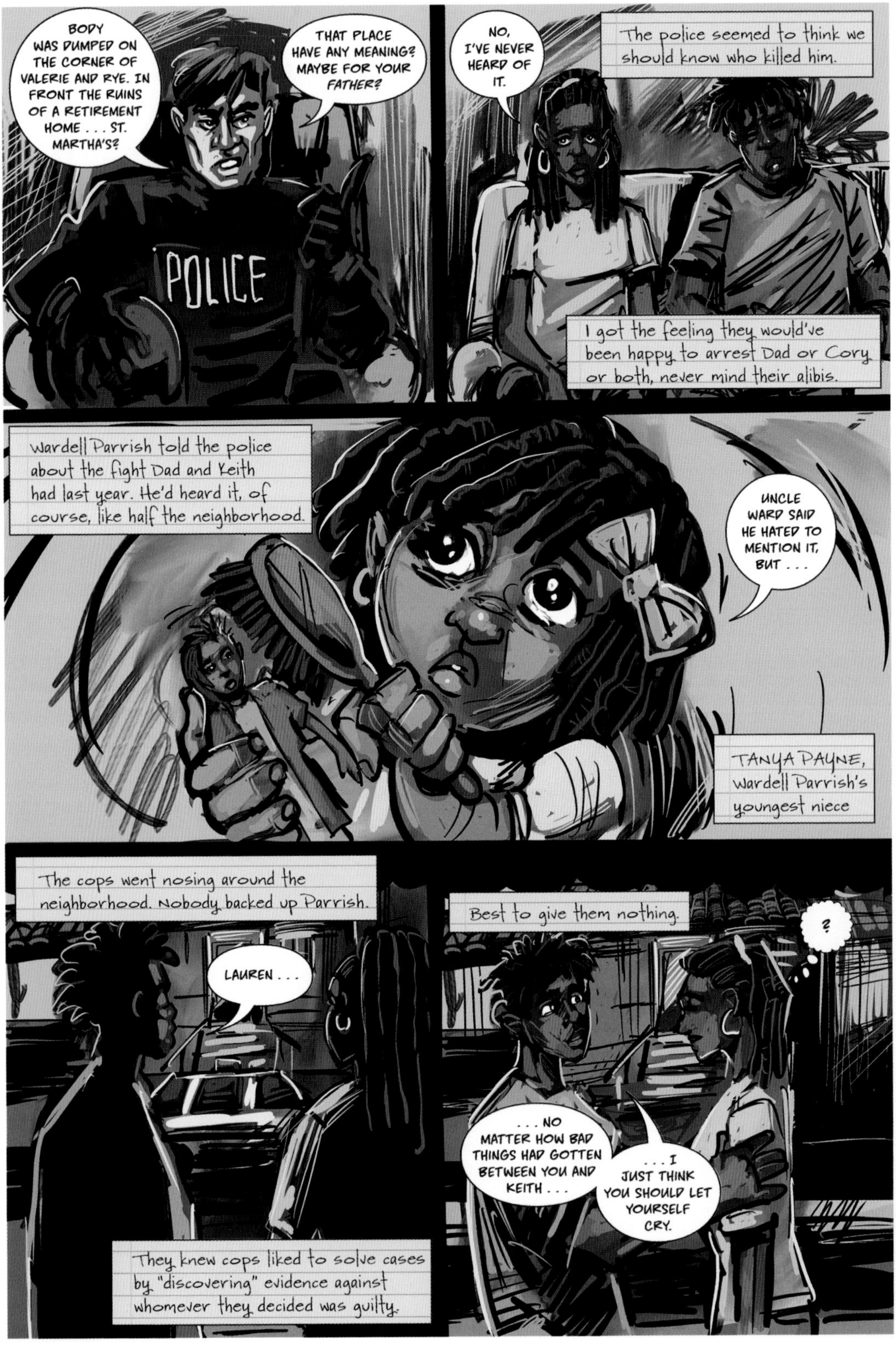
BODY WAS DUMPED ON THE CORNER OF VALERIE AND RYE. IN FRONT THE RUINS OF A RETIREMENT HOME . . . ST. MARTHA'S?
THAT PLACE HAVE ANY MEANING? MAYBE FOR YOUR FATHER?
POLICE
NO, I'VE NEVER HEARD OF IT.
The police seemed to think we should know who killed him.
I got the feeling they would've been happy to arrest Dad or Cory or both, never mind their alibis.
Wardell Parrish told the police about the fight Dad and Keith had last year. He'd heard it, of course, like half the neighborhood.
UNCLE WARD SAID HE HATED TO MENTION IT, BUT . . .
TANYA PAYNE, Wardell Parrish's youngest niece
The cops went nosing around the neighborhood. Nobody backed up Parrish.
LAUREN . . .
They knew cops liked to solve cases by "discovering" evidence against whomever they decided was guilty.
Best to give them nothing.
?
. . . NO MATTER HOW BAD THINGS HAD GOTTEN BETWEEN YOU AND KEITH . . .
. . . I JUST THINK YOU SHOULD LET YOURSELF CRY.

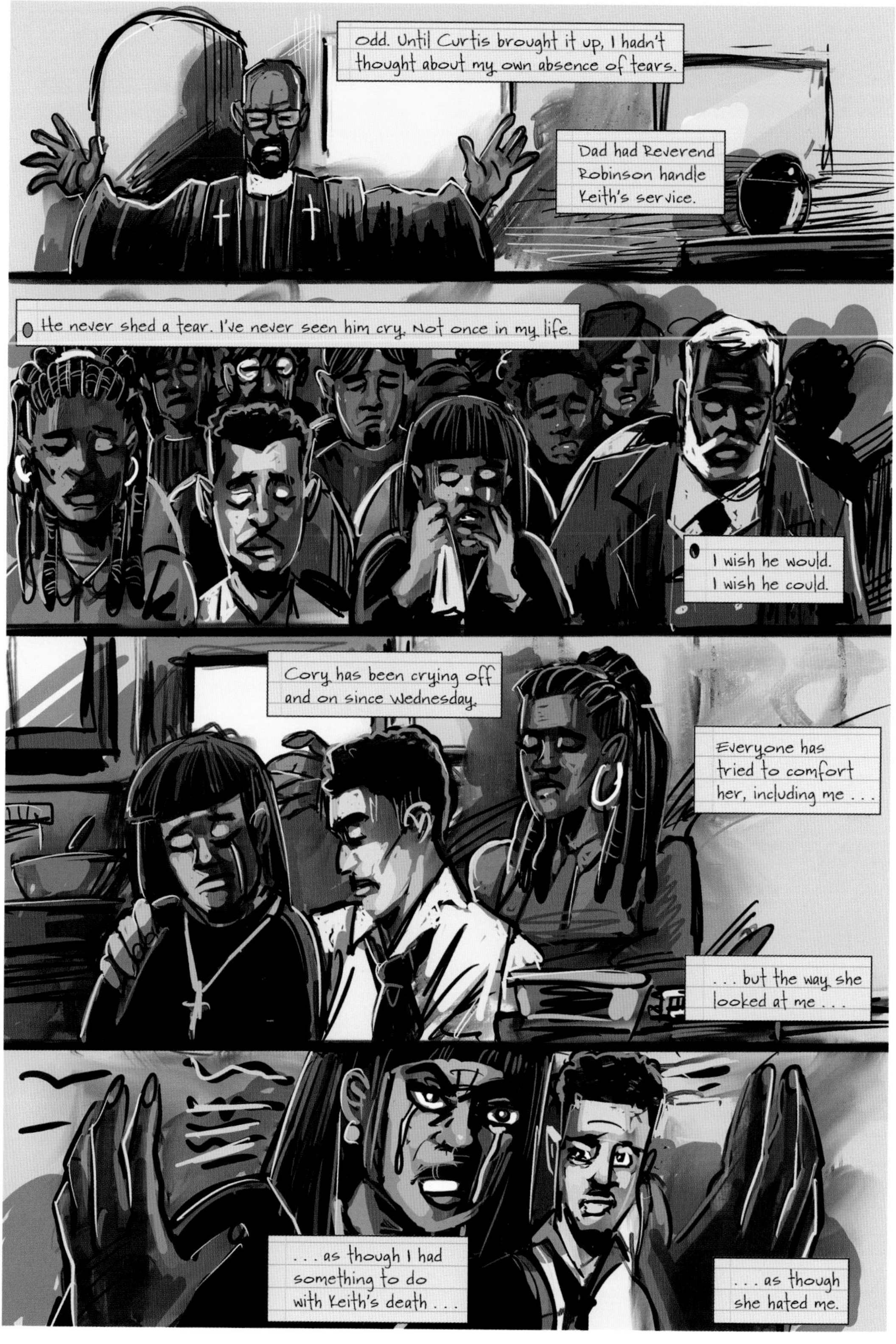
Odd. Until Curtis brought it up, I hadn't thought about my own absence of tears.
Dad had Reverend Robinson handle Keith's service.
He never shed a tear. I've never seen him cry. Not once in my life.
I wish he would. I wish he could.
Cory has been crying off and on since Wednesday.
Everyone has tried to comfort her, including me . . .
. . . but the way she looked at me . . .
. . . as though I had something to do with Keith's death . . .
. . . as though she hated me.

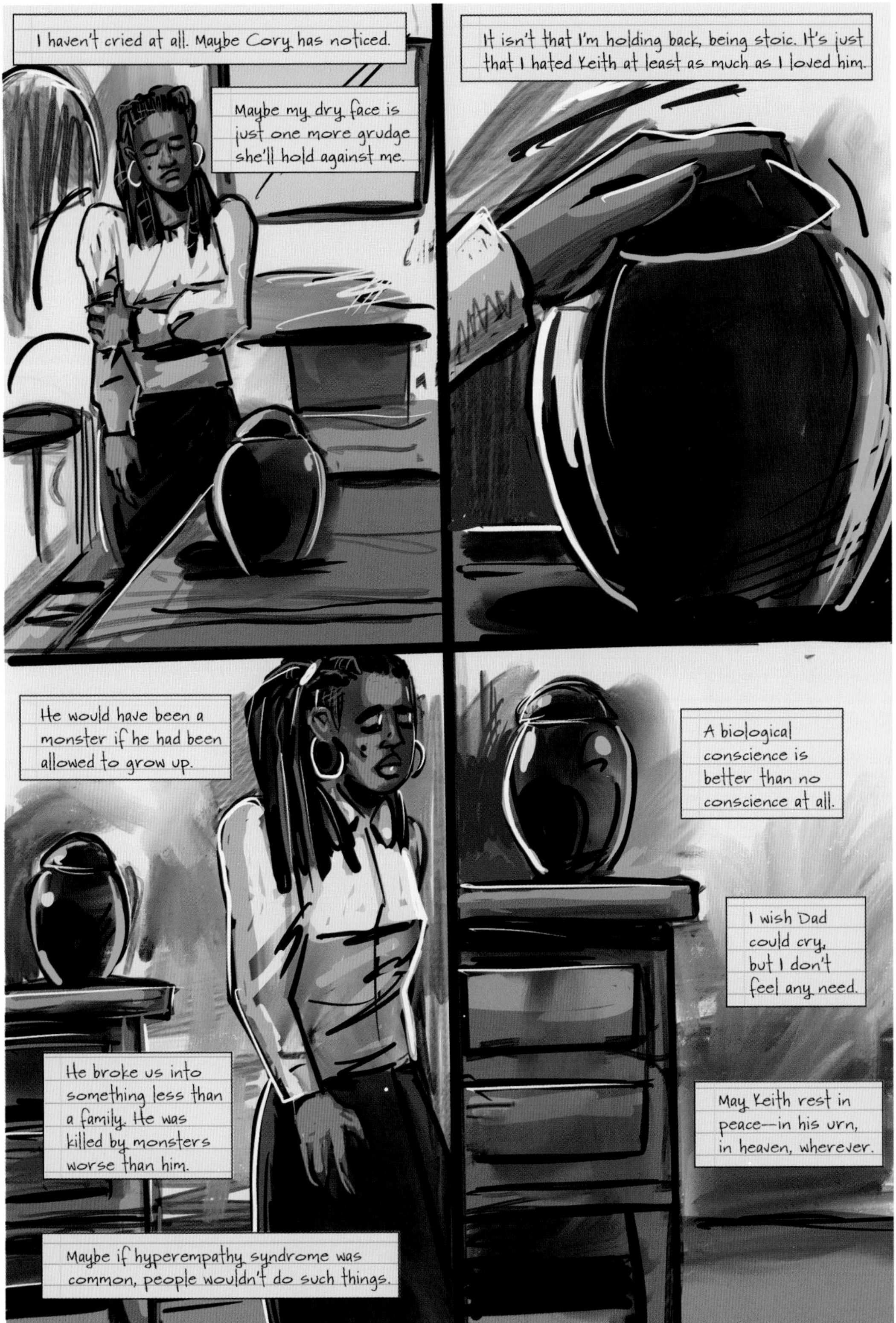
I haven't cried at all. Maybe Cory has noticed.
Maybe my dry face is just one more grudge she'll hold against me.
It isn't that I'm holding back, being stoic. It's just that I hated Keith at least as much as I loved him.
He would have been a monster if he had been allowed to grow up.
He broke us into something less than a family. He was killed by monsters worse than him.
Maybe if hyperempathy syndrome was common, people wouldn't do such things.
A biological conscience is better than no conscience at all.
I wish Dad could cry, but I don't feel any need.
May Keith rest in peace—in his urn, in heaven, wherever.

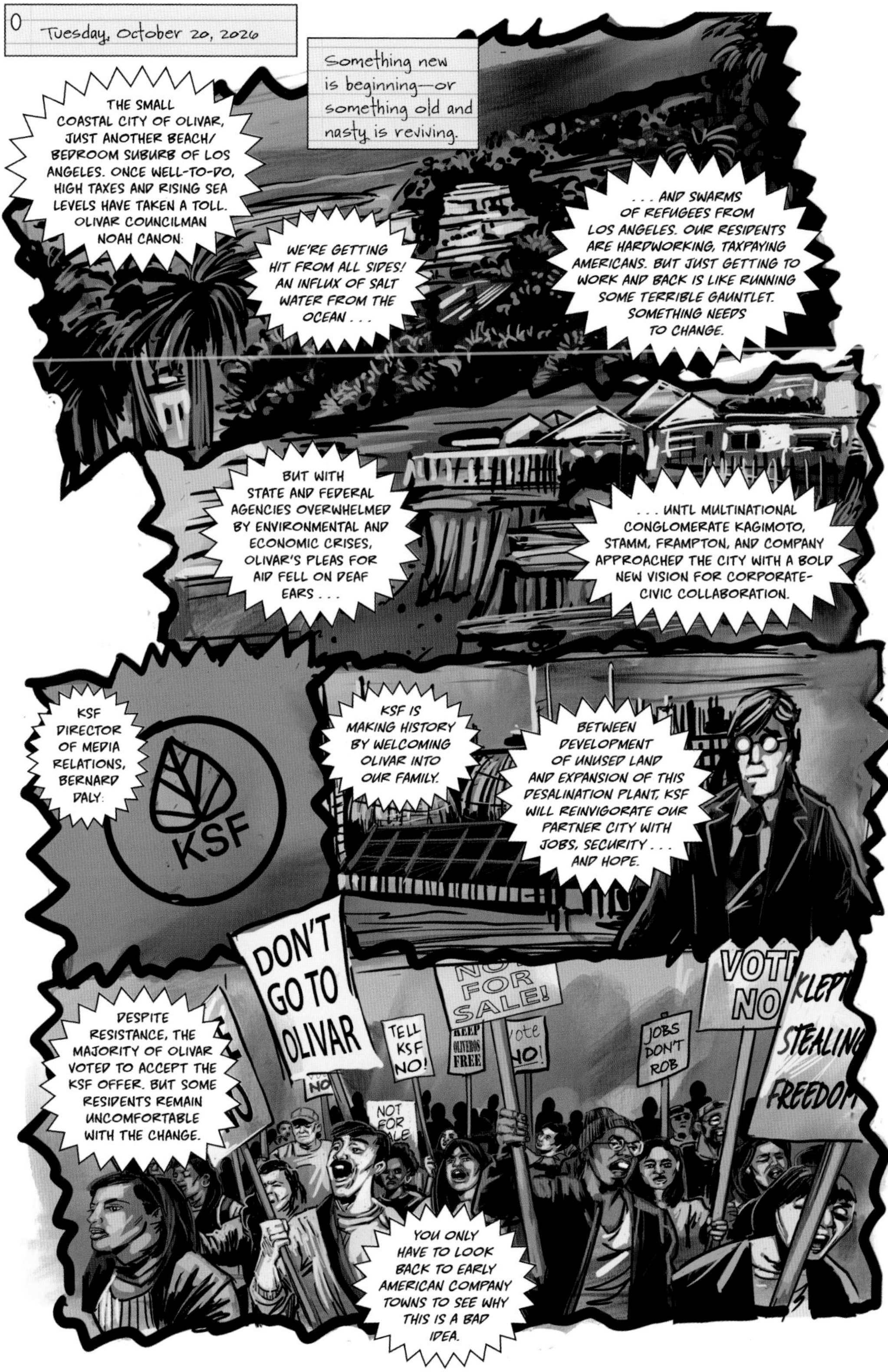

Tuesday, October 20, 2026
Something new is beginning—or something old and nasty is reviving.
THE SMALL COASTAL CITY OF OLIVAR, JUST ANOTHER BEACH/ BEDROOM SUBURB OF LOS ANGELES. ONCE WELL-TO-DO, HIGH TAXES AND RISING SEA LEVELS HAVE TAKEN A TOLL. OLIVAR COUNCILMAN NOAH CANON:
WE'RE GETTING HIT FROM ALL SIDES! AN INFLUX OF SALT WATER FROM THE OCEAN . . .
. . . AND SWARMS OF REFUGEES FROM LOS ANGELES. OUR RESIDENTS ARE HARDWORKING, TAXPAYING AMERICANS. BUT JUST GETTING TO WORK AND BACK IS LIKE RUNNING SOME TERRIBLE GAUNTLET. SOMETHING NEEDS TO CHANGE.
BUT WITH STATE AND FEDERAL AGENCIES OVERWHELMED BY ENVIRONMENTAL AND ECONOMIC CRISES, OLIVAR'S PLEAS FOR AID FELL ON DEAF EARS . . .
. . . UNTL MULTINATIONAL CONGLOMERATE KAGIMOTO, STAMM, FRAMPTON, AND COMPANY APPROACHED THE CITY WITH A BOLD NEW VISION FOR CORPORATE-CIVIC COLLABORATION.
KSF DIRECTOR OF MEDIA RELATIONS, BERNARD DALY:
KSF
KSF IS MAKING HISTORY BY WELCOMING OLIVAR INTO OUR FAMILY.
BETWEEN DEVELOPMENT OF UNUSED LAND AND EXPANSION OF THIS DESALINATION PLANT, KSF WILL REINVIGORATE OUR PARTNER CITY WITH JOBS, SECURITY . . . AND HOPE.
DESPITE RESISTANCE, THE MAJORITY OF OLIVAR VOTED TO ACCEPT THE KSF OFFER. BUT SOME RESIDENTS REMAIN UNCOMFORTABLE WITH THE CHANGE.
DON'T GO TO OLIVAR
FOR SALE!
TELL KSF NO!
Vote NO!
JOBS DON'T ROB
NO
STEALING
YOU ONLY HAVE TO LOOK BACK TO EARLY AMERICAN COMPANY TOWNS TO SEE WHY THIS IS A BAD IDEA.

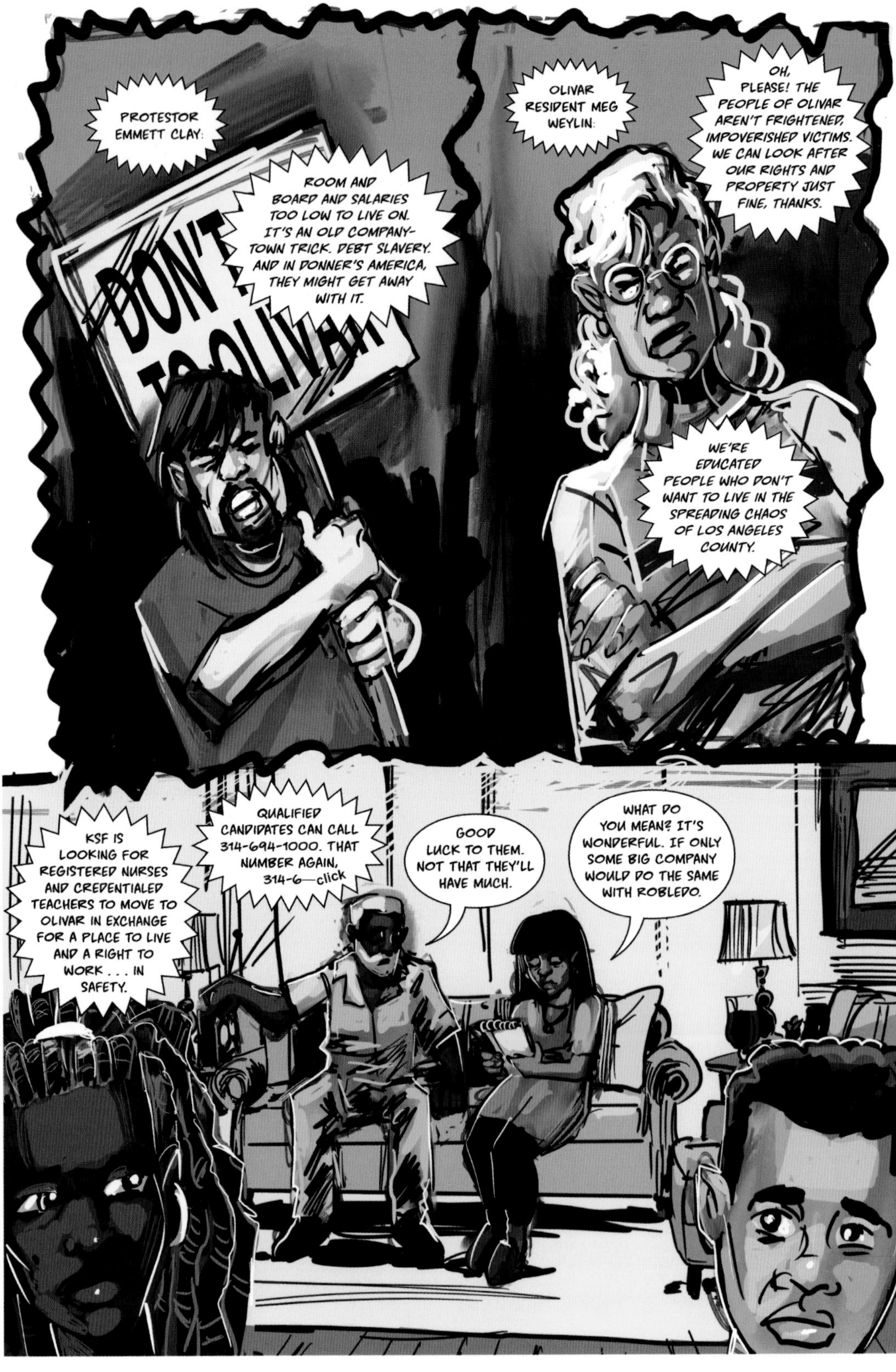
PROTESTOR EMMETT CLAY:
ROOM AND BOARD AND SALARIES TOO LOW TO LIVE ON. IT'S AN OLD COMPANY-TOWN TRICK. DEBT SLAVERY. AND IN DONNER'S AMERICA, THEY MIGHT GET AWAY WITH IT.
OLIVAR RESIDENT MEG WEYLIN:
OH, PLEASE! THE PEOPLE OF OLIVAR AREN'T FRIGHTENED, IMPOVERISHED VICTIMS. WE CAN LOOK AFTER OUR RIGHTS AND PROPERTY JUST FINE, THANKS.
WE'RE EDUCATED PEOPLE WHO DON'T WANT TO LIVE IN THE SPREADING CHAOS OF LOS ANGELES COUNTY.
KSF IS LOOKING FOR REGISTERED NURSES AND CREDENTIALED TEACHERS TO MOVE TO OLIVAR IN EXCHANGE FOR A PLACE TO LIVE AND A RIGHT TO WORK . . . IN SAFETY.
QUALIFIED CANDIDATES CAN CALL 314-694-1000. THAT NUMBER AGAIN, 314-6—click
GOOD LUCK TO THEM. NOT THAT THEY'LL HAVE MUCH.
WHAT DO YOU MEAN? IT'S WONDERFUL. IF ONLY SOME BIG COMPANY WOULD DO THE SAME WITH ROBLEDO.

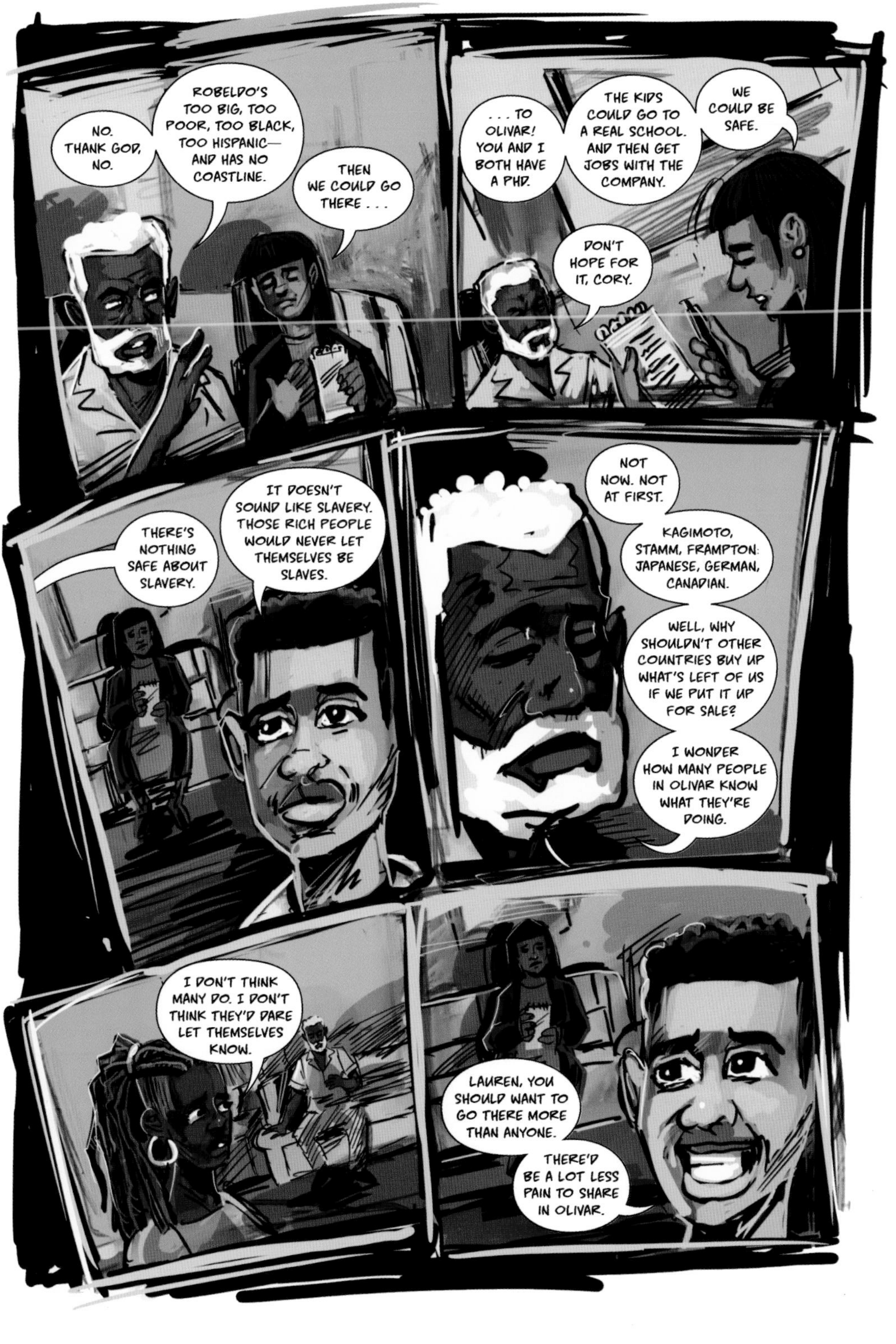
NO. THANK GOD, NO.
ROBELDO'S TOO BIG, TOO POOR, TOO BLACK, TOO HISPANIC— AND HAS NO COASTLINE.
THEN WE COULD GO THERE . . .
. . . TO OLIVAR! YOU AND I BOTH HAVE A PHD.
THE KIDS COULD GO TO A REAL SCHOOL. AND THEN GET JOBS WITH THE COMPANY.
WE COULD BE SAFE.
DON'T HOPE FOR IT, CORY.
THERE'S NOTHING SAFE ABOUT SLAVERY.
IT DOESN'T SOUND LIKE SLAVERY. THOSE RICH PEOPLE WOULD NEVER LET THEMSELVES BE SLAVES.
NOT NOW. NOT AT FIRST.
KAGIMOTO, STAMM, FRAMPTON: JAPANESE, GERMAN, CANADIAN.
WELL, WHY SHOULDN'T OTHER COUNTRIES BUY UP WHAT'S LEFT OF US IF WE PUT IT UP FOR SALE?
I WONDER HOW MANY PEOPLE IN OLIVAR KNOW WHAT THEY'RE DOING.
I DON'T THINK MANY DO. I DON'T THINK THEY'D DARE LET THEMSELVES KNOW.
LAUREN, YOU SHOULD WANT TO GO THERE MORE THAN ANYONE.
THERE'D BE A LOT LESS PAIN TO SHARE IN OLIVAR.

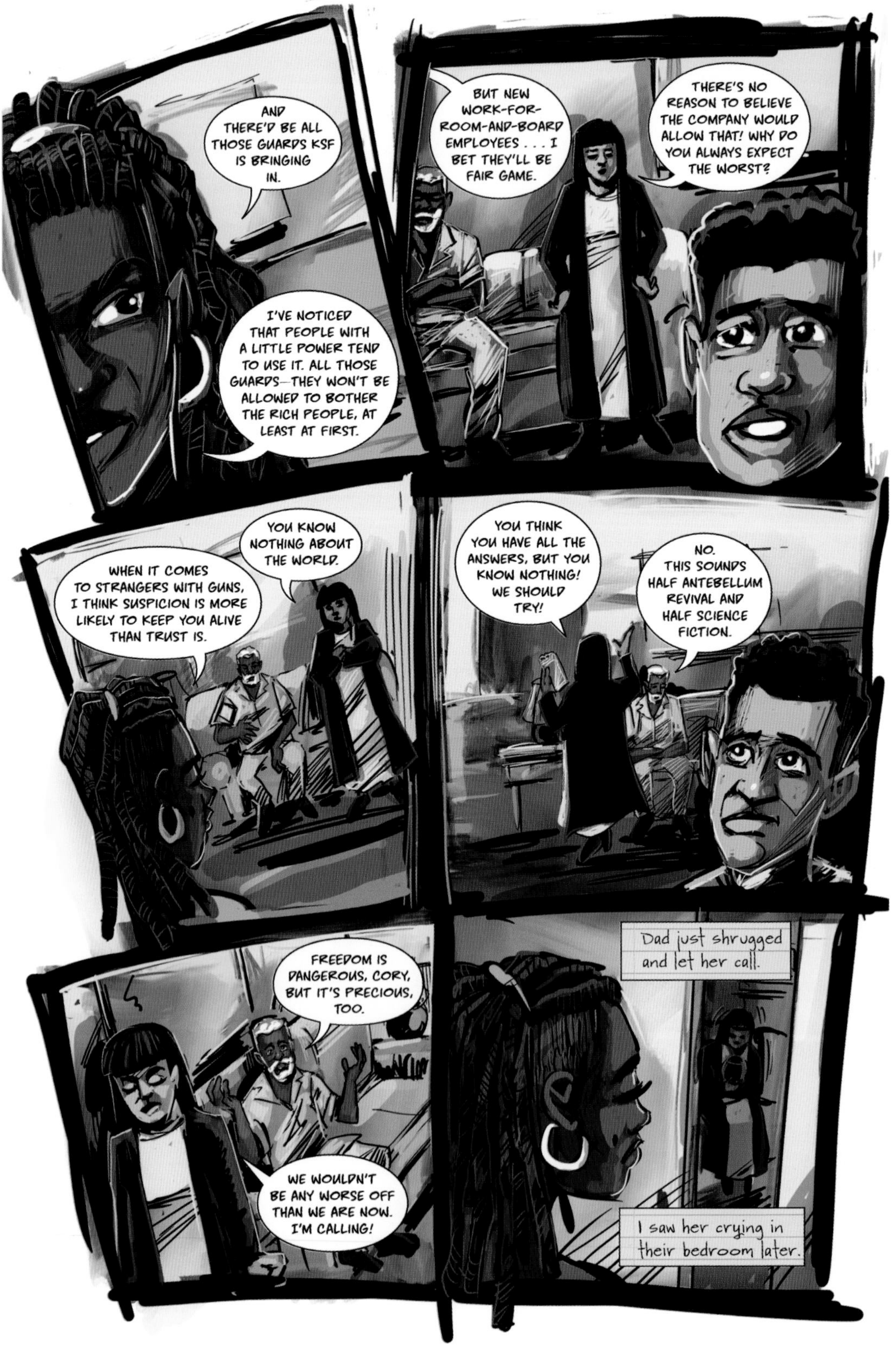
AND THERE'D BE ALL THOSE GUARDS KSF IS BRINGING IN.
I'VE NOTICED THAT PEOPLE WITH A LITTLE POWER TEND TO USE IT. ALL THOSE GUARDS—THEY WON'T BE ALLOWED TO BOTHER THE RICH PEOPLE, AT LEAST AT FIRST.
BUT NEW WORK-FOR-ROOM-AND-BOARD EMPLOYEES . . . I BET THEY'LL BE FAIR GAME.
THERE'S NO REASON TO BELIEVE THE COMPANY WOULD ALLOW THAT! WHY DO YOU ALWAYS EXPECT THE WORST?
WHEN IT COMES TO STRANGERS WITH GUNS, I THINK SUSPICION IS MORE LIKELY TO KEEP YOU ALIVE THAN TRUST IS.
YOU KNOW NOTHING ABOUT THE WORLD.
YOU THINK YOU HAVE ALL THE ANSWERS, BUT YOU KNOW NOTHING! WE SHOULD TRY!
NO. THIS SOUNDS HALF ANTEBELLUM REVIVAL AND HALF SCIENCE FICTION.
FREEDOM IS DANGEROUS, CORY, BUT IT'S PRECIOUS, TOO.
WE WOULDN'T BE ANY WORSE OFF THAN WE ARE NOW. I'M CALLING!
Dad just shrugged and let her call.
I saw her crying in their bedroom later.

Saturday, October 24, 2026

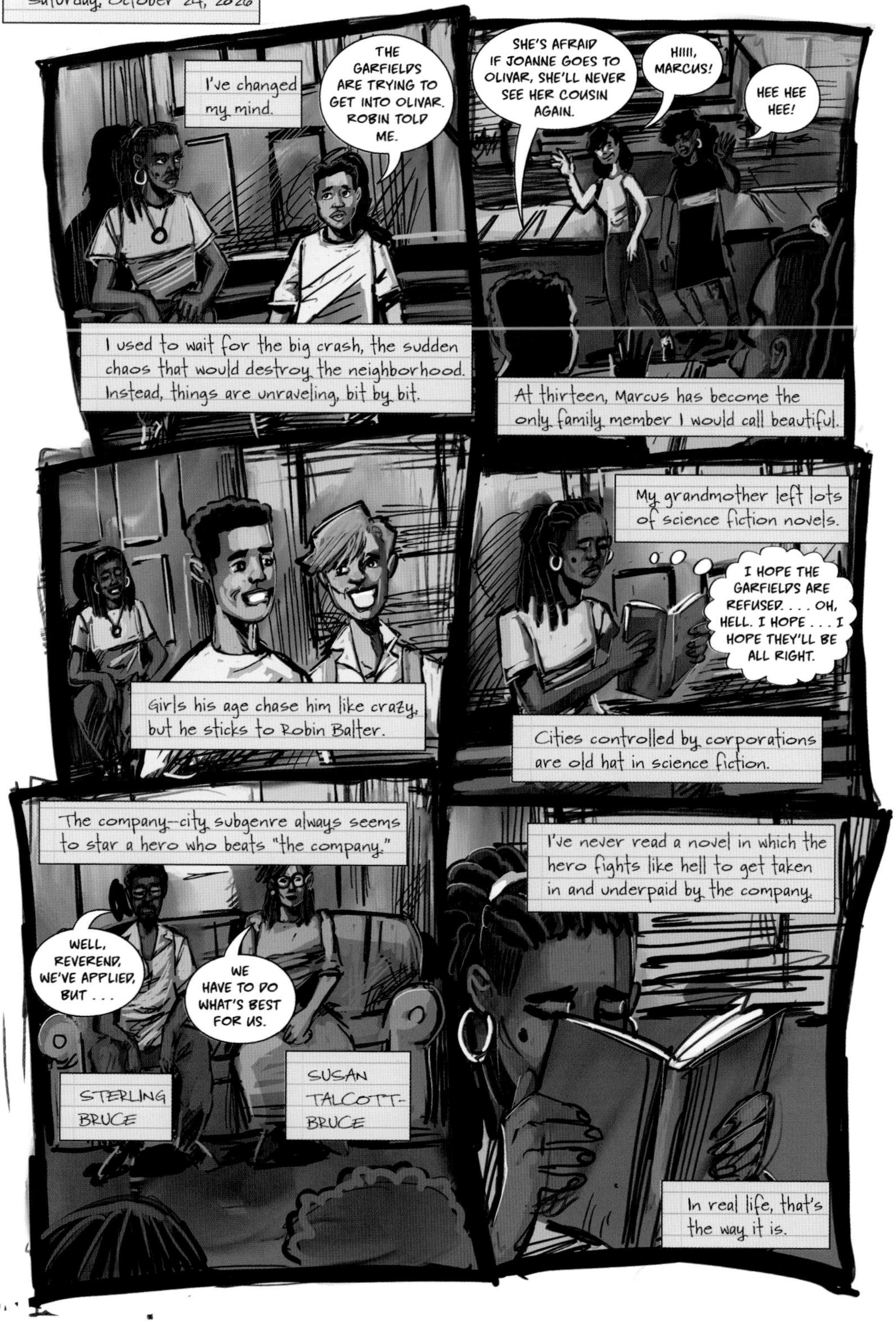

I've changed my mind.
THE GARFIELDS ARE TRYING TO GET INTO OLIVAR. ROBIN TOLD ME.
I used to wait for the big crash, the sudden chaos that would destroy the neighborhood. Instead, things are unraveling, bit by bit.
SHE'S AFRAID IF JOANNE GOES TO OLIVAR, SHE'LL NEVER SEE HER COUSIN AGAIN.
HIIII, MARCUS!
HEE HEE HEE!
At thirteen, Marcus has become the only family member I would call beautiful.
Girls his age chase him like crazy, but he sticks to Robin Balter.
My grandmother left lots of science fiction novels.
I HOPE THE GARFIELDS ARE REFUSED. . . . OH, HELL. I HOPE . . . I HOPE THEY'LL BE ALL RIGHT.
Cities controlled by corporations are old hat in science fiction.
The company-city subgenre always seems to star a hero who beats "the company."
WELL, REVEREND, WE'VE APPLIED, BUT . . .
WE HAVE TO DO WHAT'S BEST FOR US.
STERLING BRUCE
SUSAN TALCOTT-BRUCE
I've never read a novel in which the hero fights like hell to get taken in and underpaid by the company.
In real life, that's the way it is.

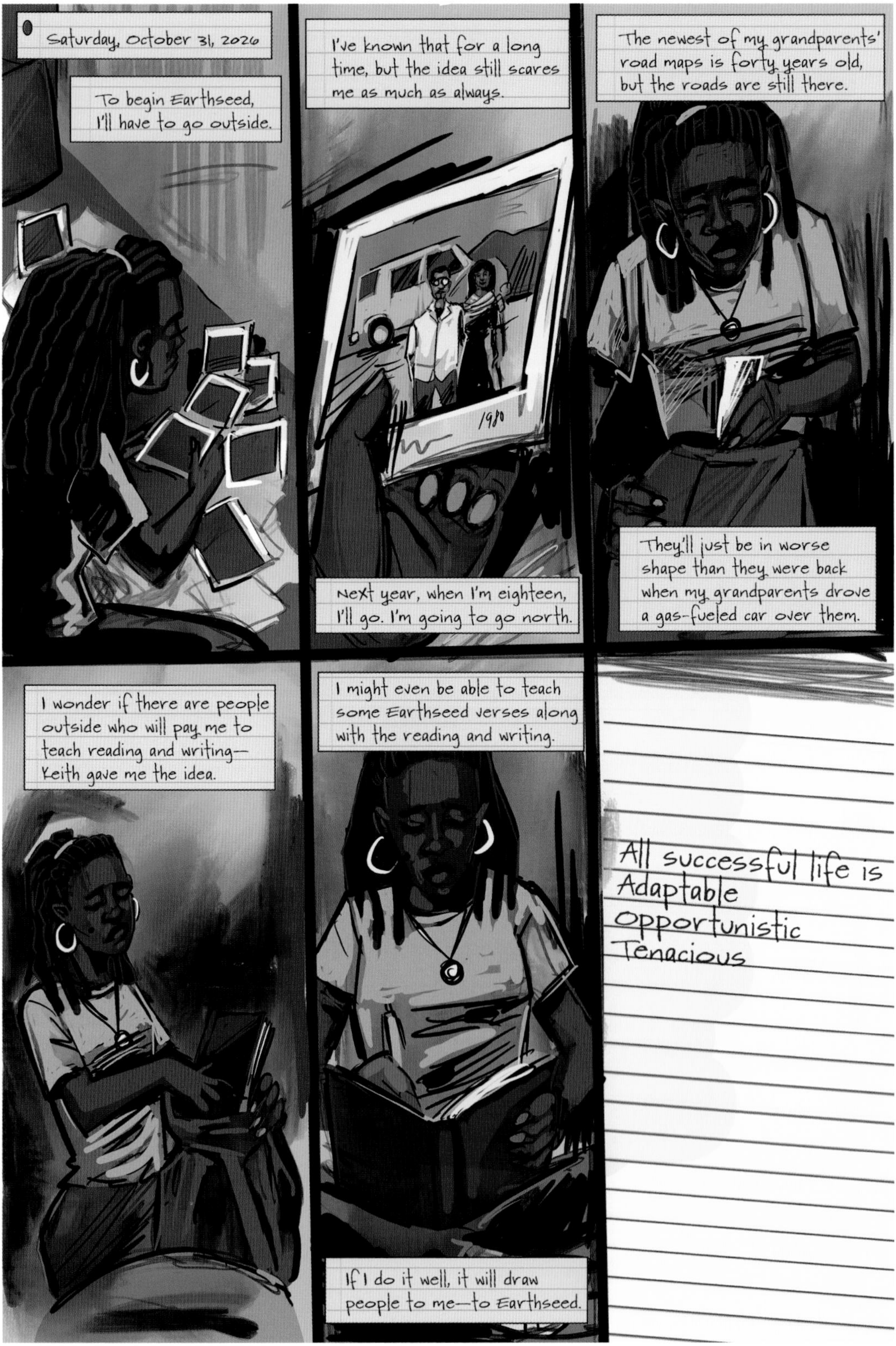
Saturday, October 31, 2026
To begin Earthseed, I'll have to go outside.
I've known that for a long time, but the idea still scares me as much as always.
1980
Next year, when I'm eighteen, I'll go. I'm going to go north.
The newest of my grandparents' road maps is forty years old, but the roads are still there.
They'll just be in worse shape than they were back when my grandparents drove a gas-fueled car over them.
I wonder if there are people outside who will pay me to teach reading and writing—Keith gave me the idea.
I might even be able to teach some Earthseed verses along with the reading and writing.
If I do it well, it will draw people to me—to Earthseed.
All successful life is
Adaptable
Opportunistic
Tenacious

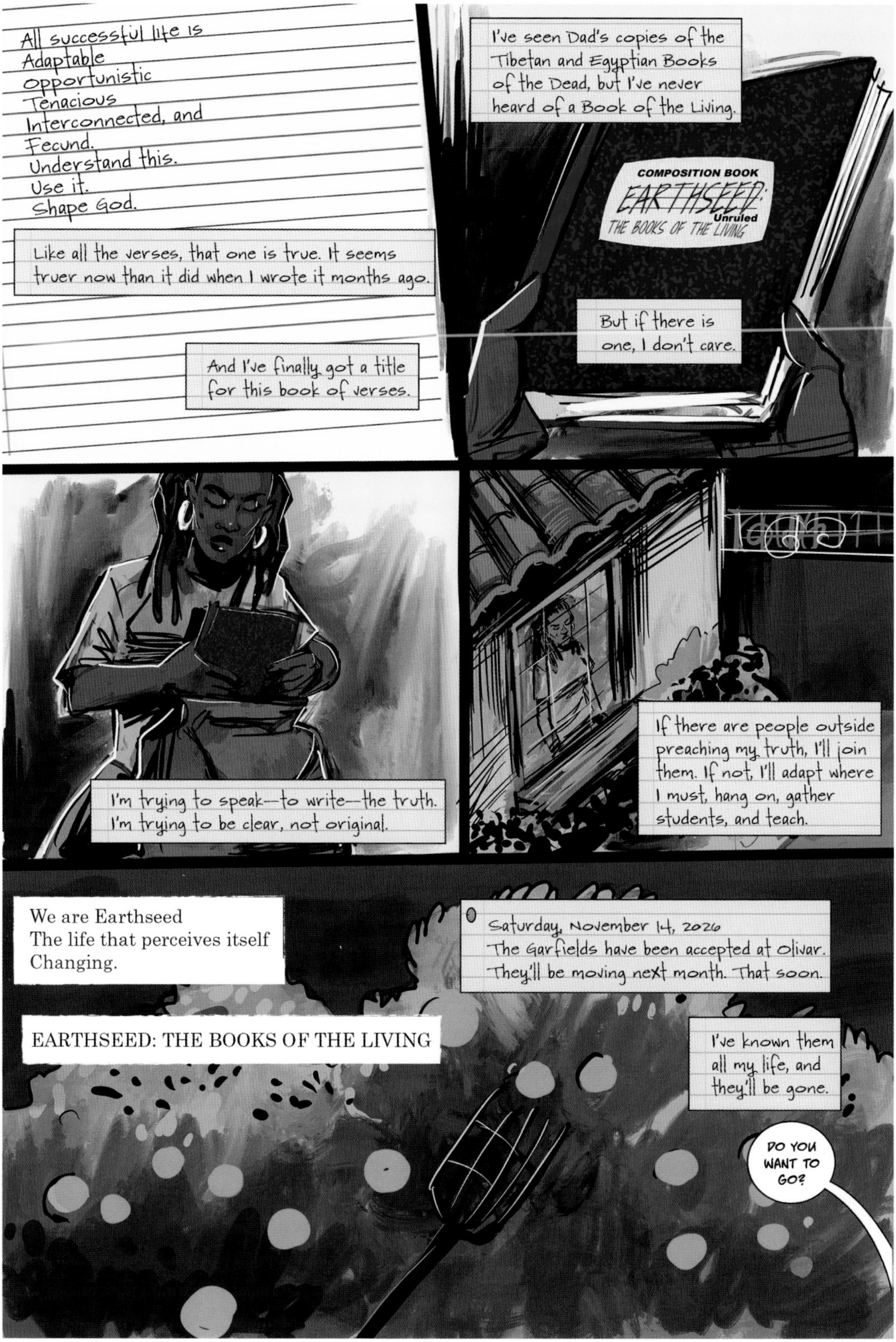

All successful life is
Adaptable
Opportunistic
Tenacious
Interconnected, and
Fecund.
Understand this.
Use it.
Shape God.
Like all the verses, that one is true. It seems truer now than it did when I wrote it months ago.
And I've finally got a title for this book of verses.
I've seen Dad's copies of the Tibetan and Egyptian Books of the Dead, but I've never heard of a Book of the Living.
COMPOSITION BOOK
EARTHSEED:
Unruled
THE BOOKS OF THE LIVING
But if there is one, I don't care.
I'm trying to speak—to write—the truth. I'm trying to be clear, not original.
If there are people outside preaching my truth, I'll join them. If not, I'll adapt where I must, hang on, gather students, and teach.
We are Earthseed
The life that perceives itself
Changing.
EARTHSEED: THE BOOKS OF THE LIVING
Saturday, November 14, 2026
The Garfields have been accepted at Olivar. They'll be moving next month. That soon.
I've known them all my life, and they'll be gone.
DO YOU WANT TO GO?

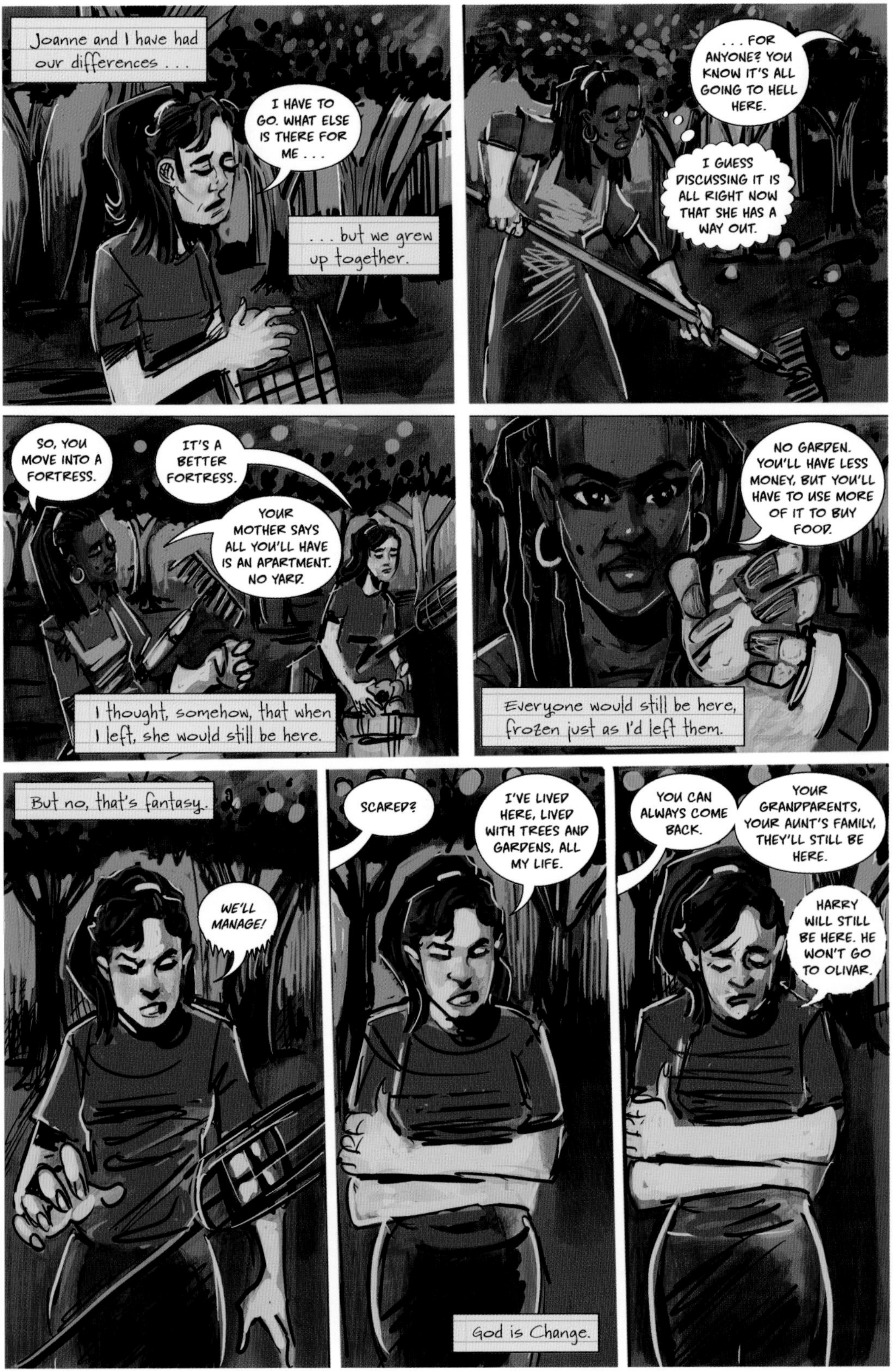

Joanne and I have had our differences . . .
I HAVE TO GO. WHAT ELSE IS THERE FOR ME . . .
. . . but we grew up together.
. . . FOR ANYONE? YOU KNOW IT'S ALL GOING TO HELL HERE.
I GUESS DISCUSSING IT IS ALL RIGHT NOW THAT SHE HAS A WAY OUT.
SO, YOU MOVE INTO A FORTRESS.
IT'S A BETTER FORTRESS.
YOUR MOTHER SAYS ALL YOU'LL HAVE IS AN APARTMENT. NO YARD.
I thought, somehow, that when I left, she would still be here.
NO GARDEN. YOU'LL HAVE LESS MONEY, BUT YOU'LL HAVE TO USE MORE OF IT TO BUY FOOD.
Everyone would still be here, frozen just as I'd left them.
But no, that's fantasy.
WE'LL MANAGE!
SCARED?
I'VE LIVED HERE, LIVED WITH TREES AND GARDENS, ALL MY LIFE.
God is Change.
YOU CAN ALWAYS COME BACK.
YOUR GRANDPARENTS, YOUR AUNT'S FAMILY, THEY'LL STILL BE HERE.
HARRY WILL STILL BE HERE. HE WON'T GO TO OLIVAR.

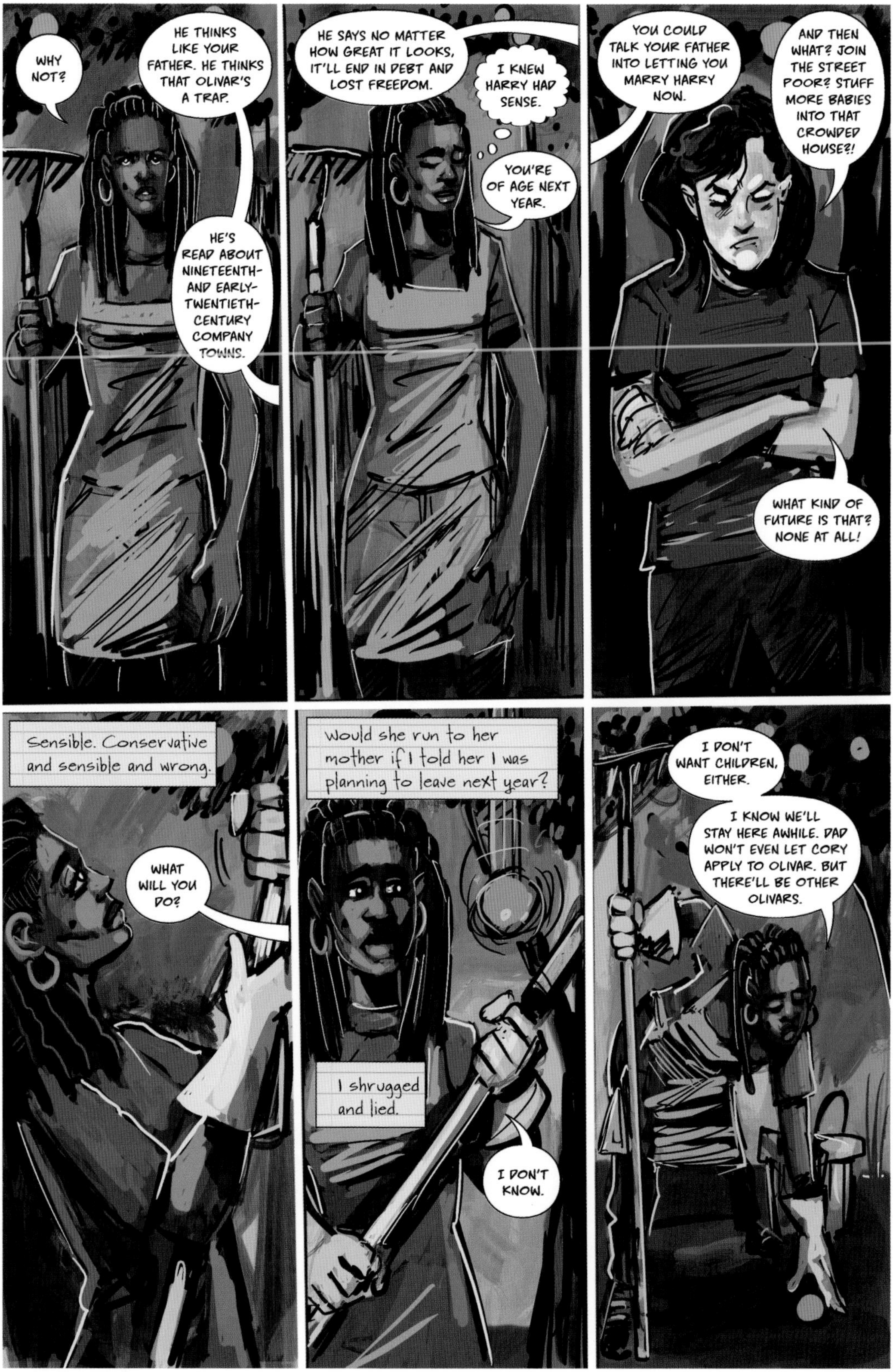
WHY NOT?
HE THINKS LIKE YOUR FATHER. HE THINKS THAT OLIVAR'S A TRAP.
HE'S READ ABOUT NINETEENTH- AND EARLY-TWENTIETH-CENTURY COMPANY TOWNS.
HE SAYS NO MATTER HOW GREAT IT LOOKS, IT'LL END IN DEBT AND LOST FREEDOM.
I KNEW HARRY HAD SENSE.
YOU'RE OF AGE NEXT YEAR.
YOU COULD TALK YOUR FATHER INTO LETTING YOU MARRY HARRY NOW.
AND THEN WHAT? JOIN THE STREET POOR? STUFF MORE BABIES INTO THAT CROWDED HOUSE?!
WHAT KIND OF FUTURE IS THAT? NONE AT ALL!
Sensible. Conservative and sensible and wrong.
WHAT WILL YOU DO?
Would she run to her mother if I told her I was planning to leave next year?
I shrugged and lied.
I DON'T KNOW.
I DON'T WANT CHILDREN, EITHER.
I KNOW WE'LL STAY HERE AWHILE. DAD WON'T EVEN LET CORY APPLY TO OLIVAR. BUT THERE'LL BE OTHER OLIVARS.

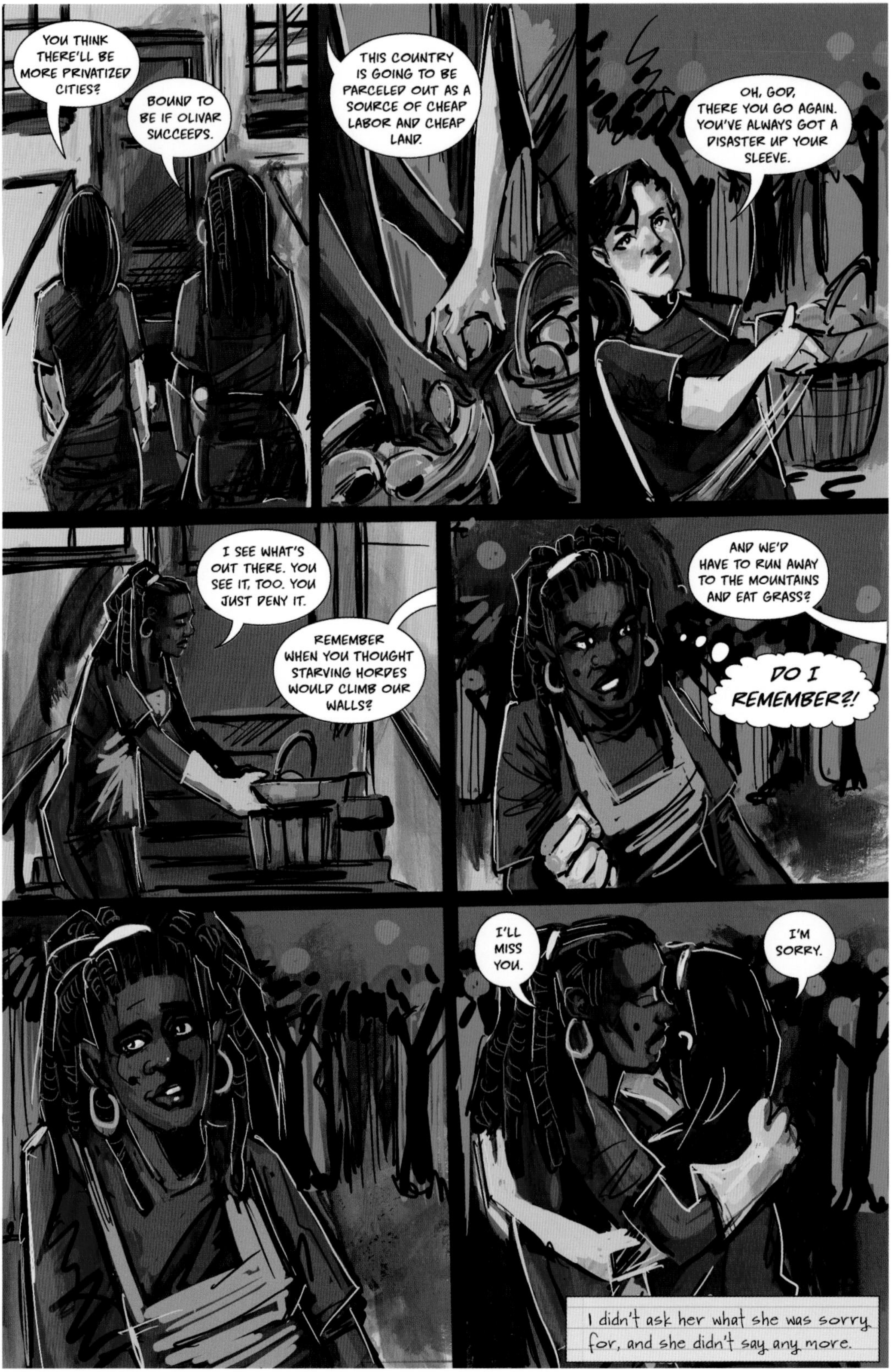

YOU THINK THERE'LL BE MORE PRIVATIZED CITIES?
BOUND TO BE IF OLIVAR SUCCEEDS.
THIS COUNTRY IS GOING TO BE PARCELED OUT AS A SOURCE OF CHEAP LABOR AND CHEAP LAND.
OH, GOD, THERE YOU GO AGAIN. YOU'VE ALWAYS GOT A DISASTER UP YOUR SLEEVE.
I SEE WHAT'S OUT THERE. YOU SEE IT, TOO. YOU JUST DENY IT.
REMEMBER WHEN YOU THOUGHT STARVING HORDES WOULD CLIMB OUR WALLS?
AND WE'D HAVE TO RUN AWAY TO THE MOUNTAINS AND EAT GRASS?
DO I REMEMBER?!
I'LL MISS YOU.
I'M SORRY.
I didn't ask her what she was sorry for, and she didn't say any more.

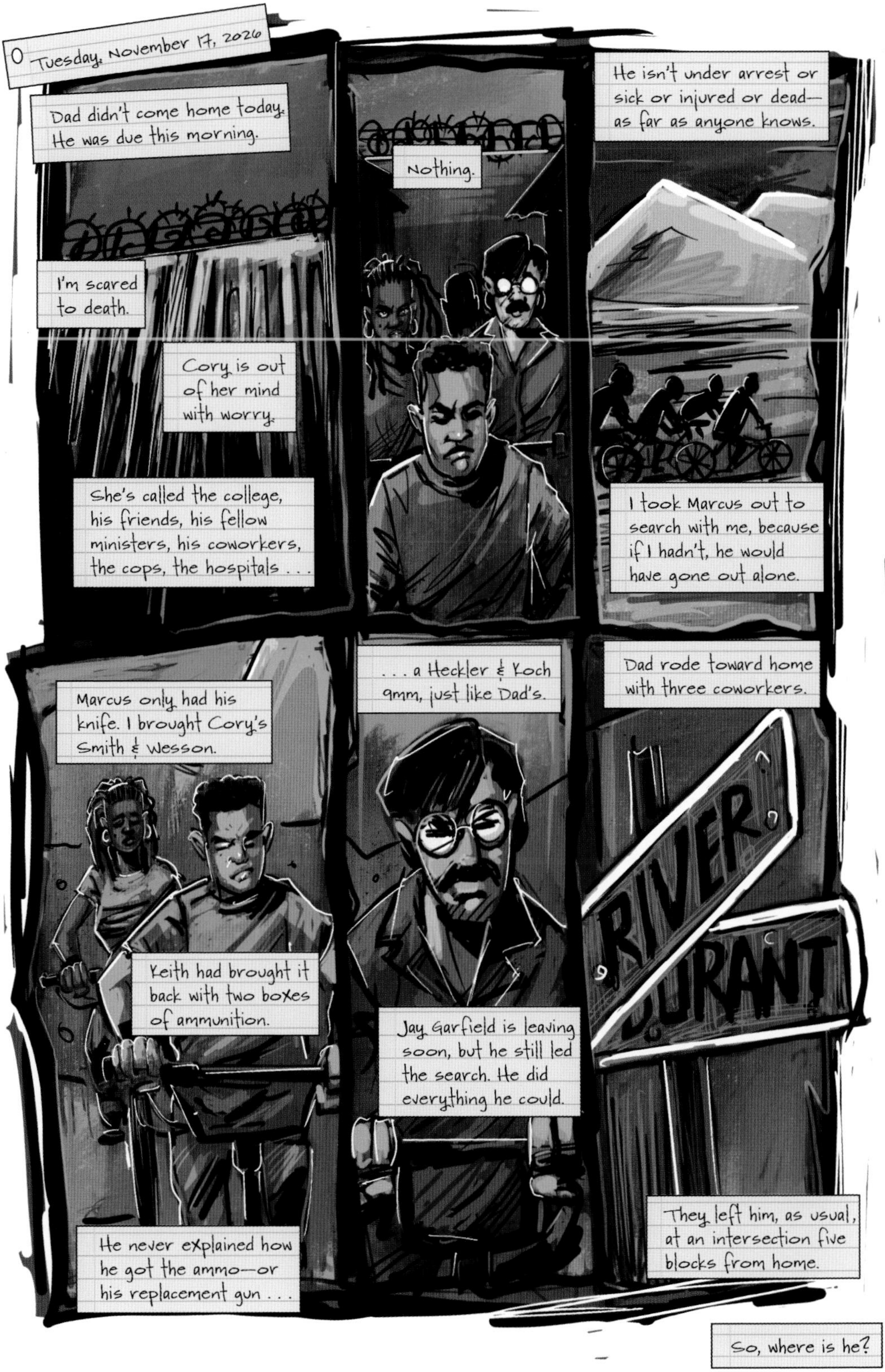
Tuesday, November 17, 2026
Dad didn't come home today. He was due this morning.
I'm scared to death.
Cory is out of her mind with worry.
She's called the college, his friends, his fellow ministers, his coworkers, the cops, the hospitals . . .
Nothing.
He isn't under arrest or sick or injured or dead—as far as anyone knows.
I took Marcus out to search with me, because if I hadn't, he would have gone out alone.
Marcus only had his knife. I brought Cory's Smith & Wesson.
Keith had brought it back with two boxes of ammunition.
He never explained how he got the ammo—or his replacement gun . . .
. . . a Heckler & Koch 9mm, just like Dad's.
Jay Garfield is leaving soon, but he still led the search. He did everything he could.
Dad rode toward home with three coworkers.
RIVER
DURANT
They left him, as usual, at an intersection five blocks from home.
So, where is he?

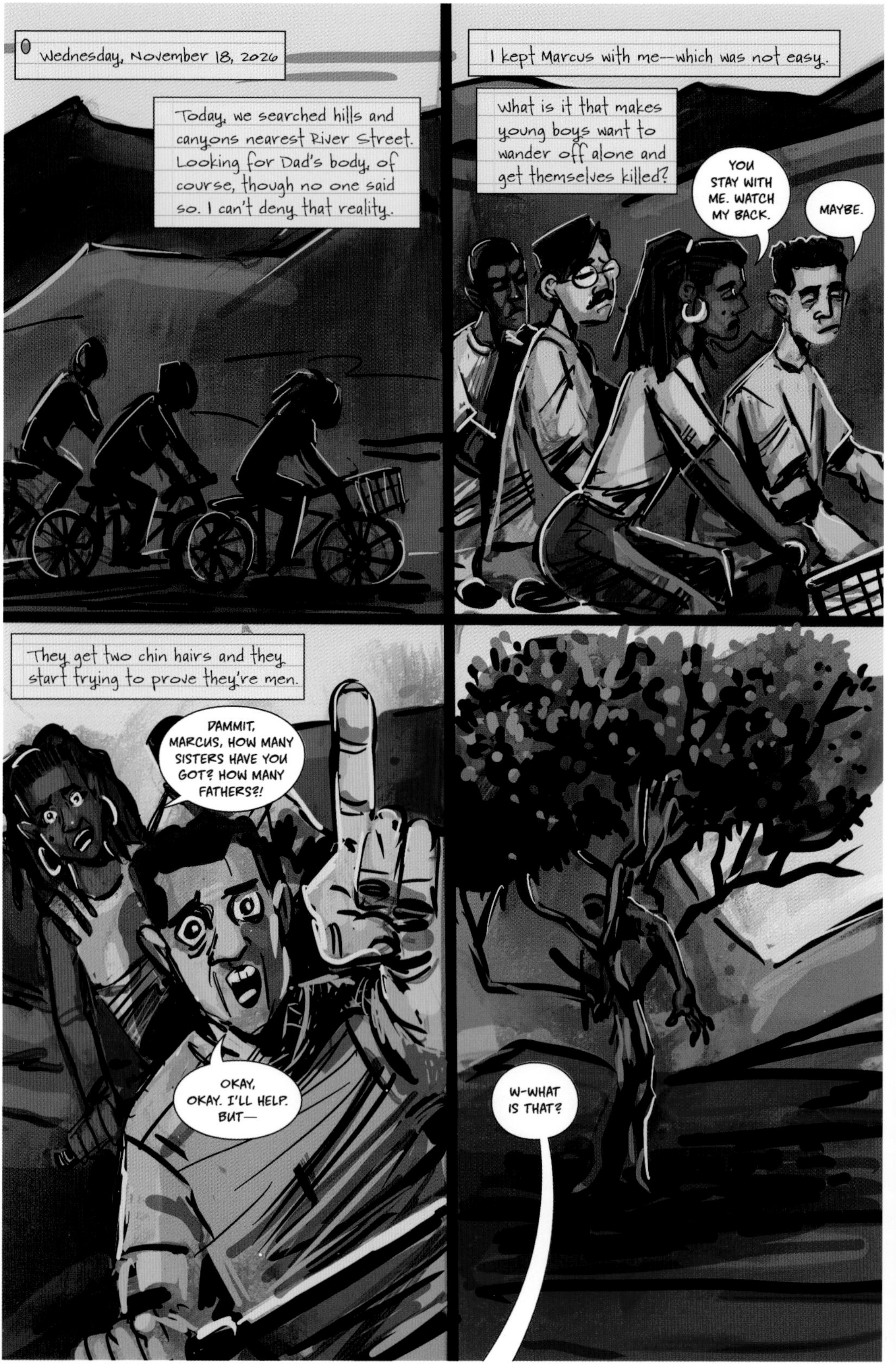
Wednesday, November 18, 2026
Today, we searched hills and canyons nearest River Street. Looking for Dad's body, of course, though no one said so. I can't deny that reality.
I kept Marcus with me—which was not easy.
What is it that makes young boys want to wander off alone and get themselves killed?
YOU STAY WITH ME. WATCH MY BACK.
MAYBE.
They get two chin hairs and they start trying to prove they're men.
DAMMIT, MARCUS, HOW MANY SISTERS HAVE YOU GOT? HOW MANY FATHERS?!
OKAY, OKAY. I'LL HELP. BUT—
W-WHAT IS THAT?

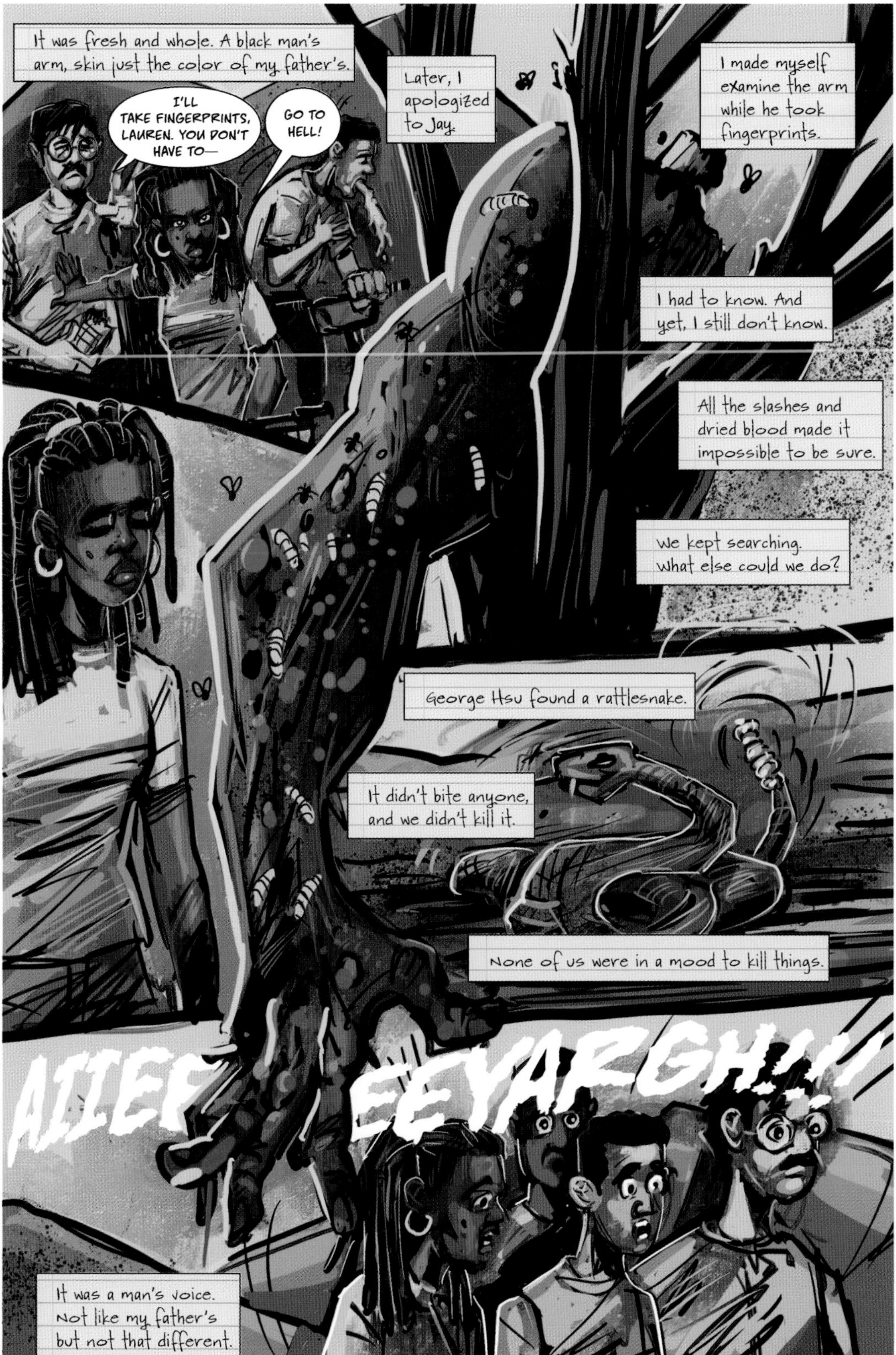

It was fresh and whole. A black man's arm, skin just the color of my father's.
I'LL TAKE FINGERPRINTS, LAUREN. YOU DON'T HAVE TO—
GO TO HELL!
Later, I apologized to Jay.
I made myself examine the arm while he took fingerprints.
I had to know. And yet, I still don't know.
All the slashes and dried blood made it impossible to be sure.
We kept searching. What else could we do?
George Hsu found a rattlesnake.
It didn't bite anyone, and we didn't kill it.
None of us were in a mood to kill things.
AIIEEEEYARGH!!!
It was a man's voice. Not like my father's but not that different.

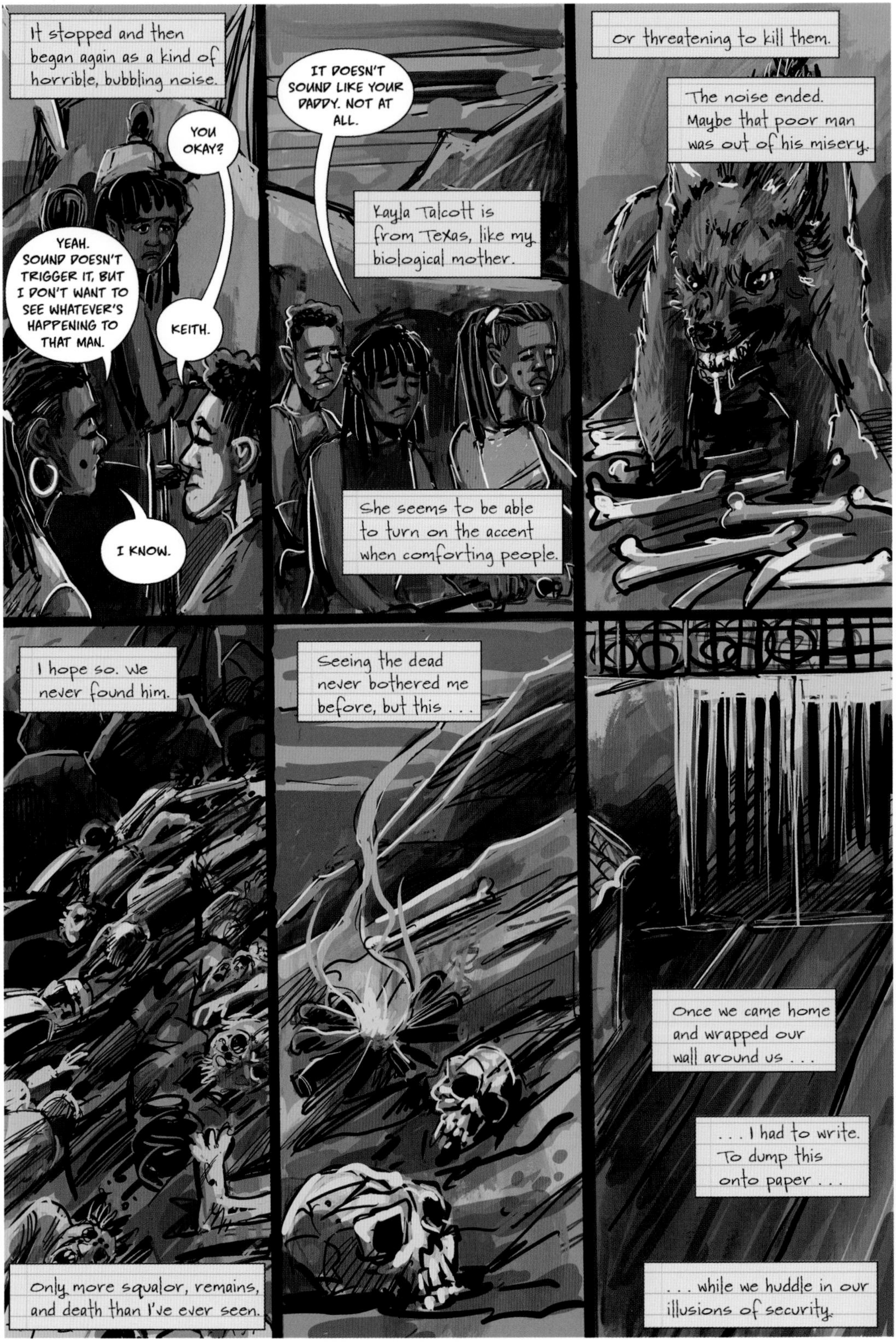
It stopped and then began again as a kind of horrible, bubbling noise.
YOU OKAY?
YEAH. SOUND DOESN'T TRIGGER IT, BUT I DON'T WANT TO SEE WHATEVER'S HAPPENING TO THAT MAN.
KEITH.
I KNOW.
IT DOESN'T SOUND LIKE YOUR DADDY. NOT AT ALL.
Kayla Talcott is from Texas, like my biological mother.
She seems to be able to turn on the accent when comforting people.
Or threatening to kill them.
The noise ended. Maybe that poor man was out of his misery.
I hope so. We never found him.
Only more squalor, remains, and death than I've ever seen.
Seeing the dead never bothered me before, but this . . .
Once we came home and wrapped our wall around us . . .
. . . I had to write. To dump this onto paper . . .
. . . while we huddle in our illusions of security.

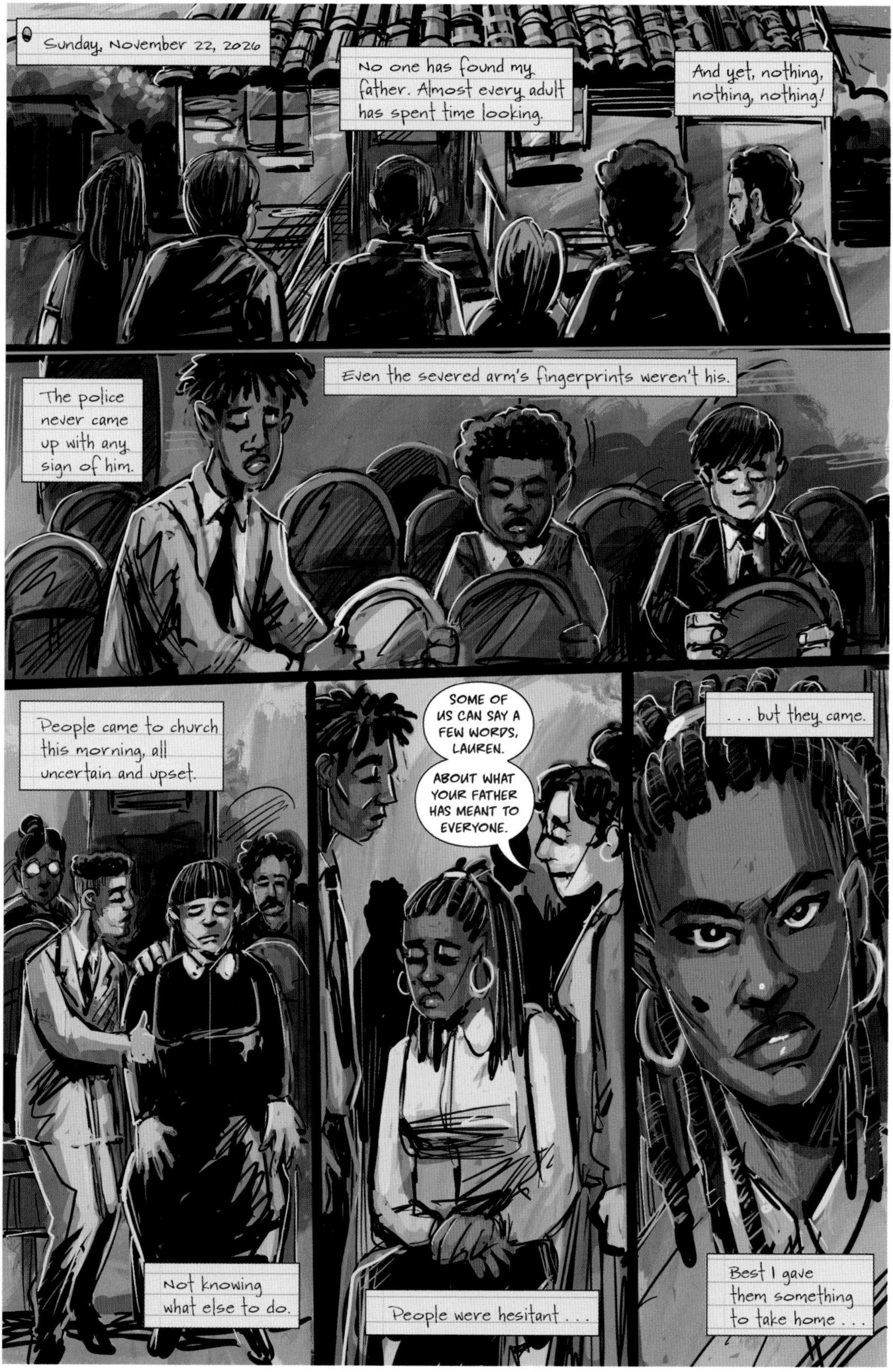

Sunday, November 22, 2026
No one has found my father. Almost every adult has spent time looking.
And yet, nothing, nothing, nothing!
The police never came up with any sign of him.
Even the severed arm's fingerprints weren't his.
People came to church this morning, all uncertain and upset.
Not knowing what else to do.
SOME OF US CAN SAY A FEW WORDS, LAUREN.
ABOUT WHAT YOUR FATHER HAS MEANT TO EVERYONE.
People were hesitant . . .
. . . but they came.
Best I gave them something to take home . . .

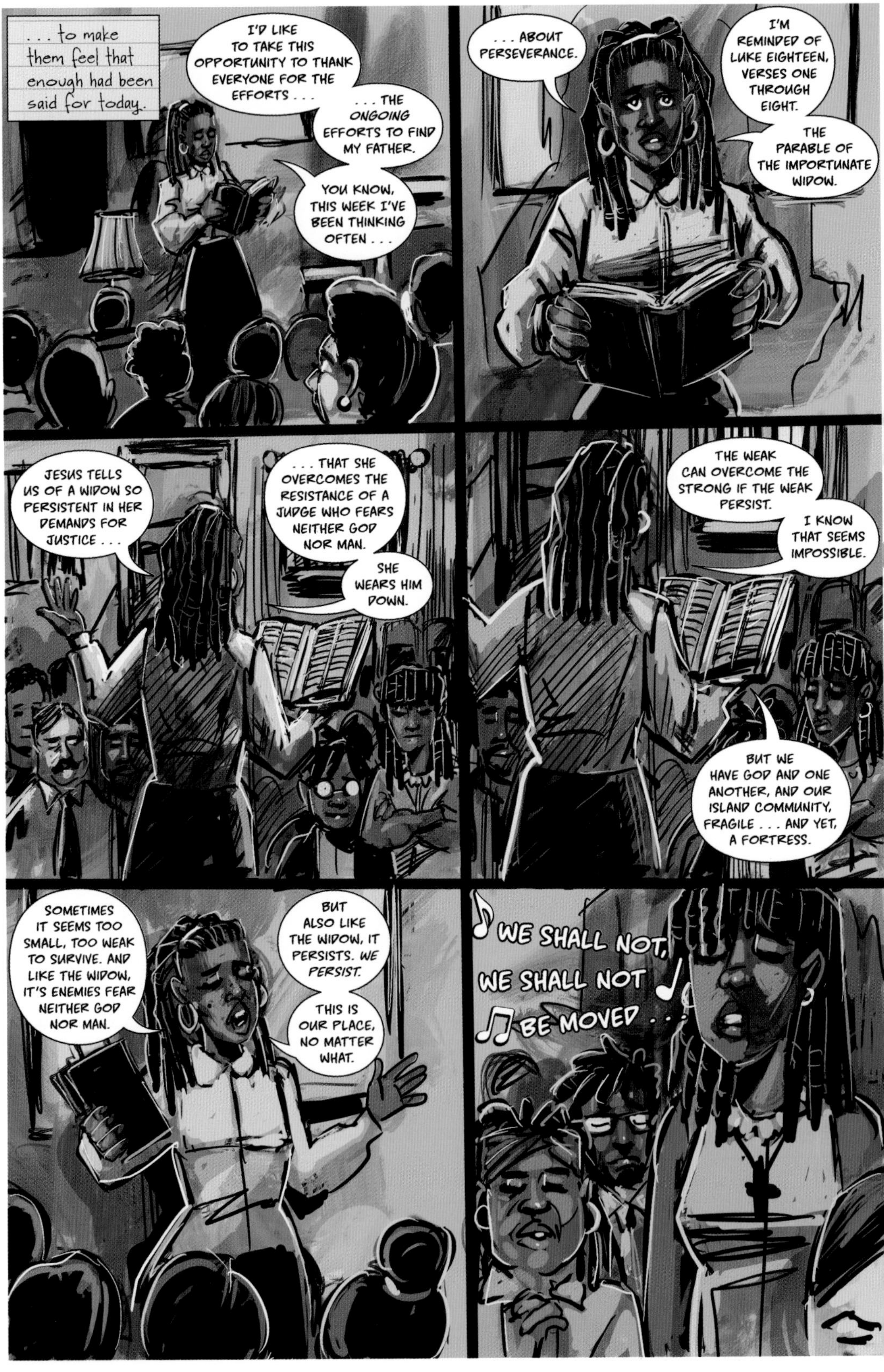
. . . to make them feel that enough had been said for today.
I'D LIKE TO TAKE THIS OPPORTUNITY TO THANK EVERYONE FOR THE EFFORTS . . .
. . . THE ONGOING EFFORTS TO FIND MY FATHER.
YOU KNOW, THIS WEEK I'VE BEEN THINKING OFTEN . . .
. . . ABOUT PERSEVERANCE.
I'M REMINDED OF LUKE EIGHTEEN, VERSES ONE THROUGH EIGHT.
THE PARABLE OF THE IMPORTUNATE WIDOW.
JESUS TELLS US OF A WIDOW SO PERSISTENT IN HER DEMANDS FOR JUSTICE . . .
. . . THAT SHE OVERCOMES THE RESISTANCE OF A JUDGE WHO FEARS NEITHER GOD NOR MAN.
SHE WEARS HIM DOWN.
THE WEAK CAN OVERCOME THE STRONG IF THE WEAK PERSIST.
I KNOW THAT SEEMS IMPOSSIBLE.
BUT WE HAVE GOD AND ONE ANOTHER, AND OUR ISLAND COMMUNITY, FRAGILE . . . AND YET, A FORTRESS.
SOMETIMES IT SEEMS TOO SMALL, TOO WEAK TO SURVIVE. AND LIKE THE WIDOW, IT'S ENEMIES FEAR NEITHER GOD NOR MAN.
BUT ALSO LIKE THE WIDOW, IT PERSISTS. WE PERSIST.
THIS IS OUR PLACE, NO MATTER WHAT.
WE SHALL NOT, WE SHALL NOT BE MOVED . . .

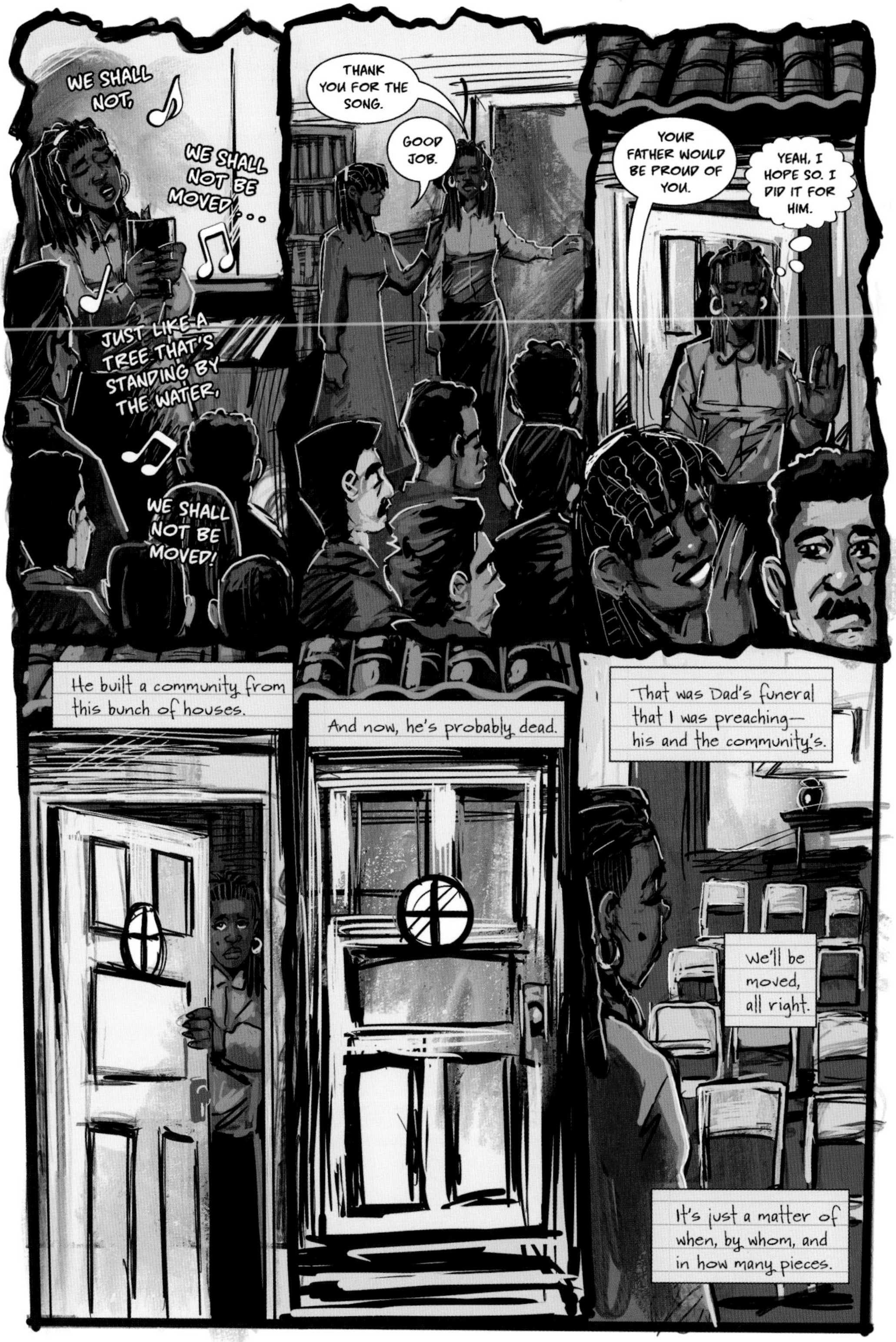
WE SHALL NOT,
WE SHALL NOT BE MOVED . . .
JUST LIKE A TREE THAT'S STANDING BY THE WATER,
WE SHALL NOT BE MOVED!
THANK YOU FOR THE SONG.
GOOD JOB.
YOUR FATHER WOULD BE PROUD OF YOU.
YEAH, I HOPE SO. I DID IT FOR HIM.
He built a community from this bunch of houses.
And now, he's probably dead.
That was Dad's funeral that I was preaching— his and the community's.
We'll be moved, all right.
It's just a matter of when, by whom, and in how many pieces.

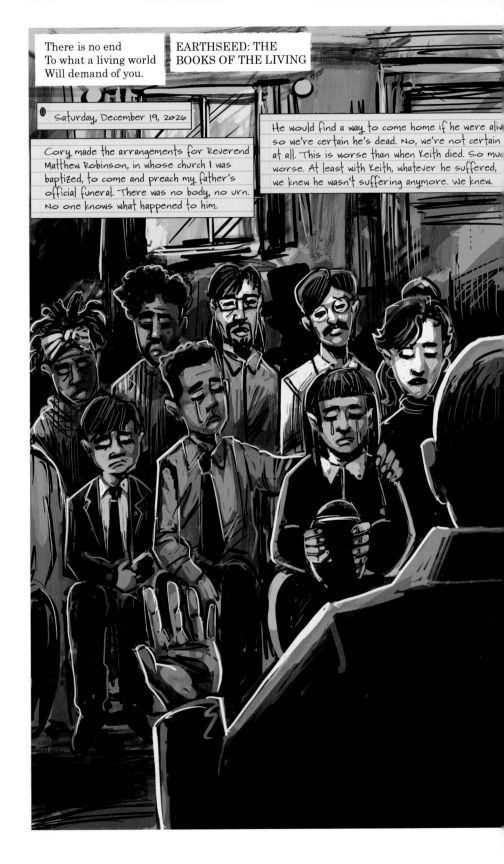

There is no end
To what a living world
Will demand of you.

EARTHSEED: THE
BOOKS OF THE LIVING

Saturday, December 19, 2026

Cory made the arrangements for Reverend
Matthew Robinson, in whose church I was
baptized, to come and preach my father's
official funeral. There was no body, no urn.
No one knows what happened to him.

He would find a way to come home if he were aliv
so we're certain he's dead. No, we're not certain
at all. This is worse than when Keith died. So muc
worse. At least with Keith, whatever he suffered,
we knew he wasn't suffering anymore. We knew.

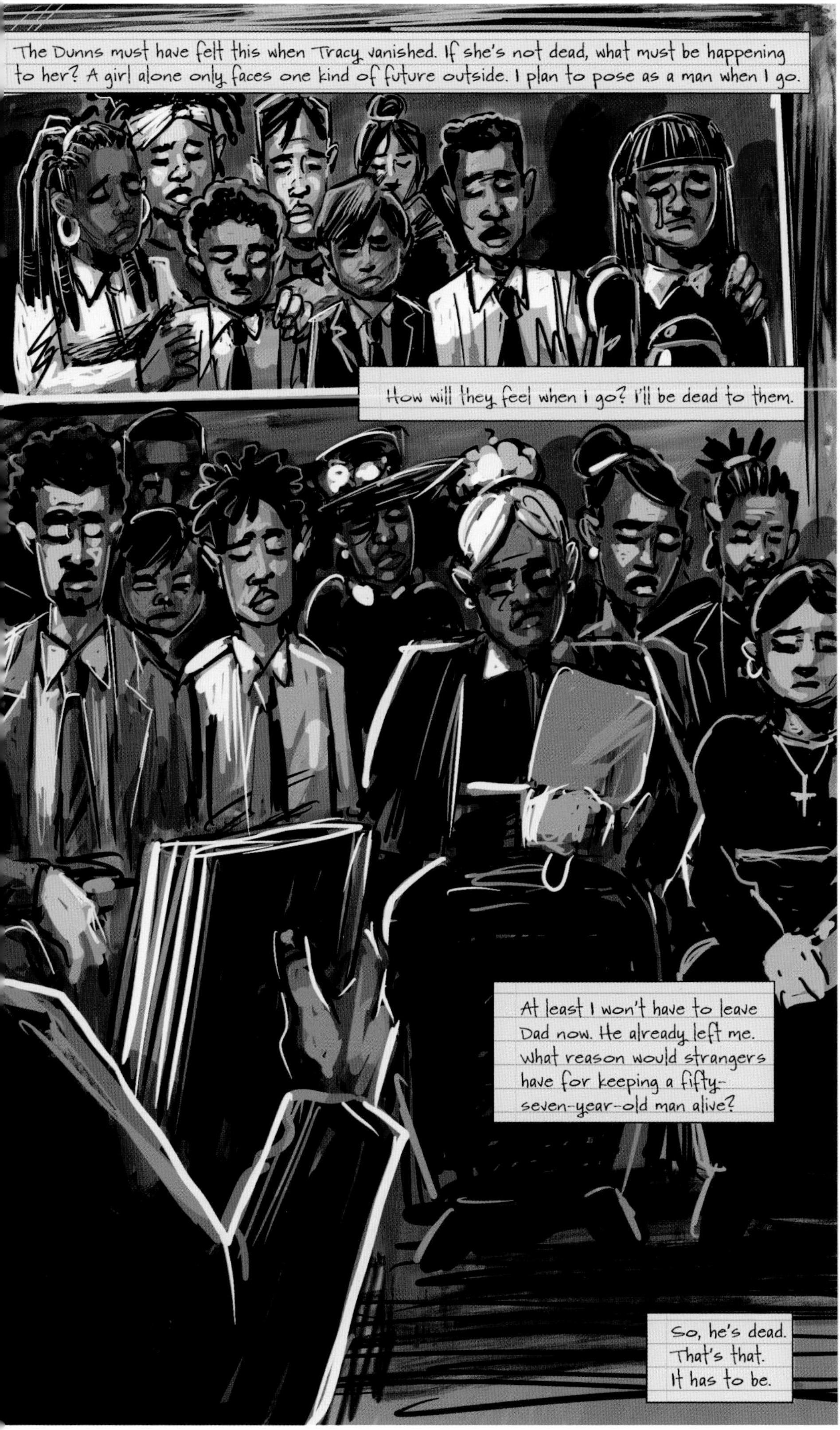
The Dunns must have felt this when Tracy vanished. If she's not dead, what must be happening to her? A girl alone only faces one kind of future outside. I plan to pose as a man when I go.
How will they feel when i go? i'll be dead to them.
At least I won't have to leave Dad now. He already left me. what reason would strangers have for keeping a fifty-seven-year-old man alive?
So, he's dead. That's that. It has to be.

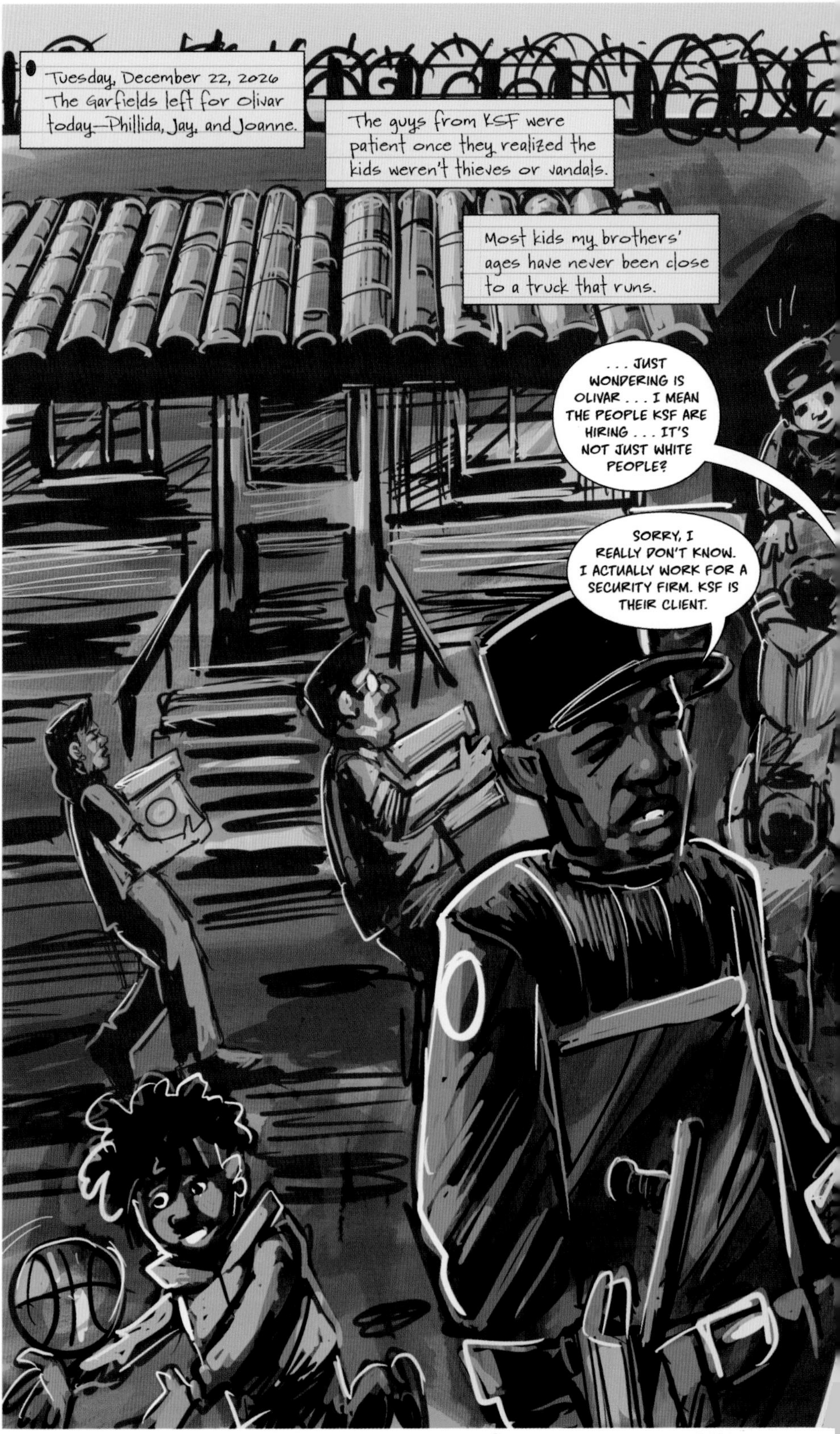
Tuesday, December 22, 2026
The Garfields left for Olivar today—Phillida, Jay, and Joanne.
The guys from KSF were patient once they realized the kids weren't thieves or vandals.
Most kids my brothers' ages have never been close to a truck that runs.
. . . JUST WONDERING IS OLIVAR . . . I MEAN THE PEOPLE KSF ARE HIRING . . . IT'S NOT JUST WHITE PEOPLE?
SORRY, I REALLY DON'T KNOW. I ACTUALLY WORK FOR A SECURITY FIRM. KSF IS THEIR CLIENT.

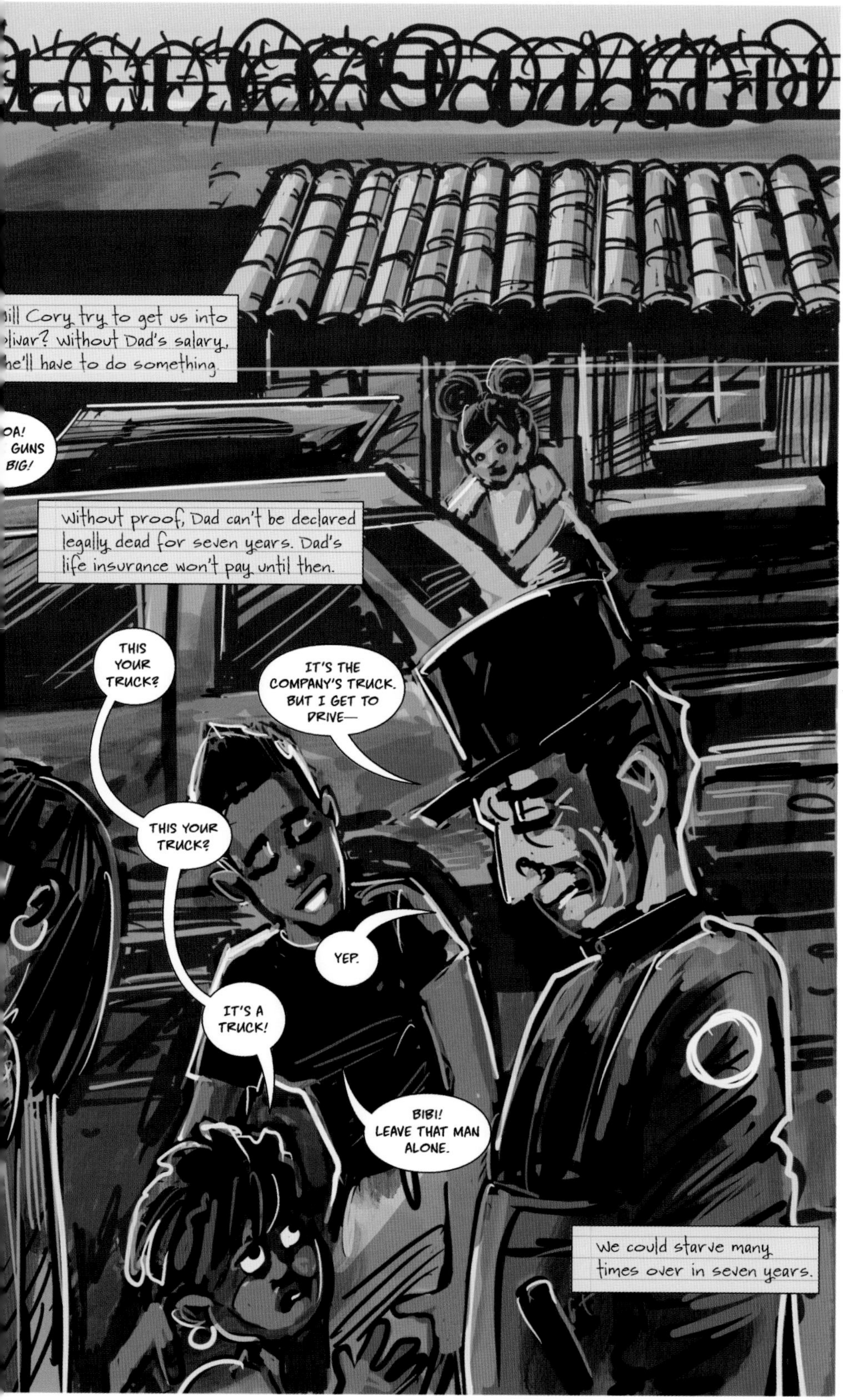

ill Cory try to get us into
livar? without Dad's salary,
he'll have to do something.
OA! GUNS BIG!
without proof, Dad can't be declared legally dead for seven years. Dad's life insurance won't pay until then.
THIS YOUR TRUCK?
IT'S THE COMPANY'S TRUCK. BUT I GET TO DRIVE—
THIS YOUR TRUCK?
YEP.
IT'S A TRUCK!
BIBI! LEAVE THAT MAN ALONE.
We could starve many times over in seven years.

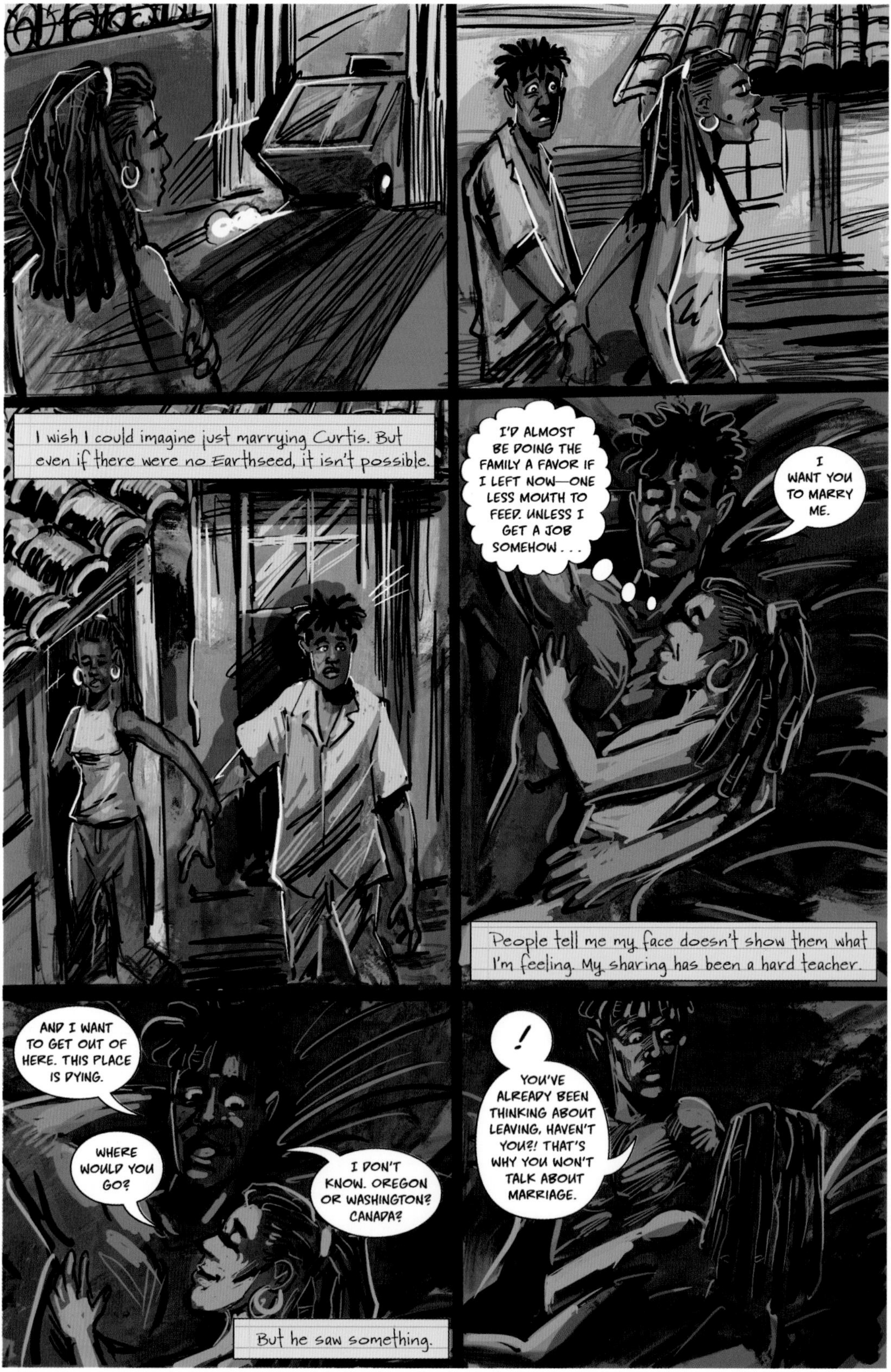
I wish I could imagine just marrying Curtis. But even if there were no Earthseed, it isn't possible.
I'D ALMOST BE DOING THE FAMILY A FAVOR IF I LEFT NOW—ONE LESS MOUTH TO FEED. UNLESS I GET A JOB SOMEHOW . . .
I WANT YOU TO MARRY ME.
People tell me my face doesn't show them what I'm feeling. My sharing has been a hard teacher.
AND I WANT TO GET OUT OF HERE. THIS PLACE IS DYING.
WHERE WOULD YOU GO?
I DON'T KNOW. OREGON OR WASHINGTON? CANADA?
But he saw something.
!
YOU'VE ALREADY BEEN THINKING ABOUT LEAVING, HAVEN'T YOU?! THAT'S WHY YOU WON'T TALK ABOUT MARRIAGE.

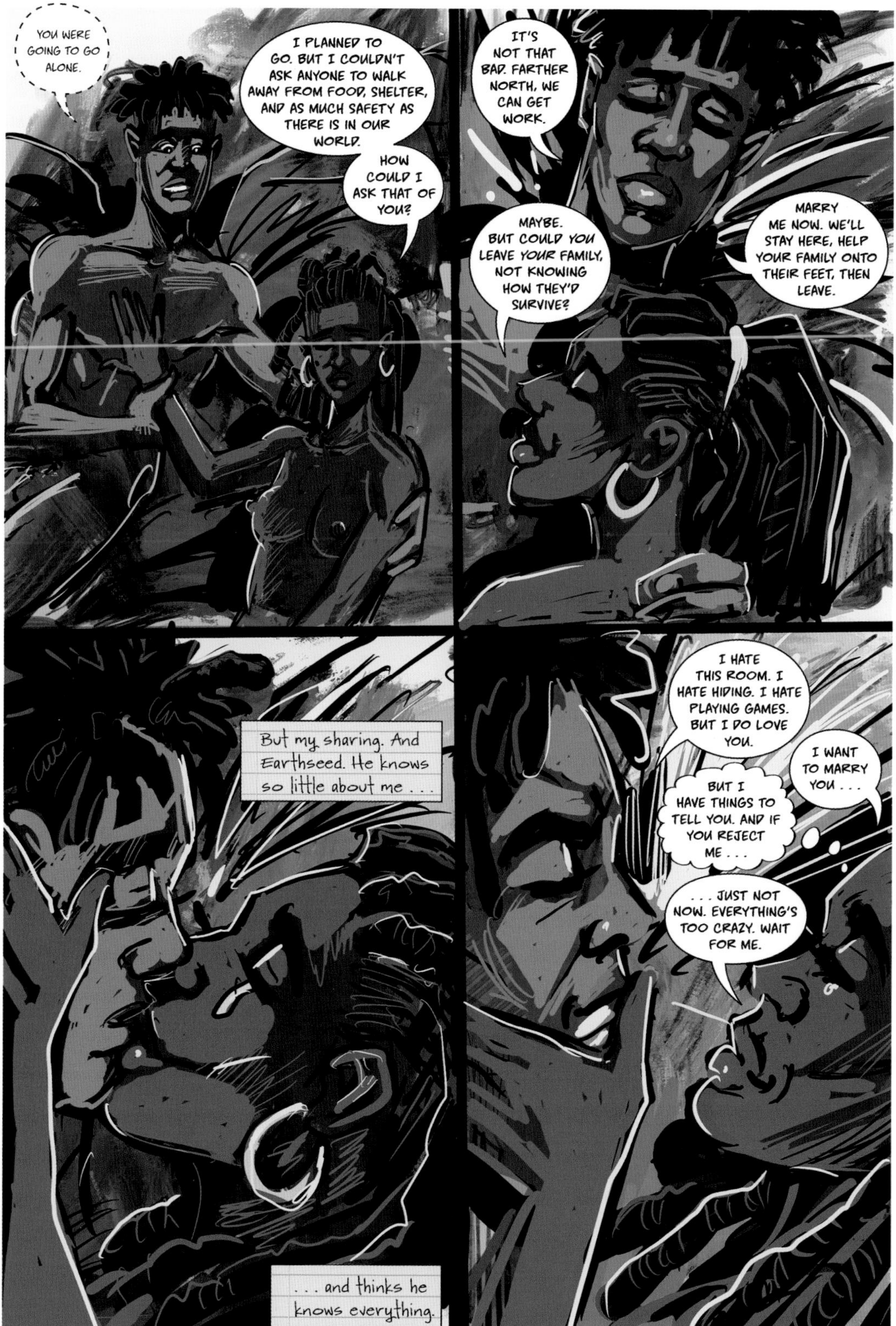
YOU WERE GOING TO GO ALONE.
I PLANNED TO GO. BUT I COULDN'T ASK ANYONE TO WALK AWAY FROM FOOD, SHELTER, AND AS MUCH SAFETY AS THERE IS IN OUR WORLD.
HOW COULD I ASK THAT OF YOU?
IT'S NOT THAT BAD. FARTHER NORTH, WE CAN GET WORK.
MAYBE. BUT COULD YOU LEAVE YOUR FAMILY, NOT KNOWING HOW THEY'D SURVIVE?
MARRY ME NOW. WE'LL STAY HERE, HELP YOUR FAMILY ONTO THEIR FEET, THEN LEAVE.
But my sharing. And Earthseed. He knows so little about me . . .
. . . and thinks he knows everything.
I HATE THIS ROOM. I HATE HIDING. I HATE PLAYING GAMES. BUT I DO LOVE YOU.
I WANT TO MARRY YOU . . .
BUT I HAVE THINGS TO TELL YOU. AND IF YOU REJECT ME . . .
. . . JUST NOT NOW. EVERYTHING'S TOO CRAZY. WAIT FOR ME.

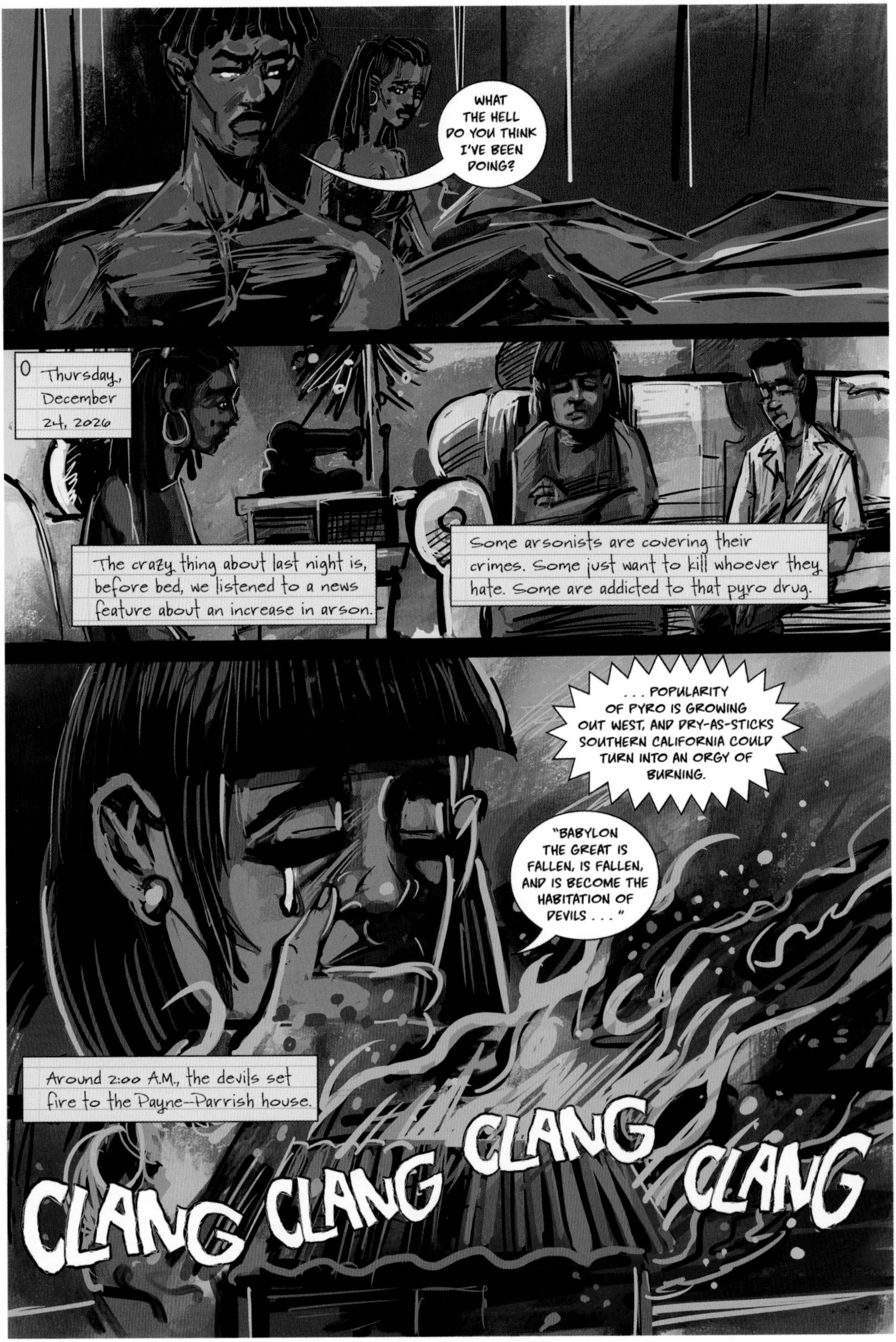
WHAT THE HELL DO YOU THINK I'VE BEEN DOING?
Thursday, December 24, 2026
The crazy thing about last night is, before bed, we listened to a news feature about an increase in arson.
Some arsonists are covering their crimes. Some just want to kill whoever they hate. Some are addicted to that pyro drug.
. . . POPULARITY OF PYRO IS GROWING OUT WEST, AND DRY-AS-STICKS SOUTHERN CALIFORNIA COULD TURN INTO AN ORGY OF BURNING.
"BABYLON THE GREAT IS FALLEN, IS FALLEN, AND IS BECOME THE HABITATION OF DEVILS . . ."
Around 2:00 A.M., the devils set fire to the Payne-Parrish house.
CLANG CLANG CLANG CLANG

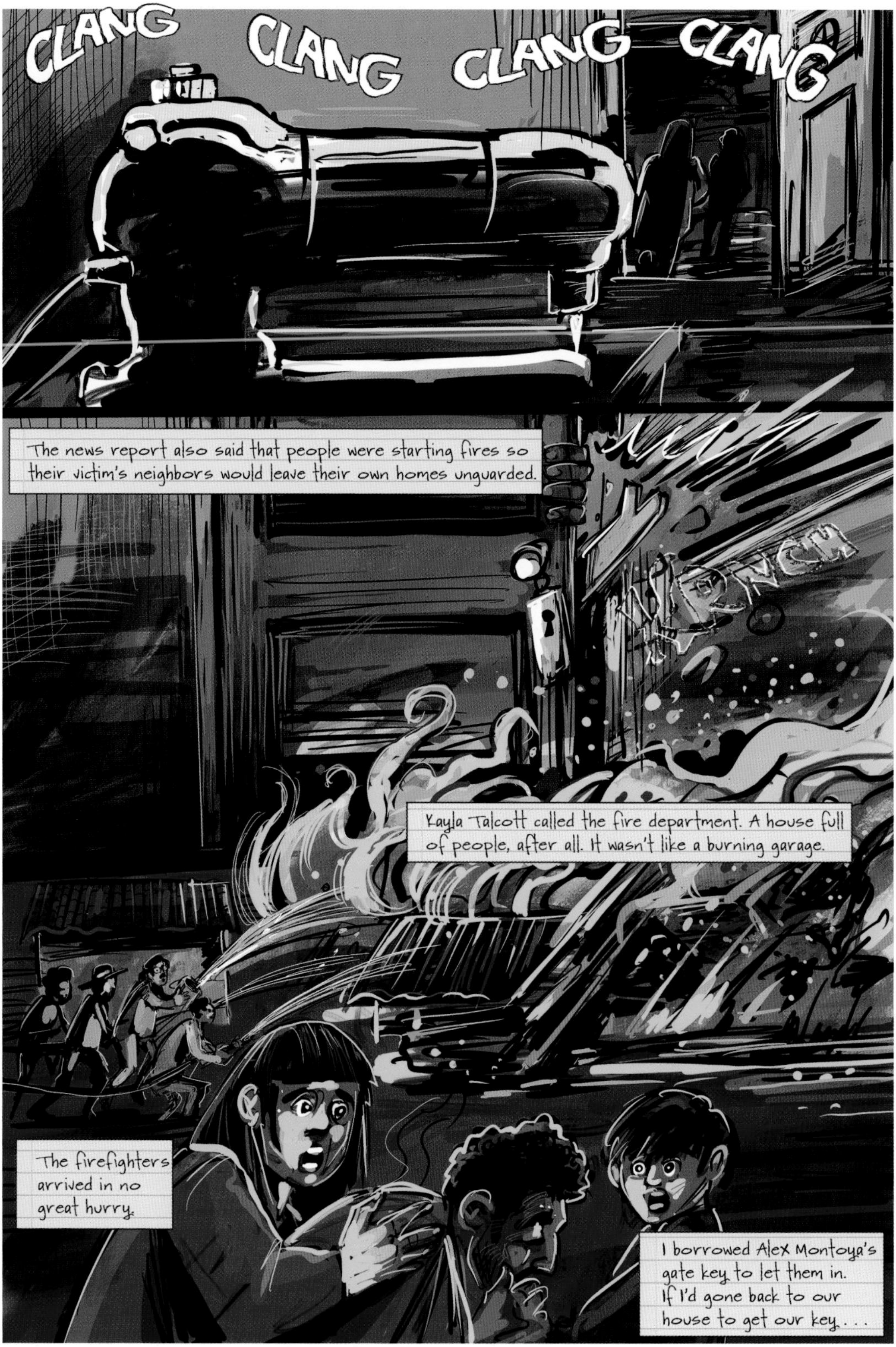
CLANG
CLANG
CLANG
CLANG
The news report also said that people were starting fires so their victim's neighbors would leave their own homes unguarded.
Kayla Talcott called the fire department. A house full of people, after all. It wasn't like a burning garage.
The firefighters arrived in no great hurry.
I borrowed Alex Montoya's gate key to let them in. If I'd gone back to our house to get our key . . .

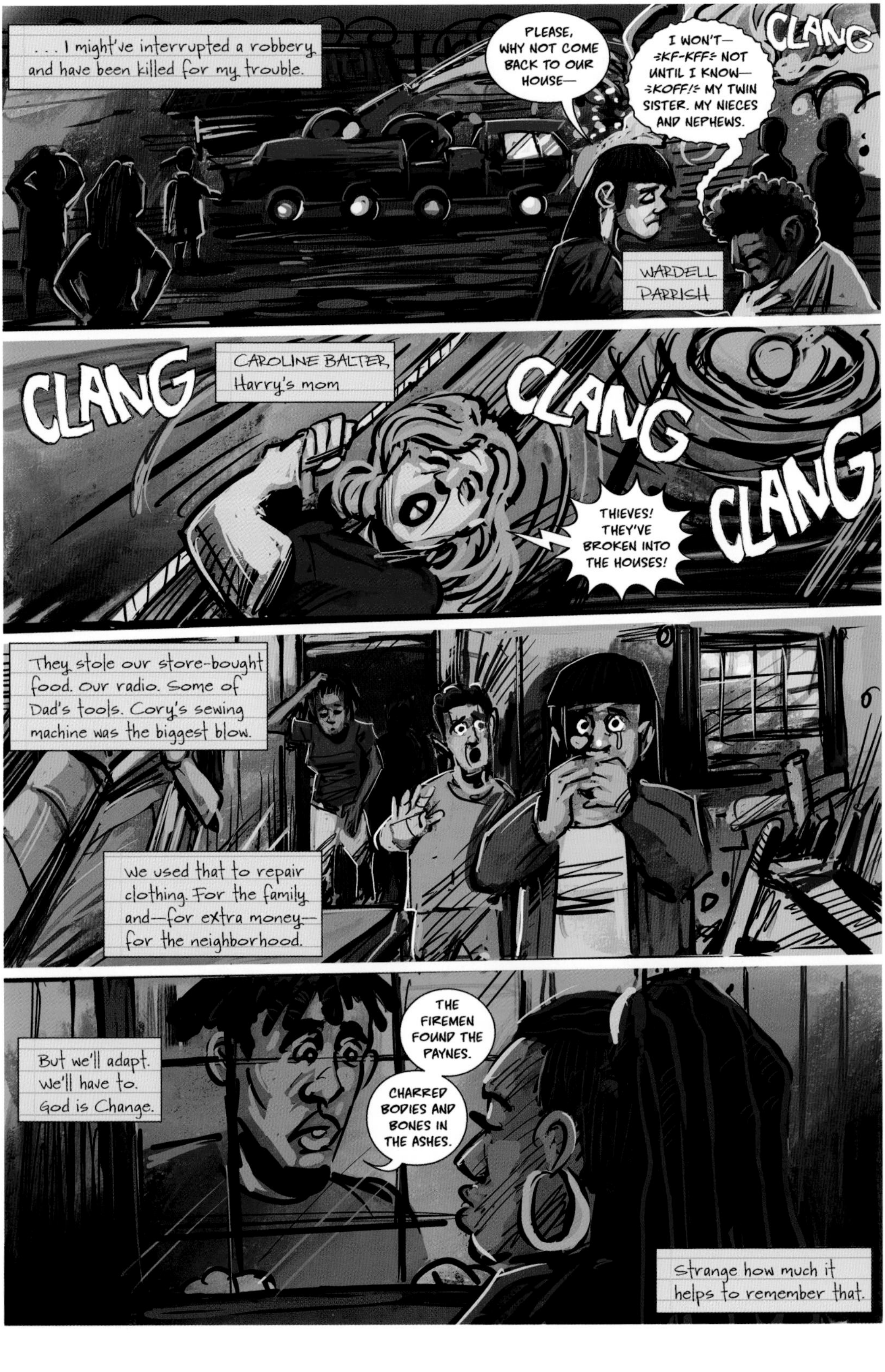
. . . I might've interrupted a robbery and have been killed for my trouble.
PLEASE, WHY NOT COME BACK TO OUR HOUSE—
I WON'T— ≈KF-KFF≈ NOT UNTIL I KNOW— ≈KOFF!≈ MY TWIN SISTER. MY NIECES AND NEPHEWS.
CLANG
WARDELL PARRISH
CLANG
CAROLINE BALTER, Harry's mom
CLANG
CLANG
THIEVES! THEY'VE BROKEN INTO THE HOUSES!
They stole our store-bought food. Our radio. Some of Dad's tools. Cory's sewing machine was the biggest blow.
We used that to repair clothing. For the family and—for extra money—for the neighborhood.
But we'll adapt. We'll have to. God is Change.
THE FIREMEN FOUND THE PAYNES.
CHARRED BODIES AND BONES IN THE ASHES.
Strange how much it helps to remember that.

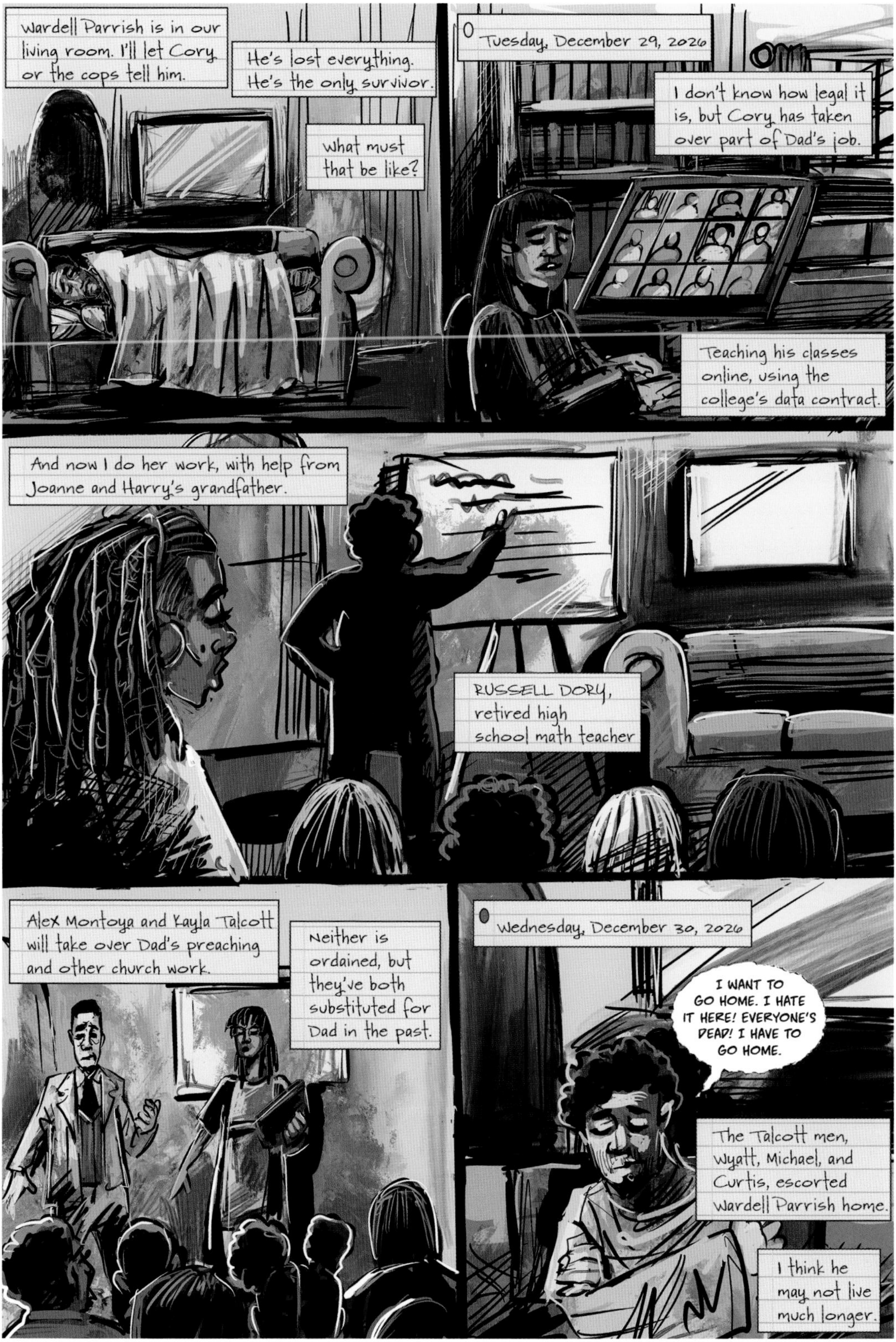
Wardell Parrish is in our living room. I'll let Cory or the cops tell him.
He's lost everything. He's the only survivor.
What must that be like?
Tuesday, December 29, 2026
I don't know how legal it is, but Cory has taken over part of Dad's job.
Teaching his classes online, using the college's data contract.
And now I do her work, with help from Joanne and Harry's grandfather.
RUSSELL DORY, retired high school math teacher
Alex Montoya and Kayla Talcott will take over Dad's preaching and other church work.
Neither is ordained, but they've both substituted for Dad in the past.
Wednesday, December 30, 2026
I WANT TO GO HOME. I HATE IT HERE! EVERYONE'S DEAD! I HAVE TO GO HOME.
The Talcott men, Wyatt, Michael, and Curtis, escorted Wardell Parrish home.
I think he may not live much longer.

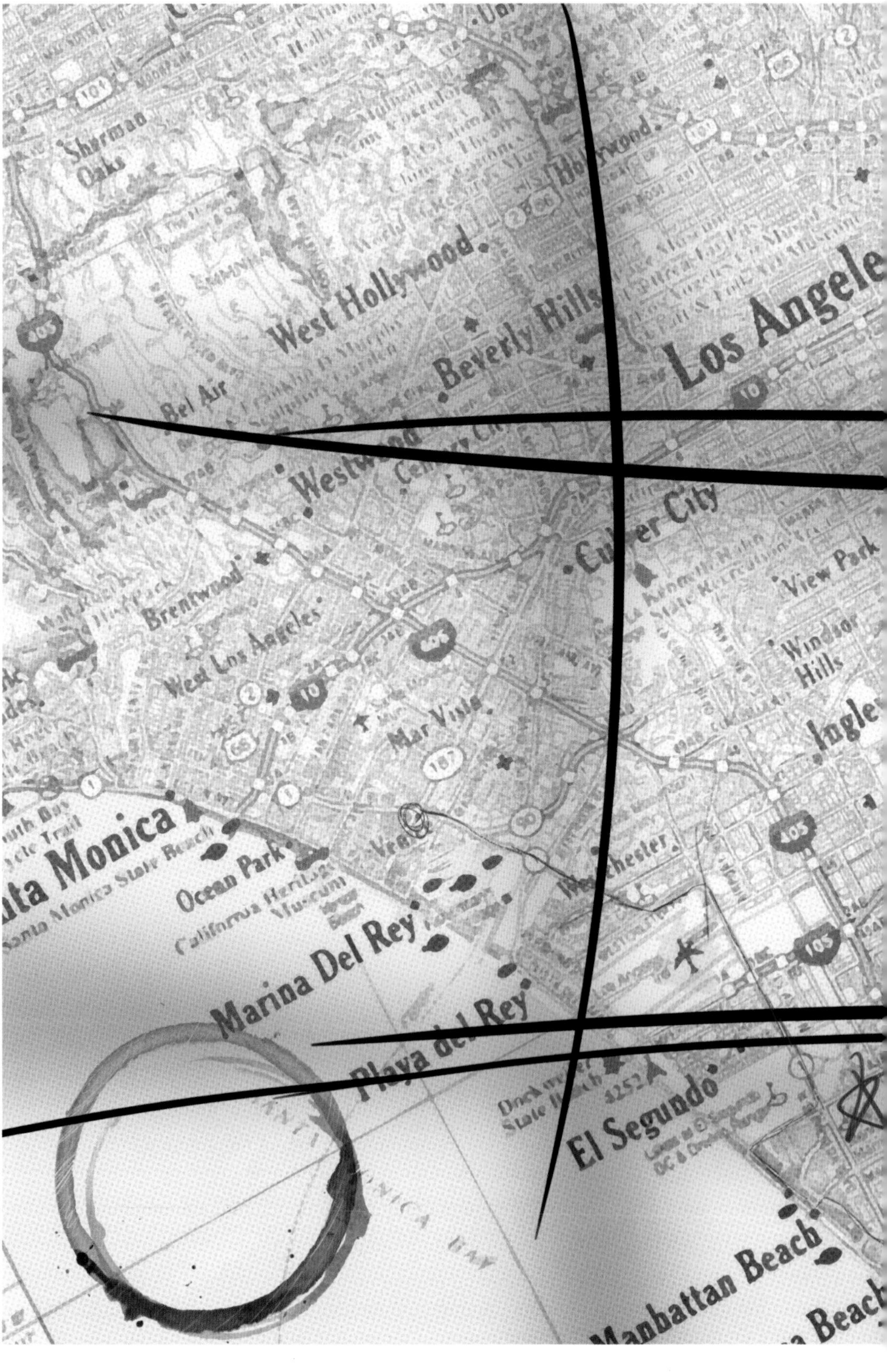
Sherman Oaks
West Hollywood
Beverly Hills
Bel Air
Brentwood
West Los Angeles
View Park
Windsor Hills
Mar Vista
Ocean Park
Santa Monica State Beach
California Heritage Museum
Marina Del Rey
Playa del Rey
El Segundo
Manhattan Beach

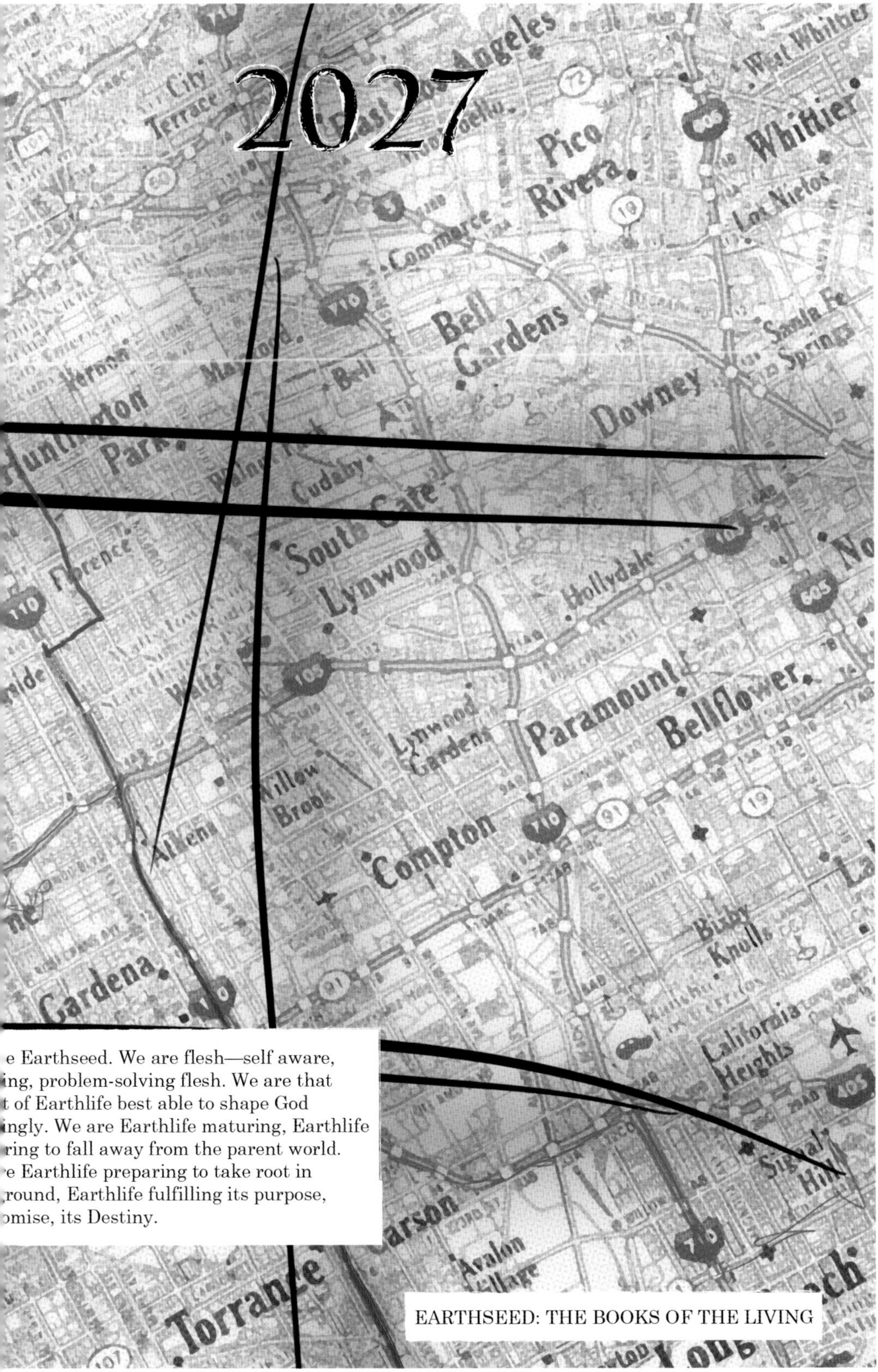

City Terrace
East Los Angeles
West Whittier
Whittier
Pico Rivera
Los Nietos
Commerce
Bell Gardens
Santa Fe Springs
Bell
Maywood
Vernon
Huntington Park
Downey
Cudahy
South Gate
Florence
Lynwood
Hollydale
Paramount
Bellflower
Lynwood Gardens
Willow Brook
Athens
Compton
Bixby Knolls
Gardena
California Heights
Signal Hill
Carson
Avalon Village
Torrance

2027

e Earthseed. We are flesh—self aware,
ing, problem-solving flesh. We are that
t of Earthlife best able to shape God
ingly. We are Earthlife maturing, Earthlife
ring to fall away from the parent world.
e Earthlife preparing to take root in
round, Earthlife fulfilling its purpose,
omise, its Destiny.

EARTHSEED: THE BOOKS OF THE LIVING

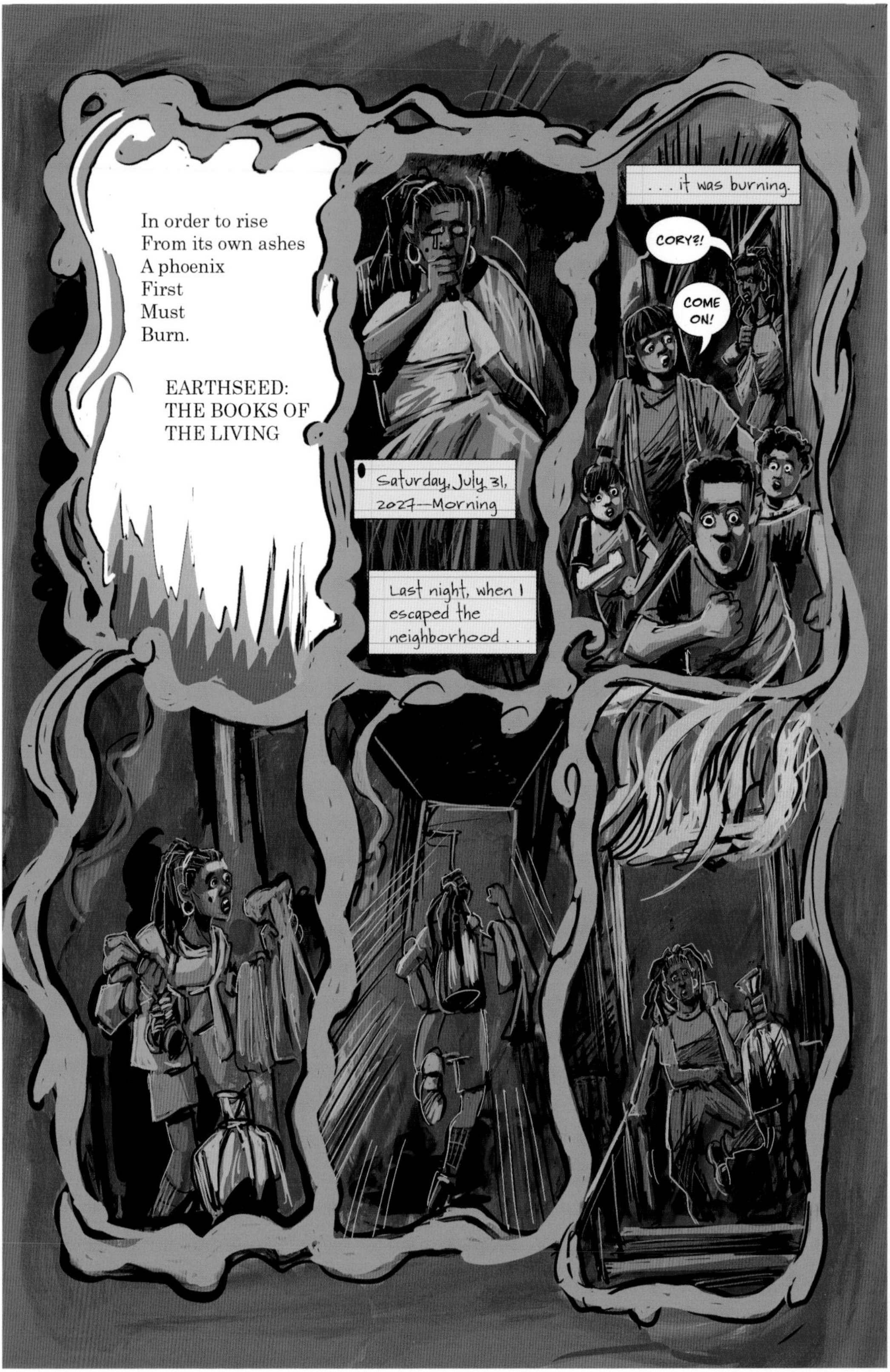

In order to rise
From its own ashes
A phoenix
First
Must
Burn.

EARTHSEED:
THE BOOKS OF
THE LIVING

Saturday, July 31, 2027—Morning
Last night, when I escaped the neighborhood . . .
. . . it was burning.
CORY?!
COME ON!

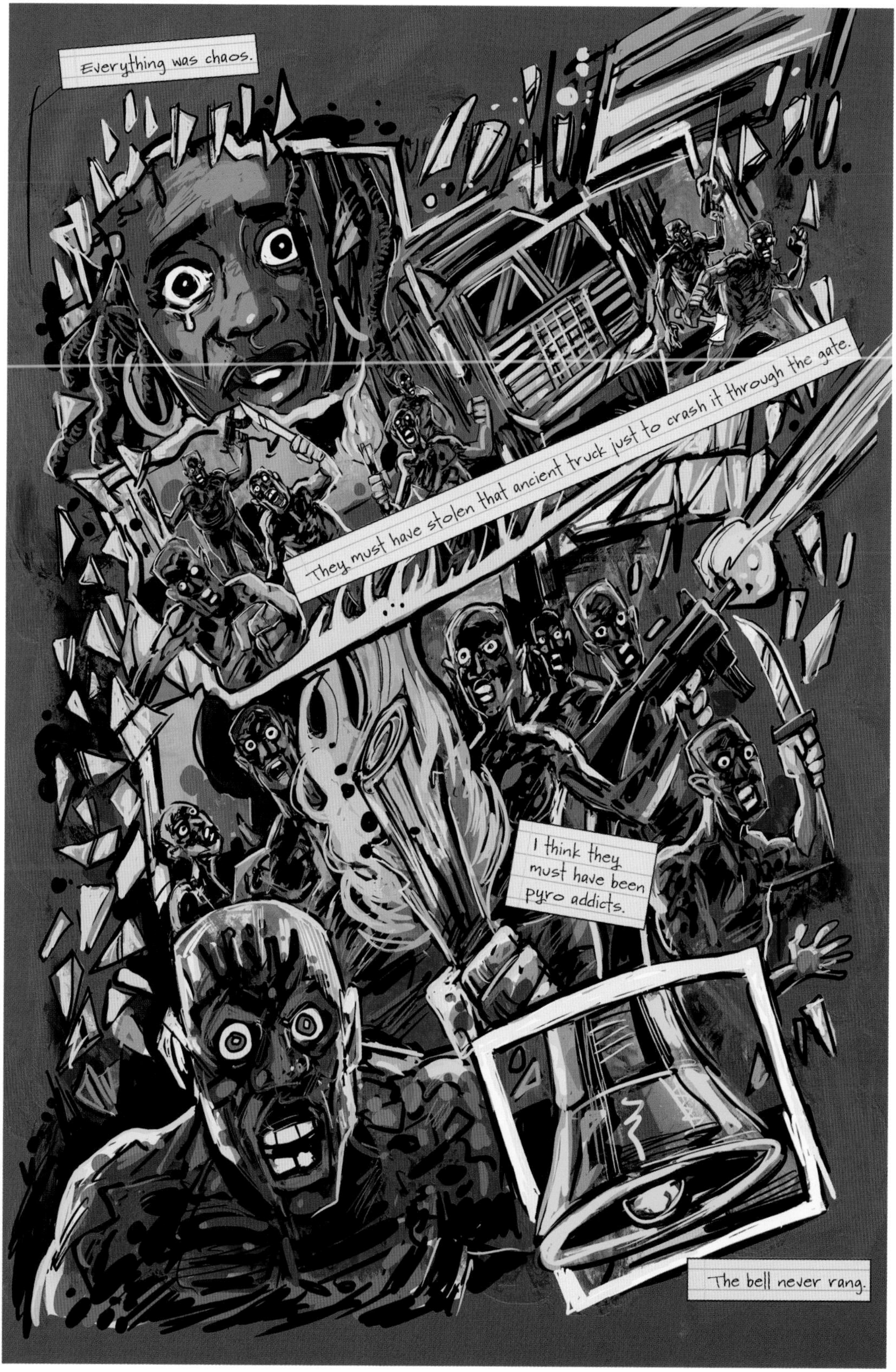
Everything was chaos.
They must have stolen that ancient truck just to crash it through the gate.
I think they must have been pyro addicts.
The bell never rang.

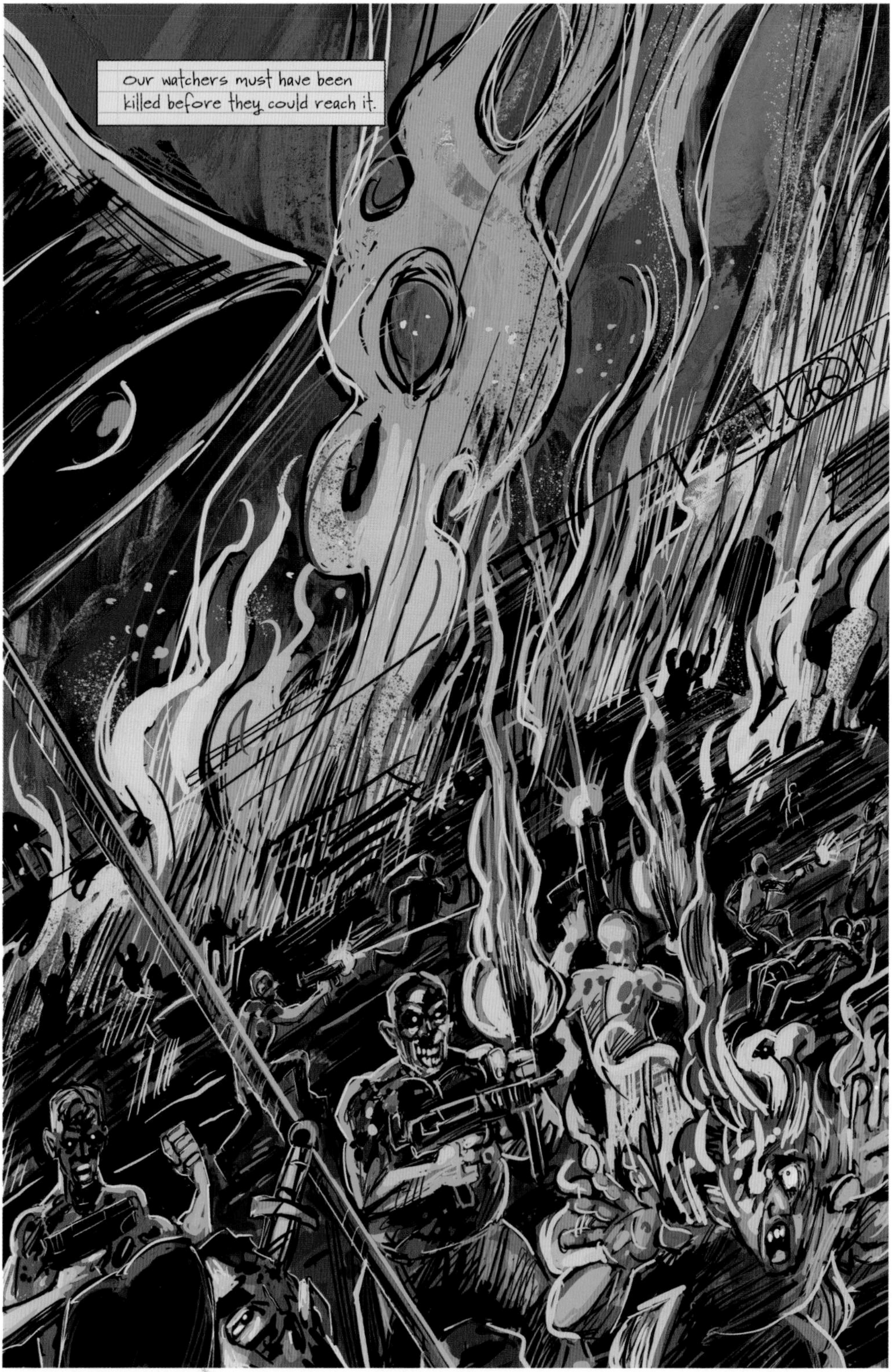
Our watchers must have been killed before they could reach it.

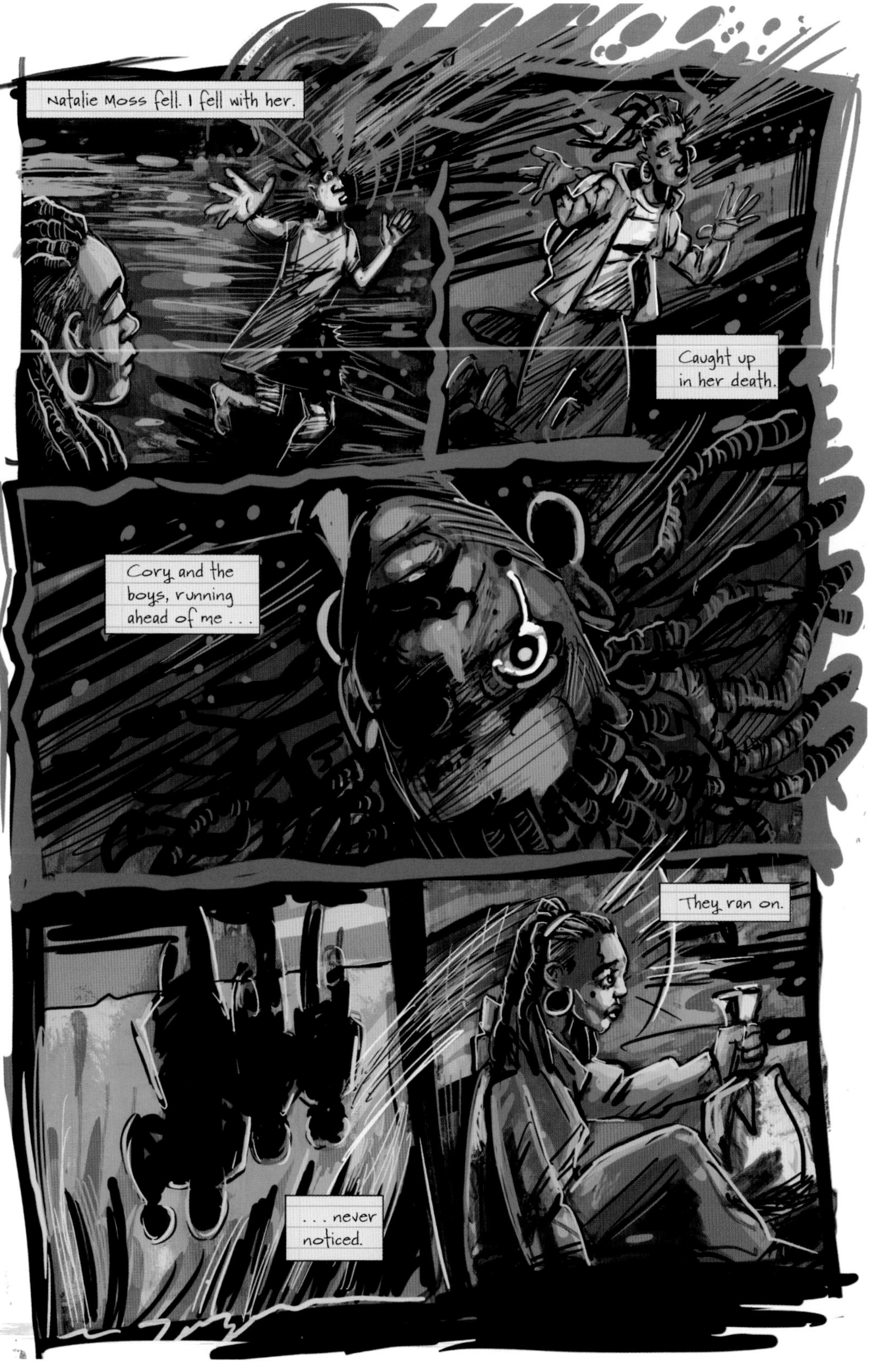
Natalie Moss fell. I fell with her.
Caught up in her death.
Cory and the boys, running ahead of me . . .
They ran on.
. . . never noticed.

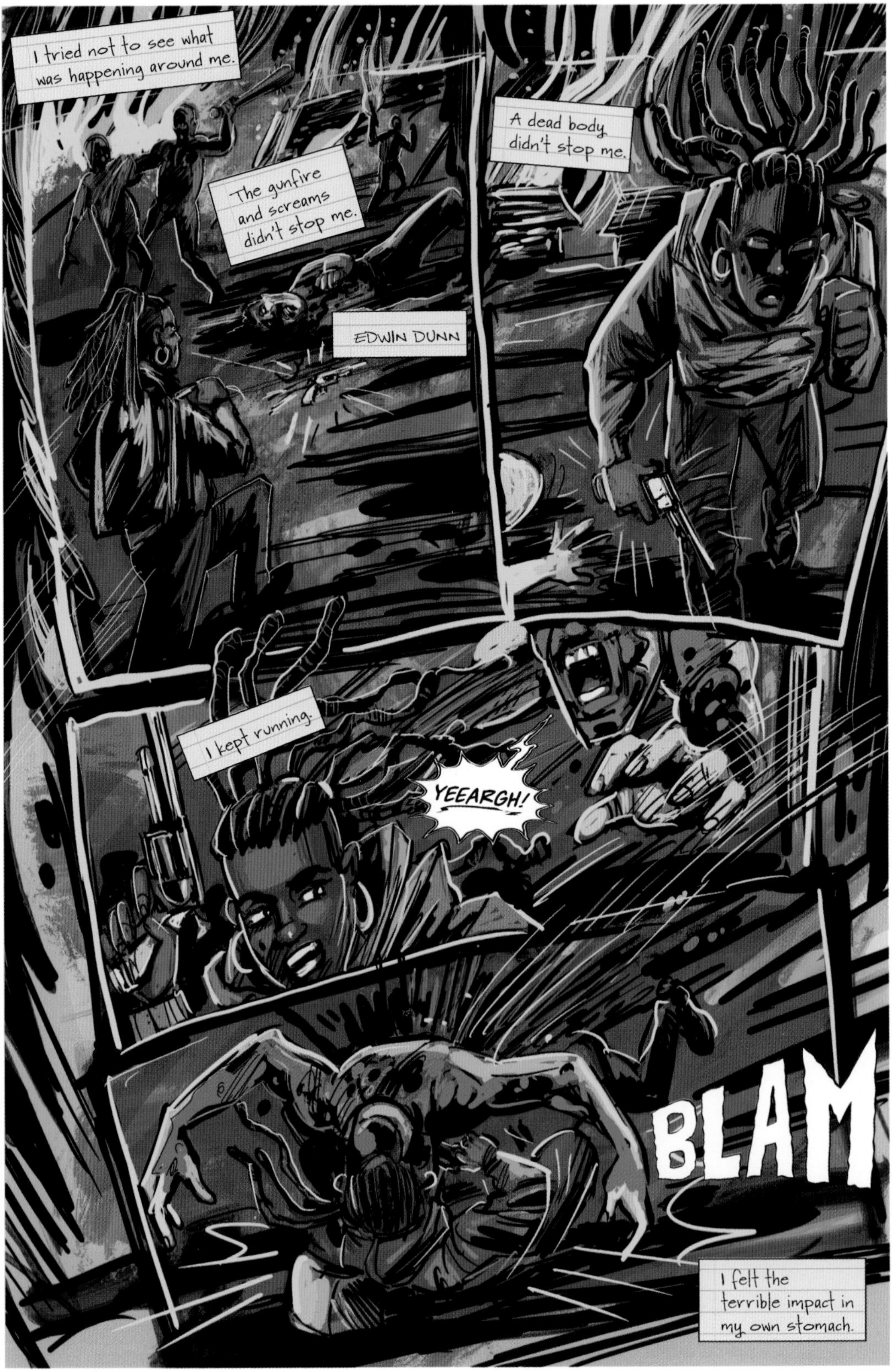
I tried not to see what was happening around me.
The gunfire and screams didn't stop me.
EDWIN DUNN
A dead body didn't stop me.
I kept running.
YEEARGH!
BLAM
I felt the terrible impact in my own stomach.

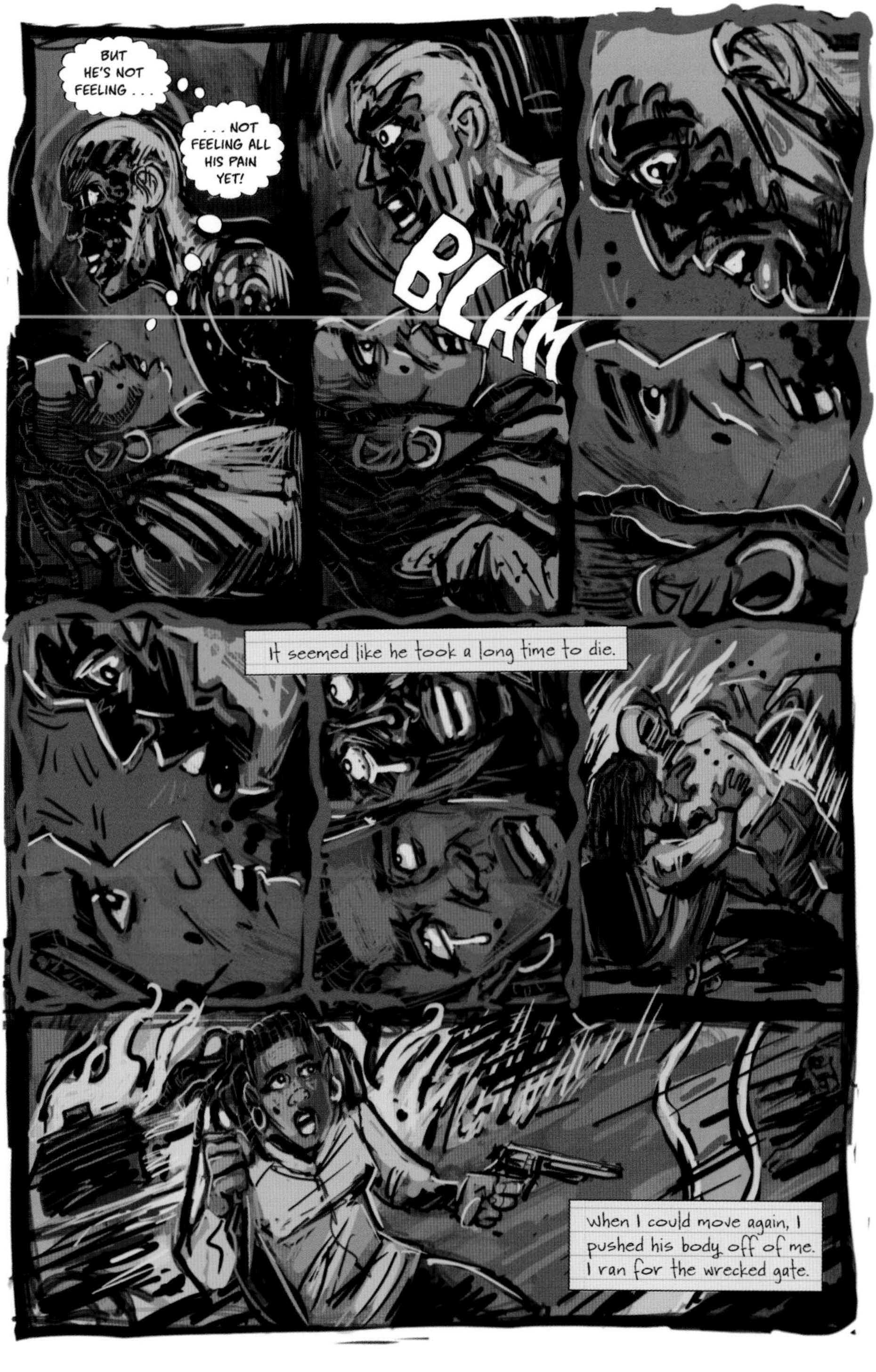
BUT HE'S NOT FEELING . . .
. . . NOT FEELING ALL HIS PAIN YET!
BLAM
It seemed like he took a long time to die.
When I could move again, I pushed his body off of me. I ran for the wrecked gate.

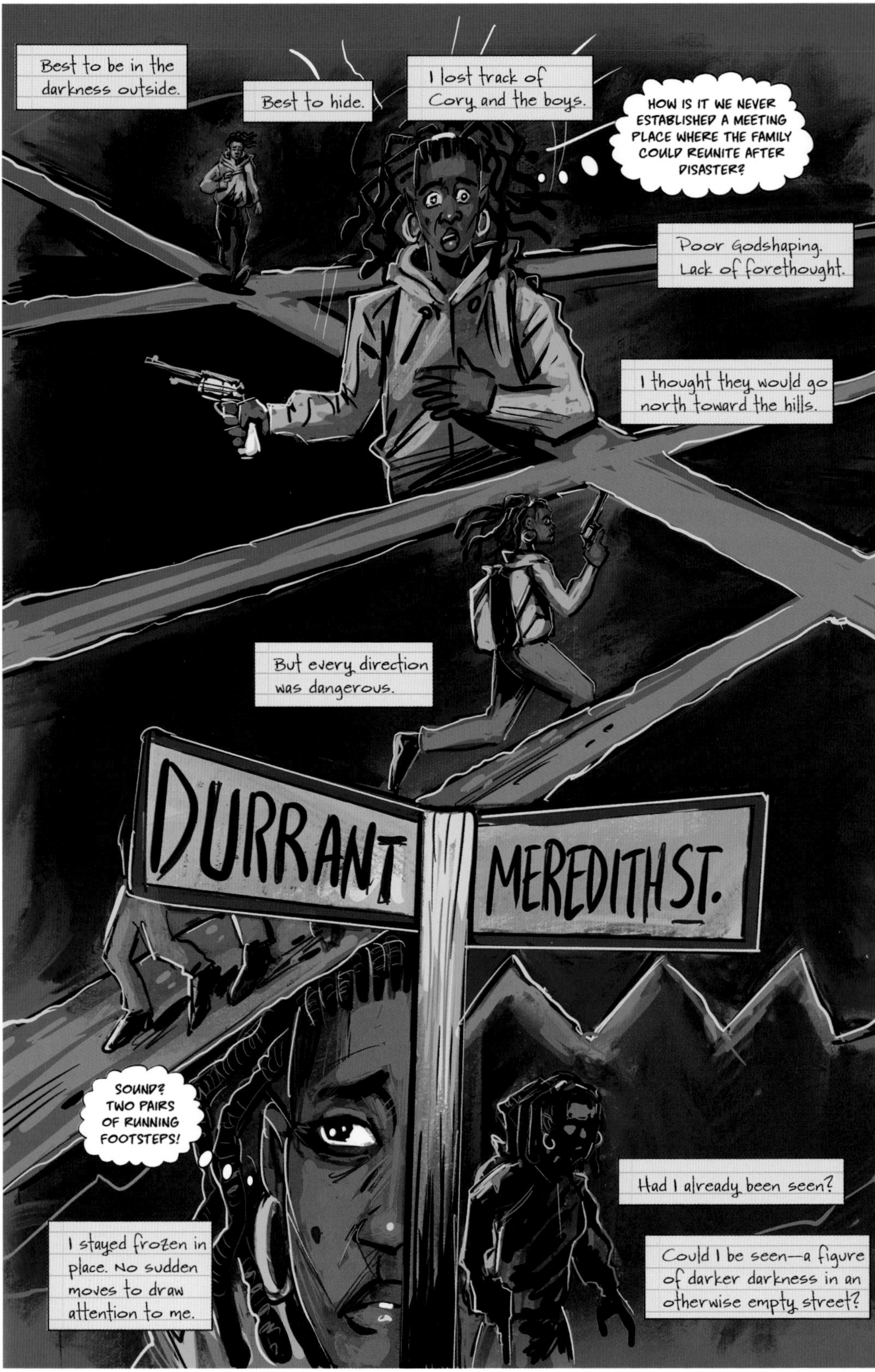
Best to be in the darkness outside.
Best to hide.
I lost track of Cory and the boys.
HOW IS IT WE NEVER ESTABLISHED A MEETING PLACE WHERE THE FAMILY COULD REUNITE AFTER DISASTER?
Poor Godshaping. Lack of forethought.
I thought they would go north toward the hills.
But every direction was dangerous.
DURRANT
MEREDITH ST.
SOUND? TWO PAIRS OF RUNNING FOOTSTEPS!
Had I already been seen?
I stayed frozen in place. No sudden moves to draw attention to me.
Could I be seen—a figure of darker darkness in an otherwise empty street?

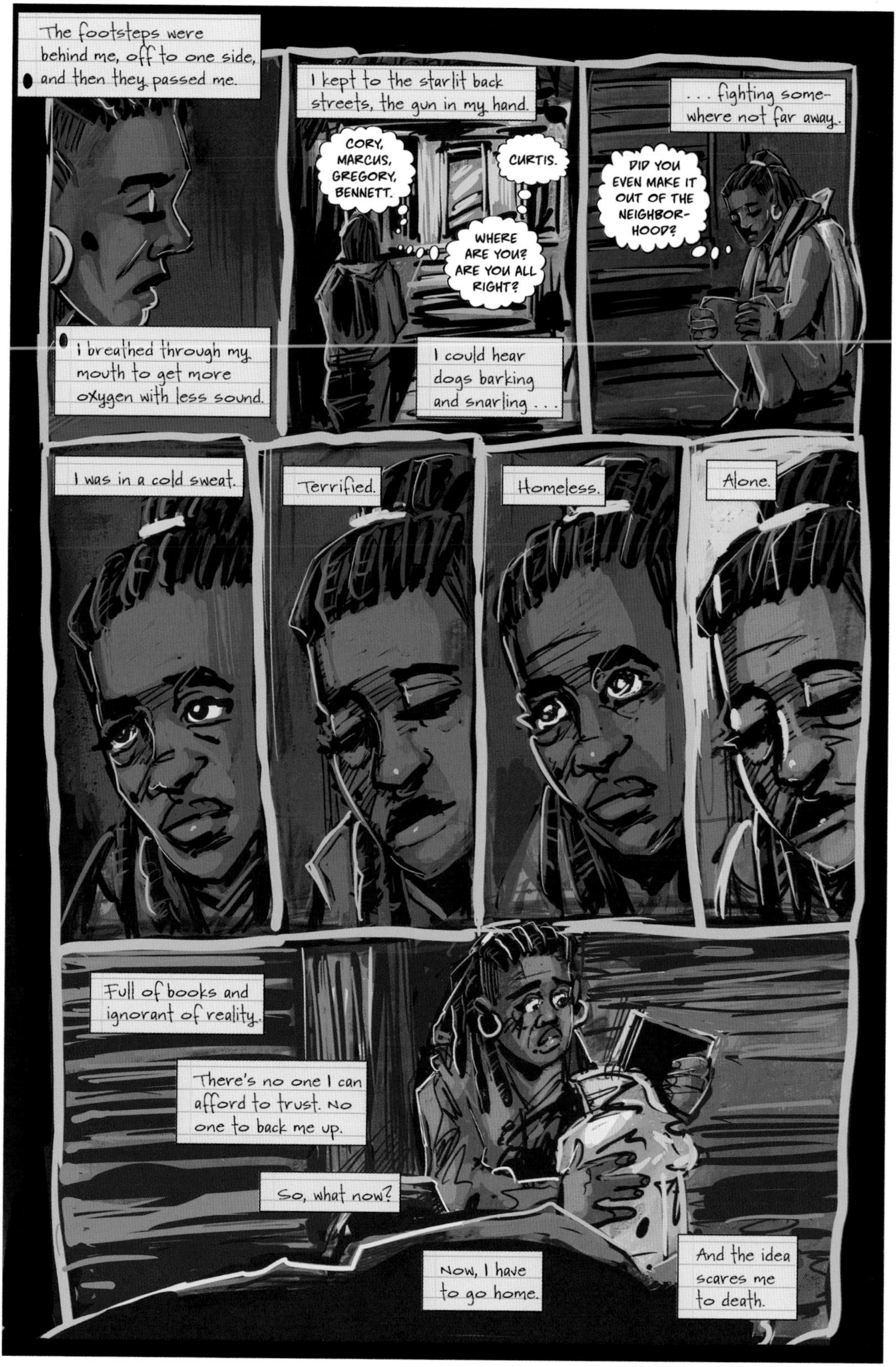
The footsteps were behind me, off to one side, and then they passed me.
I breathed through my mouth to get more oxygen with less sound.
I kept to the starlit back streets, the gun in my hand.
CORY, MARCUS, GREGORY, BENNETT.
CURTIS.
WHERE ARE YOU? ARE YOU ALL RIGHT?
I could hear dogs barking and snarling . . .
. . . fighting somewhere not far away.
DID YOU EVEN MAKE IT OUT OF THE NEIGHBORHOOD?
I was in a cold sweat.
Terrified.
Homeless.
Alone.
Full of books and ignorant of reality.
There's no one I can afford to trust. No one to back me up.
So, what now?
Now, I have to go home.
And the idea scares me to death.

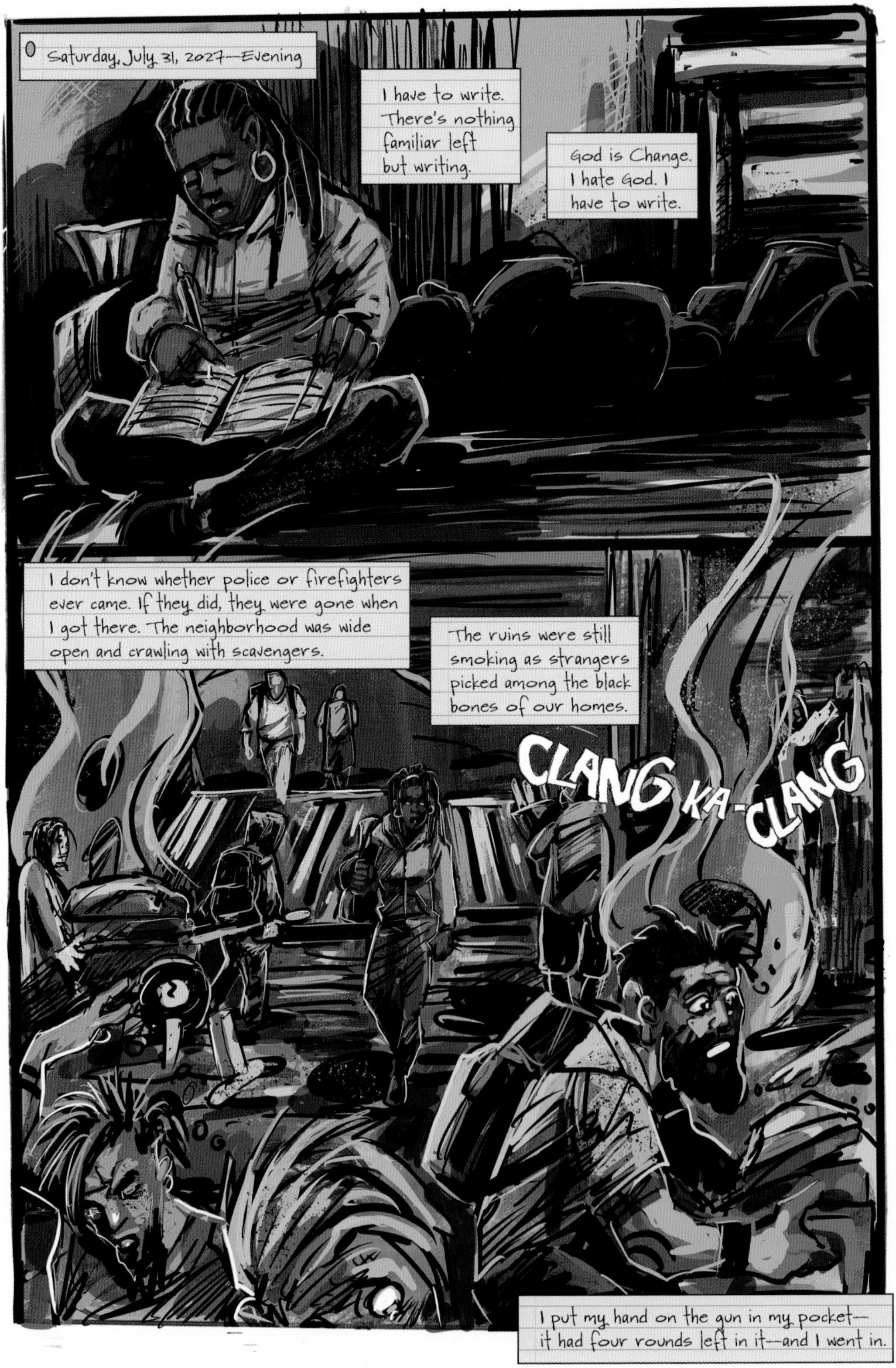
Saturday, July 31, 2027—Evening
I have to write. There's nothing familiar left but writing.
God is Change. I hate God. I have to write.
I don't know whether police or firefighters ever came. If they did, they were gone when I got there. The neighborhood was wide open and crawling with scavengers.
The ruins were still smoking as strangers picked among the black bones of our homes.
CLANG KA-CLANG
I put my hand on the gun in my pocket—it had four rounds left in it—and I went in.

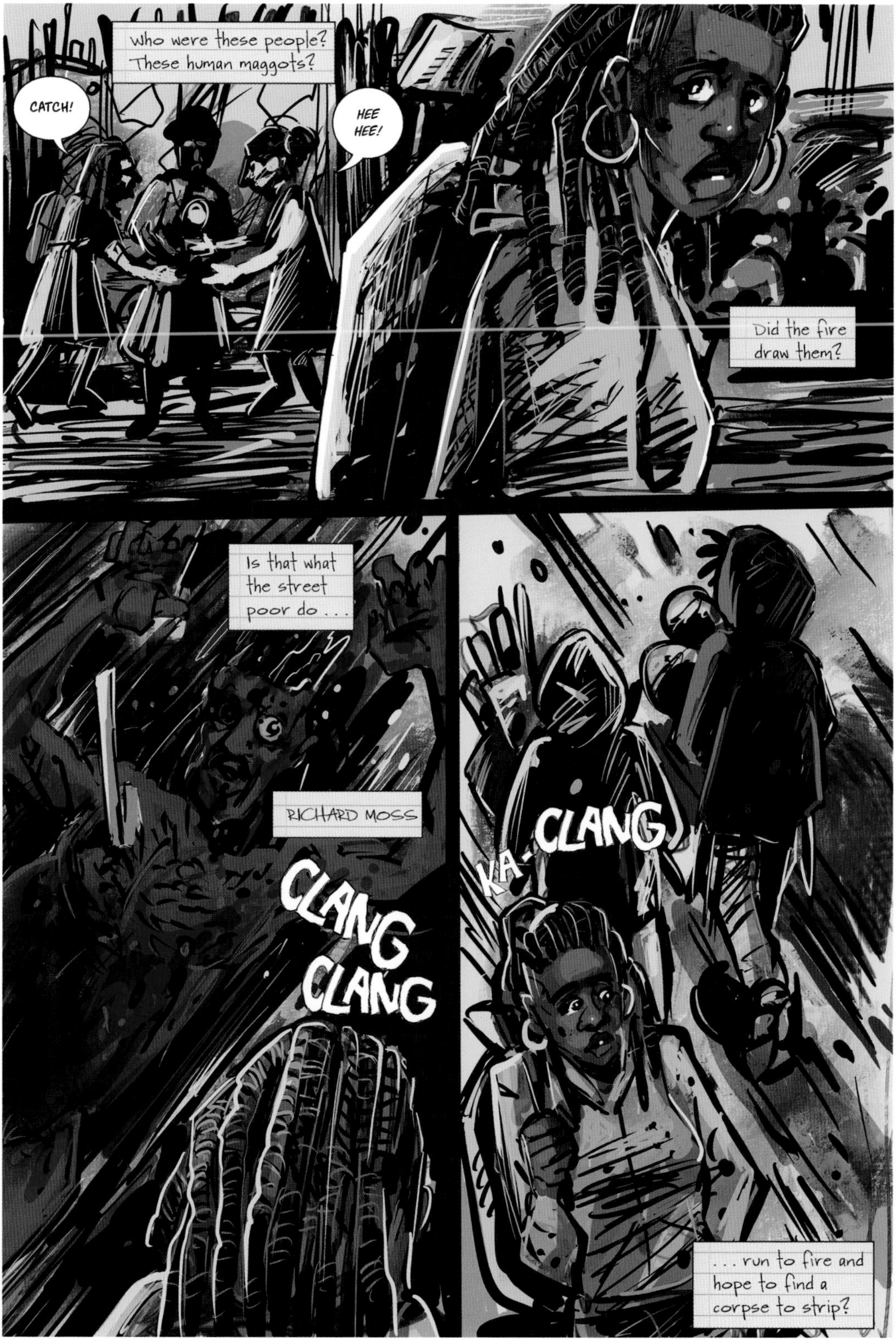
who were these people? These human maggots?
CATCH!
HEE HEE!
Did the fire draw them?
Is that what the street poor do . . .
RICHARD MOSS
CLANG CLANG CLANG
KA-CLANG
. . . run to fire and hope to find a corpse to strip?

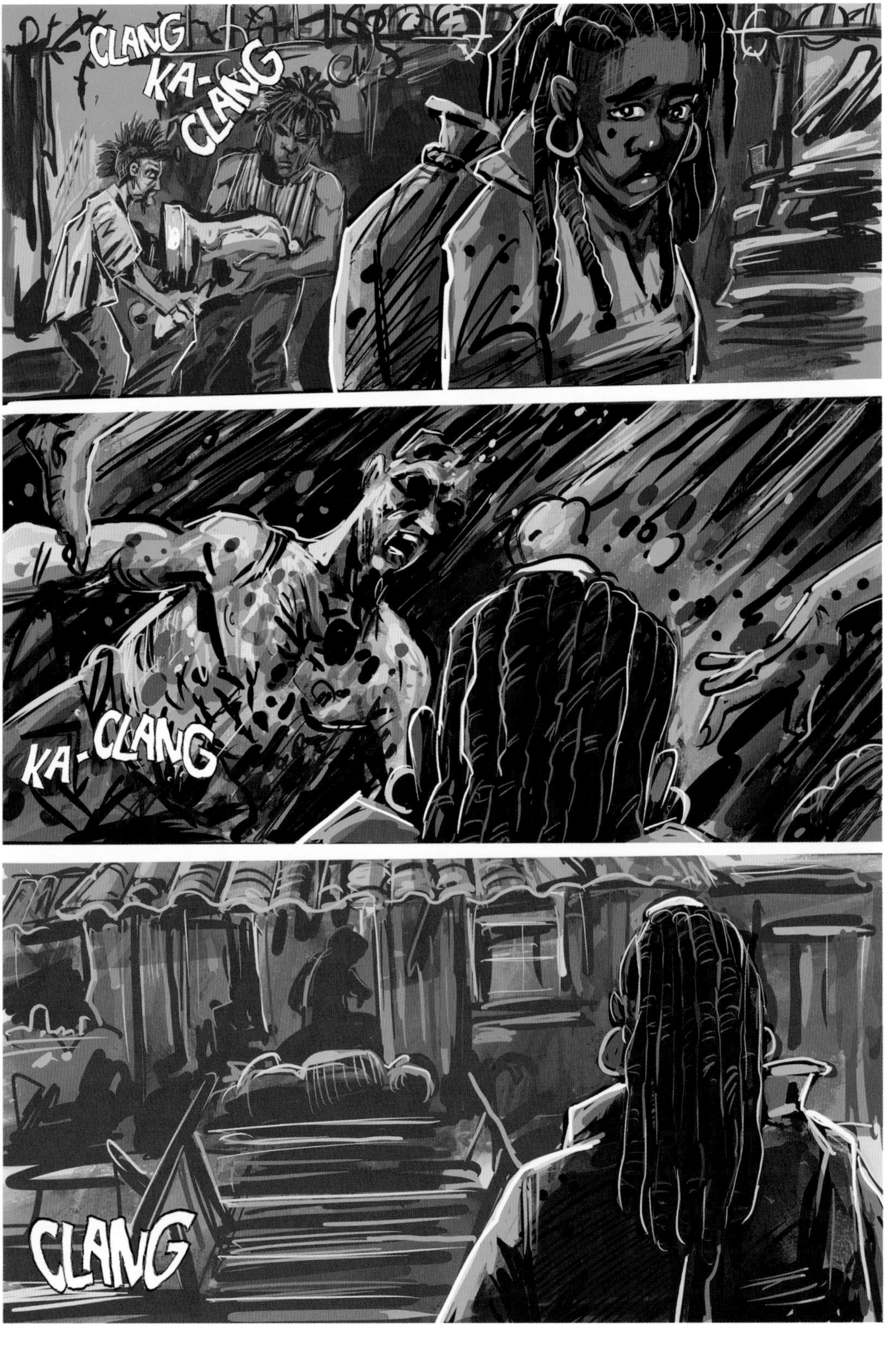
CLANG
KA-
CLANG
KA-CLANG
CLANG

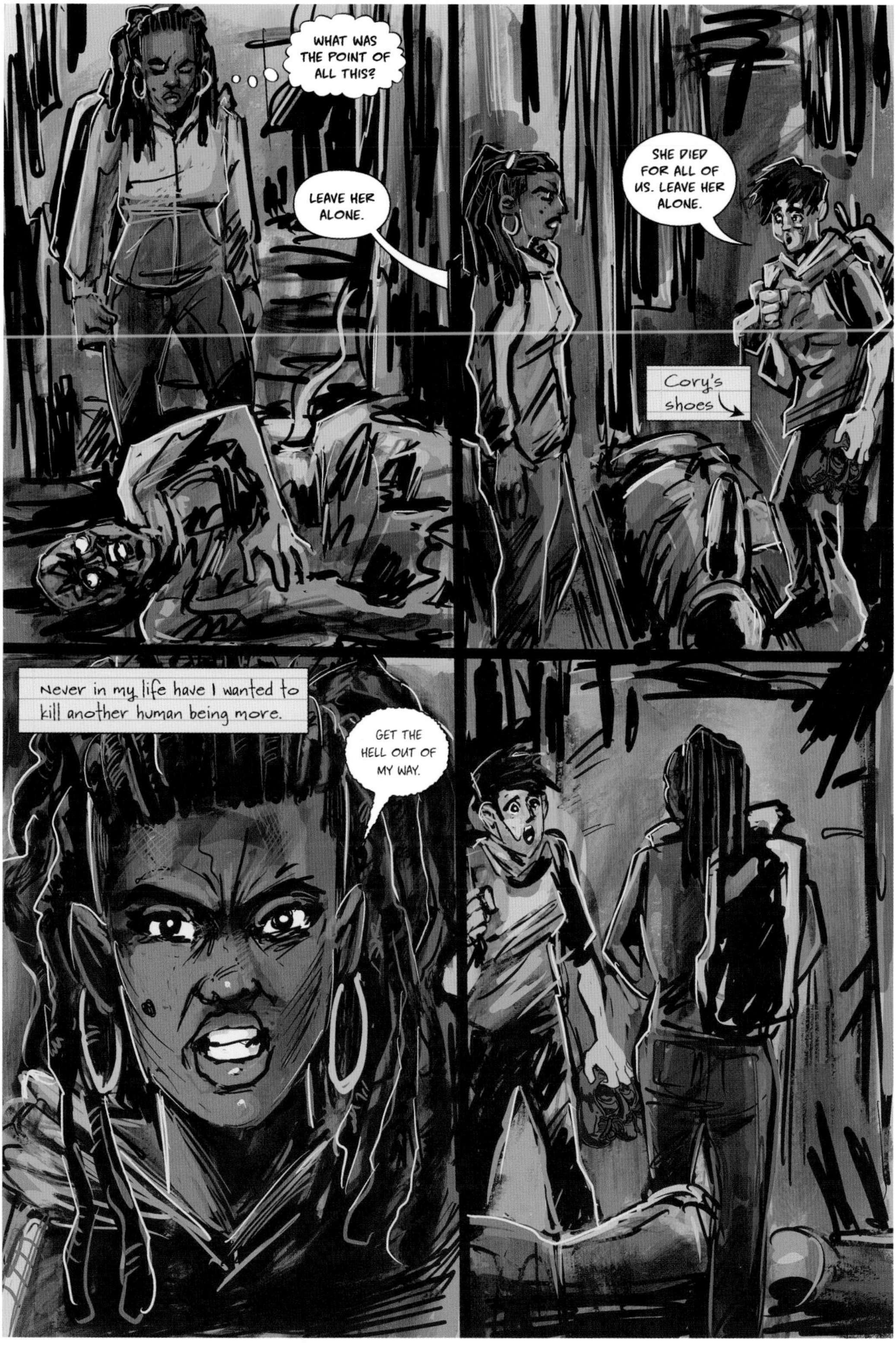
WHAT WAS THE POINT OF ALL THIS?
LEAVE HER ALONE.
SHE DIED FOR ALL OF US. LEAVE HER ALONE.
Cory's shoes
Never in my life have I wanted to kill another human being more.
GET THE HELL OUT OF MY WAY.

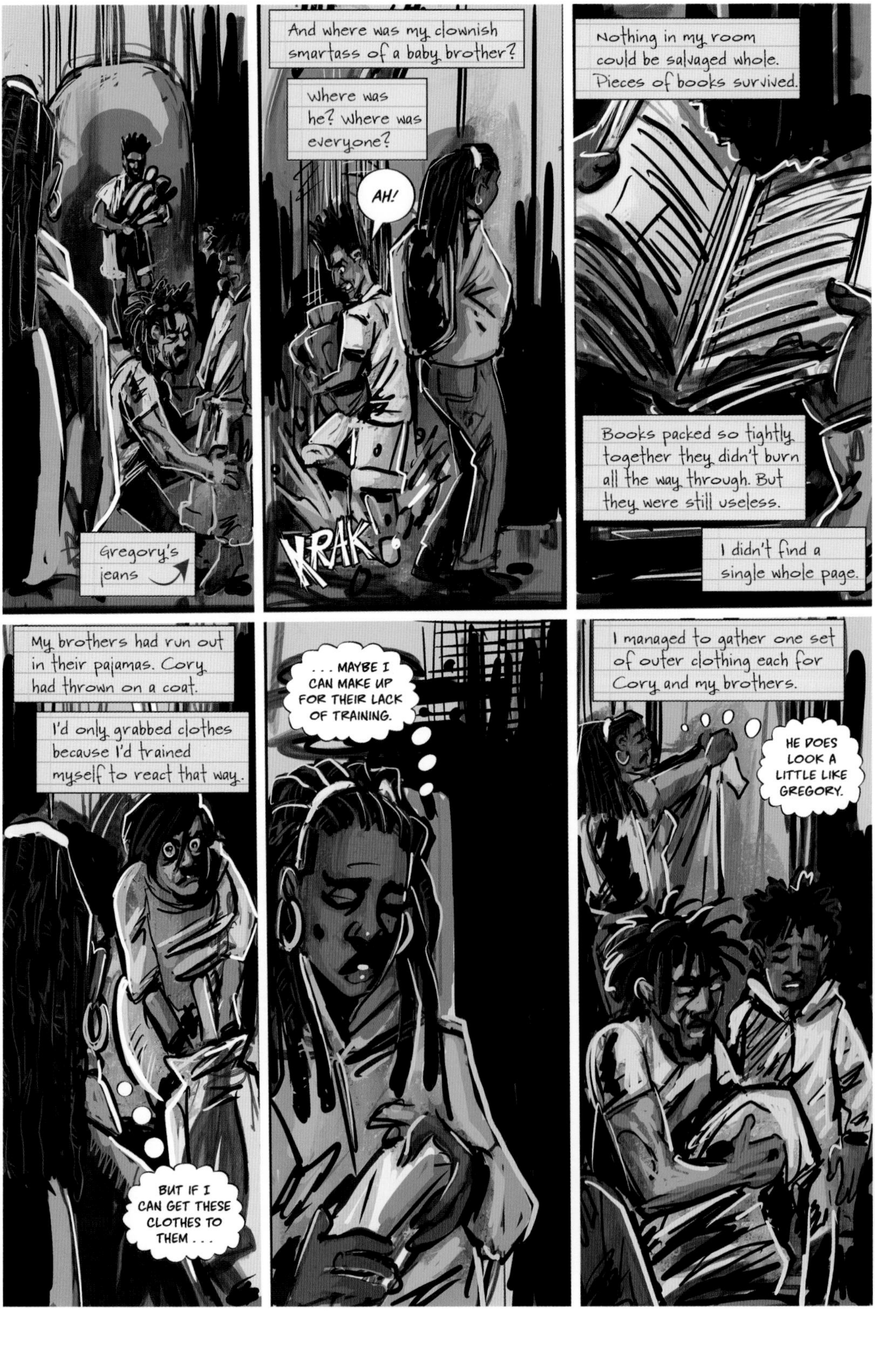
Gregory's jeans
And where was my clownish smartass of a baby brother?
Where was he? Where was everyone?
AH!
KRAK
Nothing in my room could be salvaged whole. Pieces of books survived.
Books packed so tightly together they didn't burn all the way through. But they were still useless.
I didn't find a single whole page.
My brothers had run out in their pajamas. Cory had thrown on a coat.
I'd only grabbed clothes because I'd trained myself to react that way.
BUT IF I CAN GET THESE CLOTHES TO THEM . . .
. . . MAYBE I CAN MAKE UP FOR THEIR LACK OF TRAINING.
I managed to gather one set of outer clothing each for Cory and my brothers.
HE DOES LOOK A LITTLE LIKE GREGORY.

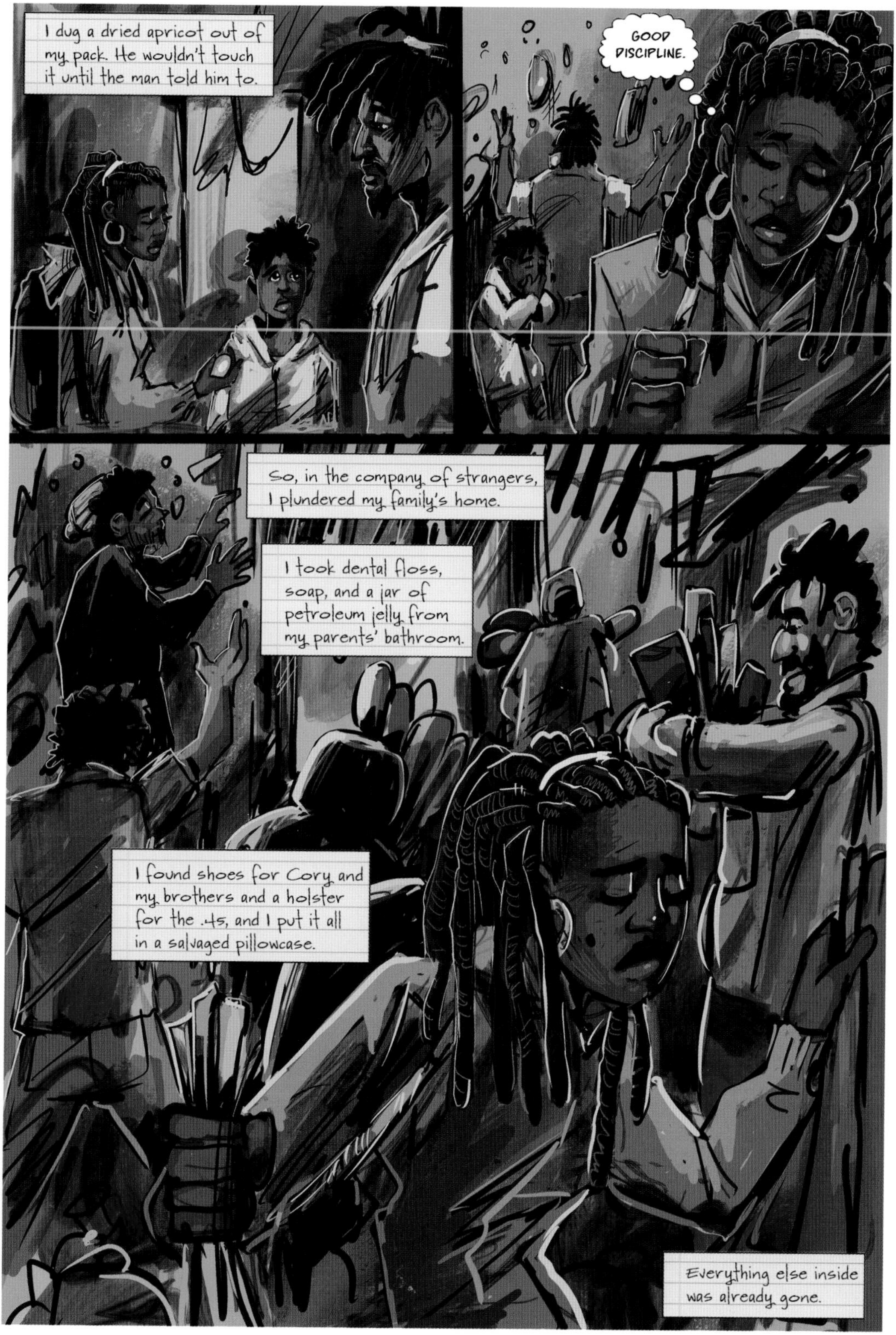
I dug a dried apricot out of my pack. He wouldn't touch it until the man told him to.
GOOD DISCIPLINE.
So, in the company of strangers, I plundered my family's home.
I took dental floss, soap, and a jar of petroleum jelly from my parents' bathroom.
I found shoes for Cory and my brothers and a holster for the .45, and I put it all in a salvaged pillowcase.
Everything else inside was already gone.

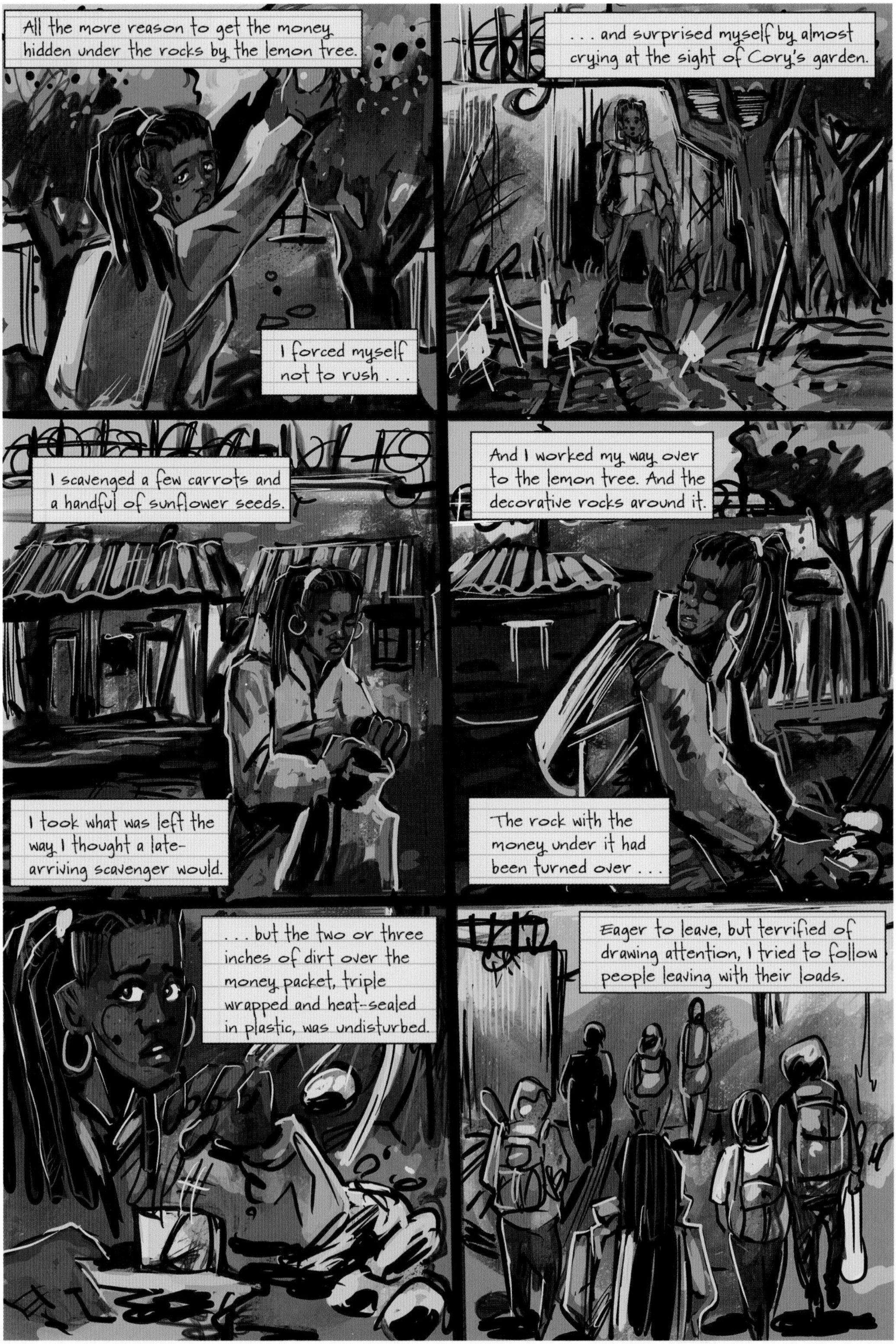
All the more reason to get the money hidden under the rocks by the lemon tree.
I forced myself not to rush . . .
. . . and surprised myself by almost crying at the sight of Cory's garden.
I scavenged a few carrots and a handful of sunflower seeds.
I took what was left the way I thought a late-arriving scavenger would.
And I worked my way over to the lemon tree. And the decorative rocks around it.
The rock with the money under it had been turned over . . .
. . . but the two or three inches of dirt over the money packet, triple wrapped and heat-sealed in plastic, was undisturbed.
Eager to leave, but terrified of drawing attention, I tried to follow people leaving with their loads.

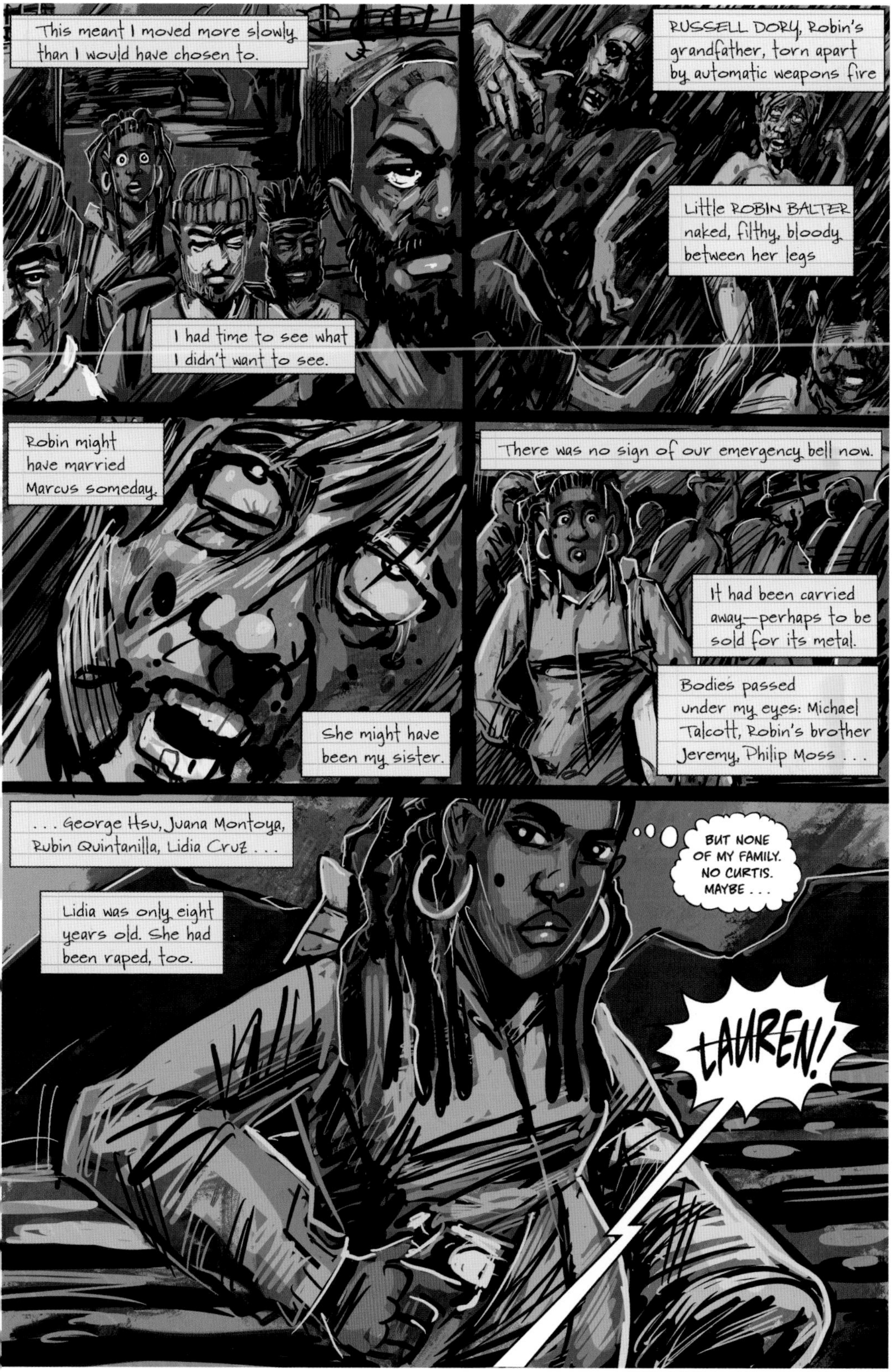
This meant I moved more slowly than I would have chosen to.
I had time to see what I didn't want to see.
RUSSELL DORY, Robin's grandfather, torn apart by automatic weapons fire
Little ROBIN BALTER naked, filthy, bloody between her legs
Robin might have married Marcus someday.
She might have been my sister.
There was no sign of our emergency bell now.
It had been carried away—perhaps to be sold for its metal.
Bodies passed under my eyes: Michael Talcott, Robin's brother Jeremy, Philip Moss . . .
. . . George Hsu, Juana Montoya, Rubin Quintanilla, Lidia Cruz . . .
Lidia was only eight years old. She had been raped, too.
BUT NONE OF MY FAMILY. NO CURTIS. MAYBE . . .
LAUREN!

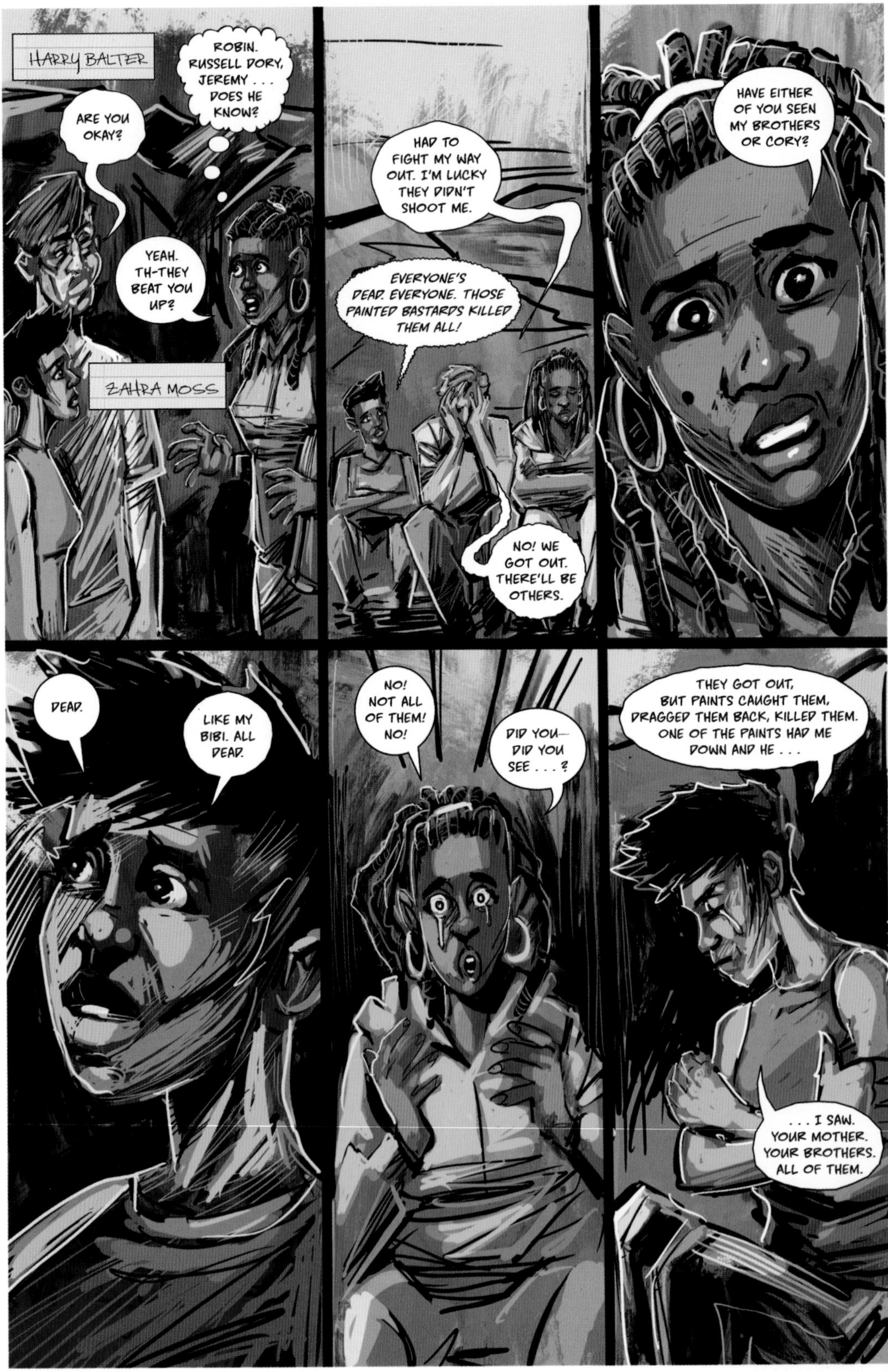
HARRY BALTER
ROBIN. RUSSELL DORY, JEREMY . . . DOES HE KNOW?
ARE YOU OKAY?
YEAH. TH-THEY BEAT YOU UP?
ZAHRA MOSS
HAD TO FIGHT MY WAY OUT. I'M LUCKY THEY DIDN'T SHOOT ME.
EVERYONE'S DEAD. EVERYONE. THOSE PAINTED BASTARDS KILLED THEM ALL!
NO! WE GOT OUT. THERE'LL BE OTHERS.
HAVE EITHER OF YOU SEEN MY BROTHERS OR CORY?
DEAD.
LIKE MY BIBI. ALL DEAD.
NO! NOT ALL OF THEM! NO!
DID YOU— DID YOU SEE . . . ?
THEY GOT OUT, BUT PAINTS CAUGHT THEM, DRAGGED THEM BACK, KILLED THEM. ONE OF THE PAINTS HAD ME DOWN AND HE . . .
. . . I SAW. YOUR MOTHER. YOUR BROTHERS. ALL OF THEM.

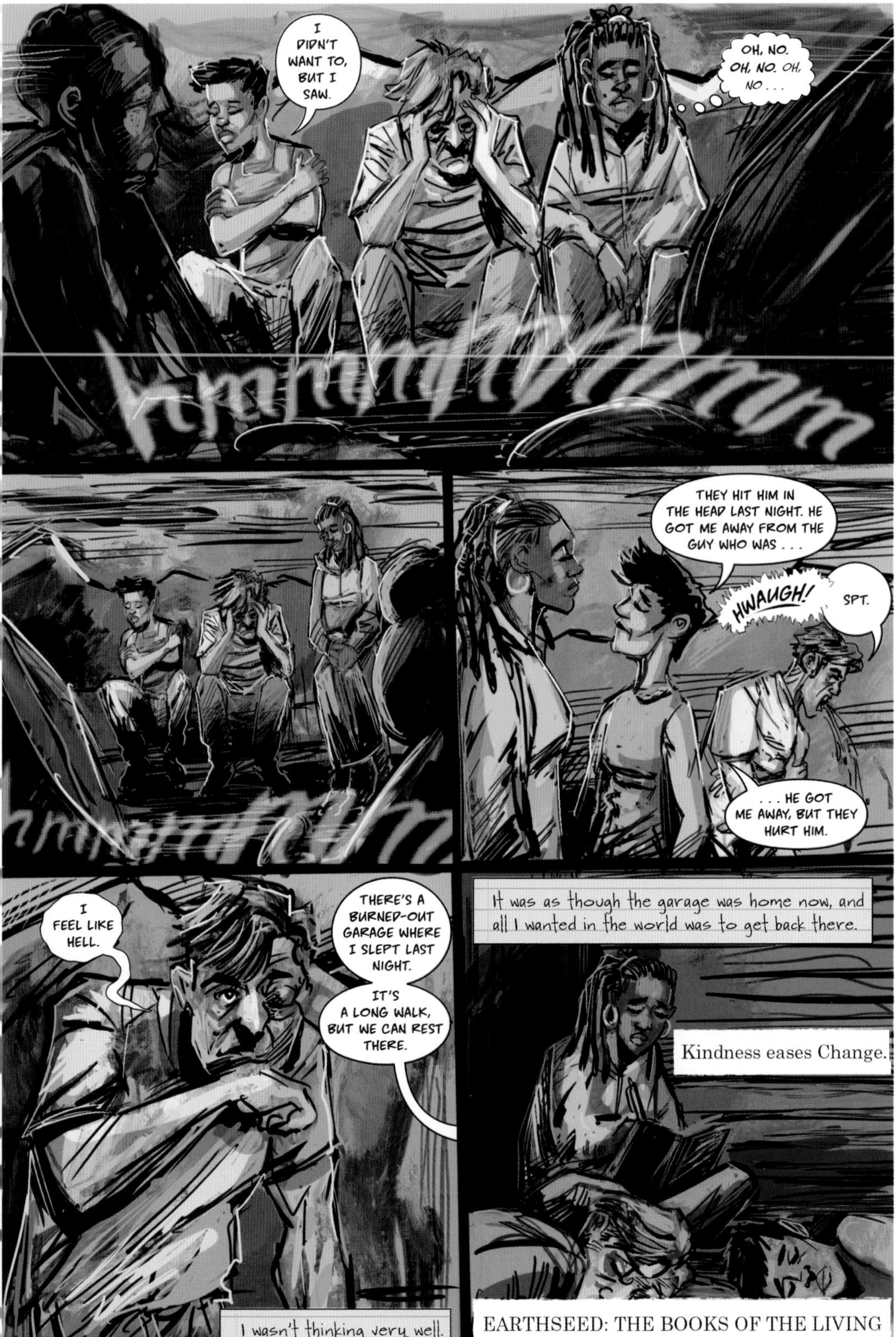
I DIDN'T WANT TO, BUT I SAW.
OH, NO. OH, NO. OH, NO . . .
hmmmmmm
THEY HIT HIM IN THE HEAD LAST NIGHT. HE GOT ME AWAY FROM THE GUY WHO WAS . . .
HWAUGH!
SPT.
. . . HE GOT ME AWAY, BUT THEY HURT HIM.
I FEEL LIKE HELL.
THERE'S A BURNED-OUT GARAGE WHERE I SLEPT LAST NIGHT.
IT'S A LONG WALK, BUT WE CAN REST THERE.
I wasn't thinking very well.
It was as though the garage was home now, and all I wanted in the world was to get back there.
Kindness eases Change.
EARTHSEED: THE BOOKS OF THE LIVING

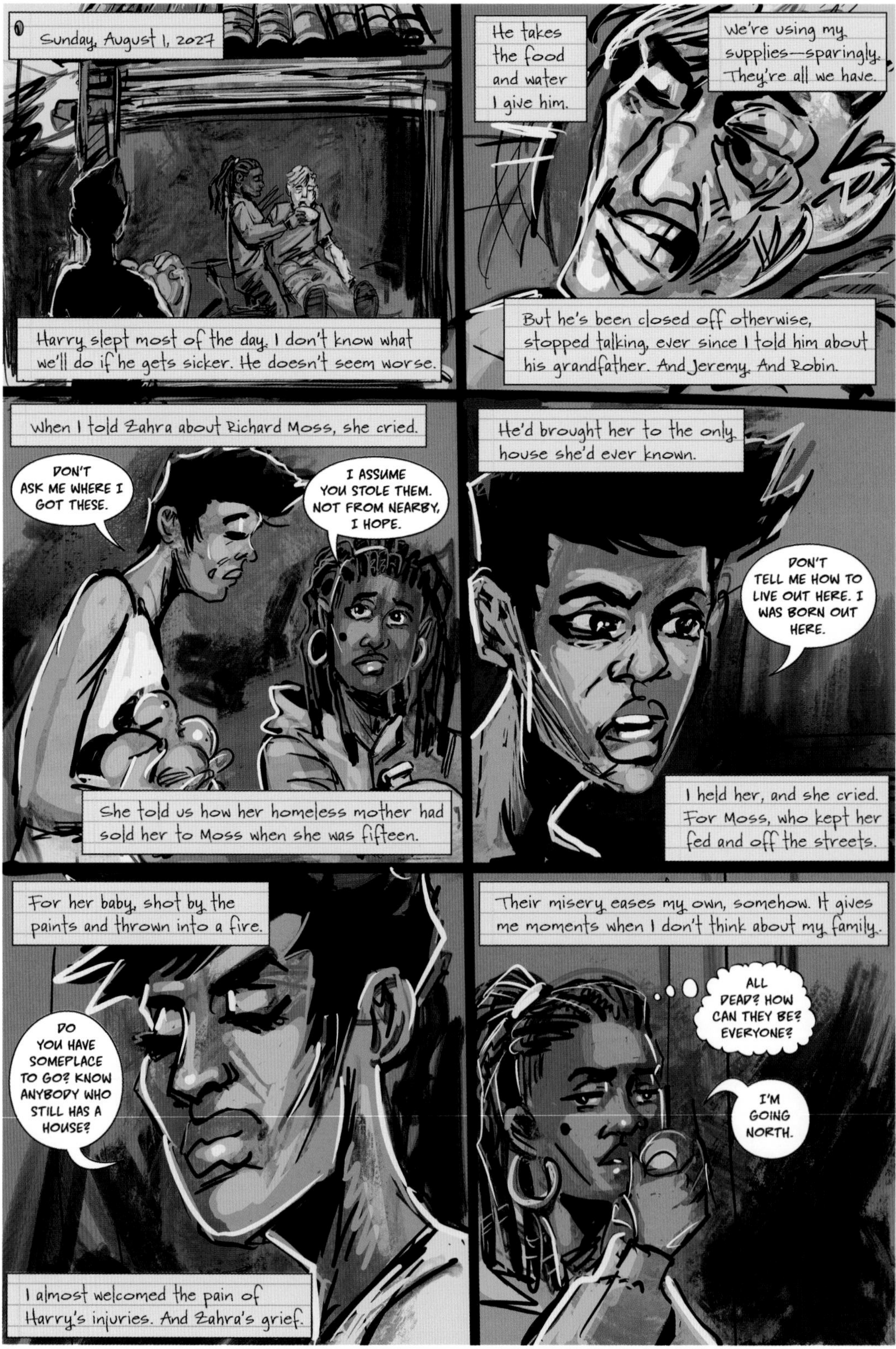
Sunday, August 1, 2027
Harry slept most of the day. I don't know what we'll do if he gets sicker. He doesn't seem worse.
He takes the food and water I give him.
We're using my supplies—sparingly. They're all we have.
But he's been closed off otherwise, stopped talking, ever since I told him about his grandfather. And Jeremy. And Robin.
When I told Zahra about Richard Moss, she cried.
DON'T ASK ME WHERE I GOT THESE.
I ASSUME YOU STOLE THEM. NOT FROM NEARBY, I HOPE.
She told us how her homeless mother had sold her to Moss when she was fifteen.
He'd brought her to the only house she'd ever known.
DON'T TELL ME HOW TO LIVE OUT HERE. I WAS BORN OUT HERE.
I held her, and she cried. For Moss, who kept her fed and off the streets.
For her baby, shot by the paints and thrown into a fire.
DO YOU HAVE SOMEPLACE TO GO? KNOW ANYBODY WHO STILL HAS A HOUSE?
I almost welcomed the pain of Harry's injuries. And Zahra's grief.
Their misery eases my own, somehow. It gives me moments when I don't think about my family.
ALL DEAD? HOW CAN THEY BE? EVERYONE?
I'M GOING NORTH.

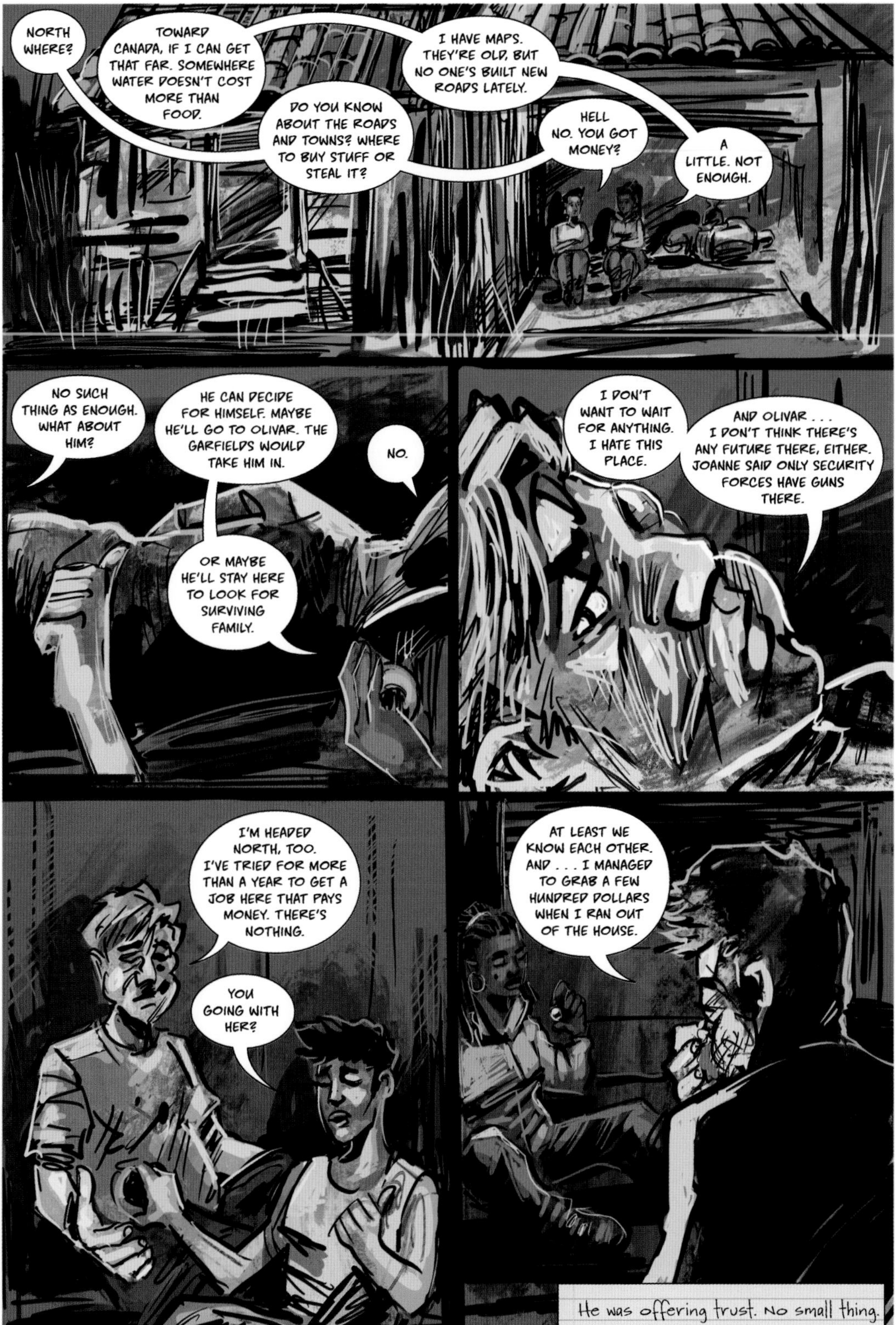

NORTH WHERE?
TOWARD CANADA, IF I CAN GET THAT FAR. SOMEWHERE WATER DOESN'T COST MORE THAN FOOD.
I HAVE MAPS. THEY'RE OLD, BUT NO ONE'S BUILT NEW ROADS LATELY.
DO YOU KNOW ABOUT THE ROADS AND TOWNS? WHERE TO BUY STUFF OR STEAL IT?
HELL NO. YOU GOT MONEY?
A LITTLE. NOT ENOUGH.
NO SUCH THING AS ENOUGH. WHAT ABOUT HIM?
HE CAN DECIDE FOR HIMSELF. MAYBE HE'LL GO TO OLIVAR. THE GARFIELDS WOULD TAKE HIM IN.
OR MAYBE HE'LL STAY HERE TO LOOK FOR SURVIVING FAMILY.
NO.
I DON'T WANT TO WAIT FOR ANYTHING. I HATE THIS PLACE.
AND OLIVAR . . . I DON'T THINK THERE'S ANY FUTURE THERE, EITHER. JOANNE SAID ONLY SECURITY FORCES HAVE GUNS THERE.
I'M HEADED NORTH, TOO. I'VE TRIED FOR MORE THAN A YEAR TO GET A JOB HERE THAT PAYS MONEY. THERE'S NOTHING.
YOU GOING WITH HER?
AT LEAST WE KNOW EACH OTHER. AND . . . I MANAGED TO GRAB A FEW HUNDRED DOLLARS WHEN I RAN OUT OF THE HOUSE.
He was offering trust. No small thing.

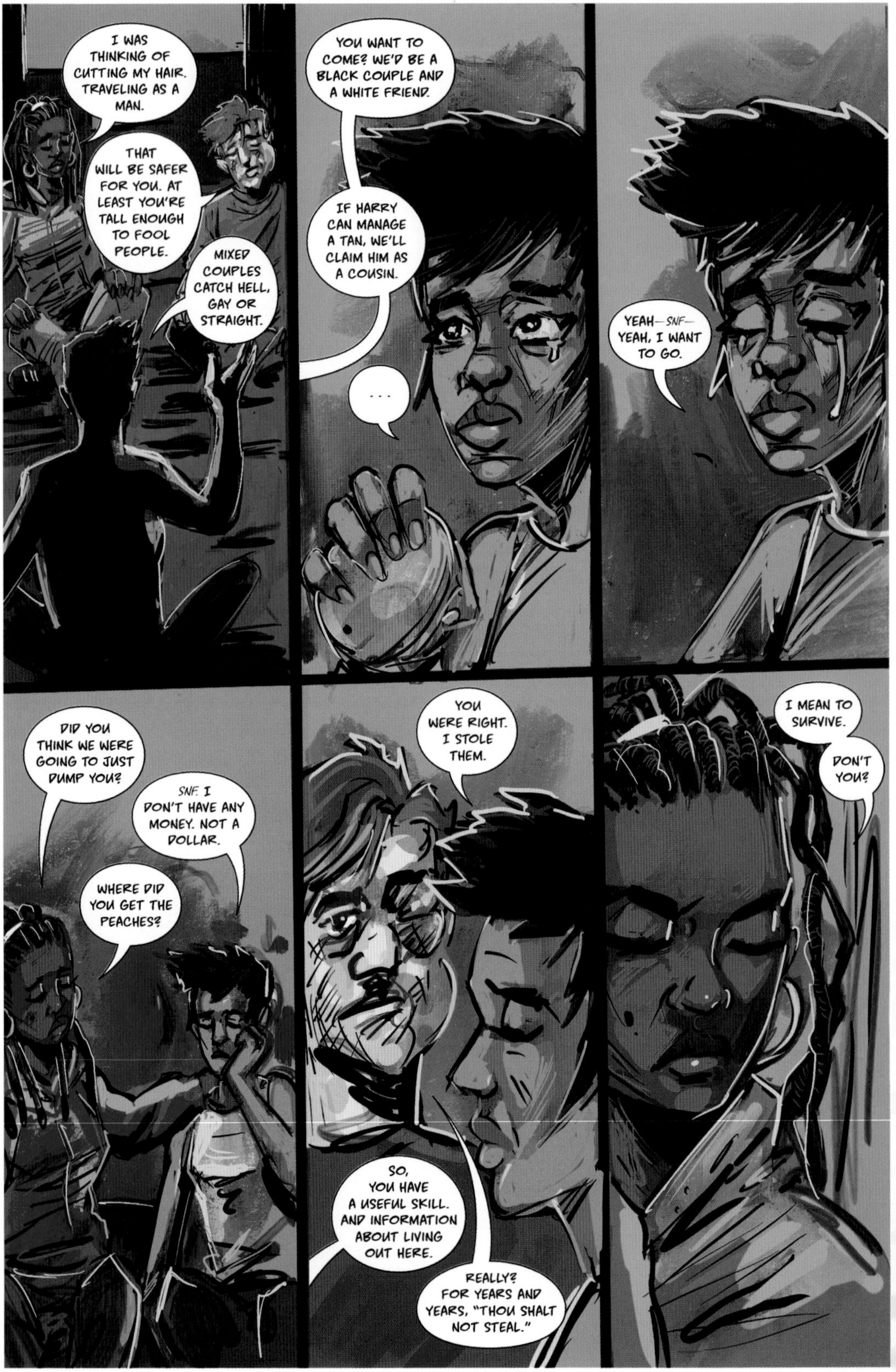
I WAS THINKING OF CUTTING MY HAIR. TRAVELING AS A MAN.
THAT WILL BE SAFER FOR YOU. AT LEAST YOU'RE TALL ENOUGH TO FOOL PEOPLE.
MIXED COUPLES CATCH HELL, GAY OR STRAIGHT.
YOU WANT TO COME? WE'D BE A BLACK COUPLE AND A WHITE FRIEND.
IF HARRY CAN MANAGE A TAN, WE'LL CLAIM HIM AS A COUSIN.
. . .
YEAH—SNF—YEAH, I WANT TO GO.
DID YOU THINK WE WERE GOING TO JUST DUMP YOU?
SNF. I DON'T HAVE ANY MONEY. NOT A DOLLAR.
WHERE DID YOU GET THE PEACHES?
YOU WERE RIGHT. I STOLE THEM.
SO, YOU HAVE A USEFUL SKILL. AND INFORMATION ABOUT LIVING OUT HERE.
REALLY? FOR YEARS AND YEARS, "THOU SHALT NOT STEAL."
I MEAN TO SURVIVE.
DON'T YOU?

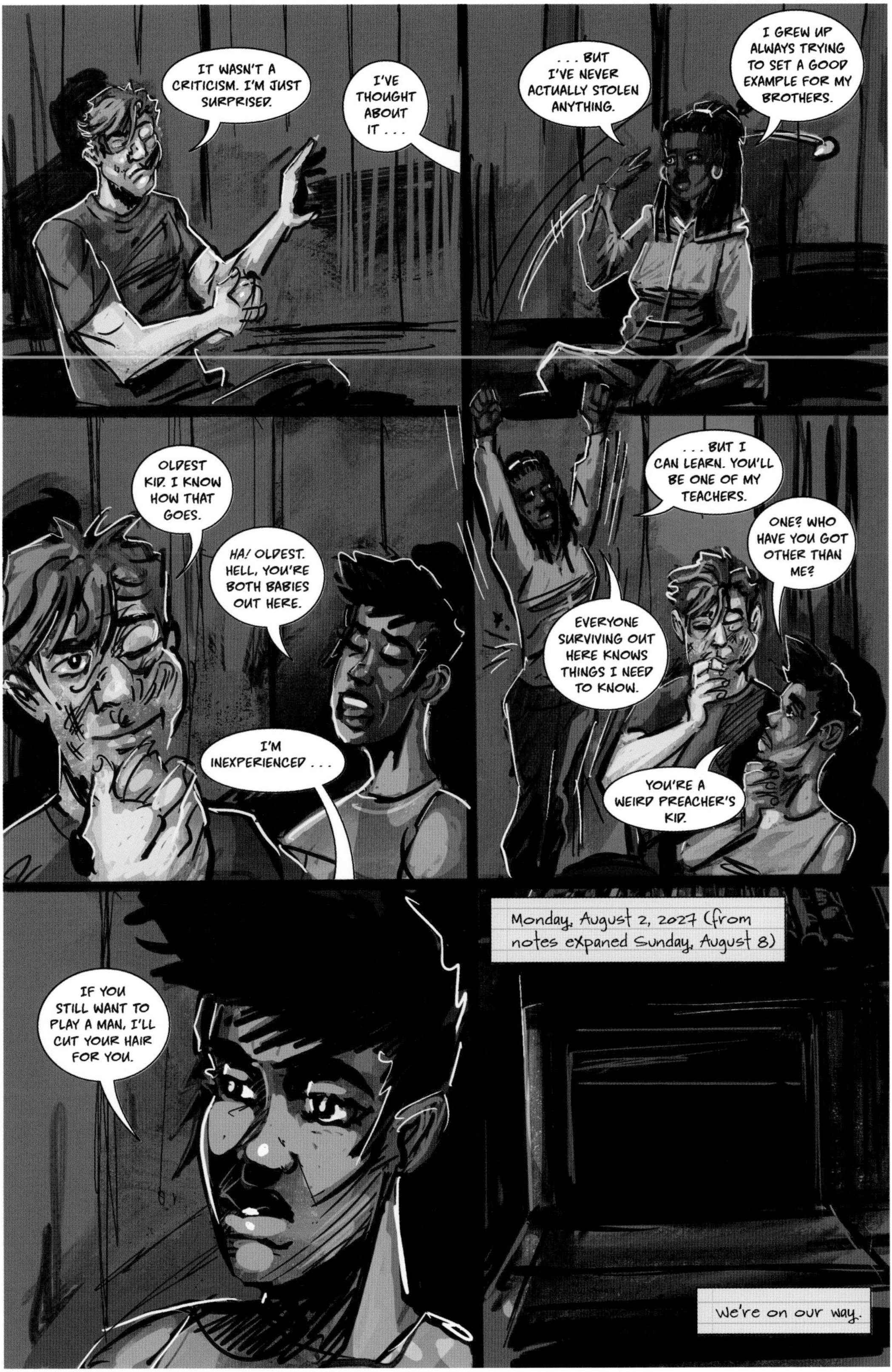

IT WASN'T A CRITICISM. I'M JUST SURPRISED.
I'VE THOUGHT ABOUT IT . . .
. . . BUT I'VE NEVER ACTUALLY STOLEN ANYTHING.
I GREW UP ALWAYS TRYING TO SET A GOOD EXAMPLE FOR MY BROTHERS.
OLDEST KID. I KNOW HOW THAT GOES.
HA! OLDEST. HELL, YOU'RE BOTH BABIES OUT HERE.
I'M INEXPERIENCED . . .
. . . BUT I CAN LEARN. YOU'LL BE ONE OF MY TEACHERS.
ONE? WHO HAVE YOU GOT OTHER THAN ME?
EVERYONE SURVIVING OUT HERE KNOWS THINGS I NEED TO KNOW.
YOU'RE A WEIRD PREACHER'S KID.
IF YOU STILL WANT TO PLAY A MAN, I'LL CUT YOUR HAIR FOR YOU.
Monday, August 2, 2027 (from notes expaned Sunday, August 8)
We're on our way.

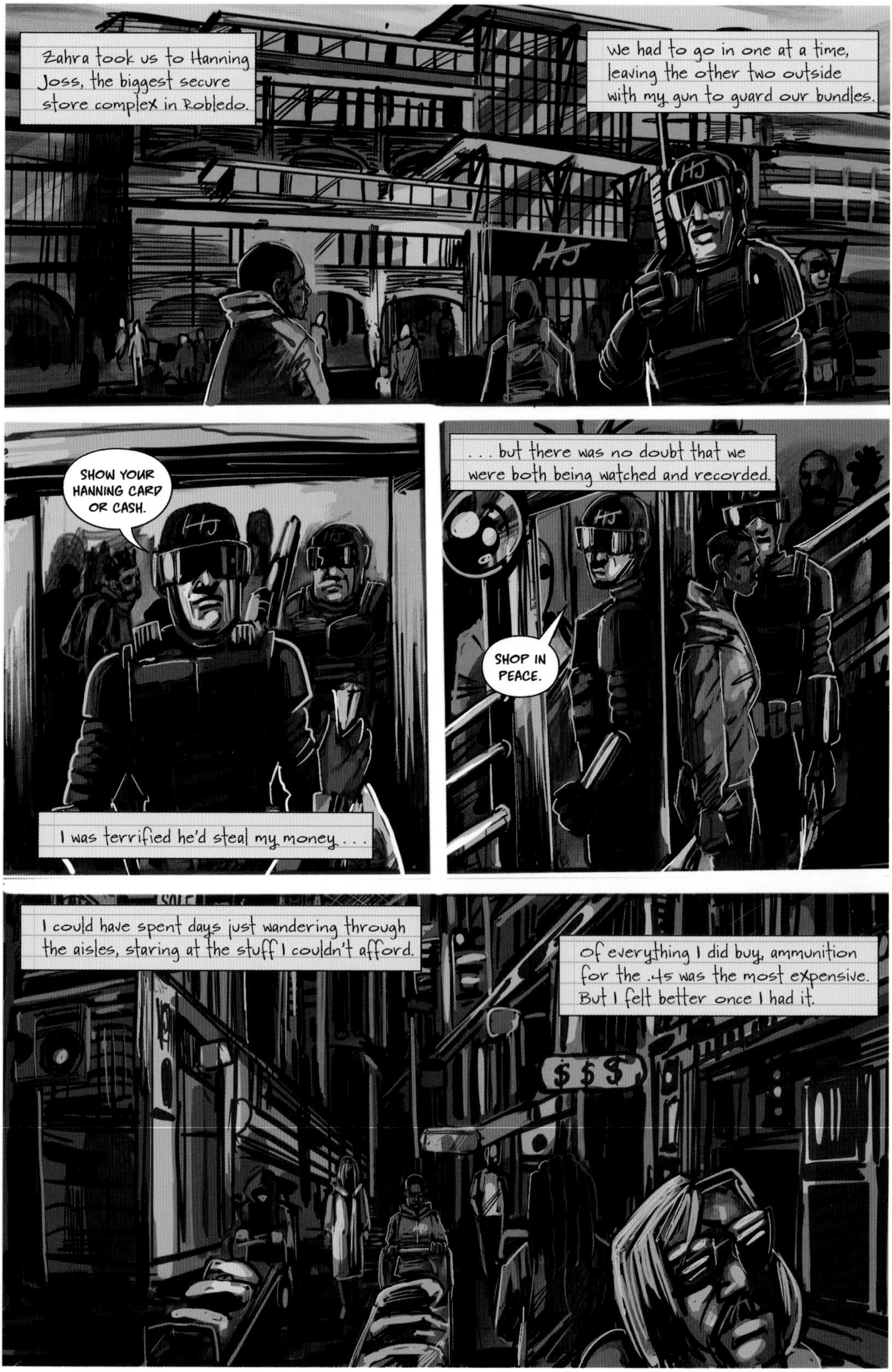
Zahra took us to Hanning Joss, the biggest secure store complex in Robledo.
We had to go in one at a time, leaving the other two outside with my gun to guard our bundles.
SHOW YOUR HANNING CARD OR CASH.
I was terrified he'd steal my money . . .
. . . but there was no doubt that we were both being watched and recorded.
SHOP IN PEACE.
I could have spent days just wandering through the aisles, staring at the stuff I couldn't afford.
Of everything I did buy, ammunition for the .45 was the most expensive. But I felt better once I had it.

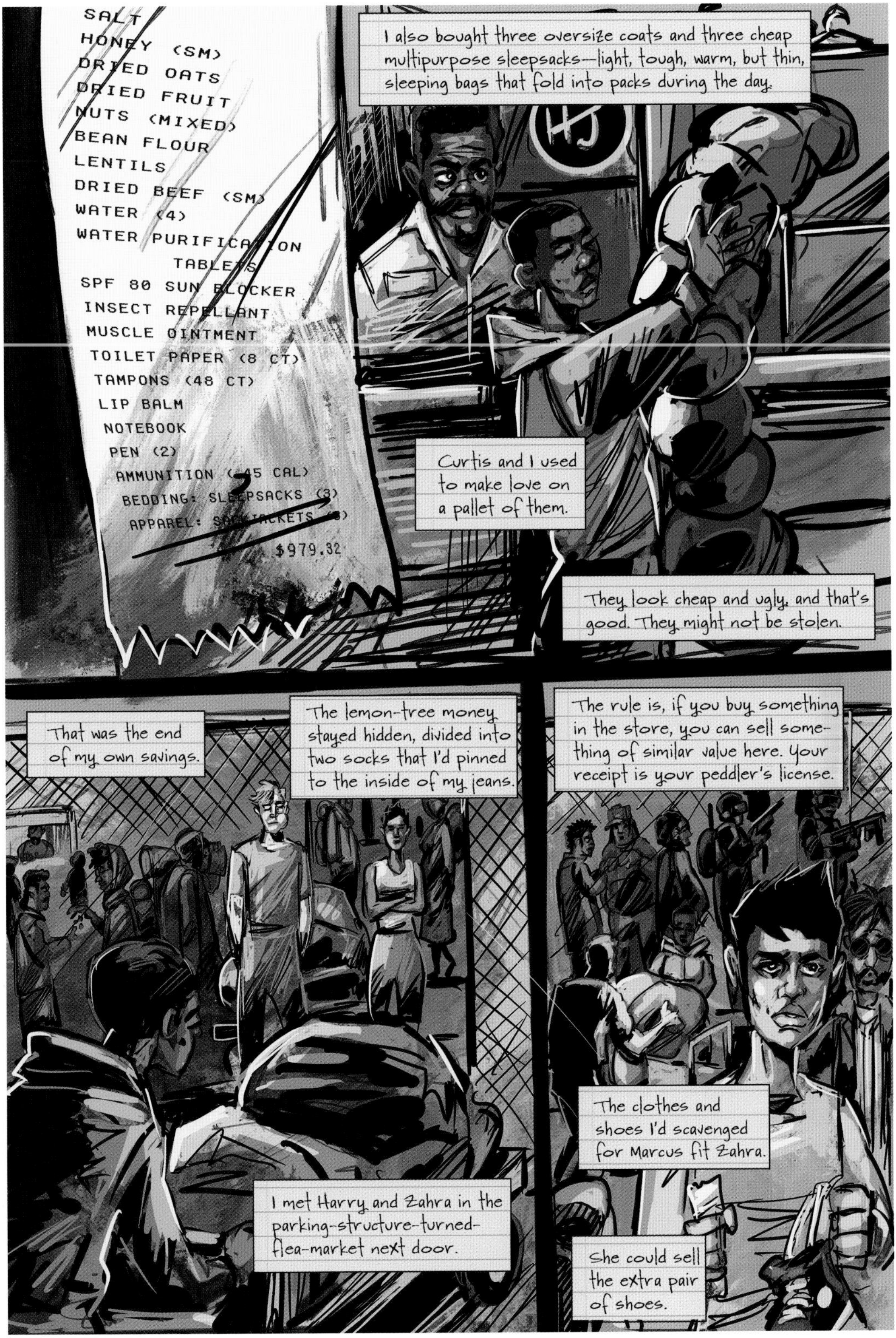
SALT
HONEY (SM)
DRIED OATS
DRIED FRUIT
NUTS (MIXED)
BEAN FLOUR
LENTILS
DRIED BEEF (SM)
WATER (4)
WATER PURIFICATION TABLETS
SPF 80 SUN BLOCKER
INSECT REPELLANT
MUSCLE OINTMENT
TOILET PAPER (8 CT)
TAMPONS (48 CT)
LIP BALM
NOTEBOOK
PEN (2)
AMMUNITION (.45 CAL)
BEDDING: SLEEPSACKS (3)
APPAREL:
$979.32
I also bought three oversize coats and three cheap multipurpose sleepsacks—light, tough, warm, but thin, sleeping bags that fold into packs during the day.
HJ
Curtis and I used to make love on a pallet of them.
They look cheap and ugly, and that's good. They might not be stolen.
That was the end of my own savings.
The lemon-tree money stayed hidden, divided into two socks that I'd pinned to the inside of my jeans.
I met Harry and Zahra in the parking-structure-turned-flea-market next door.
The rule is, if you buy something in the store, you can sell something of similar value here. Your receipt is your peddler's license.
The clothes and shoes I'd scavenged for Marcus fit Zahra.
She could sell the extra pair of shoes.

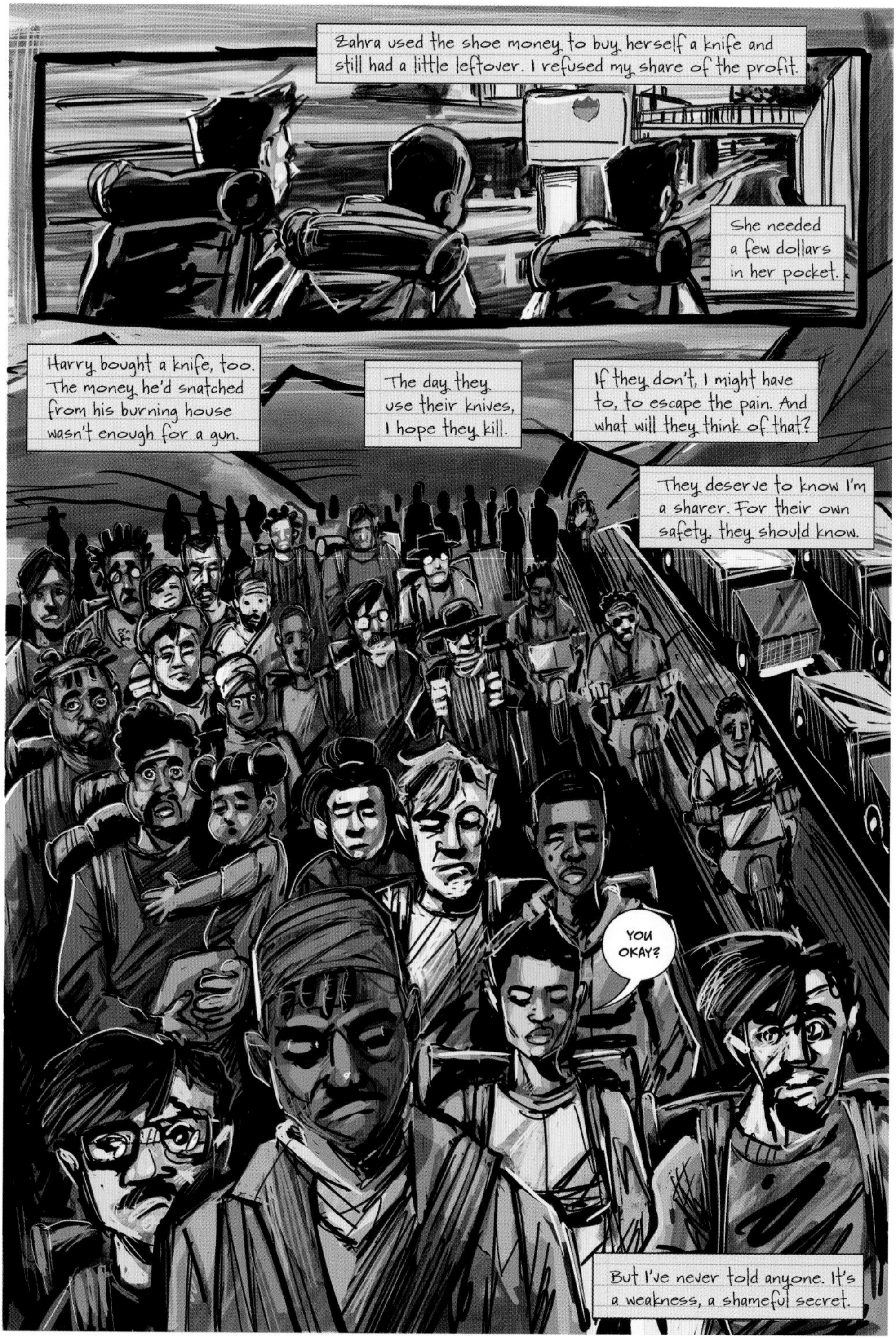
Zahra used the shoe money to buy herself a knife and still had a little leftover. I refused my share of the profit.
She needed a few dollars in her pocket.
Harry bought a knife, too. The money he'd snatched from his burning house wasn't enough for a gun.
The day they use their knives, I hope they kill.
If they don't, I might have to, to escape the pain. And what will they think of that?
They deserve to know I'm a sharer. For their own safety, they should know.
YOU OKAY?
But I've never told anyone. It's a weakness, a shameful secret.

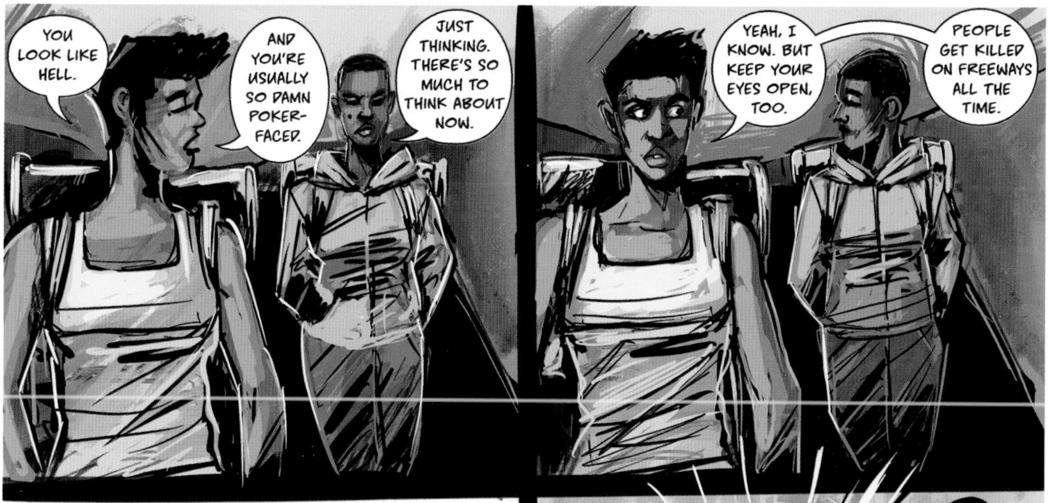
YOU LOOK LIKE HELL.
AND YOU'RE USUALLY SO DAMN POKER-FACED.
JUST THINKING. THERE'S SO MUCH TO THINK ABOUT NOW.
YEAH, I KNOW. BUT KEEP YOUR EYES OPEN, TOO.
PEOPLE GET KILLED ON FREEWAYS ALL THE TIME.

Earthseed
Cast on new ground
Must first perceive
That it knows nothing.

EARTHSEED: THE BOOKS OF THE LIVING

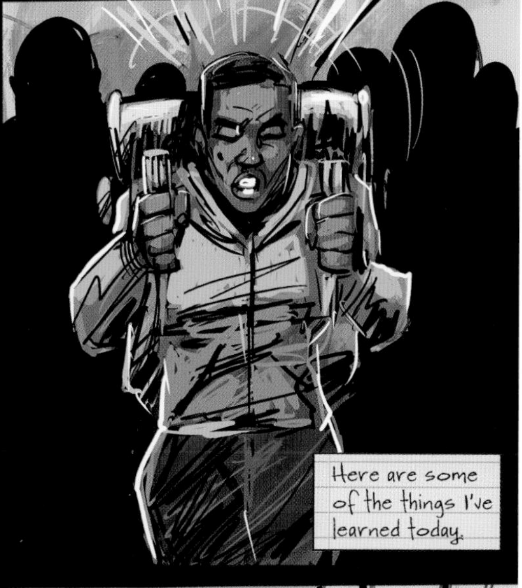
Here are some of the things I've learned today.

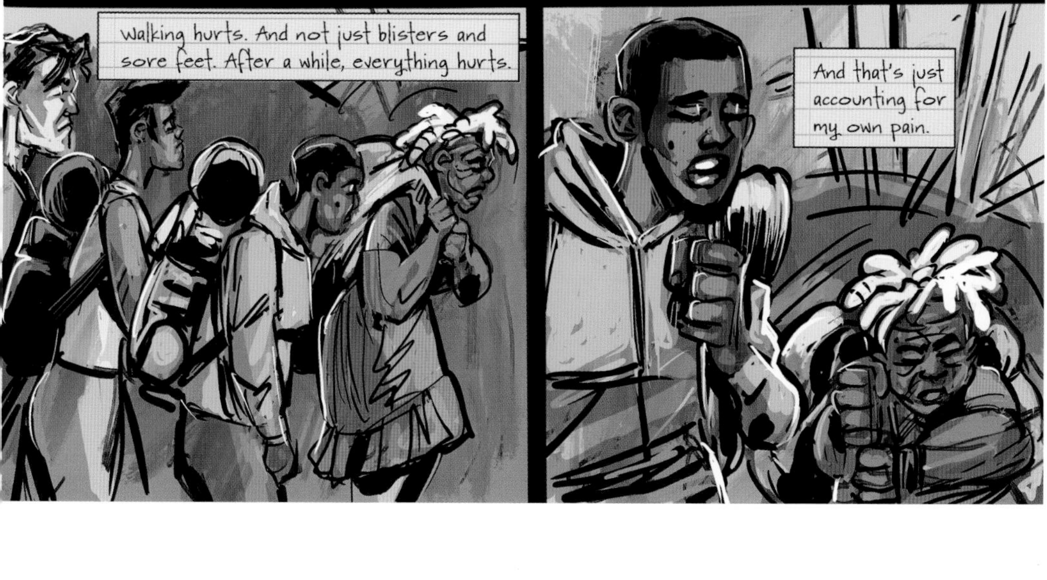
Walking hurts. And not just blisters and sore feet. After a while, everything hurts.
And that's just accounting for my own pain.

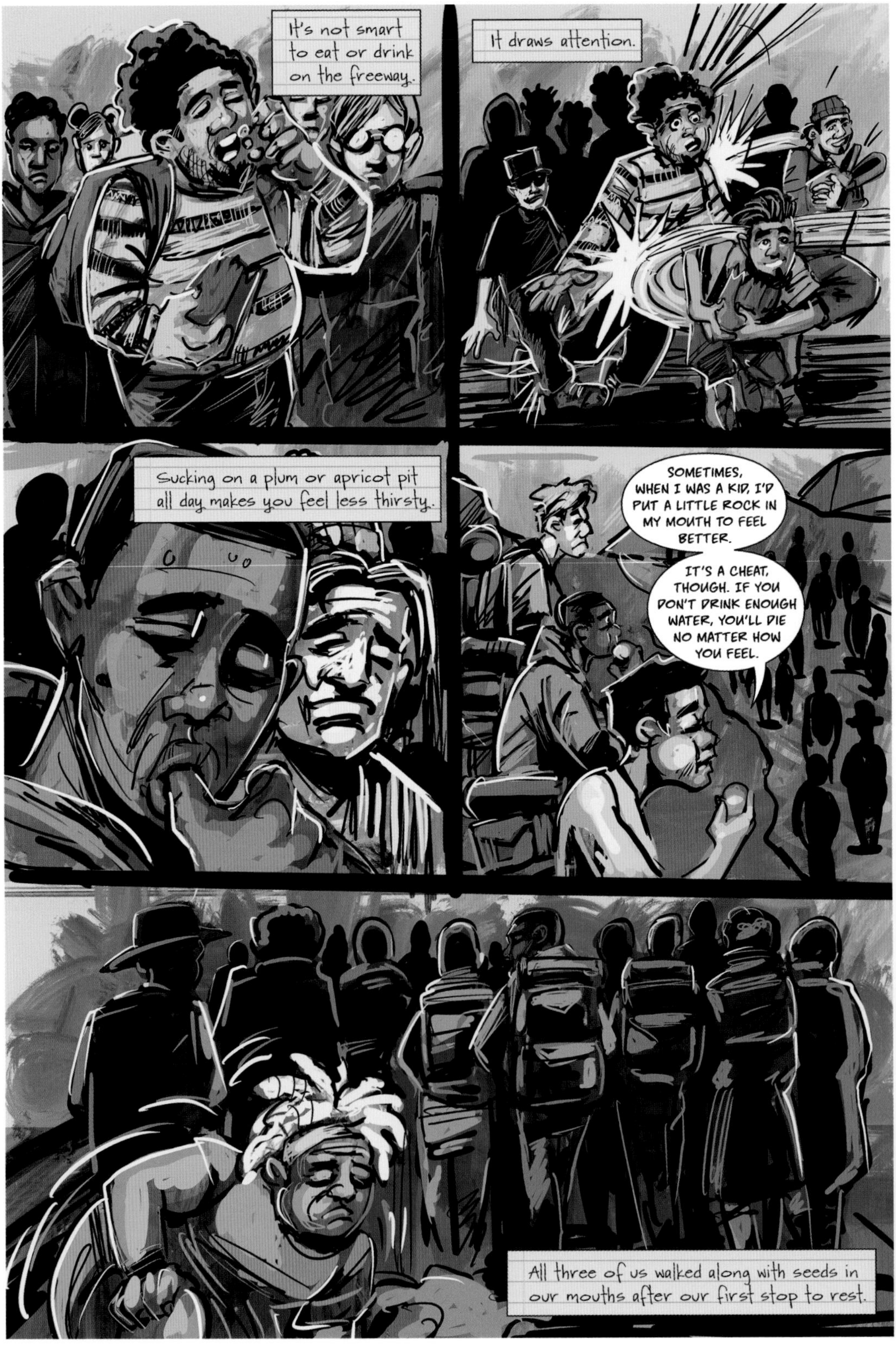
It's not smart to eat or drink on the freeway.
It draws attention.
Sucking on a plum or apricot pit all day makes you feel less thirsty.
SOMETIMES, WHEN I WAS A KID, I'D PUT A LITTLE ROCK IN MY MOUTH TO FEEL BETTER.
IT'S A CHEAT, THOUGH. IF YOU DON'T DRINK ENOUGH WATER, YOU'LL DIE NO MATTER HOW YOU FEEL.
All three of us walked along with seeds in our mouths after our first stop to rest.

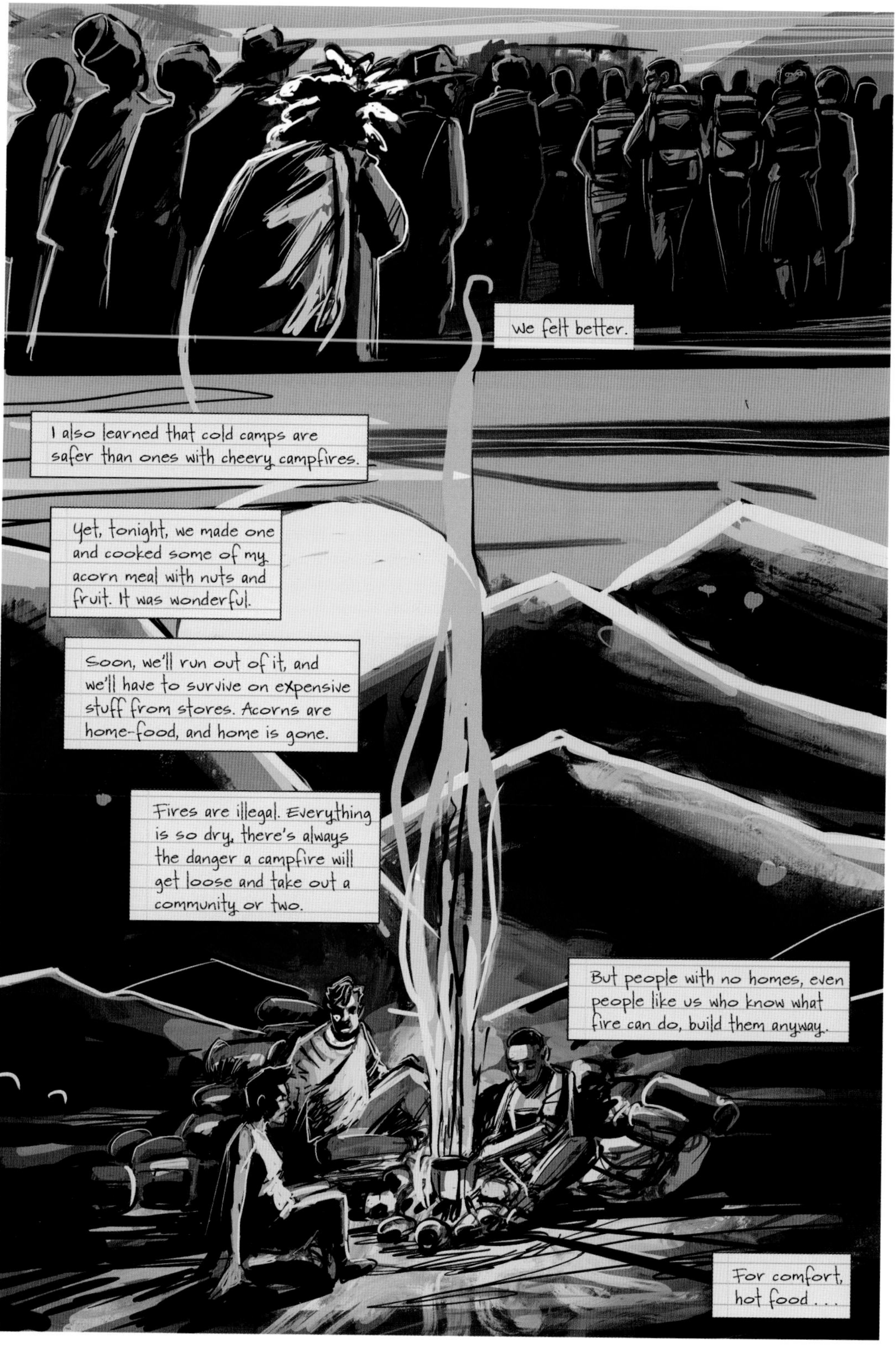
we felt better.
I also learned that cold camps are safer than ones with cheery campfires.
Yet, tonight, we made one and cooked some of my acorn meal with nuts and fruit. It was wonderful.
Soon, we'll run out of it, and we'll have to survive on expensive stuff from stores. Acorns are home-food, and home is gone.
Fires are illegal. Everything is so dry, there's always the danger a campfire will get loose and take out a community or two.
But people with no homes, even people like us who know what fire can do, build them anyway.
For comfort, hot food . . .

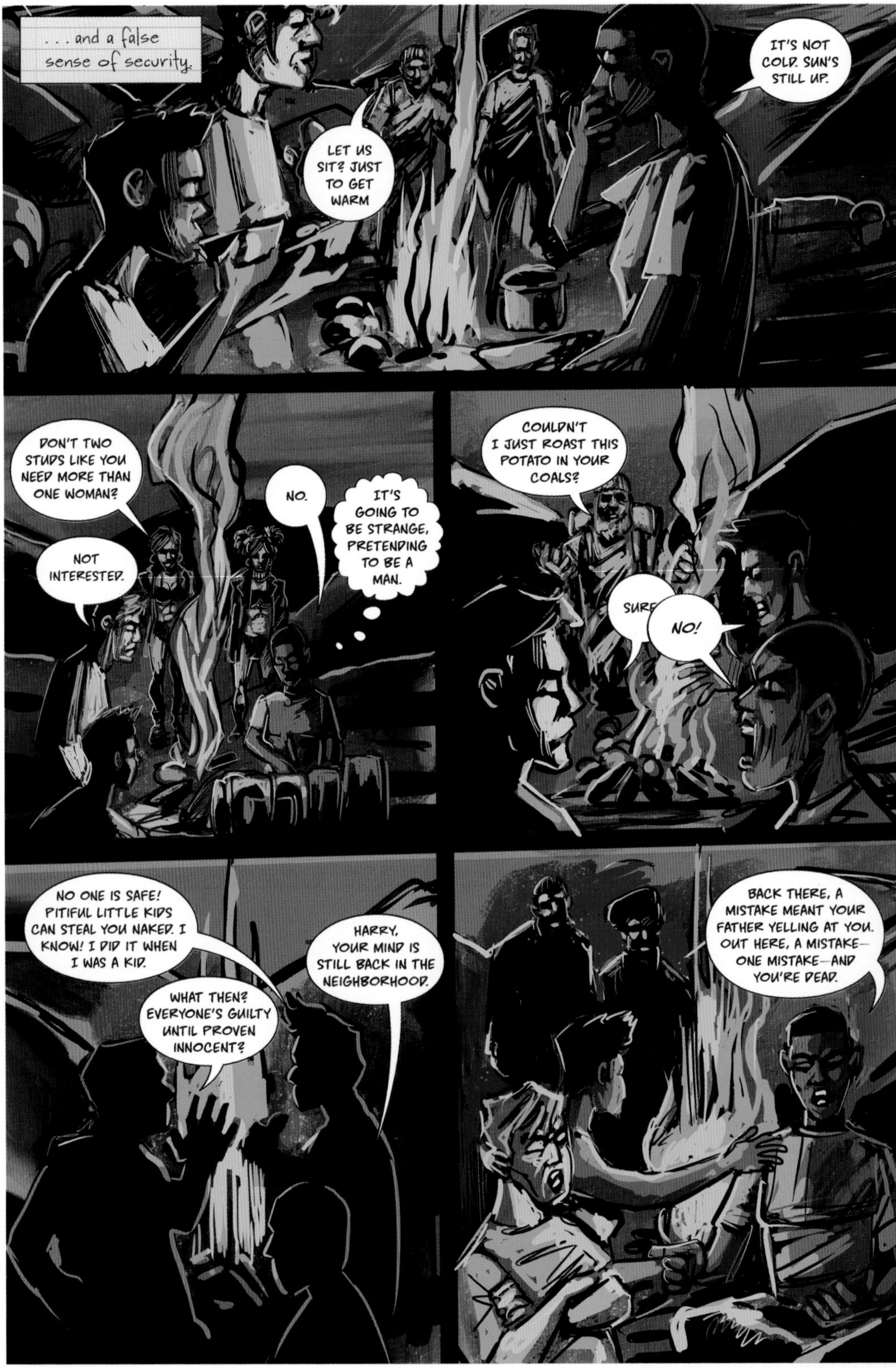
. . . and a false sense of security.
IT'S NOT COLD. SUN'S STILL UP.
LET US SIT? JUST TO GET WARM
DON'T TWO STUDS LIKE YOU NEED MORE THAN ONE WOMAN?
NOT INTERESTED.
NO.
IT'S GOING TO BE STRANGE, PRETENDING TO BE A MAN.
COULDN'T I JUST ROAST THIS POTATO IN YOUR COALS?
SURE
NO!
NO ONE IS SAFE! PITIFUL LITTLE KIDS CAN STEAL YOU NAKED. I KNOW! I DID IT WHEN I WAS A KID.
WHAT THEN? EVERYONE'S GUILTY UNTIL PROVEN INNOCENT?
HARRY, YOUR MIND IS STILL BACK IN THE NEIGHBORHOOD.
BACK THERE, A MISTAKE MEANT YOUR FATHER YELLING AT YOU. OUT HERE, A MISTAKE— ONE MISTAKE—AND YOU'RE DEAD.

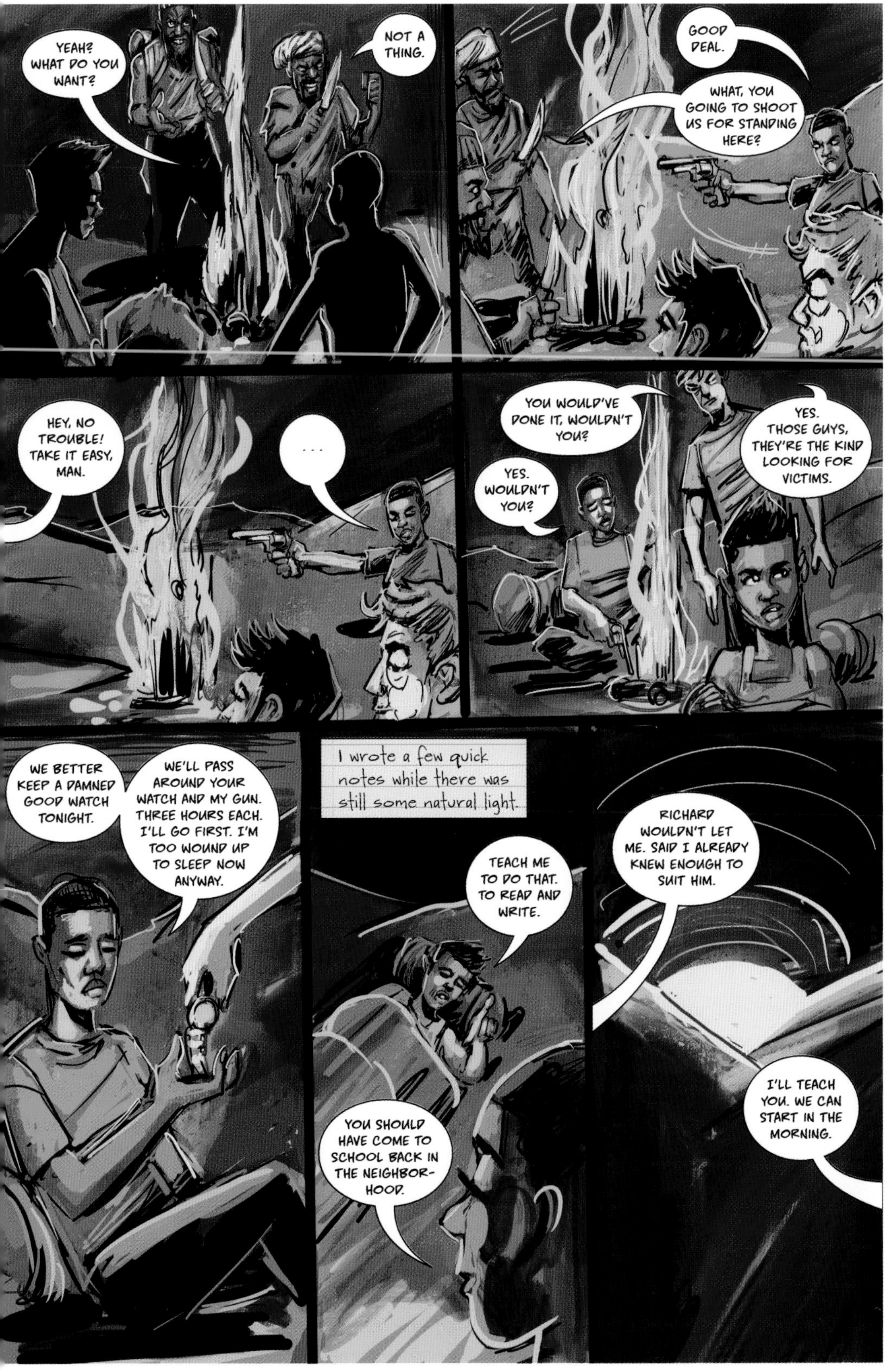
YEAH? WHAT DO YOU WANT?
NOT A THING.
GOOD DEAL.
WHAT, YOU GOING TO SHOOT US FOR STANDING HERE?
HEY, NO TROUBLE! TAKE IT EASY, MAN.
. . .
YOU WOULD'VE DONE IT, WOULDN'T YOU?
YES. WOULDN'T YOU?
YES. THOSE GUYS, THEY'RE THE KIND LOOKING FOR VICTIMS.
WE BETTER KEEP A DAMNED GOOD WATCH TONIGHT.
WE'LL PASS AROUND YOUR WATCH AND MY GUN. THREE HOURS EACH. I'LL GO FIRST. I'M TOO WOUND UP TO SLEEP NOW ANYWAY.
I wrote a few quick notes while there was still some natural light.
TEACH ME TO DO THAT. TO READ AND WRITE.
YOU SHOULD HAVE COME TO SCHOOL BACK IN THE NEIGHBORHOOD.
RICHARD WOULDN'T LET ME. SAID I ALREADY KNEW ENOUGH TO SUIT HIM.
I'LL TEACH YOU. WE CAN START IN THE MORNING.

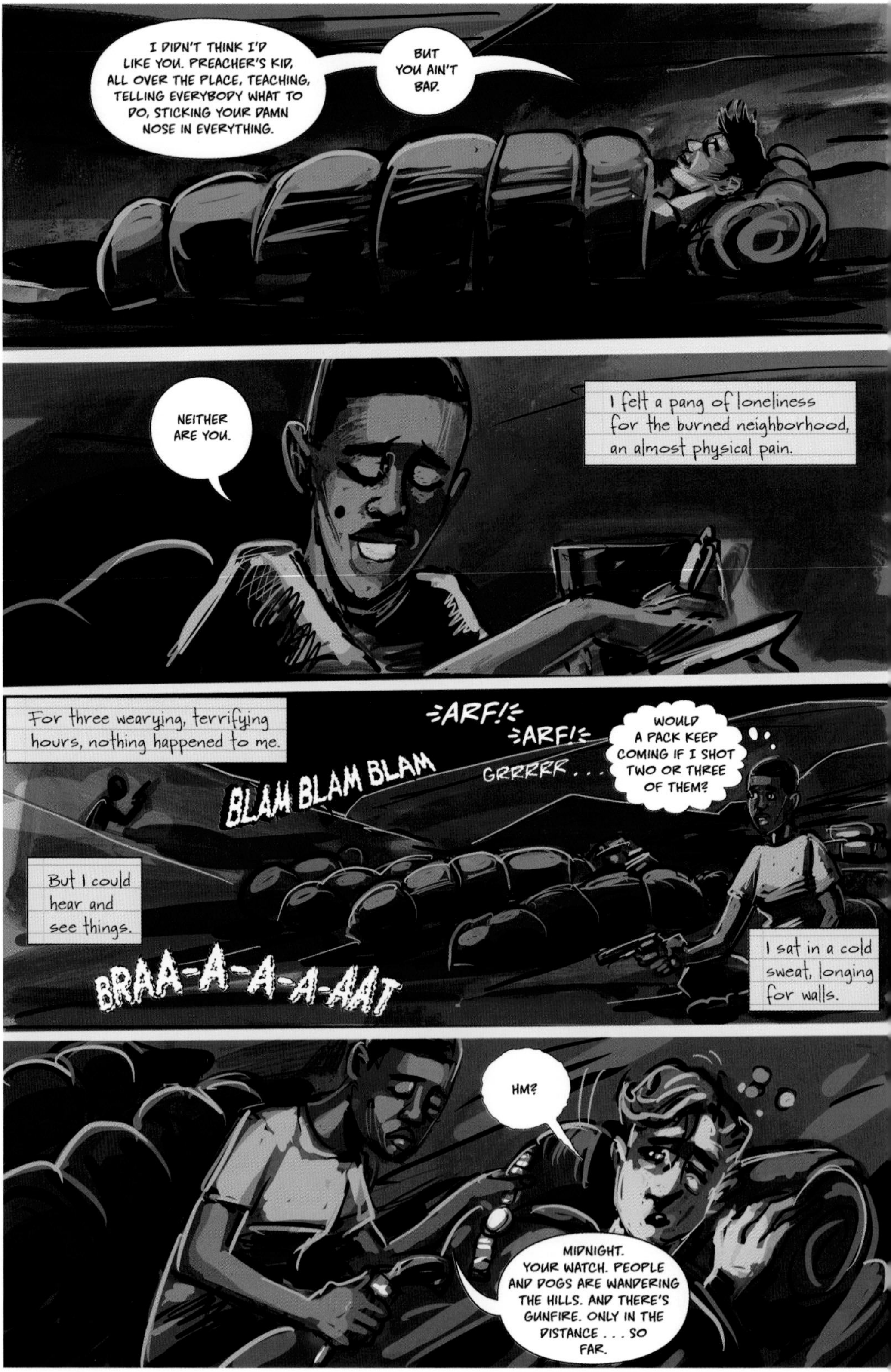

I DIDN'T THINK I'D LIKE YOU. PREACHER'S KID, ALL OVER THE PLACE, TEACHING, TELLING EVERYBODY WHAT TO DO, STICKING YOUR DAMN NOSE IN EVERYTHING.
BUT YOU AIN'T BAD.
NEITHER ARE YOU.
I felt a pang of loneliness for the burned neighborhood, an almost physical pain.
For three wearying, terrifying hours, nothing happened to me.
ARF!
ARF!
GRRRRR . . .
WOULD A PACK KEEP COMING IF I SHOT TWO OR THREE OF THEM?
BLAM BLAM BLAM
But I could hear and see things.
BRAA-A-A-A-AAT
I sat in a cold sweat, longing for walls.
HM?
MIDNIGHT. YOUR WATCH. PEOPLE AND DOGS ARE WANDERING THE HILLS. AND THERE'S GUNFIRE. ONLY IN THE DISTANCE . . . SO FAR.

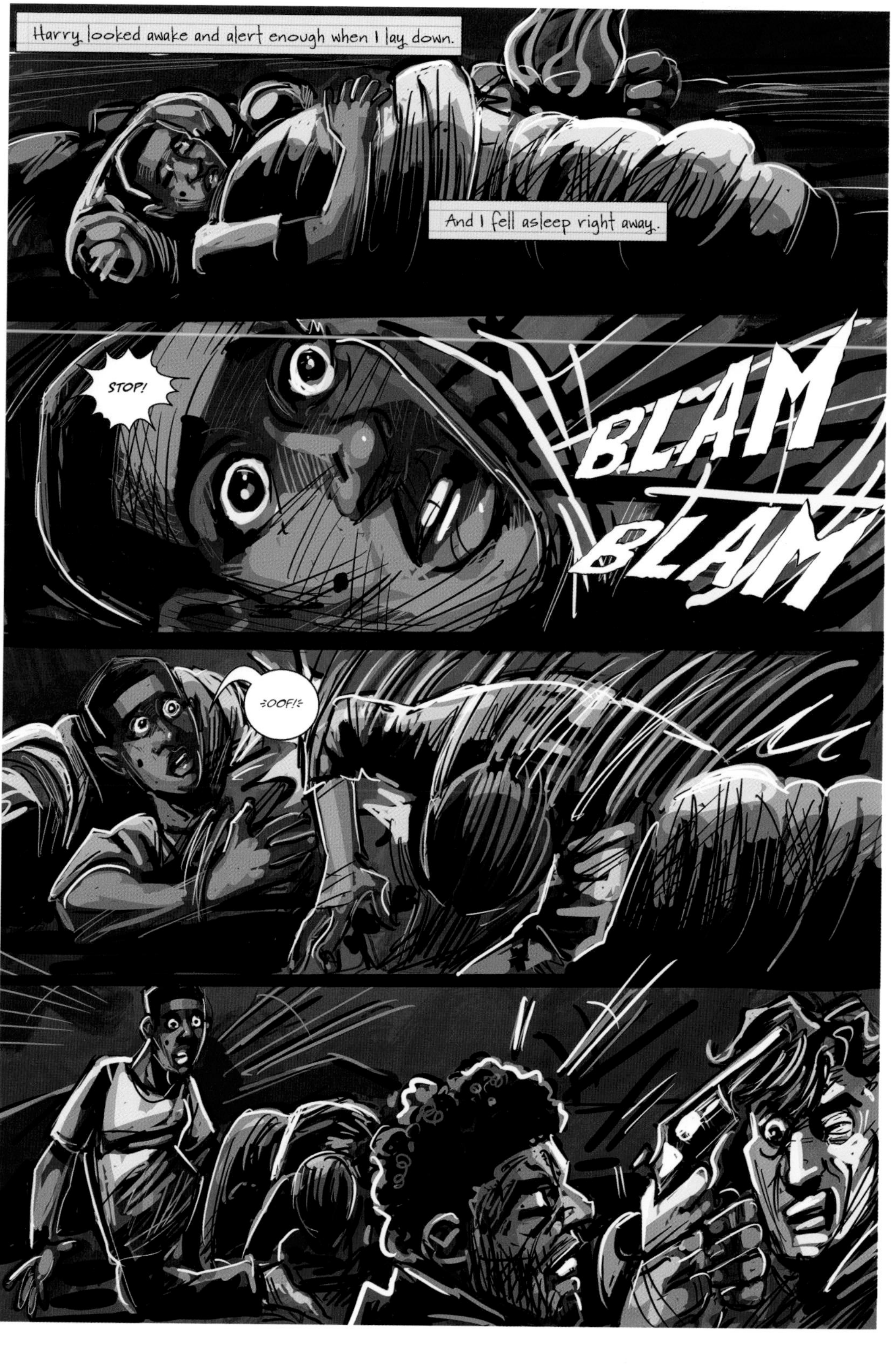
Harry looked awake and alert enough when I lay down.
And I fell asleep right away.
STOP!
BLAM
BLAM
OOF!

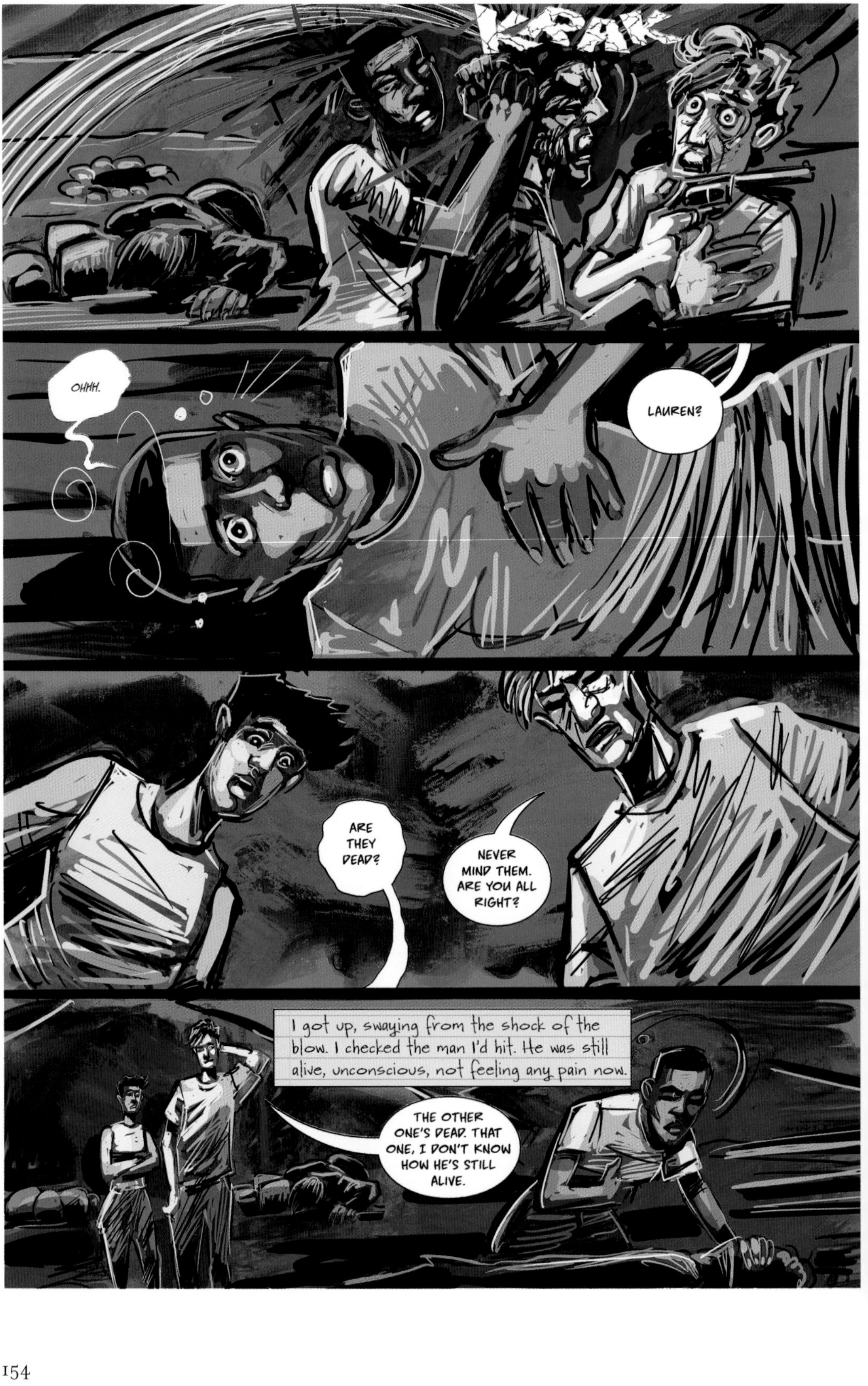
OHHH.
LAUREN?
ARE THEY DEAD?
NEVER MIND THEM. ARE YOU ALL RIGHT?
I got up, swaying from the shock of the blow. I checked the man I'd hit. He was still alive, unconscious, not feeling any pain now.
THE OTHER ONE'S DEAD. THAT ONE, I DON'T KNOW HOW HE'S STILL ALIVE.

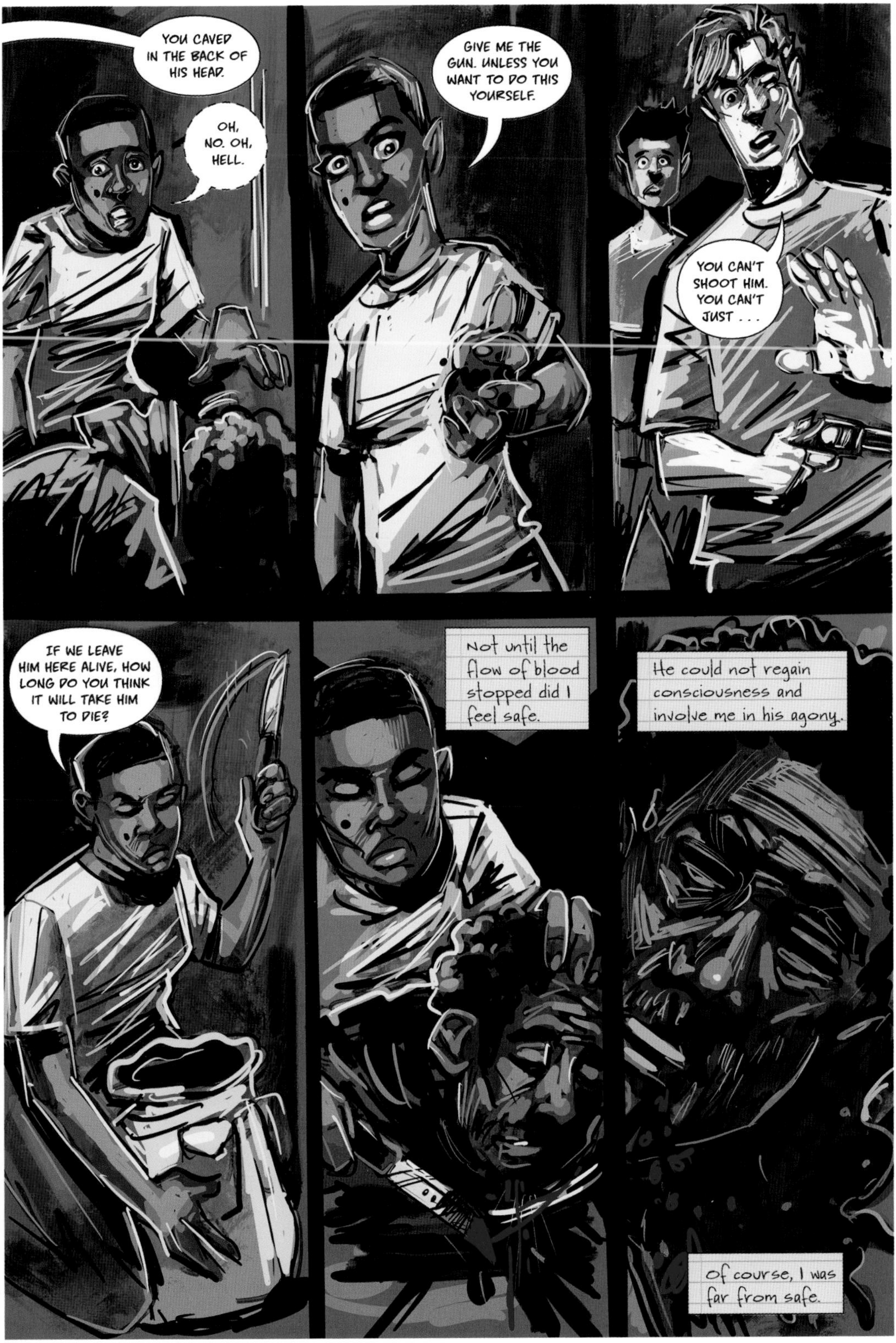
YOU CAVED IN THE BACK OF HIS HEAD.
OH, NO. OH, HELL.
GIVE ME THE GUN. UNLESS YOU WANT TO DO THIS YOURSELF.
YOU CAN'T SHOOT HIM. YOU CAN'T JUST . . .
IF WE LEAVE HIM HERE ALIVE, HOW LONG DO YOU THINK IT WILL TAKE HIM TO DIE?
Not until the flow of blood stopped did I feel safe.
He could not regain consciousness and involve me in his agony.
Of course, I was far from safe.

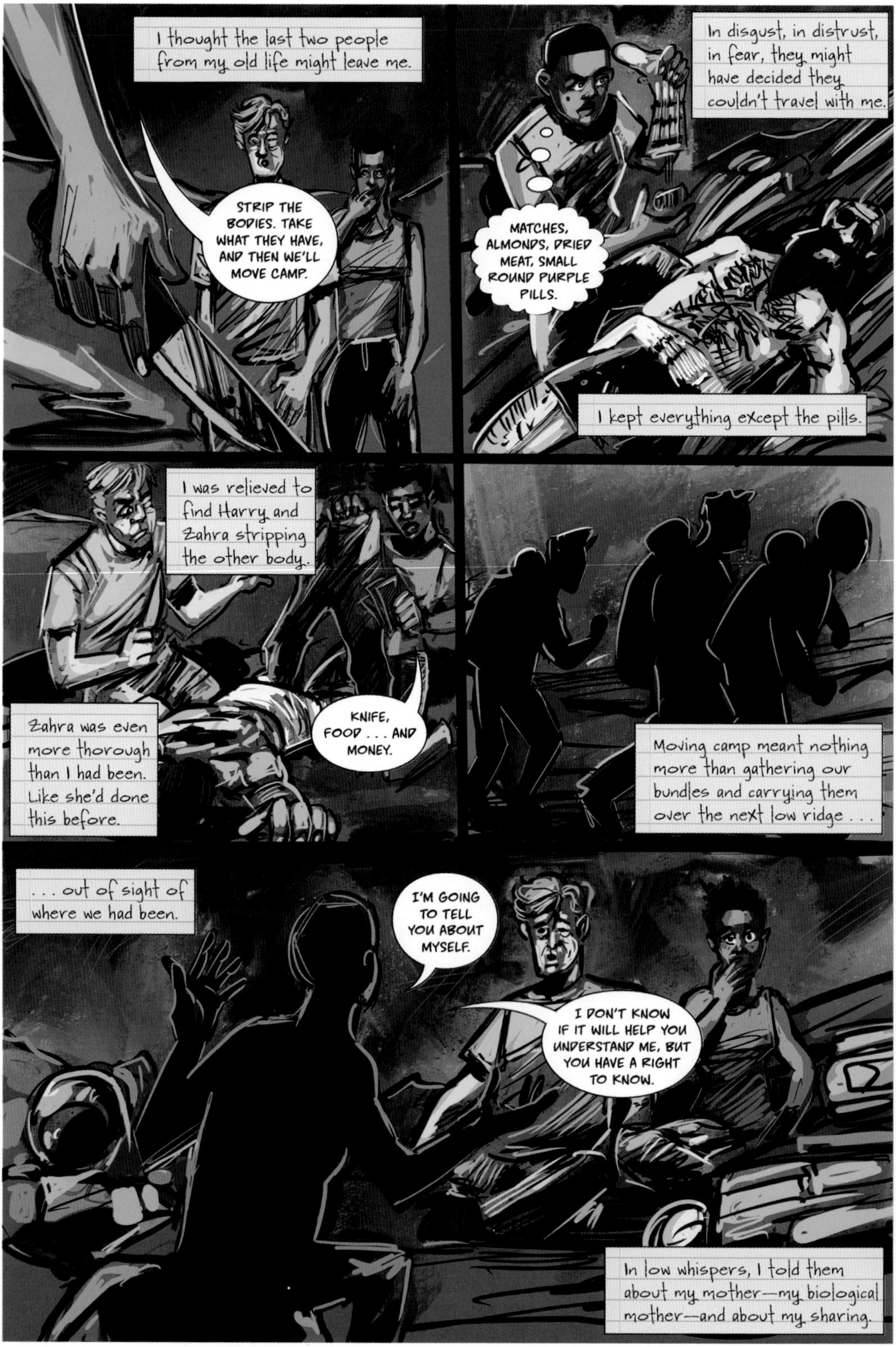
I thought the last two people from my old life might leave me.
STRIP THE BODIES. TAKE WHAT THEY HAVE, AND THEN WE'LL MOVE CAMP.
In disgust, in distrust, in fear, they might have decided they couldn't travel with me.
MATCHES, ALMONDS, DRIED MEAT, SMALL ROUND PURPLE PILLS.
I kept everything except the pills.
I was relieved to find Harry and Zahra stripping the other body.
Zahra was even more thorough than I had been. Like she'd done this before.
KNIFE, FOOD . . . AND MONEY.
Moving camp meant nothing more than gathering our bundles and carrying them over the next low ridge . . .
. . . out of sight of where we had been.
I'M GOING TO TELL YOU ABOUT MYSELF.
I DON'T KNOW IF IT WILL HELP YOU UNDERSTAND ME, BUT YOU HAVE A RIGHT TO KNOW.
In low whispers, I told them about my mother—my biological mother—and about my sharing.

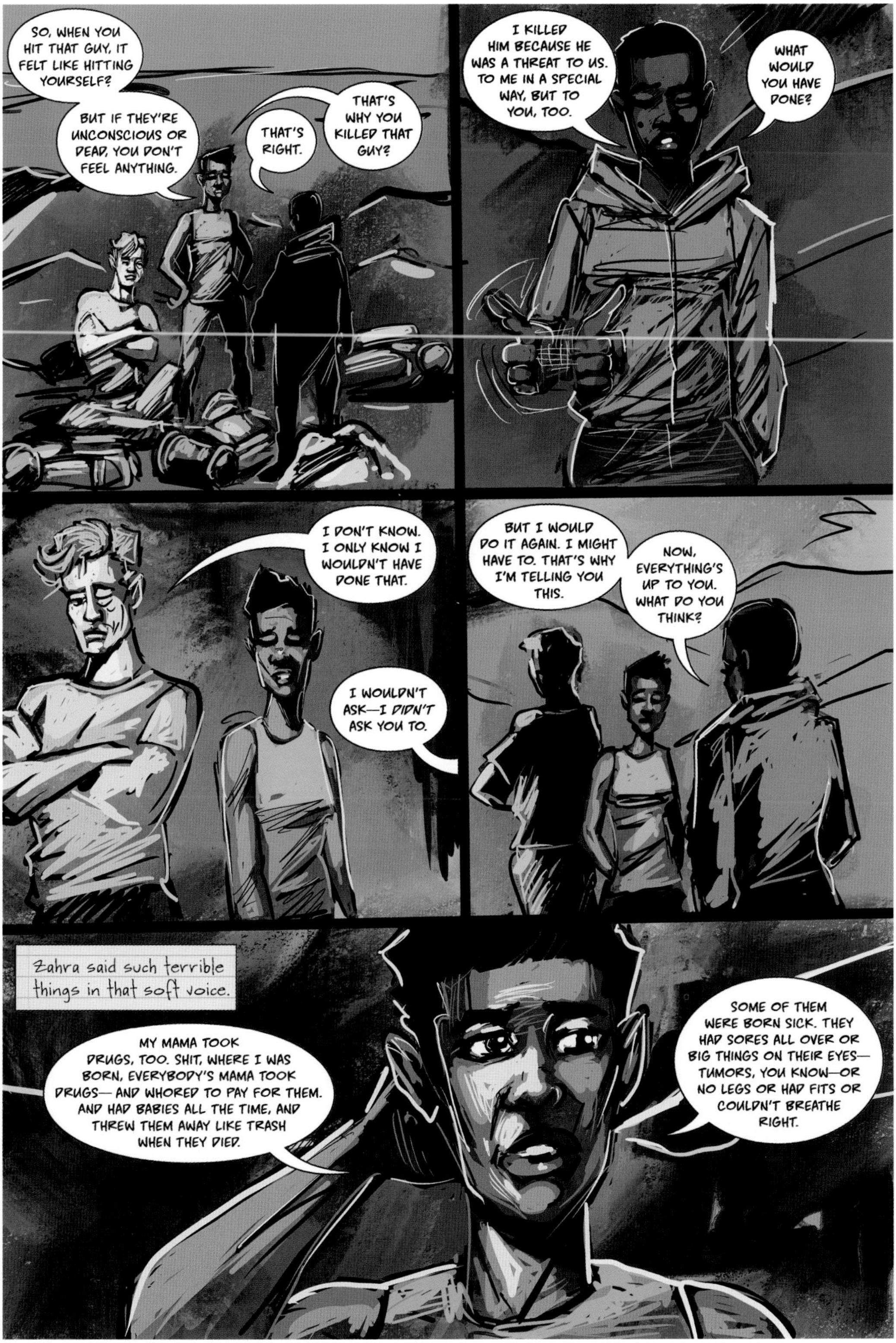
SO, WHEN YOU HIT THAT GUY, IT FELT LIKE HITTING YOURSELF?
BUT IF THEY'RE UNCONSCIOUS OR DEAD, YOU DON'T FEEL ANYTHING.
THAT'S RIGHT.
THAT'S WHY YOU KILLED THAT GUY?
I KILLED HIM BECAUSE HE WAS A THREAT TO US. TO ME IN A SPECIAL WAY, BUT TO YOU, TOO.
WHAT WOULD YOU HAVE DONE?
I DON'T KNOW. I ONLY KNOW I WOULDN'T HAVE DONE THAT.
I WOULDN'T ASK—I DIDN'T ASK YOU TO.
BUT I WOULD DO IT AGAIN. I MIGHT HAVE TO. THAT'S WHY I'M TELLING YOU THIS.
NOW, EVERYTHING'S UP TO YOU. WHAT DO YOU THINK?
Zahra said such terrible things in that soft voice.
MY MAMA TOOK DRUGS, TOO. SHIT, WHERE I WAS BORN, EVERYBODY'S MAMA TOOK DRUGS— AND WHORED TO PAY FOR THEM. AND HAD BABIES ALL THE TIME, AND THREW THEM AWAY LIKE TRASH WHEN THEY DIED.
SOME OF THEM WERE BORN SICK. THEY HAD SORES ALL OVER OR BIG THINGS ON THEIR EYES— TUMORS, YOU KNOW—OR NO LEGS OR HAD FITS OR COULDN'T BREATHE RIGHT.

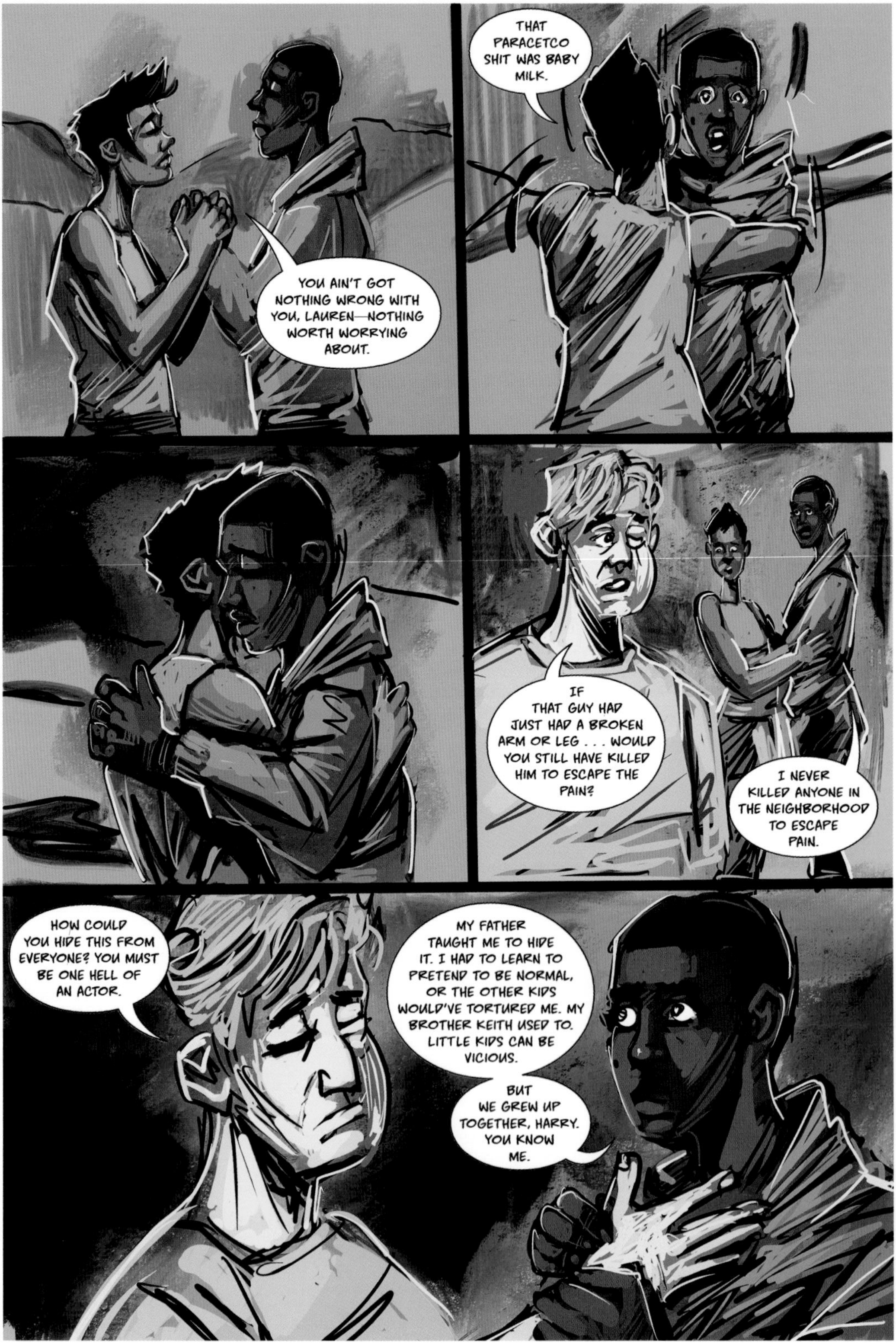
YOU AIN'T GOT NOTHING WRONG WITH YOU, LAUREN—NOTHING WORTH WORRYING ABOUT.
THAT PARACETCO SHIT WAS BABY MILK.
IF THAT GUY HAD JUST HAD A BROKEN ARM OR LEG . . . WOULD YOU STILL HAVE KILLED HIM TO ESCAPE THE PAIN?
I NEVER KILLED ANYONE IN THE NEIGHBORHOOD TO ESCAPE PAIN.
HOW COULD YOU HIDE THIS FROM EVERYONE? YOU MUST BE ONE HELL OF AN ACTOR.
MY FATHER TAUGHT ME TO HIDE IT. I HAD TO LEARN TO PRETEND TO BE NORMAL, OR THE OTHER KIDS WOULD'VE TORTURED ME. MY BROTHER KEITH USED TO. LITTLE KIDS CAN BE VICIOUS.
BUT WE GREW UP TOGETHER, HARRY. YOU KNOW ME.

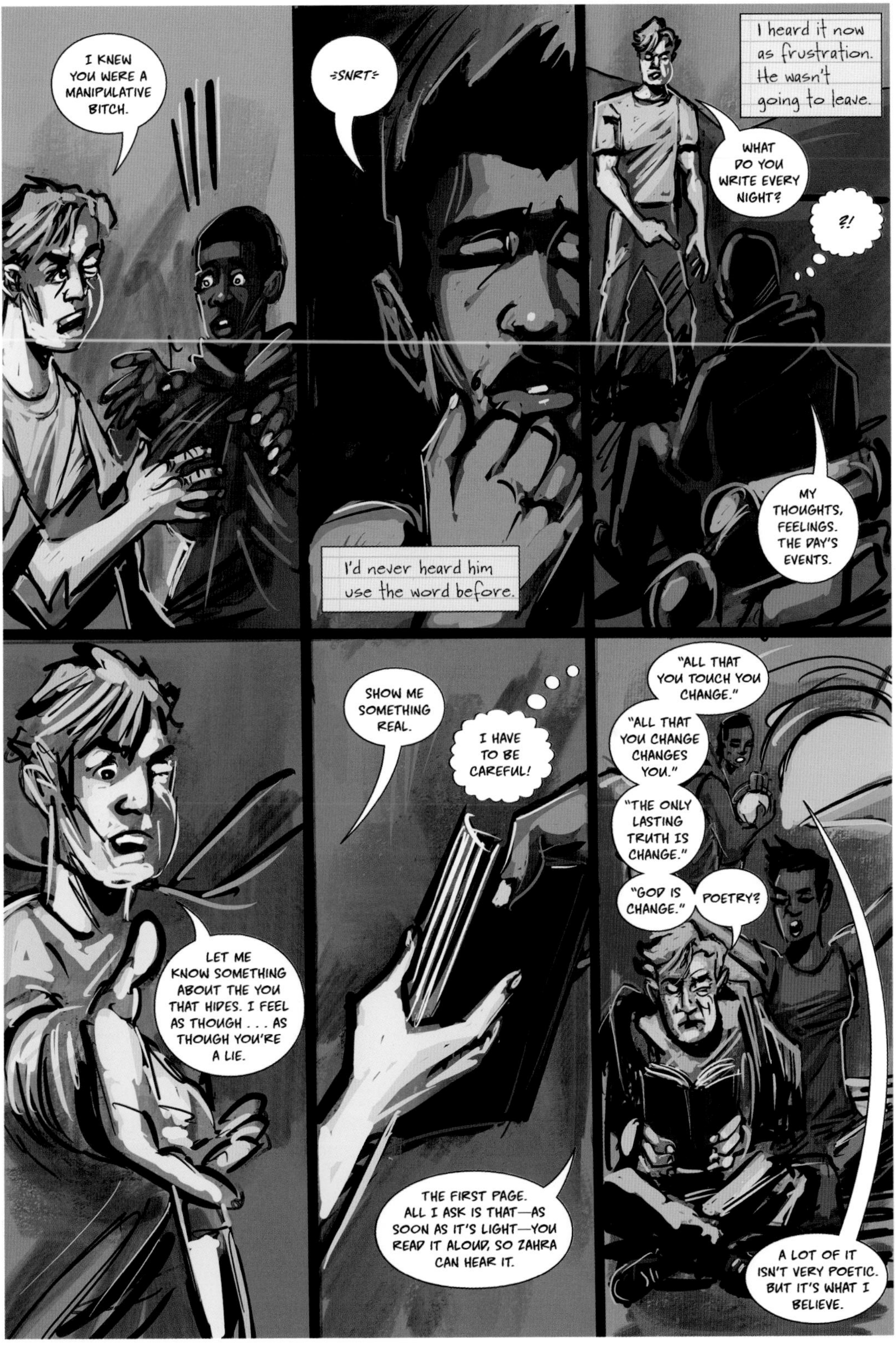
I KNEW YOU WERE A MANIPULATIVE BITCH.
=SNRT=
I'd never heard him use the word before.
I heard it now as frustration. He wasn't going to leave.
WHAT DO YOU WRITE EVERY NIGHT?
?!
MY THOUGHTS, FEELINGS. THE DAY'S EVENTS.
LET ME KNOW SOMETHING ABOUT THE YOU THAT HIDES. I FEEL AS THOUGH . . . AS THOUGH YOU'RE A LIE.
SHOW ME SOMETHING REAL.
I HAVE TO BE CAREFUL!
THE FIRST PAGE. ALL I ASK IS THAT—AS SOON AS IT'S LIGHT—YOU READ IT ALOUD, SO ZAHRA CAN HEAR IT.
"ALL THAT YOU TOUCH YOU CHANGE."
"ALL THAT YOU CHANGE CHANGES YOU."
"THE ONLY LASTING TRUTH IS CHANGE."
"GOD IS CHANGE."
POETRY?
A LOT OF IT ISN'T VERY POETIC. BUT IT'S WHAT I BELIEVE.

Embrace diversity.
Unite—
Or be divided,
robbed,
ruled,
killed
By those who see you as prey.
Embrace diversity
Or be destroyed.

EARTHSEED: THE
BOOKS OF THE LIVING

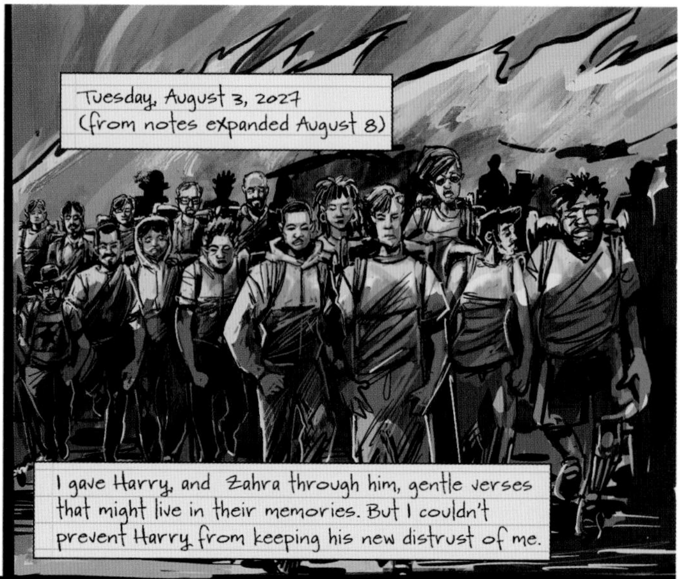

Tuesday, August 3, 2027
(from notes expanded August 8)
I gave Harry, and Zahra through him, gentle verses that might live in their memories. But I couldn't prevent Harry from keeping his new distrust of me.

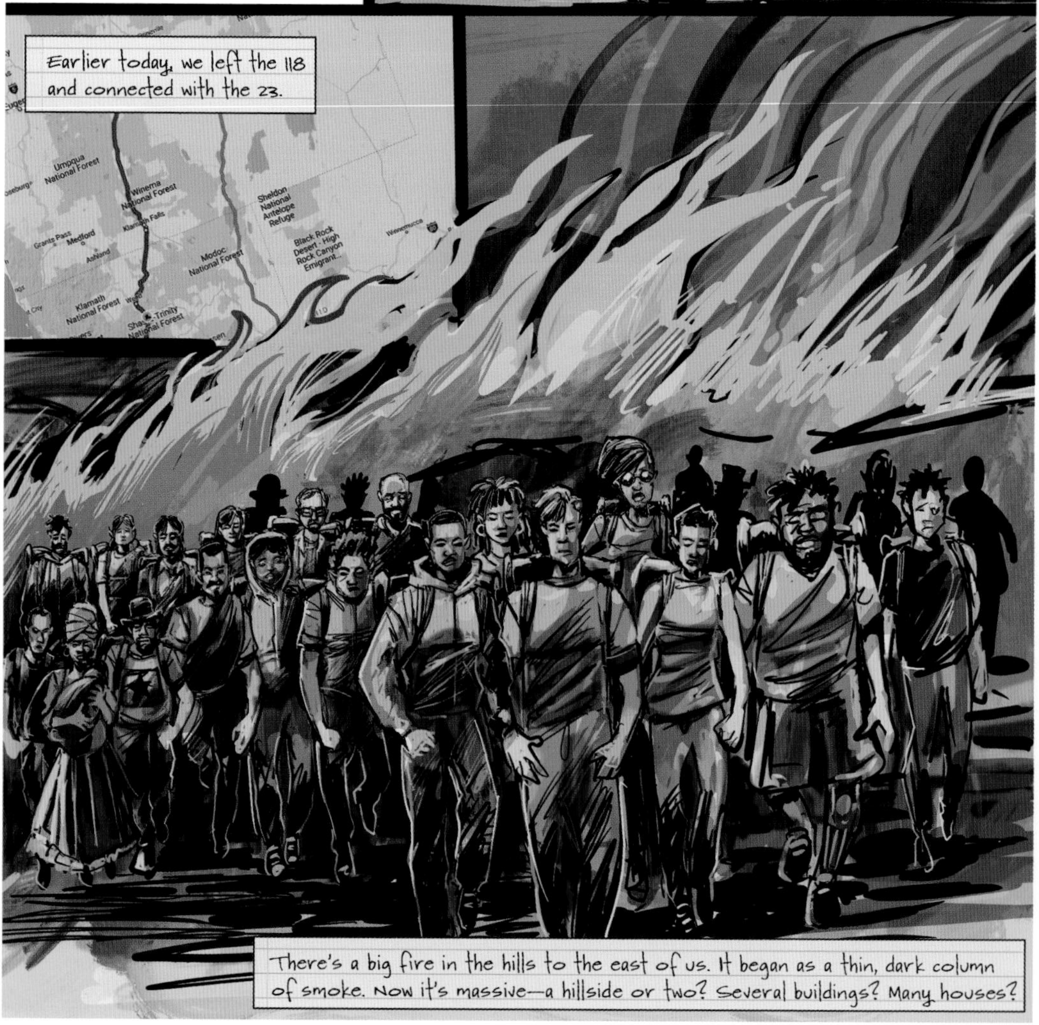

Earlier today, we left the 118 and connected with the 23.
Umpqua National Forest
Winema National Forest
Klamath Falls
Grants Pass
Medford
Ashland
Sheldon National Antelope Refuge
Modoc National Forest
Black Rock Desert - High Rock Canyon Emigrant...
Klamath National Forest
Winnemucca
There's a big fire in the hills to the east of us. It began as a thin, dark column of smoke. Now it's massive—a hillside or two? Several buildings? Many houses?

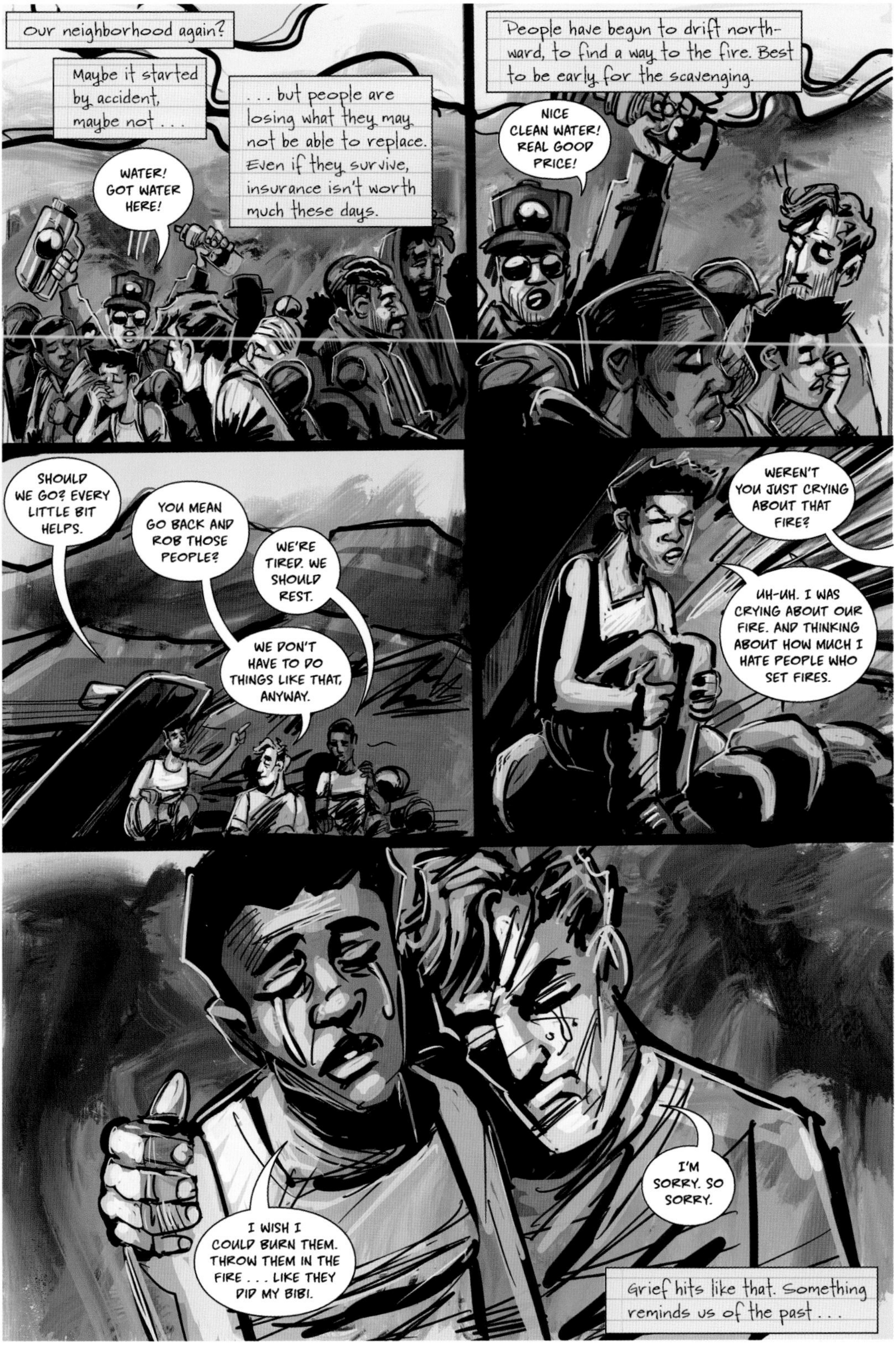
Our neighborhood again?
Maybe it started by accident, maybe not . . .
. . . but people are losing what they may not be able to replace. Even if they survive, insurance isn't worth much these days.
WATER! GOT WATER HERE!
People have begun to drift northward, to find a way to the fire. Best to be early for the scavenging.
NICE CLEAN WATER! REAL GOOD PRICE!
SHOULD WE GO? EVERY LITTLE BIT HELPS.
YOU MEAN GO BACK AND ROB THOSE PEOPLE?
WE'RE TIRED. WE SHOULD REST.
WE DON'T HAVE TO DO THINGS LIKE THAT, ANYWAY.
WEREN'T YOU JUST CRYING ABOUT THAT FIRE?
UH-UH. I WAS CRYING ABOUT OUR FIRE. AND THINKING ABOUT HOW MUCH I HATE PEOPLE WHO SET FIRES.
I WISH I COULD BURN THEM. THROW THEM IN THE FIRE . . . LIKE THEY DID MY BIBI.
I'M SORRY. SO SORRY.
Grief hits like that. Something reminds us of the past . . .

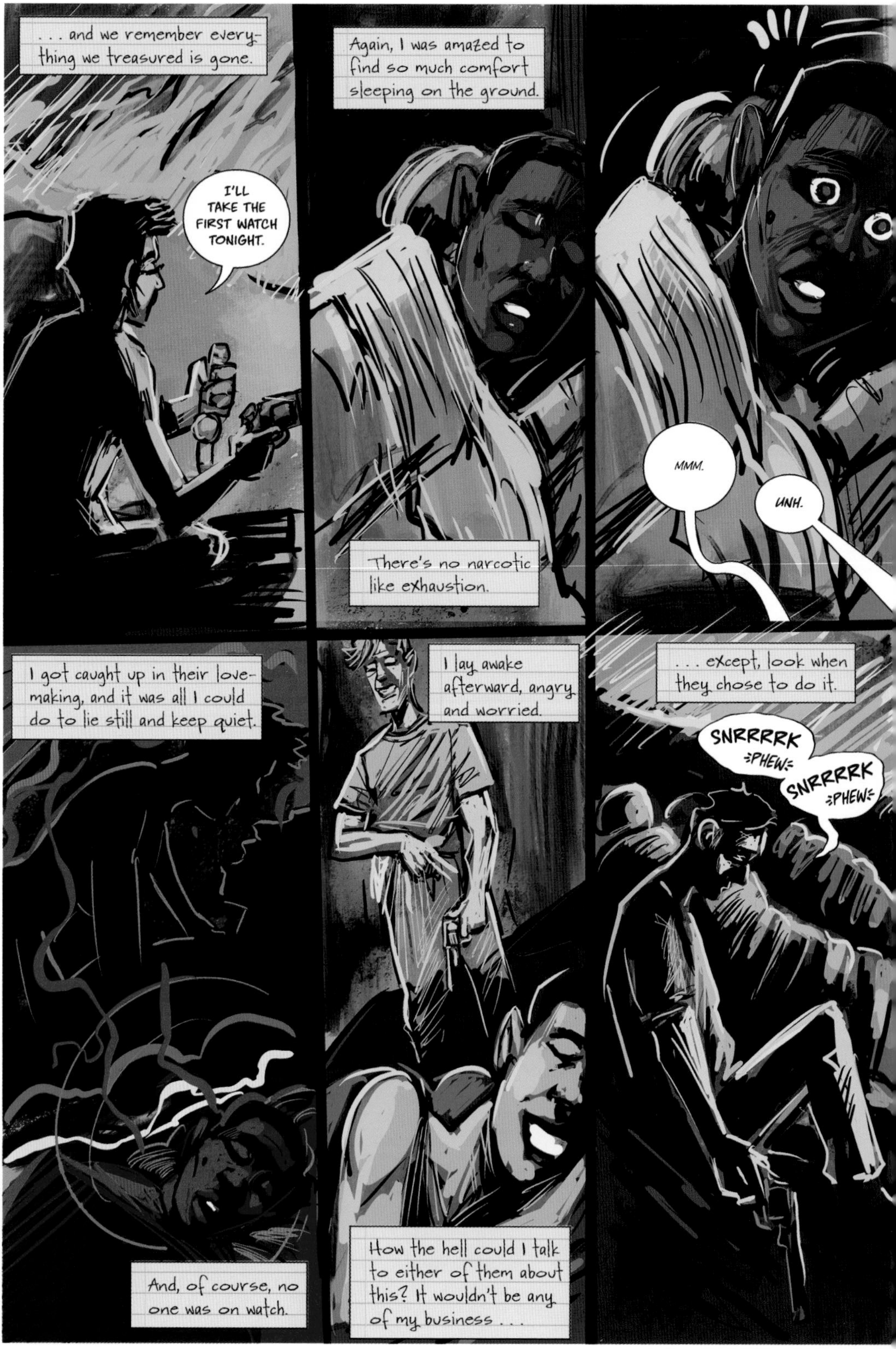
. . . and we remember everything we treasured is gone.
I'LL TAKE THE FIRST WATCH TONIGHT.
Again, I was amazed to find so much comfort sleeping on the ground.
There's no narcotic like exhaustion.
MMM.
UNH.
I got caught up in their lovemaking, and it was all I could do to lie still and keep quiet.
And, of course, no one was on watch.
I lay awake afterward, angry and worried.
How the hell could I talk to either of them about this? It wouldn't be any of my business . . .
. . . except, look when they chose to do it.
SNRRRRK
PHEW
SNRRRRK
PHEW

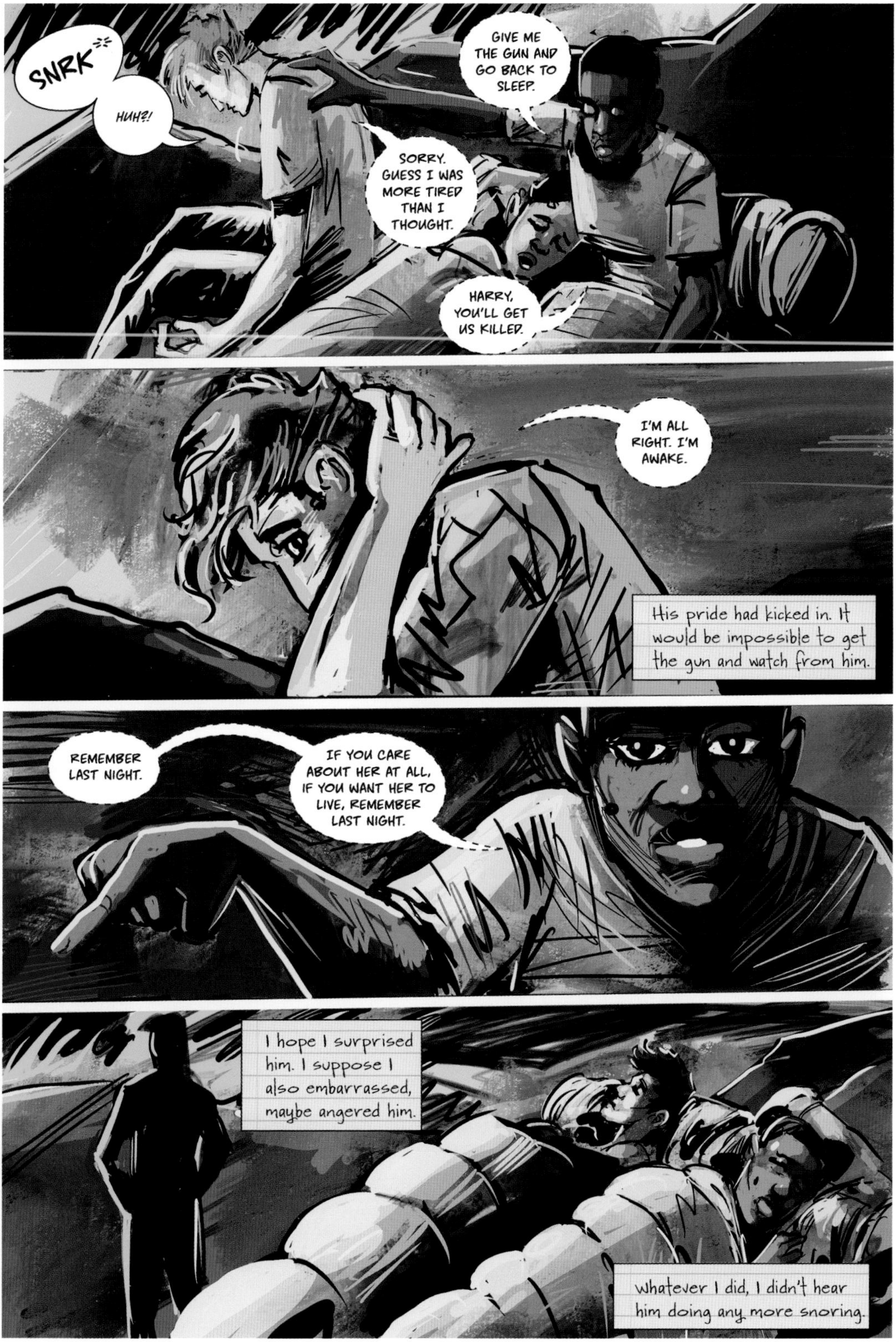
SNRK
HUH?!
GIVE ME THE GUN AND GO BACK TO SLEEP.
SORRY. GUESS I WAS MORE TIRED THAN I THOUGHT.
HARRY, YOU'LL GET US KILLED.
I'M ALL RIGHT. I'M AWAKE.
His pride had kicked in. It would be impossible to get the gun and watch from him.
REMEMBER LAST NIGHT.
IF YOU CARE ABOUT HER AT ALL, IF YOU WANT HER TO LIVE, REMEMBER LAST NIGHT.
I hope I surprised him. I suppose I also embarrassed, maybe angered him.
Whatever I did, I didn't hear him doing any more snoring.

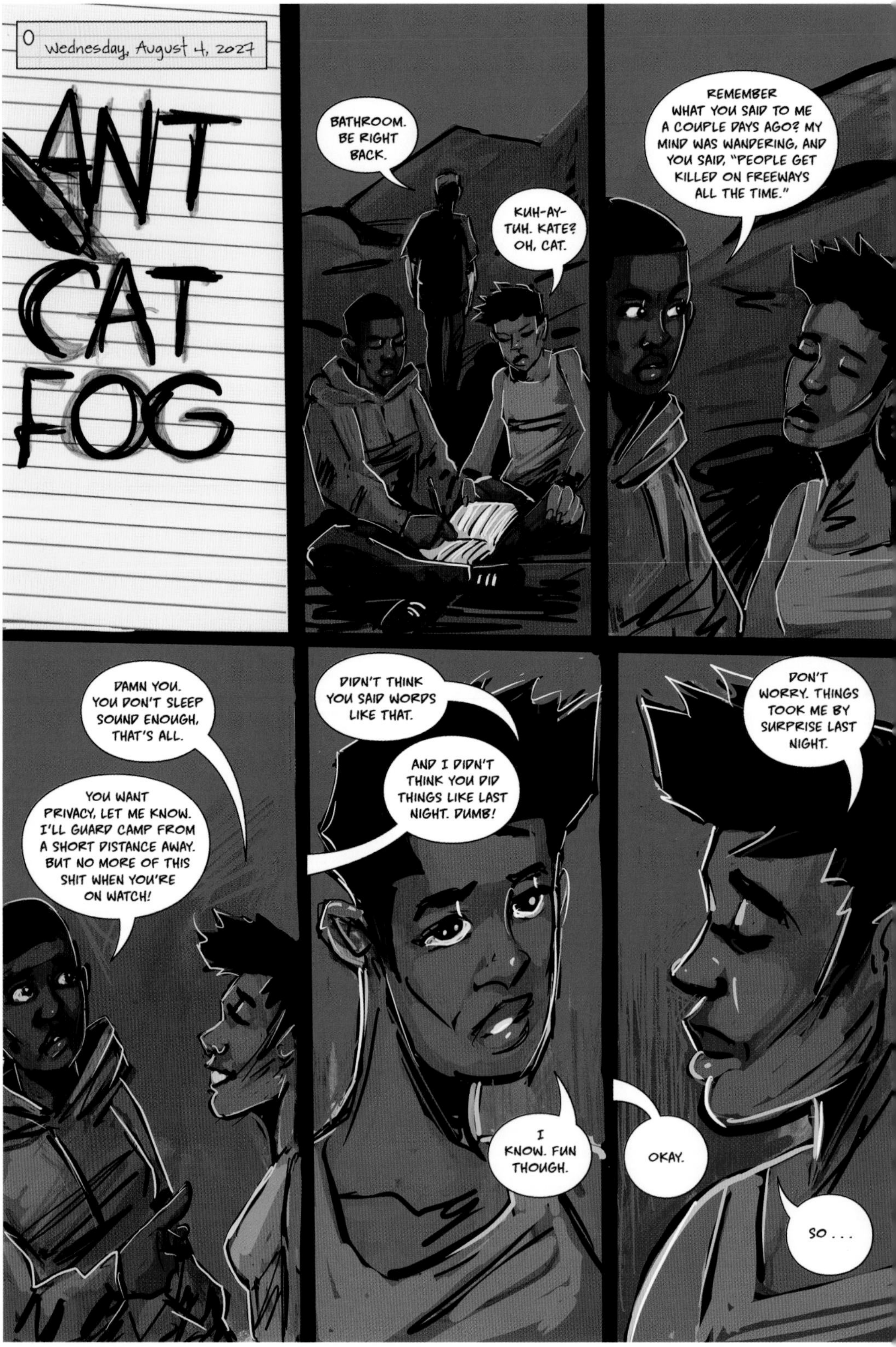
Wednesday, August 4, 2027
ANT
CAT
FOG
BATHROOM. BE RIGHT BACK.
KUH-AY-TUH. KATE? OH, CAT.
REMEMBER WHAT YOU SAID TO ME A COUPLE DAYS AGO? MY MIND WAS WANDERING, AND YOU SAID, "PEOPLE GET KILLED ON FREEWAYS ALL THE TIME."
DAMN YOU. YOU DON'T SLEEP SOUND ENOUGH, THAT'S ALL.
YOU WANT PRIVACY, LET ME KNOW. I'LL GUARD CAMP FROM A SHORT DISTANCE AWAY. BUT NO MORE OF THIS SHIT WHEN YOU'RE ON WATCH!
DIDN'T THINK YOU SAID WORDS LIKE THAT.
AND I DIDN'T THINK YOU DID THINGS LIKE LAST NIGHT. DUMB!
I KNOW. FUN THOUGH.
DON'T WORRY. THINGS TOOK ME BY SURPRISE LAST NIGHT.
OKAY.
SO . . .

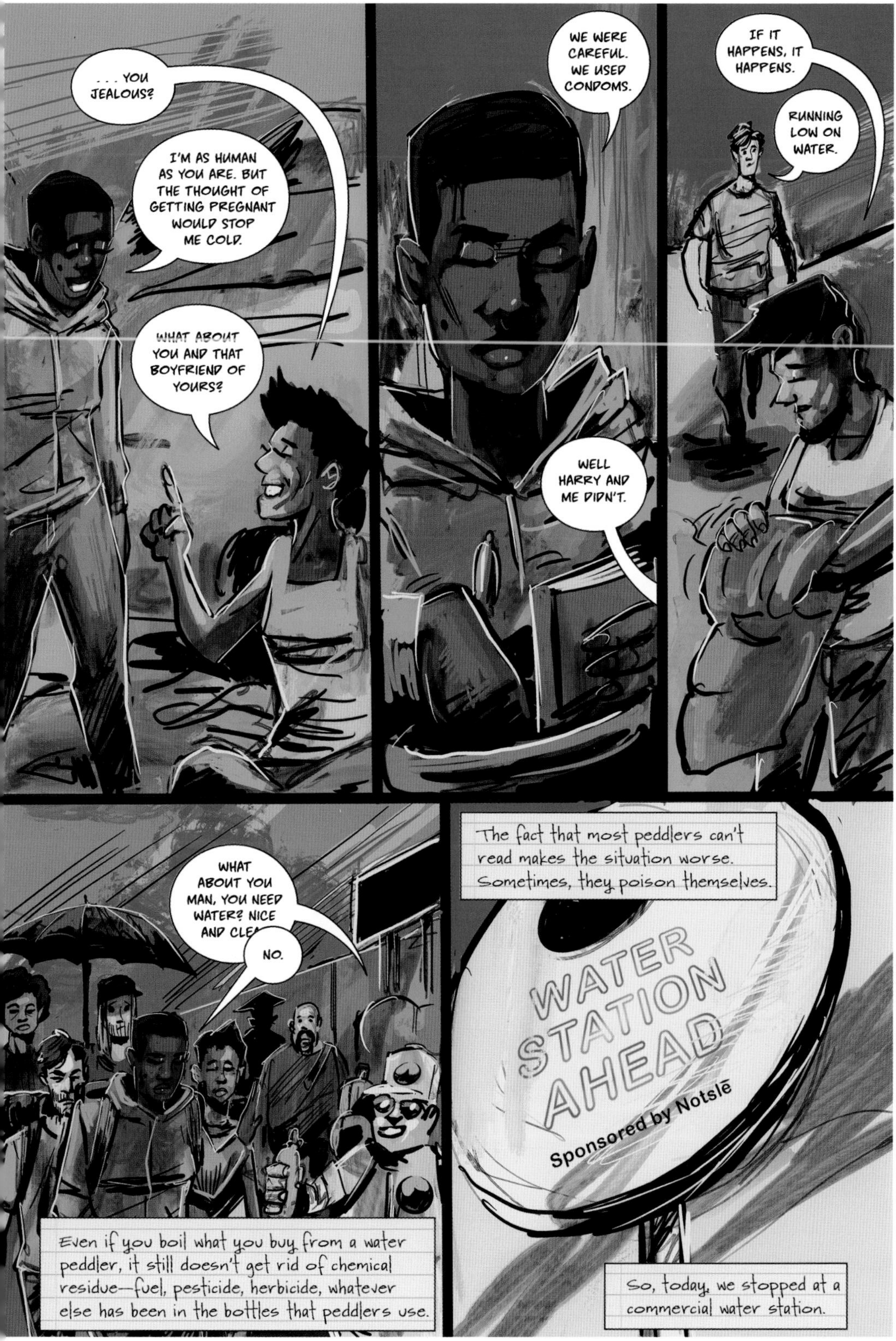

. . . YOU JEALOUS?
I'M AS HUMAN AS YOU ARE. BUT THE THOUGHT OF GETTING PREGNANT WOULD STOP ME COLD.
WHAT ABOUT YOU AND THAT BOYFRIEND OF YOURS?
WE WERE CAREFUL. WE USED CONDOMS.
WELL HARRY AND ME DIDN'T.
IF IT HAPPENS, IT HAPPENS.
RUNNING LOW ON WATER.
WHAT ABOUT YOU MAN, YOU NEED WATER? NICE AND CLE
NO.
Even if you boil what you buy from a water peddler, it still doesn't get rid of chemical residue—fuel, pesticide, herbicide, whatever else has been in the bottles that peddlers use.
The fact that most peddlers can't read makes the situation worse. Sometimes, they poison themselves.
WATER STATION AHEAD
Sponsored by Notslē
So, today, we stopped at a commercial water station.

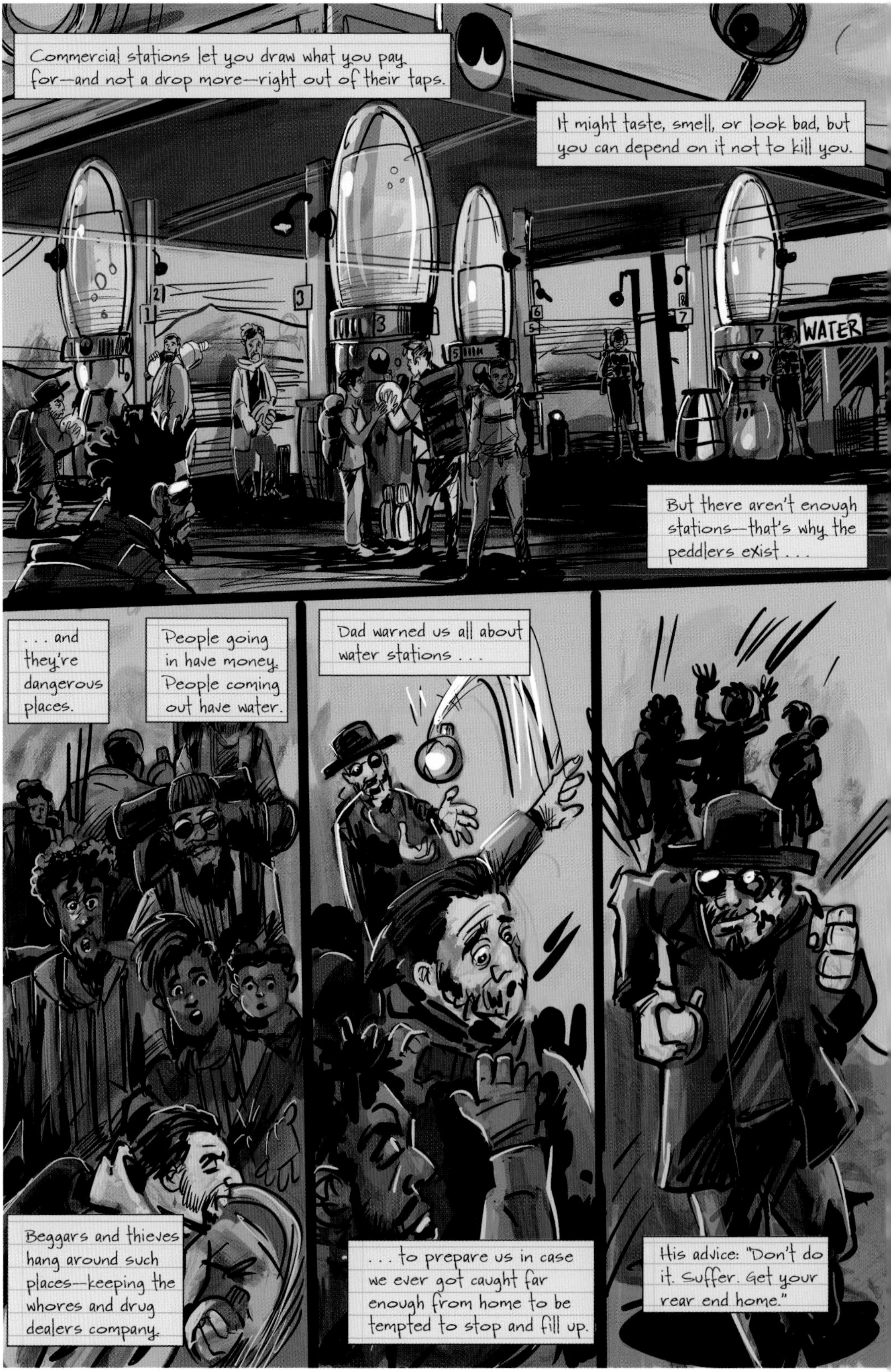
Commercial stations let you draw what you pay for—and not a drop more—right out of their taps.
It might taste, smell, or look bad, but you can depend on it not to kill you.
WATER
But there aren't enough stations—that's why the peddlers exist . . .
. . . and they're dangerous places.
People going in have money. People coming out have water.
Beggars and thieves hang around such places—keeping the whores and drug dealers company.
Dad warned us all about water stations . . .
. . . to prepare us in case we ever got caught far enough from home to be tempted to stop and fill up.
His advice: "Don't do it. Suffer. Get your rear end home."

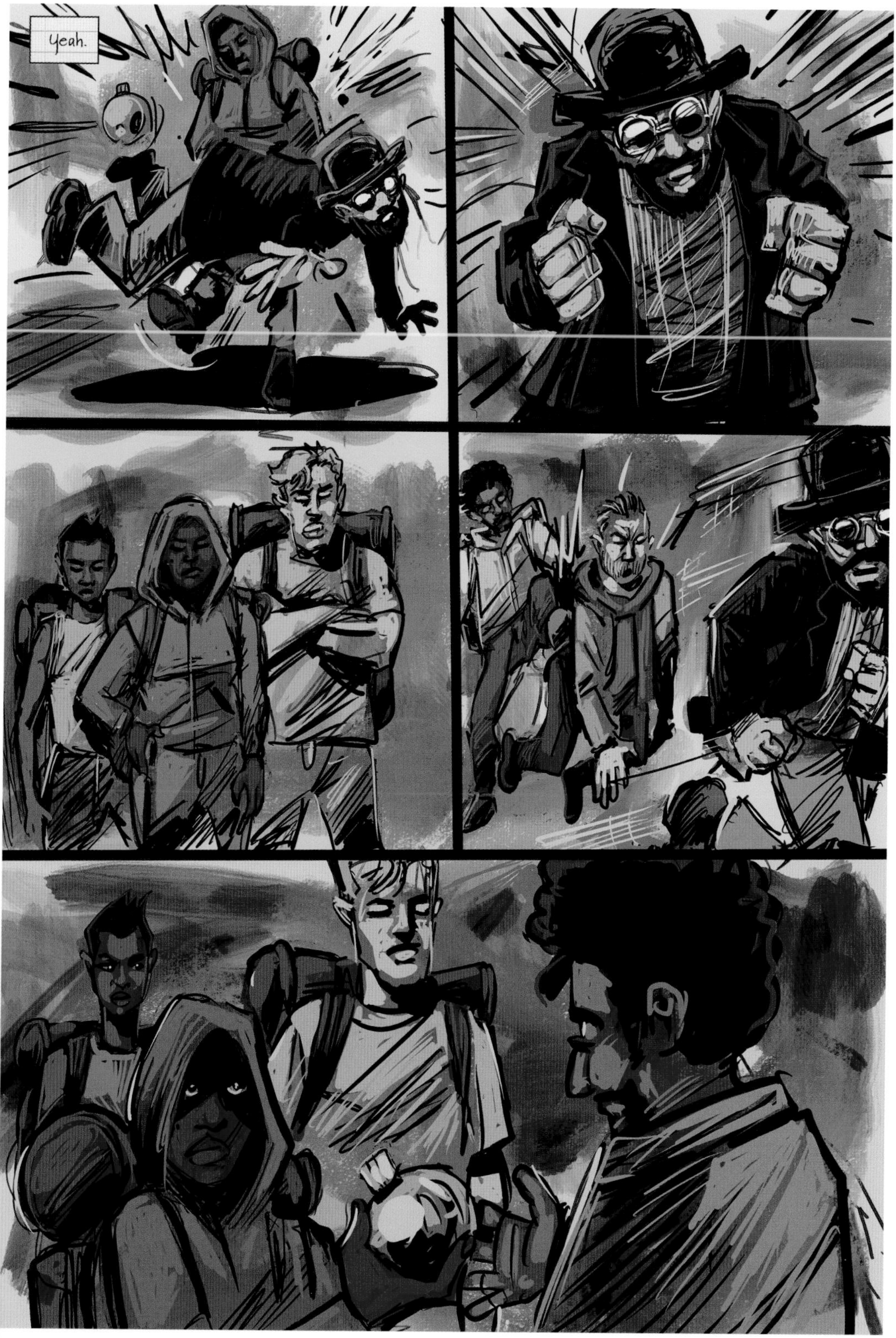
Yeah.

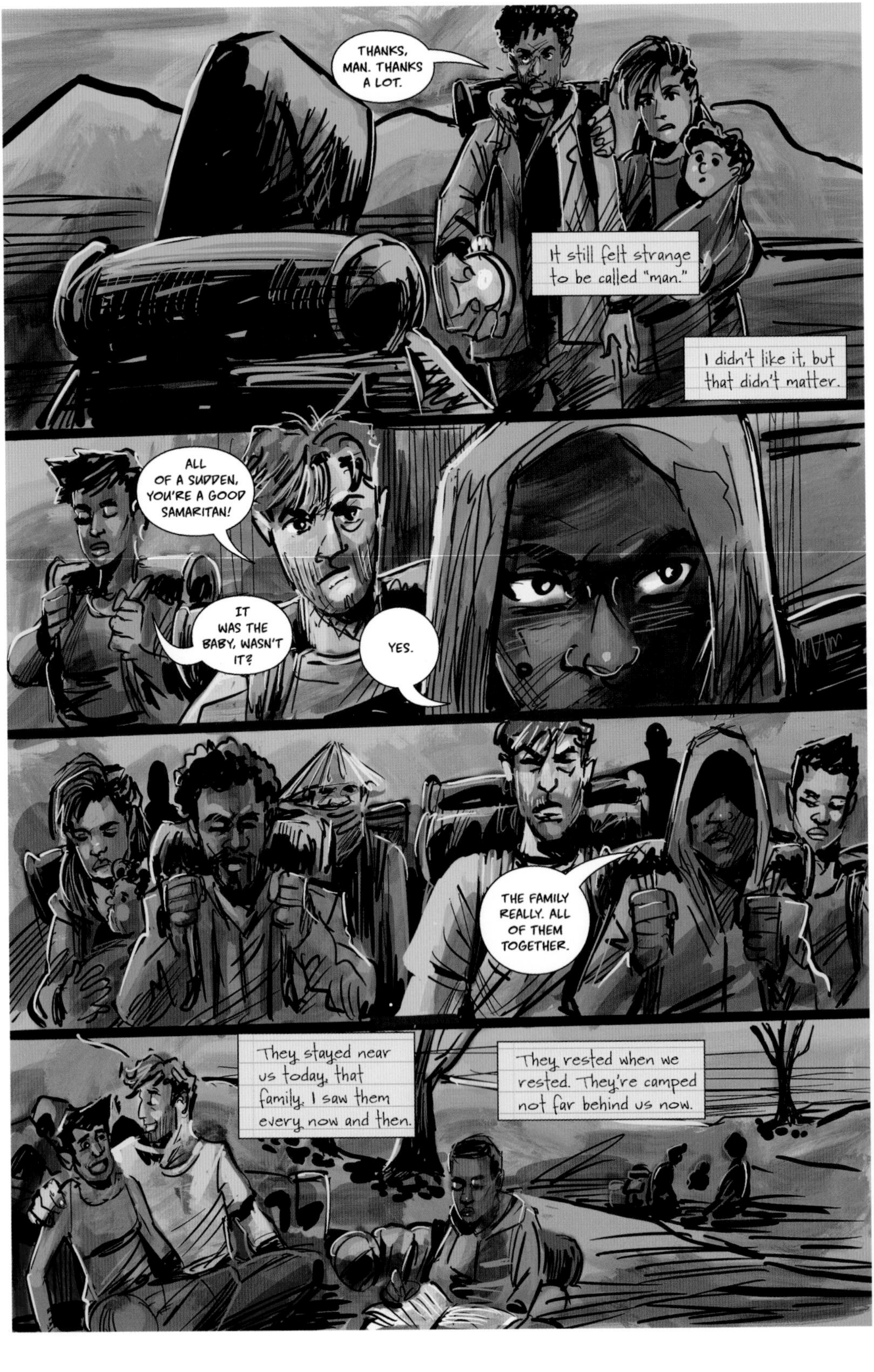
THANKS, MAN. THANKS A LOT.
It still felt strange to be called "man."
I didn't like it, but that didn't matter.
ALL OF A SUDDEN, YOU'RE A GOOD SAMARITAN!
IT WAS THE BABY, WASN'T IT?
YES.
THE FAMILY REALLY. ALL OF THEM TOGETHER.
They stayed near us today, that family. I saw them every now and then.
They rested when we rested. They're camped not far behind us now.

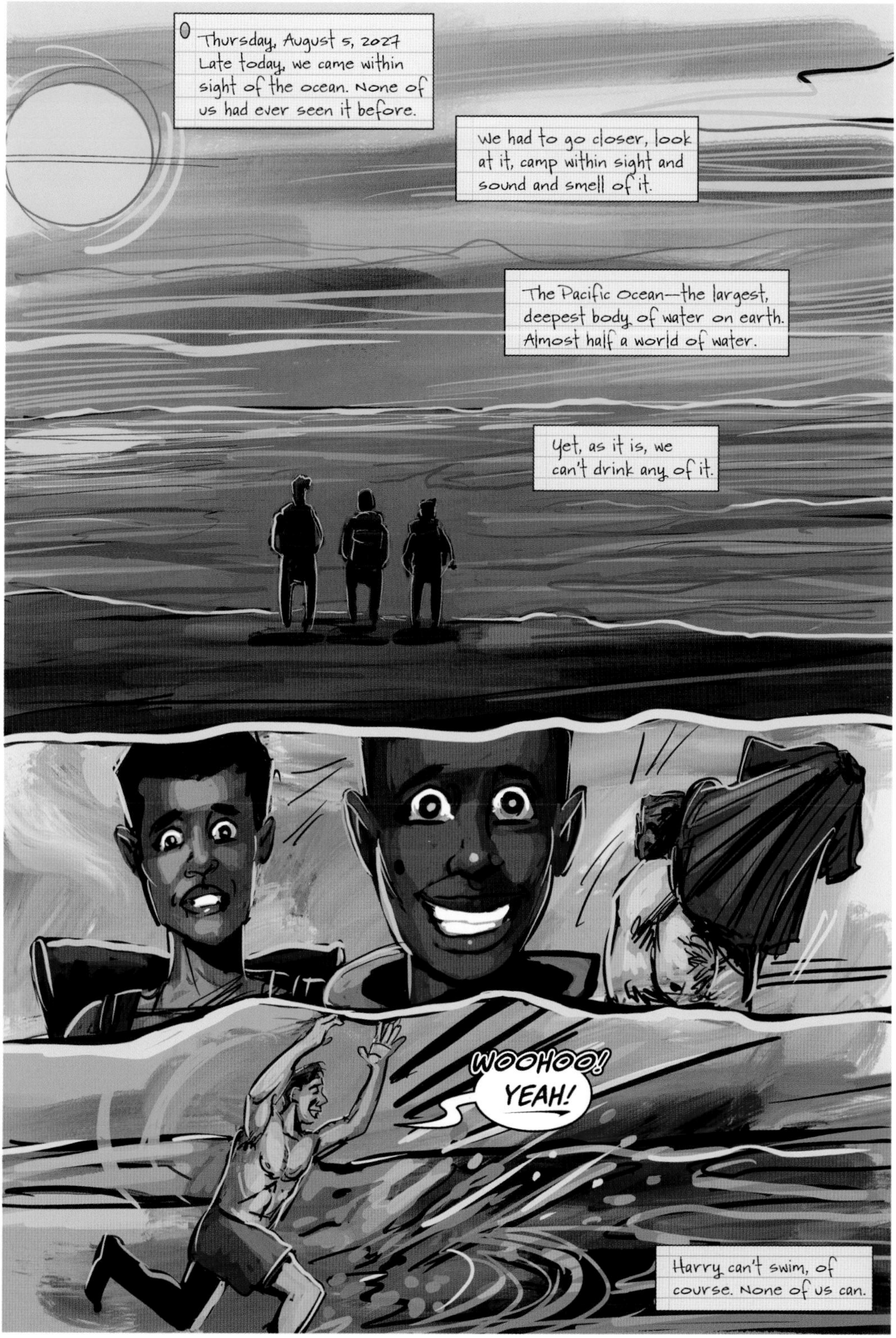
Thursday, August 5, 2027
Late today, we came within sight of the ocean. None of us had ever seen it before.
We had to go closer, look at it, camp within sight and sound and smell of it.
The Pacific Ocean—the largest, deepest body of water on earth. Almost half a world of water.
Yet, as it is, we can't drink any of it.
WOOHOO! YEAH!
Harry can't swim, of course. None of us can.

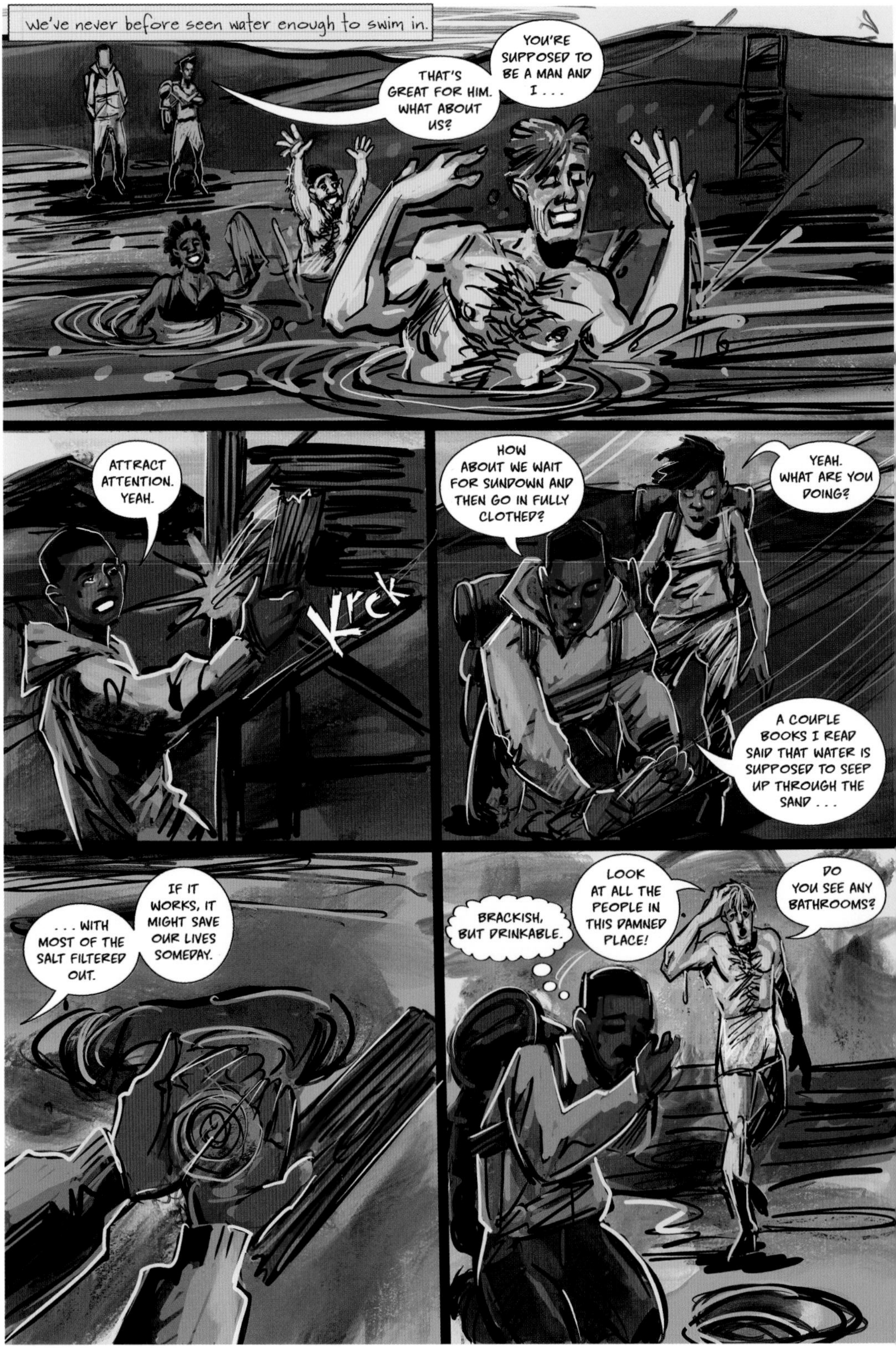
We've never before seen water enough to swim in.
YOU'RE SUPPOSED TO BE A MAN AND I . . .
THAT'S GREAT FOR HIM. WHAT ABOUT US?
ATTRACT ATTENTION. YEAH.
Krck
HOW ABOUT WE WAIT FOR SUNDOWN AND THEN GO IN FULLY CLOTHED?
YEAH. WHAT ARE YOU DOING?
A COUPLE BOOKS I READ SAID THAT WATER IS SUPPOSED TO SEEP UP THROUGH THE SAND . . .
. . . WITH MOST OF THE SALT FILTERED OUT.
IF IT WORKS, IT MIGHT SAVE OUR LIVES SOMEDAY.
BRACKISH, BUT DRINKABLE.
LOOK AT ALL THE PEOPLE IN THIS DAMNED PLACE!
DO YOU SEE ANY BATHROOMS?

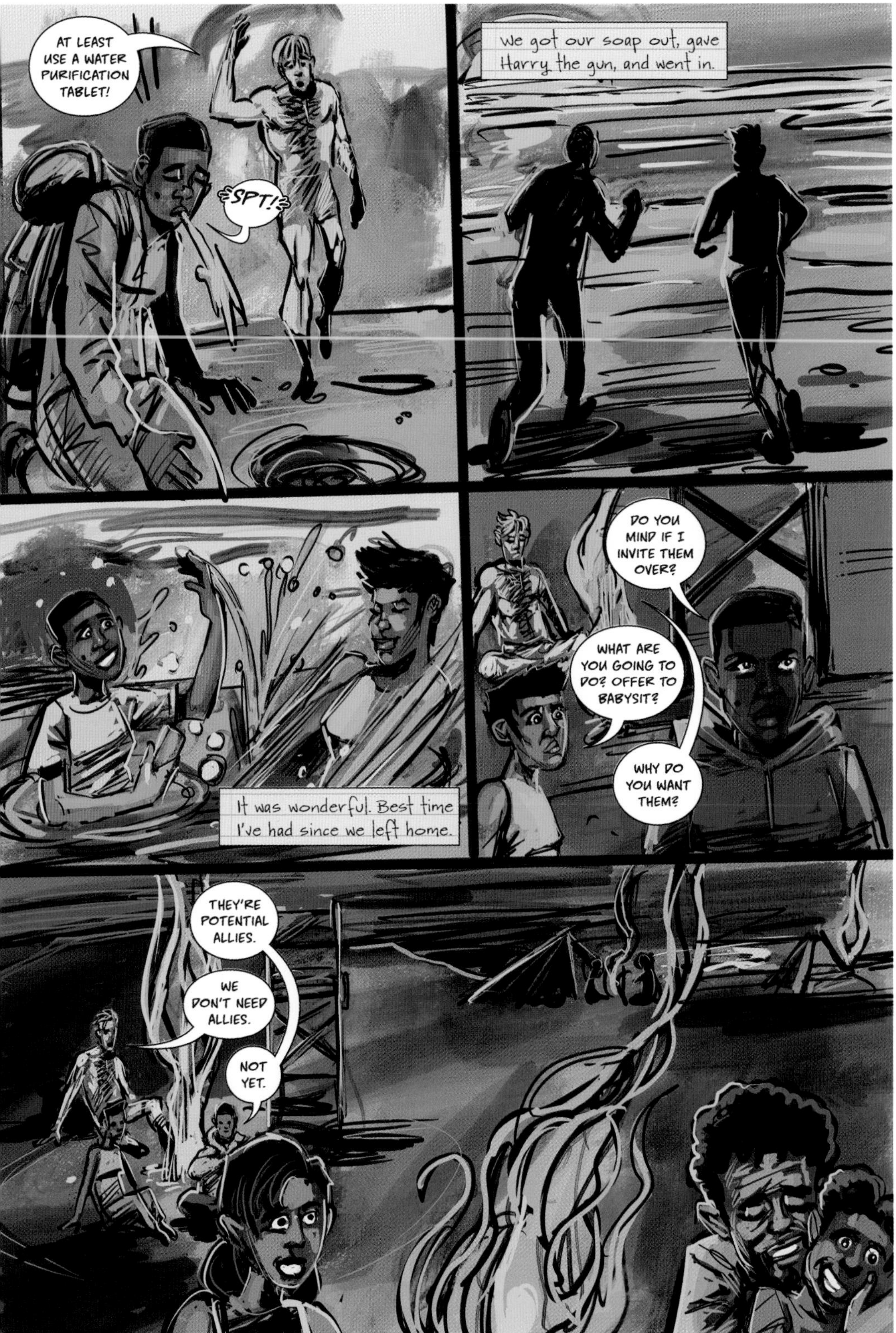
AT LEAST USE A WATER PURIFICATION TABLET!
SPT!
We got our soap out, gave Harry the gun, and went in.
It was wonderful. Best time I've had since we left home.
DO YOU MIND IF I INVITE THEM OVER?
WHAT ARE YOU GOING TO DO? OFFER TO BABYSIT?
WHY DO YOU WANT THEM?
THEY'RE POTENTIAL ALLIES.
WE DON'T NEED ALLIES.
NOT YET.

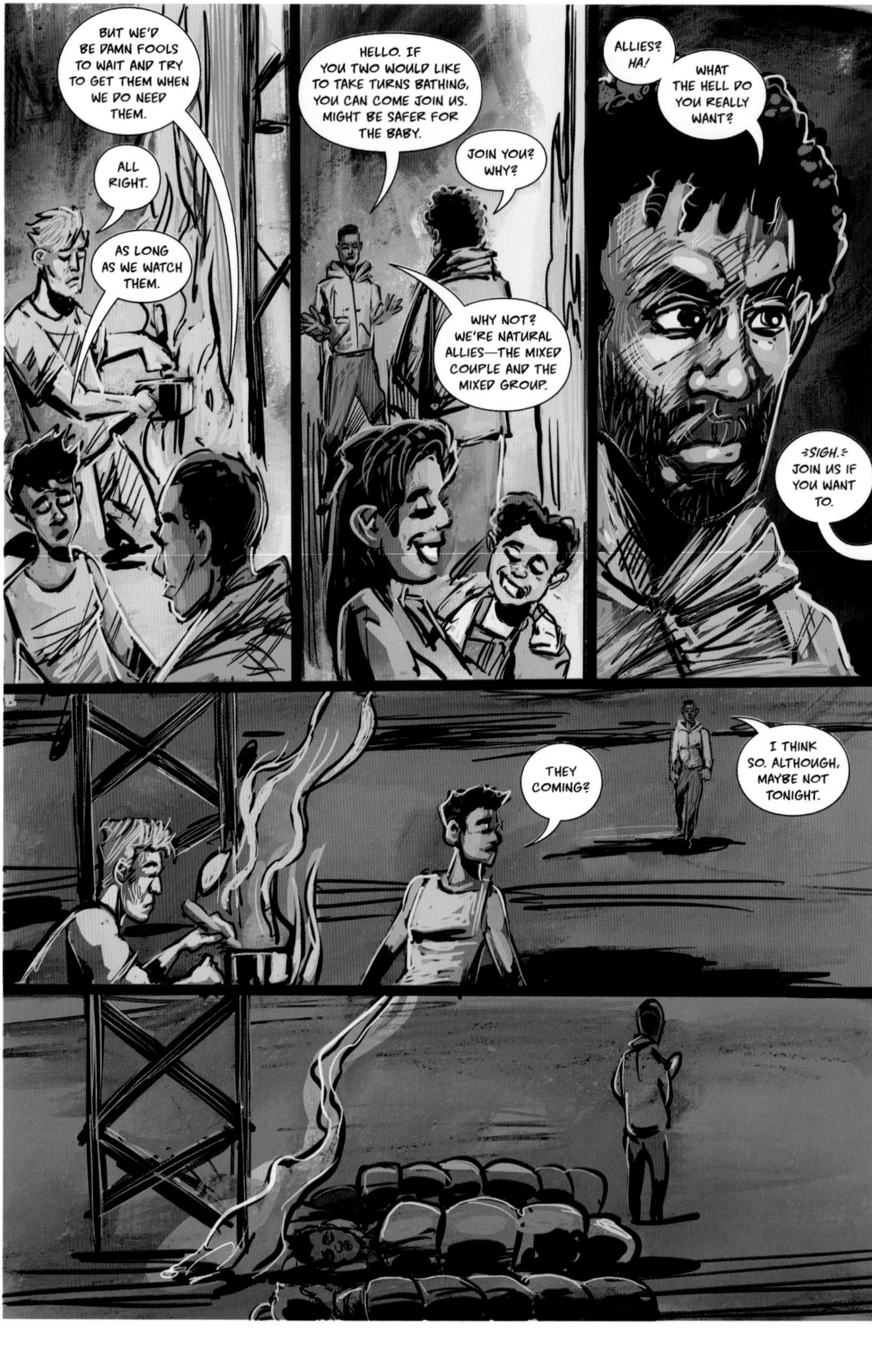

BUT WE'D BE DAMN FOOLS TO WAIT AND TRY TO GET THEM WHEN WE DO NEED THEM.
ALL RIGHT.
AS LONG AS WE WATCH THEM.
HELLO. IF YOU TWO WOULD LIKE TO TAKE TURNS BATHING, YOU CAN COME JOIN US. MIGHT BE SAFER FOR THE BABY.
JOIN YOU? WHY?
WHY NOT? WE'RE NATURAL ALLIES—THE MIXED COUPLE AND THE MIXED GROUP.
ALLIES? HA!
WHAT THE HELL DO YOU REALLY WANT?
=SIGH.= JOIN US IF YOU WANT TO.
THEY COMING?
I THINK SO. ALTHOUGH, MAYBE NOT TONIGHT.

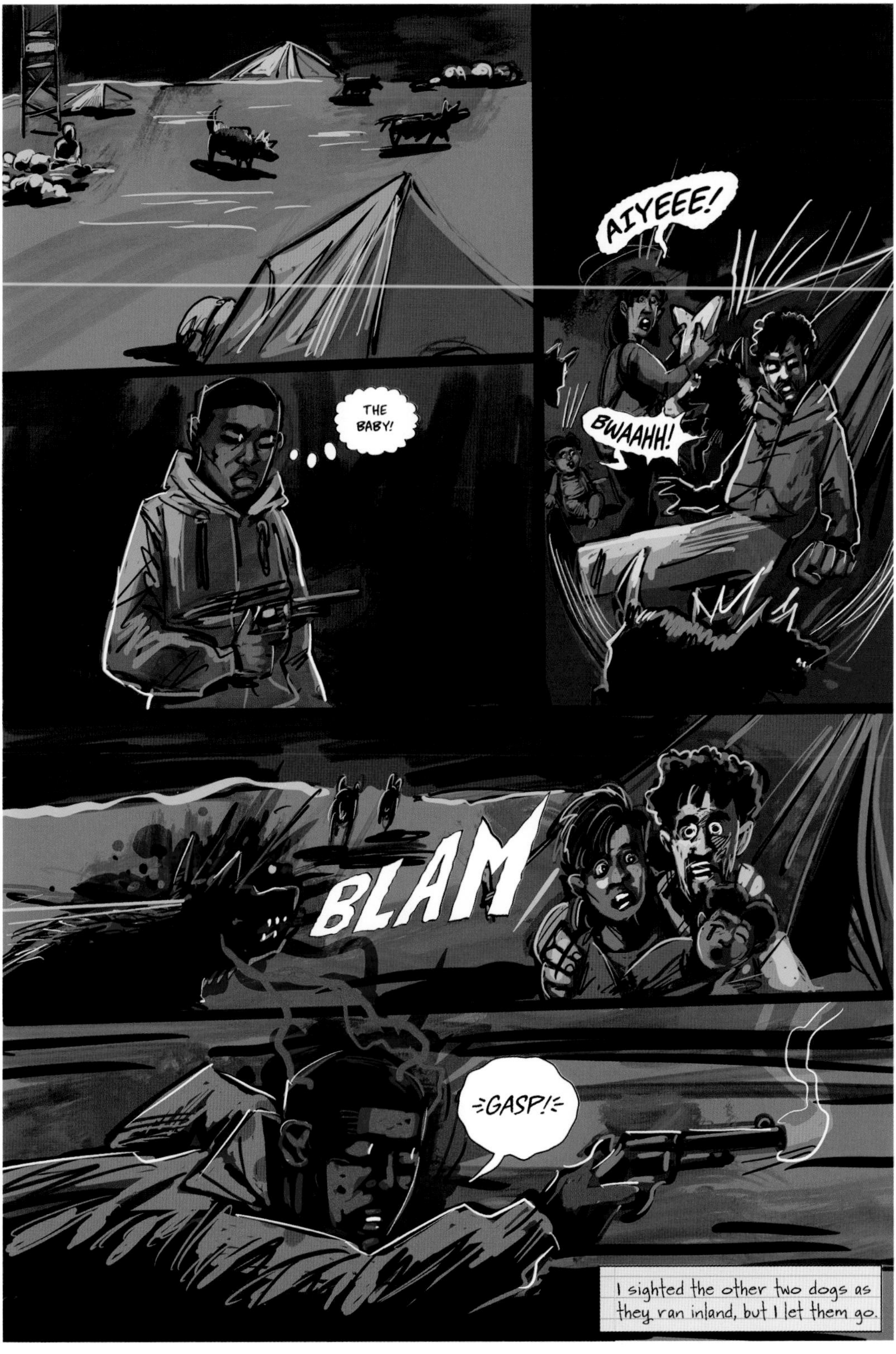
AIYEEE!
BWAAHH!
THE BABY!
BLAM
GASP!
I sighted the other two dogs as they ran inland, but I let them go.

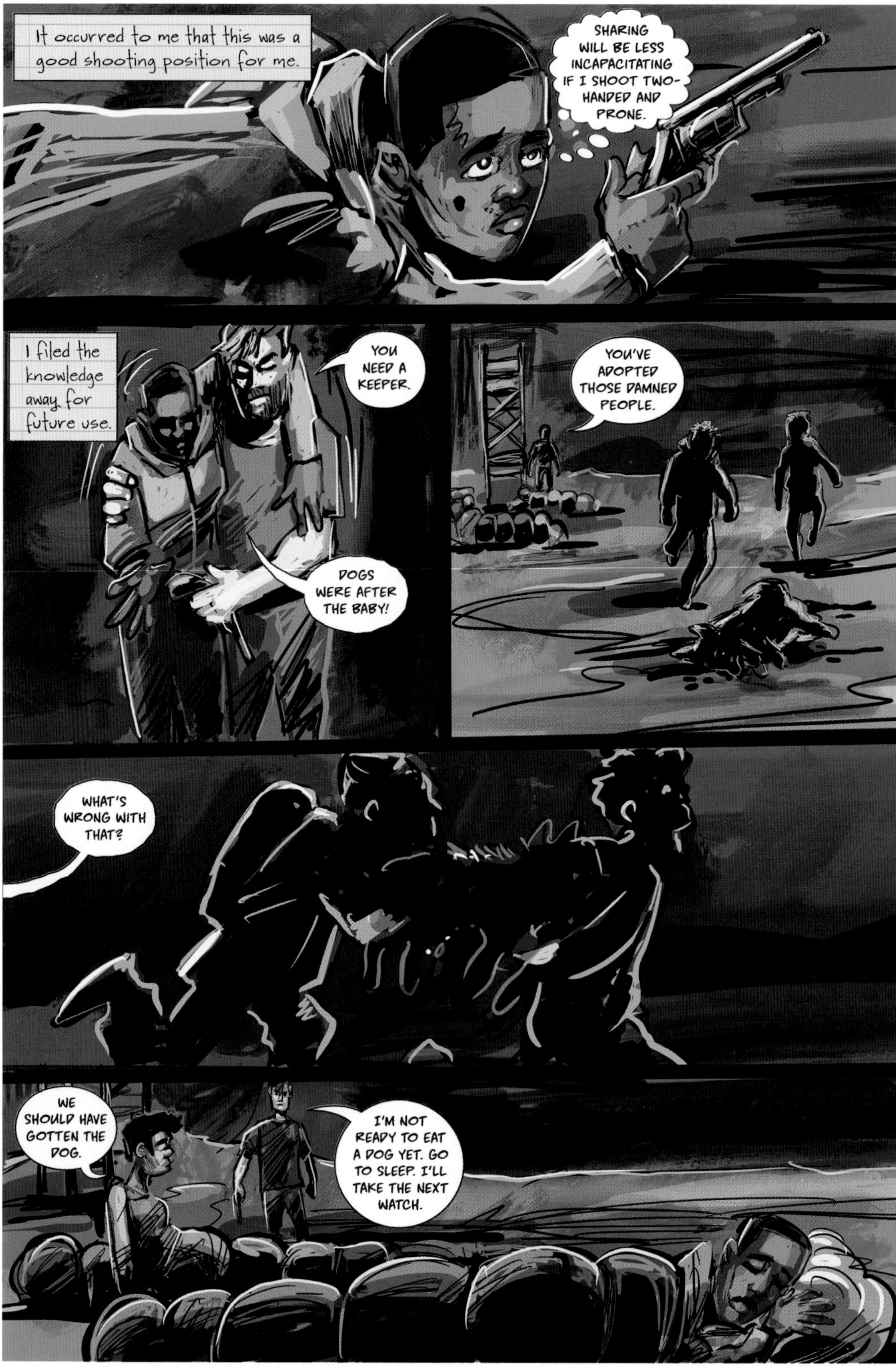
It occurred to me that this was a good shooting position for me.
SHARING WILL BE LESS INCAPACITATING IF I SHOOT TWO-HANDED AND PRONE.
I filed the knowledge away for future use.
YOU NEED A KEEPER.
DOGS WERE AFTER THE BABY!
YOU'VE ADOPTED THOSE DAMNED PEOPLE.
WHAT'S WRONG WITH THAT?
WE SHOULD HAVE GOTTEN THE DOG.
I'M NOT READY TO EAT A DOG YET. GO TO SLEEP. I'LL TAKE THE NEXT WATCH.

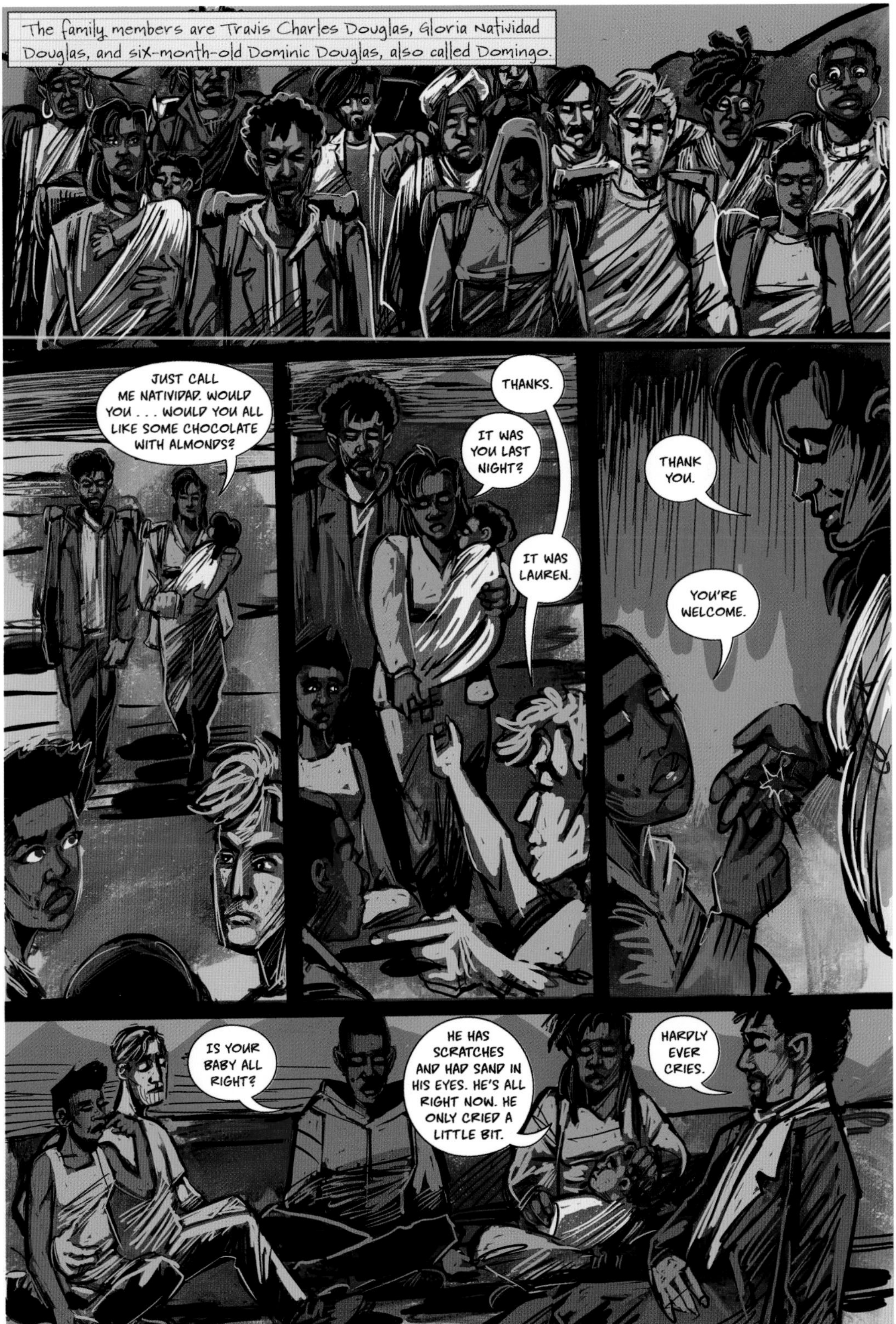

The family members are Travis Charles Douglas, Gloria Natividad Douglas, and six-month-old Dominic Douglas, also called Domingo.
JUST CALL ME NATIVIDAD. WOULD YOU . . . WOULD YOU ALL LIKE SOME CHOCOLATE WITH ALMONDS?
THANKS.
IT WAS YOU LAST NIGHT?
IT WAS LAUREN.
THANK YOU.
YOU'RE WELCOME.
IS YOUR BABY ALL RIGHT?
HE HAS SCRATCHES AND HAD SAND IN HIS EYES. HE'S ALL RIGHT NOW. HE ONLY CRIED A LITTLE BIT.
HARDLY EVER CRIES.

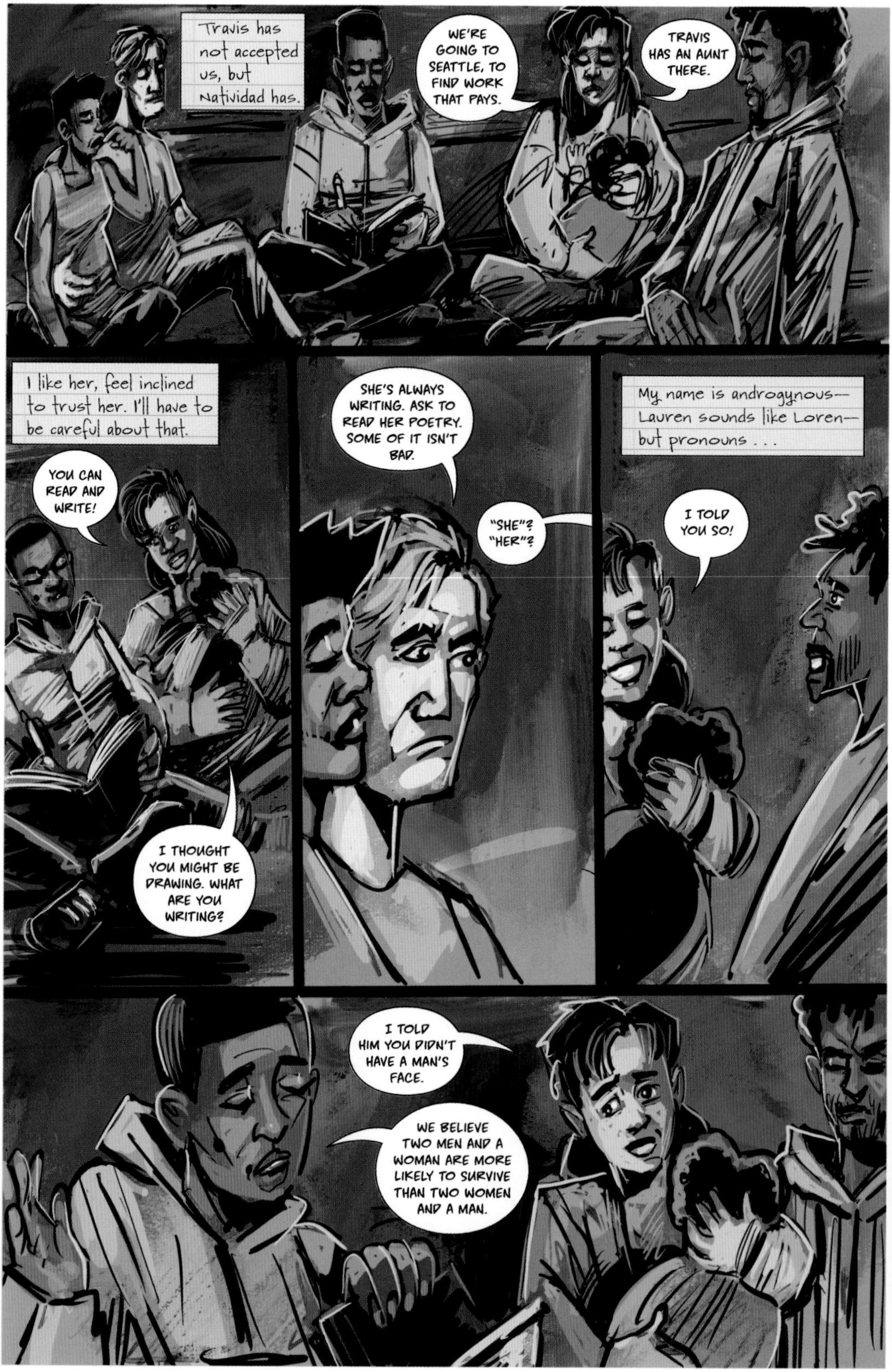
Travis has not accepted us, but Natividad has.
WE'RE GOING TO SEATTLE, TO FIND WORK THAT PAYS.
TRAVIS HAS AN AUNT THERE.
I like her, feel inclined to trust her. I'll have to be careful about that.
YOU CAN READ AND WRITE!
I THOUGHT YOU MIGHT BE DRAWING. WHAT ARE YOU WRITING?
SHE'S ALWAYS WRITING. ASK TO READ HER POETRY. SOME OF IT ISN'T BAD.
"SHE"? "HER"?
My name is androgynous— Lauren sounds like Loren— but pronouns . . .
I TOLD YOU SO!
I TOLD HIM YOU DIDN'T HAVE A MAN'S FACE.
WE BELIEVE TWO MEN AND A WOMAN ARE MORE LIKELY TO SURVIVE THAN TWO WOMEN AND A MAN.

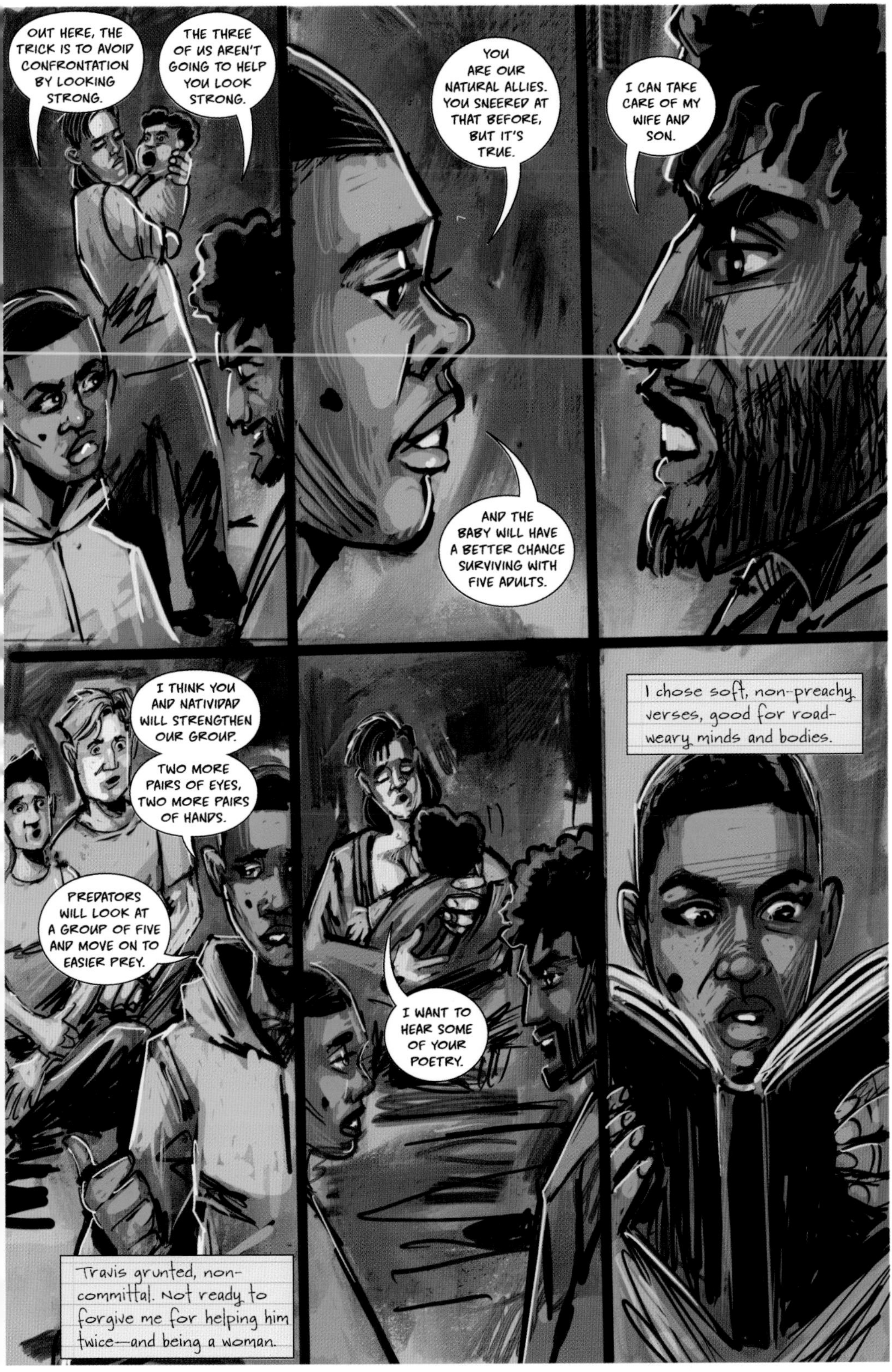

OUT HERE, THE TRICK IS TO AVOID CONFRONTATION BY LOOKING STRONG.
THE THREE OF US AREN'T GOING TO HELP YOU LOOK STRONG.
YOU ARE OUR NATURAL ALLIES. YOU SNEERED AT THAT BEFORE, BUT IT'S TRUE.
AND THE BABY WILL HAVE A BETTER CHANCE SURVIVING WITH FIVE ADULTS.
I CAN TAKE CARE OF MY WIFE AND SON.
I THINK YOU AND NATIVIDAD WILL STRENGTHEN OUR GROUP.
TWO MORE PAIRS OF EYES, TWO MORE PAIRS OF HANDS.
PREDATORS WILL LOOK AT A GROUP OF FIVE AND MOVE ON TO EASIER PREY.
Travis grunted, non-committal. Not ready to forgive me for helping him twice—and being a woman.
I WANT TO HEAR SOME OF YOUR POETRY.
I chose soft, non-preachy verses, good for road-weary minds and bodies.

Once or twice
each week
A Gathering of Earthseed
is a good and necessary thing.
It vents emotion, then
quiets the mind.
It focuses attention,
strengthens purpose,
and unifies people.

EARTHSEED: THE BOOKS OF THE LIVING

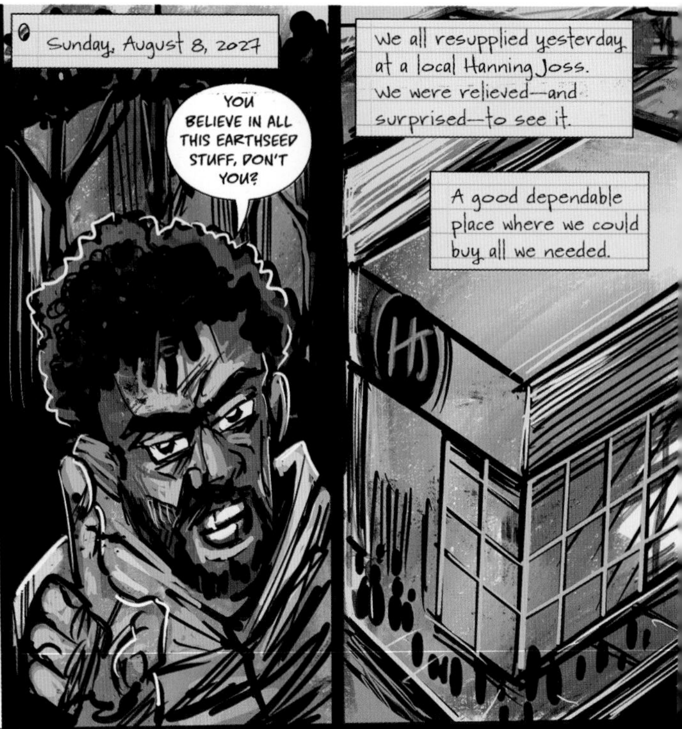
Sunday, August 8, 2027
YOU BELIEVE IN ALL THIS EARTHSEED STUFF, DON'T YOU?
We all resupplied yesterday at a local Hanning Joss. We were relieved—and surprised—to see it.
A good dependable place where we could buy all we needed.
HJ

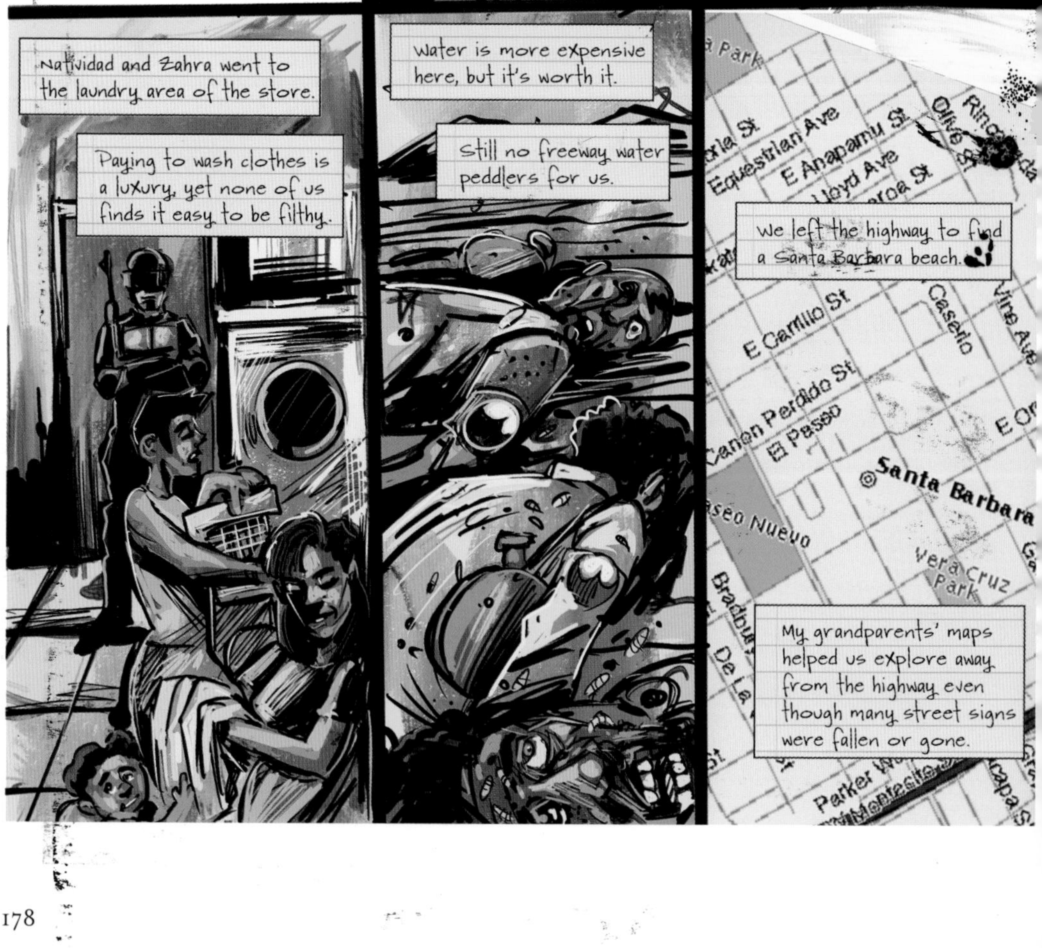
Natividad and Zahra went to the laundry area of the store.
Paying to wash clothes is a luxury, yet none of us finds it easy to be filthy.
Water is more expensive here, but it's worth it.
Still no freeway water peddlers for us.
We left the highway to find a Santa Barbara beach.
Equestrian Ave
E Anapamu St
E Carrillo St
Canon Perdido St
El Paseo
Santa Barbara
Vera Cruz Park
My grandparents' maps helped us explore away from the highway even though many street signs were fallen or gone.

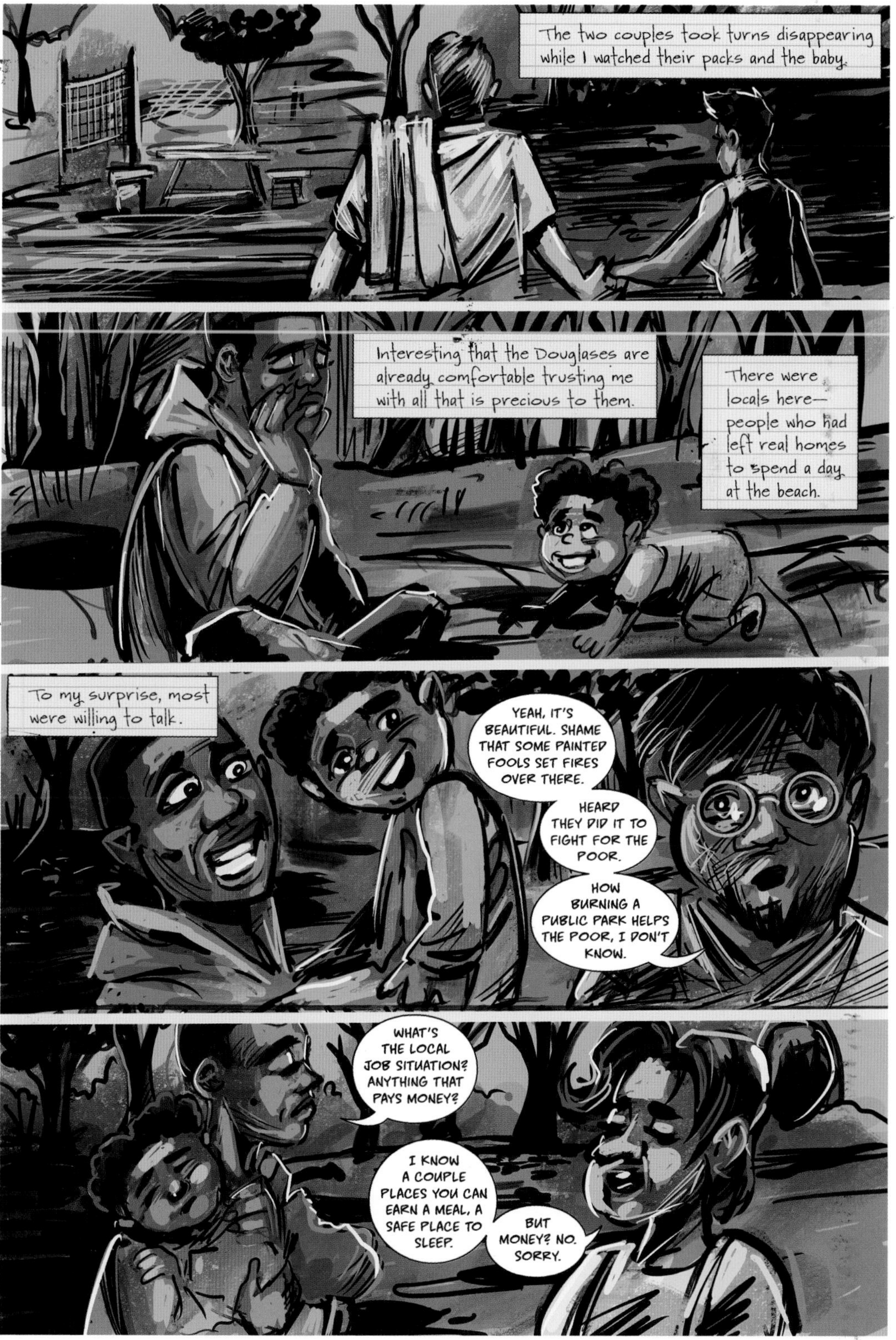
The two couples took turns disappearing while I watched their packs and the baby.
Interesting that the Douglases are already comfortable trusting me with all that is precious to them.
There were locals here—people who had left real homes to spend a day at the beach.
To my surprise, most were willing to talk.
YEAH, IT'S BEAUTIFUL. SHAME THAT SOME PAINTED FOOLS SET FIRES OVER THERE.
HEARD THEY DID IT TO FIGHT FOR THE POOR.
HOW BURNING A PUBLIC PARK HELPS THE POOR, I DON'T KNOW.
WHAT'S THE LOCAL JOB SITUATION? ANYTHING THAT PAYS MONEY?
I KNOW A COUPLE PLACES YOU CAN EARN A MEAL, A SAFE PLACE TO SLEEP.
BUT MONEY? NO. SORRY.

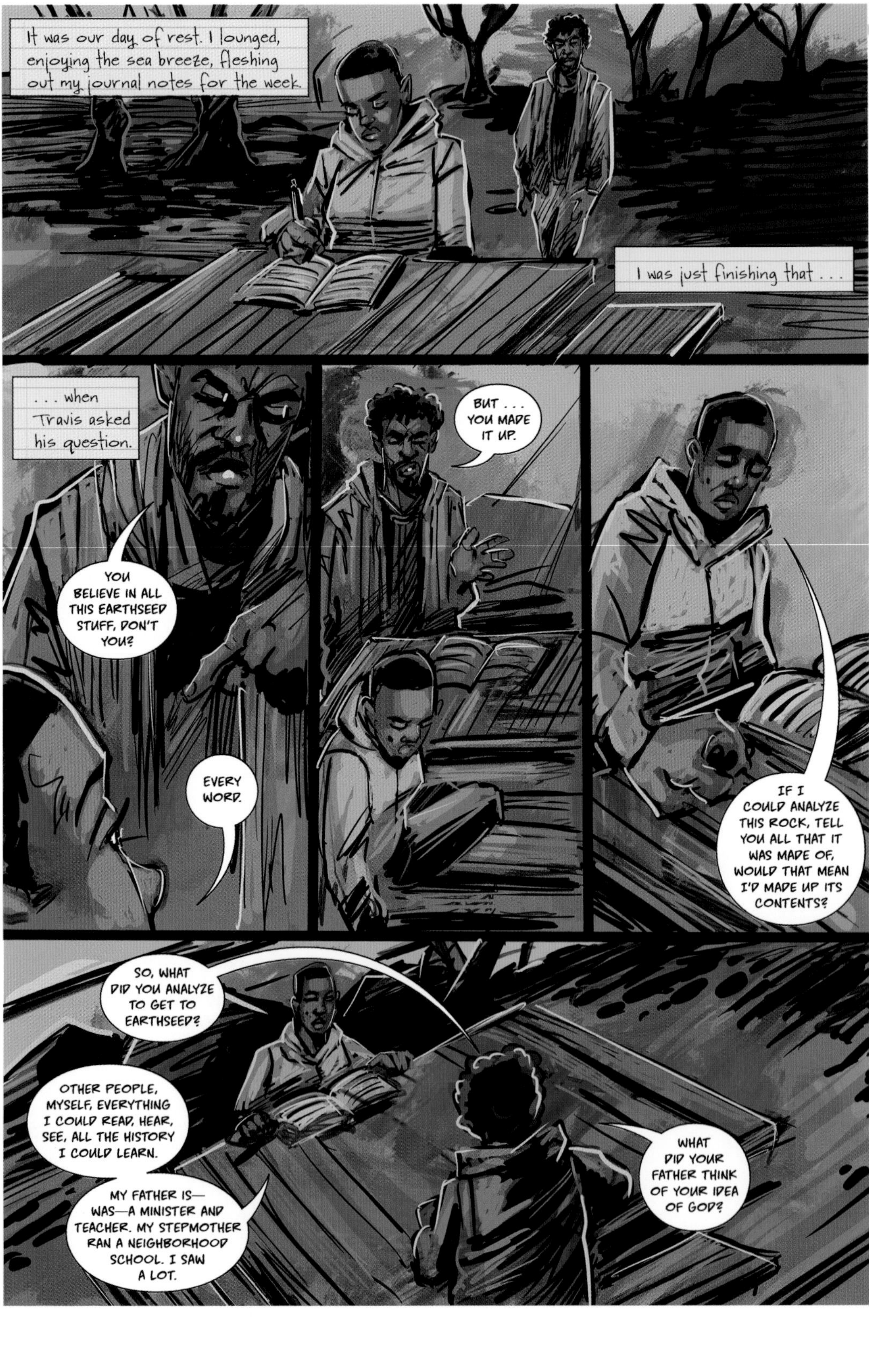

It was our day of rest. I lounged, enjoying the sea breeze, fleshing out my journal notes for the week.
I was just finishing that . . .
. . . when Travis asked his question.
YOU BELIEVE IN ALL THIS EARTHSEED STUFF, DON'T YOU?
EVERY WORD.
BUT . . . YOU MADE IT UP.
IF I COULD ANALYZE THIS ROCK, TELL YOU ALL THAT IT WAS MADE OF, WOULD THAT MEAN I'D MADE UP ITS CONTENTS?
SO, WHAT DID YOU ANALYZE TO GET TO EARTHSEED?
OTHER PEOPLE, MYSELF, EVERYTHING I COULD READ, HEAR, SEE, ALL THE HISTORY I COULD LEARN.
MY FATHER IS—WAS—A MINISTER AND TEACHER. MY STEPMOTHER RAN A NEIGHBORHOOD SCHOOL. I SAW A LOT.
WHAT DID YOUR FATHER THINK OF YOUR IDEA OF GOD?

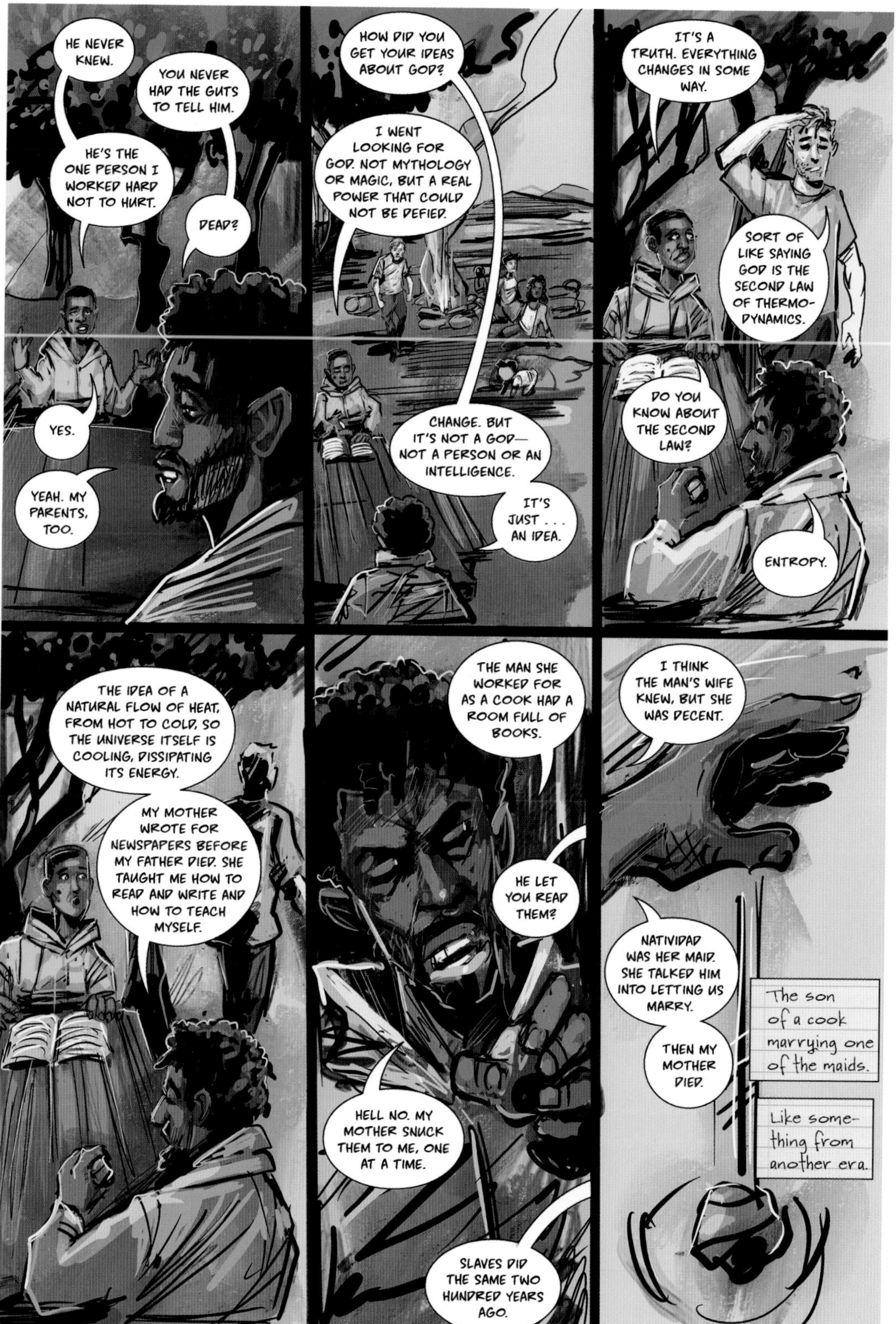
HE NEVER KNEW.
YOU NEVER HAD THE GUTS TO TELL HIM.
HE'S THE ONE PERSON I WORKED HARD NOT TO HURT.
DEAD?
YES.
YEAH. MY PARENTS, TOO.
HOW DID YOU GET YOUR IDEAS ABOUT GOD?
I WENT LOOKING FOR GOD. NOT MYTHOLOGY OR MAGIC, BUT A REAL POWER THAT COULD NOT BE DEFIED.
CHANGE. BUT IT'S NOT A GOD— NOT A PERSON OR AN INTELLIGENCE.
IT'S JUST . . . AN IDEA.
IT'S A TRUTH. EVERYTHING CHANGES IN SOME WAY.
SORT OF LIKE SAYING GOD IS THE SECOND LAW OF THERMO-DYNAMICS.
DO YOU KNOW ABOUT THE SECOND LAW?
ENTROPY.
THE IDEA OF A NATURAL FLOW OF HEAT, FROM HOT TO COLD, SO THE UNIVERSE ITSELF IS COOLING, DISSIPATING ITS ENERGY.
MY MOTHER WROTE FOR NEWSPAPERS BEFORE MY FATHER DIED. SHE TAUGHT ME HOW TO READ AND WRITE AND HOW TO TEACH MYSELF.
THE MAN SHE WORKED FOR AS A COOK HAD A ROOM FULL OF BOOKS.
HE LET YOU READ THEM?
HELL NO. MY MOTHER SNUCK THEM TO ME, ONE AT A TIME.
SLAVES DID THE SAME TWO HUNDRED YEARS AGO.
I THINK THE MAN'S WIFE KNEW, BUT SHE WAS DECENT.
NATIVIDAD WAS HER MAID. SHE TALKED HIM INTO LETTING US MARRY.
THEN MY MOTHER DIED.
The son of a cook marrying one of the maids.
Like something from another era.

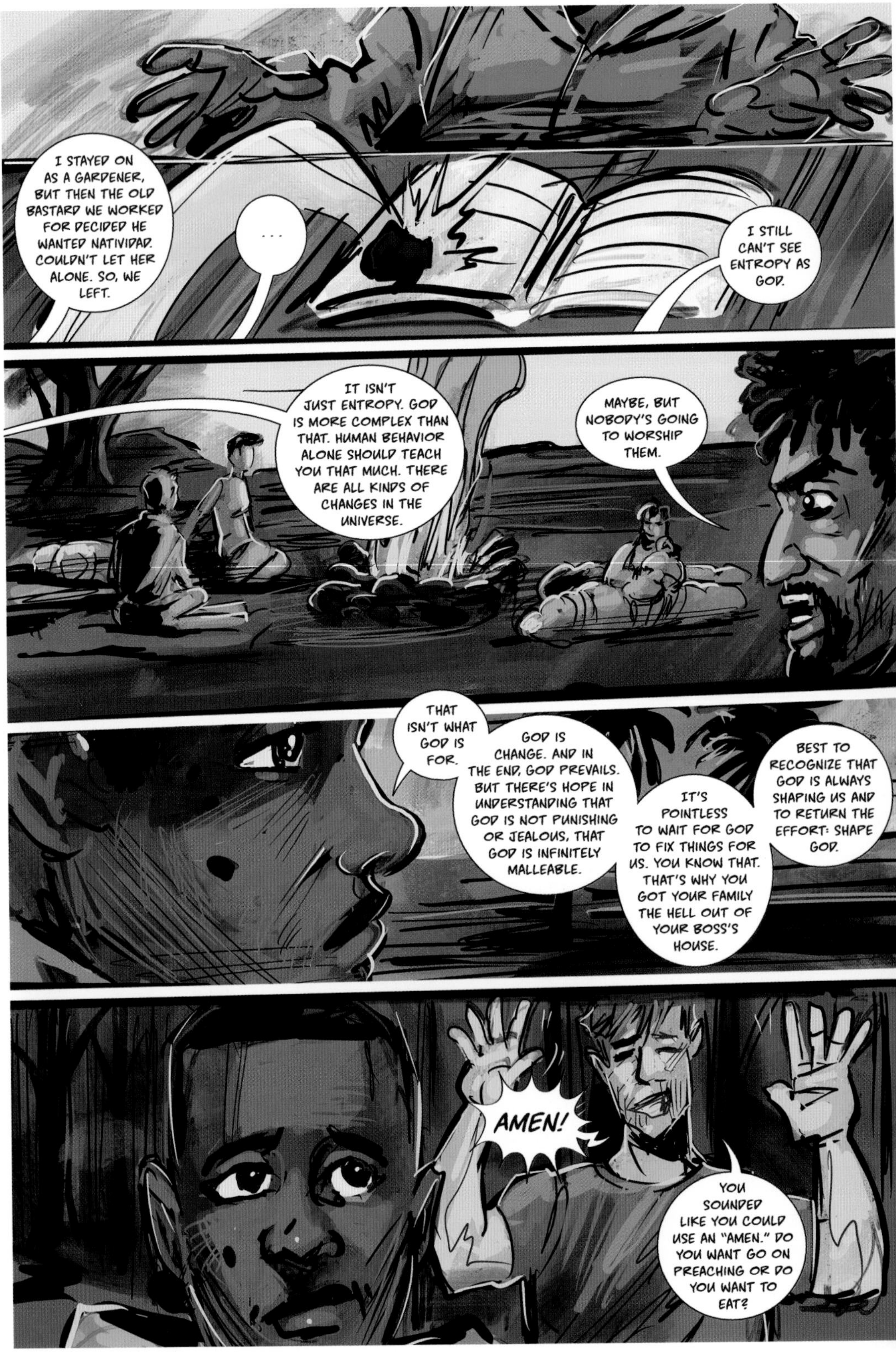
I STAYED ON AS A GARDENER, BUT THEN THE OLD BASTARD WE WORKED FOR DECIDED HE WANTED NATIVIDAD. COULDN'T LET HER ALONE. SO, WE LEFT.
. . .
I STILL CAN'T SEE ENTROPY AS GOD.
IT ISN'T JUST ENTROPY. GOD IS MORE COMPLEX THAN THAT. HUMAN BEHAVIOR ALONE SHOULD TEACH YOU THAT MUCH. THERE ARE ALL KINDS OF CHANGES IN THE UNIVERSE.
MAYBE, BUT NOBODY'S GOING TO WORSHIP THEM.
THAT ISN'T WHAT GOD IS FOR.
GOD IS CHANGE. AND IN THE END, GOD PREVAILS. BUT THERE'S HOPE IN UNDERSTANDING THAT GOD IS NOT PUNISHING OR JEALOUS, THAT GOD IS INFINITELY MALLEABLE.
IT'S POINTLESS TO WAIT FOR GOD TO FIX THINGS FOR US. YOU KNOW THAT. THAT'S WHY YOU GOT YOUR FAMILY THE HELL OUT OF YOUR BOSS'S HOUSE.
BEST TO RECOGNIZE THAT GOD IS ALWAYS SHAPING US AND TO RETURN THE EFFORT: SHAPE GOD.
AMEN!
YOU SOUNDED LIKE YOU COULD USE AN "AMEN." DO YOU WANT GO ON PREACHING OR DO YOU WANT TO EAT?

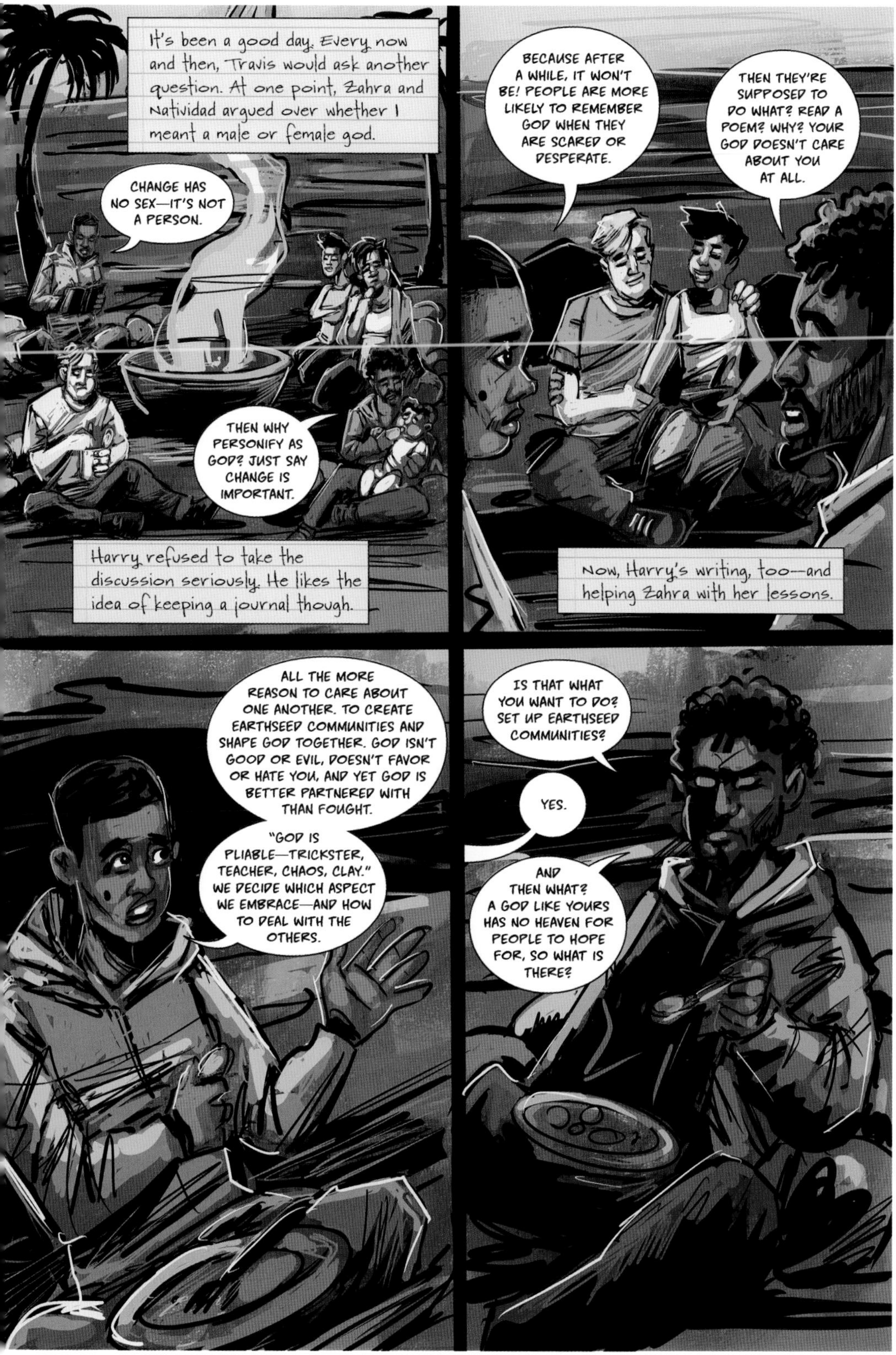
It's been a good day. Every now and then, Travis would ask another question. At one point, Zahra and Natividad argued over whether I meant a male or female god.
CHANGE HAS NO SEX—IT'S NOT A PERSON.
THEN WHY PERSONIFY AS GOD? JUST SAY CHANGE IS IMPORTANT.
Harry refused to take the discussion seriously. He likes the idea of keeping a journal though.
BECAUSE AFTER A WHILE, IT WON'T BE! PEOPLE ARE MORE LIKELY TO REMEMBER GOD WHEN THEY ARE SCARED OR DESPERATE.
THEN THEY'RE SUPPOSED TO DO WHAT? READ A POEM? WHY? YOUR GOD DOESN'T CARE ABOUT YOU AT ALL.
Now, Harry's writing, too—and helping Zahra with her lessons.
ALL THE MORE REASON TO CARE ABOUT ONE ANOTHER. TO CREATE EARTHSEED COMMUNITIES AND SHAPE GOD TOGETHER. GOD ISN'T GOOD OR EVIL, DOESN'T FAVOR OR HATE YOU, AND YET GOD IS BETTER PARTNERED WITH THAN FOUGHT.
"GOD IS PLIABLE—TRICKSTER, TEACHER, CHAOS, CLAY." WE DECIDE WHICH ASPECT WE EMBRACE—AND HOW TO DEAL WITH THE OTHERS.
IS THAT WHAT YOU WANT TO DO? SET UP EARTHSEED COMMUNITIES?
YES.
AND THEN WHAT? A GOD LIKE YOURS HAS NO HEAVEN FOR PEOPLE TO HOPE FOR, SO WHAT IS THERE?

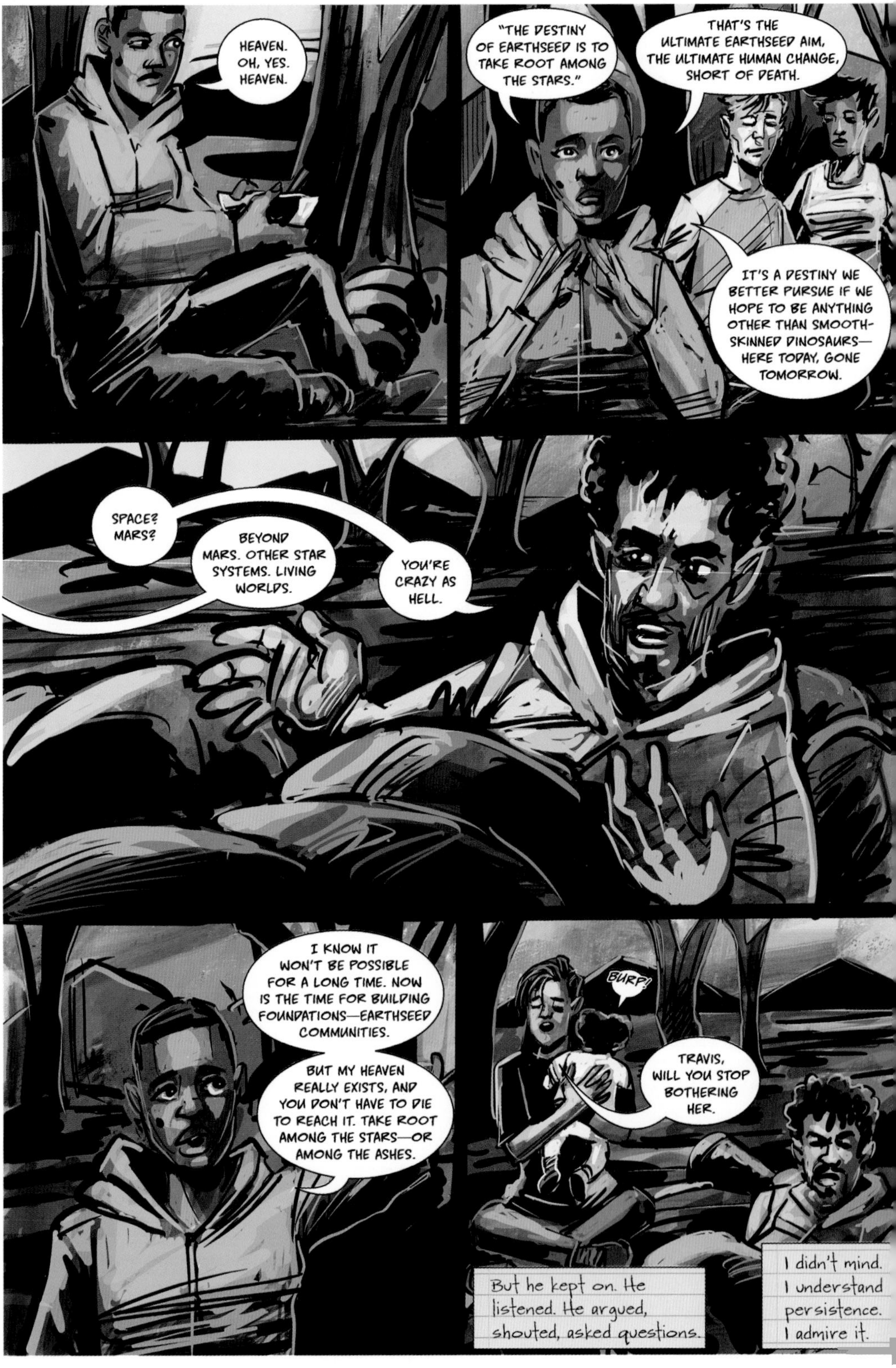
HEAVEN. OH, YES. HEAVEN.
"THE DESTINY OF EARTHSEED IS TO TAKE ROOT AMONG THE STARS."
THAT'S THE ULTIMATE EARTHSEED AIM, THE ULTIMATE HUMAN CHANGE, SHORT OF DEATH.
IT'S A DESTINY WE BETTER PURSUE IF WE HOPE TO BE ANYTHING OTHER THAN SMOOTH-SKINNED DINOSAURS—HERE TODAY, GONE TOMORROW.
SPACE? MARS?
BEYOND MARS. OTHER STAR SYSTEMS. LIVING WORLDS.
YOU'RE CRAZY AS HELL.
I KNOW IT WON'T BE POSSIBLE FOR A LONG TIME. NOW IS THE TIME FOR BUILDING FOUNDATIONS—EARTHSEED COMMUNITIES.
BUT MY HEAVEN REALLY EXISTS, AND YOU DON'T HAVE TO DIE TO REACH IT. TAKE ROOT AMONG THE STARS—OR AMONG THE ASHES.
BURP!
TRAVIS, WILL YOU STOP BOTHERING HER.
But he kept on. He listened. He argued, shouted, asked questions.
I didn't mind. I understand persistence. I admire it.

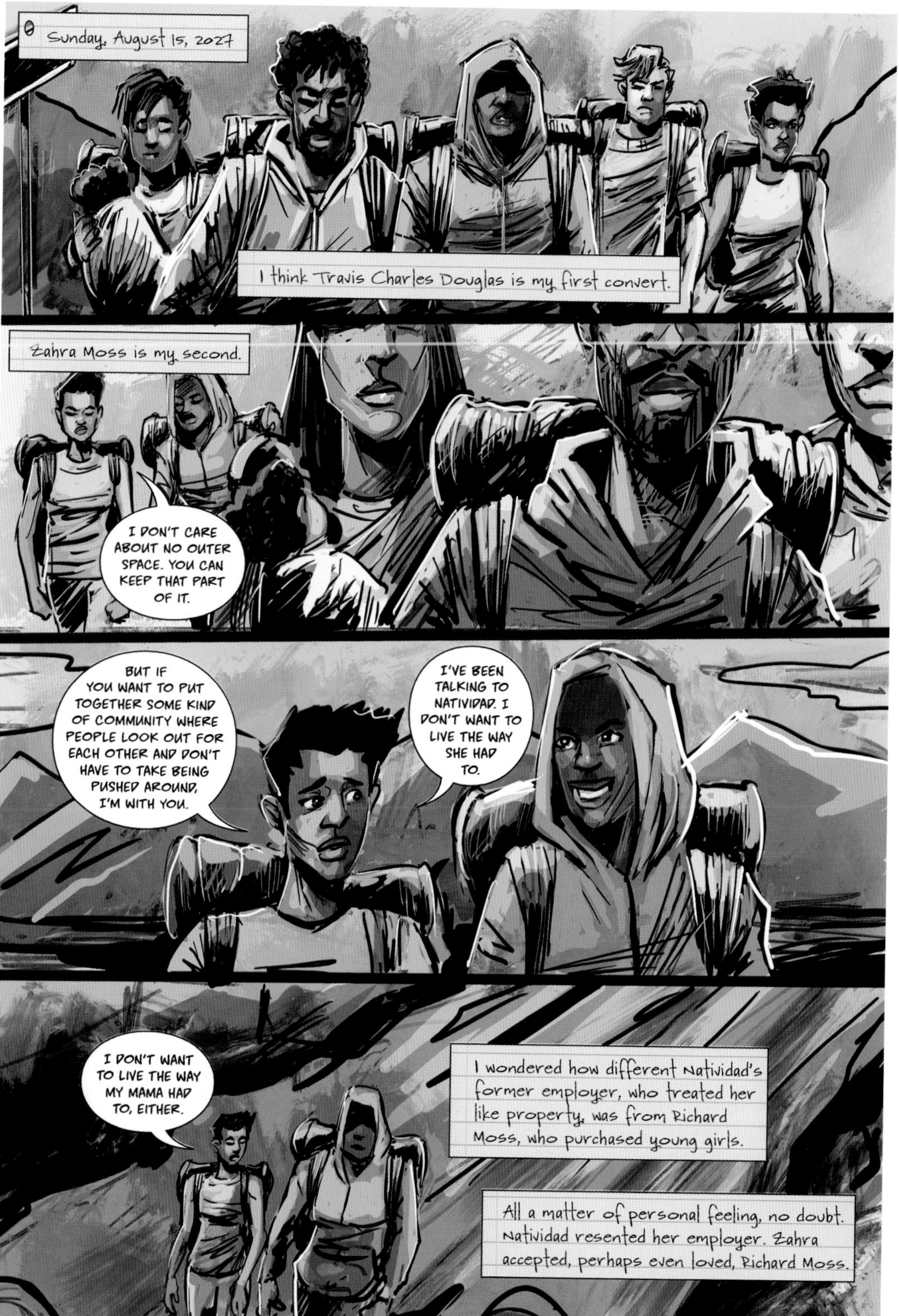

Sunday, August 15, 2027
I think Travis Charles Douglas is my first convert.
Zahra Moss is my second.
I DON'T CARE ABOUT NO OUTER SPACE. YOU CAN KEEP THAT PART OF IT.
BUT IF YOU WANT TO PUT TOGETHER SOME KIND OF COMMUNITY WHERE PEOPLE LOOK OUT FOR EACH OTHER AND DON'T HAVE TO TAKE BEING PUSHED AROUND, I'M WITH YOU.
I'VE BEEN TALKING TO NATIVIDAD. I DON'T WANT TO LIVE THE WAY SHE HAD TO.
I DON'T WANT TO LIVE THE WAY MY MAMA HAD TO, EITHER.
I wondered how different Natividad's former employer, who treated her like property, was from Richard Moss, who purchased young girls.
All a matter of personal feeling, no doubt. Natividad resented her employer. Zahra accepted, perhaps even loved, Richard Moss.

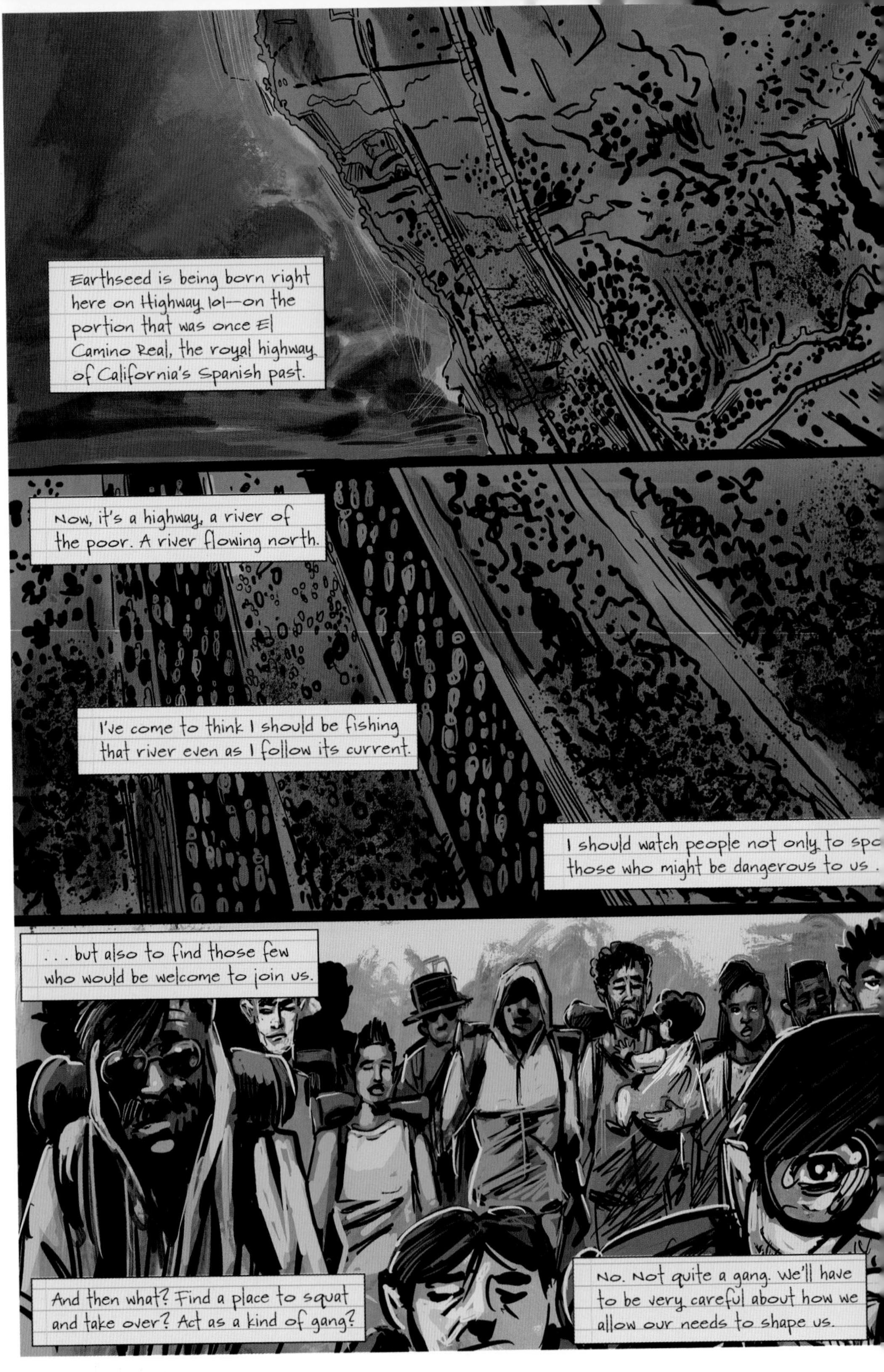
Earthseed is being born right here on Highway 101—on the portion that was once El Camino Real, the royal highway of California's Spanish past.
Now, it's a highway, a river of the poor. A river flowing north.
I've come to think I should be fishing that river even as I follow its current.
I should watch people not only to spo
those who might be dangerous to us . .
. . . but also to find those few who would be welcome to join us.
And then what? Find a place to squat and take over? Act as a kind of gang?
No. Not quite a gang. We'll have to be very careful about how we allow our needs to shape us.

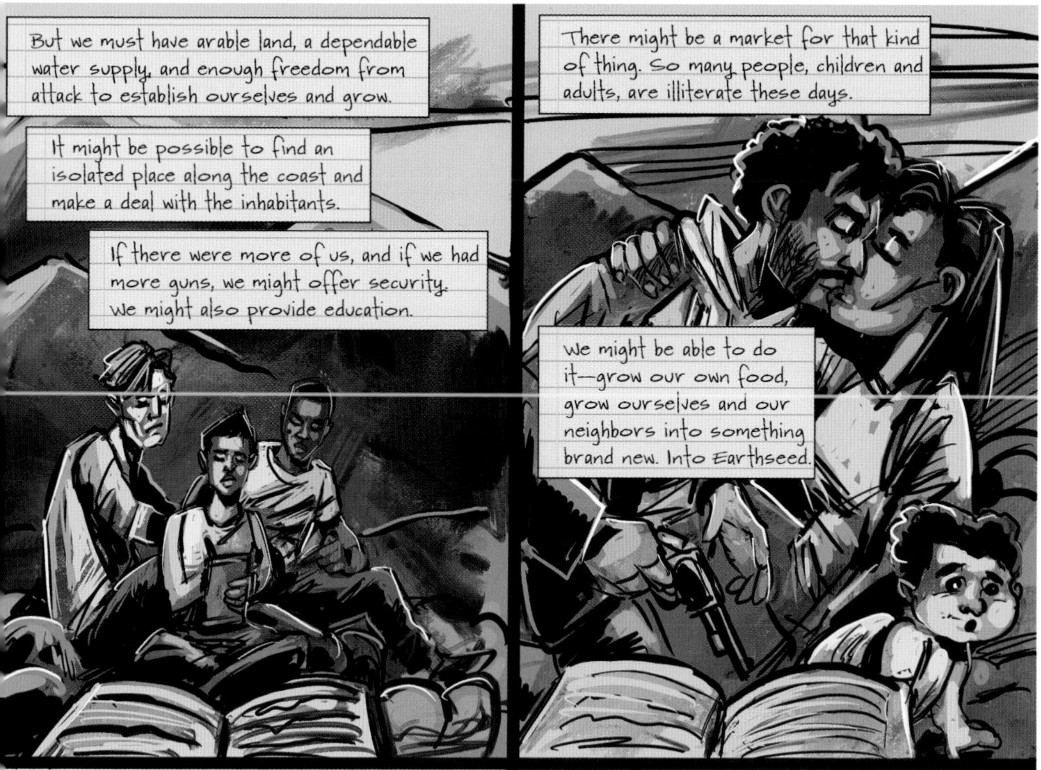
But we must have arable land, a dependable water supply, and enough freedom from attack to establish ourselves and grow.
It might be possible to find an isolated place along the coast and make a deal with the inhabitants.
If there were more of us, and if we had more guns, we might offer security. We might also provide education.
There might be a market for that kind of thing. So many people, children and adults, are illiterate these days.
We might be able to do it—grow our own food, grow ourselves and our neighbors into something brand new. Into Earthseed.

Changes.
The galaxies move through space.
The stars ignite,
burn,
age,
cool,
Evolving.
God is Change.
God prevails.

EARTHSEED: THE
BOOKS OF THE LIVING

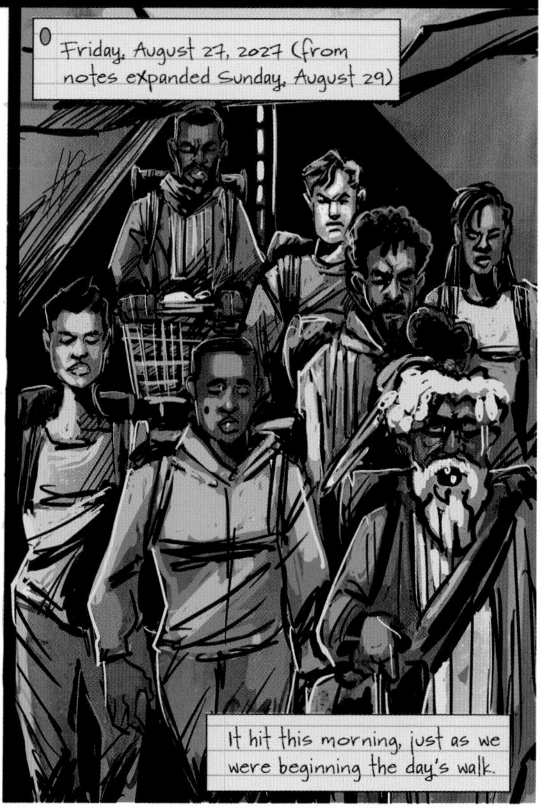
Friday, August 27, 2027 (from notes expanded Sunday, August 29)
It hit this morning, just as we were beginning the day's walk.

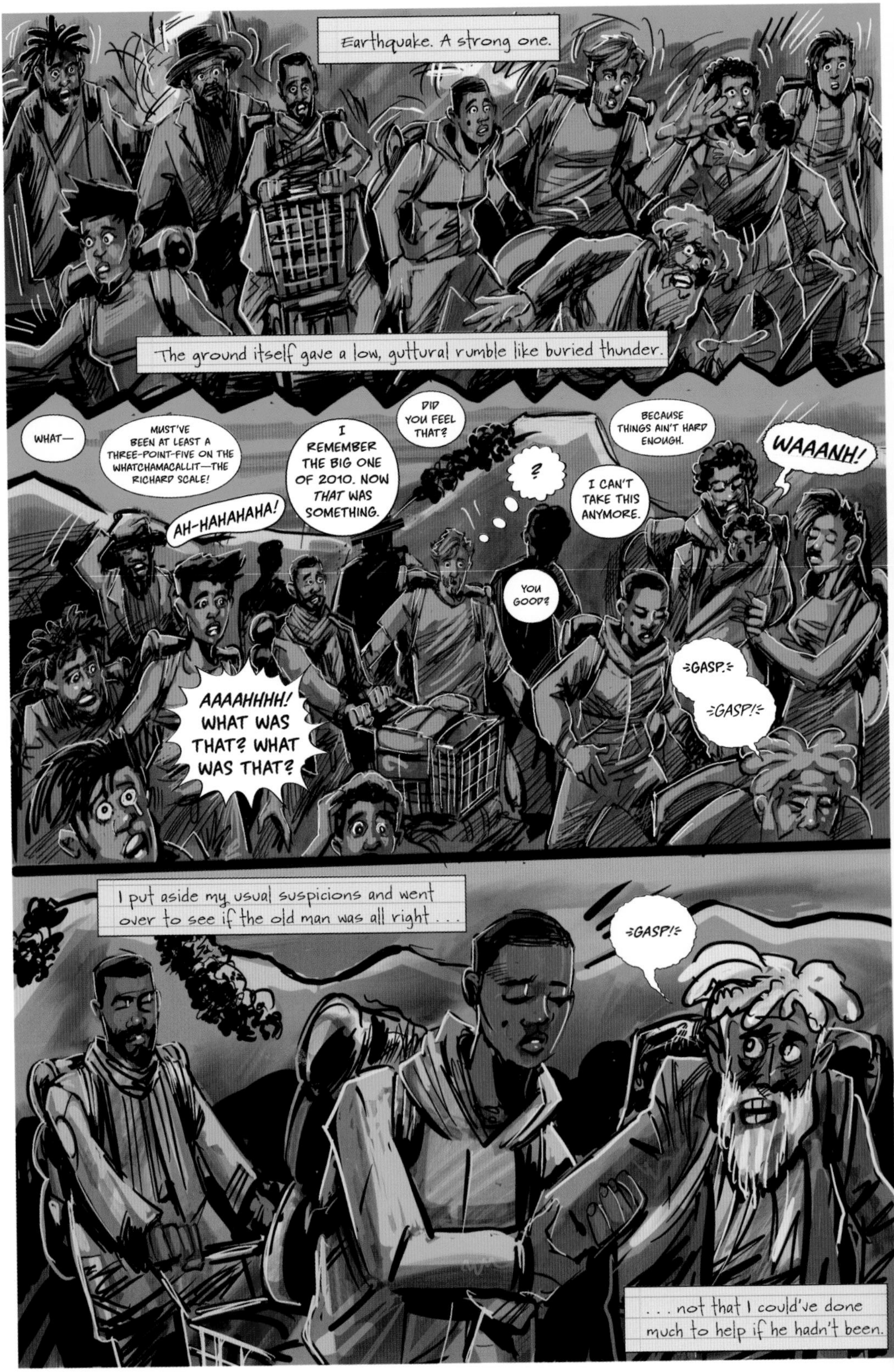
Earthquake. A strong one.
The ground itself gave a low, guttural rumble like buried thunder.
WHAT—
MUST'VE BEEN AT LEAST A THREE-POINT-FIVE ON THE WHATCHAMACALLIT—THE RICHARD SCALE!
I REMEMBER THE BIG ONE OF 2010. NOW THAT WAS SOMETHING.
DID YOU FEEL THAT?
?
BECAUSE THINGS AIN'T HARD ENOUGH.
WAAANH!
I CAN'T TAKE THIS ANYMORE.
AH-HAHAHAHA!
YOU GOOD?
AAAAHHHH! WHAT WAS THAT? WHAT WAS THAT?
GASP.
GASP!
I put aside my usual suspicions and went over to see if the old man was all right . . .
GASP!
. . . not that I could've done much to help if he hadn't been.

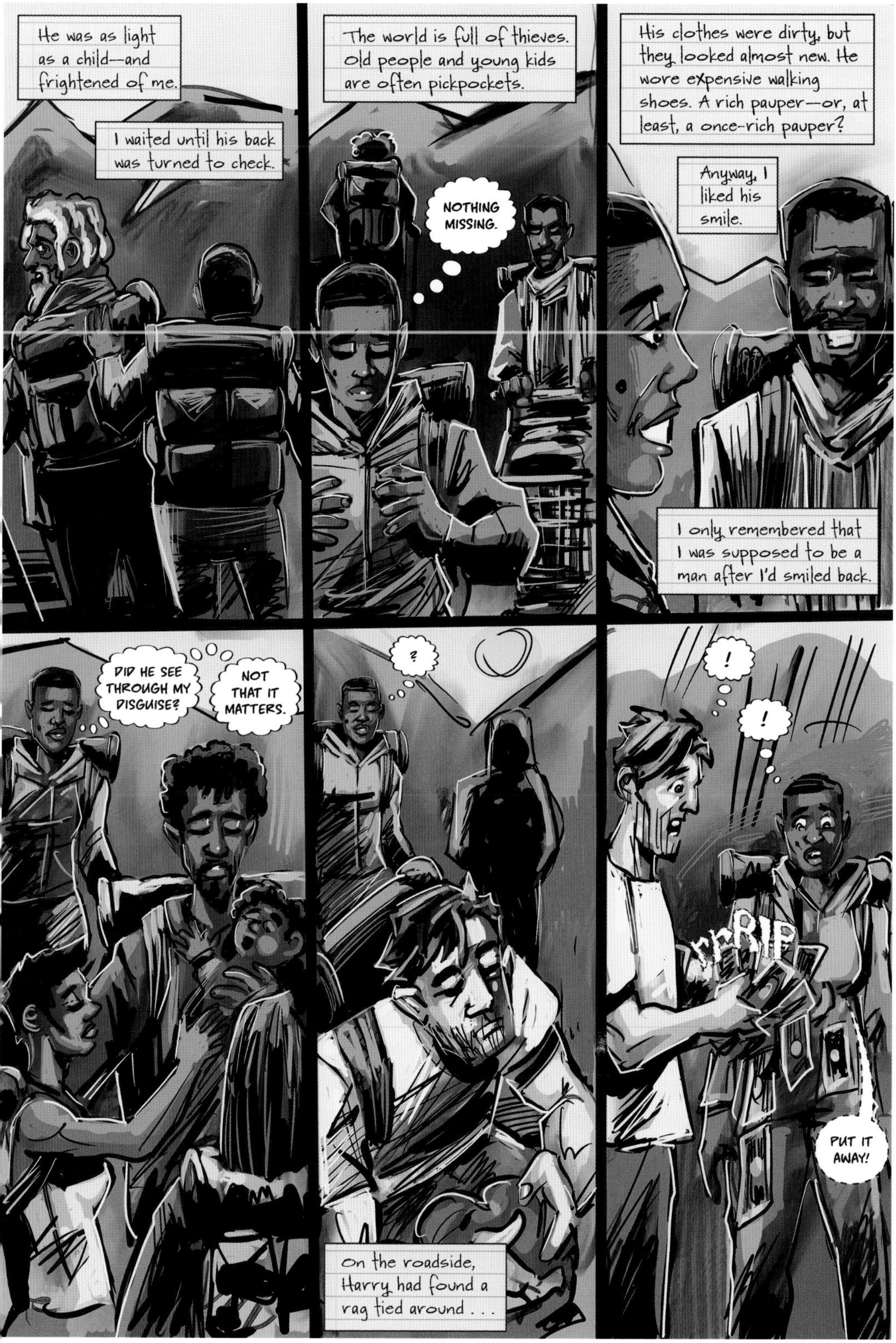
He was as light as a child—and frightened of me.
I waited until his back was turned to check.
The world is full of thieves. Old people and young kids are often pickpockets.
NOTHING MISSING.
His clothes were dirty, but they looked almost new. He wore expensive walking shoes. A rich pauper—or, at least, a once-rich pauper?
Anyway, I liked his smile.
I only remembered that I was supposed to be a man after I'd smiled back.
DID HE SEE THROUGH MY DISGUISE?
NOT THAT IT MATTERS.
?
On the roadside, Harry had found a rag tied around . . .
!
!
RRRIP
PUT IT AWAY!

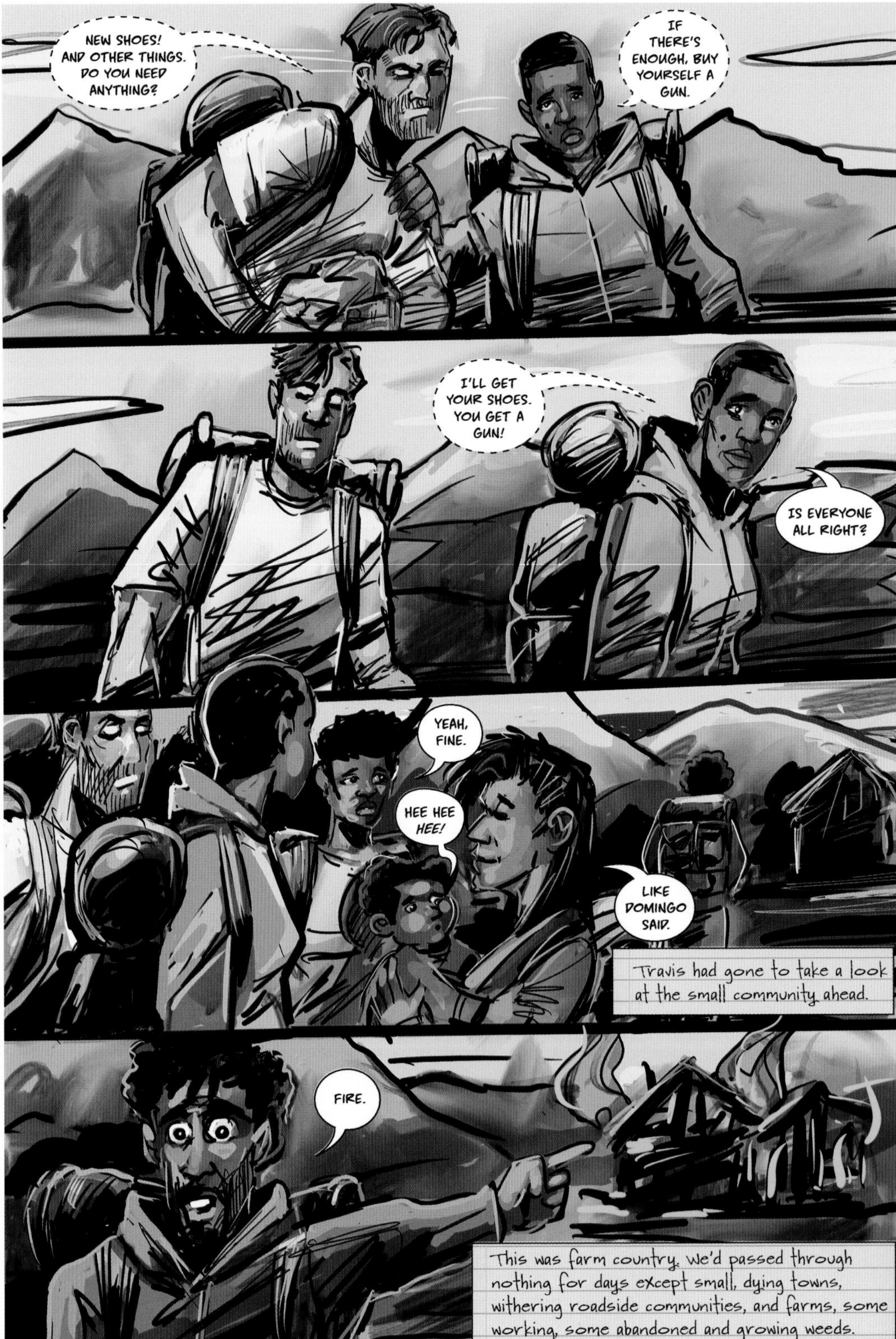
NEW SHOES! AND OTHER THINGS. DO YOU NEED ANYTHING?
IF THERE'S ENOUGH, BUY YOURSELF A GUN.
I'LL GET YOUR SHOES. YOU GET A GUN!
IS EVERYONE ALL RIGHT?
YEAH, FINE.
HEE HEE HEE!
LIKE DOMINGO SAID.
Travis had gone to take a look at the small community ahead.
FIRE.
This was farm country. We'd passed through nothing for days except small, dying towns, withering roadside communities, and farms, some working, some abandoned and growing weeds.

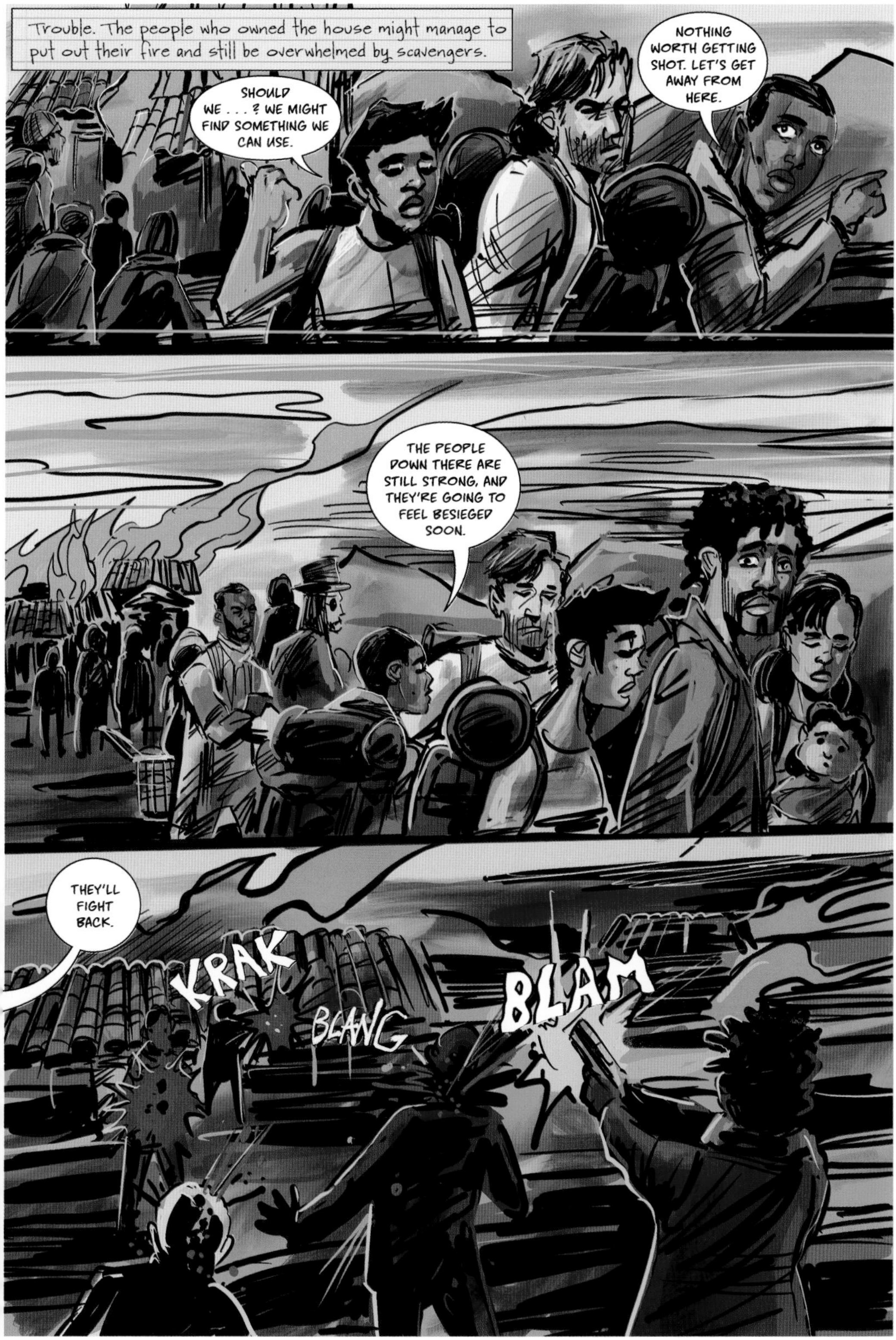
Trouble. The people who owned the house might manage to put out their fire and still be overwhelmed by scavengers.
SHOULD WE . . . ? WE MIGHT FIND SOMETHING WE CAN USE.
NOTHING WORTH GETTING SHOT. LET'S GET AWAY FROM HERE.
THE PEOPLE DOWN THERE ARE STILL STRONG, AND THEY'RE GOING TO FEEL BESIEGED SOON.
THEY'LL FIGHT BACK.
KRAK
BLANG
BLAM

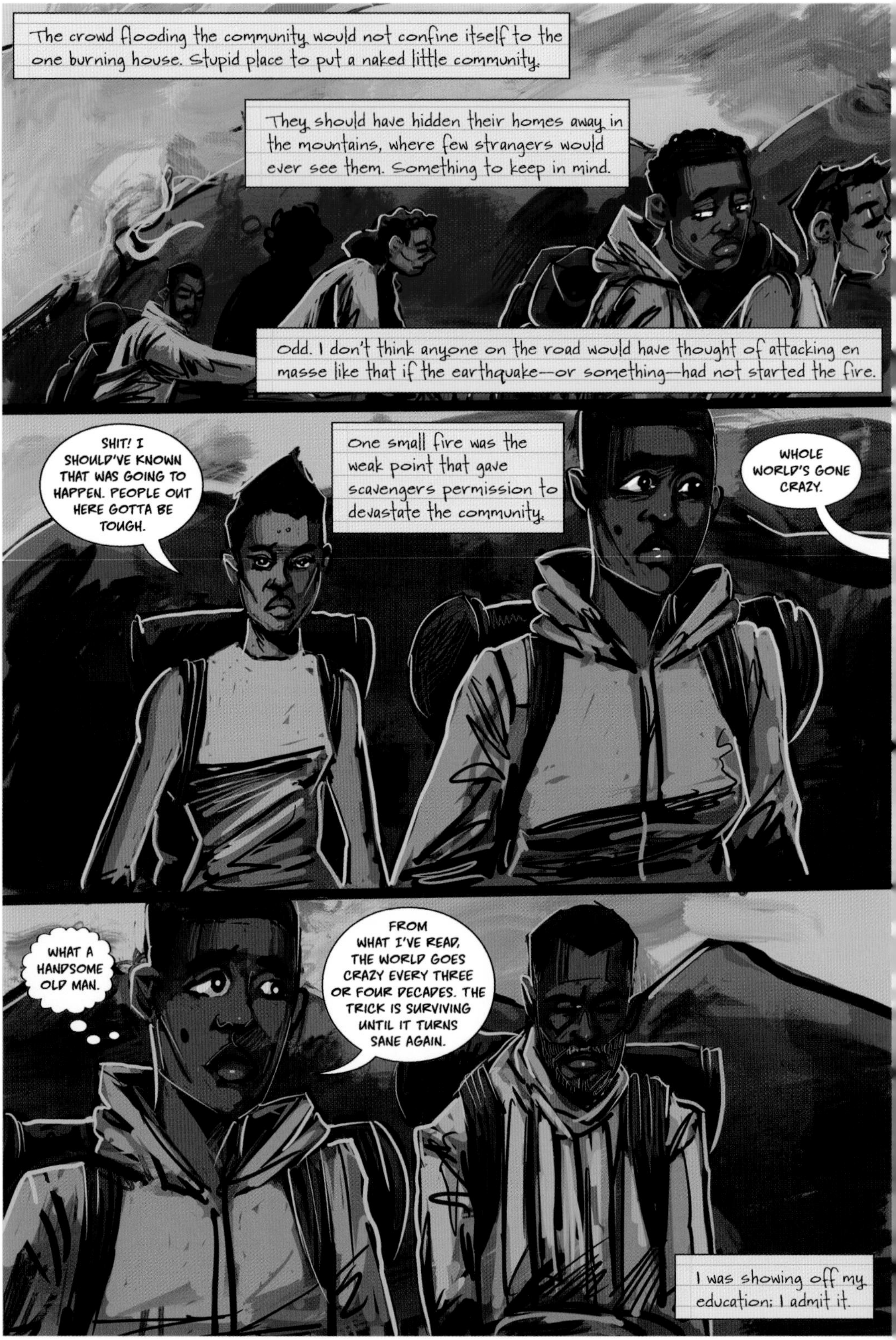

The crowd flooding the community would not confine itself to the one burning house. Stupid place to put a naked little community.
They should have hidden their homes away in the mountains, where few strangers would ever see them. Something to keep in mind.
Odd. I don't think anyone on the road would have thought of attacking en masse like that if the earthquake—or something—had not started the fire.
SHIT! I SHOULD'VE KNOWN THAT WAS GOING TO HAPPEN. PEOPLE OUT HERE GOTTA BE TOUGH.
One small fire was the weak point that gave scavengers permission to devastate the community.
WHOLE WORLD'S GONE CRAZY.
WHAT A HANDSOME OLD MAN.
FROM WHAT I'VE READ, THE WORLD GOES CRAZY EVERY THREE OR FOUR DECADES. THE TRICK IS SURVIVING UNTIL IT TURNS SANE AGAIN.
I was showing off my education; I admit it.

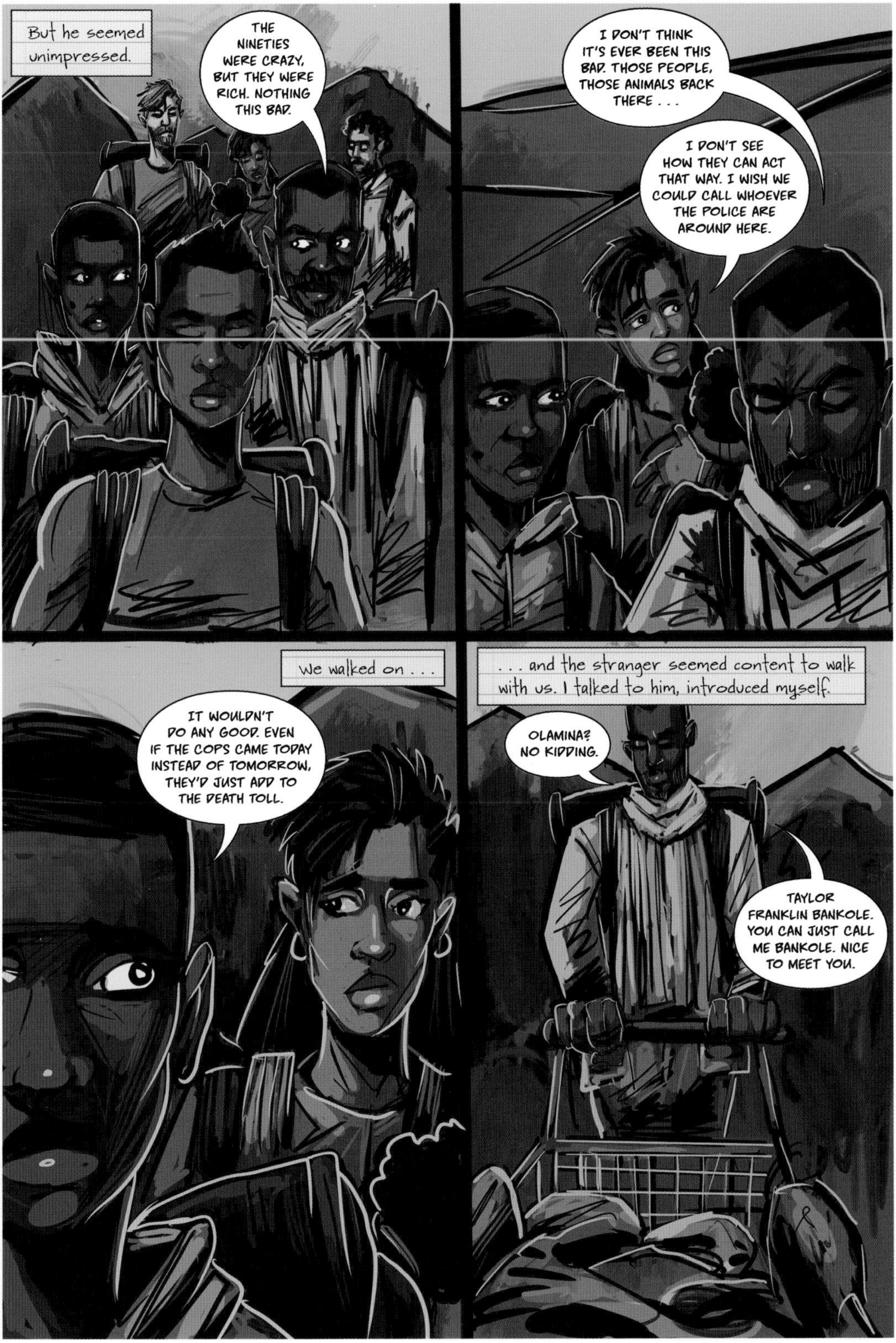
But he seemed unimpressed.
THE NINETIES WERE CRAZY, BUT THEY WERE RICH. NOTHING THIS BAD.
I DON'T THINK IT'S EVER BEEN THIS BAD. THOSE PEOPLE, THOSE ANIMALS BACK THERE . . .
I DON'T SEE HOW THEY CAN ACT THAT WAY. I WISH WE COULD CALL WHOEVER THE POLICE ARE AROUND HERE.
We walked on . . .
IT WOULDN'T DO ANY GOOD. EVEN IF THE COPS CAME TODAY INSTEAD OF TOMORROW, THEY'D JUST ADD TO THE DEATH TOLL.
. . . and the stranger seemed content to walk with us. I talked to him, introduced myself.
OLAMINA? NO KIDDING.
TAYLOR FRANKLIN BANKOLE. YOU CAN JUST CALL ME BANKOLE. NICE TO MEET YOU.

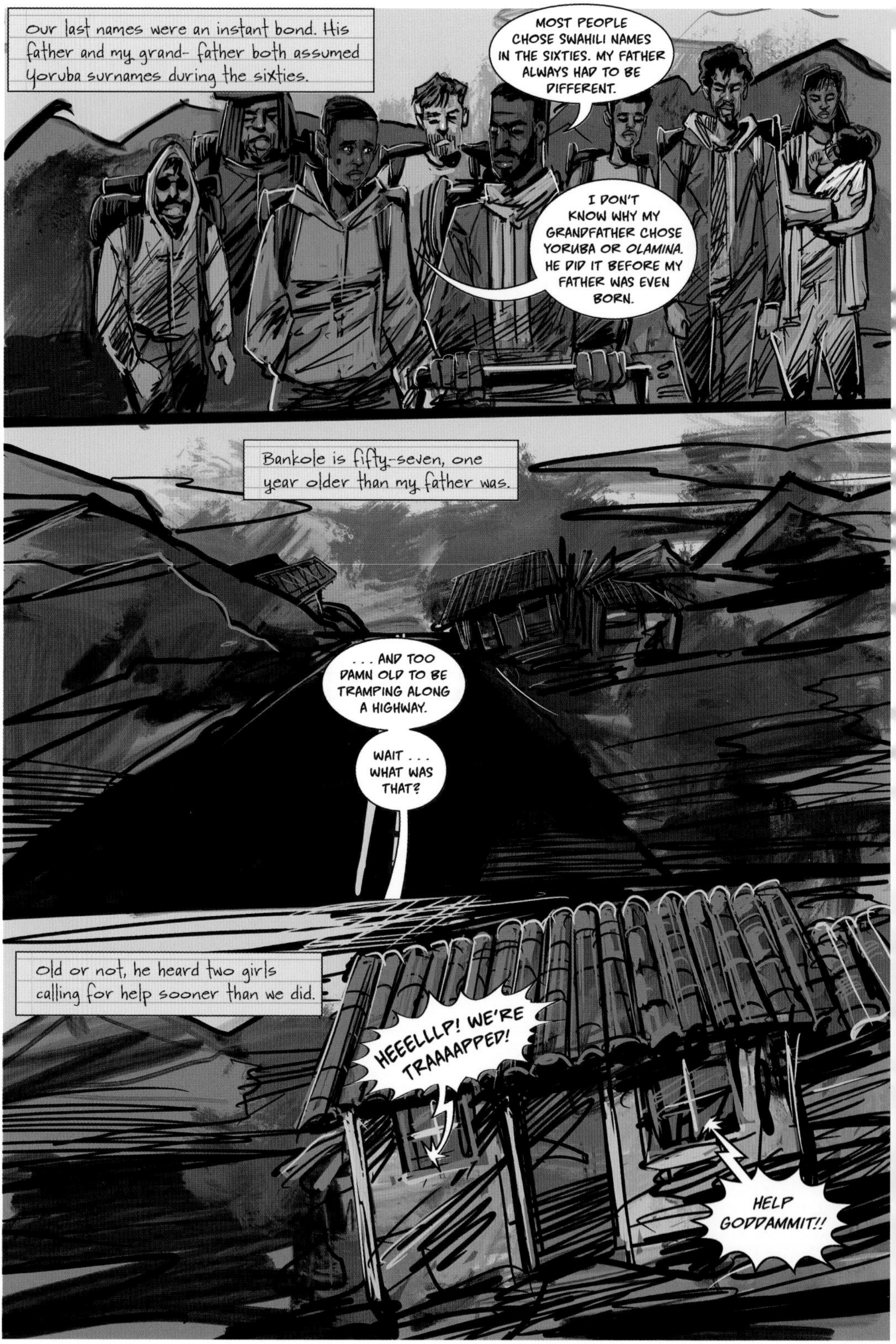

Our last names were an instant bond. His father and my grand- father both assumed Yoruba surnames during the sixties.
MOST PEOPLE CHOSE SWAHILI NAMES IN THE SIXTIES. MY FATHER ALWAYS HAD TO BE DIFFERENT.
I DON'T KNOW WHY MY GRANDFATHER CHOSE YORUBA OR OLAMINA. HE DID IT BEFORE MY FATHER WAS EVEN BORN.
Bankole is fifty-seven, one year older than my father was.
. . . AND TOO DAMN OLD TO BE TRAMPING ALONG A HIGHWAY.
WAIT . . . WHAT WAS THAT?
Old or not, he heard two girls calling for help sooner than we did.
HEEELLLP! WE'RE TRAAAAPPED!
HELP GODDAMMIT!!

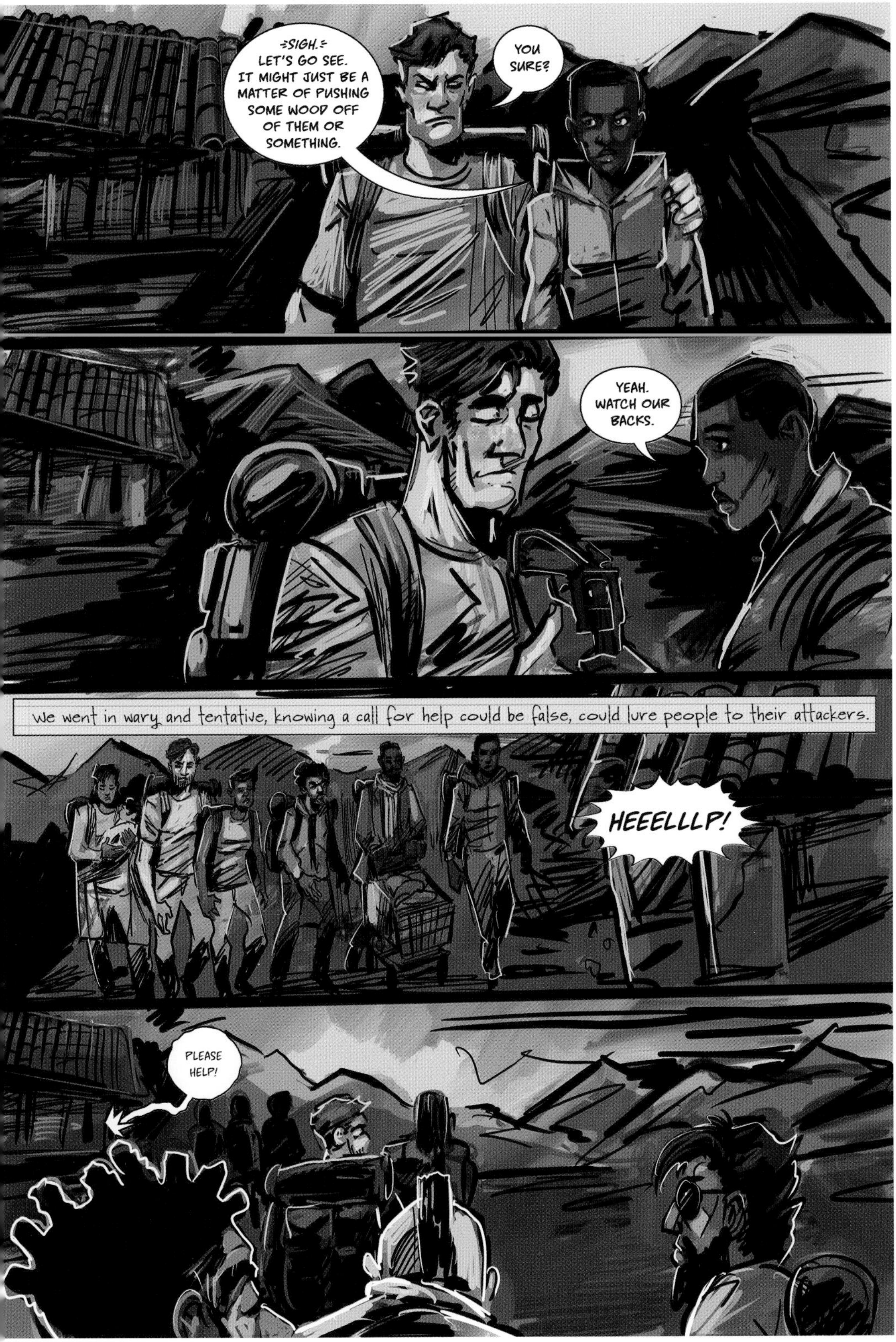

=SIGH.= LET'S GO SEE. IT MIGHT JUST BE A MATTER OF PUSHING SOME WOOD OFF OF THEM OR SOMETHING.
YOU SURE?
YEAH. WATCH OUR BACKS.
we went in wary and tentative, knowing a call for help could be false, could lure people to their attackers.
HEEELLLP!
PLEASE HELP!

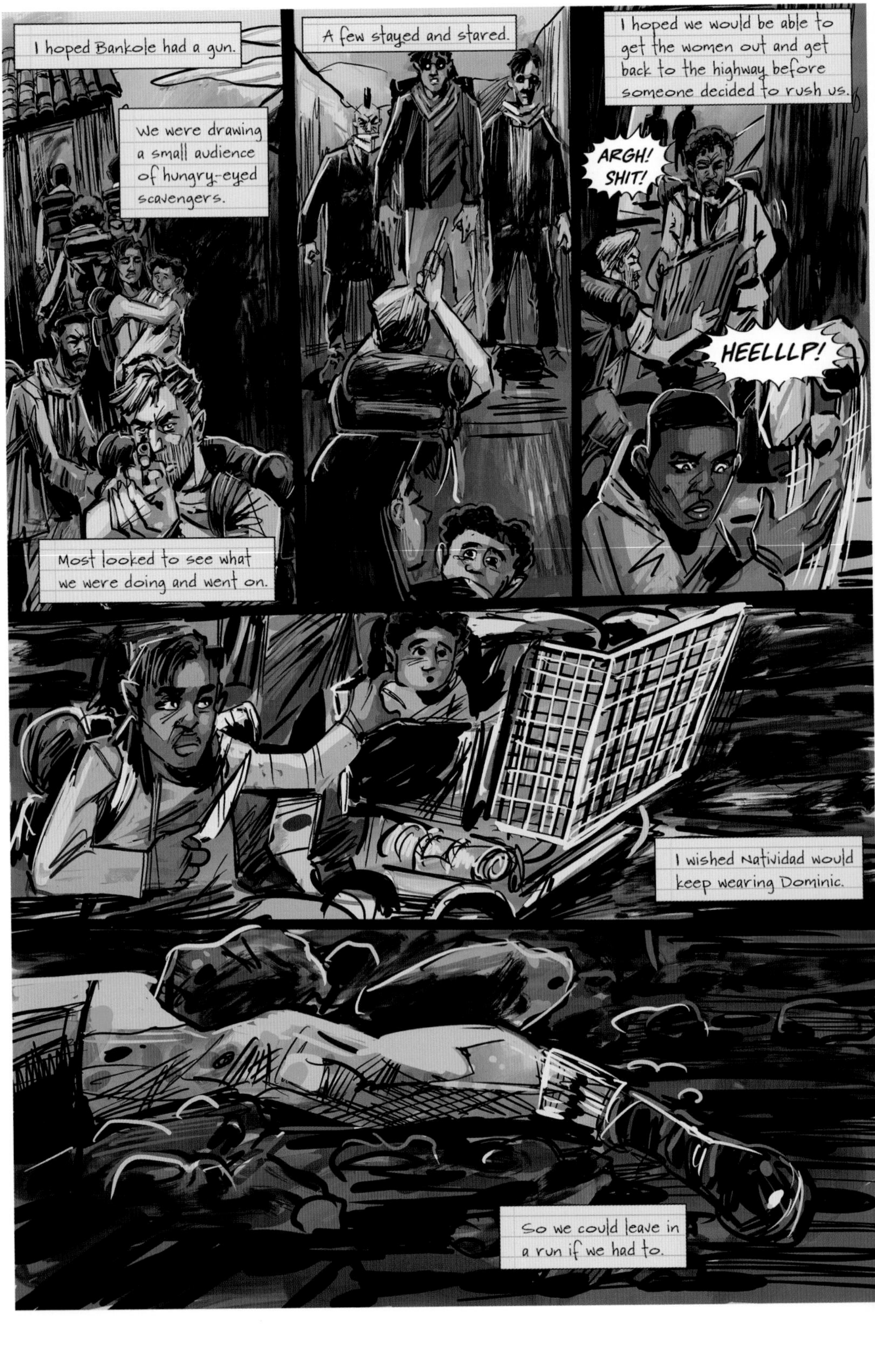
I hoped Bankole had a gun.
We were drawing a small audience of hungry-eyed scavengers.
Most looked to see what we were doing and went on.
A few stayed and stared.
I hoped we would be able to get the women out and get back to the highway before someone decided to rush us.
ARGH! SHIT!
HEELLLP!
I wished Natividad would keep wearing Dominic.
So we could leave in a run if we had to.

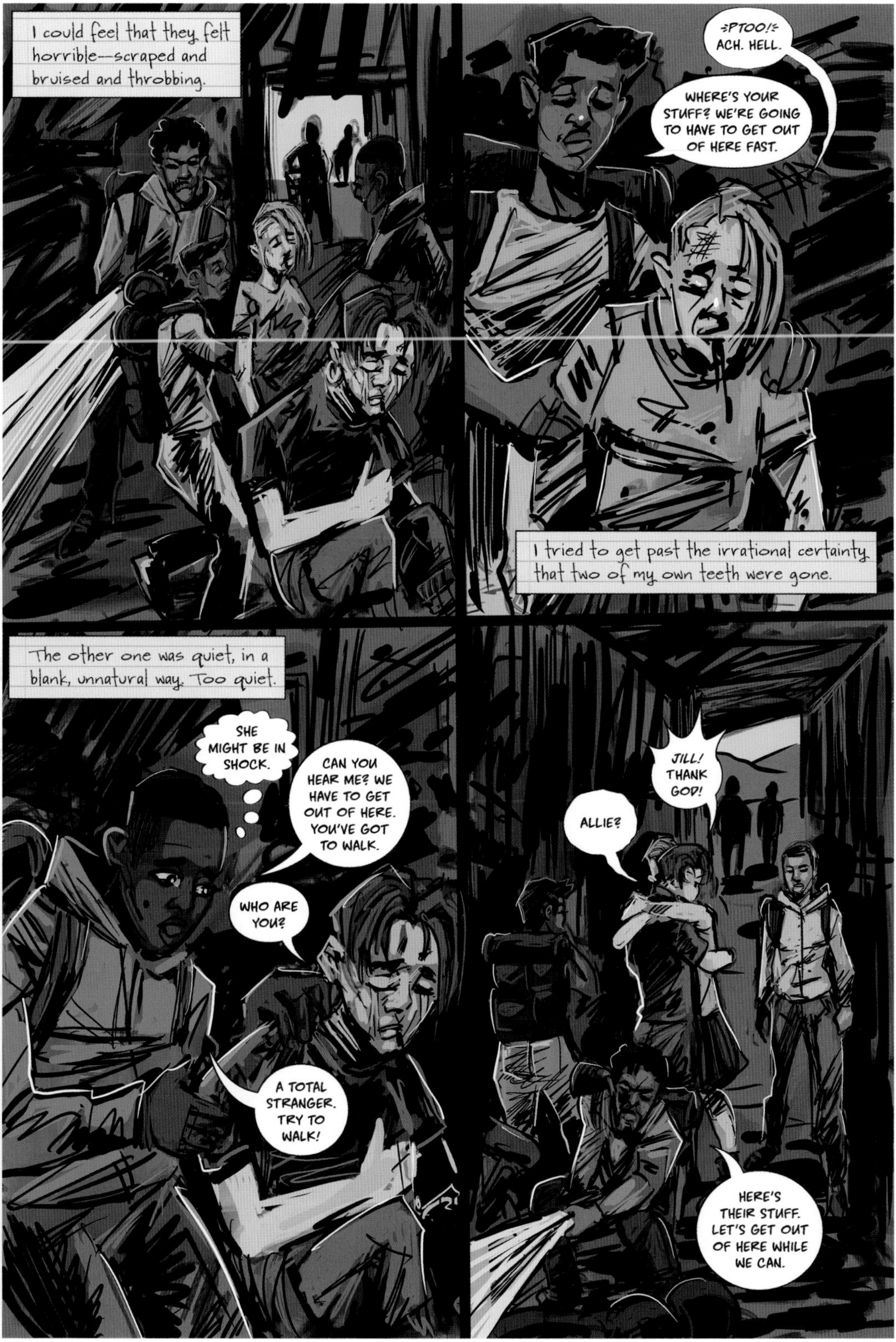
I could feel that they felt horrible—scraped and bruised and throbbing.
⪡PTOO!⪢ ACH. HELL.
WHERE'S YOUR STUFF? WE'RE GOING TO HAVE TO GET OUT OF HERE FAST.
I tried to get past the irrational certainty that two of my own teeth were gone.
The other one was quiet, in a blank, unnatural way. Too quiet.
SHE MIGHT BE IN SHOCK.
CAN YOU HEAR ME? WE HAVE TO GET OUT OF HERE. YOU'VE GOT TO WALK.
WHO ARE YOU?
A TOTAL STRANGER. TRY TO WALK!
JILL! THANK GOD!
ALLIE?
HERE'S THEIR STUFF. LET'S GET OUT OF HERE WHILE WE CAN.

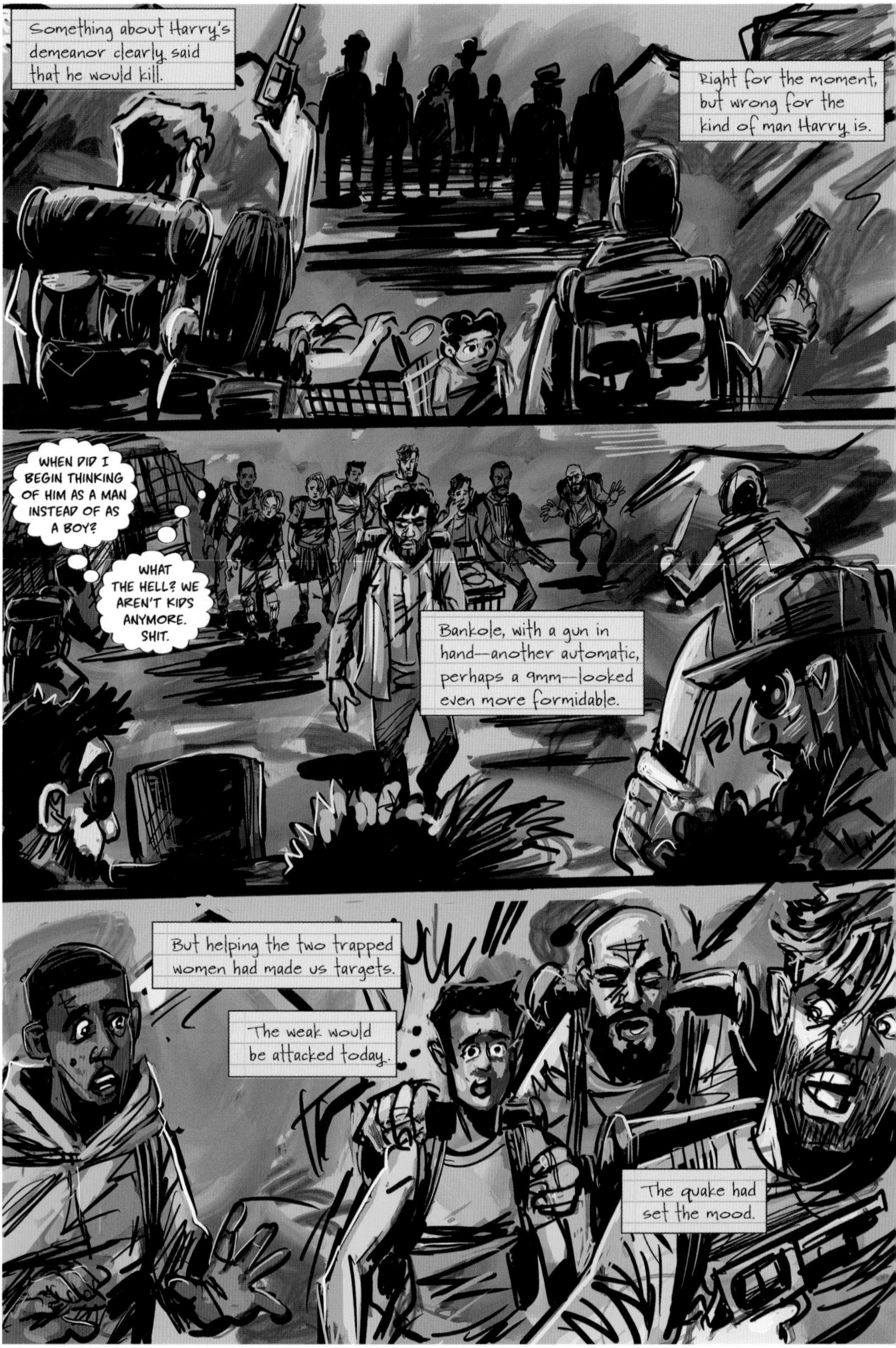
Something about Harry's demeanor clearly said that he would kill.
Right for the moment, but wrong for the kind of man Harry is.
WHEN DID I BEGIN THINKING OF HIM AS A MAN INSTEAD OF AS A BOY?
WHAT THE HELL? WE AREN'T KIDS ANYMORE. SHIT.
Bankole, with a gun in hand—another automatic, perhaps a 9mm—looked even more formidable.
But helping the two trapped women had made us targets.
The weak would be attacked today.
The quake had set the mood.

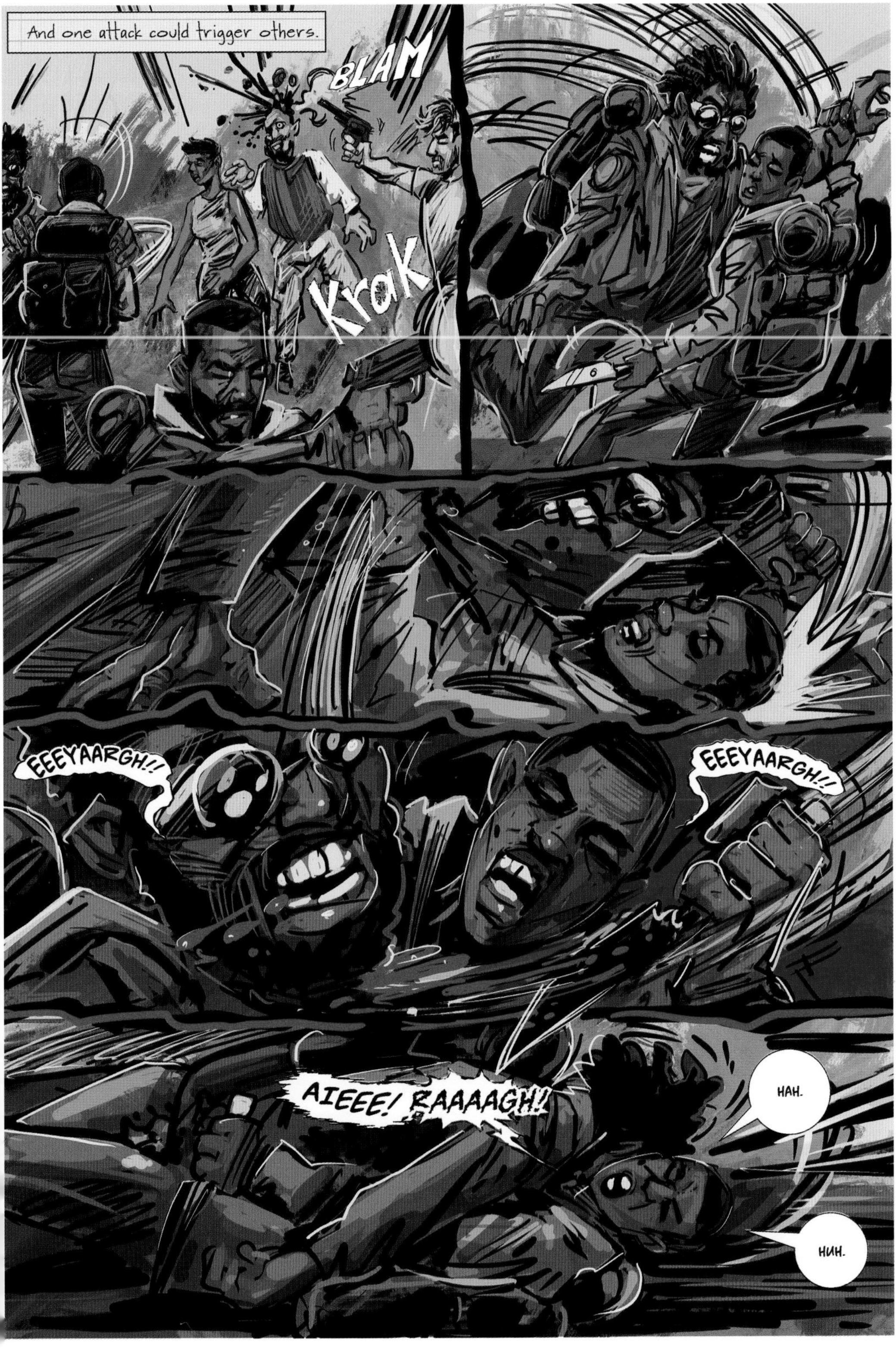
And one attack could trigger others.
BLAM
KRAK
EEEYAARGH!!
EEEYAARGH!!
AIEEE! RAAAAGH!
HAH.
HUH.

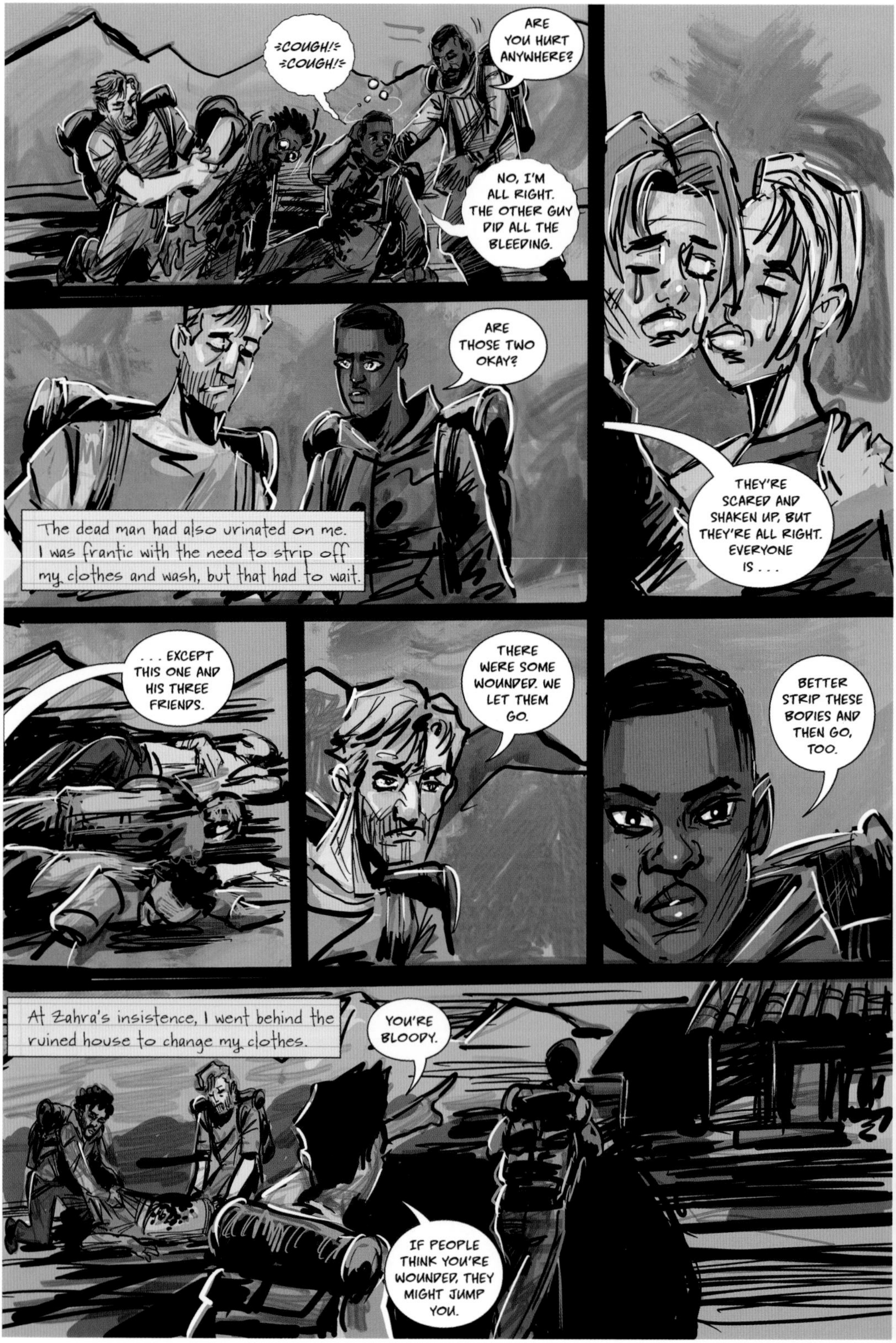

COUGH! COUGH!
ARE YOU HURT ANYWHERE?
NO, I'M ALL RIGHT. THE OTHER GUY DID ALL THE BLEEDING.
ARE THOSE TWO OKAY?
The dead man had also urinated on me. I was frantic with the need to strip off my clothes and wash, but that had to wait.
THEY'RE SCARED AND SHAKEN UP, BUT THEY'RE ALL RIGHT. EVERYONE IS . . .
. . . EXCEPT THIS ONE AND HIS THREE FRIENDS.
THERE WERE SOME WOUNDED. WE LET THEM GO.
BETTER STRIP THESE BODIES AND THEN GO, TOO.
At Zahra's insistence, I went behind the ruined house to change my clothes.
YOU'RE BLOODY.
IF PEOPLE THINK YOU'RE WOUNDED, THEY MIGHT JUMP YOU.

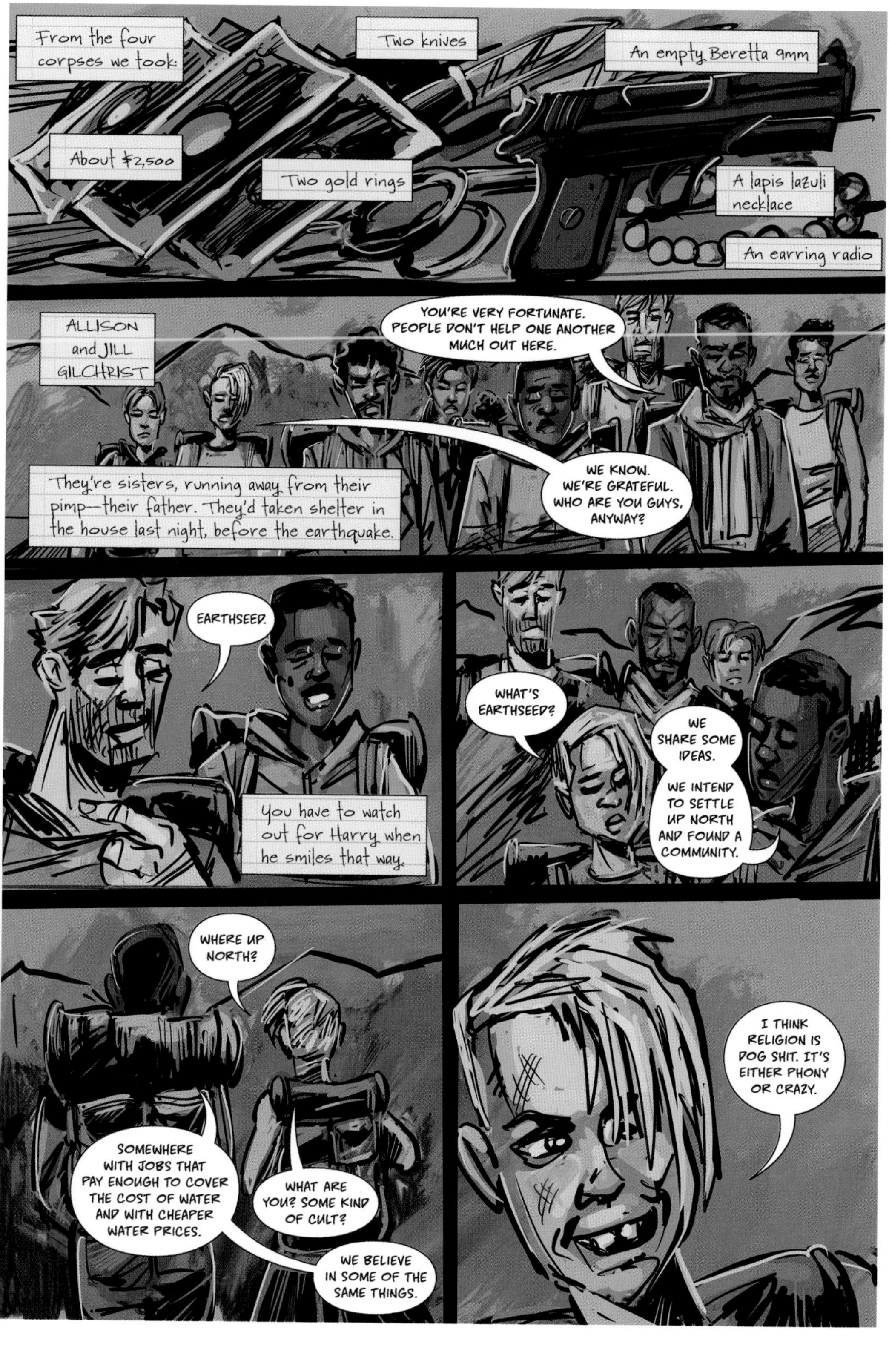
From the four corpses we took:
Two knives
An empty Beretta 9mm
About $2,500
Two gold rings
A lapis lazuli necklace
An earring radio
ALLISON and JILL GILCHRIST
YOU'RE VERY FORTUNATE. PEOPLE DON'T HELP ONE ANOTHER MUCH OUT HERE.
They're sisters, running away from their pimp—their father. They'd taken shelter in the house last night, before the earthquake.
WE KNOW. WE'RE GRATEFUL. WHO ARE YOU GUYS, ANYWAY?
EARTHSEED.
You have to watch out for Harry when he smiles that way.
WHAT'S EARTHSEED?
WE SHARE SOME IDEAS.
WE INTEND TO SETTLE UP NORTH AND FOUND A COMMUNITY.
WHERE UP NORTH?
SOMEWHERE WITH JOBS THAT PAY ENOUGH TO COVER THE COST OF WATER AND WITH CHEAPER WATER PRICES.
WHAT ARE YOU? SOME KIND OF CULT?
WE BELIEVE IN SOME OF THE SAME THINGS.
I THINK RELIGION IS DOG SHIT. IT'S EITHER PHONY OR CRAZY.

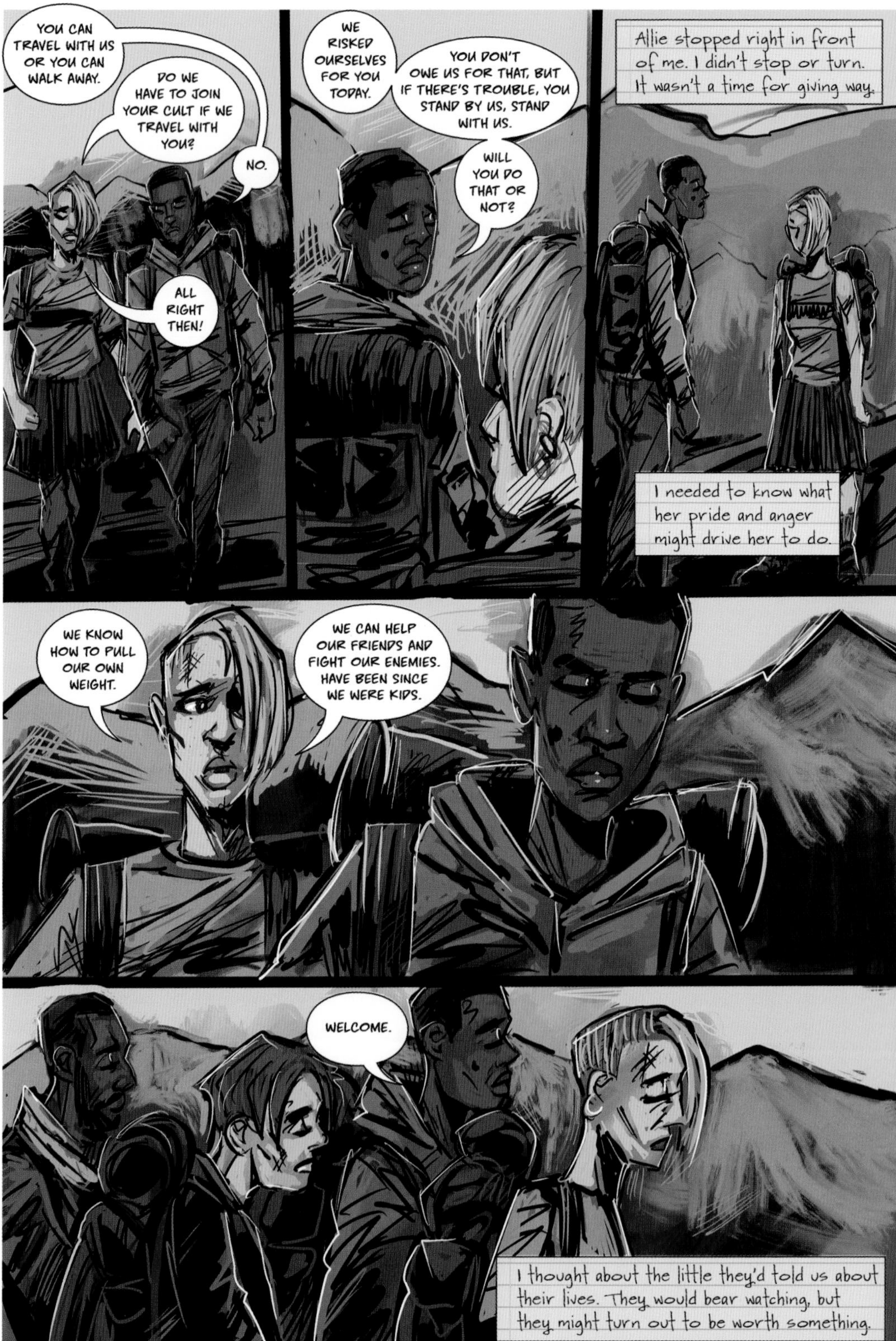
YOU CAN TRAVEL WITH US OR YOU CAN WALK AWAY.
DO WE HAVE TO JOIN YOUR CULT IF WE TRAVEL WITH YOU?
NO.
ALL RIGHT THEN!
WE RISKED OURSELVES FOR YOU TODAY.
YOU DON'T OWE US FOR THAT, BUT IF THERE'S TROUBLE, YOU STAND BY US, STAND WITH US.
WILL YOU DO THAT OR NOT?
Allie stopped right in front of me. I didn't stop or turn. It wasn't a time for giving way.
I needed to know what her pride and anger might drive her to do.
WE KNOW HOW TO PULL OUR OWN WEIGHT.
WE CAN HELP OUR FRIENDS AND FIGHT OUR ENEMIES. HAVE BEEN SINCE WE WERE KIDS.
WELCOME.
I thought about the little they'd told us about their lives. They would bear watching, but they might turn out to be worth something.

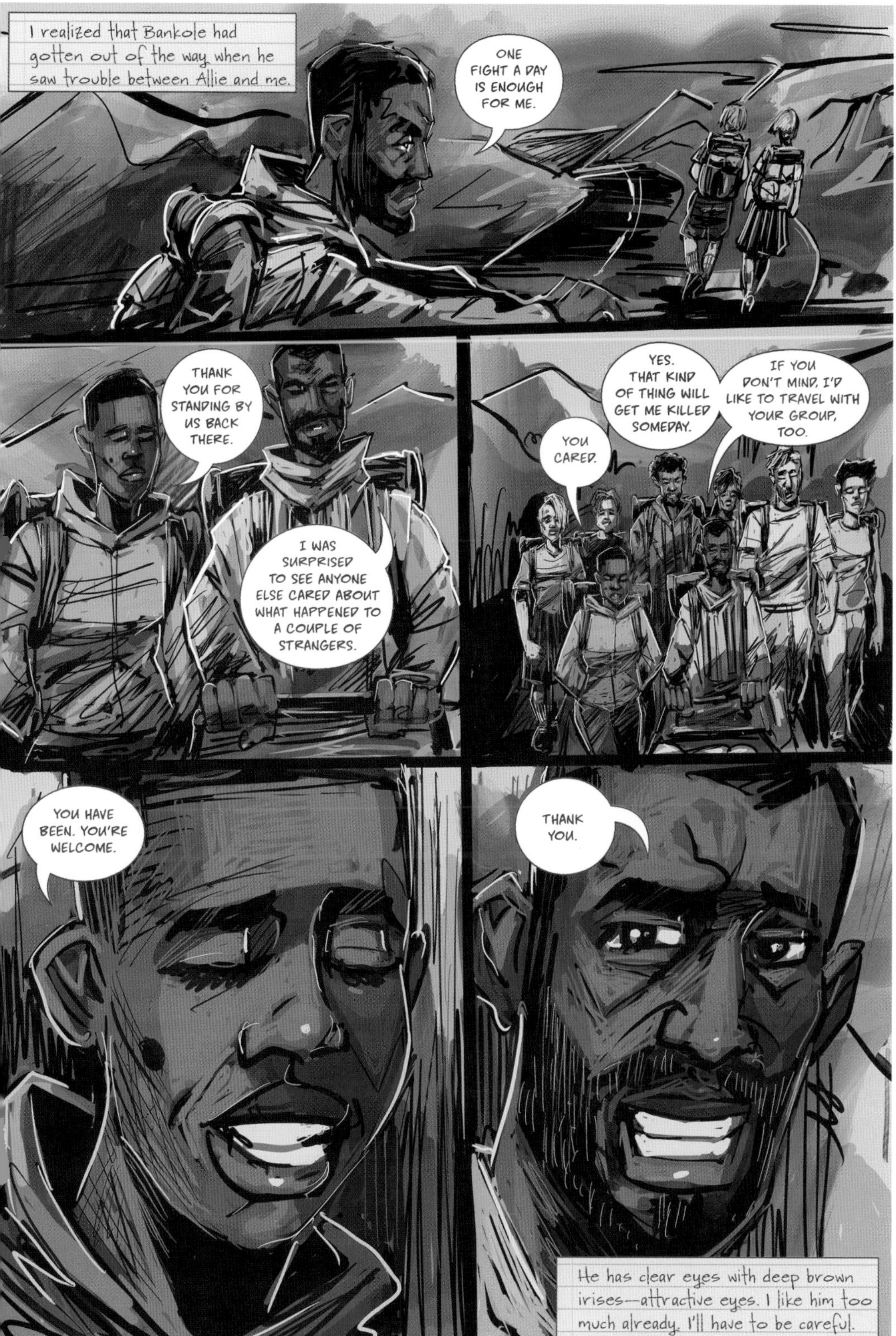
I realized that Bankole had gotten out of the way when he saw trouble between Allie and me.
ONE FIGHT A DAY IS ENOUGH FOR ME.
THANK YOU FOR STANDING BY US BACK THERE.
I WAS SURPRISED TO SEE ANYONE ELSE CARED ABOUT WHAT HAPPENED TO A COUPLE OF STRANGERS.
YOU CARED.
YES. THAT KIND OF THING WILL GET ME KILLED SOMEDAY.
IF YOU DON'T MIND, I'D LIKE TO TRAVEL WITH YOUR GROUP, TOO.
YOU HAVE BEEN. YOU'RE WELCOME.
THANK YOU.
He has clear eyes with deep brown irises—attractive eyes. I like him too much already. I'll have to be careful.

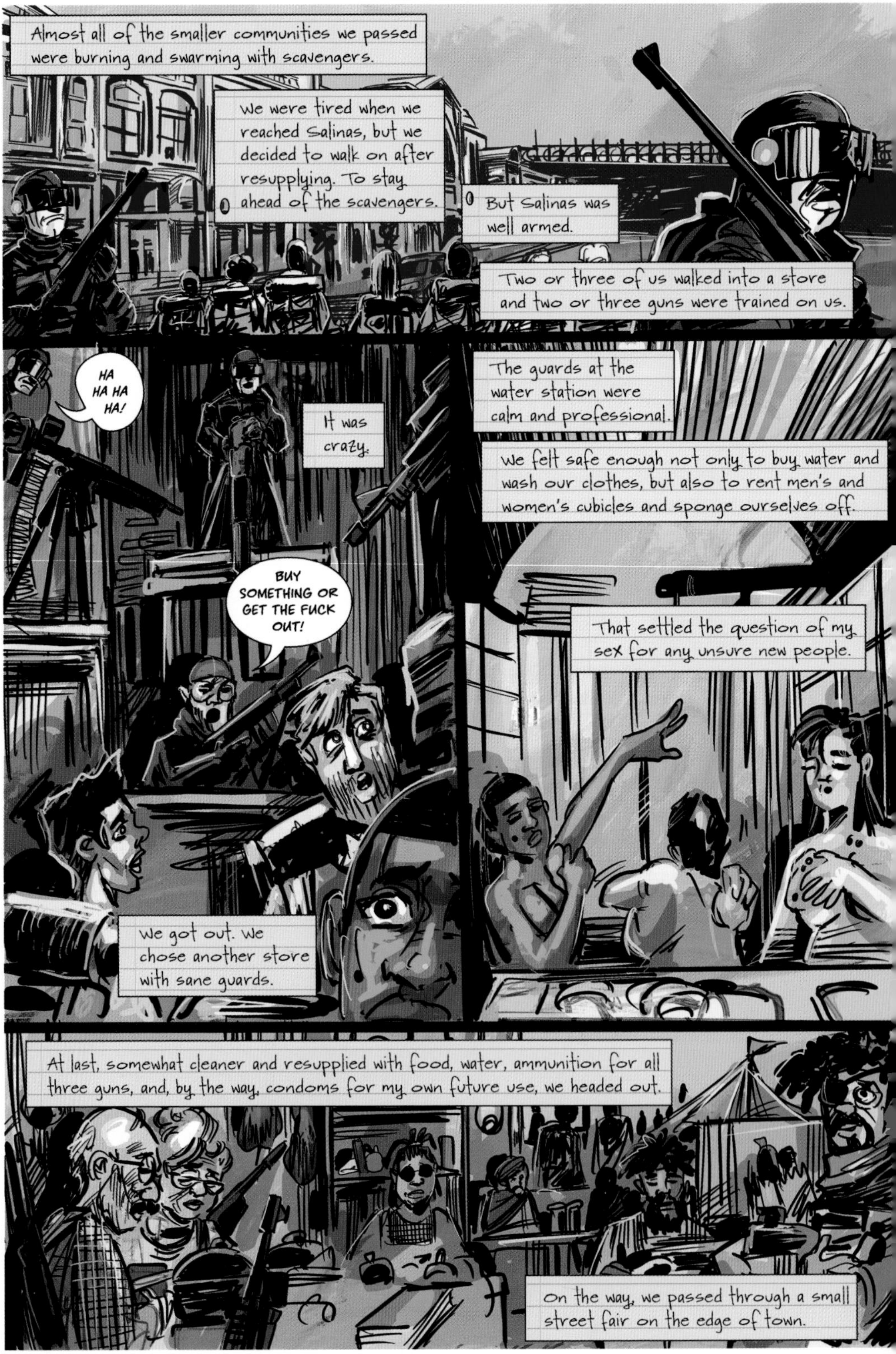

Almost all of the smaller communities we passed were burning and swarming with scavengers.
We were tired when we reached Salinas, but we decided to walk on after resupplying. To stay ahead of the scavengers.
But Salinas was well armed.
Two or three of us walked into a store and two or three guns were trained on us.
HA HA HA HA!
It was crazy.
BUY SOMETHING OR GET THE FUCK OUT!
We got out. We chose another store with sane guards.
The guards at the water station were calm and professional.
We felt safe enough not only to buy water and wash our clothes, but also to rent men's and women's cubicles and sponge ourselves off.
That settled the question of my sex for any unsure new people.
At last, somewhat cleaner and resupplied with food, water, ammunition for all three guns, and, by the way, condoms for my own future use, we headed out.
On the way, we passed through a small street fair on the edge of town.

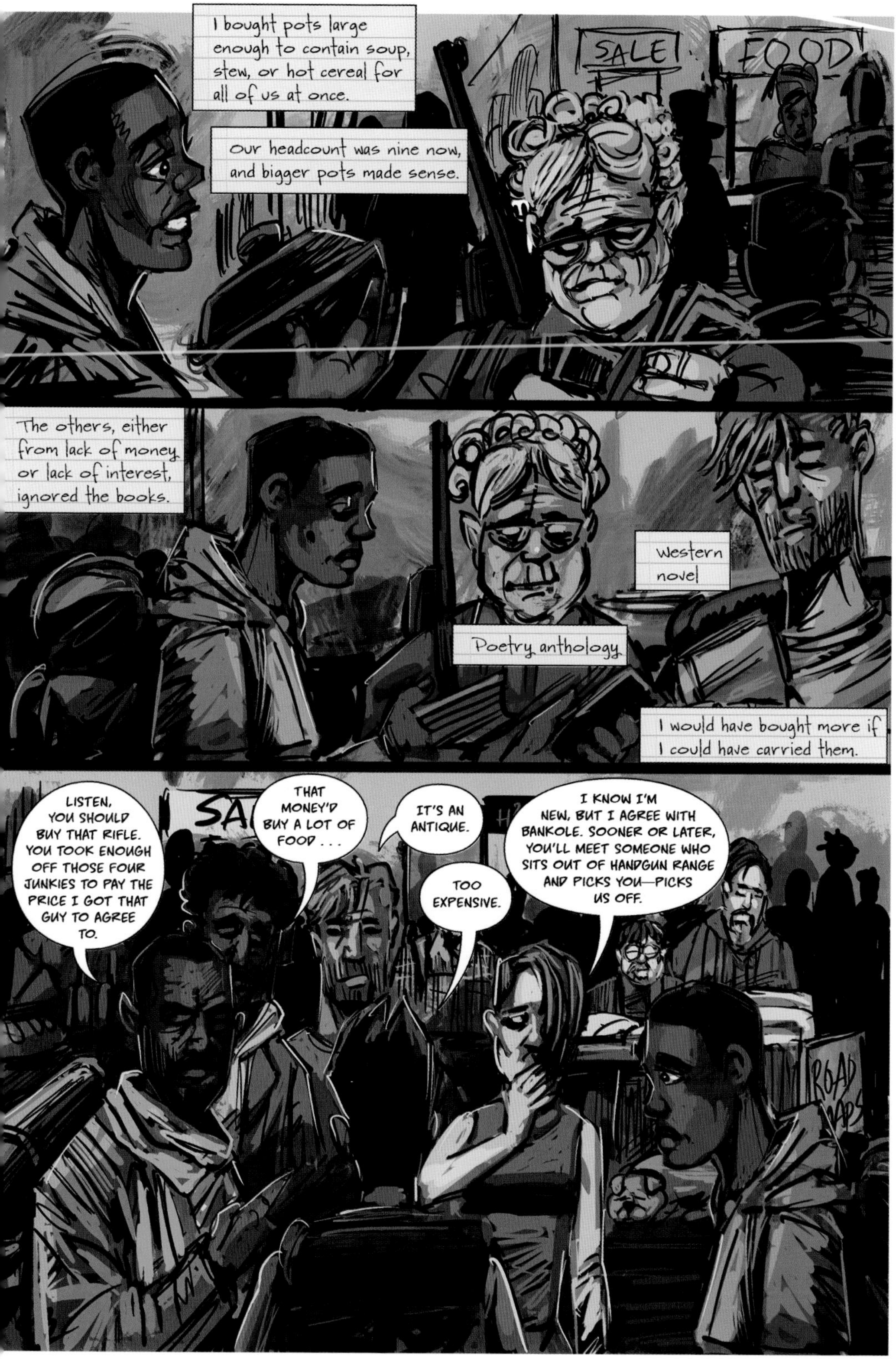
I bought pots large enough to contain soup, stew, or hot cereal for all of us at once.
Our headcount was nine now, and bigger pots made sense.
SALE
FOOD
The others, either from lack of money or lack of interest, ignored the books.
Western novel
Poetry anthology
I would have bought more if I could have carried them.
LISTEN, YOU SHOULD BUY THAT RIFLE. YOU TOOK ENOUGH OFF THOSE FOUR JUNKIES TO PAY THE PRICE I GOT THAT GUY TO AGREE TO.
THAT MONEY'D BUY A LOT OF FOOD . . .
IT'S AN ANTIQUE.
TOO EXPENSIVE.
I KNOW I'M NEW, BUT I AGREE WITH BANKOLE. SOONER OR LATER, YOU'LL MEET SOMEONE WHO SITS OUT OF HANDGUN RANGE AND PICKS YOU—PICKS US OFF.

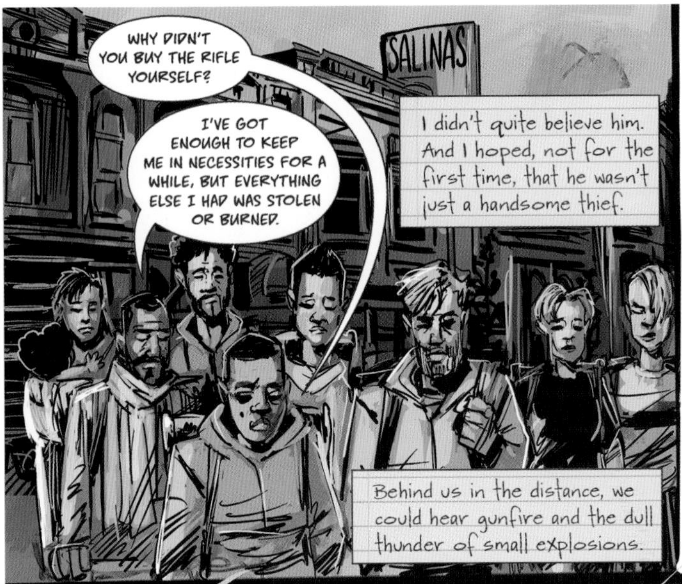
SALINAS
WHY DIDN'T YOU BUY THE RIFLE YOURSELF?
I'VE GOT ENOUGH TO KEEP ME IN NECESSITIES FOR A WHILE, BUT EVERYTHING ELSE I HAD WAS STOLEN OR BURNED.
I didn't quite believe him. And I hoped, not for the first time, that he wasn't just a handsome thief.
Behind us in the distance, we could hear gunfire and the dull thunder of small explosions.

God is neither good
nor evil,
neither loving
nor hating.
God is Power.
God is Change.
We must find the rest
of what we need
within ourselves,
in one another,
in our Destiny.

EARTHSEED:
THE BOOKS OF
THE LIVING

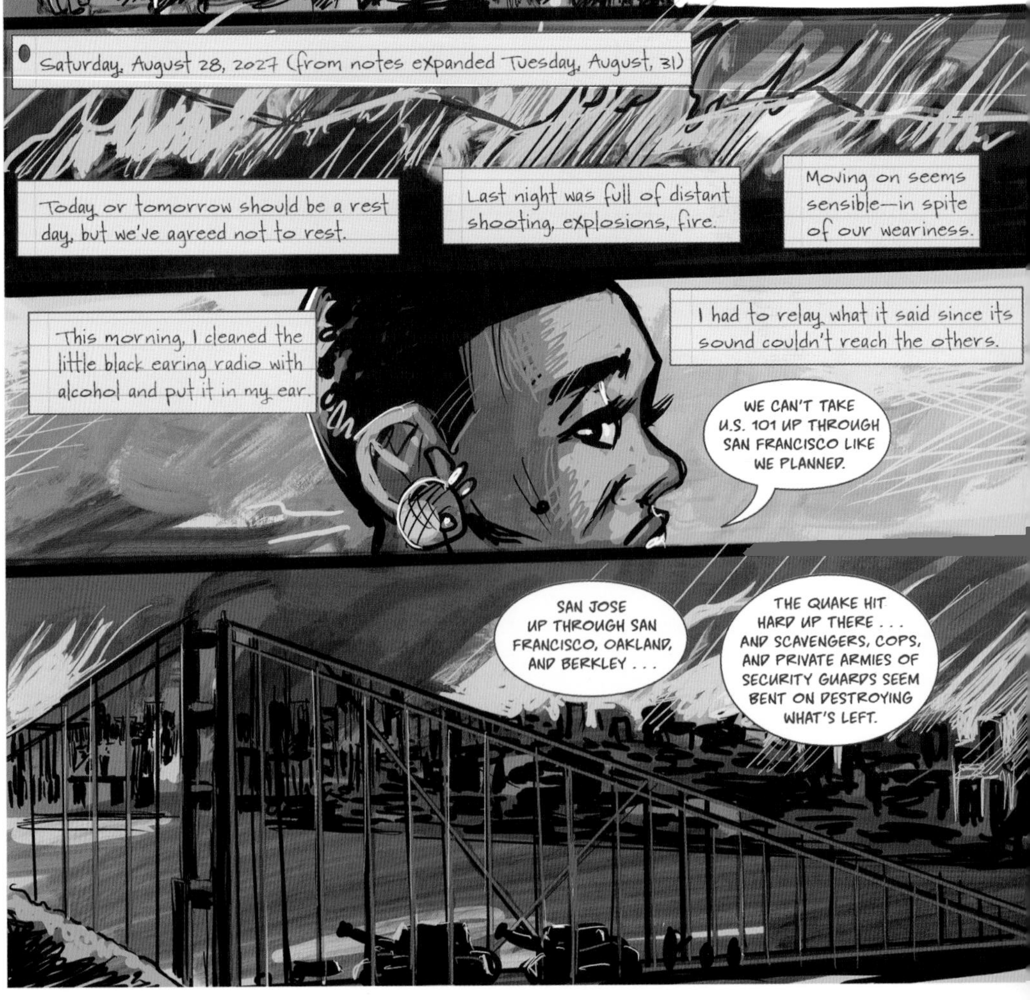
Saturday, August 28, 2027 (from notes expanded Tuesday, August, 31)
Today or tomorrow should be a rest day, but we've agreed not to rest.
Last night was full of distant shooting, explosions, fire.
Moving on seems sensible—in spite of our weariness.
This morning, I cleaned the little black earing radio with alcohol and put it in my ear.
I had to relay what it said since its sound couldn't reach the others.
WE CAN'T TAKE U.S. 101 UP THROUGH SAN FRANCISCO LIKE WE PLANNED.
SAN JOSE UP THROUGH SAN FRANCISCO, OAKLAND, AND BERKLEY . . .
THE QUAKE HIT HARD UP THERE . . . AND SCAVENGERS, COPS, AND PRIVATE ARMIES OF SECURITY GUARDS SEEM BENT ON DESTROYING WHAT'S LEFT.

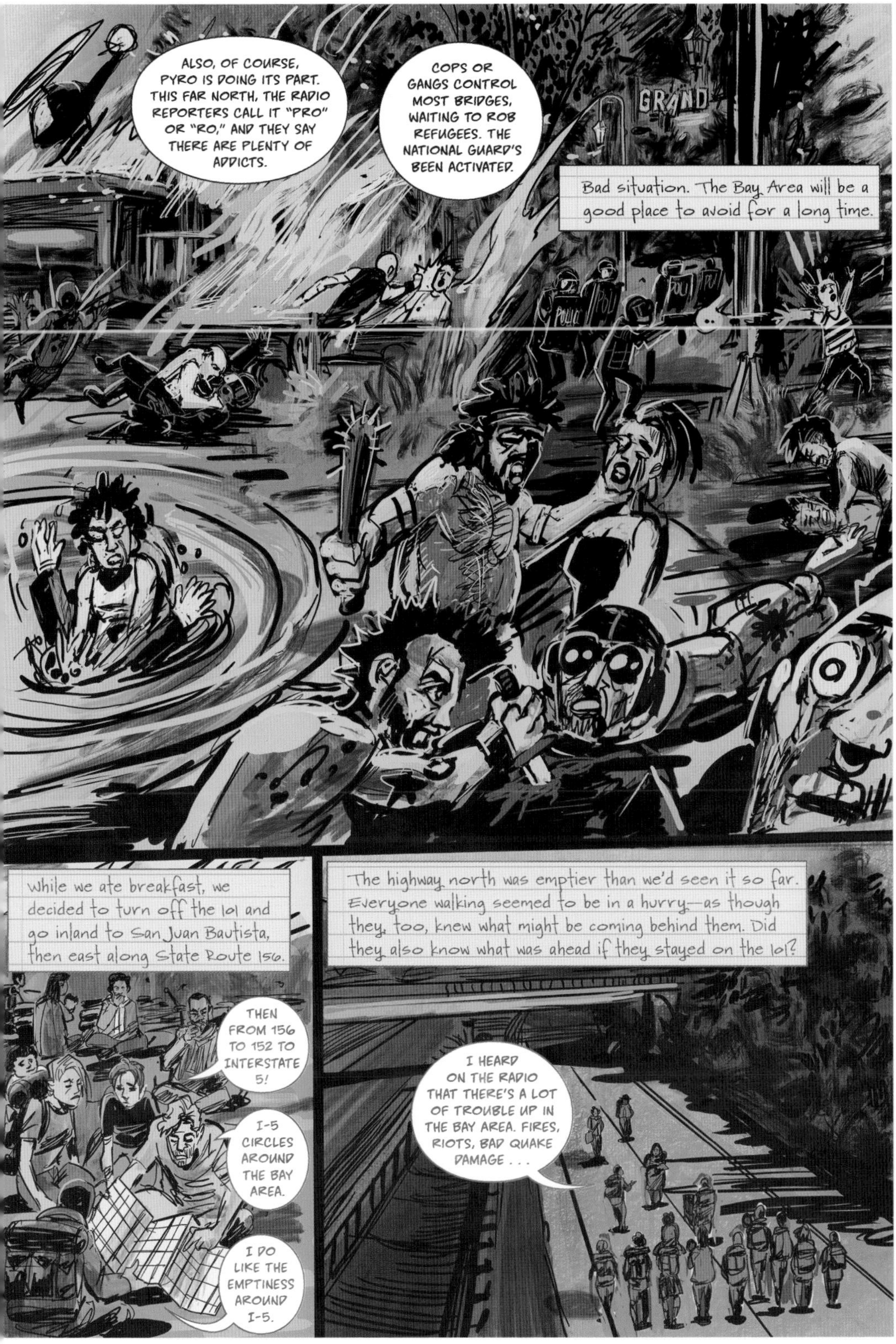
ALSO, OF COURSE, PYRO IS DOING ITS PART. THIS FAR NORTH, THE RADIO REPORTERS CALL IT "PRO" OR "RO," AND THEY SAY THERE ARE PLENTY OF ADDICTS.
COPS OR GANGS CONTROL MOST BRIDGES, WAITING TO ROB REFUGEES. THE NATIONAL GUARD'S BEEN ACTIVATED.
GRAND
Bad situation. The Bay Area will be a good place to avoid for a long time.
While we ate breakfast, we decided to turn off the 101 and go inland to San Juan Bautista, then east along State Route 156.
THEN FROM 156 TO 152 TO INTERSTATE 5!
I-5 CIRCLES AROUND THE BAY AREA.
I DO LIKE THE EMPTINESS AROUND I-5.
The highway north was emptier than we'd seen it so far. Everyone walking seemed to be in a hurry—as though they, too, knew what might be coming behind them. Did they also know what was ahead if they stayed on the 101?
I HEARD ON THE RADIO THAT THERE'S A LOT OF TROUBLE UP IN THE BAY AREA. FIRES, RIOTS, BAD QUAKE DAMAGE . . .

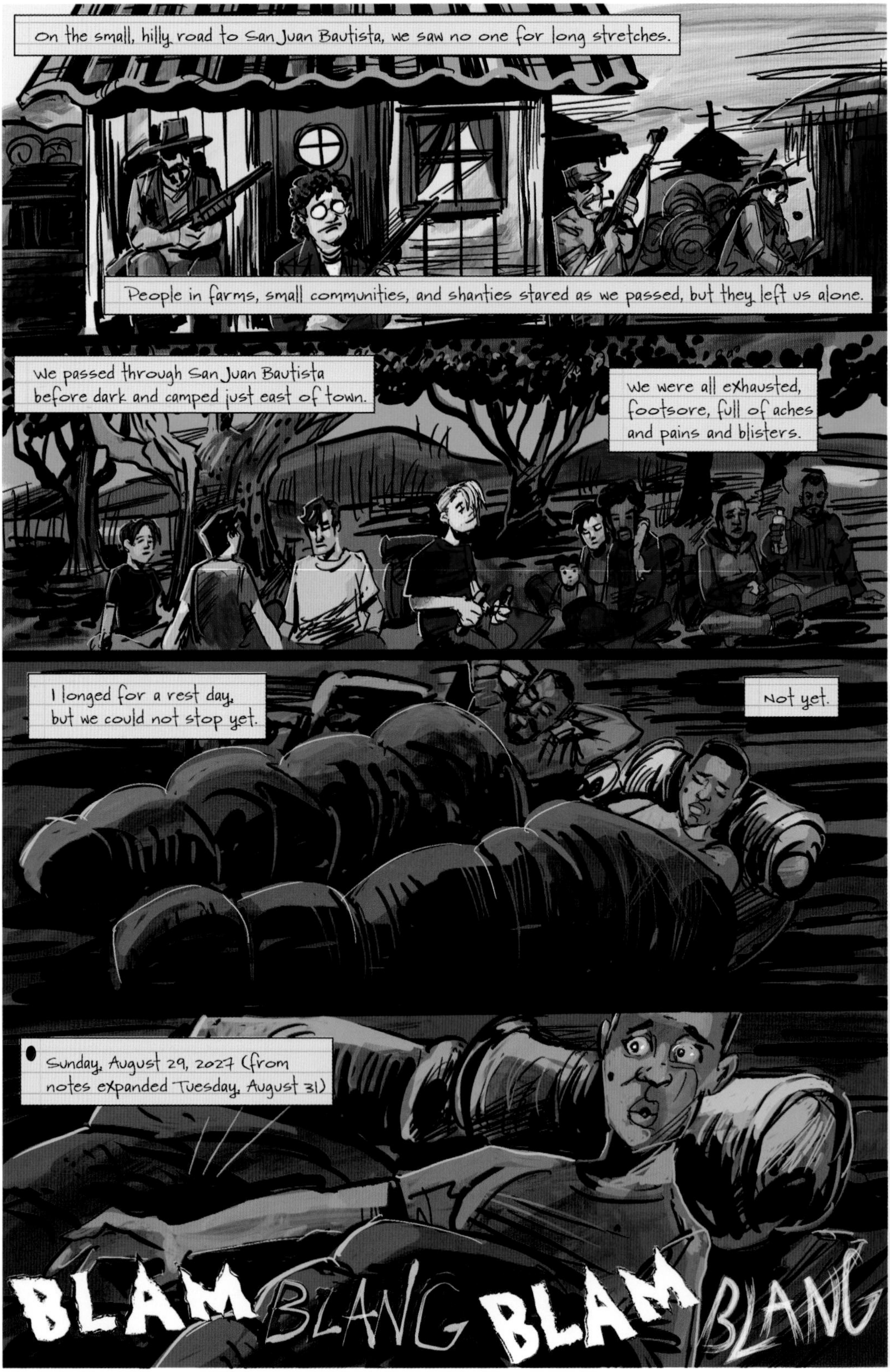

On the small, hilly road to San Juan Bautista, we saw no one for long stretches.
People in farms, small communities, and shanties stared as we passed, but they left us alone.
We passed through San Juan Bautista before dark and camped just east of town.
We were all exhausted, footsore, full of aches and pains and blisters.
I longed for a rest day, but we could not stop yet.
Not yet.
Sunday, August 29, 2027 (from notes expanded Tuesday, August 31)
BLAM BLANG BLAM BLANG

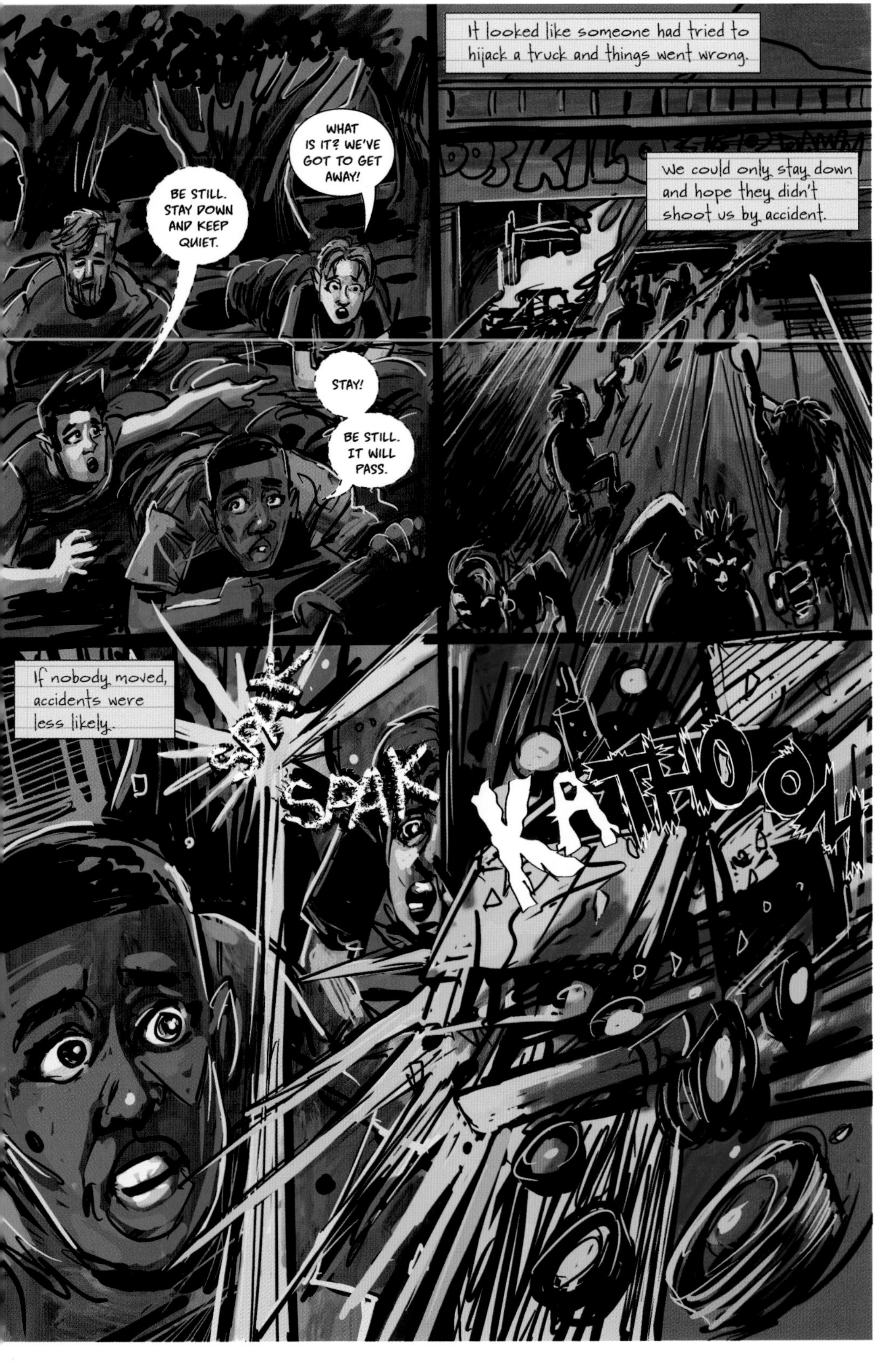
WHAT IS IT? WE'VE GOT TO GET AWAY!
BE STILL. STAY DOWN AND KEEP QUIET.
It looked like someone had tried to hijack a truck and things went wrong.
We could only stay down and hope they didn't shoot us by accident.
STAY!
BE STILL. IT WILL PASS.
If nobody moved, accidents were less likely.
SPAK
KATHOOM

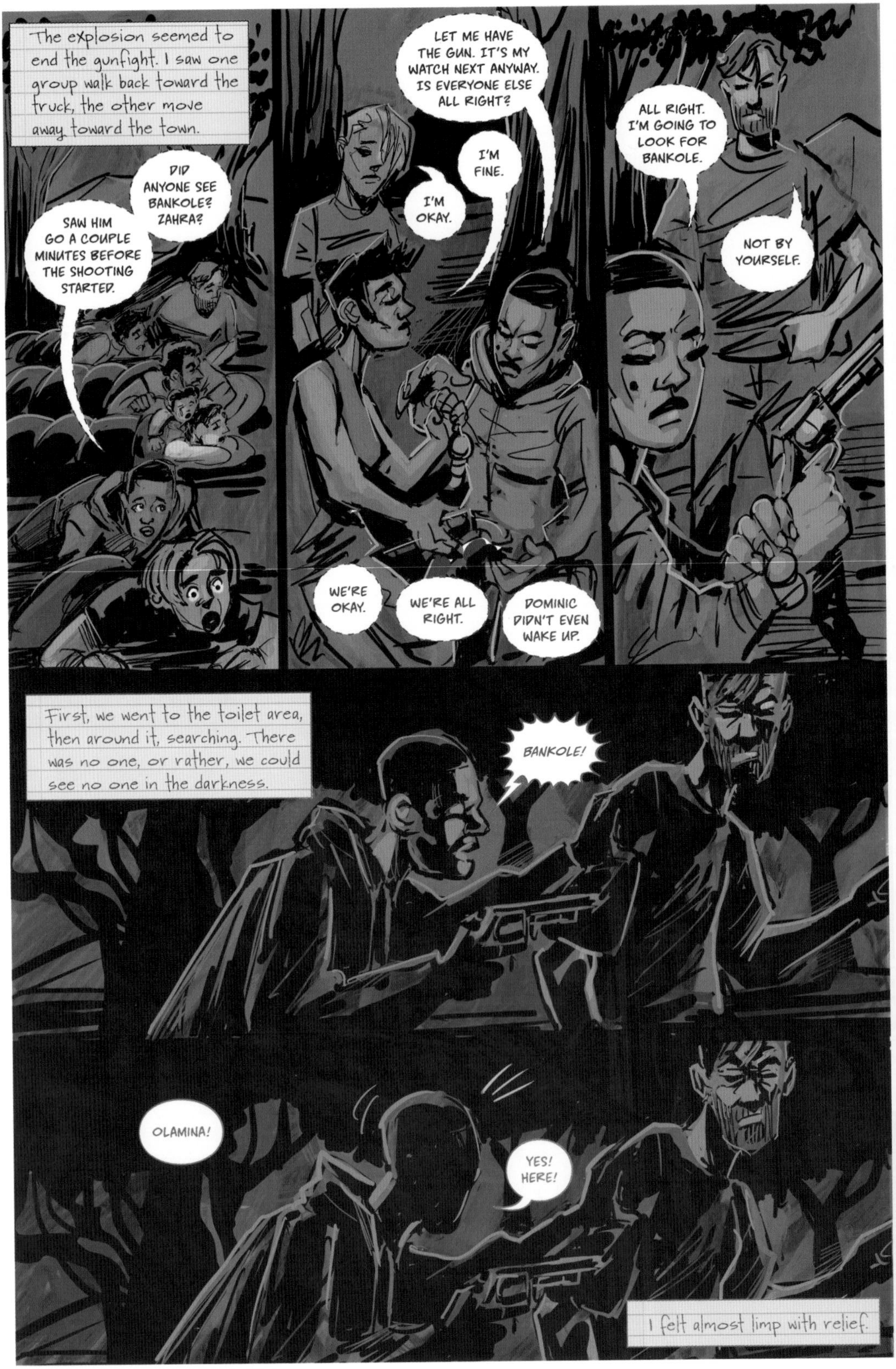
The explosion seemed to end the gunfight. I saw one group walk back toward the truck, the other move away toward the town.
DID ANYONE SEE BANKOLE? ZAHRA?
SAW HIM GO A COUPLE MINUTES BEFORE THE SHOOTING STARTED.
LET ME HAVE THE GUN. IT'S MY WATCH NEXT ANYWAY. IS EVERYONE ELSE ALL RIGHT?
I'M FINE.
I'M OKAY.
WE'RE OKAY.
WE'RE ALL RIGHT.
DOMINIC DIDN'T EVEN WAKE UP.
ALL RIGHT. I'M GOING TO LOOK FOR BANKOLE.
NOT BY YOURSELF.
First, we went to the toilet area, then around it, searching. There was no one, or rather, we could see no one in the darkness.
BANKOLE!
OLAMINA!
YES! HERE!
I felt almost limp with relief.

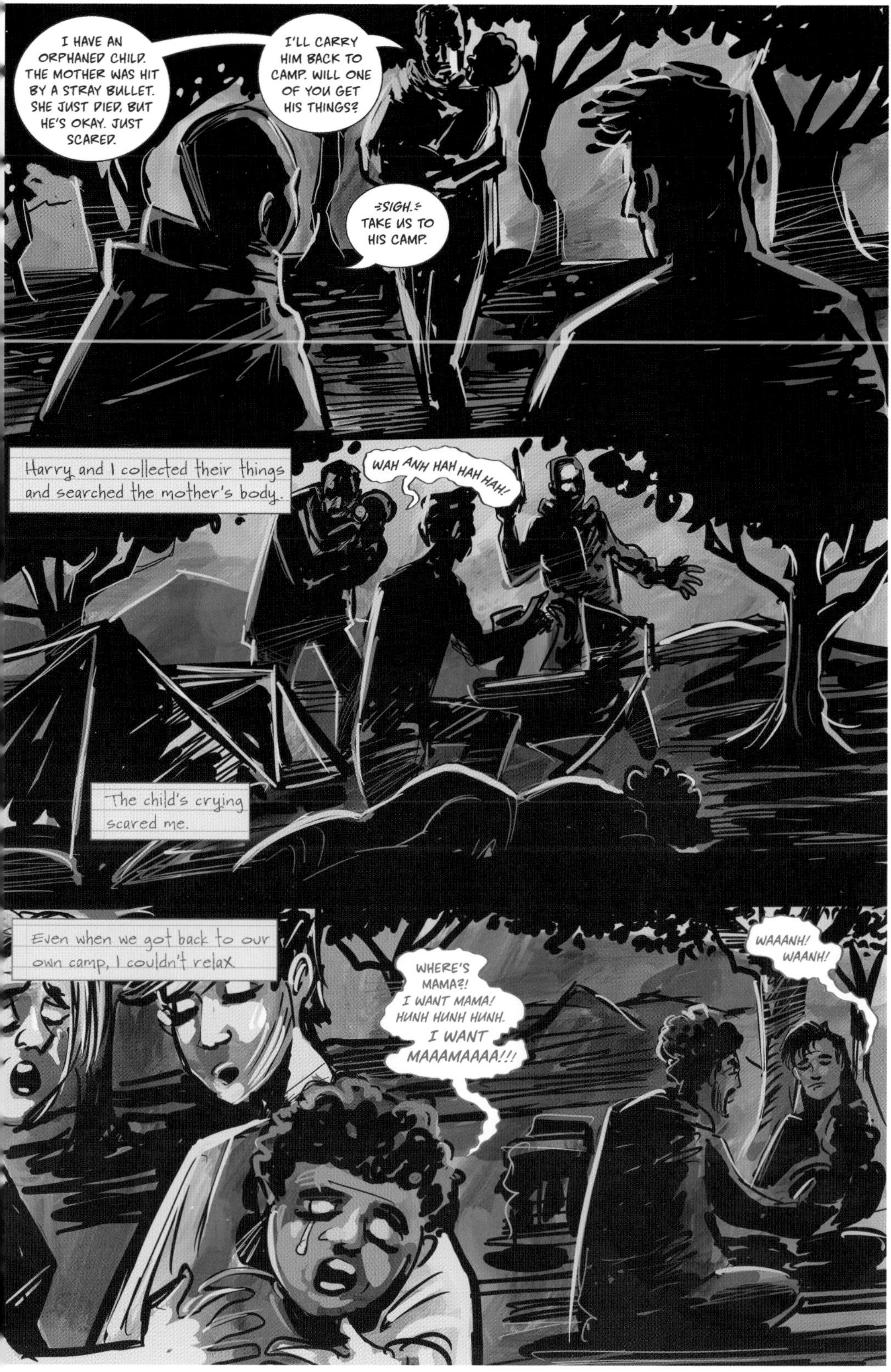
I HAVE AN ORPHANED CHILD. THE MOTHER WAS HIT BY A STRAY BULLET. SHE JUST DIED, BUT HE'S OKAY. JUST SCARED.
I'LL CARRY HIM BACK TO CAMP. WILL ONE OF YOU GET HIS THINGS?
=SIGH.= TAKE US TO HIS CAMP.
Harry and I collected their things and searched the mother's body.
WAH ANH HAH HAH HAH!
The child's crying scared me.
Even when we got back to our own camp, I couldn't relax.
WHERE'S MAMA?! I WANT MAMA! HUNH HUNH HUNH. I WANT MAAAMAAAA!!!
WAAANH! WAANH!

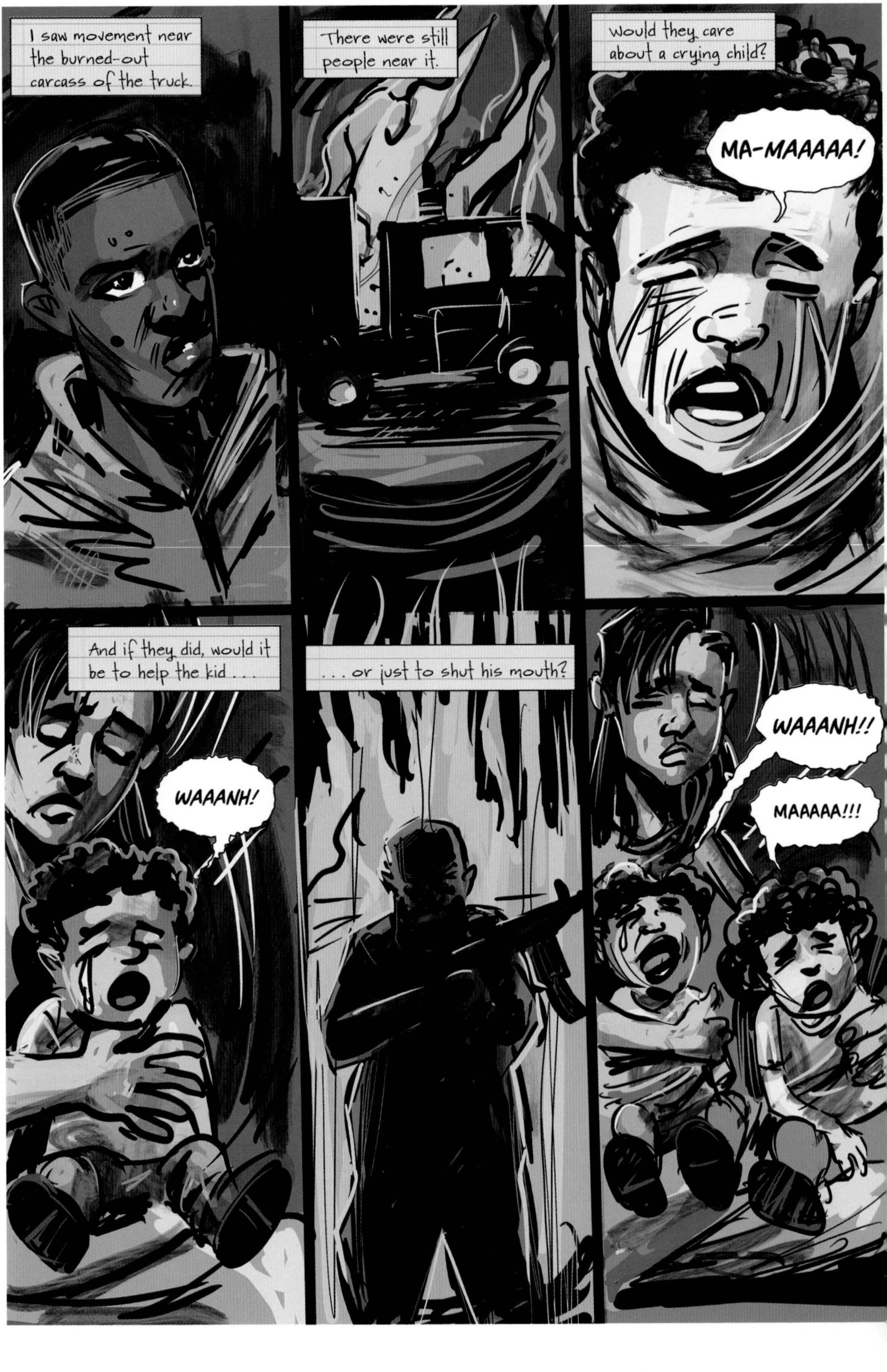
I saw movement near the burned-out carcass of the truck.
There were still people near it.
Would they care about a crying child?
MA-MAAAAA!
And if they did, would it be to help the kid . . .
. . . or just to shut his mouth?
WAAANH!
WAAANH!!
MAAAAA!!!

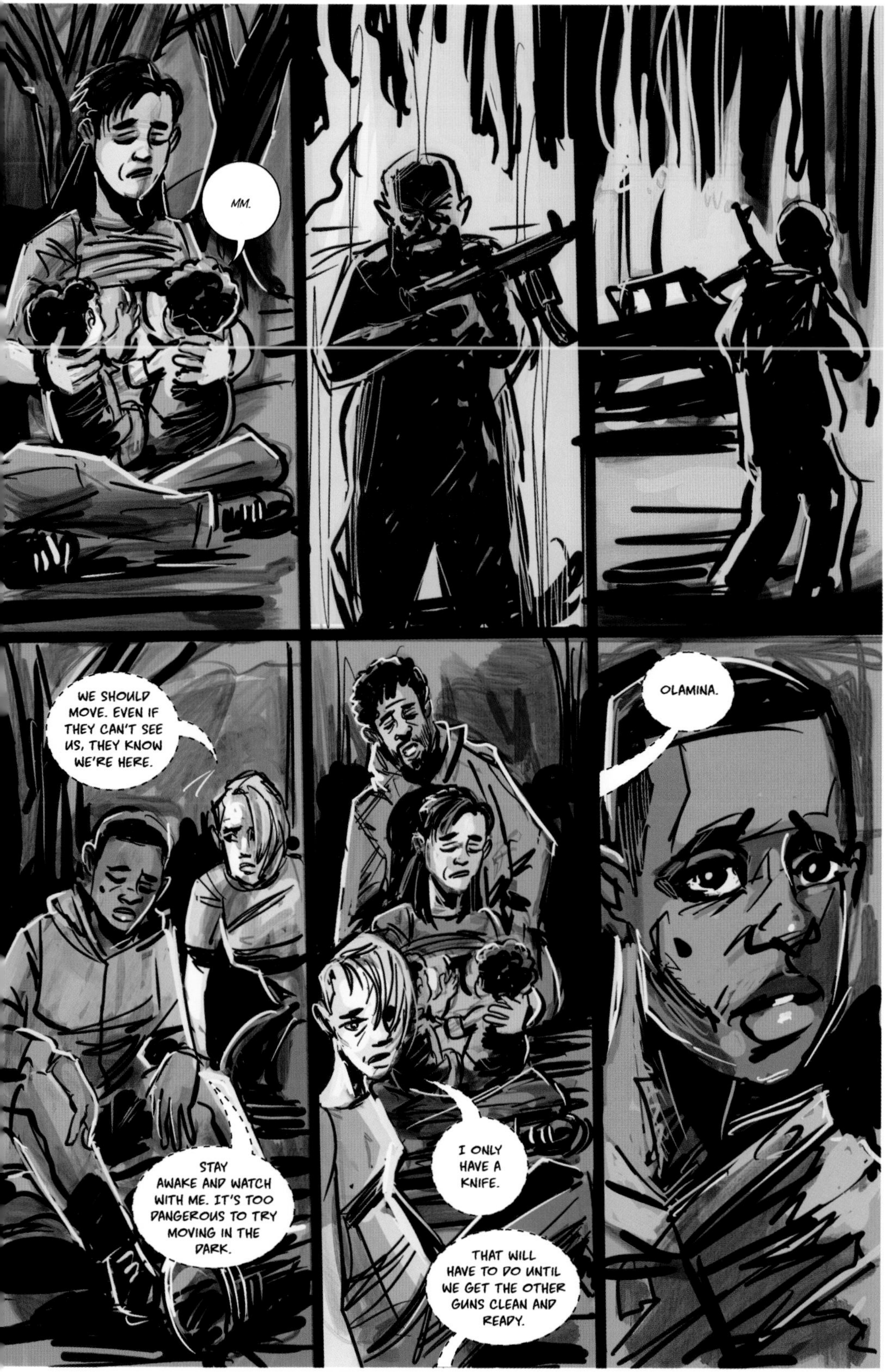
MM.
WE SHOULD MOVE. EVEN IF THEY CAN'T SEE US, THEY KNOW WE'RE HERE.
STAY AWAKE AND WATCH WITH ME. IT'S TOO DANGEROUS TO TRY MOVING IN THE DARK.
I ONLY HAVE A KNIFE.
THAT WILL HAVE TO DO UNTIL WE GET THE OTHER GUNS CLEAN AND READY.
OLAMINA.

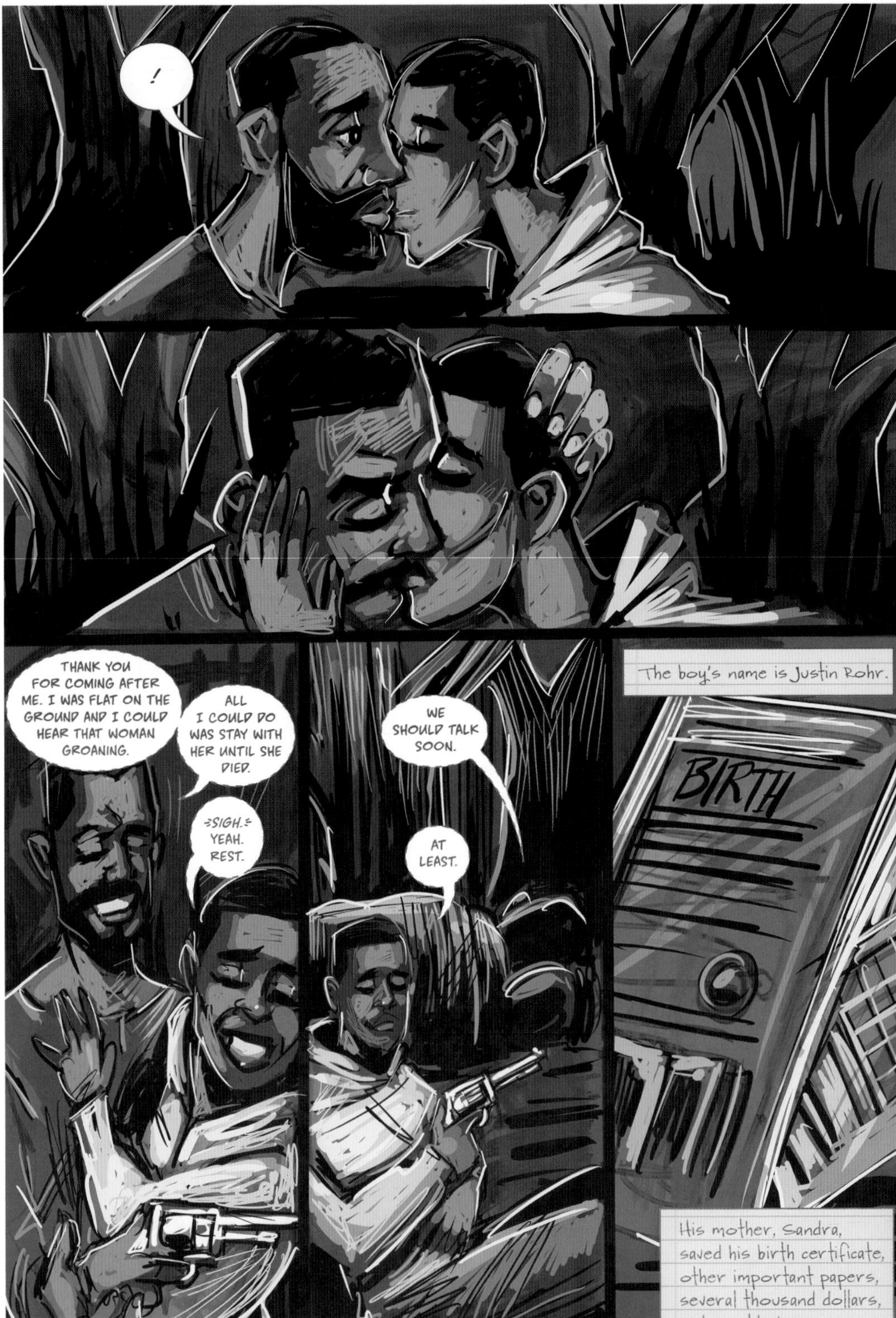
!
THANK YOU FOR COMING AFTER ME. I WAS FLAT ON THE GROUND AND I COULD HEAR THAT WOMAN GROANING.
ALL I COULD DO WAS STAY WITH HER UNTIL SHE DIED.
=SIGH.= YEAH. REST.
WE SHOULD TALK SOON.
AT LEAST.
The boy's name is Justin Rohr.
BIRTH
His mother, Sandra, saved his birth certificate, other important papers, several thousand dollars, and a gold ring.

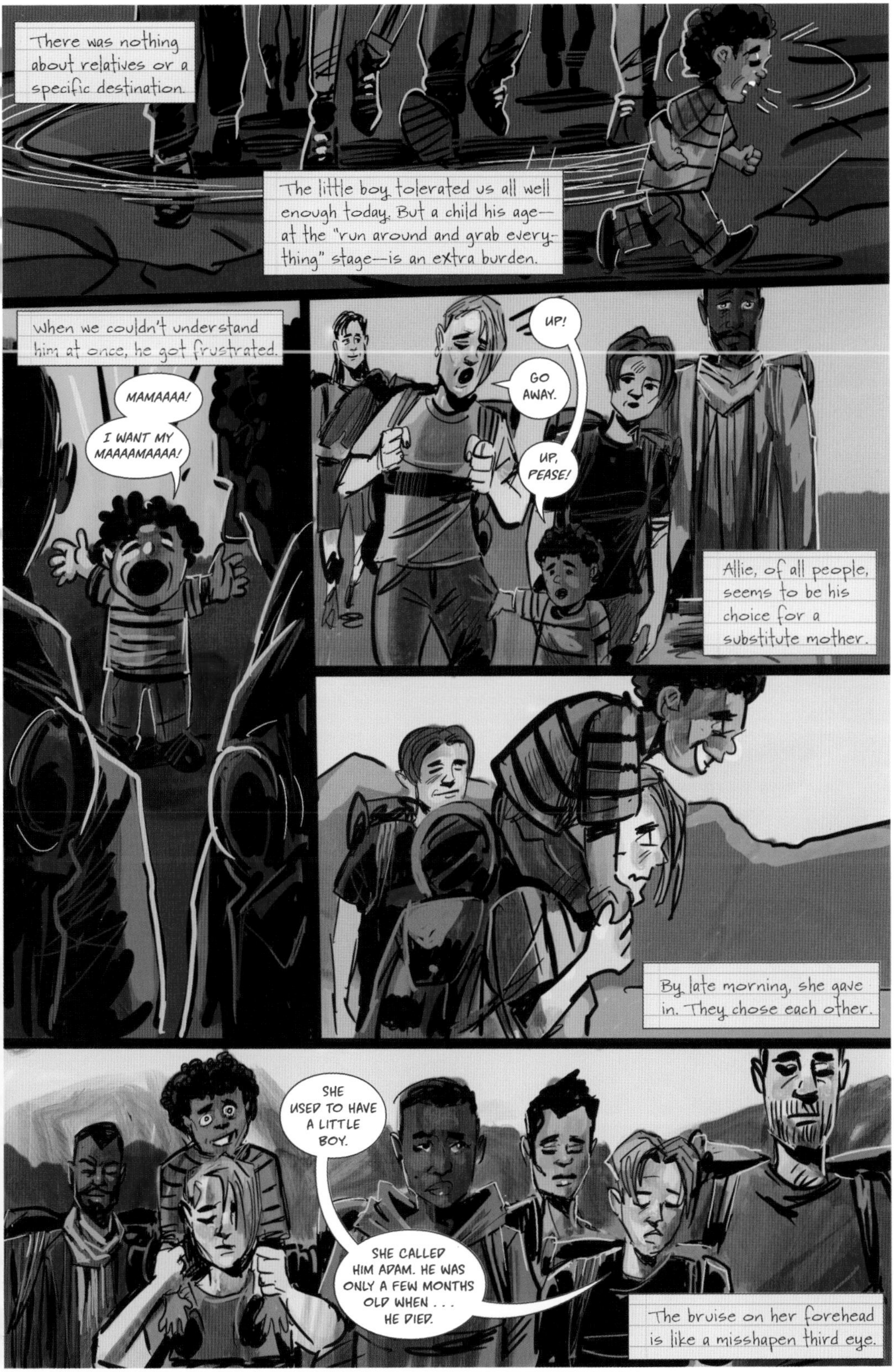
There was nothing about relatives or a specific destination.
The little boy tolerated us all well enough today. But a child his age—at the "run around and grab every-thing" stage—is an extra burden.
When we couldn't understand him at once, he got frustrated.
MAMAAAA!
I WANT MY MAAAAMAAAAA!
UP!
GO AWAY.
UP, PEASE!
Allie, of all people, seems to be his choice for a substitute mother.
By late morning, she gave in. They chose each other.
SHE USED TO HAVE A LITTLE BOY.
SHE CALLED HIM ADAM. HE WAS ONLY A FEW MONTHS OLD WHEN . . . HE DIED.
The bruise on her forehead is like a misshapen third eye.

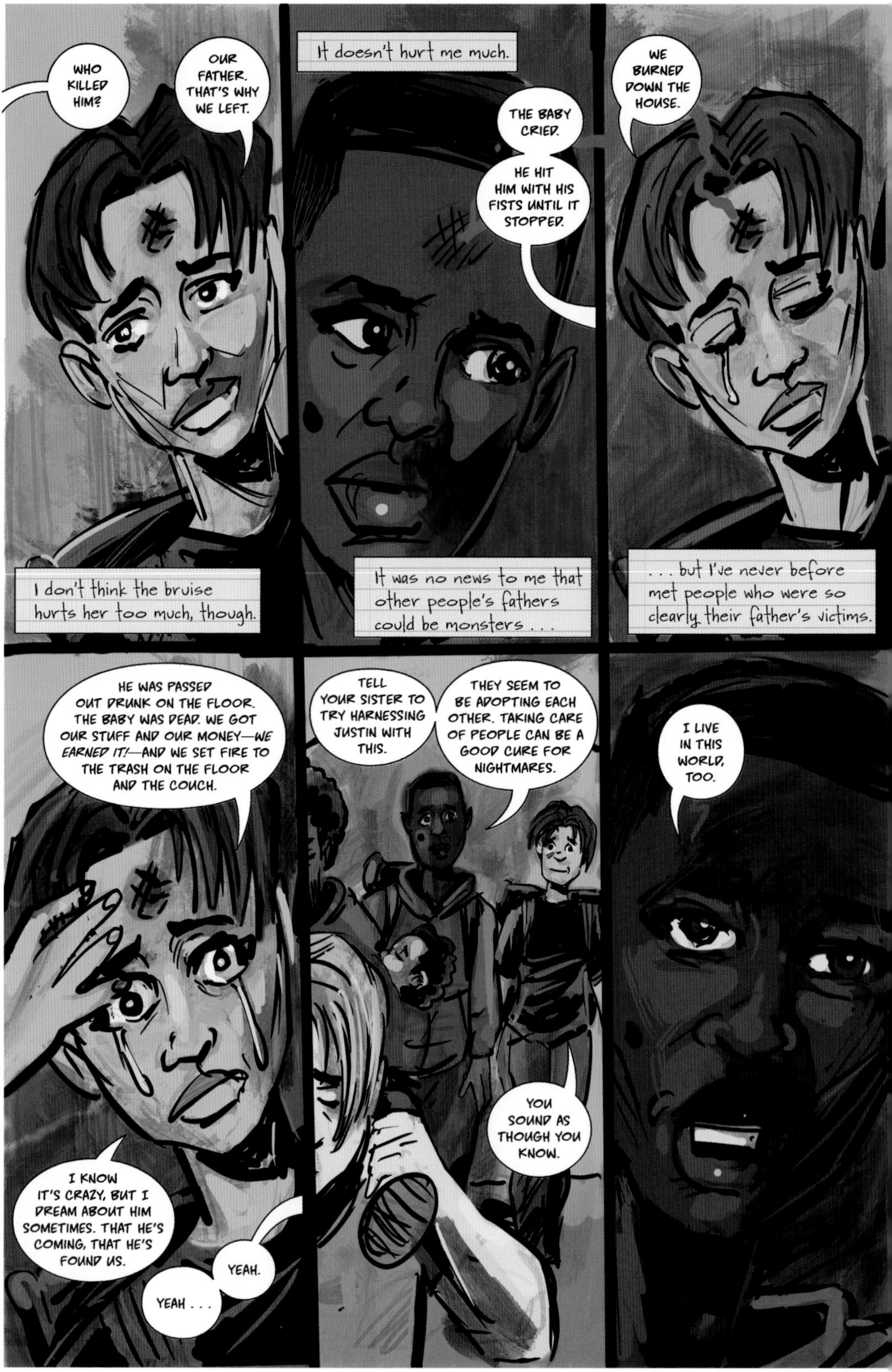

WHO KILLED HIM?
OUR FATHER. THAT'S WHY WE LEFT.
I don't think the bruise hurts her too much, though.
It doesn't hurt me much.
THE BABY CRIED.
HE HIT HIM WITH HIS FISTS UNTIL IT STOPPED.
It was no news to me that other people's fathers could be monsters . . .
WE BURNED DOWN THE HOUSE.
. . . but I've never before met people who were so clearly their father's victims.
HE WAS PASSED OUT DRUNK ON THE FLOOR. THE BABY WAS DEAD. WE GOT OUR STUFF AND OUR MONEY—*WE EARNED IT!*—AND WE SET FIRE TO THE TRASH ON THE FLOOR AND THE COUCH.
I KNOW IT'S CRAZY, BUT I DREAM ABOUT HIM SOMETIMES. THAT HE'S COMING, THAT HE'S FOUND US.
YEAH.
YEAH . . .
TELL YOUR SISTER TO TRY HARNESSING JUSTIN WITH THIS.
THEY SEEM TO BE ADOPTING EACH OTHER. TAKING CARE OF PEOPLE CAN BE A GOOD CURE FOR NIGHTMARES.
YOU SOUND AS THOUGH YOU KNOW.
I LIVE IN THIS WORLD, TOO.

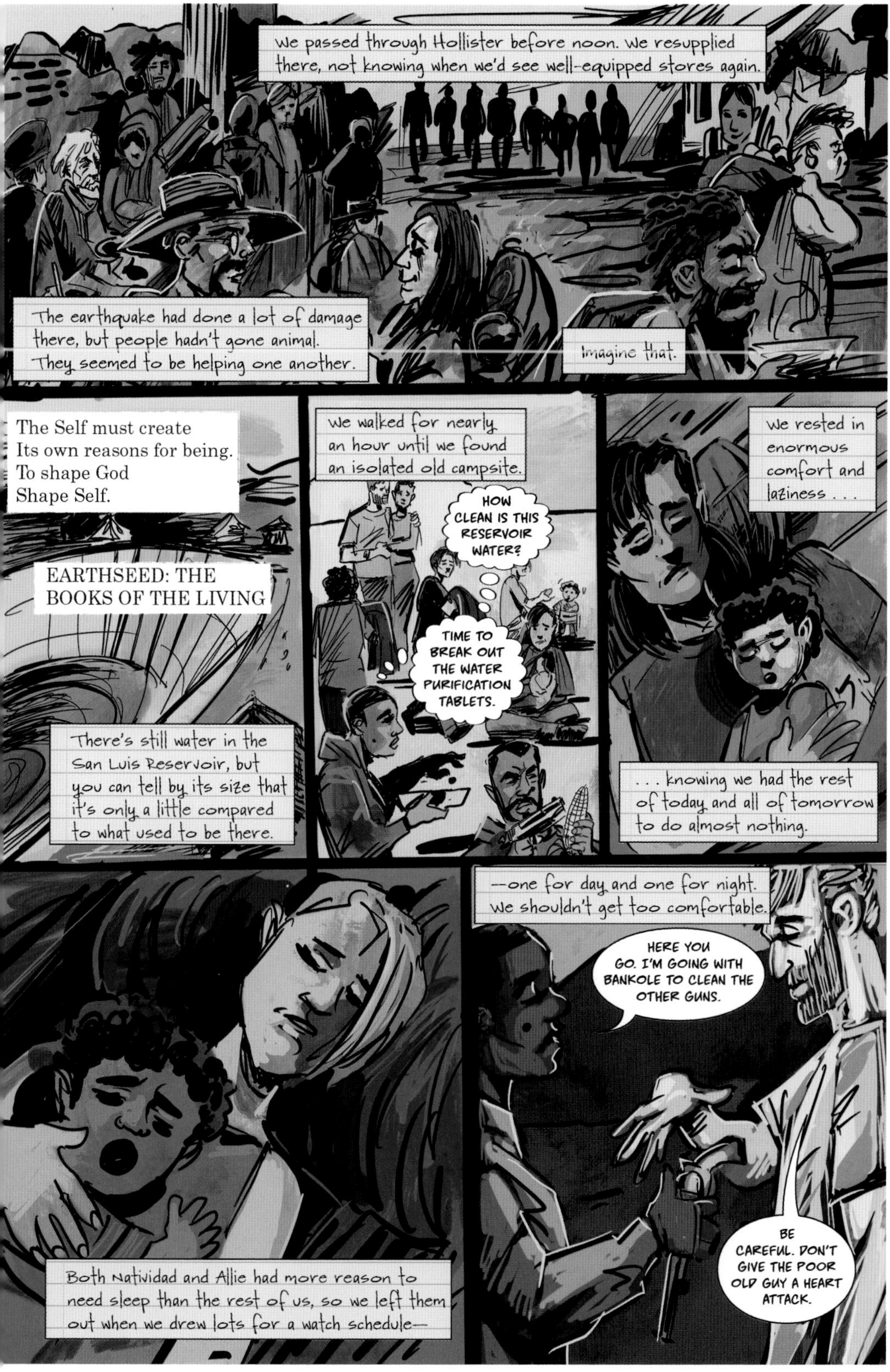
We passed through Hollister before noon. We resupplied there, not knowing when we'd see well-equipped stores again.
The earthquake had done a lot of damage there, but people hadn't gone animal. They seemed to be helping one another.
Imagine that.
The Self must create
Its own reasons for being.
To shape God
Shape Self.
EARTHSEED: THE BOOKS OF THE LIVING
There's still water in the San Luis Reservoir, but you can tell by its size that it's only a little compared to what used to be there.
We walked for nearly an hour until we found an isolated old campsite.
HOW CLEAN IS THIS RESERVOIR WATER?
TIME TO BREAK OUT THE WATER PURIFICATION TABLETS.
We rested in enormous comfort and laziness . . .
. . . knowing we had the rest of today and all of tomorrow to do almost nothing.
Both Natividad and Allie had more reason to need sleep than the rest of us, so we left them out when we drew lots for a watch schedule—
—one for day and one for night. We shouldn't get too comfortable.
HERE YOU GO. I'M GOING WITH BANKOLE TO CLEAN THE OTHER GUNS.
BE CAREFUL. DON'T GIVE THE POOR OLD GUY A HEART ATTACK.

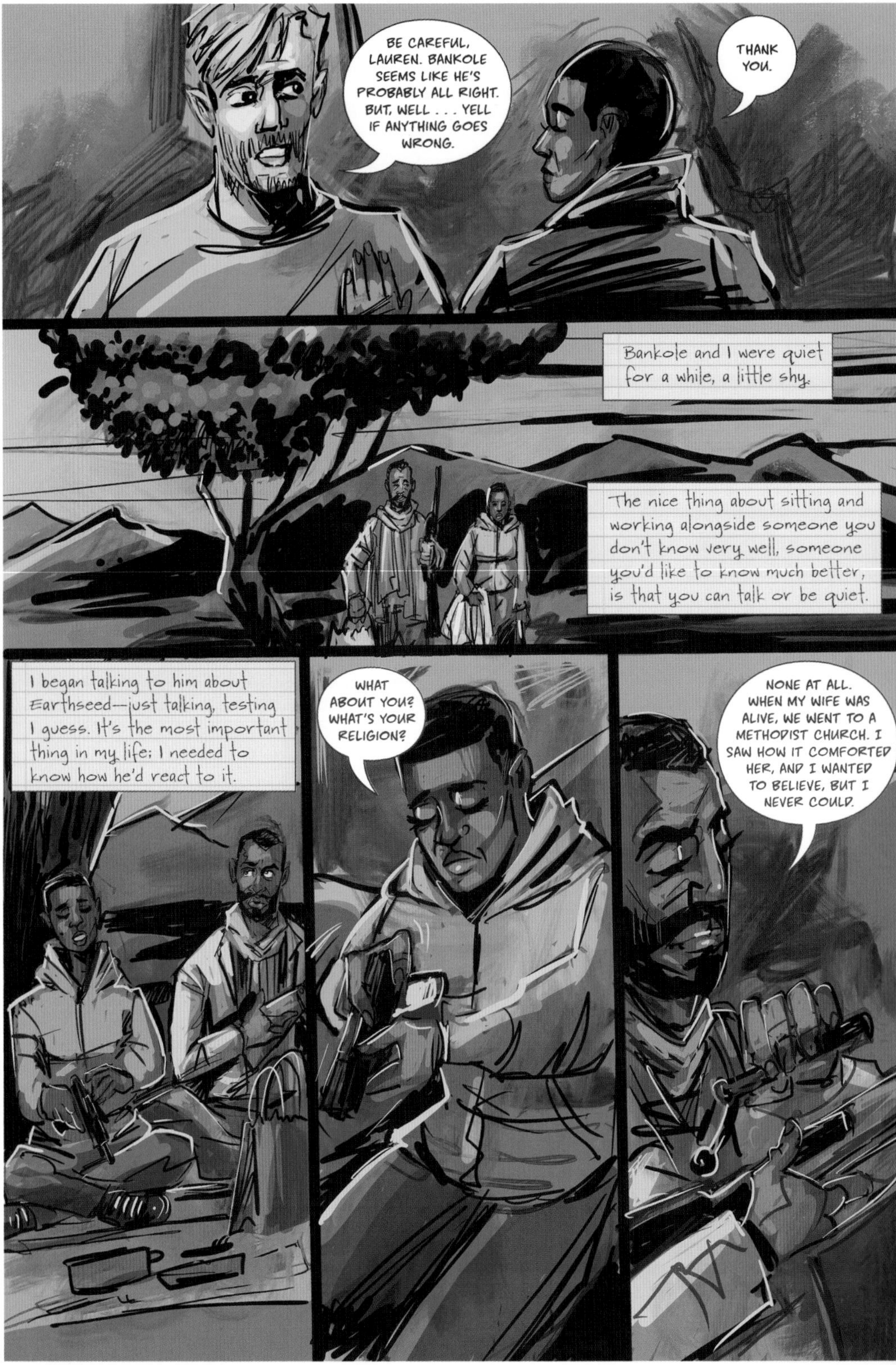
BE CAREFUL, LAUREN. BANKOLE SEEMS LIKE HE'S PROBABLY ALL RIGHT. BUT, WELL . . . YELL IF ANYTHING GOES WRONG.
THANK YOU.
Bankole and I were quiet for a while, a little shy.
The nice thing about sitting and working alongside someone you don't know very well, someone you'd like to know much better, is that you can talk or be quiet.
I began talking to him about Earthseed—just talking, testing I guess. It's the most important thing in my life; I needed to know how he'd react to it.
WHAT ABOUT YOU? WHAT'S YOUR RELIGION?
NONE AT ALL. WHEN MY WIFE WAS ALIVE, WE WENT TO A METHODIST CHURCH. I SAW HOW IT COMFORTED HER, AND I WANTED TO BELIEVE, BUT I NEVER COULD.

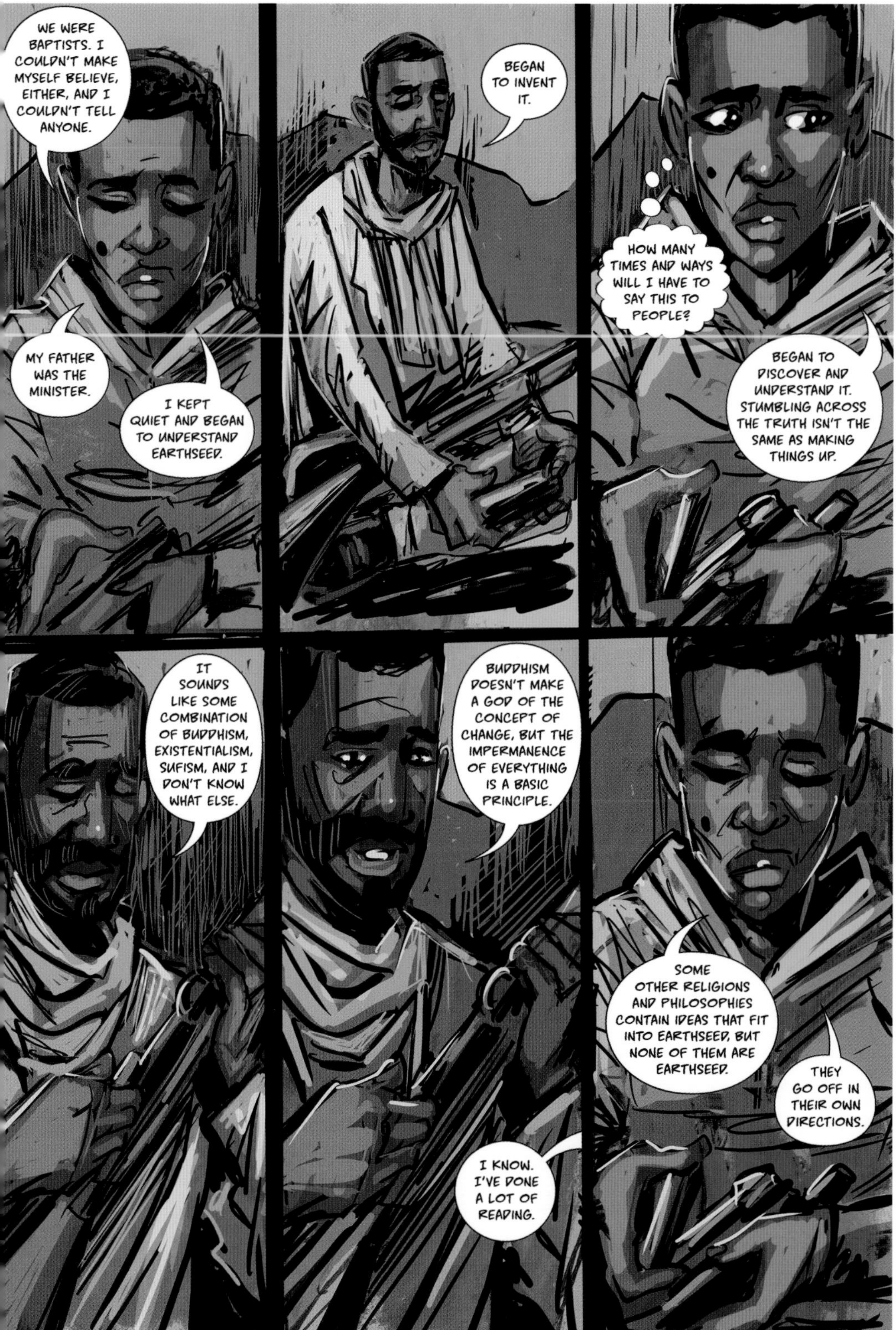
WE WERE BAPTISTS. I COULDN'T MAKE MYSELF BELIEVE, EITHER, AND I COULDN'T TELL ANYONE.
BEGAN TO INVENT IT.
HOW MANY TIMES AND WAYS WILL I HAVE TO SAY THIS TO PEOPLE?
MY FATHER WAS THE MINISTER.
I KEPT QUIET AND BEGAN TO UNDERSTAND EARTHSEED.
BEGAN TO DISCOVER AND UNDERSTAND IT. STUMBLING ACROSS THE TRUTH ISN'T THE SAME AS MAKING THINGS UP.
IT SOUNDS LIKE SOME COMBINATION OF BUDDHISM, EXISTENTIALISM, SUFISM, AND I DON'T KNOW WHAT ELSE.
BUDDHISM DOESN'T MAKE A GOD OF THE CONCEPT OF CHANGE, BUT THE IMPERMANENCE OF EVERYTHING IS A BASIC PRINCIPLE.
I KNOW. I'VE DONE A LOT OF READING.
SOME OTHER RELIGIONS AND PHILOSOPHIES CONTAIN IDEAS THAT FIT INTO EARTHSEED, BUT NONE OF THEM ARE EARTHSEED.
THEY GO OFF IN THEIR OWN DIRECTIONS.

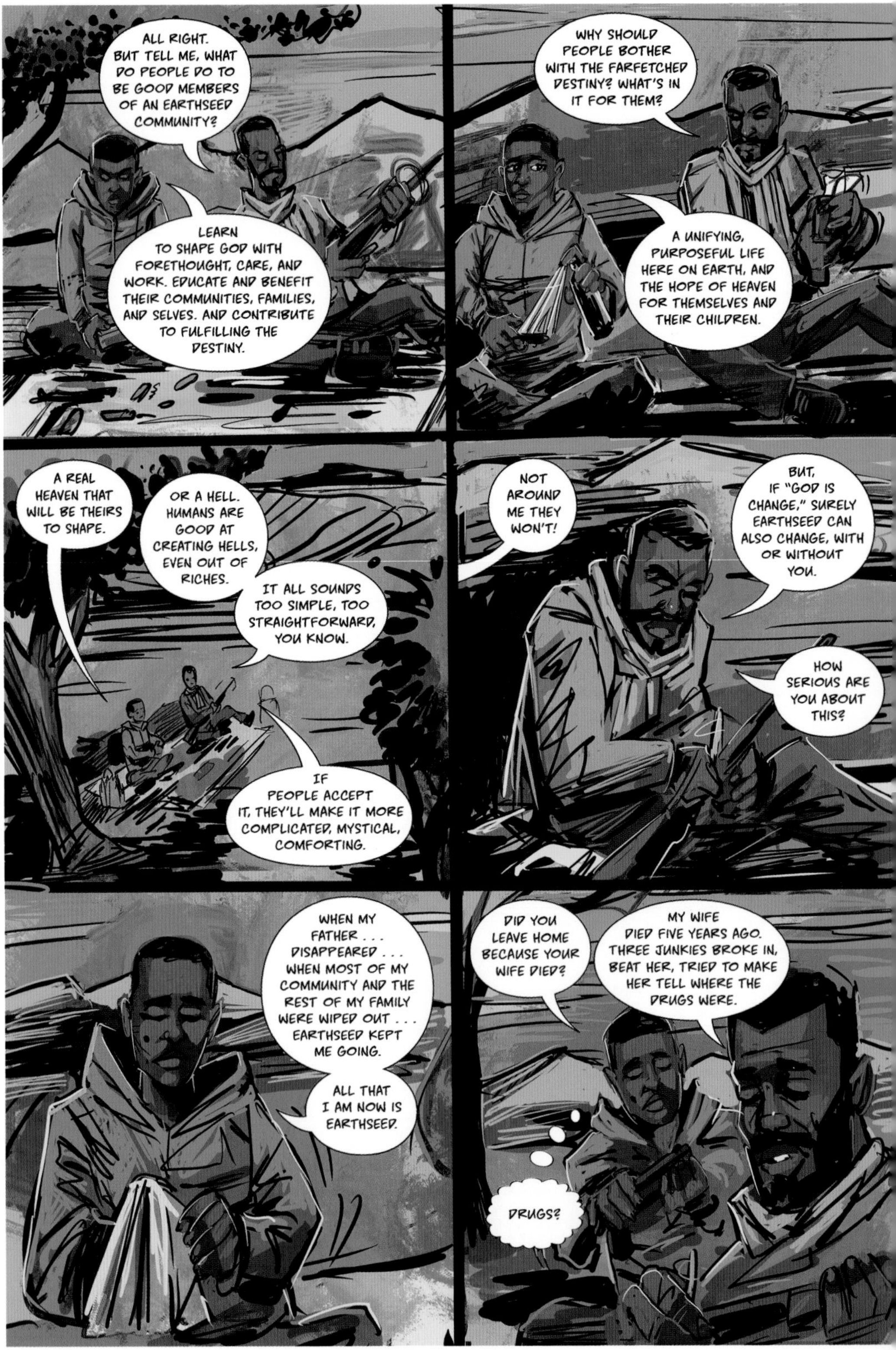
ALL RIGHT. BUT TELL ME, WHAT DO PEOPLE DO TO BE GOOD MEMBERS OF AN EARTHSEED COMMUNITY?
LEARN TO SHAPE GOD WITH FORETHOUGHT, CARE, AND WORK. EDUCATE AND BENEFIT THEIR COMMUNITIES, FAMILIES, AND SELVES. AND CONTRIBUTE TO FULFILLING THE DESTINY.
WHY SHOULD PEOPLE BOTHER WITH THE FARFETCHED DESTINY? WHAT'S IN IT FOR THEM?
A UNIFYING, PURPOSEFUL LIFE HERE ON EARTH, AND THE HOPE OF HEAVEN FOR THEMSELVES AND THEIR CHILDREN.
A REAL HEAVEN THAT WILL BE THEIRS TO SHAPE.
OR A HELL. HUMANS ARE GOOD AT CREATING HELLS, EVEN OUT OF RICHES.
IT ALL SOUNDS TOO SIMPLE, TOO STRAIGHTFORWARD, YOU KNOW.
IF PEOPLE ACCEPT IT, THEY'LL MAKE IT MORE COMPLICATED, MYSTICAL, COMFORTING.
NOT AROUND ME THEY WON'T!
BUT, IF "GOD IS CHANGE," SURELY EARTHSEED CAN ALSO CHANGE, WITH OR WITHOUT YOU.
HOW SERIOUS ARE YOU ABOUT THIS?
WHEN MY FATHER . . . DISAPPEARED . . . WHEN MOST OF MY COMMUNITY AND THE REST OF MY FAMILY WERE WIPED OUT . . . EARTHSEED KEPT ME GOING.
ALL THAT I AM NOW IS EARTHSEED.
DID YOU LEAVE HOME BECAUSE YOUR WIFE DIED?
MY WIFE DIED FIVE YEARS AGO. THREE JUNKIES BROKE IN, BEAT HER, TRIED TO MAKE HER TELL WHERE THE DRUGS WERE.
DRUGS?

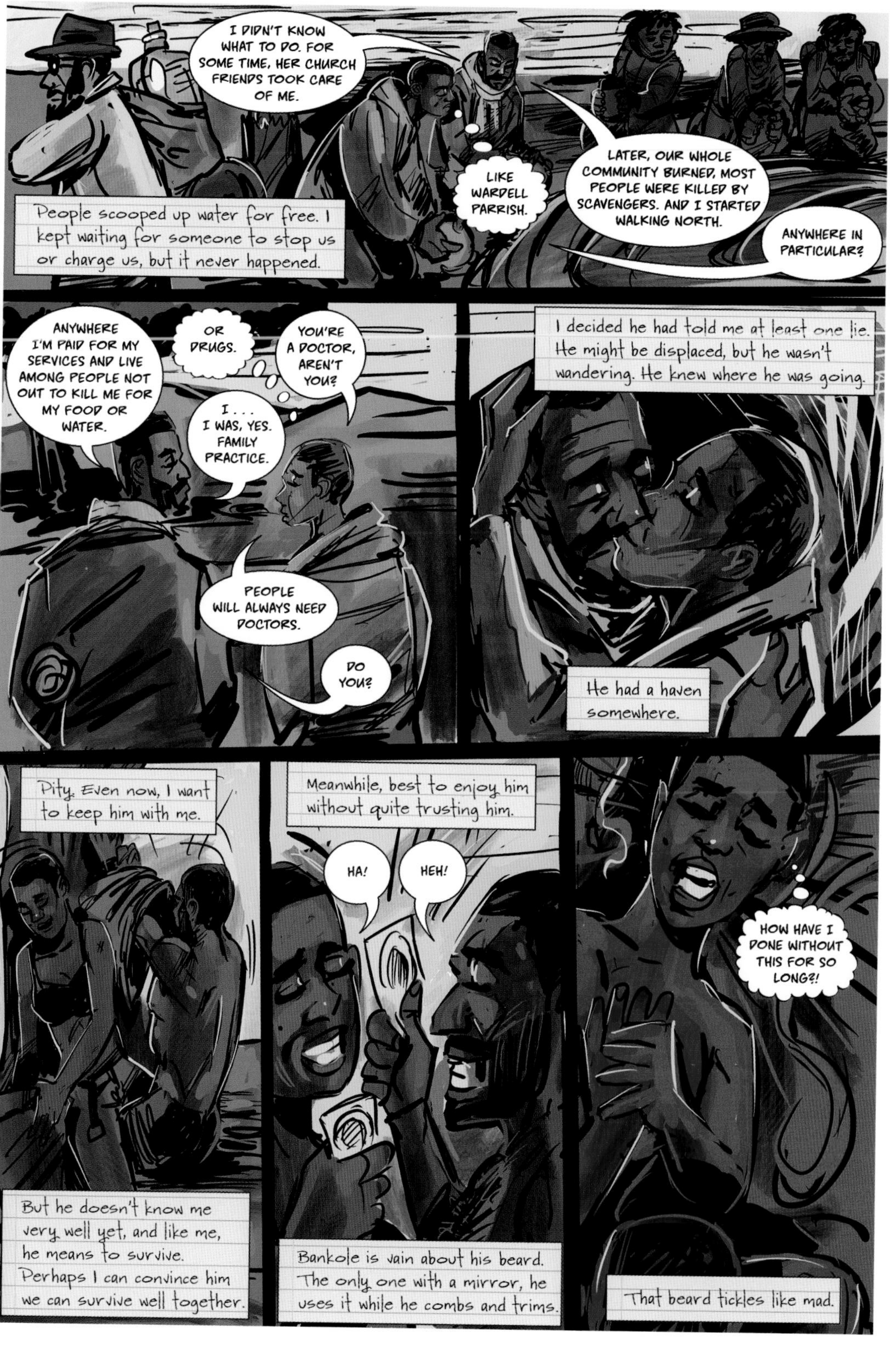

I DIDN'T KNOW WHAT TO DO. FOR SOME TIME, HER CHURCH FRIENDS TOOK CARE OF ME.
People scooped up water for free. I kept waiting for someone to stop us or charge us, but it never happened.
LIKE WARDELL PARRISH.
LATER, OUR WHOLE COMMUNITY BURNED, MOST PEOPLE WERE KILLED BY SCAVENGERS. AND I STARTED WALKING NORTH.
ANYWHERE IN PARTICULAR?
ANYWHERE I'M PAID FOR MY SERVICES AND LIVE AMONG PEOPLE NOT OUT TO KILL ME FOR MY FOOD OR WATER.
OR DRUGS.
YOU'RE A DOCTOR, AREN'T YOU?
I . . . I WAS, YES. FAMILY PRACTICE.
PEOPLE WILL ALWAYS NEED DOCTORS.
DO YOU?
I decided he had told me at least one lie. He might be displaced, but he wasn't wandering. He knew where he was going.
He had a haven somewhere.
Pity. Even now, I want to keep him with me.
But he doesn't know me very well yet, and like me, he means to survive. Perhaps I can convince him we can survive well together.
Meanwhile, best to enjoy him without quite trusting him.
HA!
HEH!
Bankole is vain about his beard. The only one with a mirror, he uses it while he combs and trims.
HOW HAVE I DONE WITHOUT THIS FOR SO LONG?!
That beard tickles like mad.

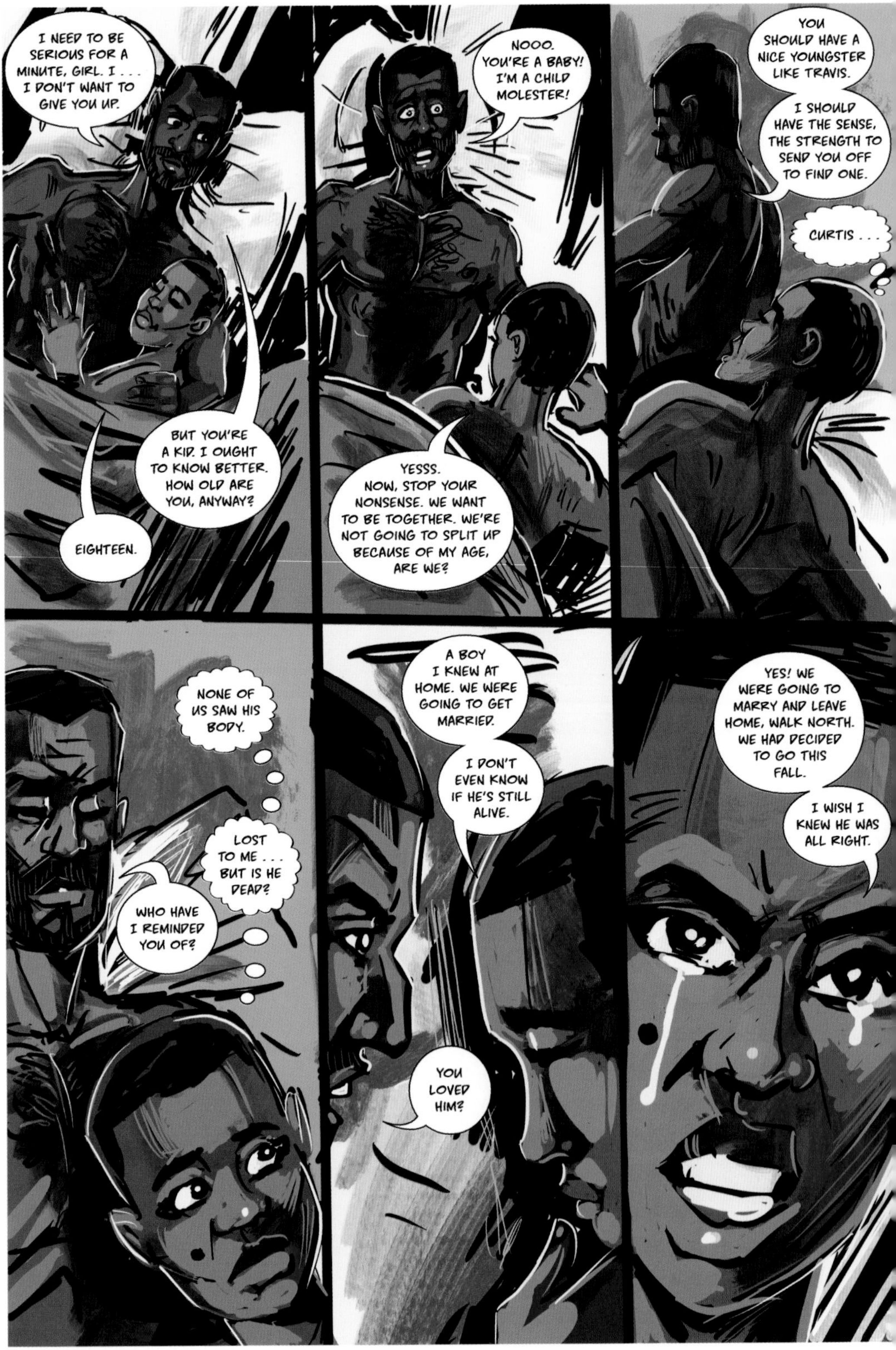
I NEED TO BE SERIOUS FOR A MINUTE, GIRL. I . . . I DON'T WANT TO GIVE YOU UP.
BUT YOU'RE A KID. I OUGHT TO KNOW BETTER. HOW OLD ARE YOU, ANYWAY?
EIGHTEEN.
NOOO. YOU'RE A BABY! I'M A CHILD MOLESTER!
YESSS. NOW, STOP YOUR NONSENSE. WE WANT TO BE TOGETHER. WE'RE NOT GOING TO SPLIT UP BECAUSE OF MY AGE, ARE WE?
YOU SHOULD HAVE A NICE YOUNGSTER LIKE TRAVIS.
I SHOULD HAVE THE SENSE, THE STRENGTH TO SEND YOU OFF TO FIND ONE.
CURTIS . . .
NONE OF US SAW HIS BODY.
LOST TO ME . . . BUT IS HE DEAD?
WHO HAVE I REMINDED YOU OF?
A BOY I KNEW AT HOME. WE WERE GOING TO GET MARRIED.
I DON'T EVEN KNOW IF HE'S STILL ALIVE.
YOU LOVED HIM?
YES! WE WERE GOING TO MARRY AND LEAVE HOME, WALK NORTH. WE HAD DECIDED TO GO THIS FALL.
I WISH I KNEW HE WAS ALL RIGHT.

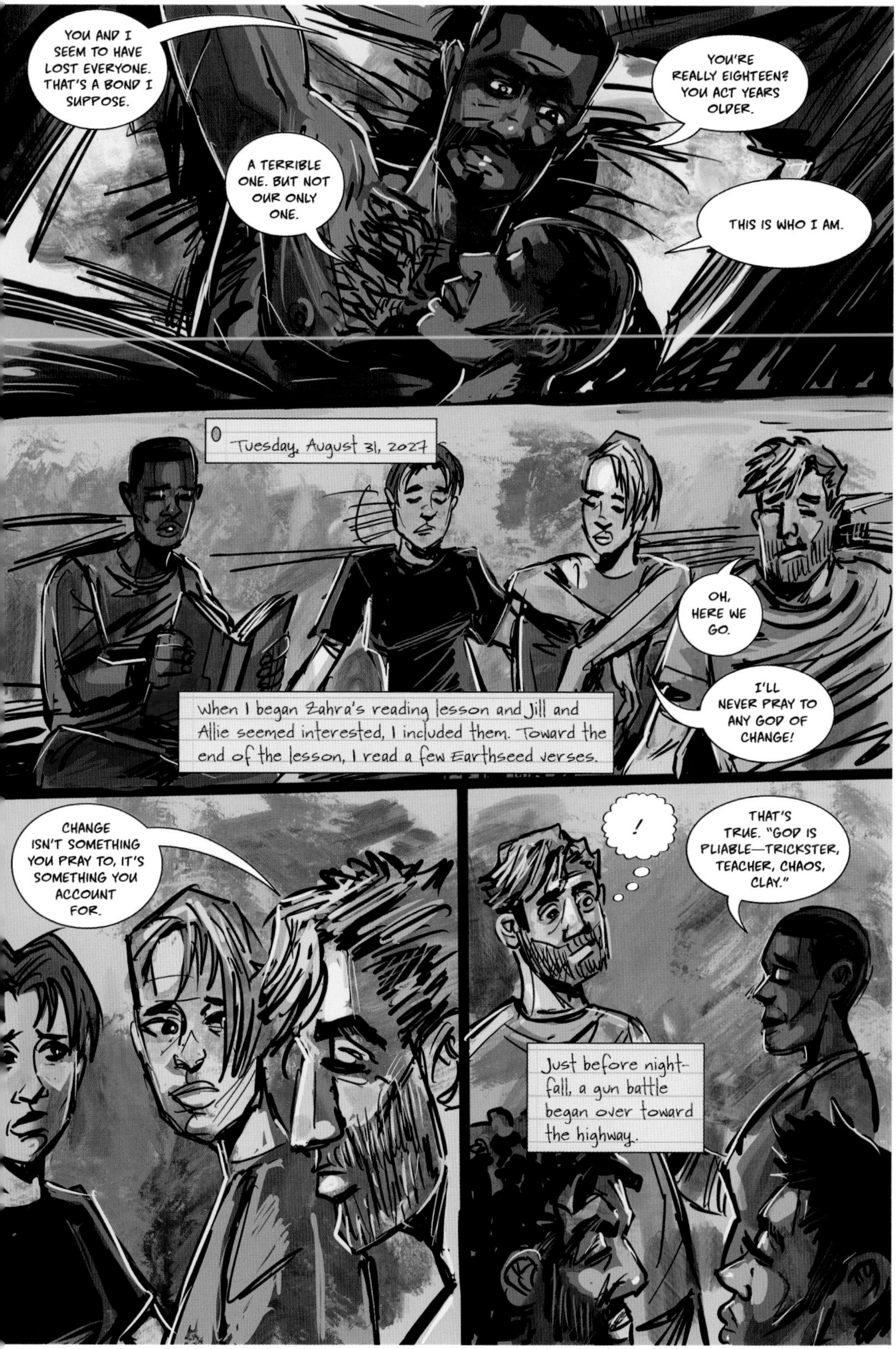
YOU AND I SEEM TO HAVE LOST EVERYONE. THAT'S A BOND I SUPPOSE.
A TERRIBLE ONE. BUT NOT OUR ONLY ONE.
YOU'RE REALLY EIGHTEEN? YOU ACT YEARS OLDER.
THIS IS WHO I AM.
Tuesday, August 31, 2027
When I began Zahra's reading lesson and Jill and Allie seemed interested, I included them. Toward the end of the lesson, I read a few Earthseed verses.
OH, HERE WE GO.
I'LL NEVER PRAY TO ANY GOD OF CHANGE!
CHANGE ISN'T SOMETHING YOU PRAY TO, IT'S SOMETHING YOU ACCOUNT FOR.
!
THAT'S TRUE. "GOD IS PLIABLE—TRICKSTER, TEACHER, CHAOS, CLAY."
Just before nightfall, a gun battle began over toward the highway.

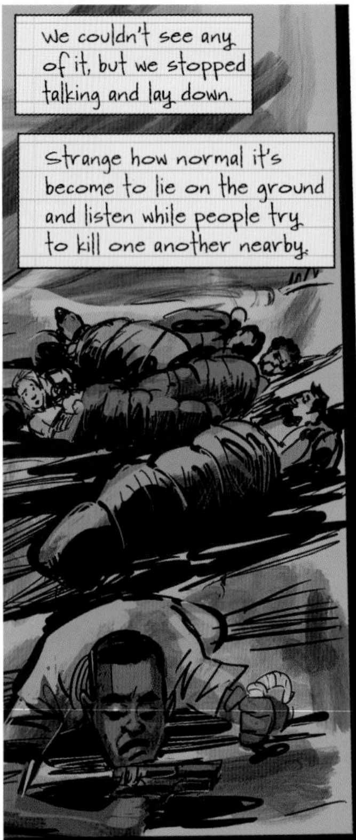
We couldn't see any of it, but we stopped talking and lay down.
Strange how normal it's become to lie on the ground and listen while people try to kill one another nearby.

As wind,
As water,
As fire,
As life,
God
Is both creative and destructive,
Demanding and yielding,
Sculptor and clay.
God is Infinite Potential:
God is Change.

EARTHSEED: THE BOOKS OF THE LIVING

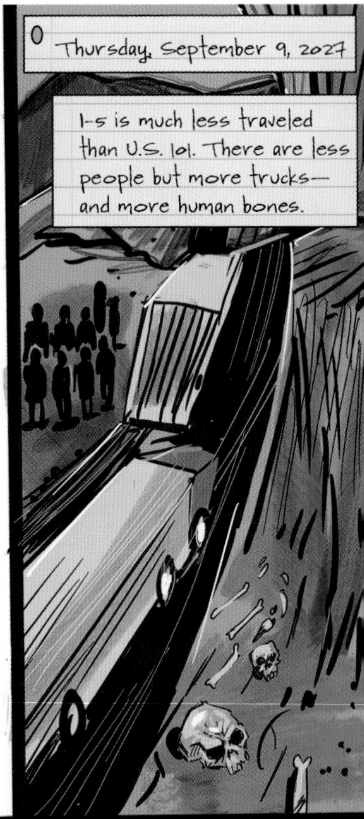
Thursday, September 9, 2027
I-5 is much less traveled than U.S. 101. There are less people but more trucks—and more human bones.

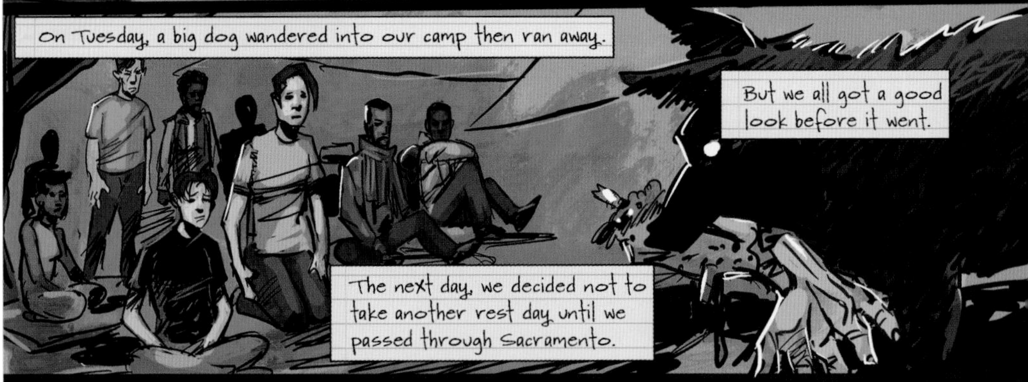
On Tuesday, a big dog wandered into our camp then ran away.
But we all got a good look before it went.
The next day, we decided not to take another rest day until we passed through Sacramento.

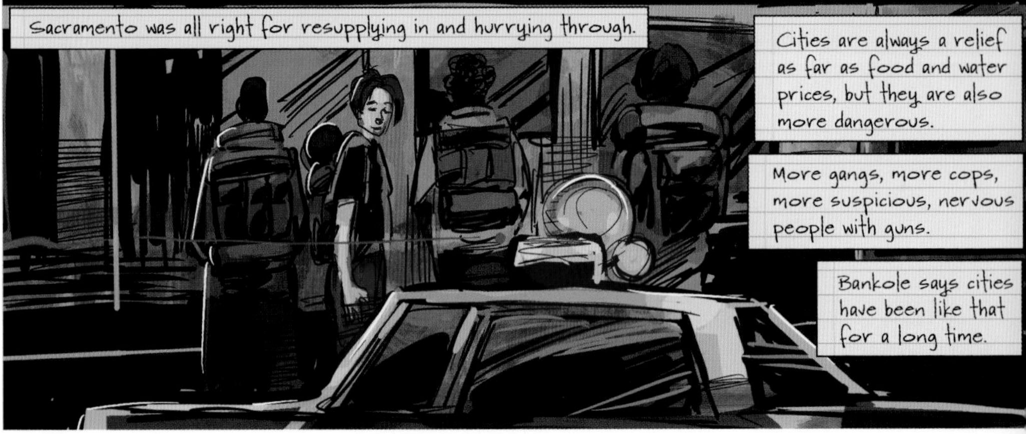
Sacramento was all right for resupplying in and hurrying through.
Cities are always a relief as far as food and water prices, but they are also more dangerous.
More gangs, more cops, more suspicious, nervous people with guns.
Bankole says cities have been like that for a long time.

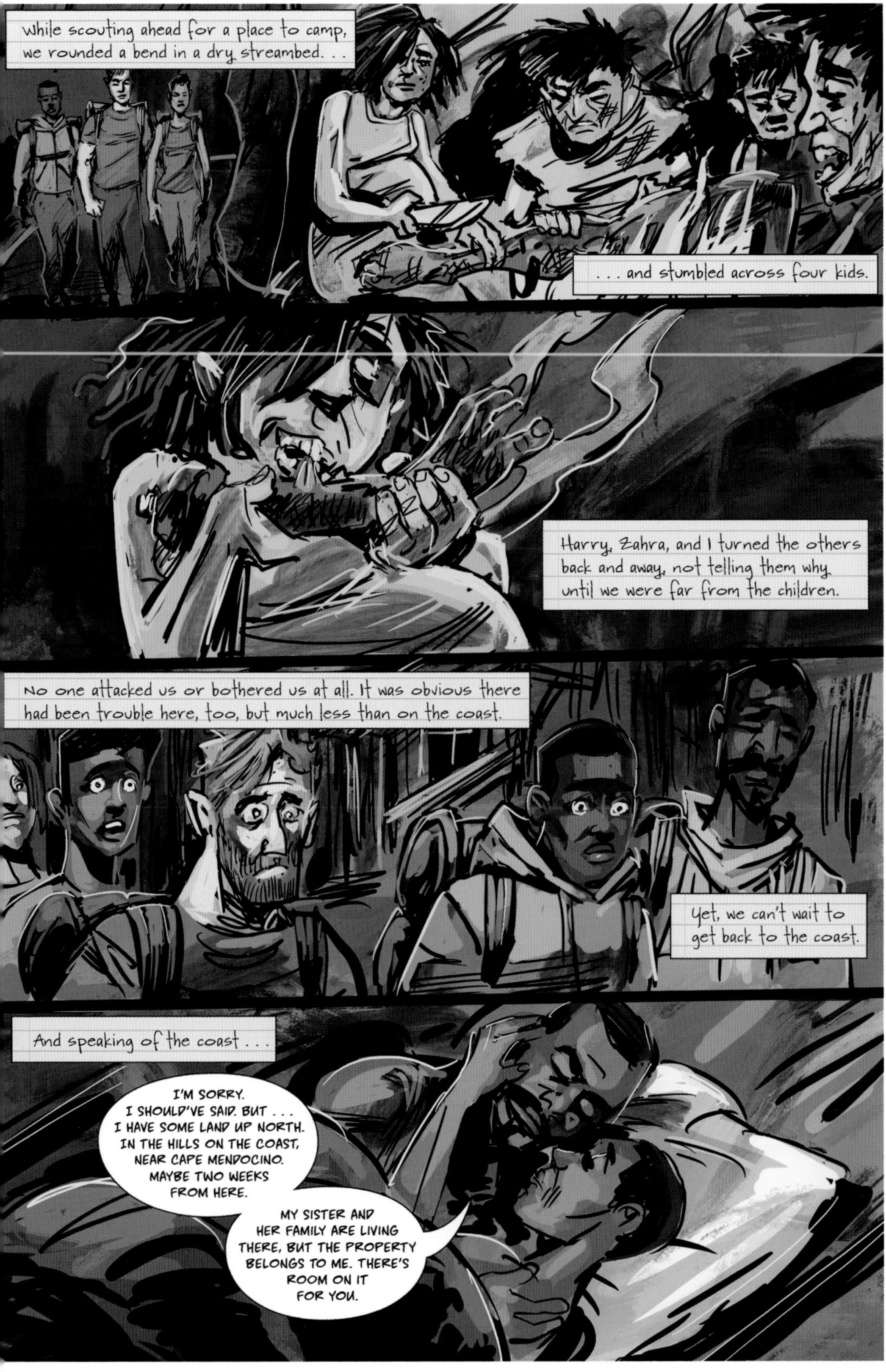
While scouting ahead for a place to camp, we rounded a bend in a dry streambed . . .
. . . and stumbled across four kids.
Harry, Zahra, and I turned the others back and away, not telling them why until we were far from the children.
No one attacked us or bothered us at all. It was obvious there had been trouble here, too, but much less than on the coast.
Yet, we can't wait to get back to the coast.
And speaking of the coast . . .
I'M SORRY. I SHOULD'VE SAID. BUT . . . I HAVE SOME LAND UP NORTH. IN THE HILLS ON THE COAST, NEAR CAPE MENDOCINO. MAYBE TWO WEEKS FROM HERE.
MY SISTER AND HER FAMILY ARE LIVING THERE, BUT THE PROPERTY BELONGS TO ME. THERE'S ROOM ON IT FOR YOU.

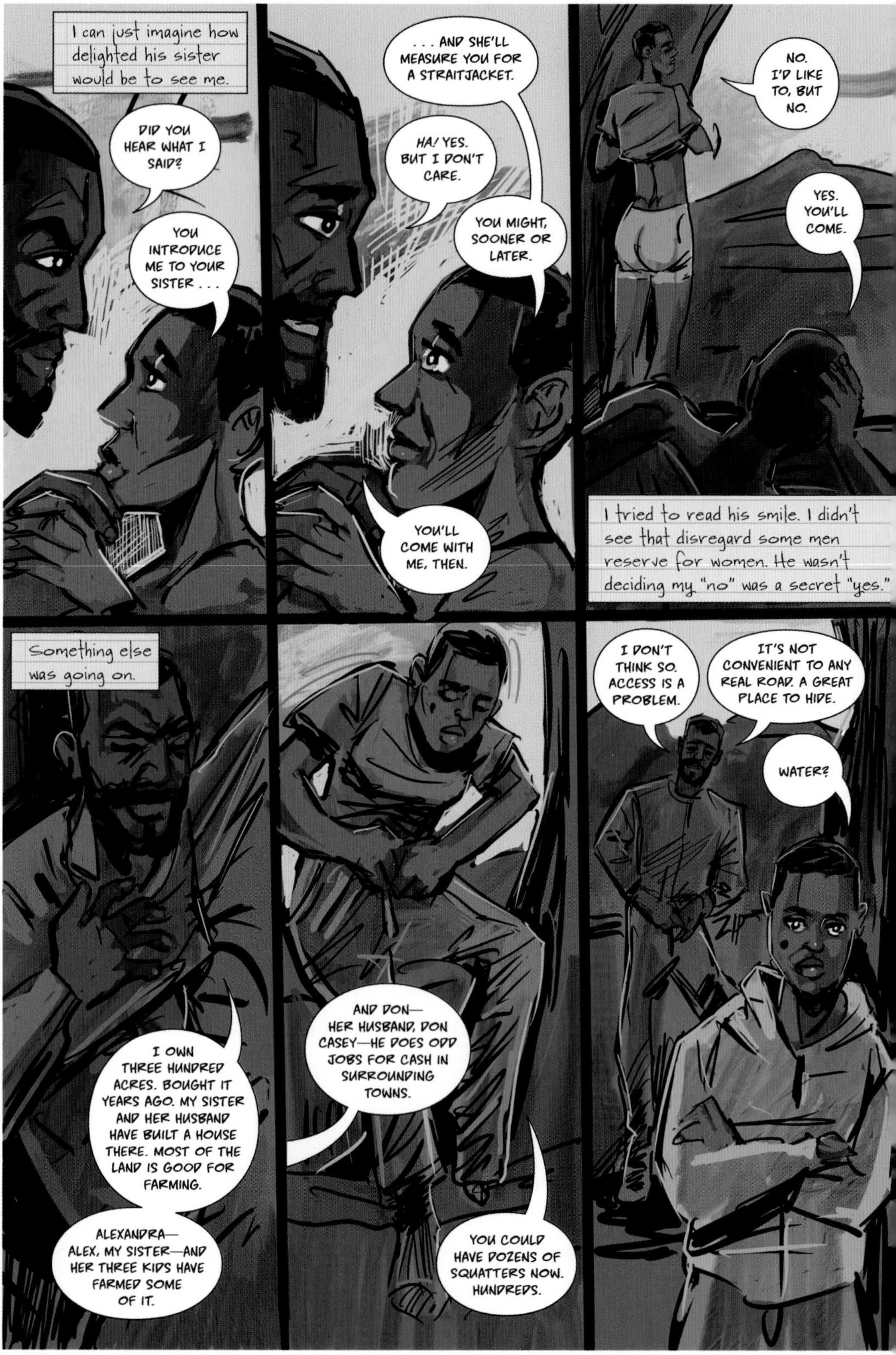

I can just imagine how delighted his sister would be to see me.
DID YOU HEAR WHAT I SAID?
YOU INTRODUCE ME TO YOUR SISTER . . .
. . . AND SHE'LL MEASURE YOU FOR A STRAITJACKET.
HA! YES. BUT I DON'T CARE.
YOU MIGHT, SOONER OR LATER.
YOU'LL COME WITH ME, THEN.
NO. I'D LIKE TO, BUT NO.
YES. YOU'LL COME.
I tried to read his smile. I didn't see that disregard some men reserve for women. He wasn't deciding my "no" was a secret "yes."
Something else was going on.
I OWN THREE HUNDRED ACRES. BOUGHT IT YEARS AGO. MY SISTER AND HER HUSBAND HAVE BUILT A HOUSE THERE. MOST OF THE LAND IS GOOD FOR FARMING.
ALEXANDRA—ALEX, MY SISTER—AND HER THREE KIDS HAVE FARMED SOME OF IT.
AND DON—HER HUSBAND, DON CASEY—HE DOES ODD JOBS FOR CASH IN SURROUNDING TOWNS.
YOU COULD HAVE DOZENS OF SQUATTERS NOW. HUNDREDS.
I DON'T THINK SO. ACCESS IS A PROBLEM.
IT'S NOT CONVENIENT TO ANY REAL ROAD. A GREAT PLACE TO HIDE.
WATER?

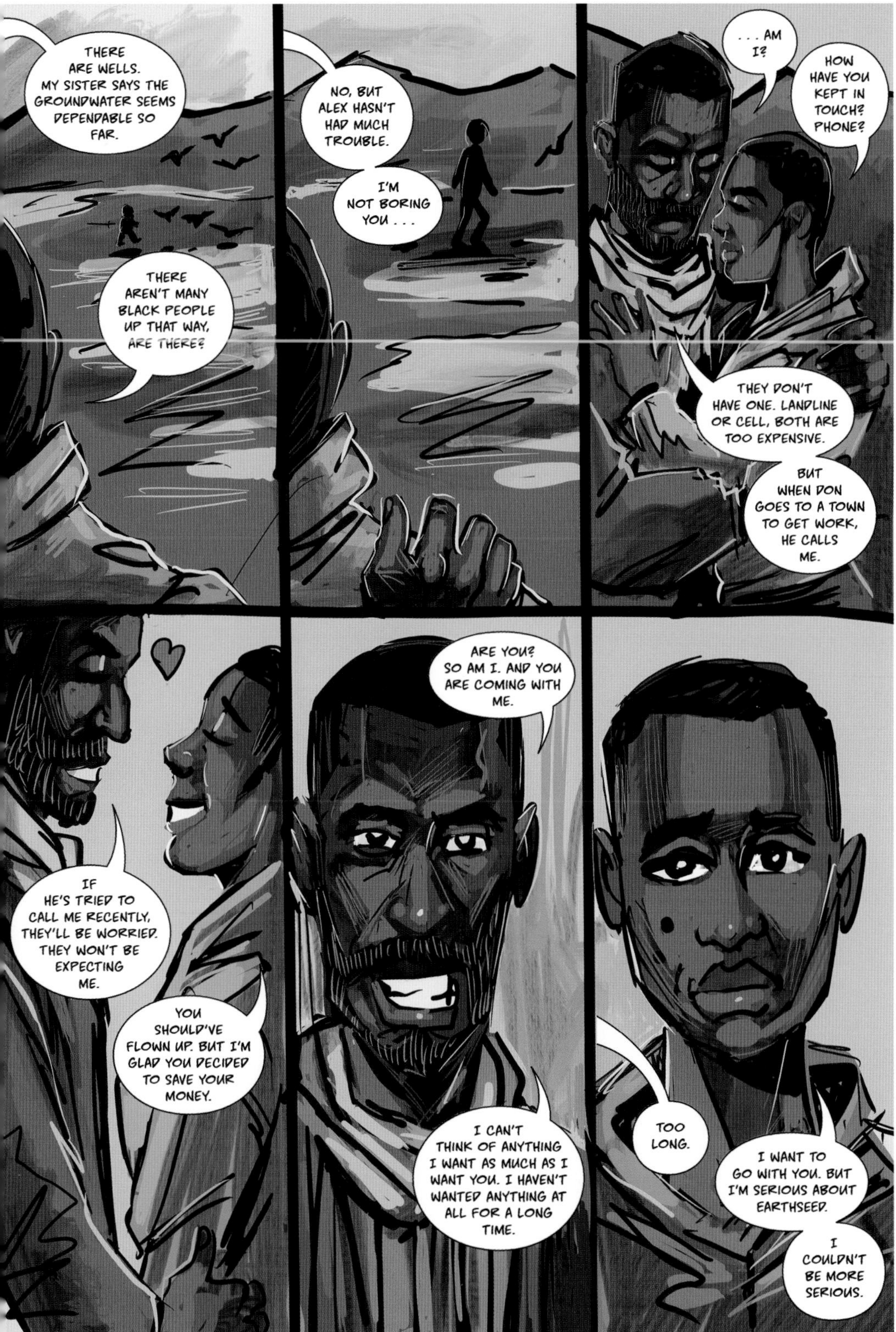
THERE ARE WELLS. MY SISTER SAYS THE GROUNDWATER SEEMS DEPENDABLE SO FAR.
THERE AREN'T MANY BLACK PEOPLE UP THAT WAY, ARE THERE?
NO, BUT ALEX HASN'T HAD MUCH TROUBLE.
I'M NOT BORING YOU . . .
. . . AM I?
HOW HAVE YOU KEPT IN TOUCH? PHONE?
THEY DON'T HAVE ONE. LANDLINE OR CELL, BOTH ARE TOO EXPENSIVE.
BUT WHEN DON GOES TO A TOWN TO GET WORK, HE CALLS ME.
IF HE'S TRIED TO CALL ME RECENTLY, THEY'LL BE WORRIED. THEY WON'T BE EXPECTING ME.
YOU SHOULD'VE FLOWN UP. BUT I'M GLAD YOU DECIDED TO SAVE YOUR MONEY.
ARE YOU? SO AM I. AND YOU ARE COMING WITH ME.
I CAN'T THINK OF ANYTHING I WANT AS MUCH AS I WANT YOU. I HAVEN'T WANTED ANYTHING AT ALL FOR A LONG TIME.
TOO LONG.
I WANT TO GO WITH YOU. BUT I'M SERIOUS ABOUT EARTHSEED.
I COULDN'T BE MORE SERIOUS.

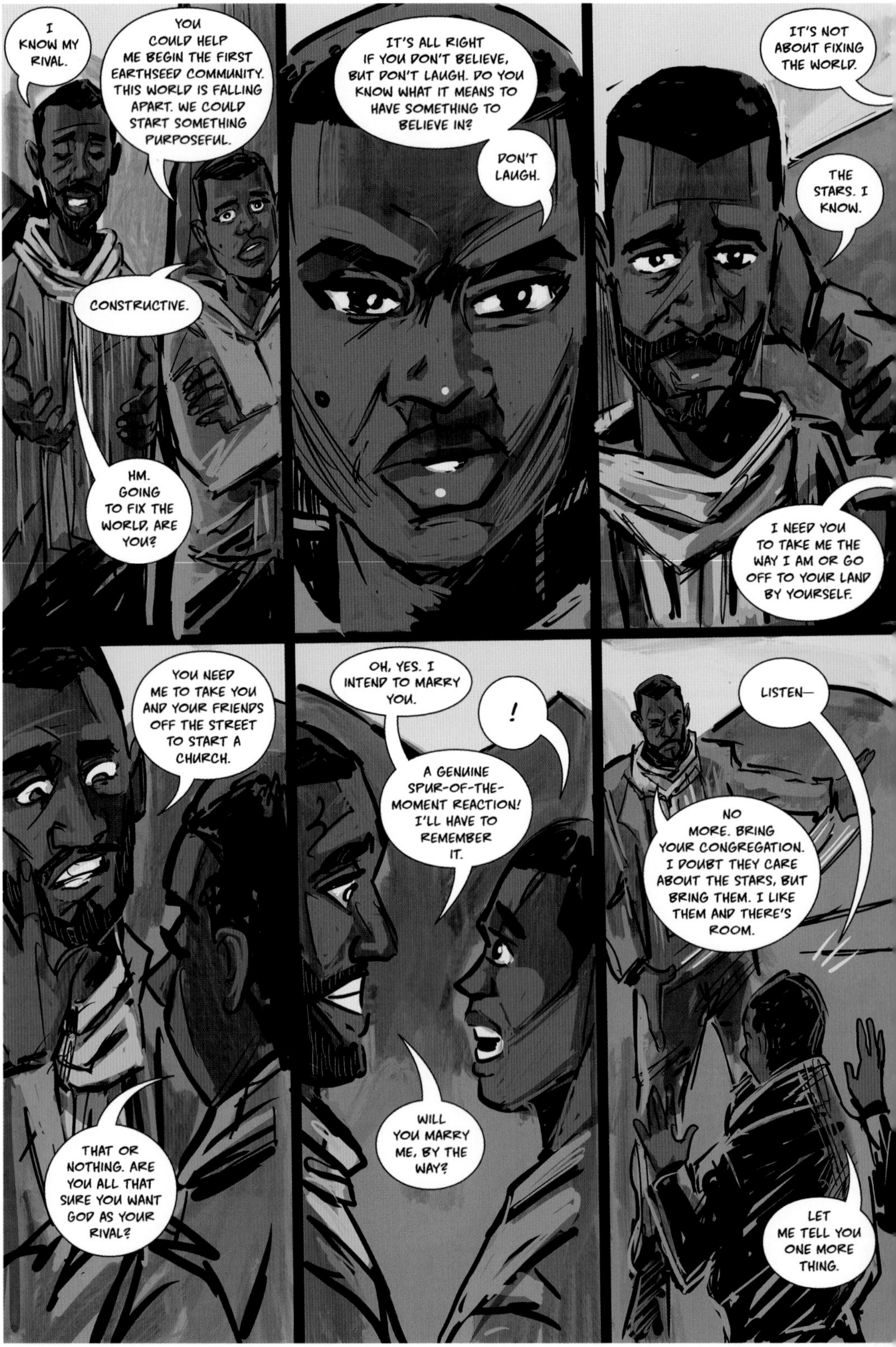
I KNOW MY RIVAL.
YOU COULD HELP ME BEGIN THE FIRST EARTHSEED COMMUNITY. THIS WORLD IS FALLING APART. WE COULD START SOMETHING PURPOSEFUL.
CONSTRUCTIVE.
HM. GOING TO FIX THE WORLD, ARE YOU?
IT'S ALL RIGHT IF YOU DON'T BELIEVE, BUT DON'T LAUGH. DO YOU KNOW WHAT IT MEANS TO HAVE SOMETHING TO BELIEVE IN?
DON'T LAUGH.
IT'S NOT ABOUT FIXING THE WORLD.
THE STARS. I KNOW.
I NEED YOU TO TAKE ME THE WAY I AM OR GO OFF TO YOUR LAND BY YOURSELF.
YOU NEED ME TO TAKE YOU AND YOUR FRIENDS OFF THE STREET TO START A CHURCH.
THAT OR NOTHING. ARE YOU ALL THAT SURE YOU WANT GOD AS YOUR RIVAL?
OH, YES. I INTEND TO MARRY YOU.
!
A GENUINE SPUR-OF-THE-MOMENT REACTION! I'LL HAVE TO REMEMBER IT.
WILL YOU MARRY ME, BY THE WAY?
LISTEN—
NO MORE. BRING YOUR CONGREGATION. I DOUBT THEY CARE ABOUT THE STARS, BUT BRING THEM. I LIKE THEM AND THERE'S ROOM.
LET ME TELL YOU ONE MORE THING.

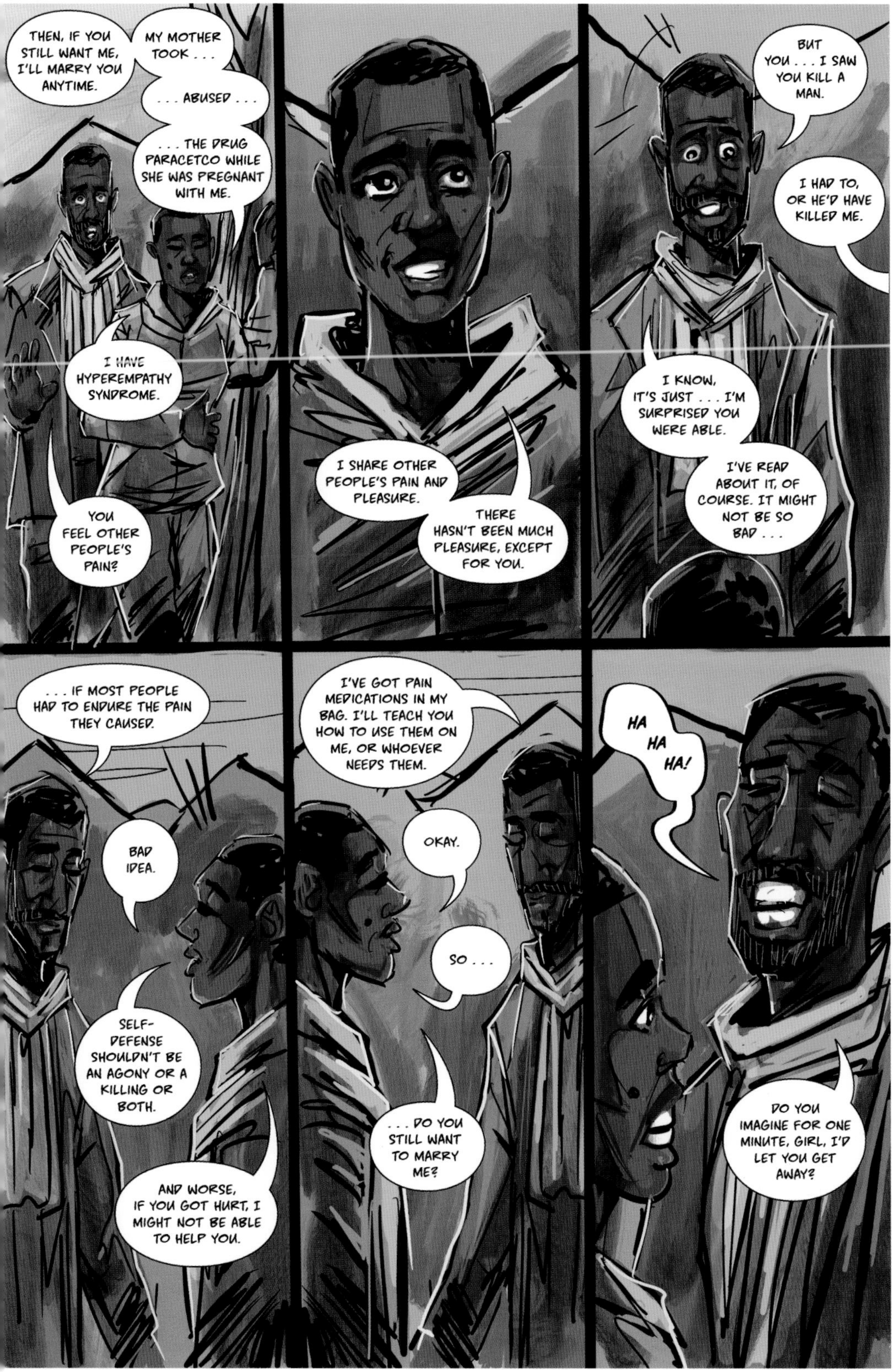
THEN, IF YOU STILL WANT ME, I'LL MARRY YOU ANYTIME.
MY MOTHER TOOK . . .
. . . ABUSED . . .
. . . THE DRUG PARACETCO WHILE SHE WAS PREGNANT WITH ME.
I HAVE HYPEREMPATHY SYNDROME.
YOU FEEL OTHER PEOPLE'S PAIN?
I SHARE OTHER PEOPLE'S PAIN AND PLEASURE.
THERE HASN'T BEEN MUCH PLEASURE, EXCEPT FOR YOU.
BUT YOU . . . I SAW YOU KILL A MAN.
I HAD TO, OR HE'D HAVE KILLED ME.
I KNOW, IT'S JUST . . . I'M SURPRISED YOU WERE ABLE.
I'VE READ ABOUT IT, OF COURSE. IT MIGHT NOT BE SO BAD . . .
. . . IF MOST PEOPLE HAD TO ENDURE THE PAIN THEY CAUSED.
BAD IDEA.
SELF-DEFENSE SHOULDN'T BE AN AGONY OR A KILLING OR BOTH.
AND WORSE, IF YOU GOT HURT, I MIGHT NOT BE ABLE TO HELP YOU.
I'VE GOT PAIN MEDICATIONS IN MY BAG. I'LL TEACH YOU HOW TO USE THEM ON ME, OR WHOEVER NEEDS THEM.
OKAY.
SO . . .
. . . DO YOU STILL WANT TO MARRY ME?
HA HA HA!
DO YOU IMAGINE FOR ONE MINUTE, GIRL, I'D LET YOU GET AWAY?

Your teachers
Are all around you.
All that you perceive,
All that you experience,
All that is given to you,
or taken from you,
All that you love or hate,
need or fear
Will teach you—
If you will learn.
God is your first
and your last teacher.
God is your harshest teacher:
subtle,
demanding.
Learn or die.

EARTHSEED: THE BOOKS OF THE LIVING

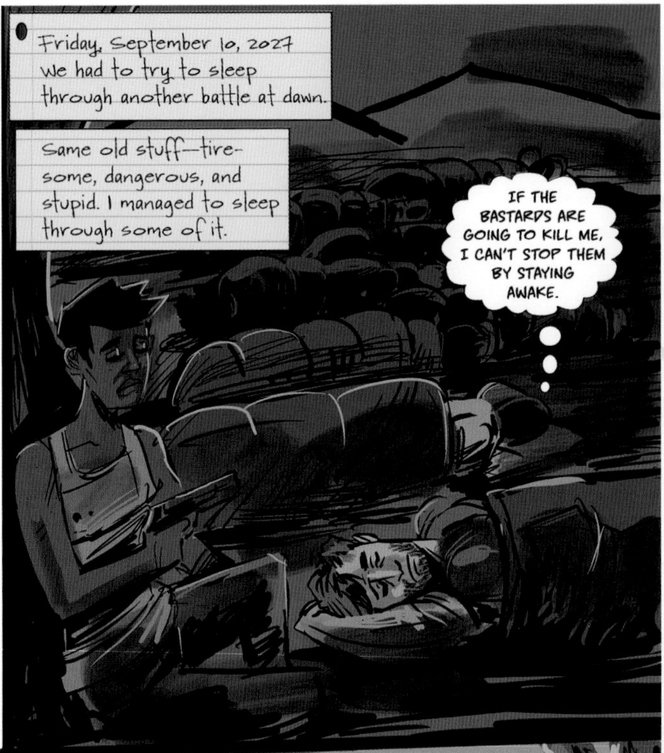
Friday, September 10, 2027
We had to try to sleep through another battle at dawn.
Same old stuff—tiresome, dangerous, and stupid. I managed to sleep through some of it.
IF THE BASTARDS ARE GOING TO KILL ME, I CAN'T STOP THEM BY STAYING AWAKE.

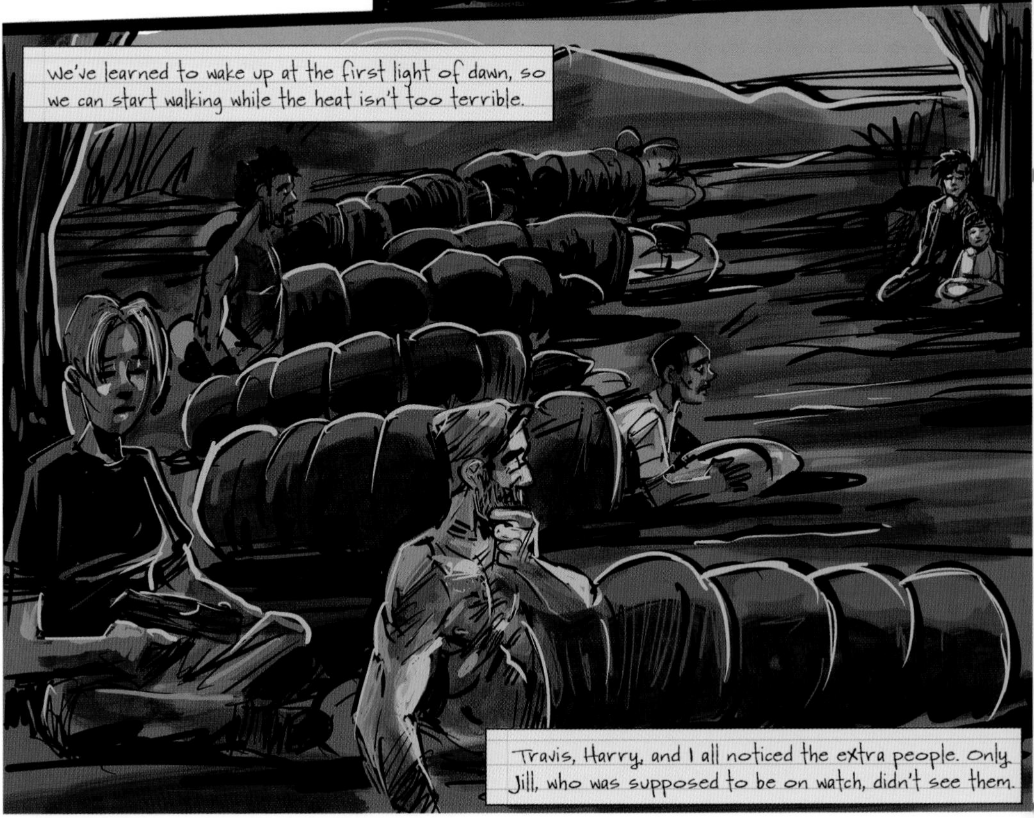
We've learned to wake up at the first light of dawn, so we can start walking while the heat isn't too terrible.
Travis, Harry, and I all noticed the extra people. Only Jill, who was supposed to be on watch, didn't see them.

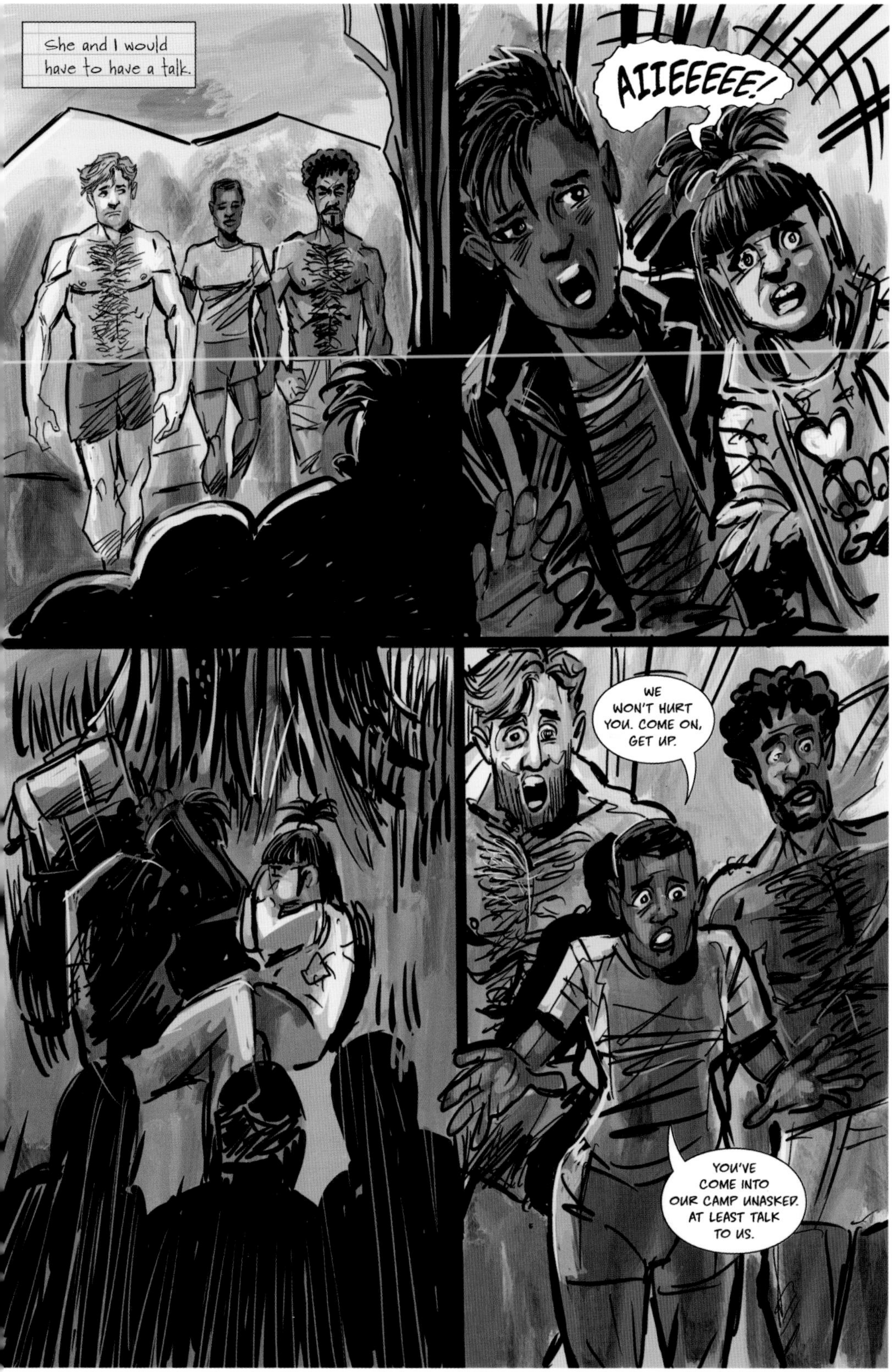
She and I would have to have a talk.
AIIEEEEE!
WE WON'T HURT YOU. COME ON, GET UP.
YOU'VE COME INTO OUR CAMP UNASKED. AT LEAST TALK TO US.

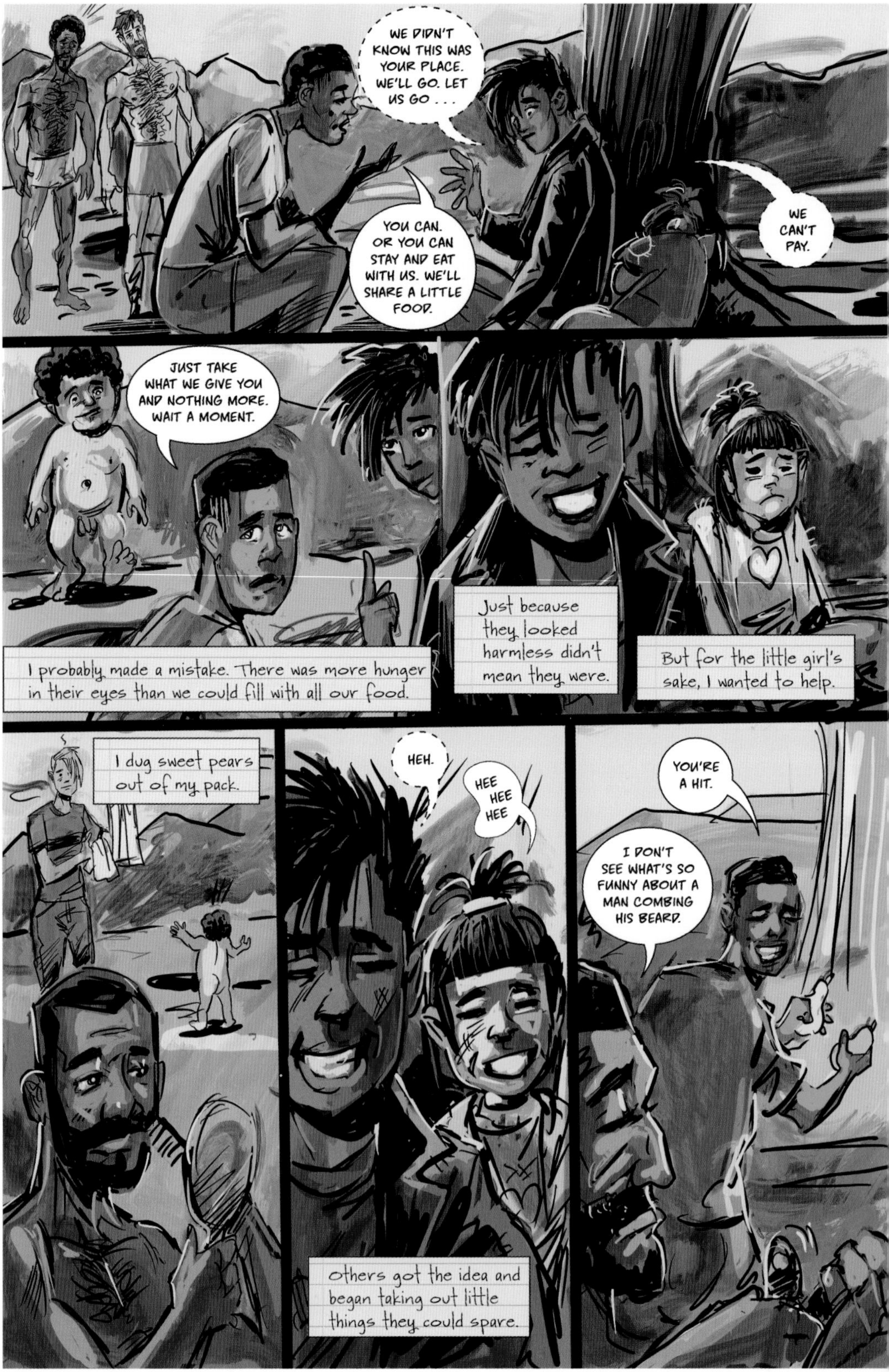
WE DIDN'T KNOW THIS WAS YOUR PLACE. WE'LL GO. LET US GO . . .
YOU CAN. OR YOU CAN STAY AND EAT WITH US. WE'LL SHARE A LITTLE FOOD.
WE CAN'T PAY.
JUST TAKE WHAT WE GIVE YOU AND NOTHING MORE. WAIT A MOMENT.
I probably made a mistake. There was more hunger in their eyes than we could fill with all our food.
Just because they looked harmless didn't mean they were.
But for the little girl's sake, I wanted to help.
I dug sweet pears out of my pack.
HEH.
HEE HEE HEE
YOU'RE A HIT.
I DON'T SEE WHAT'S SO FUNNY ABOUT A MAN COMBING HIS BEARD.
others got the idea and began taking out little things they could spare.

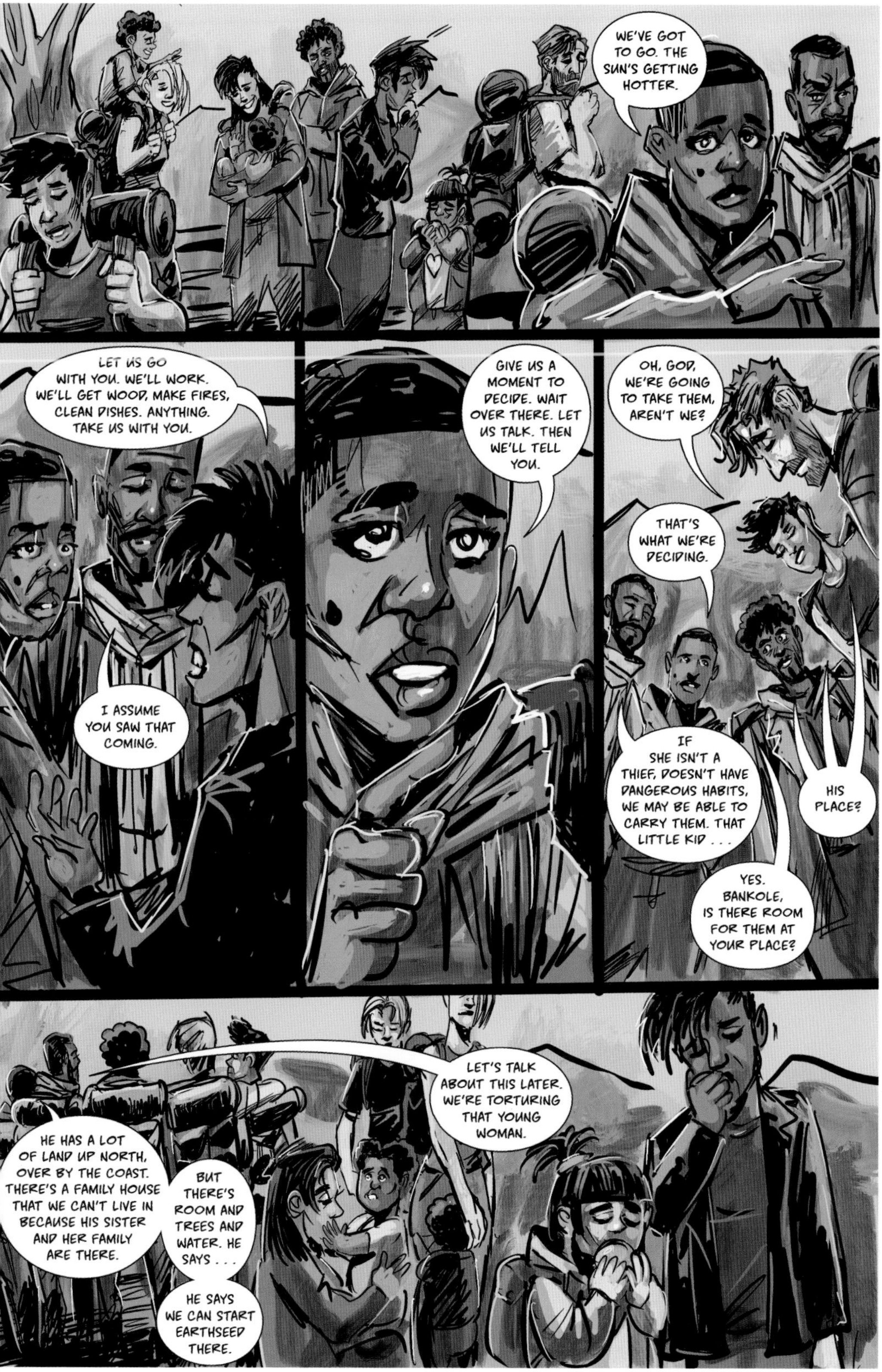
WE'VE GOT TO GO. THE SUN'S GETTING HOTTER.
LET US GO WITH YOU. WE'LL WORK. WE'LL GET WOOD, MAKE FIRES, CLEAN DISHES. ANYTHING. TAKE US WITH YOU.
I ASSUME YOU SAW THAT COMING.
GIVE US A MOMENT TO DECIDE. WAIT OVER THERE. LET US TALK. THEN WE'LL TELL YOU.
OH, GOD, WE'RE GOING TO TAKE THEM, AREN'T WE?
THAT'S WHAT WE'RE DECIDING.
IF SHE ISN'T A THIEF, DOESN'T HAVE DANGEROUS HABITS, WE MAY BE ABLE TO CARRY THEM. THAT LITTLE KID . . .
HIS PLACE?
YES. BANKOLE, IS THERE ROOM FOR THEM AT YOUR PLACE?
LET'S TALK ABOUT THIS LATER. WE'RE TORTURING THAT YOUNG WOMAN.
HE HAS A LOT OF LAND UP NORTH, OVER BY THE COAST. THERE'S A FAMILY HOUSE THAT WE CAN'T LIVE IN BECAUSE HIS SISTER AND HER FAMILY ARE THERE.
BUT THERE'S ROOM AND TREES AND WATER. HE SAYS . . .
HE SAYS WE CAN START EARTHSEED THERE.

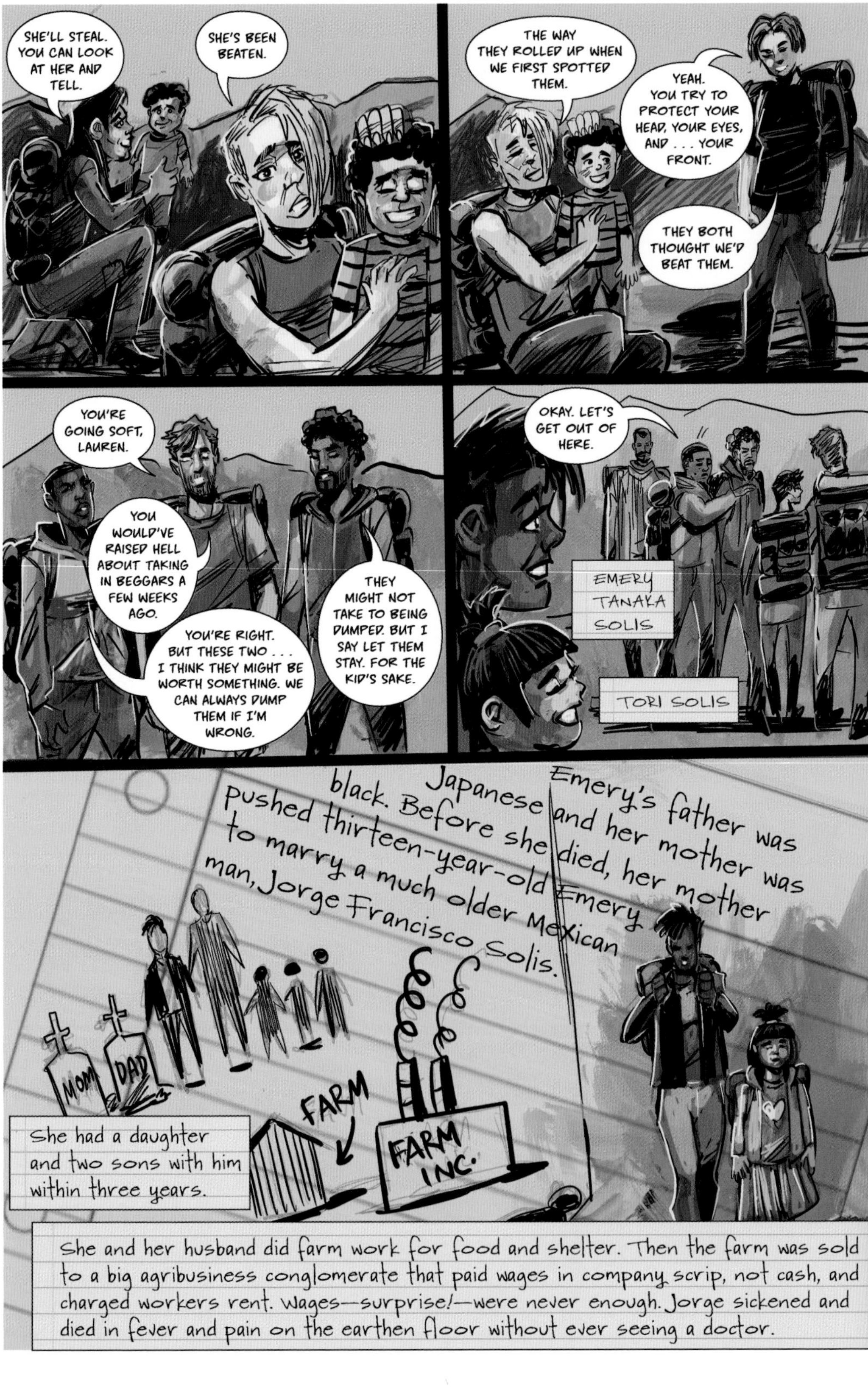
SHE'LL STEAL. YOU CAN LOOK AT HER AND TELL.
SHE'S BEEN BEATEN.
THE WAY THEY ROLLED UP WHEN WE FIRST SPOTTED THEM.
YEAH. YOU TRY TO PROTECT YOUR HEAD, YOUR EYES, AND . . . YOUR FRONT.
THEY BOTH THOUGHT WE'D BEAT THEM.
YOU'RE GOING SOFT, LAUREN.
YOU WOULD'VE RAISED HELL ABOUT TAKING IN BEGGARS A FEW WEEKS AGO.
YOU'RE RIGHT. BUT THESE TWO . . . I THINK THEY MIGHT BE WORTH SOMETHING. WE CAN ALWAYS DUMP THEM IF I'M WRONG.
THEY MIGHT NOT TAKE TO BEING DUMPED. BUT I SAY LET THEM STAY. FOR THE KID'S SAKE.
OKAY. LET'S GET OUT OF HERE.
EMERY TANAKA SOLIS
TORI SOLIS
Emery's father was Japanese and her mother was black. Before she died, her mother pushed thirteen-year-old Emery to marry a much older Mexican man, Jorge Francisco Solis.
MOM
DAD
FARM
FARM INC.
She had a daughter and two sons with him within three years.
She and her husband did farm work for food and shelter. Then the farm was sold to a big agribusiness conglomerate that paid wages in company scrip, not cash, and charged workers rent. Wages—surprise!—were never enough. Jorge sickened and died in fever and pain on the earthen floor without ever seeing a doctor.

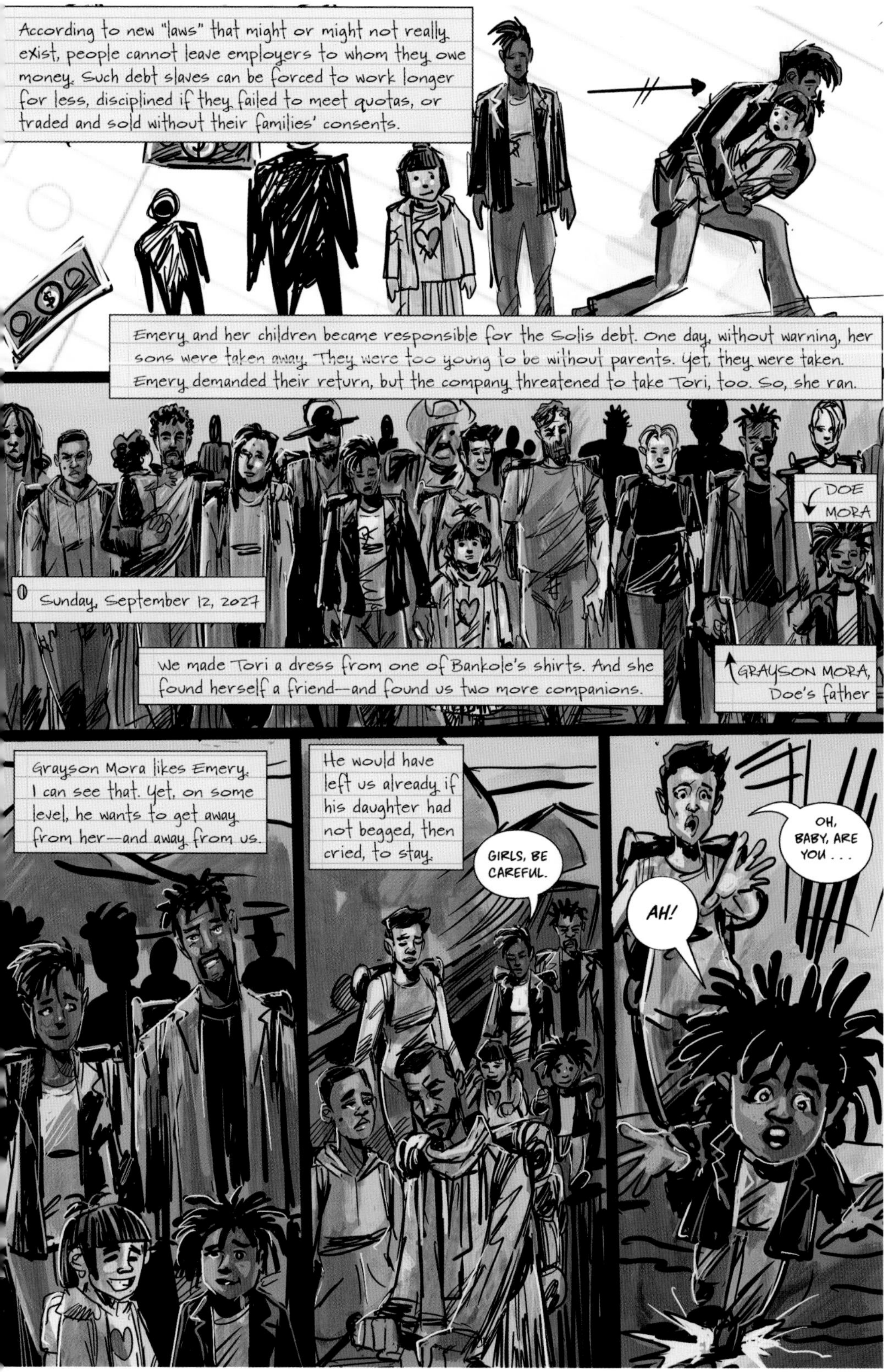

According to new "laws" that might or might not really exist, people cannot leave employers to whom they owe money. Such debt slaves can be forced to work longer for less, disciplined if they failed to meet quotas, or traded and sold without their families' consents.
Emery and her children became responsible for the Solis debt. One day, without warning, her sons were taken away. They were too young to be without parents. Yet, they were taken. Emery demanded their return, but the company threatened to take Tori, too. So, she ran.
Sunday, September 12, 2027
DOE MORA
We made Tori a dress from one of Bankole's shirts. And she found herself a friend—and found us two more companions.
GRAYSON MORA, Doe's father
Grayson Mora likes Emery. I can see that. Yet, on some level, he wants to get away from her—and away from us.
He would have left us already if his daughter had not begged, then cried, to stay.
GIRLS, BE CAREFUL.
OH, BABY, ARE YOU . . .
AH!

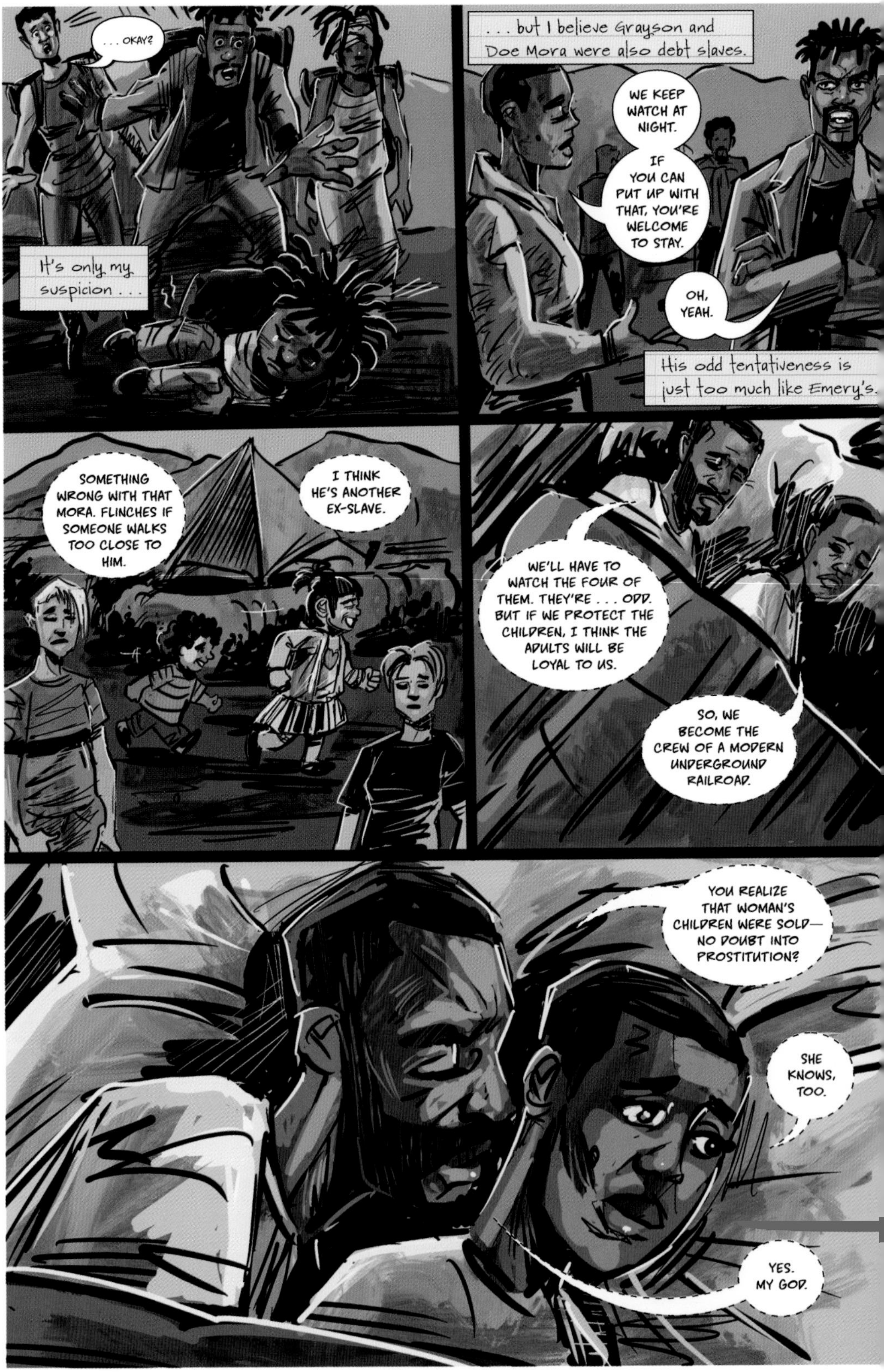
. . . OKAY?
It's only my suspicion . . .
. . . but I believe Grayson and Doe Mora were also debt slaves.
WE KEEP WATCH AT NIGHT.
IF YOU CAN PUT UP WITH THAT, YOU'RE WELCOME TO STAY.
OH, YEAH.
His odd tentativeness is just too much like Emery's.
SOMETHING WRONG WITH THAT MORA. FLINCHES IF SOMEONE WALKS TOO CLOSE TO HIM.
I THINK HE'S ANOTHER EX-SLAVE.
WE'LL HAVE TO WATCH THE FOUR OF THEM. THEY'RE . . . ODD. BUT IF WE PROTECT THE CHILDREN, I THINK THE ADULTS WILL BE LOYAL TO US.
SO, WE BECOME THE CREW OF A MODERN UNDERGROUND RAILROAD.
YOU REALIZE THAT WOMAN'S CHILDREN WERE SOLD—NO DOUBT INTO PROSTITUTION?
SHE KNOWS, TOO.
YES. MY GOD.

Respect God:
Pray working.
Pray learning,
planning,
doing.
Pray creating,
teaching,
reaching.
Pray working.
Pray to focus your thoughts,
still your fears,
strengthen your purpose.
Respect God.
Shape God.
Pray working.

EARTHSEED: THE BOOKS OF THE LIVING

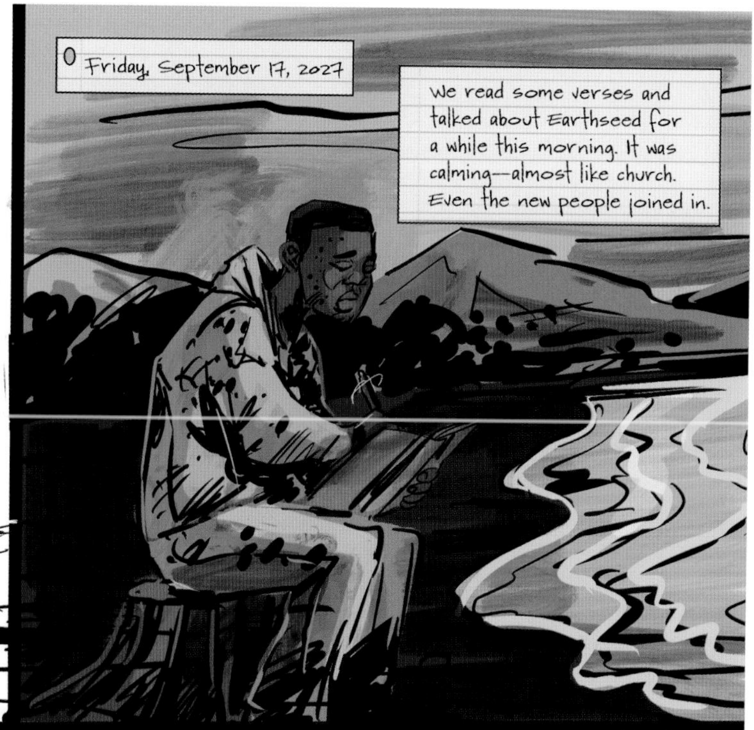
Friday, September 17, 2027
We read some verses and talked about Earthseed for a while this morning. It was calming—almost like church. Even the new people joined in.

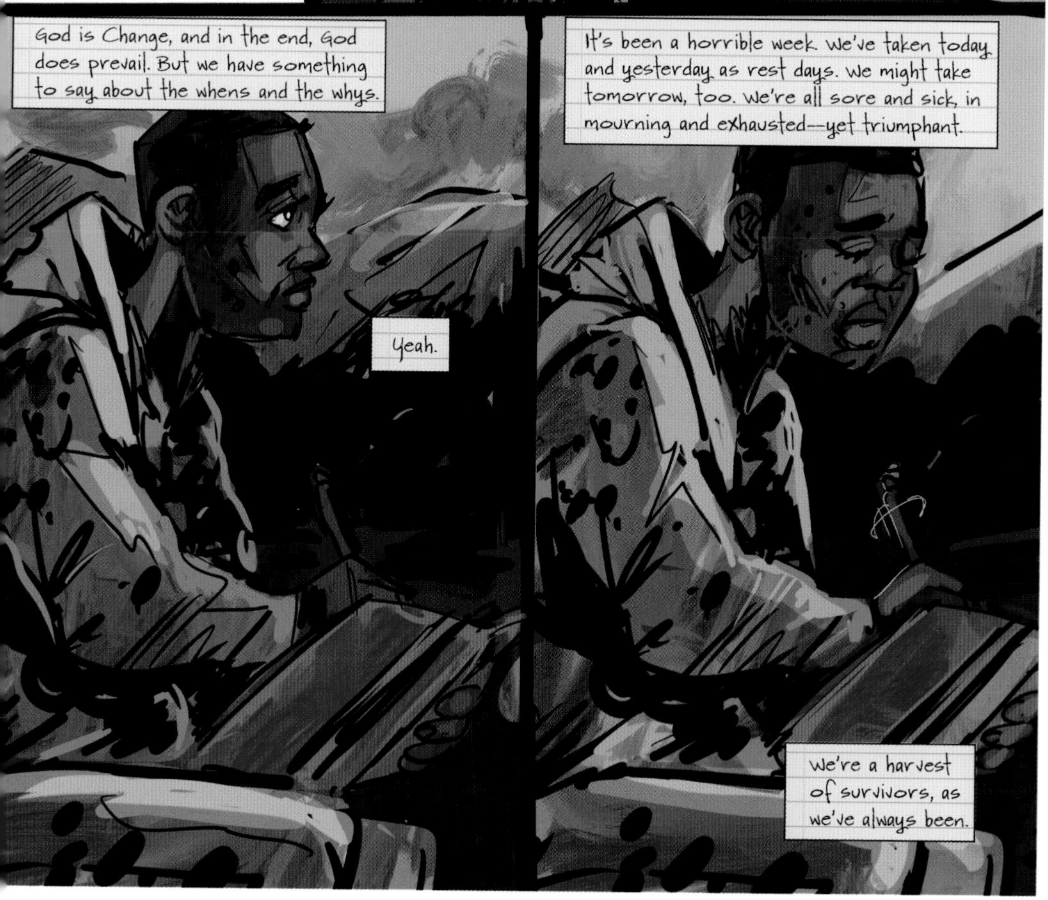
God is Change, and in the end, God does prevail. But we have something to say about the whens and the whys.
Yeah.
It's been a horrible week. We've taken today and yesterday as rest days. We might take tomorrow, too. We're all sore and sick, in mourning and exhausted—yet triumphant.
We're a harvest of survivors, as we've always been.

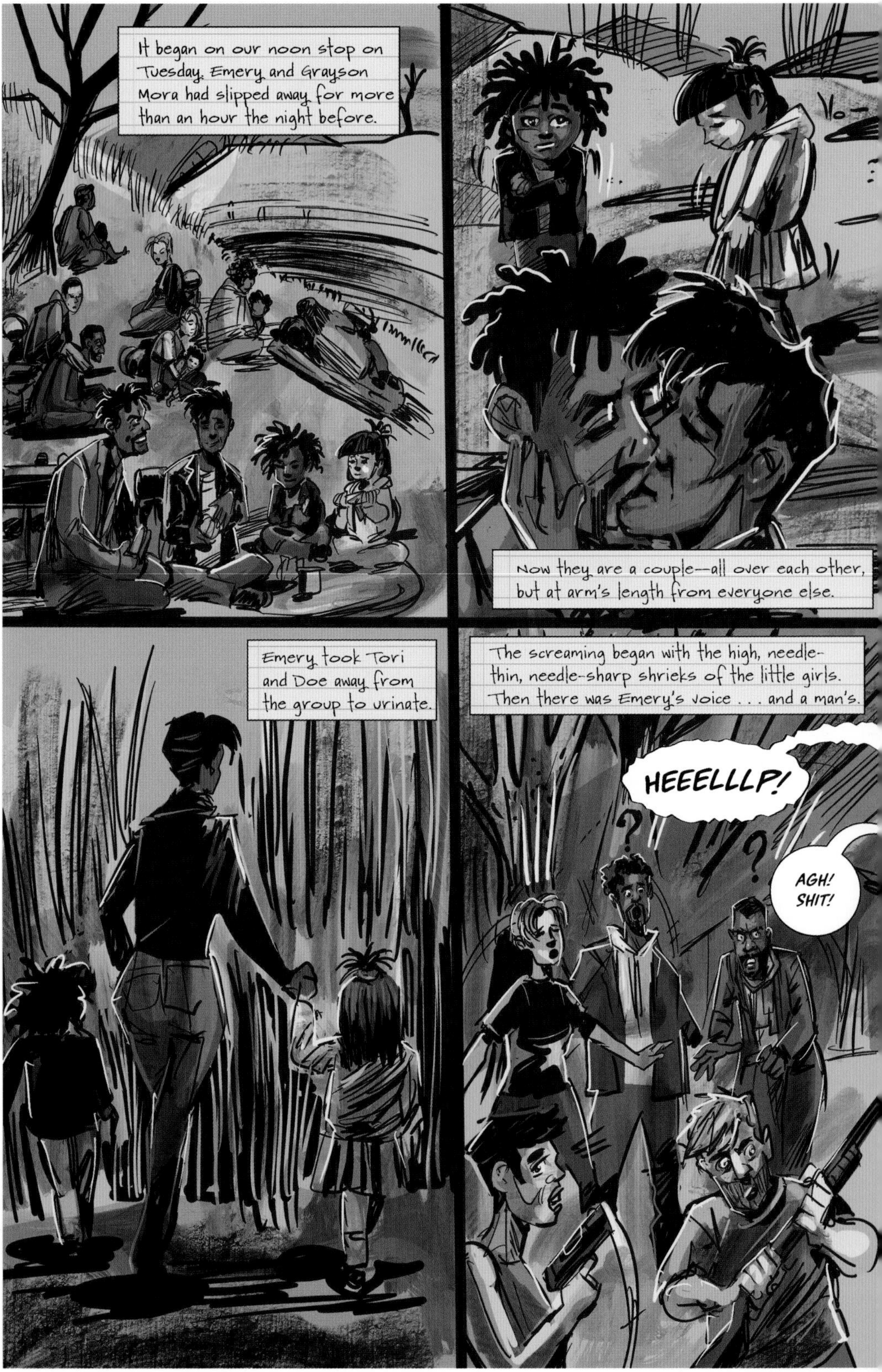
It began on our noon stop on Tuesday. Emery and Grayson Mora had slipped away for more than an hour the night before.
Now they are a couple—all over each other, but at arm's length from everyone else.
Emery took Tori and Doe away from the group to urinate.
The screaming began with the high, needle-thin, needle-sharp shrieks of the little girls. Then there was Emery's voice . . . and a man's.
HEEELLLP!
?
?
AGH! SHIT!

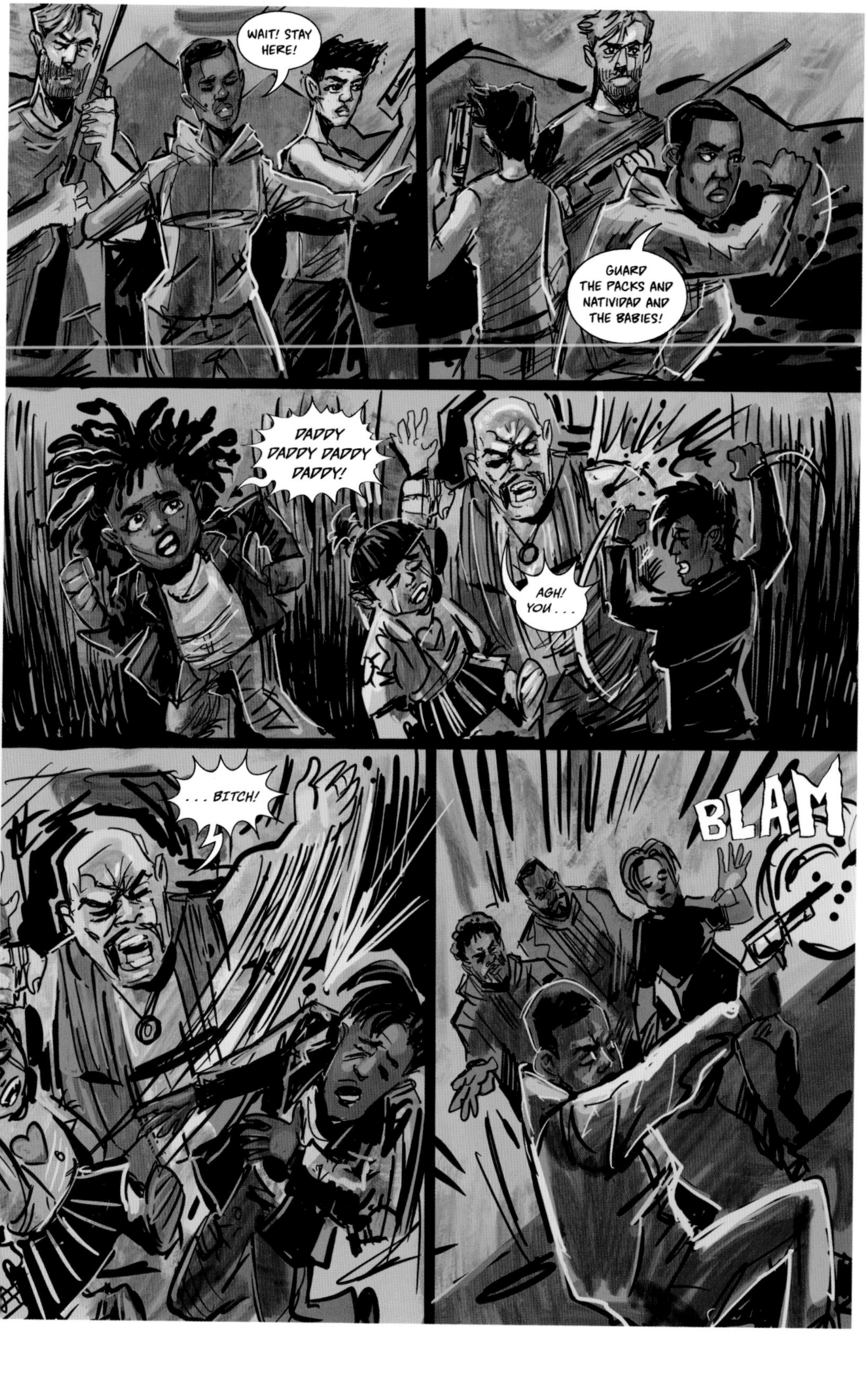
WAIT! STAY HERE!
GUARD THE PACKS AND NATIVIDAD AND THE BABIES!
DADDY DADDY DADDY DADDY!
AGH! YOU . . .
. . . BITCH!
BLAM

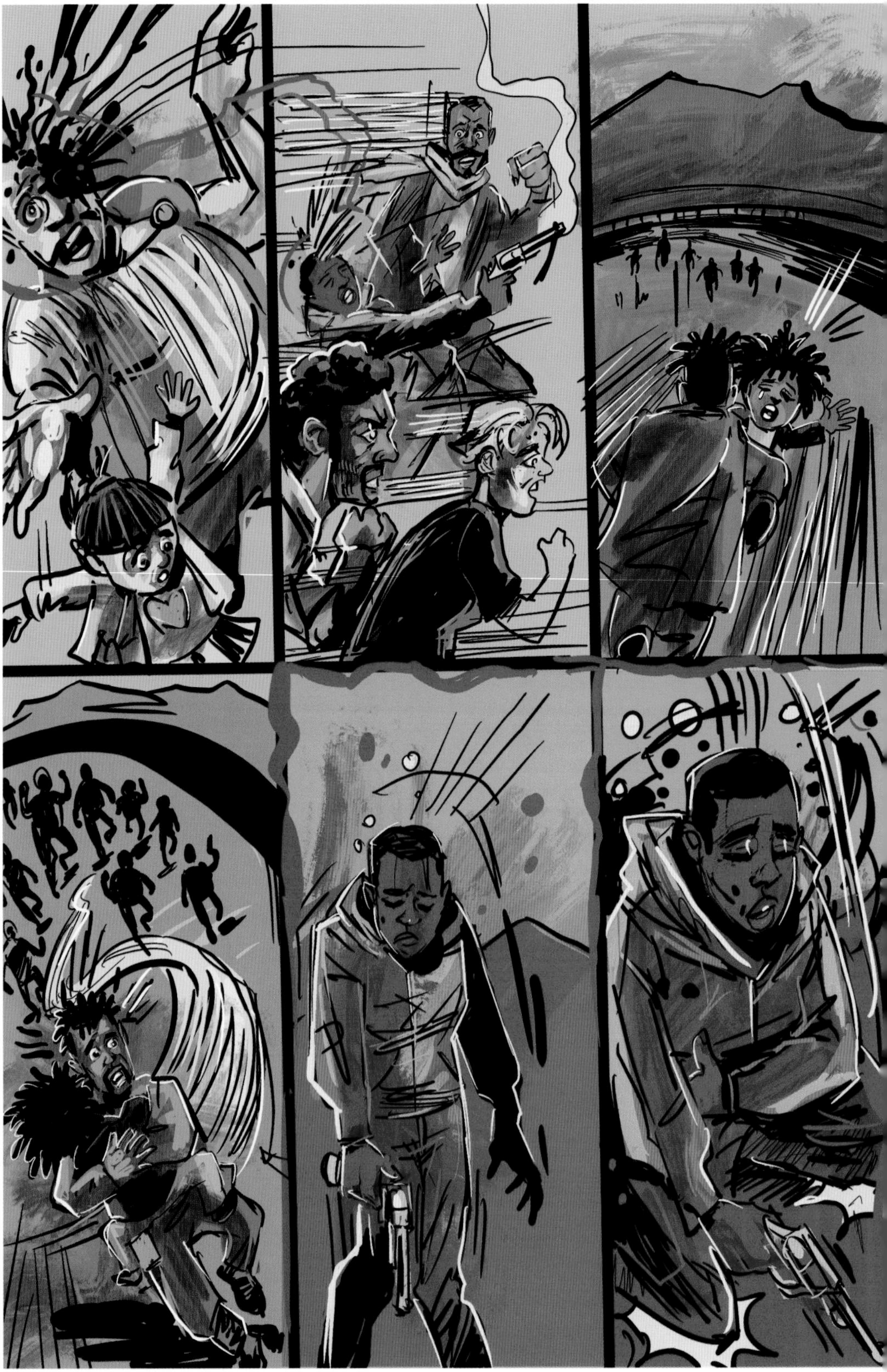

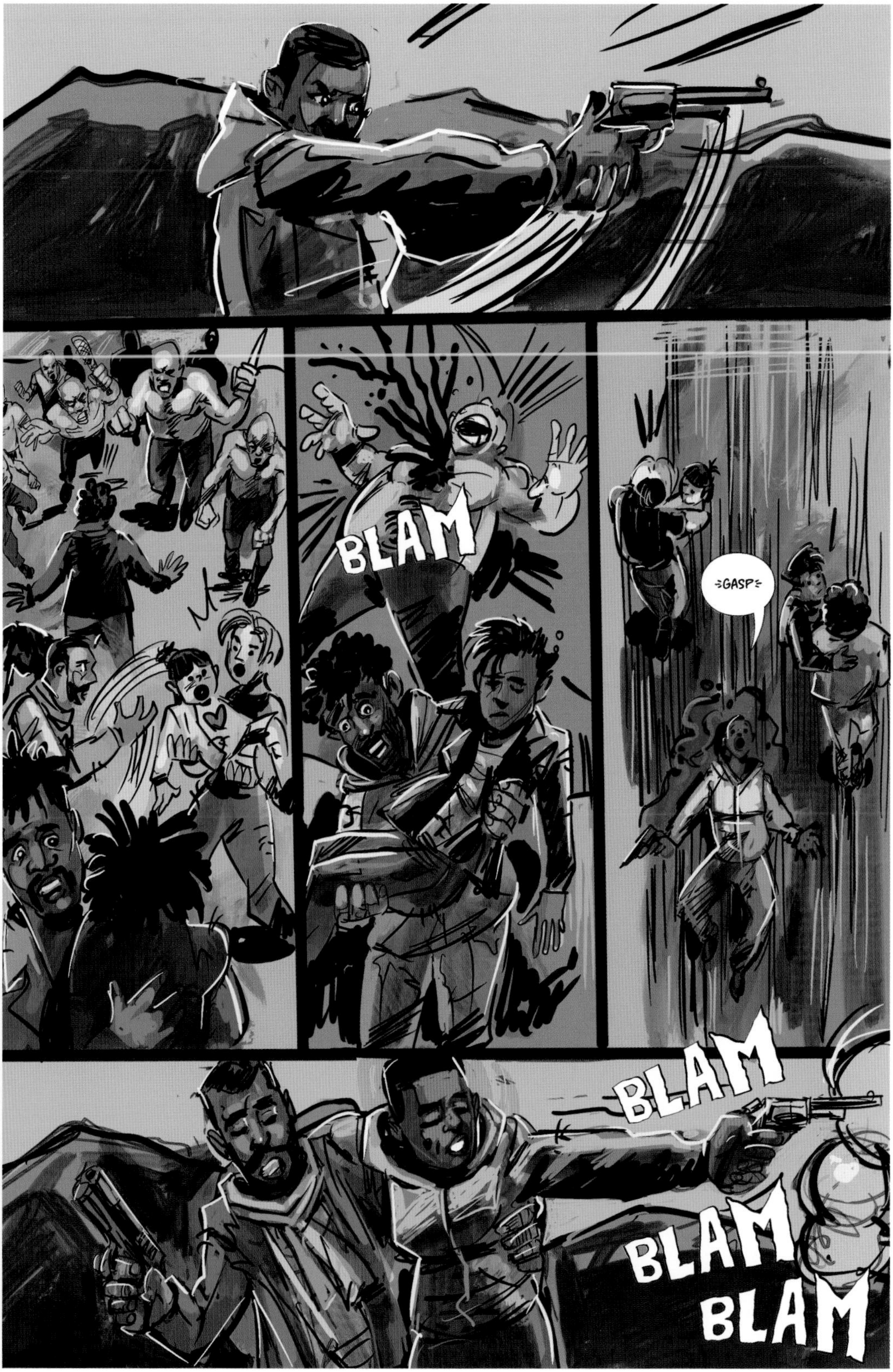
BLAM
GASP
BLAM
BLAM
BLAM

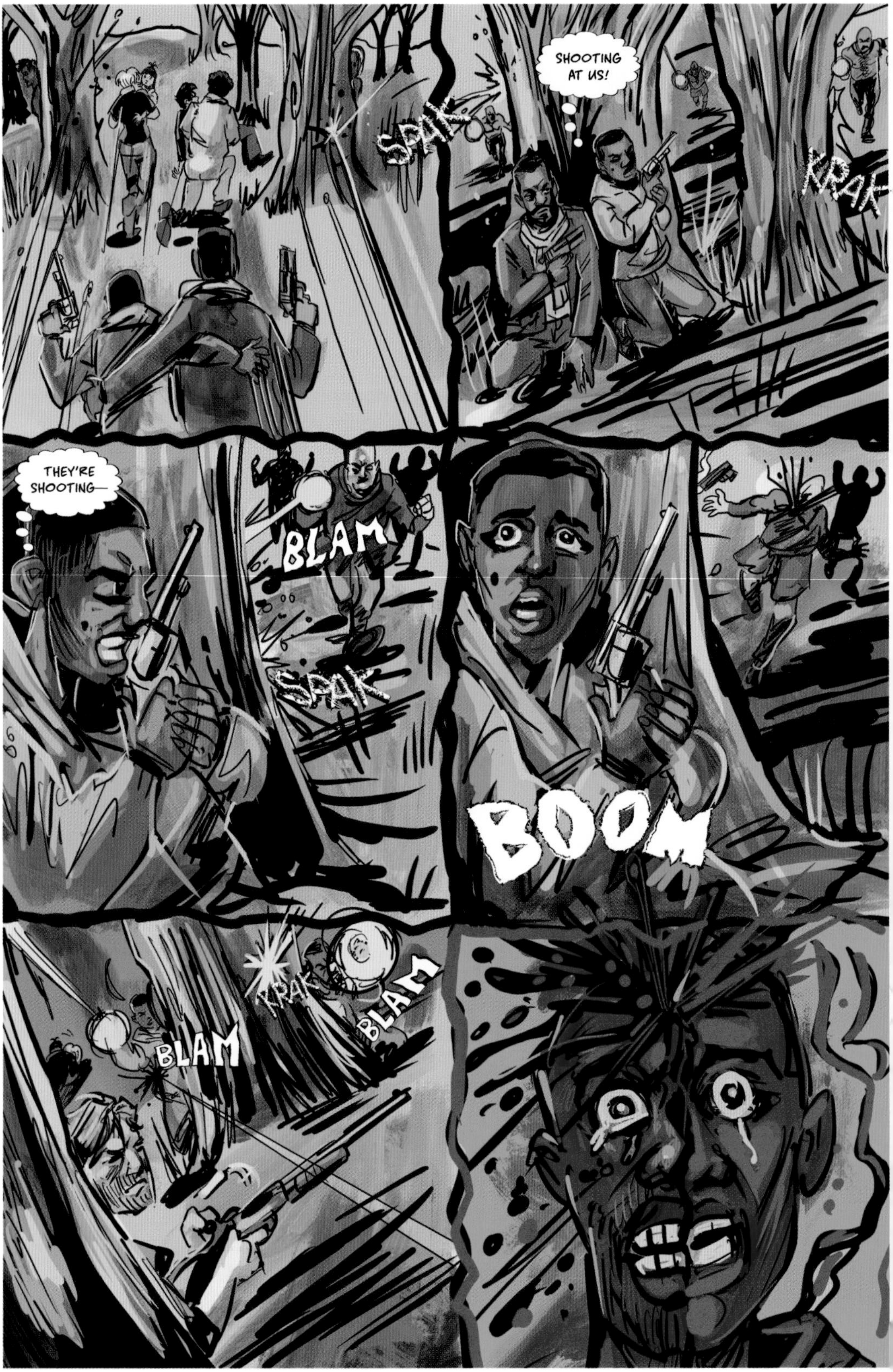
SPAK
SHOOTING AT US!
KRAK
THEY'RE SHOOTING—
BLAM
SPAK
BOOM
BLAM
KRAK
BLAM

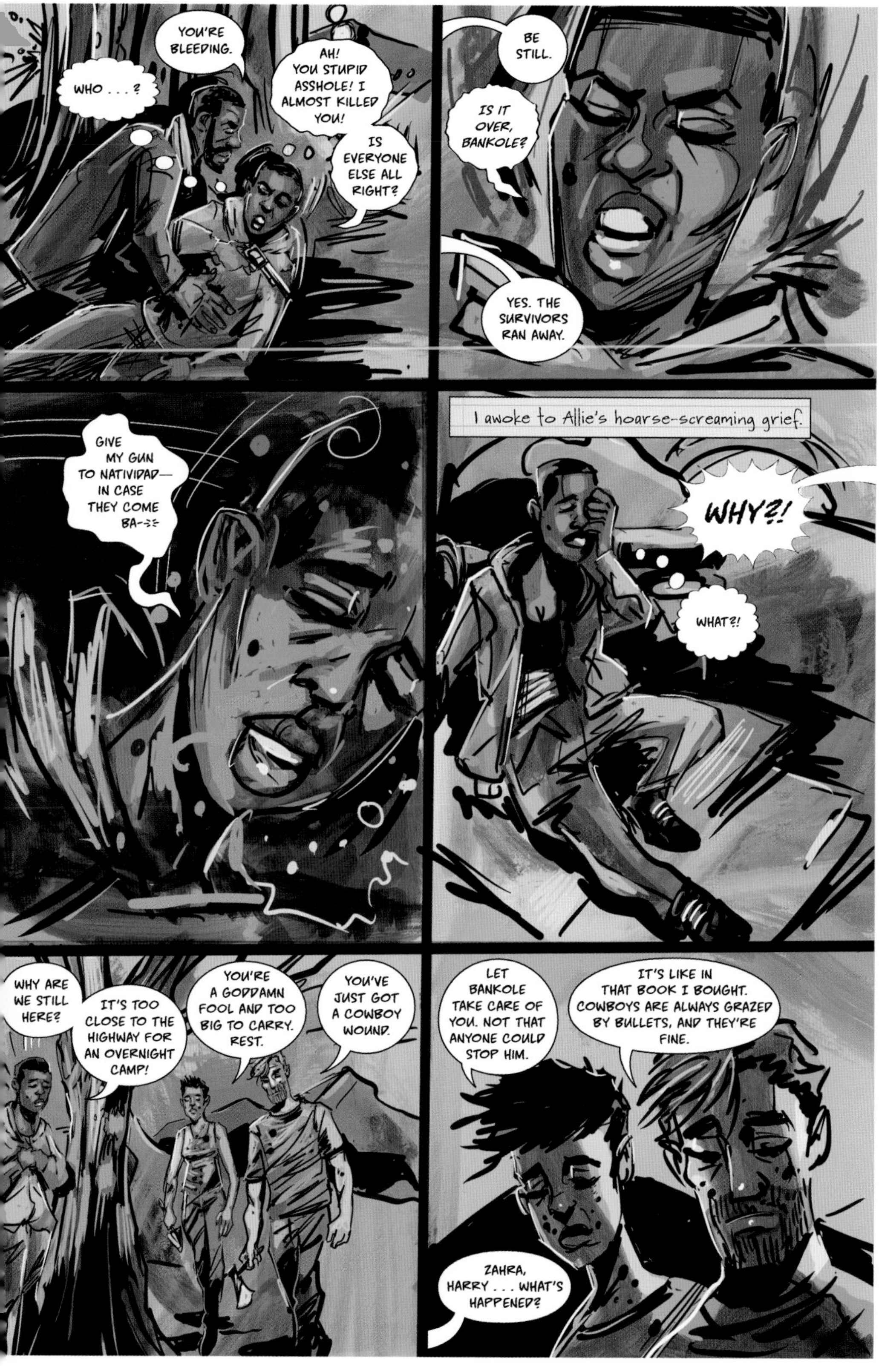
YOU'RE BLEEDING.
WHO . . . ?
AH! YOU STUPID ASSHOLE! I ALMOST KILLED YOU!
IS EVERYONE ELSE ALL RIGHT?
BE STILL.
IS IT OVER, BANKOLE?
YES. THE SURVIVORS RAN AWAY.
GIVE MY GUN TO NATIVIDAD— IN CASE THEY COME BA-
I awoke to Allie's hoarse-screaming grief.
WHY?!
WHAT?!
WHY ARE WE STILL HERE?
IT'S TOO CLOSE TO THE HIGHWAY FOR AN OVERNIGHT CAMP!
YOU'RE A GODDAMN FOOL AND TOO BIG TO CARRY. REST.
YOU'VE JUST GOT A COWBOY WOUND.
LET BANKOLE TAKE CARE OF YOU. NOT THAT ANYONE COULD STOP HIM.
IT'S LIKE IN THAT BOOK I BOUGHT. COWBOYS ARE ALWAYS GRAZED BY BULLETS, AND THEY'RE FINE.
ZAHRA, HARRY . . . WHAT'S HAPPENED?

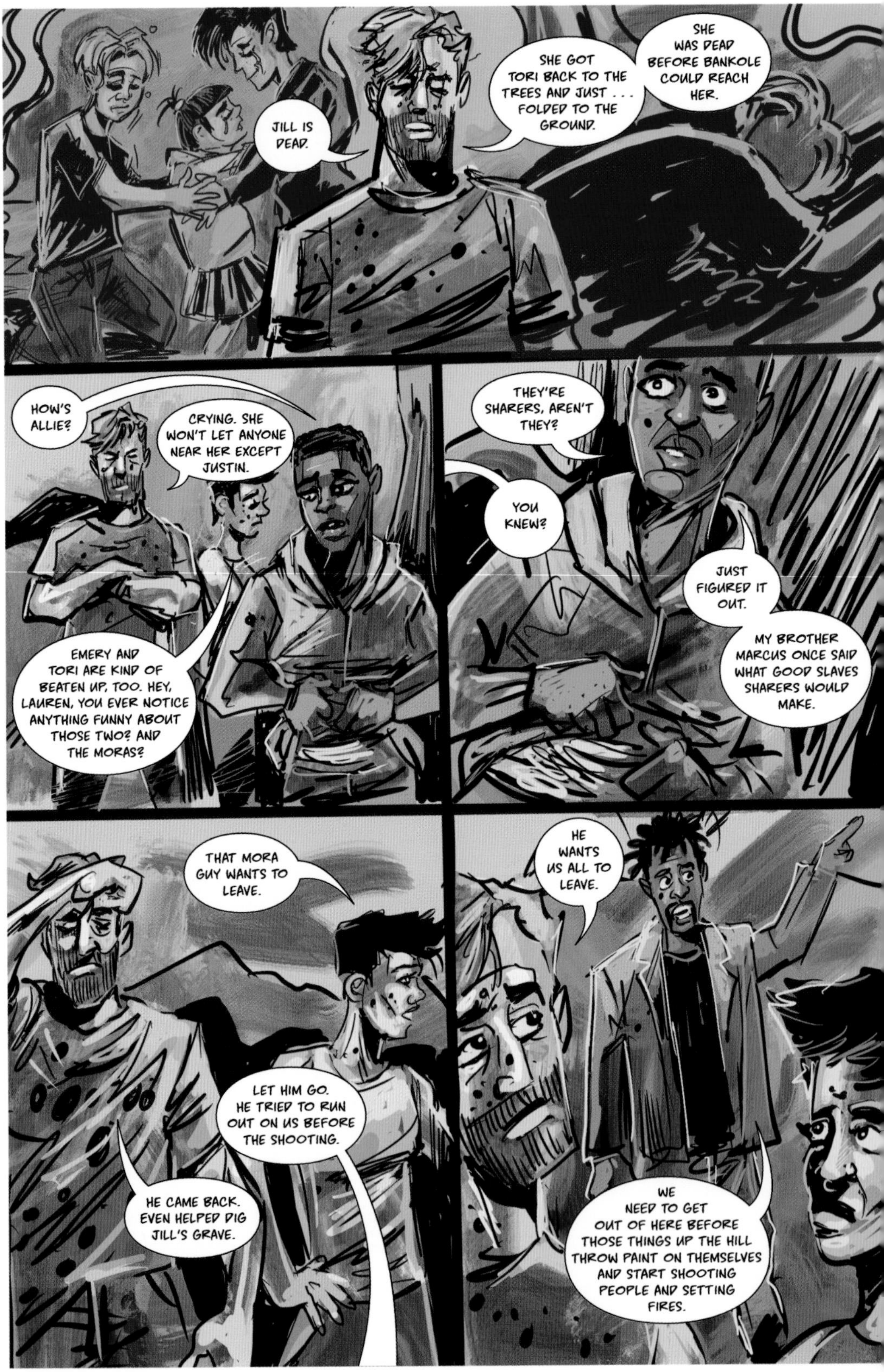
JILL IS DEAD.
SHE GOT TORI BACK TO THE TREES AND JUST . . . FOLDED TO THE GROUND.
SHE WAS DEAD BEFORE BANKOLE COULD REACH HER.
HOW'S ALLIE?
CRYING. SHE WON'T LET ANYONE NEAR HER EXCEPT JUSTIN.
EMERY AND TORI ARE KIND OF BEATEN UP, TOO. HEY, LAUREN, YOU EVER NOTICE ANYTHING FUNNY ABOUT THOSE TWO? AND THE MORAS?
THEY'RE SHARERS, AREN'T THEY?
YOU KNEW?
JUST FIGURED IT OUT.
MY BROTHER MARCUS ONCE SAID WHAT GOOD SLAVES SHARERS WOULD MAKE.
THAT MORA GUY WANTS TO LEAVE.
LET HIM GO. HE TRIED TO RUN OUT ON US BEFORE THE SHOOTING.
HE CAME BACK. EVEN HELPED DIG JILL'S GRAVE.
HE WANTS US ALL TO LEAVE.
WE NEED TO GET OUT OF HERE BEFORE THOSE THINGS UP THE HILL THROW PAINT ON THEMSELVES AND START SHOOTING PEOPLE AND SETTING FIRES.

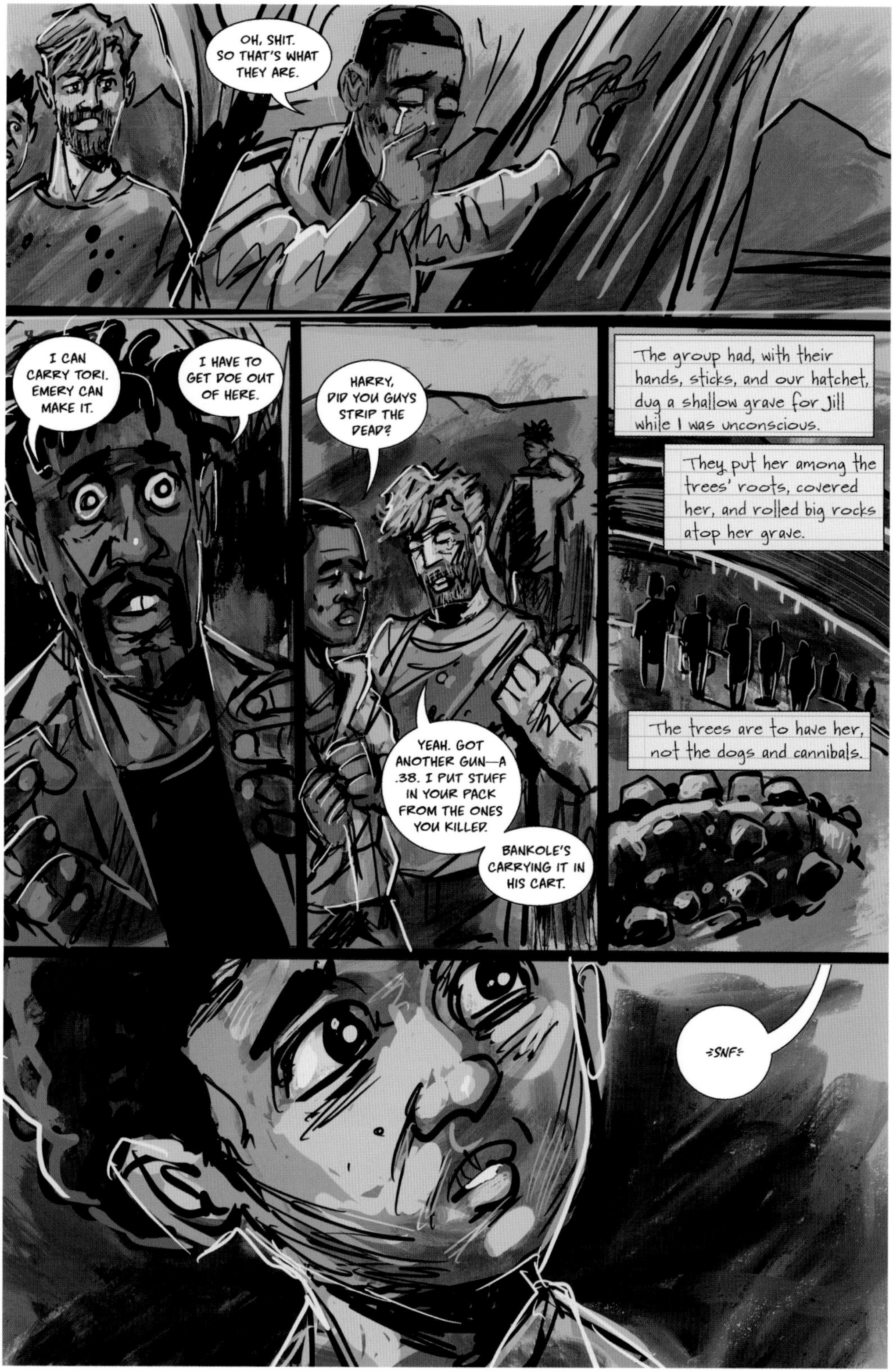
OH, SHIT. SO THAT'S WHAT THEY ARE.
I CAN CARRY TORI. EMERY CAN MAKE IT.
I HAVE TO GET DOE OUT OF HERE.
HARRY, DID YOU GUYS STRIP THE DEAD?
YEAH. GOT ANOTHER GUN—A .38. I PUT STUFF IN YOUR PACK FROM THE ONES YOU KILLED.
BANKOLE'S CARRYING IT IN HIS CART.
The group had, with their hands, sticks, and our hatchet, dug a shallow grave for Jill while I was unconscious.
They put her among the trees' roots, covered her, and rolled big rocks atop her grave.
The trees are to have her, not the dogs and cannibals.
SNF

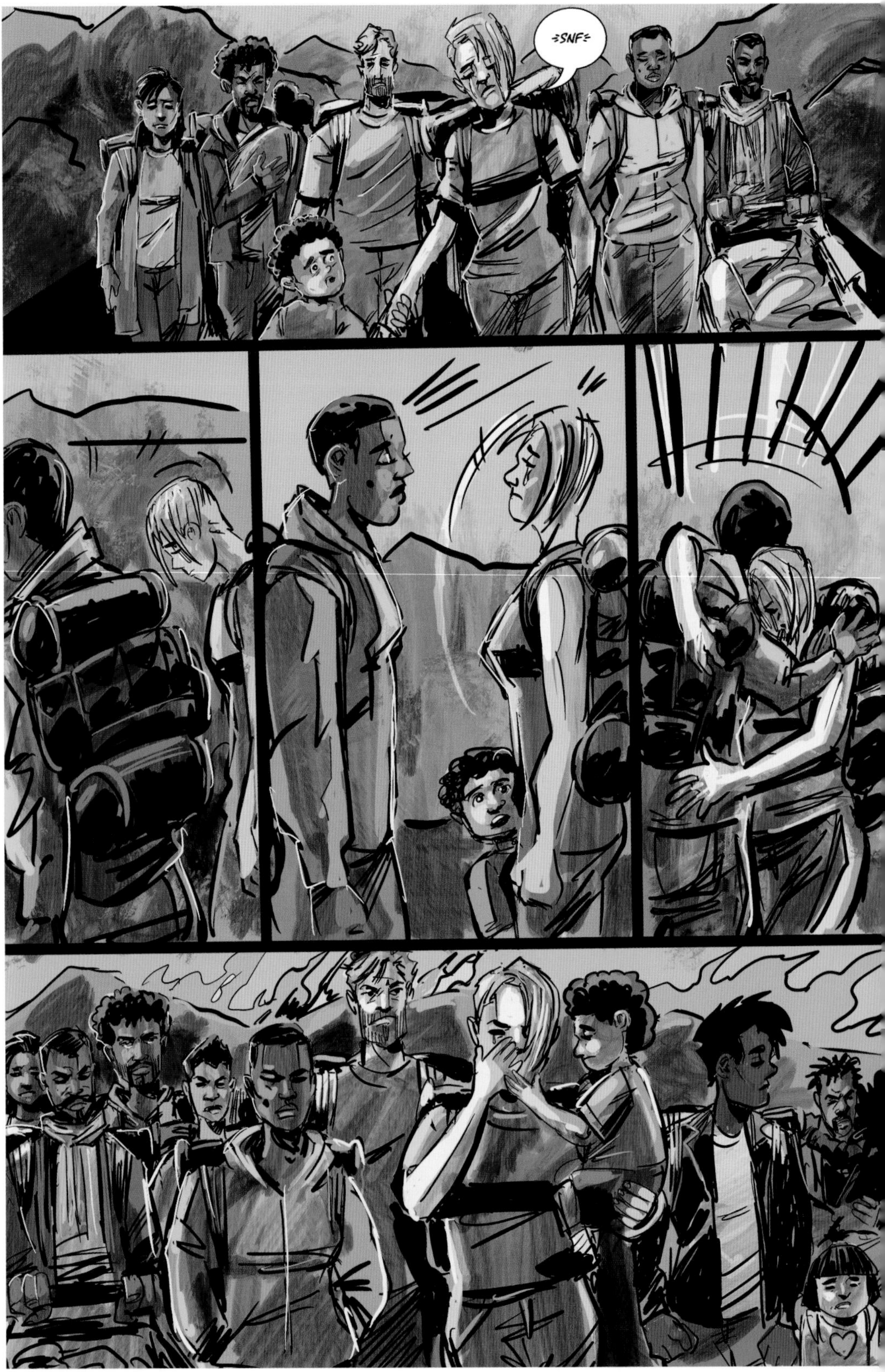
SNF

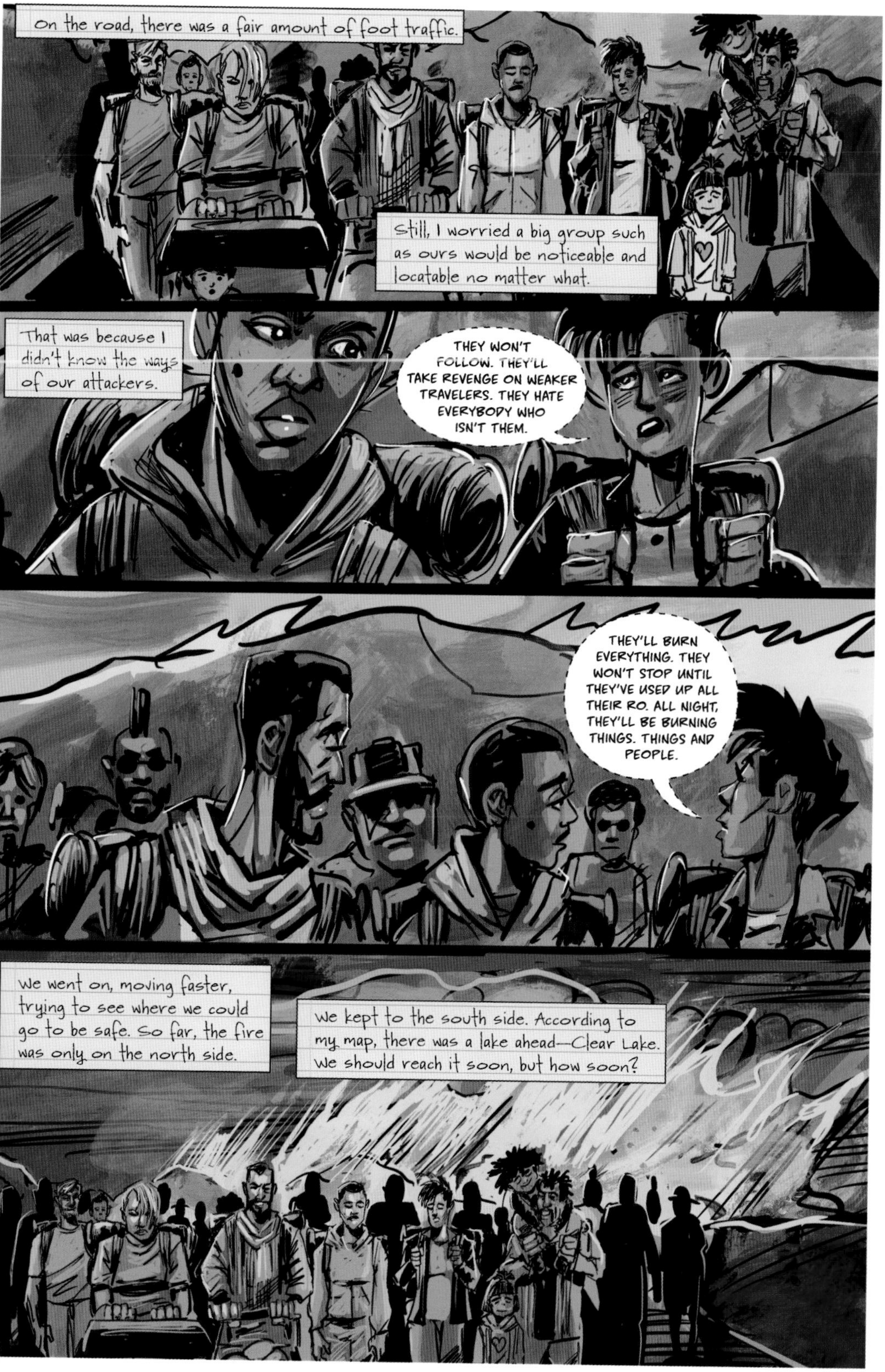
On the road, there was a fair amount of foot traffic.
Still, I worried a big group such as ours would be noticeable and locatable no matter what.
That was because I didn't know the ways of our attackers.
THEY WON'T FOLLOW. THEY'LL TAKE REVENGE ON WEAKER TRAVELERS. THEY HATE EVERYBODY WHO ISN'T THEM.
THEY'LL BURN EVERYTHING. THEY WON'T STOP UNTIL THEY'VE USED UP ALL THEIR RO. ALL NIGHT, THEY'LL BE BURNING THINGS. THINGS AND PEOPLE.
We went on, moving faster, trying to see where we could go to be safe. So far, the fire was only on the north side.
We kept to the south side. According to my map, there was a lake ahead—Clear Lake. We should reach it soon, but how soon?

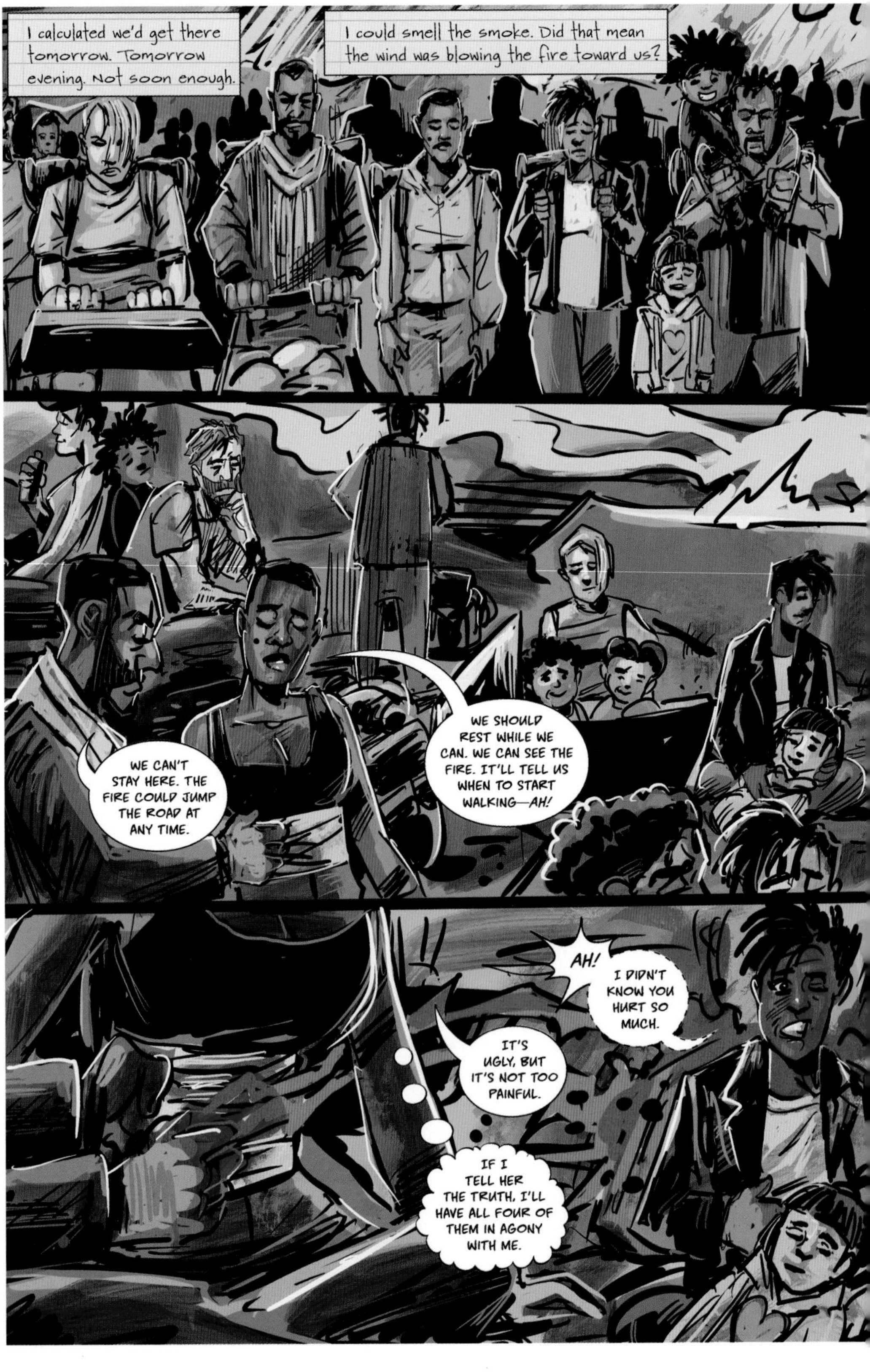
I calculated we'd get there tomorrow. Tomorrow evening. Not soon enough.
I could smell the smoke. Did that mean the wind was blowing the fire toward us?
WE CAN'T STAY HERE. THE FIRE COULD JUMP THE ROAD AT ANY TIME.
WE SHOULD REST WHILE WE CAN. WE CAN SEE THE FIRE. IT'LL TELL US WHEN TO START WALKING—AH!
AH!
I DIDN'T KNOW YOU HURT SO MUCH.
IT'S UGLY, BUT IT'S NOT TOO PAINFUL.
IF I TELL HER THE TRUTH, I'LL HAVE ALL FOUR OF THEM IN AGONY WITH ME.

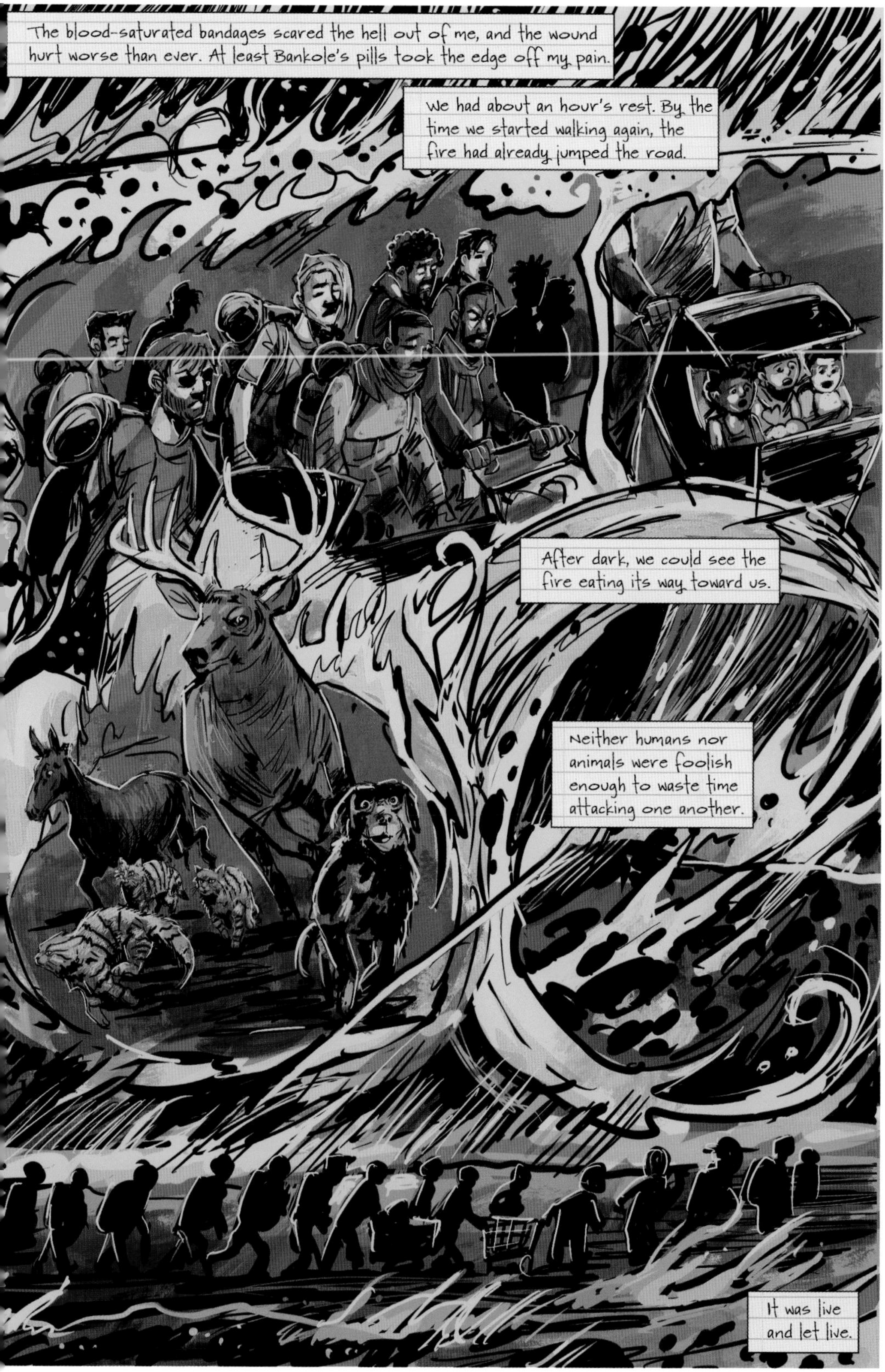
The blood-saturated bandages scared the hell out of me, and the wound hurt worse than ever. At least Bankole's pills took the edge off my pain.
We had about an hour's rest. By the time we started walking again, the fire had already jumped the road.
After dark, we could see the fire eating its way toward us.
Neither humans nor animals were foolish enough to waste time attacking one another.
It was live and let live.

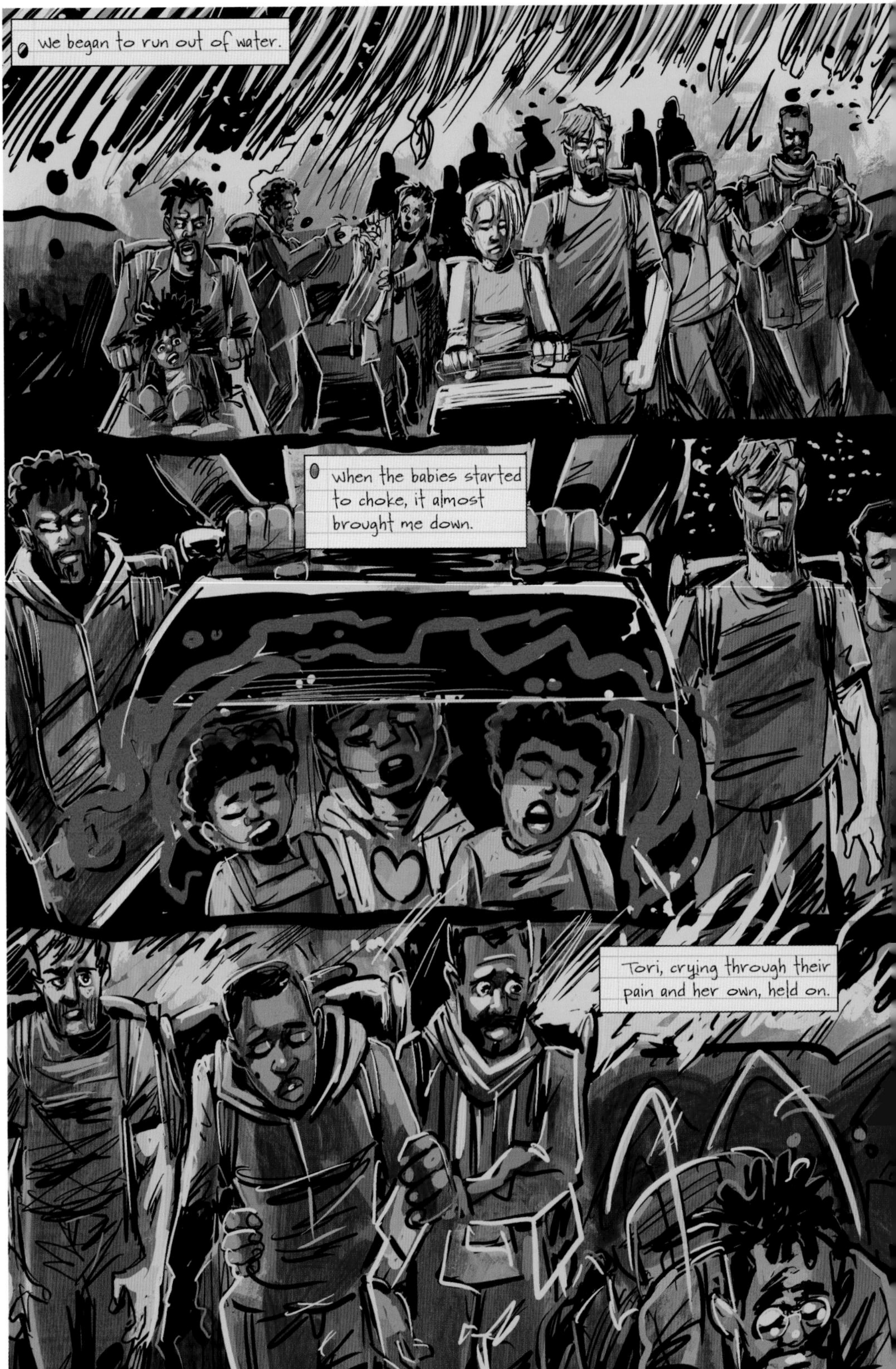
we began to run out of water.
when the babies started to choke, it almost brought me down.
Tori, crying through their pain and her own, held on.

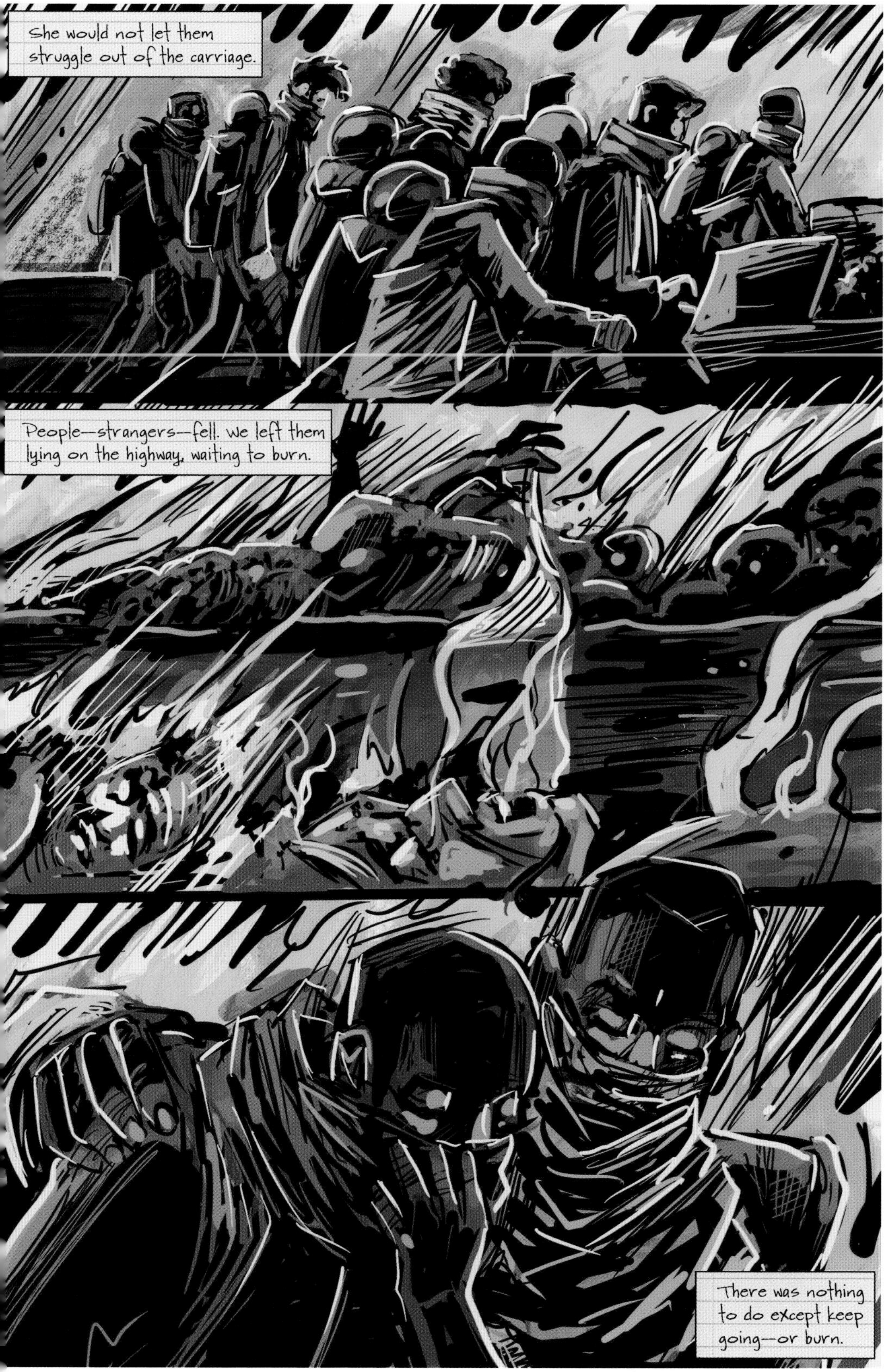
She would not let them struggle out of the carriage.
People—strangers—fell. we left them lying on the highway, waiting to burn.
There was nothing to do except keep going—or burn.

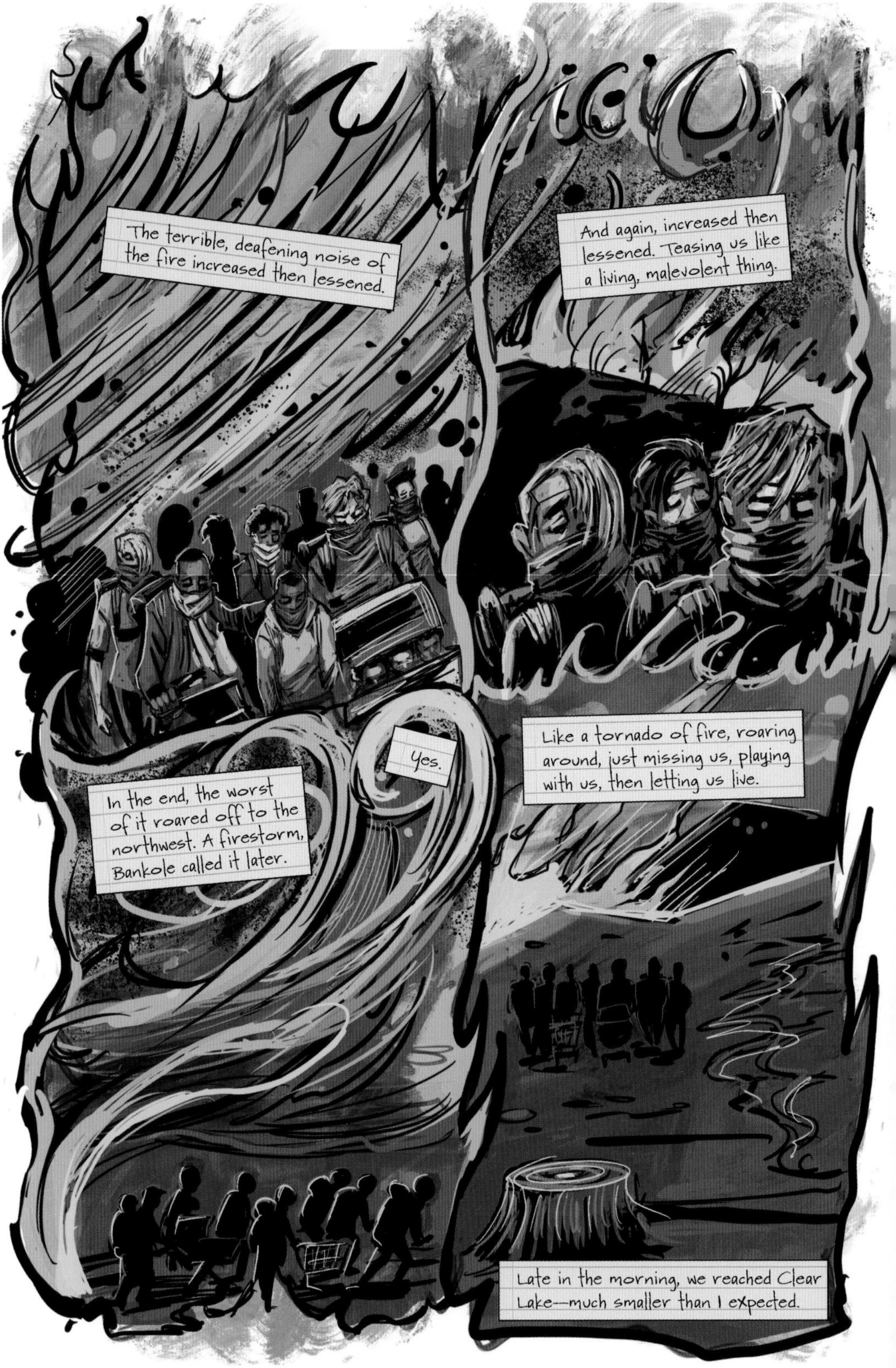
The terrible, deafening noise of the fire increased then lessened.
And again, increased then lessened. Teasing us like a living, malevolent thing.
Yes.
In the end, the worst of it roared off to the northwest. A firestorm, Bankole called it later.
Like a tornado of fire, roaring around, just missing us, playing with us, then letting us live.
Late in the morning, we reached Clear Lake—much smaller than I expected.

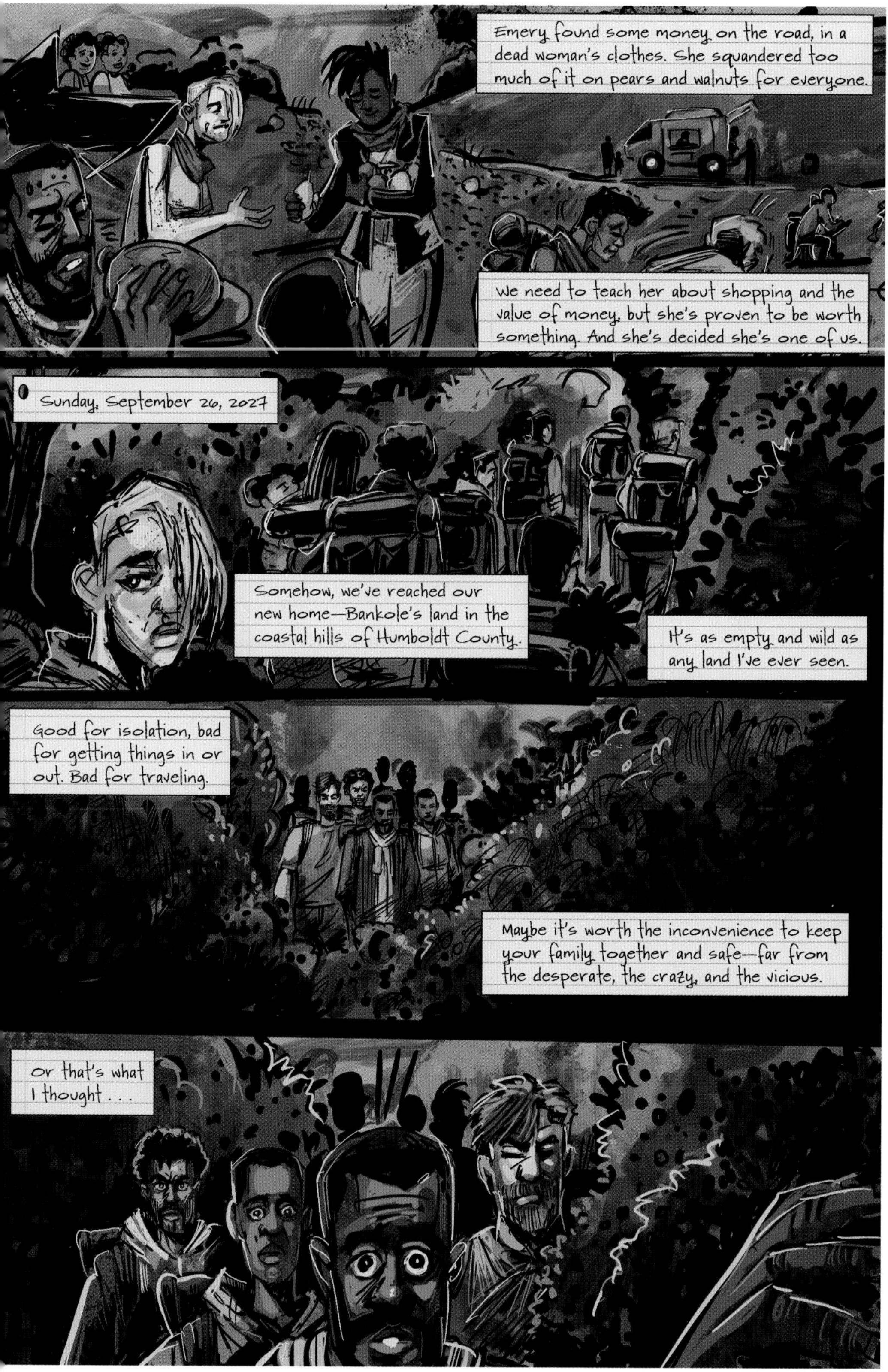
Emery found some money on the road, in a dead woman's clothes. She squandered too much of it on pears and walnuts for everyone.
We need to teach her about shopping and the value of money, but she's proven to be worth something. And she's decided she's one of us.
Sunday, September 26, 2027
Somehow, we've reached our new home—Bankole's land in the coastal hills of Humboldt County.
It's as empty and wild as any land I've ever seen.
Good for isolation, bad for getting things in or out. Bad for traveling.
Maybe it's worth the inconvenience to keep your family together and safe—far from the desperate, the crazy, and the vicious.
Or that's what I thought . . .

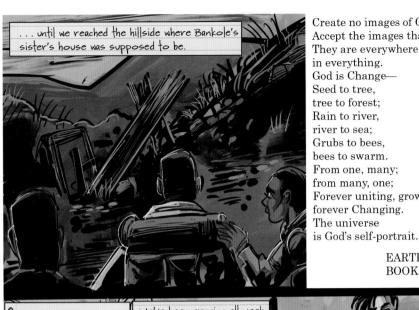

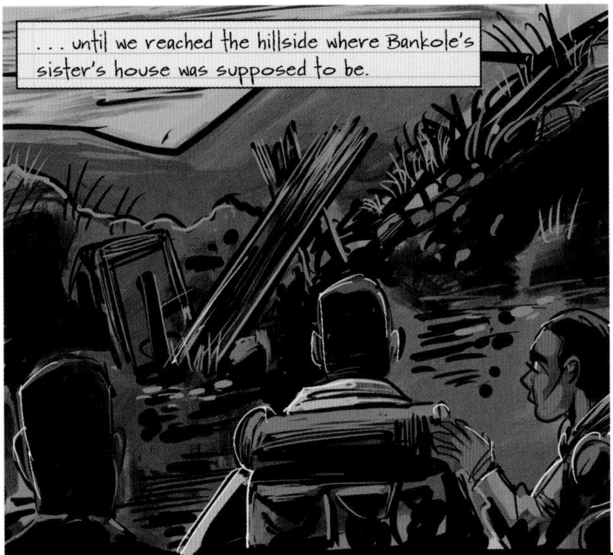
. . . until we reached the hillside where Bankole's sister's house was supposed to be.

Create no images of God.
Accept the images that God has provided.
They are everywhere,
in everything.
God is Change—
Seed to tree,
tree to forest;
Rain to river,
river to sea;
Grubs to bees,
bees to swarm.
From one, many;
from many, one;
Forever uniting, growing, dissolving—
forever Changing.
The universe
is God's self-portrait.

EARTHSEED: THE BOOKS OF THE LIVING

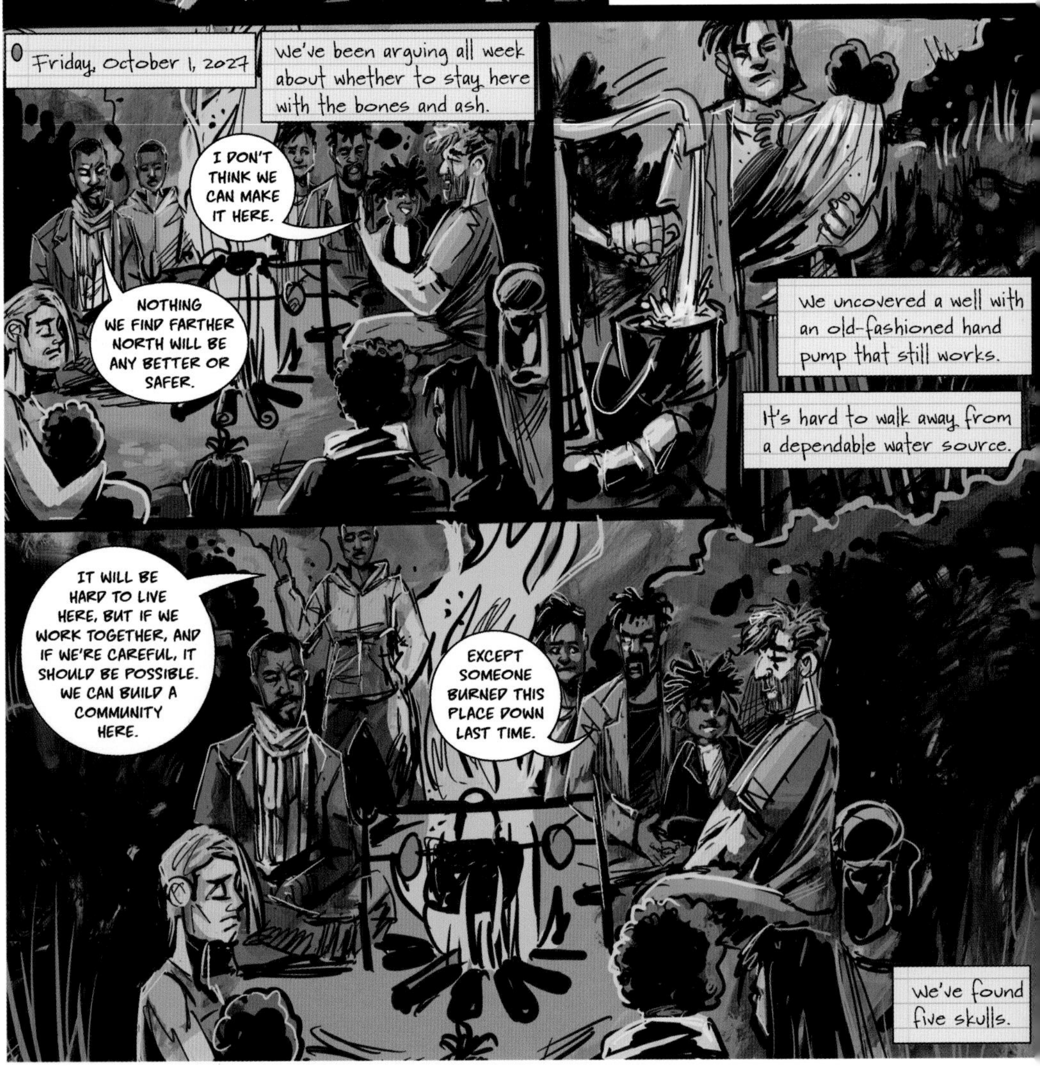
Friday, October 1, 2027
We've been arguing all week about whether to stay here with the bones and ash.
I DON'T THINK WE CAN MAKE IT HERE.
NOTHING WE FIND FARTHER NORTH WILL BE ANY BETTER OR SAFER.
We uncovered a well with an old-fashioned hand pump that still works.
It's hard to walk away from a dependable water source.
IT WILL BE HARD TO LIVE HERE, BUT IF WE WORK TOGETHER, AND IF WE'RE CAREFUL, IT SHOULD BE POSSIBLE. WE CAN BUILD A COMMUNITY HERE.
EXCEPT SOMEONE BURNED THIS PLACE DOWN LAST TIME.
We've found five skulls.

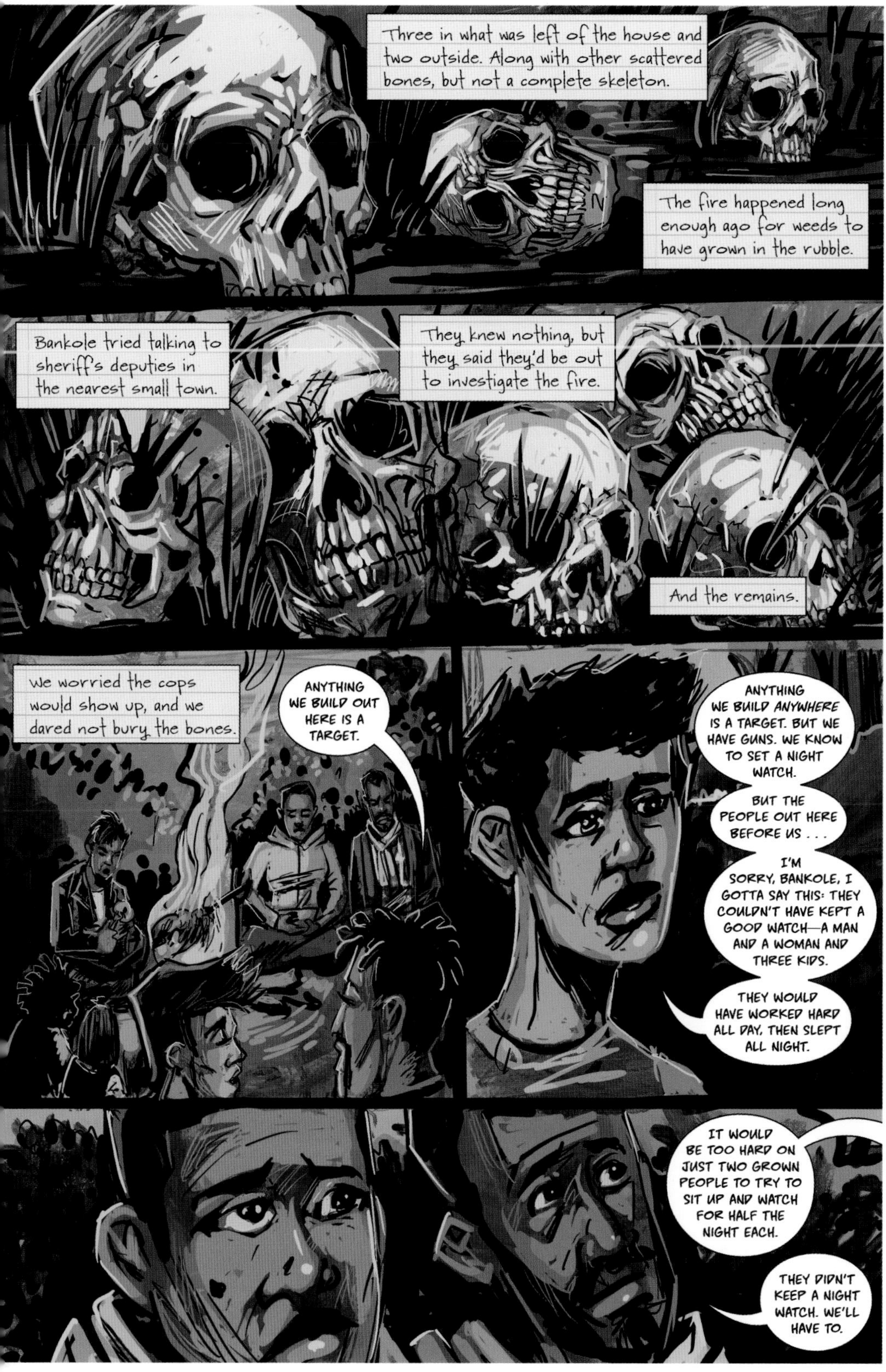
Three in what was left of the house and two outside. Along with other scattered bones, but not a complete skeleton.
The fire happened long enough ago for weeds to have grown in the rubble.
Bankole tried talking to sheriff's deputies in the nearest small town.
They knew nothing, but they said they'd be out to investigate the fire.
And the remains.
We worried the cops would show up, and we dared not bury the bones.
ANYTHING WE BUILD OUT HERE IS A TARGET.
ANYTHING WE BUILD ANYWHERE IS A TARGET. BUT WE HAVE GUNS. WE KNOW TO SET A NIGHT WATCH.
BUT THE PEOPLE OUT HERE BEFORE US . . .
I'M SORRY, BANKOLE, I GOTTA SAY THIS: THEY COULDN'T HAVE KEPT A GOOD WATCH—A MAN AND A WOMAN AND THREE KIDS.
THEY WOULD HAVE WORKED HARD ALL DAY, THEN SLEPT ALL NIGHT.
IT WOULD BE TOO HARD ON JUST TWO GROWN PEOPLE TO TRY TO SIT UP AND WATCH FOR HALF THE NIGHT EACH.
THEY DIDN'T KEEP A NIGHT WATCH. WE'LL HAVE TO.

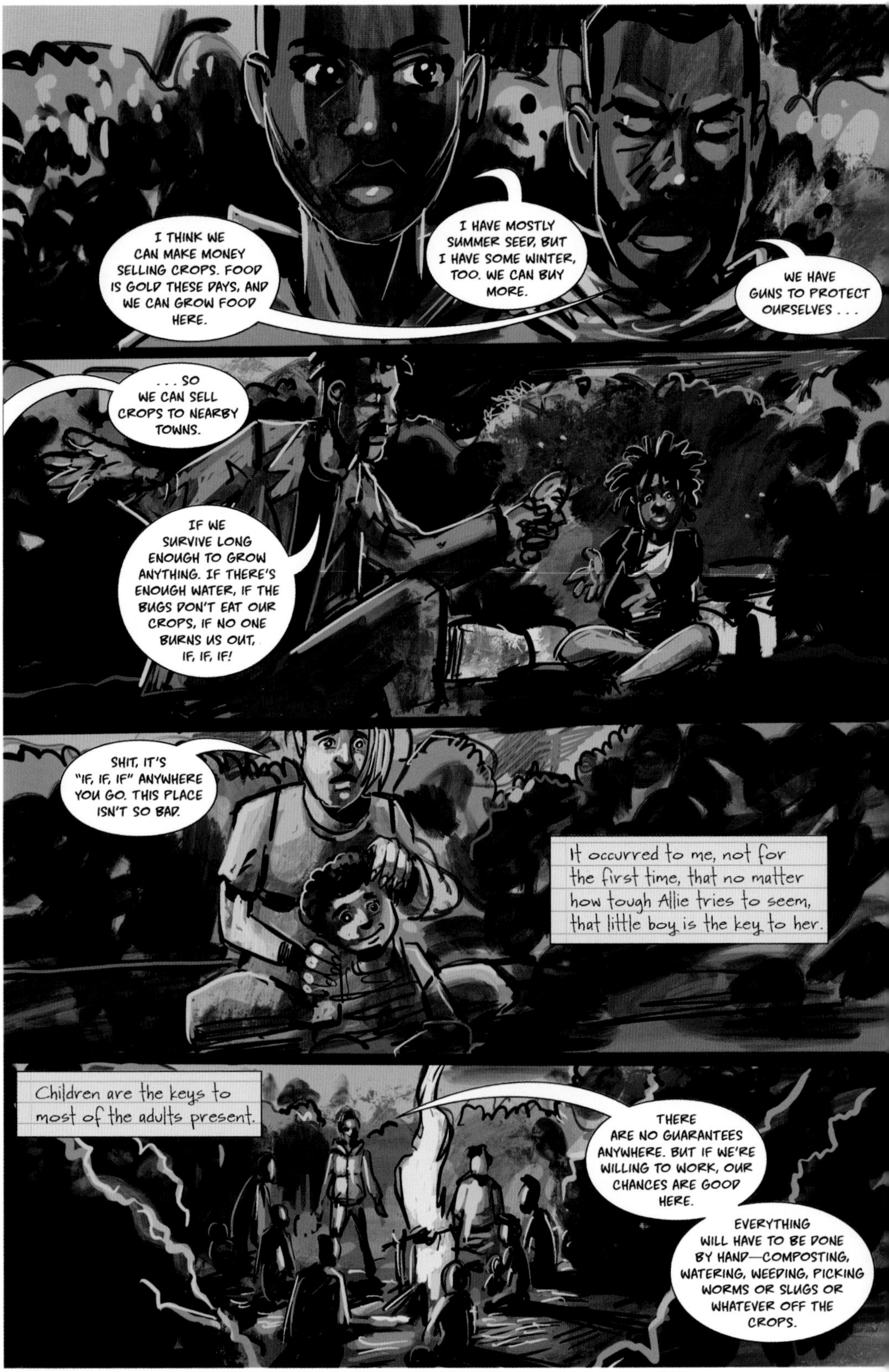
I THINK WE CAN MAKE MONEY SELLING CROPS. FOOD IS GOLD THESE DAYS, AND WE CAN GROW FOOD HERE.
I HAVE MOSTLY SUMMER SEED, BUT I HAVE SOME WINTER, TOO. WE CAN BUY MORE.
WE HAVE GUNS TO PROTECT OURSELVES . . .
. . . SO WE CAN SELL CROPS TO NEARBY TOWNS.
IF WE SURVIVE LONG ENOUGH TO GROW ANYTHING. IF THERE'S ENOUGH WATER, IF THE BUGS DON'T EAT OUR CROPS, IF NO ONE BURNS US OUT, IF, IF, IF!
SHIT, IT'S "IF, IF, IF" ANYWHERE YOU GO. THIS PLACE ISN'T SO BAD.
It occurred to me, not for the first time, that no matter how tough Allie tries to seem, that little boy is the key to her.
Children are the keys to most of the adults present.
THERE ARE NO GUARANTEES ANYWHERE. BUT IF WE'RE WILLING TO WORK, OUR CHANCES ARE GOOD HERE.
EVERYTHING WILL HAVE TO BE DONE BY HAND—COMPOSTING, WATERING, WEEDING, PICKING WORMS OR SLUGS OR WHATEVER OFF THE CROPS.

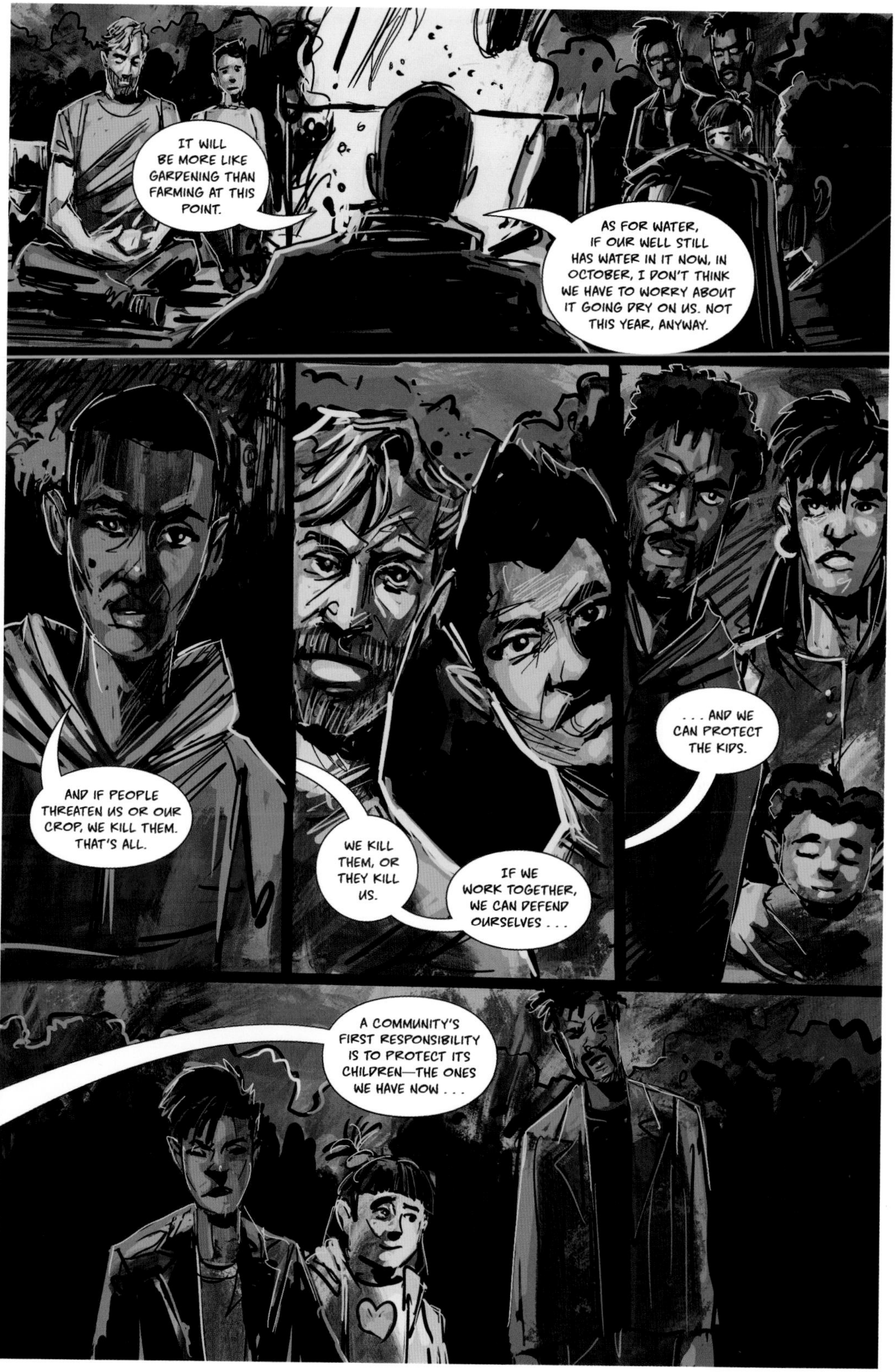

IT WILL BE MORE LIKE GARDENING THAN FARMING AT THIS POINT.
AS FOR WATER, IF OUR WELL STILL HAS WATER IN IT NOW, IN OCTOBER, I DON'T THINK WE HAVE TO WORRY ABOUT IT GOING DRY ON US. NOT THIS YEAR, ANYWAY.
AND IF PEOPLE THREATEN US OR OUR CROP, WE KILL THEM. THAT'S ALL.
WE KILL THEM, OR THEY KILL US.
IF WE WORK TOGETHER, WE CAN DEFEND OURSELVES . . .
. . . AND WE CAN PROTECT THE KIDS.
A COMMUNITY'S FIRST RESPONSIBILITY IS TO PROTECT ITS CHILDREN—THE ONES WE HAVE NOW . . .

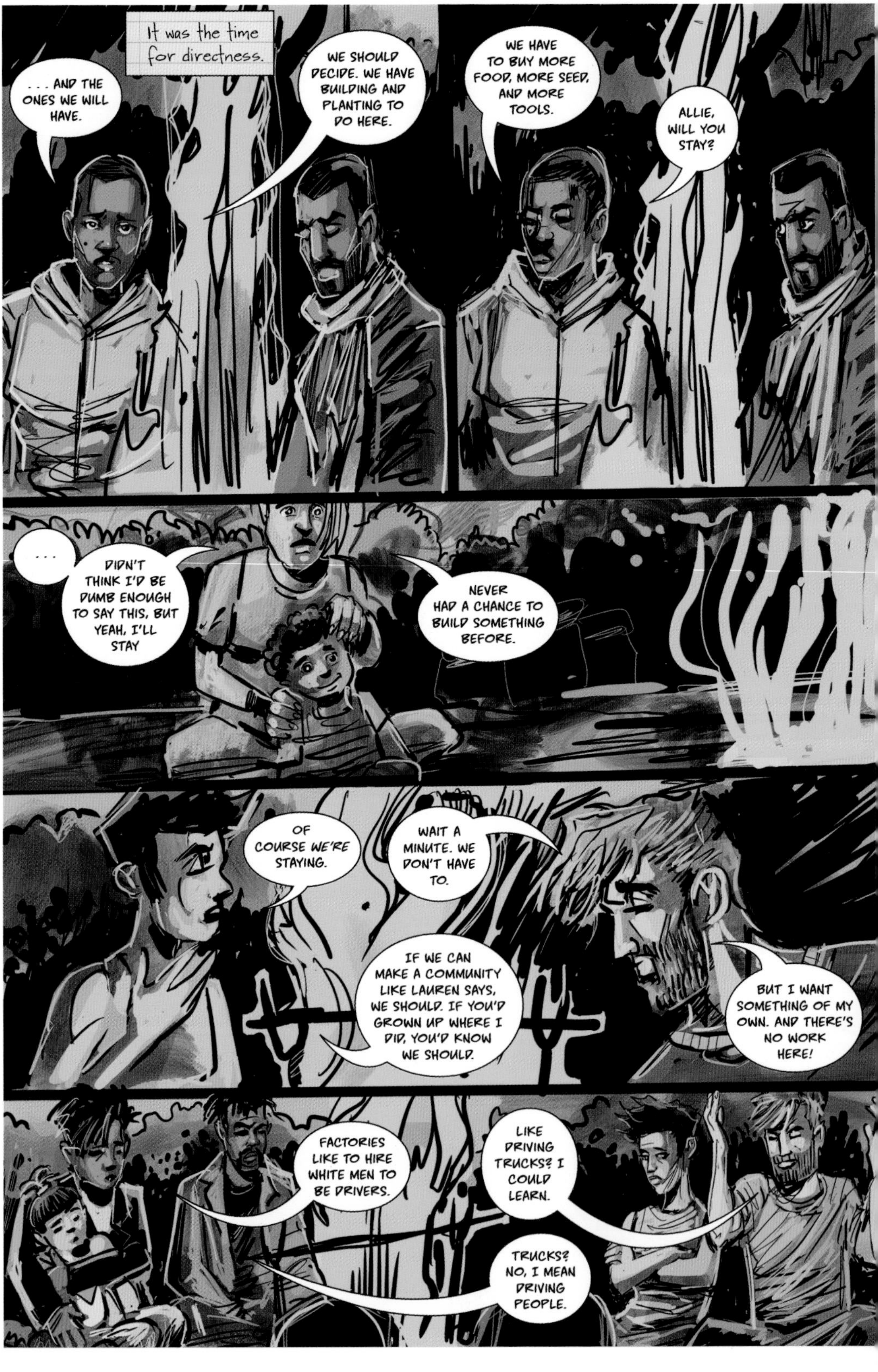

It was the time for directness.
. . . AND THE ONES WE WILL HAVE.
WE SHOULD DECIDE. WE HAVE BUILDING AND PLANTING TO DO HERE.
WE HAVE TO BUY MORE FOOD, MORE SEED, AND MORE TOOLS.
ALLIE, WILL YOU STAY?
. . .
DIDN'T THINK I'D BE DUMB ENOUGH TO SAY THIS, BUT YEAH, I'LL STAY
NEVER HAD A CHANCE TO BUILD SOMETHING BEFORE.
OF COURSE WE'RE STAYING.
WAIT A MINUTE. WE DON'T HAVE TO.
IF WE CAN MAKE A COMMUNITY LIKE LAUREN SAYS, WE SHOULD. IF YOU'D GROWN UP WHERE I DID, YOU'D KNOW WE SHOULD.
BUT I WANT SOMETHING OF MY OWN. AND THERE'S NO WORK HERE!
FACTORIES LIKE TO HIRE WHITE MEN TO BE DRIVERS.
LIKE DRIVING TRUCKS? I COULD LEARN.
TRUCKS? NO, I MEAN DRIVING PEOPLE.

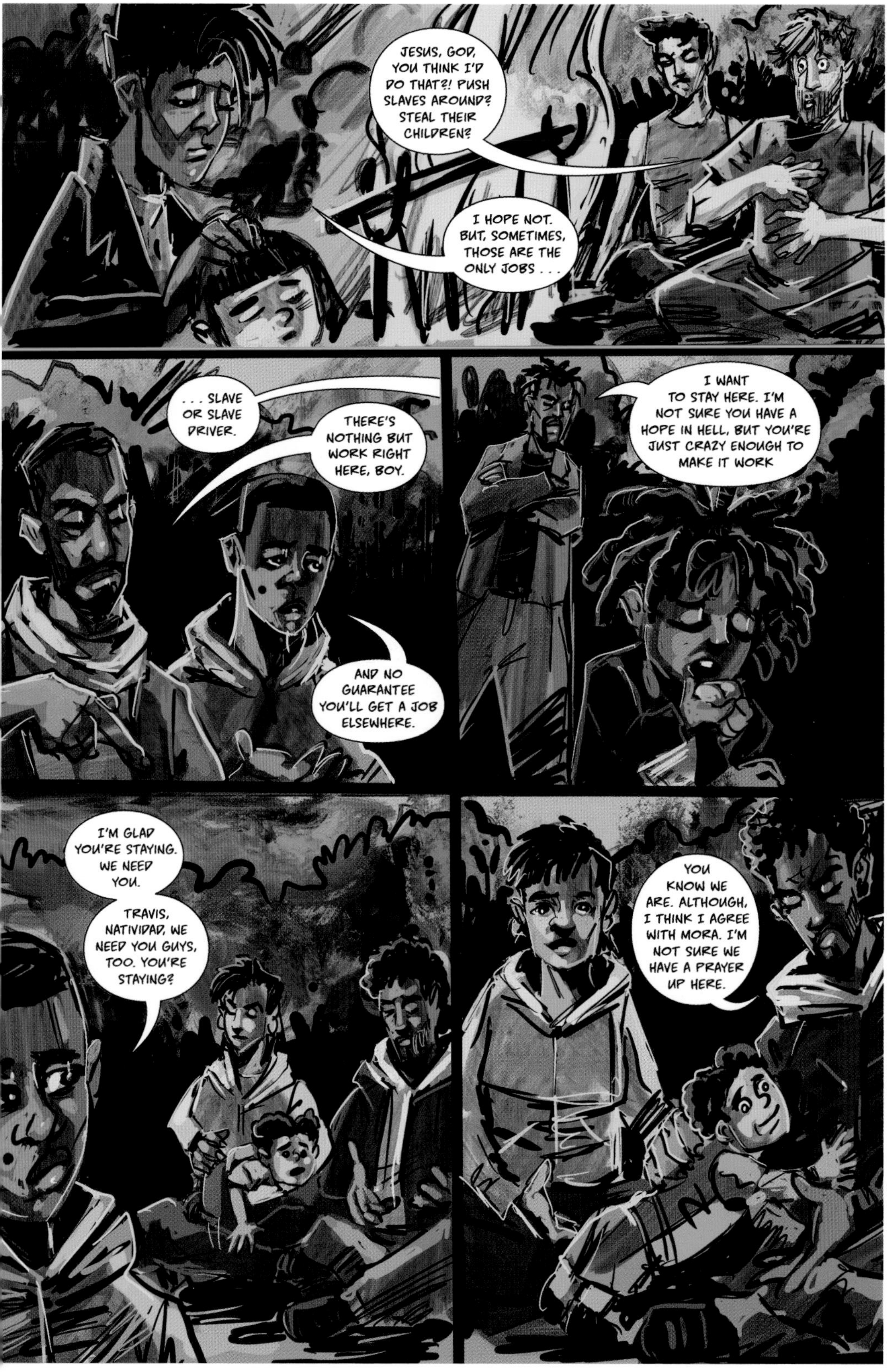
JESUS, GOD, YOU THINK I'D DO THAT?! PUSH SLAVES AROUND? STEAL THEIR CHILDREN?
I HOPE NOT. BUT, SOMETIMES, THOSE ARE THE ONLY JOBS . . .
. . . SLAVE OR SLAVE DRIVER.
THERE'S NOTHING BUT WORK RIGHT HERE, BOY.
AND NO GUARANTEE YOU'LL GET A JOB ELSEWHERE.
I WANT TO STAY HERE. I'M NOT SURE YOU HAVE A HOPE IN HELL, BUT YOU'RE JUST CRAZY ENOUGH TO MAKE IT WORK
I'M GLAD YOU'RE STAYING. WE NEED YOU.
TRAVIS, NATIVIDAD, WE NEED YOU GUYS, TOO. YOU'RE STAYING?
YOU KNOW WE ARE. ALTHOUGH, I THINK I AGREE WITH MORA. I'M NOT SURE WE HAVE A PRAYER UP HERE.

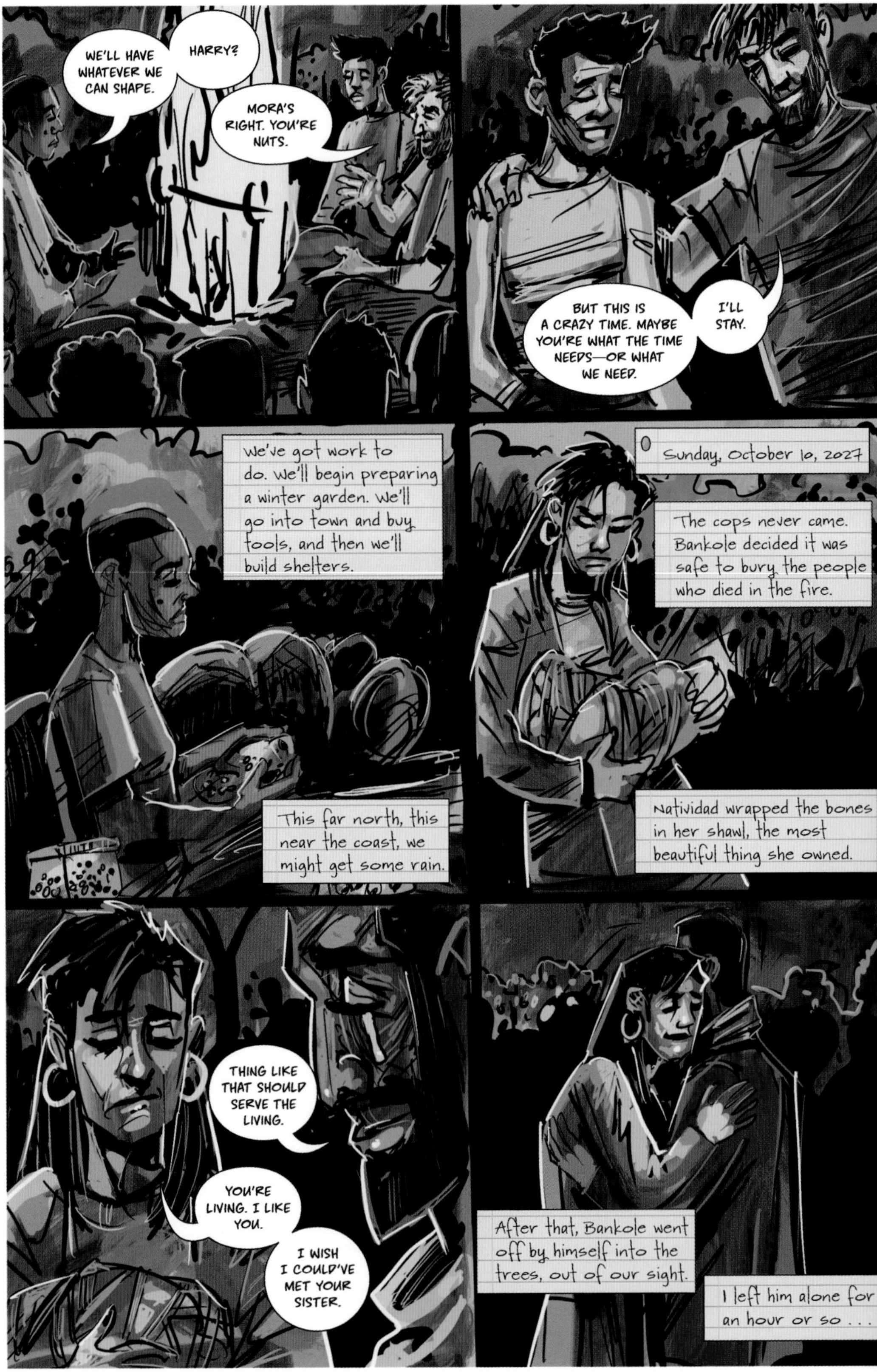
WE'LL HAVE WHATEVER WE CAN SHAPE.
HARRY?
MORA'S RIGHT. YOU'RE NUTS.
BUT THIS IS A CRAZY TIME. MAYBE YOU'RE WHAT THE TIME NEEDS—OR WHAT WE NEED.
I'LL STAY.
We've got work to do. We'll begin preparing a winter garden. We'll go into town and buy tools, and then we'll build shelters.
This far north, this near the coast, we might get some rain.
Sunday, October 10, 2027
The cops never came. Bankole decided it was safe to bury the people who died in the fire.
Natividad wrapped the bones in her shawl, the most beautiful thing she owned.
THING LIKE THAT SHOULD SERVE THE LIVING.
YOU'RE LIVING. I LIKE YOU.
I WISH I COULD'VE MET YOUR SISTER.
After that, Bankole went off by himself into the trees, out of our sight.
I left him alone for an hour or so . . .

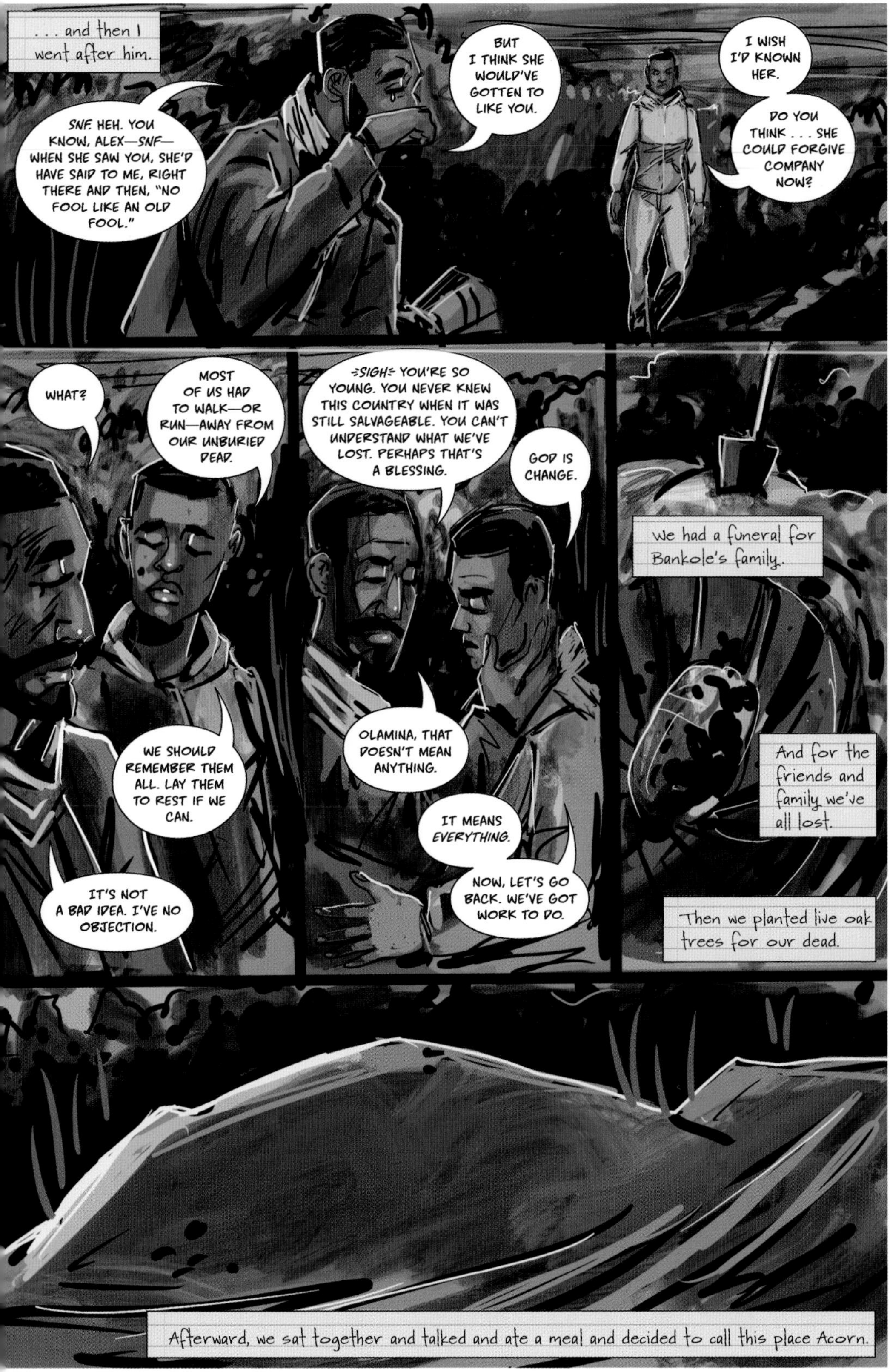

. . . and then I went after him.
SNF. HEH. YOU KNOW, ALEX—SNF—WHEN SHE SAW YOU, SHE'D HAVE SAID TO ME, RIGHT THERE AND THEN, "NO FOOL LIKE AN OLD FOOL."
BUT I THINK SHE WOULD'VE GOTTEN TO LIKE YOU.
I WISH I'D KNOWN HER.
DO YOU THINK . . . SHE COULD FORGIVE COMPANY NOW?
WHAT?
MOST OF US HAD TO WALK—OR RUN—AWAY FROM OUR UNBURIED DEAD.
WE SHOULD REMEMBER THEM ALL. LAY THEM TO REST IF WE CAN.
IT'S NOT A BAD IDEA. I'VE NO OBJECTION.
=SIGH= YOU'RE SO YOUNG. YOU NEVER KNEW THIS COUNTRY WHEN IT WAS STILL SALVAGEABLE. YOU CAN'T UNDERSTAND WHAT WE'VE LOST. PERHAPS THAT'S A BLESSING.
GOD IS CHANGE.
OLAMINA, THAT DOESN'T MEAN ANYTHING.
IT MEANS EVERYTHING.
NOW, LET'S GO BACK. WE'VE GOT WORK TO DO.
We had a funeral for Bankole's family.
And for the friends and family we've all lost.
Then we planted live oak trees for our dead.
Afterward, we sat together and talked and ate a meal and decided to call this place Acorn.

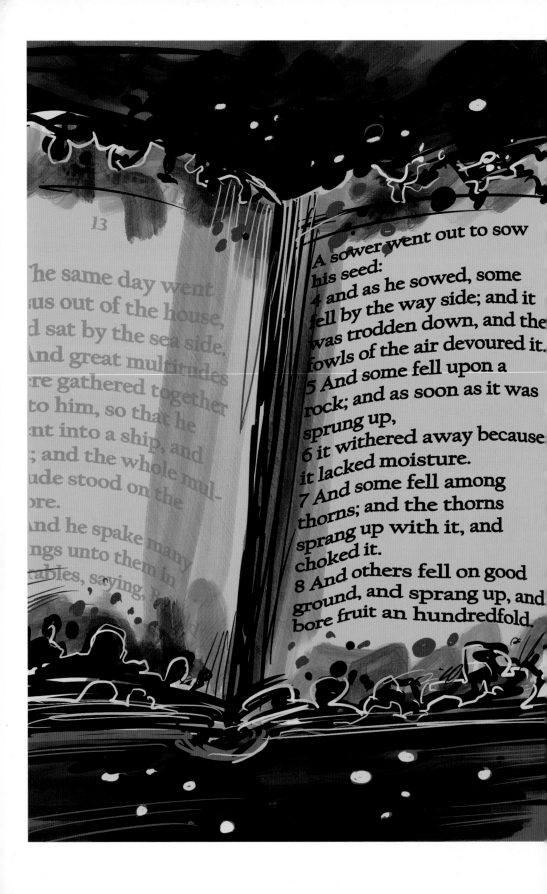

13

he same day went
sus out of the house,
d sat by the sea side.
And great multitudes
re gathered together
to him, so that he
nt into a ship, and
; and the whole mul-
ude stood on the
ore.
nd he spake many
ngs unto them in
rables, saying,

A sower went out to sow
his seed:
4 and as he sowed, some
fell by the way side; and it
was trodden down, and the
fowls of the air devoured it.
5 And some fell upon a
rock; and as soon as it was
sprung up,
6 it withered away because
it lacked moisture.
7 And some fell among
thorns; and the thorns
sprang up with it, and
choked it.
8 And others fell on good
ground, and sprang up, and
bore fruit an hundredfold.

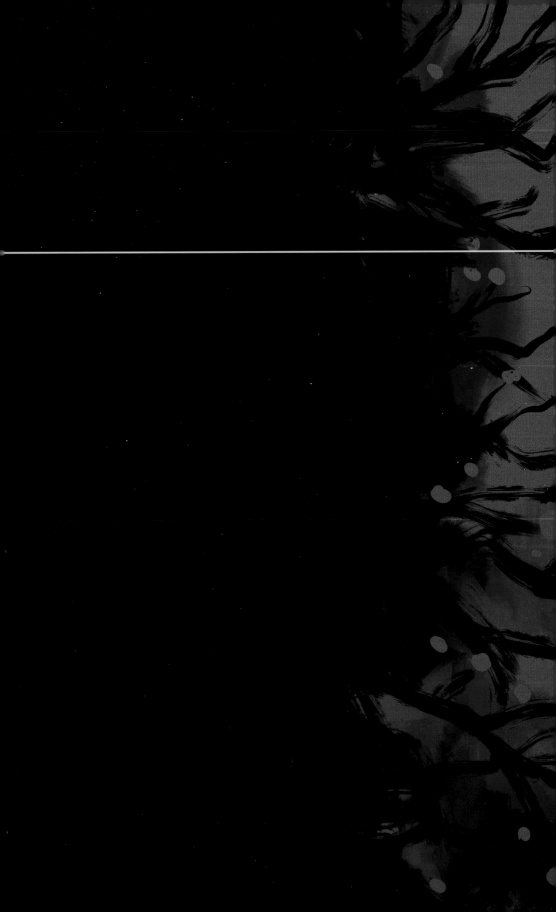

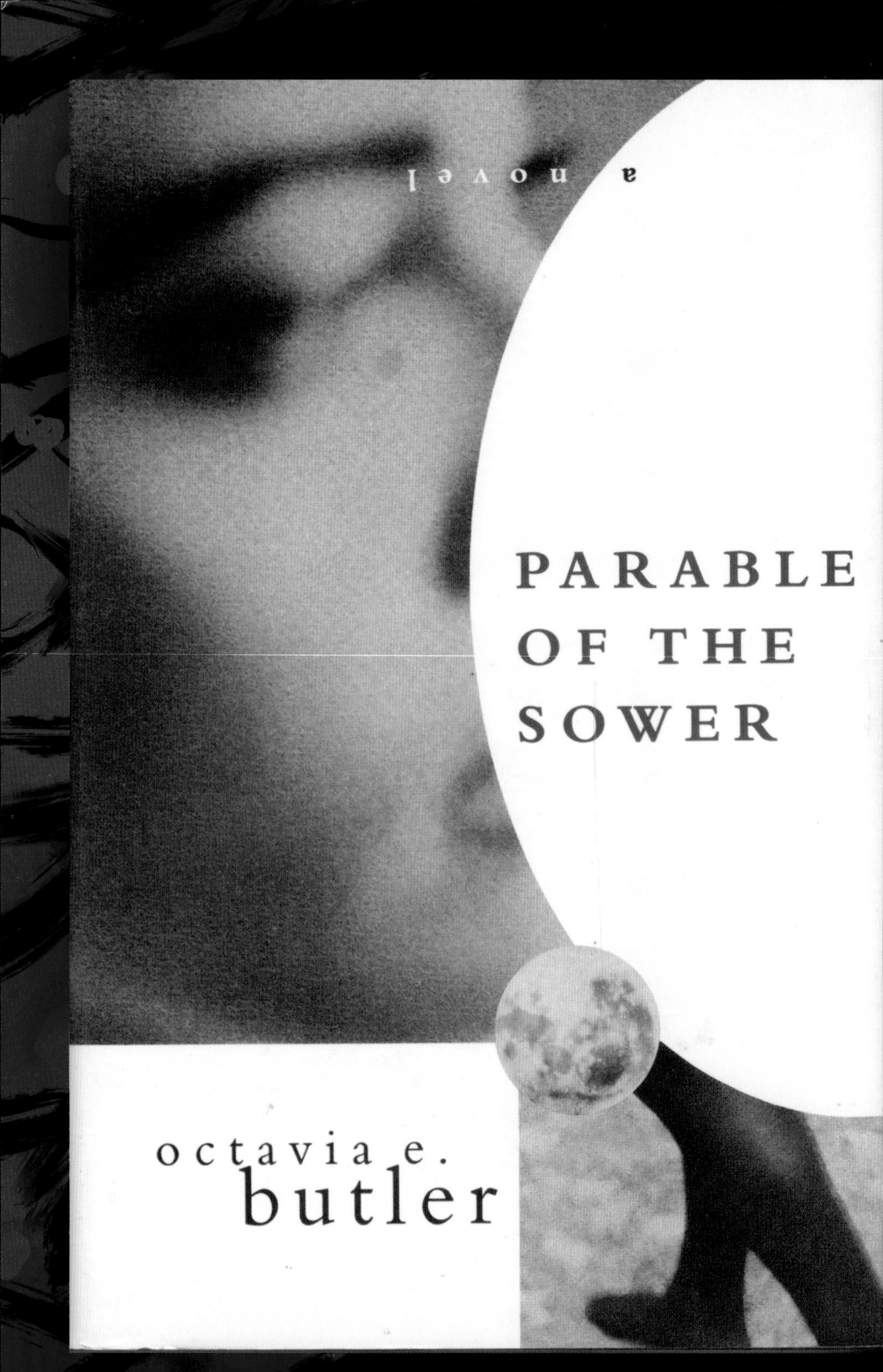
a novel
PARABLE
OF THE
SOWER
octavia e.
butler

First edition hardcover of Octavia E. Butler's *Parable of the Sower*, published by Seven Stories Press in 1993. Jacket design by Stark Design, photos by Barry Marcus.

Q&A WITH DAMIAN DUFFY AND JOHN JENNINGS

What drew you to this series?

Damian Duffy: The first time I tried to read *Parable of the Sower*, years ago, I made it maybe one hundred pages in and had to put it down. And I didn't pick it up again for a good long while. That book shook me. I had to *make* myself read it, because it's a little too real. So, I think I took that as kind of a personal creative challenge—write the thing you're afraid to write.

But, more than that, I knew we had to do the Earthseed series because the novels take place basically now. *Parable of the Sower* starts in 2024, but I don't mean that the arbitrary date matters; *1984* is still *1984*, even though we've passed 1984. But Octavia Butler chose the time period deliberately, because she set out to write a story in the "if-this-goes-on" category of science fiction (with a nod to Robert Heinlein). Butler wrote these dystopian fictional warnings at the end of the 20th century about a 21st ravaged by climate change and income inequality and fascistic authoritarians taking over the American government—a kind of America where xenophobia is on the rise, where public education is dismantled, where disease runs rampant, where people are separated from their children and housed in internment camps, and, yes, where the US president—in the sequel, *Parable of the Talents*—is elected with the slogan "Make America Great Again," just in case the rest of that wasn't on the nose enough.

All of Butler's novels are timeless in their brilliance, but these novels in particular have a timeliness that's impossible to ignore.

John Jennings: After the election of Donald Trump to the presidency in 2016, I think it was almost predetermined that this story would have to be the one that followed *Kindred*. It's prescience and power were so palpable that Damian and I felt that it was a duty to bring the story to life. So, I think *necessity* drew me to the series.

What was the most challenging part of adapting this story?

DD: Depression. I have depression and anxiety anyway, but the peculiar feeling of dramatizing dystopian fiction while the daily news renders it documentary—in real time—added a whole new flavor. It is both heart wrenching and calmly surreal to adapt a story so prescient it hurts. And, look, Octavia Butler was an amazing writer, a certified genius, but I think it does her a disservice to pretend like she was psychic. She was just paying attention. She looked at how the world was thirty years ago and projected those human practices to their logical conclusion. It is a testament not only to her imagination, but also to her masterful skills as a researcher that the book feels so prophetic. But it also underlines how some catastrophes are predictable and avoidable, which is its own kind of tragedy—something avoidable treated as inevitable. Part of what makes *Parable of the Sower* so powerful is that it makes you live a Cassandra complex by proxy. It gives you the intimate understanding of that awful feeling, being Lauren behind the walls of Robledo, knowing it's not "if" but "when."

JJ: While we were working on this book, my wife Tawana became pregnant. Also, we are now living in the area where a lot of the *Parable* books happened. There's actually a character in *Parable of the Talents* that is from Riverside, California, where we now reside. I think that fact, plus the birth of our son Jaxon, really made the themes of the story more relevant and reified. Making comics has become second nature to me. However, the anxiety of having to raise a little Black boy in an country that he was never supposed to be able to survive in become a bit too real while producing the book sometimes.

Do either of you have a favorite character?

DD: I don't want to play favorites. Lauren is the obvious answer, since you spend so much time inside her head, but even she has her human flaws. There are certainly characters I passionately hate. Keith is a sociopath. I will say, though, I have a soft spot for Bibi, Zahra Moss's child in Robledo, because hers is one of the very few bits of dialog that I invented completely—dialog that's not in the novel. I had her ask about a truck in the guileless, bossy way of little kids to give her some presence—to add some resonance earlier in the story, for when Zahra mourns her later on, and to sort of make up for having to truncate Zahra's mourning because of space constraints.

JJ: I think that Zahra Moss is my favorite character. She's tough as nails, no nonsense, and very practical. I like a lot of the characters, but I think I really liked her the best. She reminds me of a few folks that I've met.

There are a lot of parallels between Lauren's America and our America. Did the state of current events inspire you?

DD: Even in early 2017, when we pitched adapting the novel, it was clear that Lauren's America was, and would continue to be, highly evocative of day-to-day life in the United States. By the time I was working on the script, there were pictures of fire tornadoes along California highways that I could send John as photo reference. The failures in leadership and institutions, the attacks on poor and vulnerable people by systems of white supremacy and late capitalism—those cracks in the social foundation were already well underway in the United States when Butler was writing in the 1980s and '90s. Both Lauren and the rest of us are living in an America reaping what it has sown, so the story of Lauren's survival in that world felt like an important one to introduce or reintroduce to readers.

JJ: I'm not sure if "inspire" is the right word. It was hard to be continually working on the book while watching our country slide into a similar state in real time. Sometimes I felt as if our book was conjuring this insane state of events in America. I know that isn't the case but, I can't express how surreal it was to be making the book and watch certain "truths" unravel every night on cable news.

Damian, how do you deal with turning Octavia E. Butler's complex prose novels into a graphic format?

DD: *Sower* was a bit easier to adapt than *Kindred* in its technical aspects, just because I had more experience taking Butler's prose apart and putting it back together as a visual dramatization. I also felt a little freer to be more experimental in my suggestions to John for page and panel compositions—having panels mimic the emotional or narrative content of the story—like when smoke from the fire in Robledo becomes the panel borders. Since Lauren's religion is all about change, having more fluid panel structures seemed appropriate.

I also stole from Alan Moore, who took Superman editor Mort Weisinger's edict that every panel in a six-panel page could have no more than thirty-five words, and mathed that out to a maximum 210 words per page. So, for every panel, I'd type out the original prose I was working with, check the word count, and cut and condense based on how many panels I had on each page. Setting those restrictions helped me be more decisive about what text I would have to cut, which still seems like sacrilege, cutting the prose of Octavia E. Butler.

Most of all, I just strive to use the unique narrative powers of comics to tell Lauren Oya Olamina's story with the same depth and intensity that Butler achieved in the original novels.

John, drawing so many different characters is a huge burden on any artist. Was there any particular thing that helped you keep track of everyone?

JJ: I went through and made character sheets and tried to design each character according to the descriptions in the script and original story. I then tried to draw them over and over to "get to know" them on some level. There's a number of online fan pages on *Parable of the Sower* that had great breakdowns of character descriptions. I found those very, very helpful.

Your partnership has been going strong for years now. Can you give us a glimpse into how you collaborate?

DD: Yeah, fifteen-to-sixteen years, give or take. I mean, I met John in like 2005, and had him in my wedding party in 2006, so it's always just felt like a foregone conclusion that we're family. We both love comics, and we love horror and hip hop and using art to attack social injustice, and we're both willing to be flexible in our roles and creative processes—to change how we work to fit the project we're working on. What else can I say? J2D2 in full effect. We don't mess around.

JJ: Finding Damian to collaborate with was a blessing. We have very similar ideas about comics, politics, and focus on the story a great deal. Our egos take the backseat to what the story needs. I think that's what makes us a great creative team. We have the skillset to take a comic from very basic ideation to full blown production. It gives us a lot of flexibility and I think it's a rare thing to find such a perfect union of interests.

Were there any differences between working on the graphic novel adaptations of *Parable of the Sower* and *Kindred*?

DD: Well, as I said, just having the prior experience working on the *Kindred* helped me come to terms with having to cut things from Octavia Butler's original work. I've often said that, while writing *Kindred*, I worried Octavia's spirit was standing over my shoulder, shaking her head, like, "No, white boy, you're screwing this up." With the script for *Sower*, it felt more like she'd stopped shaking her head, and was maybe just giving me the side-eye.

Beyond that, just the scope of *Sower*, the sprawling cast of Robledo, and then the whole other sprawling cast of Lauren's travels north, offered new logistical challenges—figuring out how best to include as many characters as possible to make Lauren's world feel as realistic and lived-in as it is in the book.

JJ: I think the major differences were the really large scale of *Sower*. *Kindred* almost seems like a play because it was so tight regarding the main characters. *Sower* is a massive undertaking and seems to combine so many more genres into its storyline. So, there were more characters, more themes, and more challenges to illustrate.

Also, we had more time to do *Sower* so, hopefully, that shows in the work. Sower also marks a major change for me in my illustration because I switched to a totally digital production method via the Apple iPad Pro and the Procreate drawing app. This gave me a lot more flexibility and ease with production. This allowed me to focus on the work a lot more. This was really important to me because I hurt my shoulder drawing *Kindred* as fast as I did. I learned a lot about producing large works and I'm grateful for the opportunity to grow as an artist.

What is the plan for the sequel, *Parable of the Talents?*

DD: I finished writing the first draft of the script for *Parable of the Talents: A Graphic Novel Adaptation* right before the COVID-19 shelter-in-place orders started to come down, and that was a weird experience, because it felt a little like I finished adapting the story, and then I went to go live in it. It's a harrowing tale, and, I think, echoes our present reality in ways that are even more haunting than we see in *Sower*. As I mentioned before, it even has the president who campaigns to "Make America Great Again," which was actually an old Reagan slogan, because 45 couldn't do anything without some kind of theft involved.

It is definitely larger in scope than *Sower*, probably the largest graphic novel project John and I have attempted thus far. But hopefully John and I will make comics that rise to the challenge. It will include some even more dynamic visual storytelling, particularly when it comes to incorporating the dream masks—virtual reality environments created by the other major narrator in *Talents*, Lauren's daughter.

JJ: I plan to draw the book to best of my ability while having a small human hanging off of me. ∎

TES ON PROCESS

A page of LAUREN's notebook. The art on the paper is drawn in ballpoint, a sequence of LAUREN starting out as a stick figure, becoming a fully rendered ballpoint pen sketch of LAUREN, flying. She flies toward a warpy, Tim Burton-ish door, outlined with glowing blue light. A few flames have just begun to appear on the wall beside the door.
Then she flies into the flames, which serve as a sort of meta-gutter for the bottom scene. Close-up of a fully rendered 7-year-old LAUREN drawn in ballpoint. And, at the very bottom of the page (a labeled stick figure of?) 7-year-old LAUREN standing next to (a labeled stick figure of?) CORY. They're taking down laundry on a summer night, the sky full of stars, the wall looming large.
NARRATION: Saturday, July 20, 2024
NARRATION: I had my recurring dream last night.
NARRATION [*above fire*]: I guess I should have expected it. It comes to me when I struggle.
NARRATION [*below fire*]: When I try to be my father's daughter.
NARRATION/I.D.: Me, seven years old
NARRATION/I.D.: My stepmother
Dialog, 7yo LAUREN: *Prefiero tener las estrellas.*
Dialog, Stick Figure CORY: *Las estrellas son gratis. Prefiero tener las luces de la ciudad de vuelta.*
NARRATION: So, last night, I dreamed a reminder that it's all a lie

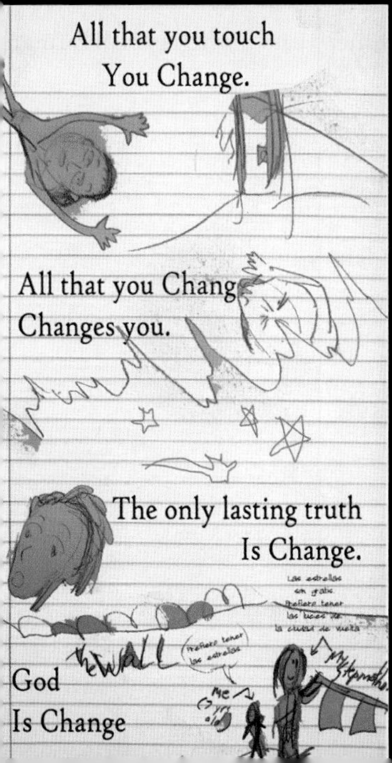

All that you touch
You Change.
All that you Chang
Changes you.
The only lasting truth
Is Change.
God
Is Change
the WALL

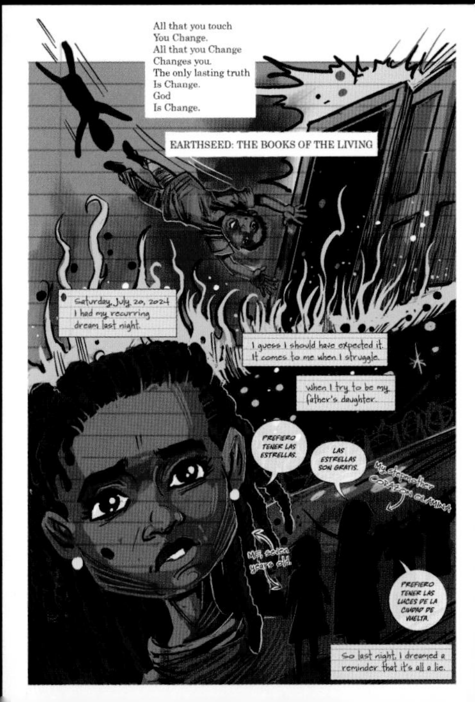

All that you touch
You Change.
All that you Change
Changes you.
The only lasting truth
Is Change.
God
Is Change.
EARTHSEED: THE BOOKS OF THE LIVING
Saturday, July 20, 2024
I had my recurring dream last night.
I guess I should have expected it.
It comes to me when I struggle.
when I try to be my father's daughter.
PREFIERO TENER LAS ESTRELLAS.
LAS ESTRELLAS SON GRATIS.
My stepmother CORAZON OLAMINA
ME, seven years old.
PREFIERO TENER LAS LUCES DE LA CIUDAD DE VUELTA.
So last night, I dreamed a reminder that it's all a lie.

MARCUS, in the background, vomits. LAUREN is walking toward the arm in the foreground. JAY GARFIELD, a pocket notebook in one hand, tries to stop LAUREN. She pushes him away.
NARRATION: It was fresh and whole. A black man's arm, skin just the color of my father's.
JAY: I'll take fingerprints, Lauren. You don't have to—
LAUREN: Go to hell!
Low angle shot, close-up on LAUREN looking down.
NARRATION: Later, I apologized to Jay.
NARRATION: I made myself examine the arm while he took fingerprints.
NARRATION: I had to know. And yet, I still don't know.
The SEVERED ARM, centered in the page, taking up the majority of it. It is described in the novel thusly: "The arm was fresh and whole—a hand, a lower, and an upper arm. A black man's arm, just the color of my father's where color could be seen. It was slashed and cut all over, yet still powerful looking—long-boned, long fingered, yet muscular and massive . . . " and later as " . . . too slashed and covered in dried blood" to be able to tell for sure if it belonged to the Rev.
NARRATION: All the slashes and dried blood made it impossible to be sure.
A shot of a coiled rattle snake, sitting beside a rock and some indeterminate bones, shaking its rattle.
NARRATION: We kept searching. What else could we do?
NARRATION: George Hsu found a rattlesnake.
NARRATION: It didn't bite anyone, and we didn't kill it.
Widescreen panel at the bottom of the page. The search party looks to the right of the panel, in various versions of fear, disgust, and horror. LAUREN is in the far left
NARRATION: None of us were in a mood to kill things.

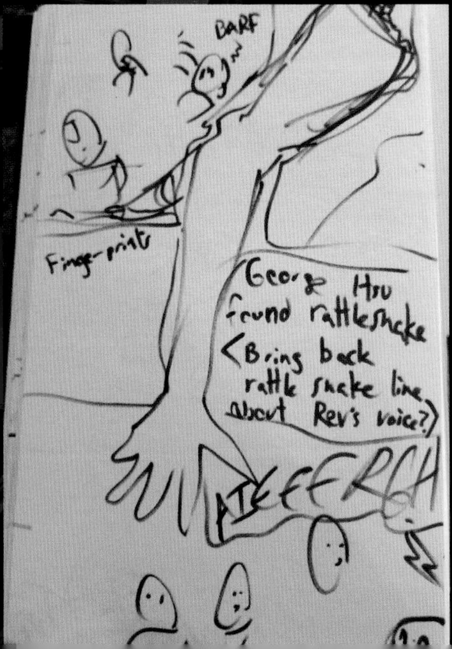
BARF
Finger-prints
George Hsu found rattlesnake
<Bring back rattle snake line about Rev's voice?>
AIEEERGH

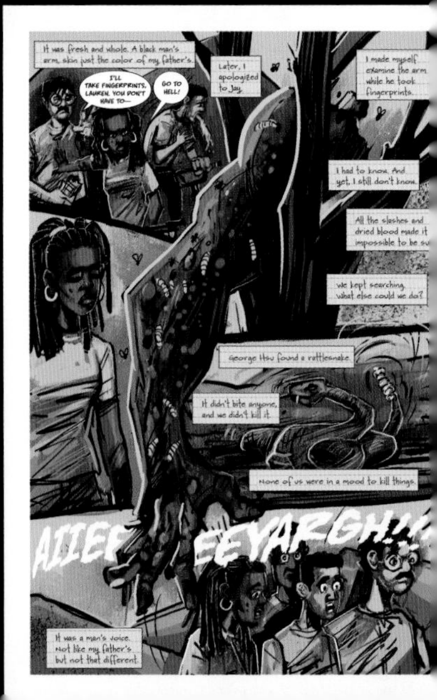
It was fresh and whole. A black man's arm, skin just the color of my father's.
I'LL TAKE FINGERPRINTS, LAUREN. YOU DON'T HAVE TO—
GO TO HELL!
Later, I apologized to Jay.
I made myself examine the arm while he took fingerprints.
I had to know. And yet, I still don't know.
All the slashes and dried blood made it impossible to be su
We kept searching. What else could we do?
George Hsu found a rattlesnake.
It didn't bite anyone, and we didn't kill it.
None of us were in a mood to kill things.
AIIEE
EEYARGH!!
It was a man's voice. Not like my father's but not that different.

VISUAL DEVELOPMENT

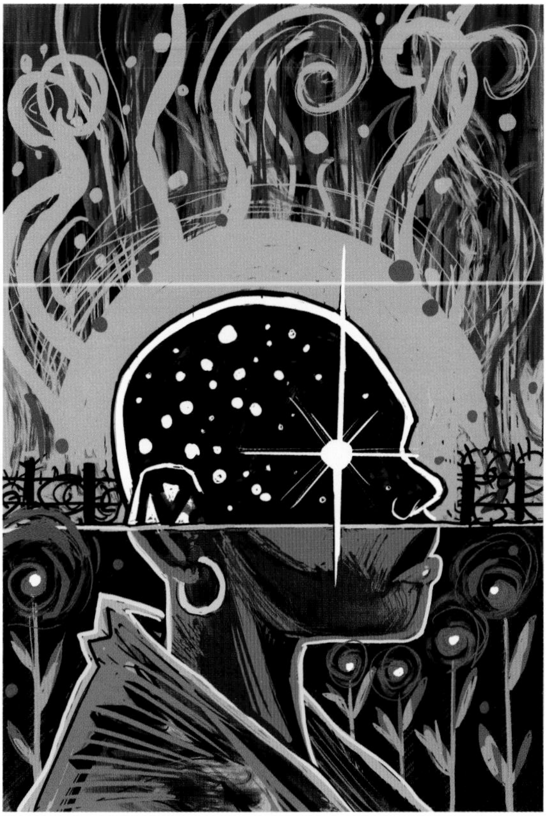

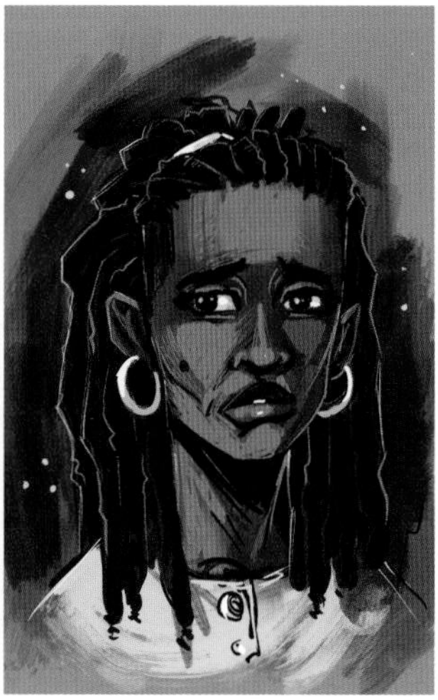

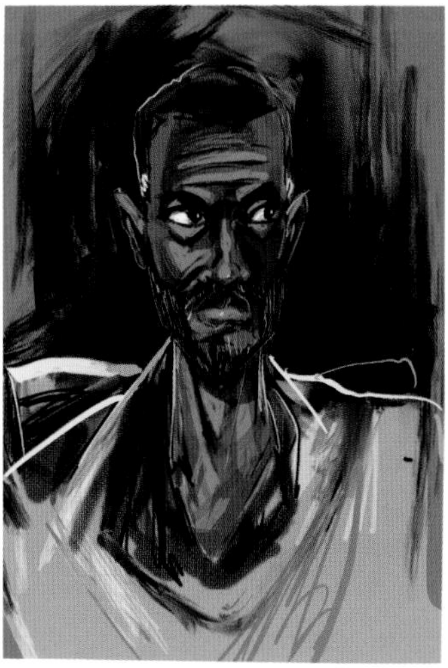

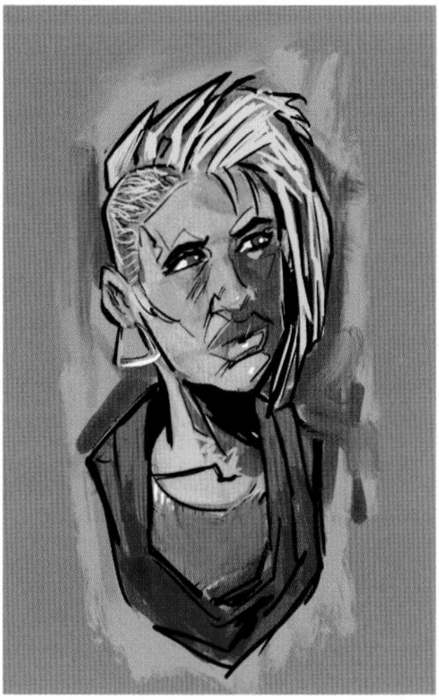

ABOVE Sketch by John Jennings produced during the cover design process.
BELOW Initial character studies of Lauren, Bankole, and Jill (2019).

PARABLE OF THE SOWER

A GRAPHIC NOVEL ADAPTATION

By Damian Duffy and Illustrated by John Jennings

BOOK INTRODUCTION

Overview

Parable of the Sower: A Graphic Novel Adaptation, by Damian Duffy and John Jennings, is a powerful update to award-winning author Octavia E. Butler's original. African American protagonist Lauren Olamina comes of age in 2024 amidst a dystopian reality that is simultaneously horrifying and uncomfortably possible. The graphic novel explores a range of themes relevant to young people and our current world. Readers will find many compelling reasons to relate to Lauren as she establishes her own religion, Earthseed, and gathers a diverse community of believers.

Supporting the national Common Core State Standards (CCSS) in Reading Literature for high school curriculums, *Parable of the Sower: A Graphic Novel Adaptation* is an appropriate selection for Grades 11-12 in Language Arts, Advanced Placement Literature and Composition, and Advanced Placement Language and Composition classes. At the college level, the book is appropriate for Composition and Literature classes and Environmental

Science classes and is also ideal for first year and common reading programs.

The following prompts provide for a critical analysis of *Parable of the Sower: A Graphic Novel Adaptation* using the CCSS for Reading Literature for Grades 11 and 12. In addition, classroom activities are provided to enhance analysis of the text.

STANDARDS

Key Ideas and Details

CCSS.ELA-LITERACY.RL.11-12.1 Cite strong and thorough textual evidence to support an analysis of what the text says explicitly, as well as an analysis based of of inferences from the text. Include specifications where the text leaves matters uncertain.

Craft and Structure

CCSS.ELA-LITERACY.RL.11-12.5 Analyze how an author's choices on structuring specific parts of a text (e.g., the choice of where to begin or end a story, or to provide a comedic or tragic resolution) contribute to its overall structure and meaning as well as its aesthetic impact.

Pre-reading Ideas

These pre-reading ideas are intended to help educators create an environment that enables students to deeply engage with the text. By drawing from students' prior knowledge, educators prepare young people to understand this complex text on multiple levels.

Teachers can spend time familiarizing students with the works of the award-winning author Octavia E. Butler and her importance as an African American science fiction writer. Examining her Google Doodle and her *New York Times* obituary provides an overview of her life and career (see Resources) that can acquaint students with her accomplishments. Teachers can also share pictures and interview clips of Butler, where she talks candidly about her writing process, her influences, and her reasons for selecting the topics of her texts. During these introductory activities, teachers can reinforce the importance of Butler's voice in the world of science fiction, especially given the predominance of white authors in the genre. Teachers might also choose to have an extended discussion about the Afrofuturism and the influences they notice between Butler, Parable of the Sower, and contemporary popular culture, with consideration to how some have cited her importance as an early influencer for Afrofuturism.

Graphic novels are works of sequential art, which "features a series of panels that convey a single story" (Kelley, p. 3) and benefit from multiple readings. A teacher can guide students through these revisits with a focus on images, words, and how the two work together in each reading. The article "Sequential Art, Graphic Novels, and Comics" asserts:

> In sequential art and visual narrative . . . the pictures conveyed through multiple panels work together with words to tell a story or provide information to a reader. While the image sometimes enhances the meaning of the text, frequently the image and text work in concert throughout multiple panels and are symbiotic in nature. The reader must pay careful attention to both image and word, understanding how the two work together, to clearly comprehend worded graphic novels. (p. 5)

Students will most likely have a range of familiarity with reading graphic novels. To make their reading of the text successful, teachers should spend time helping students first understand that graphic novels are rigorous texts, and the same active reading strategies they incorporate for other genres of texts are applicable when reading graphic novels. For instance, to prepare readers for thinking about and analyzing how text and images work together, teachers can pull images of Lauren from diferent parts of the text for analysis. Then, teachers can use the following questions to guide discussions based of of one panel or image:

> "What is the story in this panel? How do we know? Is there more to this story than we're aware of? How do we know?" (Kelley, p. 10)

Next, teachers can build students' competence for close reading of the text by adding a second image, asking: "Have we learned anything new about the character, the setting, or the situation from the addition of a second panel?" (Kelley, p. 11), and use their responses as the basis for thoughtful discussion.

The concept of change is a central one. Teachers can select page 2 to begin a conversation about the various meanings of change in students' own lives and guide them through making predictions about Lauren and the changes afecting her. As they read, they can either confirm or correct predictions based on textual evidence.

The text spans several years and locations, a potential challenge for readers. Collaboratively construct a timeline of key dates to help students keep track of plot points. Teachers can also have students sketch or chart the names and other identifying information in each community Lauren lives within as she travels. These tools will assist students in keeping track of settings and characters as they read.

Lauren has hyperempathy, a condition in which she feels the emotions and pain of others. It is worthwhile to lead students in a robust discussion of their beliefs and misunderstandings about people with disabilities so they can begin to understand Lauren from a strengths- based perspective (see Resources).

Earthseed, the religion Lauren creates, grounds the book. Lauren also embraces community as important to this religion. Spending some time considering students' personal religious beliefs—especially how they came to have them—and their ideas about community could be additional topics for discussion.

Finally, teachers can define terms with students to help them frame the text, adding vocabulary as the novel study progresses based on student interest, input, and areas of confusion. Keeping these terms and definitions available while reading the text allows students to reference them regularly. Some suggested words include: dystopia, survivalism, climate change, climate action, ableism.

Note to readers: *Parable of the Sower: A Graphic Novel Adaptation* features images of nudity and scenes of physical and sexual violence. A teacher must preview the book before reading it with students, noting what parts of the text could be triggering for readers and where to take necessary precautions.

DISCUSSION QUESTIONS
Coming of Age
Lauren is a complex character. Identify plot points in the text that challenge Lauren's beliefs and make her think diferently. **Who is she before these moments of conflict, and how does she continue to mature and change throughout the novel? How does she exemplify Earthseed?**

Lauren initially lives at home with her father, stepmother, and siblings. **What does Lauren's family expect from her? What does Curtis want from her? What does Lauren want for herself? How does she handle these expectations and the conflict between them?**

Following a fight with their father, Keith leaves home and returns to tell Lauren about his life outside the community, providing other details for his sister about a world that is unknown to her. Later, Keith is killed and Lauren's father uses his death as a warning for others. **How does Keith's death, his fate, and her father's response to her brother impact Lauren's view of the world?**

Lauren's home and family are destroyed in a fire. She returns to collect her family's belongings in the presence of scavengers. **Consider the impact of this moment on Lauren's personal development.**

Ability/Disability/Critical Disability

Outside the gates, Lauren observes the street poor and explains her hyperempathy. Analyze the image on page 9. **How do the illustrations work together to help the reader understand the severity of Lauren's disability? In what ways is her hyperempathy seen by others as a limitation, and is it indicative of how people with a disability have historically been treated? In what ways is Lauren's hyperempathy a strength? Provide evidence from other parts of the text to support your claims.** Later, Lauren learns that Emery, Tori, and the Moras are also "sharers," and escaped enslavement. **What are the dangers of others knowing about their hyperempathy?**

Shortly after shopping for provisions at a Hanning Joss, Lauren is conflicted about telling her companions about her hyperempathy, calling it her "weakness" and a "shameful secret" (p. 146). **When Lauren does eventually tell Zahra and Harry, determine the significance of their reactions on Lauren and on their group dynamics.**

Religion and Belief

Lauren is often in conflict with her father, a Baptist minister, particularly around issues about God and religion. She grapples with thinking her father's religion is a lie and with her desire to start her own religion, which she eventually does. **How does Lauren cope with the tension between her father's expectations and her own dreams? What do her reactions suggest about her maturity?**

Lauren's father goes missing and is assumed dead. Lauren preaches a sermon in remembrance of him. **Analyze her message, its impact on their community, and her own understandings about this change in her life.**

"All struggles are essentially power struggles" Lauren writes (p. 74). **Assess the power struggle between Keith and his father as well as Keith's internal struggles, taking into account how toxic masculinity, pride, and family dynamics come into play.**

Community

When the novel begins, Lauren lives inside a gated community in Robledo, California. **Examine how the community is supported within this society, the diferent people within it, and the roles they play. How is safety constructed and enforced? What limitations does this safety have?**

Analyze the impact of Amy Dunn's death on Lauren (pp. 39–40), especially her resignation over how the community will respond. What conclusions can the reader draw about unpredictable violence and safety within the gated community?

Once she is outside of the gates, Lauren must create her own community. **What aspects of this new community are similar and diferent to her previous one?**

What is the significance of Lauren's determination to forge a community in such challenging circumstances? What do her actions suggest about her character?

Earthseed

Consider Lauren's beliefs about Earthseed on page 21. What is the relationship between God and change? What does Lauren mean when she says, "My God just IS" (p. 21). Why does she say that the question "Is any of this real?" is "dangerous"? What systems and beliefs are threatened by acknowledging these truths?

Joanne is the first person that Lauren tells about Earthseed (pp. 42-44). What does Joanne's skepticism suggest about Lauren's ideas? Why is Lauren devastated later when her father tells her she can no longer talk about Earthseed? What is the importance of this rejection by two people she loves? What does her father mean when he later encourages her to change her approach to teaching people, from making them "look into the abyss" (p. 50) to encouraging them to be more hopeful? Why are Earthseed's concepts scary to imagine?

Assess the relationship between Lauren and Bankole and their negotiation about moving to Bankole's farm (p. 228). What do these negotiations suggest about their relationship? What does Lauren's insistence about what she wants suggest about the importance of Earthseed?

Lauren's understandings of Earthseed take shape the more she writes about them. Determine the events throughout the book that encourage her to articulate her thoughts and her beliefs. How do these events serve as catalysts for her writing? What is the importance of literacy, especially writing, to help her process her thoughts?

Dystopia

"Dystopias, through an exaggerated worst-case scenario, make a criticism about a current trend, societal norm, or political system" (ReadWriteThink). **Compare examples of dystopian elements in the novel.** Some might include climate change, policing, approaches to space travel, debt slavery, Olivar, and others. **What criticisms are being made in the text?**

Extension Activities

Parable of the Sower has resonance to our present day and offers many interdisciplinary links for deeper study. Students can demonstrate their understanding of a theme in the text that they want to explore further by creating their own graphic novel panel. To prepare students for success, select several panels for close reading to study as mentor texts, using some of the same questions from the pre-reading section. Then, have students aim for similar cohesion in their own illustrations.

Lauren's hyperempathy can be the basis for understanding Critical Disability Studies. As a Black, disabled young person, Lauren can also be a way for teachers to introduce "intersectionality," a term created by Dr. Kimberlé Crenshaw to define the overlapping ways that one's race, gender identity, ability, and other traits interact and function. These two frameworks can center discussions about decisions Lauren makes in the text, how others respond to her decisions, and the significance of these decisions and actions.

Is Lauren an activist? Students can first establish a working definition of the term, then participate in either a Socratic Seminar or a debate, drawing on the text to support their claims.

Lauren's activism and unyielding desire to forge a new world is a key reason she is able to start Earthseed. Similarly, young BIPOC (Black, Indigenous, and People of Color) climate activists are leading movements to challenge people to change. Teachers can encourage students to research these young climate activists, then create their own personal action plans for an issue of interest to them. Sherronda Brown's article "19 Youth Climate Activists of Color Who Are Fighting to Protect the Earth" for Wear Your Voice magazine ofers a starting place.

Supplemental Reading
Students are strongly encouraged to read the original *Parable of the Sower* novel for an even deeper and enriching experience.

Parable of the Talents, Octavia E. Butler

Children of Blood and Bone, Tomi Adeyimi

Harriet Tubman: Demon Slayer, David Crownson and Courtland Ellis

The Broken Earth series, N. K. Jemison

Who Fears Death, Nnedi Okorafor

RESOURCES

Brown, Sherronda J. "19 Youth Climate Activists of Color Who Are Fighting to Protect the Earth." *Wear Your Voice*, September 25, 2019. https://www.wearyourvoicemag.com/youth-climate-activists-of-color.

Butler, Octavia E. "Interview with Octavia Butler." By Charlie Rose. *Charlie Rose*, June 1, 2000. https://www.charlierose.com/videos/28978.

Crenshaw, Kimberlé. "The Urgency of Intersectionality." TED Talk, October 2016. https://www.ted.com/talks/kimberle_crenshaw_the_urgency_of_intersectionality.

"Dystopias: Definition and Characteristics." ReadWriteThink. 2006. http://www.readwritethink.org/files/resources/lesson_images/lesson926/DefinitionCharacteristics.pdf.

Fox, Margalit. "Octavia E. Butler, Science Fiction Writer, Dies at 58." *New York Times*, March 1, 2006. https://www.nytimes.com/2006/03/01/books/octavia-e-butler-science-fiction-writer-dies-at-58.html.

Kelley, Brian. "Sequential Art, Graphic Novels, and Comics." *SANE journal: Sequential Art Narrative in Education* 1, no. 1 (2010): 10. http://www.digitalcommons.unl.edu/cgi/viewcontent.cgi?article=1009&context=sane.

Kingett, Robert. "6 Anthologies Written By, For, and About Disabled People." Electric Literature. January 13, 2020. https://www.electricliterature.com/6-anthologies-written-by-for-and-about-disabled-people.

"Understanding Disabilities Lesson Plan." Teaching Tolerance. https://www.tolerance.org/classroom-resources/tolerance-lessons/understanding-disabilities.

About this Guide's Writer
Dr. Kimberly N. Parker currently prepares pre-service teachers at Shady Hill School in Cambridge, MA. She taught English in a variety of school settings for sixteen years, is active in the National Council of Teachers of English, and is a co-founder of #DisruptTexts. Dr. Parker holds a PhD in Curriculum and Instruction from the University of Illinois—Urbana Champaign.

ABOUT OCTAVIA E. BUTLER

Octavia E. Butler said of herself, "I'm Black, I'm solitary, I've always been an outsider," but she left off "extraordinary."

Octavia Estelle Butler was indeed a most extraordinary writer. Often referred to as the "grande dame of science fiction," she is the author of a short story collection and more than a dozen novels that have been translated into ten languages. Her work garnered two Hugo Awards, two Nebula Awards, and the PEN Lifetime Achievement Award. She was the first science fiction writer to win a MacArthur Genius Fellowship.

Butler was born in Pasadena, California, on June 22, 1947. A graduate of Pasadena Community College, she also attended California State University and UCLA. When she participated in the Clarion Science Fiction Writing Workshop, she attracted the attention of the famous science fiction writer and editor Harlan Ellison, who gave her a typewriter and bought Butler's first professional story.

Butler began writing as a child and was an avid reader of science fiction—which she couldn't help but notice never included characters like herself. Many of her novels, such as *Kindred*, feature strong, Black, female protagonists struggling with complicated issues of survival. She was a master of powerful, realistic prose that supported inventive genre narratives, and, most important, explored the deepest, most disturbing possibilities of human relationships.

A list of Octavia E. Butler's books can be found on the next page.

FOR FURTHER READING BY OCTAVIA E. BUTLER

Patternist Series

Patternmaster

Mind of My Mind

Survivor

Wild Seed

Clay's Ark

Seed to Harvest (omnibus edition, excluding *Survivor*)

Xenogenesis Series

Dawn

Adulthood Rites

Imago

Xenogenesis (Omnibus)

Earthseed Series

Parable of the Sower

Parable of the Talents

Standalone Novels

Kindred

Fledgling

Short Story Collections

Bloodchild and Other Stories

Unexpected Stories

ABOUT THE ADAPTOR

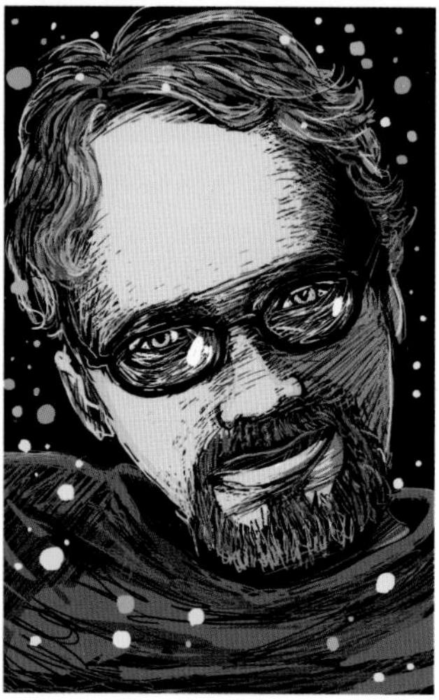

Damian Duffy, author of the #1 *New York Times* bestselling *Kindred: A Graphic Novel Adaptation*, is a cartoonist, scholar, writer, and teacher. The co-editor of *Black Comix Returns*, he holds a MS and PhD in library and information sciences from the University of Illinois at Urbana–Champaign, where he teaches classes on computers and culture, and social media and global change.

ABOUT THE ARTIST

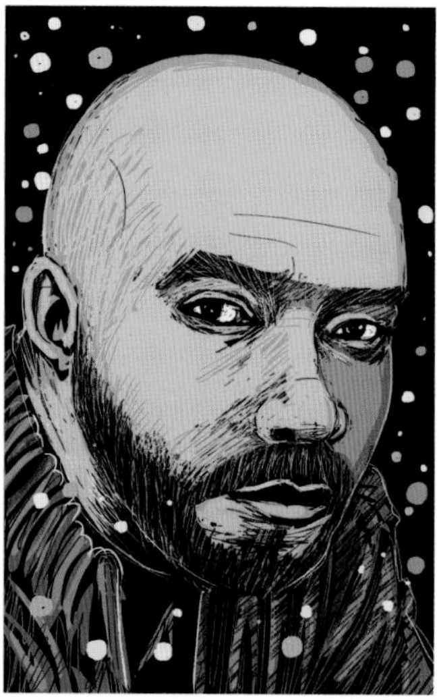

John Jennings co-edited the Eisner-winning anthology *The Blacker the Ink: Constructions of Black Identity in Comics and Sequential Art*. He is professor of media and cultural studies at the University of California at Riverside and was awarded the Nasir Jones Hiphop Fellowship at Harvard's Hutchins Center for African and American Research. He has written several works on African American comics creators, and illustrated *Kindred: A Graphic Novel Adaptation*. He is also the curator of Megascope, a new imprint under Abrams ComicArts that will publish a variety of graphic novels showcasing speculative and nonfiction works by and about people of color, with a focus on science fiction, fantasy, horror, and stories of magical realism.

ACKNOWLEDGMENTS

Damian and John say thank you forever to Octavia E. Butler for her genius and unflinching honesty, and thank you always to the Butler Estate for allowing us to contribute to her monumental legacy. Thanks also to Charlotte Greenbaum, Charlie Kochman, Pamela Notarantonio, Erin Vanderveer, Maya Bradford, and Max Temescu.

Damian also thanks Jen, Simon, and Gwen for keeping life possible, his parents for making life possible, and Tananarive Due for making sure we do Earthseed justice.

John would additionally like to thank his amazing wife, Tawana, for putting up with him. He'd also like to thank Tananarive Due for her watchful eye. John would also like to thank this book's color production artists Solomon Williamson, Cinique LeNoir, Anthony Moncada, Alexandria Batchelor, Alex Bradley, Kiyhari Sabree, and Solomon Robinson. Finally, he wants to acknowledge his son Jaxon, who was brought into the world during the production of the book. John sincerely hopes that people use this book as a guide for what *not* to do and that Jaxon inherits a better world.

COMING SOON

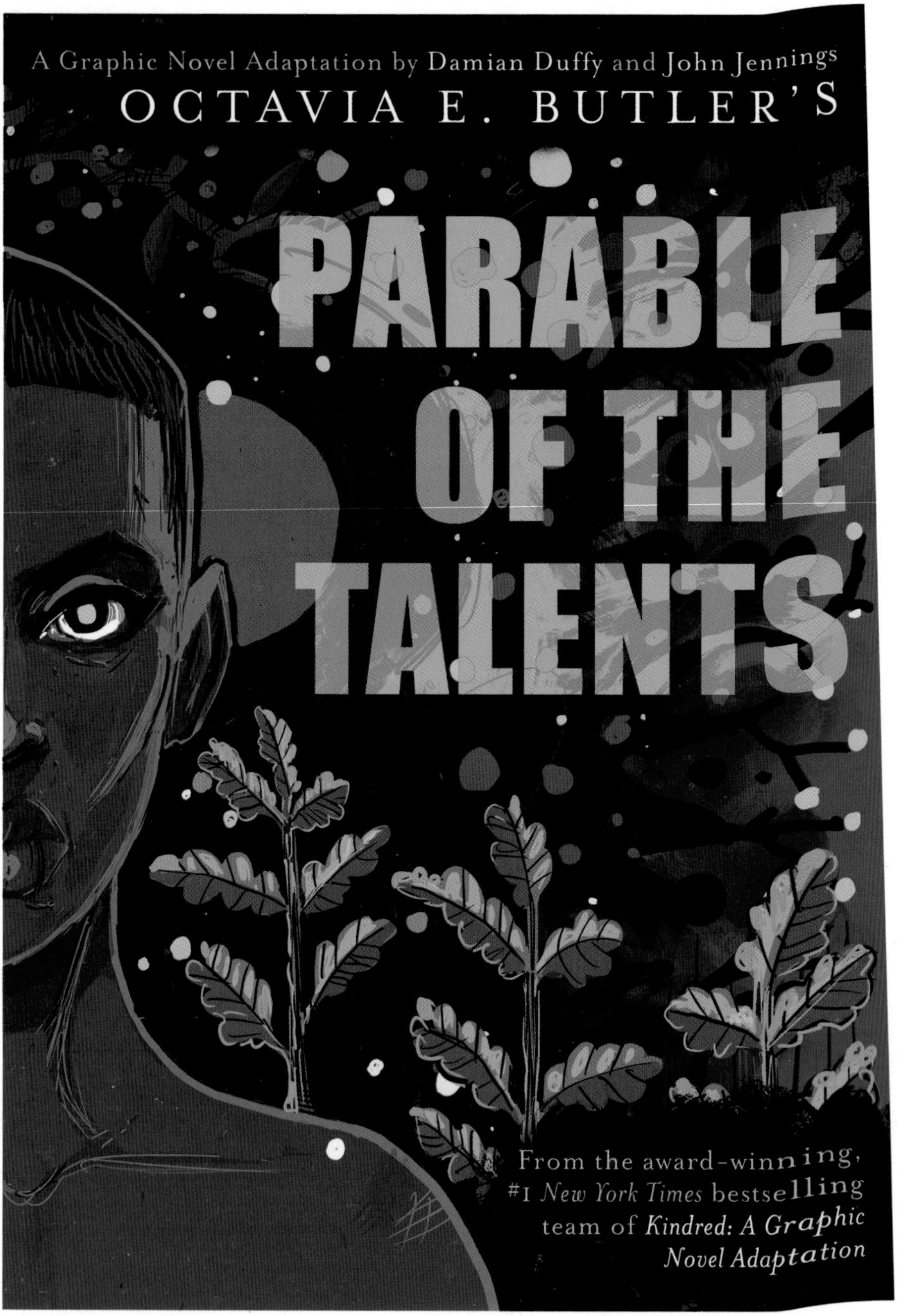
A Graphic Novel Adaptation by Damian Duffy and John Jennings
OCTAVIA E. BUTLER'S
PARABLE OF THE TALENTS
From the award-winning, #1 *New York Times* bestselling team of *Kindred: A Graphic Novel Adaptation*